OUR EMILY
and
KING OF CAMBERWELL

Also by Mary Jane Staples

The Adams Books

DOWN LAMBETH WAY
OUR EMILY
KING OF CAMBERWELL
ON MOTHERBROWN'S DOORSTEPS
A FAMILY AFFAIR
MISSING PERSON
PRIDE OF WALWORTH
ECHOES OF YESTERDAY
THE YOUNG ONES
THE CAMBERWELL RAID
THE LAST SUMMER
THE FAMILY AT WAR
FIRE OVER LONDON
CHURCHILL'S PEOPLE
BRIGHT DAY, DARK NIGHT
TOMORROW IS ANOTHER DAY
THE WAY AHEAD
YEAR OF VICTORY

Other titles in order of publication

TWO FOR THREE FARTHINGS
THE LODGER
RISING SUMMER
THE PEARLY QUEEN
SERGEANT JOE
THE TRAP
THE GHOST OF WHITECHAPEL

and published by Corgi Books

OUR EMILY
and
KING OF
CAMBERWELL

Mary Jane Staples

CORGI BOOKS

OUR EMILY and KING OF CAMBERWELL
A CORGI BOOK : 0 552 14983 7

This edition first published by Corgi Books 2002
Copyright © Mary Jane Staples 2001

1 3 5 7 9 10 8 6 4 2

including
OUR EMILY
Originally published in Great Britain by Corgi Books,
a division of Transworld Publishers
Copyright © Mary Jane Staples 1989
Set in 10/11pt Mallard.

KING OF CAMBERWELL
Originally published in Great Britain by Bantam Press,
a division of Transworld Publishers
Copyright © Mary Jane Staples 1990
Corgi edition published 1990
Set in 10/11½pt California by
Colset Private Limited, Singapore.

The right of Mary Jane Staples to be identified as the author
of this work has been asserted in accordance with sections 77
and 78 of the Copyright Designs and Patents Act 1988.

Corgi Books are published by Transworld Publishers,
61–63 Uxbridge Road, London W5 5SA,
a division of The Random House Group Ltd,
in Australia by Random House Australia (Pty) Ltd,
20 Alfred Street, Milsons Point, Sydney, NSW 2061, Australia,
in New Zealand by Random House New Zealand Ltd,
18 Poland Road, Glenfield, Auckland 10, New Zealand
and in South Africa by Random House (Pty) Ltd,
Endulini, 5a Jubilee Road, Parktown 2193, South Africa.

Printed and bound in Great Britain by
Cox & Wyman Ltd, Reading, Berkshire.

OUR EMILY

REFLECTIONS

To be born blind was one thing, he supposed, to be struck blind was another. Damn that day on the Somme. Could anyone who had known light ever be reconciled to permanent darkness? A day could be unendurably long, except there were no days in the usual sense, only night, for to the unseeing eyes days were no different from night.

He existed in frustration and helplessness, despite all the efforts he made to surmount the handicap that shut him off from the world. People came in, friends came in, and they all said, in one way or another, how well he was bearing up, how cheerful he was keeping. What was on the surface, of course, was never quite what was underneath.

The family did what they could. During the day, Chinese Lady was always there to keep him going.

'You all right, Boots? Here's a nice cup of tea, just made. Here.' She would place the cup and saucer carefully in his groping hands, then talk in her own way. Like, 'It's a good thing you don't take sugar, they're rationing us something chronic. Time they got this war over and finished with, it's a wicked waste of men's lives. If all the politicians had to go and fight it, it'ud be over in five minutes. D'you want to come to the shops with me today? Be nice for you to get out, you like gettin' out. You can hold my arm and we'll take it steady.'

Sammy, his younger brother, who had just left school at fourteen, was earning coppers and small silver in the

East Street market by making himself useful in a hundred ways to stallholders. He too would do his best whenever he was in the house.

'Got yer some apples, Boots, and they ain't specked, neither. 'Ere y'ar. D'you want anything at the shops, anything I can get for yer? I won't charge yer for goin', and would yer like a walk up the park on Sunday? Me and Tommy'll take yer. It ain't no bother, Boots.'

And Tommy, sixteen, when he came home from his job, he did his best too.

'Watcher, Boots, it's me, just got in from me daily slog. Look, I picked up a banjo from a bloke at work, it just needs a bit of mendin'. I can do it easy. Yer used to like playin' a banjo when you was at school till someone 'alf-inched it, and yer only play it by touch, don't yer? 'Ere, yer need a bit of coal on the fire. I'll do it. D'yer want to go out? I'll come with yer.'

They all knew how much he needed to get out of the house, and it was not their fault that there were moments they felt were embarrassing to him. Such as when he emerged from the house and noisy street kids fell silent. Or when neighbours were encountered and became loudly, heartily and cheerfully reassuring.

'Ain't he managing well, Mrs Adams? Who'd of thought it? It just shows what persevering can do. Yer look fine, Boots, yer gettin' along grand, we're proud of yer.'

Lizzy, his married sister, was always willing to take him on little walks whenever she came to see him. She invariably seemed more emotional than the rest of the family. He would feel that emotion in the warmth of her greetings kiss, and once he felt wetness on her cheek. She had her own hard time to endure. Her husband Ned had lost a leg in Flanders.

'Chinese Lady's bringing you on the bus to us on Friday, Boots. Ned can't wait to see you an' have a chat with you. He'd come an' see you here if he could, only he can't manage gettin' on trams or buses yet, nor can't he manage walkin' all the way on his crutches. He sent you his regards. Oh, and me baby's comin' on fine.'

Lizzy was pregnant with her first child.

Then there was Emily, the girl he was going to marry, the girl from next door who now lodged with them. She had a wartime factory job, and he always knew when she was arriving home. She always moved quickly, and he would hear the whisper and rustle of her clothes, and feel the loving encouragement of a hug and a kiss. And then her own kind of words.

'What you been doing all day, Boots? Oh, ain't that a silly question? But you been out with Chinese Lady, p'raps, or to the blind men's clinic to learn more things? We'll go out at the weekend, shall we? You like gettin' out and about as much as you can. Oh, now you got a grin on your face. I know why, yer goin' to tease me in a minute for all me silly questions.'

Without Emily, without her love and her own kind of help, reconciliation to blindness would have existed in his mind as an impossibility. She gave him moments when they were laughing together, and she gave him other moments when, during an adventurous outing, he was able to suggest throwing away his stick, a blind man's stick, because she was, he said, a surer defence against aggressive lamp-posts than any stick. And in addition to what Emily meant to him, there was what he chose to infer from the mutterings of the RAMC eye surgeon who gave him a monthly check-up.

'Um – ah – that hurt?'

'Bloody hell.'

'Good, good. Still a – um – little – um – ah – um.'

'A little what?'

'Inflamed. Well, mmm, we'll see, we'll see.'

'Wish I could.'

But those mutterings gave him a small ray of hope.

CHAPTER ONE

Doctor McManus had many patients in Walworth, South London, and Miss Emily Castle was one of them. He liked Emily. It was true she had been a holy terror up to the age of fourteen, but in the four years since then, the twists, turns and events of life had uncovered what had always been there, a warm heart and a caring nature. Perhaps her irritating ways and her aggressive prickliness had been due to the fact that she knew she was plain. And even now, at eighteen, she was still no beauty with her thin face, peaky nose and pointed chin. But in her love of life she was engagingly infectious, and she did own an abundant crown of dark auburn hair and luminous green eyes that sometimes seemed to be swimming in wonder at what life could offer even in the middle of the decimating Great War. What it was offering at the moment was marriage to the eldest son of her kind landlady, Mrs Adams, a widow. His name was Robert, but he had only ever been called Boots. He had been blinded five months ago during the first battle of the Somme, and this added compassion to her love for him.

It was crippling the country, the awful war. It was the beginning of December, 1916, and it had been going on for two years. The soldiers were having a dreadful time in the trenches of France and Flanders, and no one knew how many sailors and merchant seamen were being lost at sea. You could tell how awful it was in the trenches by the casualty figures, although the daily papers printed more things about deeds of heroism than about what would make the people downhearted. All the same, you could tell, and people said in towns where there were war hospitals you could see hundreds and hundreds of wounded soldiers in hospital blues, soldiers on crutches with only one leg, or soldiers with only one arm, and things like that. And anyone who happened to be at Victoria station when a hospital train came in could see hundreds of stretcher cases being unloaded and put into ambulances.

On the Home Front, food was worryingly short, especially meat and butter and cheese and eggs. Not that the people of Walworth missed butter too much, because it had always been a luxury, but you could only get a certain amount of margarine. It was rationed, like lots of other foods, and you had to give up coupons for these things. Mind, lots of girls and women had jobs they wouldn't have had normally, because of so many men away at the war, so there was money coming in. Emily herself had a job in a factory in Bermondsey, where khaki uniforms were being made. The factory warehouse was stacked with great huge rolls of khaki serge, which made you wonder if the government expected it to go on for ever, or at least until there were no more men left. She was so lucky Boots wouldn't have to do any more fighting, although it was an awful price he'd had to pay. Mind, her future mother-in-law had said them politicians wouldn't be past calling up blinded ex-soldiers and pointing them at the Germans.

In regard to her forthcoming marriage on the Saturday before Christmas, Emily had a problem of an intimate kind. So she decided to consult Doctor McManus, a general practitioner devoted to the physical welfare of the poor people of Walworth. He listened while she confusedly introduced the subject of marital conjugality. Except she didn't call it that.

She interrupted herself to say, 'It's that embarrassing, doctor, havin' to come and talk to you like this.'

'Emily,' said Doctor McManus, who had known her

10

since childhood, 'some embarrassments are exclusive to nice people.'

'Well, I'm touched if yer think – if you think I'm nice,' said Emily, who was always striving to speak more proper, like Boots did. Because of his good education, Boots spoke so much more proper that in his younger days the street kids called him Lord Muck, which title he had accepted without turning a hair. 'You always been kind to me, doctor, even when I was a wretched little terror and come out in mumps, which I was sure would be fateful. I don't know how I deserve Boots askin' me to marry him after I was such a pest to him as a schoolkid. Still, the Lord smiles on all of us sometimes, I suppose. Imagine it, the wedding three weeks from now.'

'That's not a problem, I hope,' smiled Doctor McManus.

'Oh, no. It's Boots's wishful desire. Well, he's said awful nice things to me like he means it is. But with him being blinded in the war, and me being the one to go out to work, well, yer see, doctor, we shouldn't have babies yet. When they give Boots his eye operation, which they said they might, which we hope they will, then it'll be different, like, he'll be able to get a job himself. He don't go on about it, but I know it's 'urtful to a man not being the breadwinner, specially when he shouldn't be a father yet, either.'

'I'm sure it's hurtful to both of you,' said Doctor McManus, 'but it's a very sensible decision.' He wished certain other patients would show similar sense.

'I've come to you, doctor, because I don't want Boots 'avin' to go to the chemist's. He said he would, but I didn't like that idea at all, nor did his mother when I mentioned it to her. I mean, Boots being blind he wouldn't know who was in the shop listening to him, and I'd die if I 'ad to go and ask the chemist meself. His mother and me, we been havin' some little talks.' Emily blushed perceptibly.

11

'Some little talks, yes.' Doctor McManus smiled in understanding. 'Mrs Adams is a wise and practical lady.'

Emily swallowed and said pinkly, 'She was very explanat'ry about – about – oh, you know, doctor.'

'About how to avoid pregnancy? Good.' Doctor McManus, despite a busy surgery, was prepared to give Emily time.

'So I said I better come and see you. Could you help, doctor, instead of Boots or me havin' to go to the chemist's and ask out loud? Boots said he really don't mind goin', but oh Lor', if someone 'eard him it might get about that him and me was being illicit before being married.'

'Illicit, yes,' said Doctor McManus gravely. 'Well, we don't want that. I'm willing to give you a prescription for fine quality washables.'

'Washables?' Emily was pink again. She knew, as most grown girls in Walworth did, what a wedding night was all about, and she also knew from her little talks with Boots's mother, how babies were made and how to stop that happening. But only the fatherly kindness of Doctor McManus made it possible for her to consult with him on the matter.

'Washables are on the market now, Emily. The Government has covertly condoned the availability of these things.' Doctor McManus meant, of course, that the Government did not want men coming home on leave to find their lonely wives had fallen from grace and were in a state of unhappy expectancy. 'The washables are more expensive, ninepence each—'

'Oh, lor', that much?' said Emily, pinker.

'Well, they're safer and, in the long run, cheaper. They can easily be washed after use, and if you bought two they would last Boots quite a long time.'

'Yes, I see, doctor. Oh, lor', Doctor, does givin' me a prescription still mean I got to go to the chemist's?'

Doctor McManus smiled. So many poor people liked

to be respectable, and to hand a chemist a prescription of that kind would not have been considered respectable at all.

'We don't usually manufacture them in my dispensary, Emily. But come along in three days and my dispenser will have them ready for you. Under the circumstances, I'm pleased you and Boots have agreed to contraception.'

'What?' asked Emily, startled.

'That's what you and I are talking about, you know. Contraception. It isn't generally approved of, and is forbidden to Roman Catholics.'

'Oh, Lord above,' breathed Emily, wondering if she and Boots were being unsacred. 'But does it help, Boots and me being Church of England?'

'It's your sensible attitude that helps, Emily. Have no misgivings.'

'You're so kind and informing,' said Emily. 'Do you think some people don't approve because they think stoppin' babies from happening ain't religious?'

Doctor McManus smiled again.

'Never mind what other people think,' he said. 'You and Boots have made a very sound decision. Have you heard of Doctor Marie Stopes? She calls it constructive birth control.'

'Oh, help,' breathed Emily, 'don't that sound awful?'

'Not to me.'

'Well, if it don't to you, doctor, then it won't to me,' said Emily firmly.

'Good. What time is the wedding? I should like to be at the service, to see you and Boots married. I've known both of you for many years.'

'Oh, it's twelve o'clock at St John's,' said Emily in pleasure. 'You and Mrs McManus could come to the weddin' breakfast at Mrs Adams's house, if yer like. It's where I been lodging since me mum went to live with her sister after me dad died.'

'That's very nice of you, Emily, and if I can find the

13

time, I'll bring myself and my wife to the house. The last Saturday before Christmas, you said?'

'Well, yer see,' said Emily, 'Boots wanted it as close to Christmas as convenient, like. He's so funny. Not funny peculiar, but lots of laughs. He said he wants me for Christmas, so I'd be his best Christmas present ever. Don't you think that's funny, doctor?'

'Do you think it is?'

'Oh, I think it's lovely, really,' said Emily.

'So do I,' said Doctor McManus.

So on the Saturday before Christmas, when Mr Lloyd George had taken over the premiership from Mr Asquith to give the country hope in his Welsh wizardry, Emily was getting ready for her marriage to Robert Alfred Adams, whom everyone called Boots. She was willing to promise to love, honour and obey in the giddiness of being a bride.

His mother, whom the family called Chinese Lady because she had lovely almond eyes and had once taken in washing, was giving her some last words of advice.

'When you say you'll obey, Em'ly love, it only means to agree with Boots when he's right, and to help him see what's right when he's wrong. Don't let him go ordering you about, our Lord don't expect any wife to accept being ordered about. That's nothing to do with obeying. Obeying just means keepin' the peace, which a woman can do better than a man. There wouldn't be no war on if things had been left to women to settle. Oh, and don't go doing things for Boots that he can do for hisself.'

'I don't mind doing some things, really I don't.'

'I know you don't, love. You're a godsend to all of us, you've turned into a lovin' girl, you have. But it's best Boots does as much as he can, best for you and best for him.'

'Oh, I know what you mean,' said Emily, 'only I do feel I'm lucky gettin' him.'

'Lucky?' said Chinese Lady.

'Some of the girls round 'ere – round here – would give their right arm to have Boots.'

'No, they wouldn't. Be a waste of a good arm. If anyone's lucky out of the two of you, it's Boots. You'll have a lot to put up with, him goin' off to the war and gettin' hisself blinded, when he shouldn't of. But you'll manage, you're a sensible girl, you are. Now, take that old dressing-gown off, or whatever it is, and let's get you into your wedding gown. That's it – why, Em'ly Castle, you already look a real bridal picture in that new corset. If your mum was here—' Chinese Lady immediately wished she hadn't mentioned Emily's loud and blowsy mother, for Mrs Castle was quite capable of saying something shockingly bawdy. 'Well, never mind, she's not here, love, and I'm proud to do the honours myself.'

'Oh, I don't hardly know how to tell you how glad I am I'm goin' to be your daughter,' breathed Emily. 'Mrs Adams, I do love yer, really I do, you been wonderful to me.'

Chinese Lady coughed and busied herself with the wedding gown and underskirt. But when she had Emily fully dressed, and wearing the veil she herself had worn when marrying Boots's father, she could not hold back words of affection.

'Why, Em'ly, now just look at yourself. You're a lovely Christmas bride, that you are.'

Emily, emotional, said, 'Oh, you and Boots and the boys've all been a blessing to me, and now I'm goin' to be one of the fam'ly.'

'There, Em'ly pet, don't let's have no tears now, not on your weddin' day. Your mum should be here any minute, with your aunt and uncle, and Boots will be goin' off to church with Ned, so dry them eyes now and perk up sweet and pretty.'

Whatever Boots thought about Emily's looks, he did not

cast her in his mind as plain. Emily had proved to be a girl loving and loyal, and he thought it had shone out of her on the last occasion he had seen her, at Lizzy's wedding nine months ago. He wondered if that was to remain his last physical sight of her. In November, the specialist at the eye hospital had said keep hoping, it's going to be some time before we'll be able to decide if you're a promising case or not.

He could not contemplate living in darkness for the rest of his life without feeling it was going to drain his last reserves of tolerance of his condition. It was bad enough being unable to see Emily on their wedding day. He did not see her advancing up the aisle in her bridal gown of virgin white, on the arm of her Uncle Bert, who was to give her away, and he did not even see her when she reached his side. But he felt her put her hand in his, and he felt the warm clasp of her fingers.

He was in his uniform, the uniform of a sergeant of the West Kents. His battalion was still out there, still fighting and dying. Emily had asked him to wear his uniform. She had asked because she was proud he had volunteered to serve his country. He might have said he was no longer entitled to wear it, for he had received his official discharge from the Army ten days ago, together with a few months back pay and a pension to compensate him for losing his sight. But for Emily he put on his khaki for the last time.

St John's Church, Larcom Street, was crowded, the gentle-mannered vicar, the Reverend Edwards, officiating. The whole of Caulfield Place seemed to be there, and many other people. Chinese Lady was in the front pew with her younger sons Tommy and Sammy, and her daughter Lizzy, the mother of a baby girl born a month premature but already, at four weeks, gurgling and healthy, and presently in the care of the daughter of Lizzy's district nurse at the house in Caulfield Place.

Tommy and Sammy were in their best suits, second-hand buys from East Street market and good as new, nearly. Sammy, now fourteen, was a bit upset that Boots couldn't see. Tommy, sixteen, thought Emily looked like she'd been turned into a princess by some fairy godmother. Lizzy, glowing in a bright red coat and a black hat trimmed with astrakhan, had a fixed smile on her face, disguising the pain she felt because Boots was blind and her husband Ned was on crutches. Ned had very much wanted to be Boots's best man, and she had been very emotional on the day Boots asked him. Well, it was so right that they should stand together in the church. They were friends, they had both been soldiers, they had both fought, and they had both been so badly wounded. Boots had lost his eyesight, and Ned had lost his left leg. He was to be fitted with an artificial one as soon as the stump was fully healed and toughened up.

He went about on crutches, and had been hobbling about at home on the day she experienced the alarming sensations signifying the possibility of premature birth. Thank goodness he'd had the telephone installed in their house off Denmark Hill. She had shouted in panic, and Ned simply threw his crutches down, hopped like a one-legged wonder to the telephone, and the district nurse had come round in no time, delivering her of an eight-month baby girl who was six pounds and perfect.

There he was, standing not far from Boots, using just one crutch to keep himself upright. Like Boots, he was in uniform, his left trouser leg neatly pinned up above his stump. He was drawing his pay, a captain's pay. He had not yet been discharged, although Boots had. Lizzy was sentimentally proud of both of them.

In the other front pew sat Emily's mother, Mrs Castle, with her sister Mabel. Mrs Castle had done her best with herself, but still looked a boozy, red-faced woman beneath a shrieking pink hat. She was generous and open-hearted, but loud, raucous and bulging with fat. Her husband had died of cancer in the summer, and she had gone to live with her sister, leaving Emily to lodge with the Adams family, much to Emily's bliss.

17

Emily's eyes behind her veil were emotionally moist throughout the ceremony, and dangerously moist when Boots finally slipped the ring on her finger. She turned her veil up and lifted her face.

'Boots?' It was the tiniest whisper to let him know where her mouth was, and Boots had no trouble in locating it. He kissed her, firmly.

War or no war, everyone seemed to have confetti, and the bride and groom were showered with it as they came out of the church, Emily tightly arm-in-arm with Boots, guiding him. Chinese Lady may have refused to shed tears, but her almond eyes were over-bright as she saw Emily looking up at Boots like a girl dizzy with wonder. Boots, who always seemed to have a smile lurking, as if life and people were far more amusing than tragic, had the broadest grin on his face as he felt the light touch of the showering confetti.

Sammy darted.

'Oi, Mr Greenberg, yer can bring Toby an' yer cart in!' he yelled to the bowler-hatted rag and bone man. Lizzy and Ned had been driven to the house from the church in Mr Greenberg's open cart on the occasion of their wedding. Emily had begged that she and Boots might do the same. The cold weather wouldn't matter, it was only a short ride. Sammy said he'd speak to his friend, Mr Greenberg. Mr Greenberg would charge five bob, he said, seeing the cart would have to be cleaned up and done up, and there'd be his own commission of twenty per cent, which meant a bob. Emily willingly paid. Sammy, of course, did not tell her he was also getting twenty per cent commission from Mr Greenberg. The indefatigable and ageless rag and bone man was now outside the church, his green-painted cart clean, holly adorning it, and his tireless horse spruced up. 'Mr Greenberg!' yelled Sammy. 'Oi, wake up! Yer can bring the cart right in, the vicar says it's a Christian gester to Boots.'

'I'm 'earing yer, Sammy,' called Mr Greenberg, 'and

vould Abraham's people not make a likevise gesture, my poy?'

The crowd in the forecourt of the church made way as Mr Greenberg brought his horse and cart in at a moment when a neighbour, Mr Franks, had just finished taking half a dozen wedding plates with a camera on a tripod, both items borrowed from a firm of photographers. Emily and Boots detached themselves from their mothers, the best man and the bridesmaid Vi, cousin to Boots. Emily, hitching her gown, stepped up into the cart. Boots followed, carefully feeling his way, Emily with one hand at the ready in case he stumbled. There was a seat fixed, and they sat down on it, Emily clutching her bouquet and slipping her free arm inside Boots's left arm.

'Oh, ain't we doing well?' she whispered. 'But can yer believe it, can yer believe we're married?'

'Are ve ready, my dears?' enquired Mr Greenberg.

'Wait, old cock,' said Boots. 'Emily, where's Lizzy?'

'I'm here, Boots,' said Lizzy, close by.

'Good on yer, sis. Look, d'you think Ned would like to come up with us? Save him clumping all the way back, and he is the best man.'

'Oh, you're lovely,' said Lizzy, 'I'll get him, he won't have any pride about riding with you and Em'ly.'

'Ask Vi to come up too. Best man and bridesmaid. Ned can sit on the other side of Emily, and Vi can sit on my lap.'

Emily laughed. Nothing could take away the bliss she felt.

'See if I care,' she said.

Ned got aboard on his one leg, with help from Tommy, and Vi, excited, climbed on too. All four of them found room on the seat, Emily and Vi in the middle, Boots next to Emily, and Ned next to Vi, his crutches grounded.

'Vell, my dears, are you ready now?' enquired Mr Greenberg. He turned his head and looked at Emily.

19

Her veil was up, her eyes dizzy with excitement, her face glowing in the midday light. The December day was as kind as it could be in its clear crispness. Mr Greenberg lifted his bowler hat to the radiant bride. 'Ah, my pretty lady, vill you give the vord?'

'Oh, yer may kindly proceed, Mr Greenberg,' said Emily in inspired graciousness.

'Very good, Mrs Adams,' said Mr Greenberg, 'proceed I vill.'

Emily laughed, hugging her husband's arm in delight. Mr Greenberg had been the first one to call her Mrs Adams.

'Oh, Boots, ain't it sheer heaven?' she said.

Boots found her ear and whispered amid the cheers that went up as the horse and cart moved off.

'It will be, Mrs Adams, when I get you to myself.'

As Mr Greenberg drove out into Larcom Street, close observers might have noticed that the bride was blushing. Mr Greenberg let his horse move at an amble, and everyone either walked behind or swarmed at the sides of the cart. Chinese Lady and Lizzy followed, escorted by Sammy and Tommy. Aunt Victoria, Chinese Lady's cousin, and her husband Tom, also followed. They were the parents of Vi, the bridesmaid. Aunt Victoria might have seemed a little aloof had she not been proud of how pretty Vi looked in bridesmaid's pink. Also, she was very fond of Boots, her favourite nephew.

Emily waved to people looking on from their open street doors or from their windows. Cries of 'Good luck!' rang in her ears. Oh, if only peace would come, if only the war would finish, if only Boots could get his eyesight back, life would be just lovely.

Mr Greenberg turned left into Walworth Road, and trams came clanging up to pass them. The passengers looked, the pedestrians looked, the shoppers looked. People waved, Emily waved, and Vi waved. Ned laughed. Boots smiled. He could see nothing, but he smiled all the same, for he could hear and feel how rapturous Emily was. It was her day, Emily's day. She had once been a ragged, urchin-like school-kid, a terrible menace to boys with her kicking feet and her scratching fingernails. But one day she had grown up. Now which day was that? He could not put his finger on it. He supposed it was one day among the many days he had been in France. No, it was before the war.

He must be careful not to let his blindness become a bitter thing, for her sake. He knew he had his bad days. He felt it was impossible to escape the moments when the thought of being blind for the rest of his life was unbearable. He would take his stick then and get out of the house, to tap his way around the streets he knew so well. Emily worried about that kind of thing, but Chinese Lady told her not to worry, and not to go after him.

Along Walworth Road, someone in the wedding procession produced a mouth-organ and played the tune of one of Marie Lloyd's most popular songs. The procession began to sing.

'My old man said foller the van
And don't dilly-dally on the way.
Orf went the van with me 'ome packed in it,
I follered on with me old cock linnet,
I dillied, I dallied, dallied and I dillied
Lorst me wav and don't know where to roam,
Oh, yer can't trust the specials like the old-
    time coppers
When yer can't find your way 'ome.'

The people of Walworth and some soldiers on leave stood and watched and cheered. Chinese Lady glanced at the soldiers, one or two of whom were wearing their greatcoats on this fine but cold December day. Emily worked in a factory that made soldiers' uniforms.

Chinese Lady supposed that most of them were for new recruits. There were always new recruits. There had to be when trained soldiers were being blown to pieces every day. If the war just went on and on, Tommy would have to go, and then Sammy. The government wouldn't do her any favours on account of having sent Boots home blinded. It would take her other sons in time if the war didn't end. It would reckon that in returning a blinded son and a crippled son-in-law to her, it had done her a favour, anyway. Lizzy was going to have a hard time seeing Ned through to the time when he could cope with his infirmity, and Emily was going to have an even harder time as the wife of a blind husband. And Lizzy with a baby to look after as well now, poor lamb. The war was a disgrace, that's what it was. Chinese Lady sighed.

'You all right, Maisie?' asked Mrs Castle, wheezing along beside her. 'Yer look a bit sad, yer do.'

'Yes, I'm all right,' said Chinese Lady. Girls in the procession were singing 'Why Am I Always The Bridesmaid And Never The Blushing Bride?'

And when the procession turned into Browning Street, everyone sang, 'Pack Up Your Troubles', the morale-raising song of the war.

On the cart, Ned glanced at Boots, and he knew Boots was remembering, as he was himself, the innocent first-timers going up the line to the trenches and singing as they went.

Emily, all nerves gone now, was singing in extrovert style. Her mother and her Aunt Mabel veered towards the Browning Street pub, on the corner of King and Queen Street. Her mother was informing Aunt Mabel that her feet were killing her, so a little sit-down in the pub before the wedding breakfast would do her plates of meat a power of good. They both had a little sit-down and a nourishing stout.

CHAPTER TWO

The wedding breakfast inevitably turned into a rousing party. Friends, neighbours and relatives crowded into the kitchen, the parlour and the passage. It all meant a few hours escape from the doldrums of war. There was plenty of beer and lemonade, and even some bottles of port, the latter a favourite with the ladies. And there was food, as much as could be decently provided. A good part of it had been provided by kind neighbours, all willing to help Chinese Lady do the bride and bridegroom proud. Emily, having received the guests with Boots, and been overwhelmed by so many wedding gifts, swept and darted about in her quicksilver fashion, helping the family to see to the wants of people. Her white gown rustled and rushed, the brilliance of her eyes and the spontaneity of her laughter born of her gladness. This, to Emily, was the happiest day of her life. Like most London cockneys she saw all things in clear simple black and white. There was the good and the bad, there was celebration and sorrow, and in the midst of poverty there was always tomorrow and its hopes. She was sure Boots was the nicest man in the world, and nothing was ever going to change her feelings for him, not even if he took to drink, which was the worst thing that could happen to a wife.

Emily did not realise that for all her peaky looks, she radiated a love of life so expressively that it made her a completely engaging girl. It had been a dream of hers for years, to belong to Mrs Adams and her family, for she loved them all. She felt she'd been privileged.

Chinese Lady would have told her the family had come best out of it.

But for all her gladness, there were painful little moments for Emily whenever she looked at Boots and realised he could see nothing of all this. Behind his smile there must be awful bitterness. How could there not be? She frequently went over to him. 'Oh, it's a lovely weddin' party, Boots. Are you all right?' And each time Boots said he was fine, except the place sounded as if hooligans had taken over. Or something like that.

Ned was with him most of the time. They had a great liking for each other, which was a happiness to Lizzy. Ned was seated, taking the weight off his one leg, and Boots stood beside him, listening to him and to people who came up to talk to them.

'Boots?' It was Vi, his cousin, the daughter of Aunt Victoria and quiet Uncle Tom. Uncle Tom had been the brother-in-law of Corporal Daniel Adams, Chinese Lady's deceased husband. Vi was shy and retiring and sixteen, a girl dominated by her mother, a woman of erratic moods, who could be expansive one day and carping the next, and who sometimes treated her inoffensive husband as if his existence was an annoyance. 'Boots, it's me, Vi.'

'I heard you, Vi,' said Boots, keeping his problems under the surface because it was Emily's day. 'Can I do something for you? Like give you a kiss for being the bridesmaid?'

'As best man, that's my privilege,' said Ned.

'Oh, go on,' said Vi. 'Boots, I just wanted to say – oh, you know.'

'Do I know?' asked Boots.

'Oh, just that yer grand, honest you are, because—' Vi checked. 'I mean, Em'ly looks lovely, really she does. You can be proud of her. Even me mum – I mean, Mum thinks so too.'

'Well, I think I'm proud of you, Vi, seeing you look lovely too.'

'Oh, yer can't know that,' said Vi.

'I do know it,' said Boots. 'I asked Tommy. "How's Cousin Vi as a bridesmaid?" I asked. And Tommy said, "Crikey, our Vi's a corker." '

Vi laughed softly. 'You're good for a girl, you are,' she said.

Boots remembered Emily had said that to him once. More than once. But he could not see there was any point in being bad for people, especially women, who got the roughest end of the stick.

'Well, give us a kiss,' he said. Vi laughed again. Then he felt her arms around his neck and the warm pressure of a soft mouth against his.

'Crikey, look at our Vi,' called Sammy, his sunny face expressing shock. 'She's kissin' Boots. Help, all the kissin' that's been goin' on. I'll be suffering next. That's death, that is.'

'I'll kiss yer, Sammy love,' bawled Mrs Castle, whose bulk was a trial to every seam of her tight dress.

'Oh, gawd 'elp us,' breathed Sammy, and vanished before death overtook him.

At half-past three the wedding cake was cut. Chinese Lady had not been able to make it herself because of the criminal shortage of dried fruit and other coveted ingredients. She had had to order it a month in advance from Hall's the bakers. She suspected there was not much fruit in it, but it was quite nicely iced. Mrs Castle had aplogised for not being able to have the wedding breakfast at her sister's place, and Chinese Lady had skated tactfully around the obligations of the bride's mother. The last thing she wanted was the mess Mrs Castle would make of everything. The one thing she did want was to do right by Emily and Boots, because Emily was a godsend and Boots her only oldest son

Things had cost money, and even Sammy had contributed something from his treasured hoard of savings. He handed five bob to his mother with a sacrificial air, telling her she could pay him back a bob a week and a penny a week interest. Chinese Lady told him he was a good boy. Tommy said no, he ain't, and I'll run him out of the house.

The cake shone whitely on its stand on the parlour table. Emily and Boots held the knife together, Emily guiding it. His hand was strong around hers, and her heart turned over, her head bent as they pushed the knife in, her eyes brimming.

There was a piece of cake for everyone, the kitchen bursting outwards with people. Ned made a winning little speech, toasting the bridesmaid. Vi looked shyly pleased. Boots began his own speech, in his own way, suggesting that a wedding was a highly serious occasion for a bride and a highly responsible occasion for a bridegroom. Accordingly, he couldn't think why his bride was laughing about it.

Chinese Lady was soon provoked into protest.

'Oh, that comedian son of mine,' she said, 'I don't know where he gets it from. I'm sure, not from me or his dad.'

To which Boots said, 'I don't know where I get it from, either, and I don't even know what it is. I didn't even realise I had it—'

'Oh, you've got it all right,' called Lizzy, and that brought yells of laughter.

'Goin' to give it to Em'ly now, he is,' said Uncle Tom, and received a severe look from Aunt Victoria.

'But if he don't know what it is,' said Tommy, 'how's he goin' to give it to Em'ly?'

Mrs Castle exploded out of her dress, nearly.

'Who's making this speech?' asked Boots.

'You are,' said Ned, 'we're just giving you some help.'

'Much obliged,' said Boots, hearing everything but seeing nothing. 'But I'll try without help to say some kind words about our mother.'

'You watch your tongue, my lad,' said Chinese Lady.

'Come on, Boots,' said Sammy.

'Well,' said Boots. 'I'm glad my mother and departed

26

father decided to have me. If they'd had second thoughts, I wouldn't be here, I'd only be a might-have-been, a twinkle that didn't come to anything.'

'Oh, you implorable hooligan,' gasped Chinese Lady as pandemonium set in.

'I never seen a twinkle what come to be more like a lit-up circus than Boots,' said Mr Blake, a neighbour.

'Ain't 'e a caution?' bawled Mrs Castle, and Emily sighed a little for her mum's loudness. It was only a transient sigh, however, for Boots was helping to bring the house down, helping everyone to forget the war.

'I have to thank my mother for being a mother to me,' he said.

'Well, she ain't yer uncle, that's fer sure,' grinned Emily's Uncle Bert.

'That's true,' said Boots, 'and without her I'd have been an orphan. Can't say I'd have liked that very much. It's been a good life here at home. I've even been able to put up with Sammy—'

'That's done it,' said Sammy, 'I ain't loanin' you no money, Boots, when yer gets 'ard-up, not even a farthing. I might loan Em'ly, I ain't loanin' you.'

'Now don't talk like that to your only oldest brother, Sammy,' admonished Chinese Lady, her wedding hat glossy and resplendent.

'Me?' said Sammy, blue eyes round with indignation. 'What've I said? What about what Boots said?'

'That's different,' said Chinese Lady, 'it's his weddin' day and we all got to put up with his comic turns.'

'I like the fact it's Emily's wedding day too,' said Boots, 'it's the kind of coincidence that could only happen once. I'm accordingly very appreciative. Emily's my kind of girl. Is she still here, by the way, or has she gone up to bed?'

'Boots!' Emily shrieked.

'Oh, ain't 'e wicked?' cried her Aunt Mabel.

'Order, if you please,' said Ned, best man. 'Emily, we'll excuse you if you want to go up, and we'll do what we can to see Boots doesn't keep you waiting.'

'Oh, it ain't fair,' gasped Emily, blushing, but she was in joy that Boots could make such fun of everything when the war had been so cruel to him.

'It won't last long, Em,' said Boots.

'Oh, yer demon!' shouted Lizzy in laughter.

'The rest of my speech, I mean, sis,' said Boots. 'I want to thank my mother for what she means to all of us. I want to thank Lizzy for being my sister, and I want to thank Tommy and Sammy for all the support they've given me when I most needed it, including several loans of a bob from Sammy at minimum interest rates.'

' 'Ere, I didn't charge no interest,' protested Sammy, 'Well, not much.'

Boots continued, 'I want to thank Mrs Castle for giving me Emily, and I want to thank everyone here for being here and for all their gifts to Emily and me. And I want to thank Emily for being lovely to me, and for taking me on.' He paused. There was a remoteness about speaking to people whom he couldn't see, about being in darkness while they were in light. But he had to keep going for a few seconds more. 'Emily is very special. I'll drink to that, and I hope you'll all drink with me, and include in the toast a mention of her departed dad and my departed dad. I'm sure they both think she's special too.'

There were boisterous cheers and much drinking. A hand touched Boots's fingers and squeezed them lovingly. Mrs Castle declared it had been a lovely speech and everyone agreed. The applause had a rousing cockney ring to it, and no one said Boots had got a bit posh for Walworth. He was still one of them, whatever he sounded like, and for a blinded man he'd stood up and spoke up like a regular bloke.

'Good on yer, Boots!'

'Good luck, Em!'

Mrs Castle heaved herself forward, wrapped Boots in a hot, beefy hug and kissed him smackingly.

Sammy rolled his eyes and said, 'If there's goin' to be more kissin' again we might as well all fall down dead.'

Uncle Tom made himself heard. 'Could I say something?'

'Of course you can't,' said Aunt Victoria, 'you'll only make a fool of yourself.'

Bravely Vi said, 'Go on, Dad.'

Uncle Tom spoke to Chinese Lady. 'I'd like to say something, Maisie.'

'All right, Tom,' said Chinese Lady, who knew he found Aunt Victoria a trial sometimes.

'Well,' said Uncle Tom, addressing the multitude, 'I'd like to say on be'alf of everyone – well, I hope it's everyone—'

'Get on with it,' said Aunt Victoria.

'I'd like to say that Mrs Adams, who's my distant cousin Maisie, has done us all proud,' said Uncle Tom. 'I'm pleasured to speak up in praise of 'er 'ospitality which, considering what the war's doin' to our larders, is something remarkable. She tells me gen'rous neighbours 'ere 'ave kindly contributed, for which I'm sure we'd all like to thank them. Still, it's her welcome 'ospitality we're all enjoying. I know it's Boots and Em'ly's day, we all know it, that we do, but I 'ope everyone'll agree it's Mrs Adam's day too, and I'm raisin' me glass of beer to her, which I trust yer'll all do likewise.'

'God bless yer, Maisie!' bawled Mrs Castle.

'And so say all of us!' cried Aunt Mabel.

'And so say all of us!' cried everyone else.

Chinese Lady fussed at her dress and looked as if she'd like to be somewhere else. Lizzy kissed Uncle Tom.

'You sweet old thing, you embarrassed our mum,' she said.

'But I thought someone ought to thank her,' said Uncle Tom.

'Yes, and you did,' said Lizzy, 'so you're a sweetie.'

At this point there was a call for Tommy to play the piano. Tommy had acquired the gift without being able to read a note of music. The house took on an atmosphere of musical gaiety as he began to play a selection of favourites. Lizzy repaired to her mother's bedroom, where the daughter of her district nurse was keeping a caring eye on the infant baby. Emily joined her and they cooed together over the sleeping mite. Ned and Boots seated themselves in the kitchen to reminisce quietly.

Emily was soon pulled into the parlour to show herself again in her white finery and to be greeted by the song, 'I'll Be Your Sweetheart'. Lizzy went into the kitchen to speak to Boots.

'All right?' she said, giving him a light, affectionate pat.

'Well, I've walked into most people here,' said Boots, 'I haven't been able to find any empty spaces until now.'

'Oh, you've been marvellous all day,' said Lizzy, 'hasn't he, Ned?'

'He's managing,' said Ned.

'No, but you've done wonders for Emily, Boots,' said Lizzy. 'She was worried in case things got too much for you. If you'd asked for a quiet weddin', just the family, she wouldn't have minded. But you've given her a real weddin', so you can take a bow.'

'It's not a one-sided thing, sis,' said Boots.

'I should hope not,' said Lizzy. 'What's the eye doctors been saying to you lately?'

'Hello when I arrive and goodbye when I push off,' said Boots. Ned smiled faintly. Lizzy looked at her husband. He grimaced.

'But they still tell you there's hope, don't they, Boots?' she said.

'They tell me to keep coming for check-ups,' said Boots. 'That's hope, I suppose.'

'That's good,' said Lizzy, and gave him another pat.

'Now, I'll nip up to Em'ly's room and pack some of her things, shall I, while you make sure she stays in the parlour? I'll take you to her. Oh, I know what to pack. And don't forget it's a quarter to eight that Ned and me'll be meetin' you at the theatre. Em'ly's goin' to jump over the moon when she finds out about everything.'

From the parlour came the sound of piano, song and revelry.

Tommy, still at the piano, was in the mood. The guests were in the mood. Tommy, using his natural talents, played the songs that were loved, Victorian ballads and Edwardian music-hall numbers. Outside, the December afternoon was dark. In France and Flanders the guns were silent in some sectors. Boots stood in the passage, listening to an uproarious rendering of 'I've Got A Lovely Bunch Of Coconuts', and thinking about a man who had been his drill sergeant at training camp, his company commander in the trenches and during the opening battles of the Somme, and who had bled to death in Trones Wood.

Ned was sitting on the stairs with Lizzy, she proud that their baby daughter was sleeping like an angel through all the noise after being fed thirty minutes ago.

'Are you tired, Ned? Is your leg aching a bit?'

'I'm fine,' said Ned, 'and I'm damned pleased for Boots and Emily.'

'You don't mind the racket?'

'It's people having a good time,' said Ned.

'My kind of people,' said Lizzy.

'Our kind,' said Ned. 'I'm people too, you know.'

'Glad to hear it,' said Lizzy, 'you being a captain officer and all.'

'Three-quarters of one,' said Ned, at which Lizzy was instantly fierce.

'Don't you say things like that,' she whispered in angry distress, 'don't you ever!'

Ned, who thought Lizzy living proof that a rose

31

could blossom in the smoky grey of Walworth, said, 'Not another word, sweetheart.'

'Oh, you silly,' said Lizzy, 'look what you give me, a lovely house and garden, and a darling baby. What more could a girl want?'

'Ask me again, when we're rich,' said Ned.

Boots was interrupted in his reflections by the touch of a hand on his arm.

'Who's that?' he asked.

'Me,' said Emily.

'Good. What's the time?'

'Ten to five.'

'Right.' Boots put an arm around her. Her wedding gown whispered as she turned in on him. 'Would you like to go upstairs, Mrs Emily Adams, and change into your best costume, put on your best hat and coat, and be down here again by twenty past five and no later?'

'What you talkin' about?' asked Emily, making herself heard above the noise. 'We're all goin' to do the knees-up later, and I want to do it with you.'

'Well, be down here sharp at twenty-past, and you can do a short knees-up. You and I are going up West for the evening.'

'What?' Emily stared at him. His blind eyes seemed so clear in the light of the passage lamp. He had a smile on his face. 'Up West?'

'To celebrate, Em.'

'Honest?' Her eyes filled with excitement. 'You and me? Round Piccadilly Circus and Trafalgar Square?'

'You and me, lovey.'

'Oh, ain't you nice? Hot chestnuts and everything?'

'I like the sound of everything. Up you go, sweetie.'

'Oh, yer darling,' said Emily, and hitched her gown and flew up the stairs, Lizzy making way for her, then following her to help her make herself look like a bride in a going-away outfit. Emily had understood she and Boots couldn't go away on honeymoon, not in December, and not with all the difficulties a strange place would mean to Boots. It hadn't worried her at all. The simple alternative of going up West with her bridegroom, when London on Saturday evenings was always fun, with soldiers and sailors on leave giving it an atmosphere of wartime excitement, was happiness enough for Emily.

But in her room, the one she had taken over from a previous lodger, a Mr Finch, she stopped to think.

'What's up?' asked Lizzy.

'It won't be any fun for Boots,' said Emily. 'I mean, the shops and everything, and watching the toffs goin' into the theatres, they won't be exciting to him or any blind man.'

'I told him you'd say something like that,' said Lizzy, going to work on hooks and eyes, 'so I've got to tell you it won't be just walkin' about, you're goin' to have a lovely weddin' evening.'

'What, Lizzy, what?'

'Ask Boots.'

'Oh, now you got me on tenterhooks,' said Emily, green eyes full of swimming light.

Freshened-up, made-up, and dressed in her best costume of dark maroon, a new hat on her head and carrying her winter coat over her arm, Emily was down again at twenty past five. Everyone was waiting for her, and as Tommy struck the chords, 'Knees Up, Mother Brown' began. This piece of cockney ebullience had been featured at the wedding of Lizzy and Ned, and the family knew Emily wanted it for her own wedding. So Tommy played it, and almost everyone sang it and danced it, in the parlour, in the passage and in the kitchen. Emily and Vi and Lizzy kicked up their legs, skirts hitched. Ned watched, laughing at the uninhibited gusto of men, women and young people. He glanced at Boots, who was standing close to the front door, his Army greatcoat on. In the right-hand corner stood a small suitcase, on top of which was Boots's peaked cap. Ned saw the expression on his brother-in-law's face.

It was introspective, as if he was looking inward at mental pictures he was conjuring up. They were as much as he could see, his mental pictures. He could see nothing of Emily, her legs flashing in new stockings. He could not see his sister Lizzy or his cousin Vi. Ned wondered if losing a leg was a lot more preferable to losing one's eyesight. He thought the answer could only be yes.

'Knees up, Mother Brown, knees up, Mother Brown . . .'

Amid the din, only Boots heard the knock on the front door. He opened it. A man's hearty voice said, 'Taxi, guv?'

'Right,' said Boots. 'Would you take this case first?' He bent, he groped, he picked up his cap, put it on, and then lifted the suitcase. The taxi driver took it from him.

'Clock's tickin', sergeant.'

'Never mind,' said Boots, 'be with you in a few moments.'

Ned, leaning on a crutch, called, 'Emily!' Tommy stopped playing.

Flushed, excited, Emily detached herself, and Chinese Lady helped her on with her coat. The passage swarmed with people as the bride called goodbye to everyone. A girl shrieked.

'Em'ly! Yer bouquet!'

'Here it is, love.' Chinese Lady rendered further assistance. Emily took the bouquet and tossed it into a forest of uplifted hands.

'I thought they wasn't goin' on no honeymoon,' wheezed Mrs Castle, red from heat and beer.

'Well, they got to go somewhere to do their kissin',' said Sammy. 'Well, I s'pose they 'ave. Bloomin' 'orrible, I call it.'

'Mind yer business,' said Tommy, and trod on his brother's foot.

Emily kissed her mother, then hugged Chinese Lady, Lizzy, Tommy and Sammy in quick succession.

'Now all of us are fam'ly, ain't we?' she said. 'Don't

go to bed till me an' Boots come back tonight, will yer? Then – oh, I left Ned out, he's fam'ly too.' She swooped on Ned and hugged him. Manfully, Ned remained upright.

Boots called from the front gate.

'Tommy, you there?'

'I'm 'ere, Boots,' called Tommy.

'Well, as Emily can't make up her mind, ask Cousin Vi if she'd like to come with me instead.'

'Still a comedian,' said Chinese Lady, but her mouth twitched.

Emily darted out, flew at Boots and gave him a hug too.

'You been havin' fun with me all day,' she said, 'and I just love yer for it.' She took his hand and they entered the taxi. People swarmed from the house to the gate, and waved and cheered and sang as the taxi moved off in the darkness to take the newly-weds into the excitement of the West End.

CHAPTER THREE

'Boots, what're you doing, and where are we goin'?'

They were out of the taxi and the portals of the Northumberland Hotel in Northumberland Avenue confronted them.

'I don't know where we're going,' said Boots, 'I can't see a thing. I'm relying on you, Mrs Adams.'

'Boots, the taxi's put us down outside the Northumberland Hotel, and what's that case you're carrying?'

'Well, you'll need your nightdress and I'll need my pyjamas. Come along now, lovey, and hold my arm or I'll walk into the wall instead of through the doors. They're swing doors, aren't they?'

'Oh, help,' said Emily faintly, 'we can't go in there, Boots, it's too posh – oh, what d'you mean, nightdress and pyjamas?'

'For bedtime,' said Boots.

'It's a joke,' gasped Emily.

'Bedtime for you and me ain't going to be any joke, Mrs Adams.'

'Oh, don't get me more worked up than I am. We're goin' in there, in the Northumberland? Boots, we're going to bed in there?'

'Not in the lobby,' said Boots, 'in a reserved room. Chinese Lady and I came here two weeks ago and reserved it. For one night. Our wedding night, Em. Lizzy packed some things for you, your nightie, a change of undies and so on. Right, then, shall we go in and be Lord and Lady Muck?'

'Oh, in such a posh place?' Emily took a deep breath.

36

'Won't that be lovely, me and you in the Northumberland? Oh, I never had anyone be as lovely to me as you. Come on, then.' She bravely linked her arm in his. She advanced with him. The uniformed commissionaire stepped forward.

'Sir?'

'We've a room reserved,' said Boots, and Emily thought, oh, don't I have a grand husband, speaking up like a real swell.

They entered the hotel, Emily experiencing a moment of panic because she had to get Boots through swing doors. But she managed it, and the lobby opened up to them. Her eyes opened wide. It was a carpeted, lofty grandeur to her. Dizzily she saw the reception desk. A porter came and took the case from Boots's hand. At the reception desk, Boots was addressed by the clerk.

'Mr and Mrs Adams, sir?'

The manager was there, looking on. He and his clerk knew this Army sergeant was blind. He and his wife were to receive the kindest attention. Emily experienced both awe and excitement. Imagine her and Boots having their wedding night here, in all this luxury, which was really only for upper-class people. There were Army officers in the lobby, and some terribly well-dressed ladies, with gorgeous feathers in their hats. She heard Boots speaking, she heard the clerk speaking.

She heard Boots say, 'My wife will sign the register.'

'Of course. Mrs Adams?' The clerk turned the register her way, and handed her a fountain pen. A rush of exaltation seized Emily. Her lovely husband was showing her he loved her. To bring her here, to give her a beautiful surprise like this, something she would remember for ever and ever, it was all for her. It couldn't mean anything to him, the hotel and its grandness, and not one of the seven wonders of the world could, either, not to a blind man. He had done it for her. Oh, she would not let him down, no, never.

'Thank you,' she said, and took the pen. But what should she write, what did one have to write? Her quick intelligence came to her help, and she scanned entries. She wrote then, in her neat, well-formed, sloping characters.

Mr and Mrs Robert Alfred Adams.

'Thank you, Mrs Adams,' said the clerk.

'Oh, not at all,' said Emily proudly. 'How good the weather is for the time of the year.' She wanted Boots to know how properly she could speak when she tried.

Boots smiled. The manager stepped forward.

'May I congratulate you, Mrs Adams, on having had such fine weather today?'

'Oh, aren't you nice?' said Emily in typical impulsiveness, and the manager smiled. Then, feeling perhaps she shouldn't have said that, she coloured a little. 'I mean—'

'I am delighted, Mrs Adams, to be thought nice,' said the manager. 'The key, William,' he said to the clerk.

An officer arrived, a major. He looked at Emily, then at Boots and at the sergeant's stripes on the sleeves of his greatcoat. He rapped on the desk with gloved knuckles.

'Major Morrison,' he said.

The clerk did not show the resentment he felt at such high-handedness. But he did say politely, 'One moment, sir.' He gave the key of room 11 to the manager.

The manager said, 'Allow me, Mr Adams – Mrs Adams – to show you to your room myself.'

Emily could never help being responsive.

'How kind,' she said, and she said it like a perfect lady. Boots smiled again. It was Emily's day, and she was handling the reception business proudly. She smiled at the clerk. 'Thank you,' she said. And the clerk smiled. He did not think her plain. He thought her lovely in her obvious shyness, in her sweetly engaging manners. She had today married a blind sergeant. The world was full of all sorts. It could do with more of her kind. He did not care where she came from. The manager had said Walworth. Good luck to her. And to him, the sergeant with the blind eyes and the whimsical smile.

'Oh,' said Emily, when the manager had opened the door of room 11 and she had stepped inside. It was beautiful to her unsophisticated eyes, its patterned red carpet and its velvet curtains rich and splendid. And it was so spacious, the double bed and blue upholstered furniture comfortably welcoming. The dressing-table was breathtakingly lovely. 'Oh,' she said again, enthralled, and the manager felt she had made his day. She saw bright yellow chrysanthemums in a tall blue vase on a table. 'Boots, oh, look – flowers.'

'Goodness gracious me,' said Boots, his hand around hers, 'flowers.'

The manager had never heard an Army sergeant speak like that.

'With the management's compliments, Mrs Adams,' he said.

'Oh, thank you, thank you,' said the enraptured Emily.

'Red ones?' enquired Boots.

'No, they're – oh, silly me, I'm sorry, darling. They're yellow chrysanths.'

'Dinner will be served at seven, Mr Adams,' said the manager.

'Thank you,' said Boots, turning to face the sound of the voice. 'We appreciate everything.'

'It is a pleasure, Mr Adams. If there is anything you want, please ring the desk. Mrs Adams?'

'Thank you ever so,' said Emily, and he smiled and withdrew.

Returning to reception, he said to the clerk, 'Tell Mrs Wilson first thing in the morning, no charge for room 11.'

'No charge, sir?' said the clerk.

'Sometimes, William, this kind of thing happens.'

'I'm all for it in this case, sir.'

Emily explored. She opened a door and was confronted by a huge bath.

'Oh, Boots, we even got a bathroom, with a real bath and hot taps and everything.'

'Is that a fact, Emily?' Boots was living in a world restricted to the sound of Emily's voice and Emily's reactions. 'Well, shall we use it, shall we have a bath? I'd like one.'

'Oh, wouldn't it be lovely, wouldn't it? Oh, you've done all this for me, you made me feel like a queen. It's so big, enormous, I never seen a room like this and a bathroom as well.'

Boots himself did not realise the impression he and Chinese Lady had made on hotel reception when they came to reserve a room two weeks ago. They had asked for a double room for a single night. They had been given a suite for himself and Emily, at no extra charge. Nor did he realise there was now to be no charge at all, because of the engaging qualities of Emily.

Feeling his way around the room and arriving at the bed, he said, 'Shall we get in together, Mrs Adams?'

Emily swallowed. She knew what everything was leading to. But she had no qualms. She was going to leave it all to Boots. She was sure he would know how to love her. Although she owned all the inexperience and uncertainty of a virgin, she wasn't so naïve as to believe Boots had not known French girls during his time in France. He had gone to France as a young man of eighteen, and his two years of fighting for his country had made him all of a man. Her own feelings for him were such that it was all too easy for her to imagine French girls throwing themselves at him. She did not really mind that too much, for she felt that all the men of the trenches deserved whatever pleasures they could find when they came out of the line for their rests. She did not mind anything Boots had done in France or Flanders as long as he loved her alone. It was just that she was naturally sensitive about the night ahead.

'Boots – oh, we can't go to bed now – it's for when we go to sleep.'

'I meant shall we get in the bath together,' said Boots.

'What?' Emily turned rosy. 'Oh, you cheeky devil, I never heard anything more saucy. Chinese Lady would have fits.'

'Why, is she coming to look?' asked Boots, beginning to undress.

'Oh, yer silly thing, course she isn't.' Emily grew a little hot and a little tingly as she saw him undressing. 'Oh, we can't bath together, it's shameless.'

'Could be fun as well,' said Boots, bare-chested and sitting on the bed to remove his shoes and socks. 'And it would save time. They're serving dinner to us at seven, here in the room.'

'Oh, that's nice. I expect everyone in the restaurant will be in their posh dinner clothes, makin' us feel common. It'll be cosy in here, just us, won't it?' Emily was talking to hide her confusion. Boots was down to just his short woollen underpants now. Confusion was inescapable. 'There's lovely big towels in the bathroom, you can finish undressing in there.'

'Lead me there, lovey,' said Boots, and Emily could not help thinking he looked a nice man, a really nice man. He had such a good body. 'After dinner, by the way, we're going to see *Chu Chin Chow*. Would you like that, Em? Lizzy and Ned are meeting us there.' Emily stared. 'Well, they're our best friends and help to make us a lively foursome, don't you think so? Em?'

'Oh!' Emily, emotional, rushed and wound herself around him. He felt her trembling quite violently against him. He felt for her hair. He caressed it.

'Don't you like the idea, Mrs Adams?'

'Like it? Boots, I love it. Don't yer see what you're doing for me, takin' me to the theatre with Lizzy and Ned, and havin' our weddin' night here?'

'I'm thinking about what you've done for me,' said

41

Boots. Chinese Lady, Tommy and Sammy had all given him their own kind of help since he had returned home blind three months ago. Emily had given him that much more, including uncompromising love and encouragement. 'I love you, Em. Would you now point me to the bath?'

She guided him to the bathroom.

'You have yours,' she said, 'and I'll have a quick one after you. There, I'll fill it for you. Soon as you've finished, I'll show you where the towel is.'

'Sounds fair,' said Boots.

Afterwards, dinner proved almost a feast, considering it was wartime and the hotel menu was necessarily restricted. It was served to them from a trolley and they ate it at the table, with a bottle of white wine. The waiter was all smiles, leaving them to enjoy each course, of which there were only two, the main course and a dessert, for that was all they had time for. Emily realised the smiles meant the waiter was aware they were newly-weds. She didn't mind, and she liked it that he was awfully nice to Boots, calling him sir.

She was very happy a little later, when the hotel doorman called up a taxi for them and it took them to the theatre where Lizzy and Ned were waiting with welcoming smiles on their faces. Lizzy was as happy as Emily. Her baby had been fed last thing before she left the house with Ned, and Chinese Lady was now in charge of the contented infant. Lizzy and Ned were to stay the night, using Emily's room.

The foyer of the theatre was crowded. There were gentlemen in top hats, tails and silk-lined cloaks, ladies in gowns, furs and jewels, and Army and Navy officers. And there were no zeppelins over London. Lizzy and Ned could think of nothing more enjoyable than sharing the excitement of *Chu Chin Chow* with Emily and Boots on such a special occasion.

Ned was in his uniform and on his crutches. He was

given very solicitous attention by the programme girl who showed them to their seats in the stalls. With the lights up, the chatter of conversation among members of the audience lapsed to a sympathetic murmur when Ned appeared. That affected Lizzy. It made Ned grimace. It made him feel like an object. It was a fact that badly wounded men did not like a surfeit of looks and whispers.

When they were seated, the atmosphere took its hold on Emily. She was enchanted by the grandeur of the theatre, with its red and gilt boxes, its imposing stage, its glittering audience and its air of excited anticipation. Chu Chin Chow, a musical, was everybody's wartime favourite, and one of the country's more exultant weapons in the fight against Germany.

A thought struck her, a thought that made her wince.

'Boots,' she whispered, 'I just realised, it's only for me and Ned and Lizzy, not for you. You won't see a thing.'

'It's for all of us, lovey,' said Boots. 'I know the story, and I'll be listening to the dialogue and the musical numbers. So don't worry.'

The lights were lowered, the orchestra began the gay and infectious overture, the curtain went up at the end of it, and everything became colourful magic to Emily. She was drawn heart and soul into the famed splendour of the show. It was up to every expectation, and it represented a world wholly enchanting to her. To Emily as a child, fairyland had been real, not imaginary. It was real to all cockney children, and some part of its appeal remained with them all their lives, which was why cockneys were great lovers of pantomime and music hall, but found straight plays dull.

Emily had never before sat in the stalls of a West End theatre, among posh people. Mostly she had been up in the gods, the sixpenny gallery seats high above the stage. She could hear the cockney girls, with their

43

soldier sweethearts, up in the gallery now, typically exuberant in their appreciation. Imagine her being down here, in the stalls, with Ned and Lizzy and her husband, who was treating her to such a wonderful wedding evening.

Chu Chin Chow was breathtaking magic.

At the interval Ned insisted on using his crutches to go with them to the bar. Lizzy guarded him watchfully, and Emily guided Boots, her arm through his. Ned wanted to stand treat in the bar, and did. Emily and Lizzy had port. Ned and Boots acknowledged the nature of the occasion by opting for a whisky each chased down by a Guinness. Emily asked Boots how he managed to get the tickets.

'Sammy queued up for them a month ago,' he said.

'Oh, I could kiss him,' said Emily.

'I don't think he'd think much of that,' said Ned, occupying a chair. 'Doesn't he fall about and die a death whenever he's kissed?'

'Oh, he manages to survive if you give him a penny first,' said Lizzy.

'The tickets must've been awful expensive,' said Emily. 'I mean, stall tickets and all.'

'Well, the tickets were reasonable,' said Boots, 'it was Sammy who was expensive. He charged for the journey, for the queueing and for getting them.'

'That boy's a shocker,' said Lizzy, 'I don't know where Chinese Lady got him from. But it's nice to splash out once in a while, specially on your wedding day, Boots, and it's a heavenly show.'

'I think I've got a few odd bobs left for another drink,' said Boots. 'My round, Ned. Another port for you girls?'

Both girls were quite happy with what they had left of their port. Emily watched Boots exercising independence. They were fairly close to the bar, but there was an awful crowd around it. She bit her lip as she saw him pushing himself gently through. He couldn't see anyone, he couldn't know where the barmaids were,

44

but somehow he drew one of them in his direction and she heard him order two whiskies.

'Oh,' she said, 'he's already had one whisky and a Guinness. Lizzy, it's awful for him, I know, being blind, but you and Ned don't think he's takin' to drink, do you? Oh, lor', I hope he isn't.'

People in the crowded bar turned to look and to wonder what had so amused a lovely young brunette and a crippled Army officer, for they were laughing their heads off. And another young lady, with glorious auburn hair, was looking at them as if she was mystified by what had set them off.

When the show was over, they came out of the theatre in a state of exhilaration. It was Lizzy who darted about and secured a taxi that would drop Emily and Boots at their hotel, and take herself and Ned back to Walworth and blow the expense. In the taxi, Lizzy and Emily both talked at once about the wonders of *Chu Chin Chow*, which some cockneys referred to as *Chu Chin Chop Suey*.

'One at a time, girls,' said Ned.

'Oh, but wasn't it lovely?' said Emily. 'Boots, you managed to enjoy it, didn't you?'

'Best evening I ever had,' said Boots, so Emily hugged his arm. They said goodbye to Lizzy and Ned when the taxi stopped outside the Northumberland Hotel. Ned made a lingering business of kissing the bride.

Which made Lizzy say, 'Wait till I get you home, you flash ha'porth.'

'Lots of luck, you two,' said Ned.

'Lots and lots,' said Lizzy.

When the newly-weds finally got to bed, Emily did what she had promised herself she would. She left it all to Boots. Boots's experience was limited to two occasions of harmony with a lady ambulance driver who happily excelled in pleasuring Tommies, and to three occasions with a young French war widow in Albert, just before the first battle of the Somme. But he remembered the only thing Chinese Lady had ever said to him in the way of advice. Be nice to your bride, and loving.

Perhaps that worked well enough, for a little while afterwards, when she was able to find her voice, Emily whispered, 'Oh, I couldn't hardly believe it, lovey, you an' me together like that.'

'Was it bearable, then? It's not always too good for a girl the first time, so I've heard.'

'Oh, you were nice to me, I could tell. Ain't it bliss, you and me cuddled up in bed like this?'

'Well, I like it, Em. Shall we cuddle up again tomorrow night?'

'Oh, yer daft thing, course we will. We're married now. We can cuddle up every night.'

'What a very nice thought, Em.'

Emily only ever had one regret about her wedding day, and that was that her beery and lovable old dad hadn't lived to see her married to Boots. He had liked Boots so much.

Boots always tried to remember the occasion as Emily's day, and as the day when she accepted without a single murmur of doubt all the responsibilities she was taking on and all the difficulties she was going to face. For him it was a teeth-gritting day of darkness. But he always remembered there had been one light.

Emily.

CHAPTER FOUR

On a May morning in 1920, Sammy Adams, Emily's brother-in-law, had charge of a china and glassware stall in the East Street market, Walworth. He was eighteen, and had a half-share in the stall with his partner, Bert Lomax.

A cadaverous-looking man trundled a handcart along the pavement behind the stalls and let it come to rest close to Sammy's legs. Sammy turned. The man drew back a covering sack, disclosing a full load of shining brass and copper, mainly ornaments.

Sammy took a keen look and said, 'Four nicker.'

'I didn't hear that,' said the man.

'Three nicker, I said.'

'I'm hearing worse'n I did before.'

'All right, I'll make it four,' said Sammy.

'I'm bleedin' dreamin'. Yer couldn't of said four.'

'It's me generous heart,' said Sammy, who was five feet ten and had grown fast out of every pair of trousers since the age of thirteen. He had a healthy brown face and the blue eyes of an angel. He had always been brown-faced. His mother said it was because he was born nine months after his dad had come home with a ruddy face from the Boer War.

'Gen'rous?' said the gaunt man. 'You're lookin' at val'able copper an' brass, Sammy mate, not a cartful of rusty nails, and nor ain't there no gilded iron. Seven pun ten I'm askin' an' wantin'.'

'I'm not saying you can't ask,' said Sammy, who dealt in various sidelines. He smiled at a comely woman who

47

had arrived to look at some brown china teapots. 'Sevenpence to you, missus, it's me birthday. Give yer one free if yer can show me a cheaper price anywhere.' He glanced again at the copper and brass. 'Never goin' to be worth more'n five quid, Ernie, if that. War's over. There's no market any more for old iron.'

'Old iron? Use yer mince pies, this ain't old iron.'

'No market, Ernie, just told yer so,' said Sammy. 'Bet you know it, too. Bet you've been trying to flog it all over the place. Bet I'm your last hope. I'd have to hang on to it if I did buy it. Be a risk, but I'm not yer friend for nothing, Ernie, not when times are cruel.'

'Times ain't as perishing cruel as you, yer young bleeder,' said Ernie. 'That's it, then, I ain't doing no more business with you. Even Ikey Mo 'ud give me five an' half, and that's still gorblimey robbery.'

'Sixpence,' said the comely woman, adjusting her crocheted shawl.

'Now, now, missus,' said Sammy, 'you know all my prices are fair cut to the bone.'

'Get 'em cheaper at Marks an' Spencer's bazaar, but I'll give yer sixpence for that one.'

Sammy laid sighing blue eyes on her.

'I don't mind yer breakin' me heart, love,' he said, 'but I do mind yer breakin' me pocket. I'm not keen on starvin' to death.'

'Nor am I,' said Ernie, 'an' there's me kids too, an' me suffering old Dutch.'

'Come on,' said the woman, 'a tanner, and not a farthing more.'

'I'm a mug, I am,' said Sammy, 'but all right, a tanner I'll take, God bless yer, lady. It's yer smiling face that's done me down.'

'I bet,' said the woman, but she was smiling as she went on her way, the wrapped teapot clasped to her bosom.

'Well, what's it to be, robbery or fair do's?' asked Ernie. 'It's a full load of the best I'm offering, it ain't no can of marbles. Look, whadjer say to six quid?'

'Four,' said Sammy, 'and that's me only offer.'

'Not bleedin' likely,' said Ernie, and trundled his cart away. But he was back inside ten minutes. 'Look, yer Shylock, I been cartin' this load about all morning.'

'I know that,' said Sammy. 'I said so, didn't I? War's over. Scrap metal's at rock bottom.'

'Curse yer,' said Ernie. 'All right, five pun ten, and I'll bring yer a load o' lead in a couple of days.'

'Where from?' asked Sammy, searching the market crowds for a sign of his partner, Bert Lomax.

'Ask no questions, 'ear no lies,' said Ernie.

'Listen,' said Sammy, 'I don't handle hot stuff, you know that. And listen again, if you knock off any lead from the roof of my church, I'll get the rozzers to run you in. I've heard what you and yer cousin Bill have been getting up to in yer own parish yard, but don't you get up to it in mine.'

'Blimey, you got religion?' asked Ernie.

'No, but St John's has got a place in me loving heart,' said Sammy. 'Me sister and brother both got married there, and I still get blessed by the vicar when we meet.'

'Didn't know skinflints got blessed,' said Ernie. 'Thought they only got done up by war widders they victimised. Oh, all right, give us five smackers, then.'

'Four.'

'You're bleedin' kickin' me when I'm down,' said Ernie. 'An' I'm down all right, on me back. So I got to take four. But it ain't goin' to make me love yer, Sammy.'

Amid the hoarse voices of stallholders crying their wares, Sammy said, 'I'm glad to hear it. Take the stuff to the yard. Fred'll pay yer.' He scribbled in pencil on a pad, ripped the little sheet off and gave it to Ernie. 'That's me promiss'ry note.'

'Yer what?'

'Promise to pay on delivery. Give it to Fred, and he'll pay.'

'Yer a hard one for yer age, Sammy, you ain't got a bit o' lovin' milk and human kindness.'

'Can't afford it,' said Sammy, 'not in these hard times.'

Times were very hard in May, 1920, with the war over and the country suffering from an expensive and hollow victory. A million dead had been very expensive. And there were no jobs for many of the returning men. Some suffragettes protested at the unfairness of the system whenever women were sacked to make way for ex-servicemen. But Lloyd George and his Government were too busy trying to lift the economic depression to listen to women.

Ernie disappeared with his handcart, and Sammy sold some cups and saucers from a job lot. Some saucers matched cups, some didn't. But at a penny each they were very acceptable for everyday use to the people of Walworth, who kept their best china, if they had any, for when relatives came to tea.

At the next stall, run by a character called Ma Earnshaw, a girl was buying three pounds of potatoes and a cabbage. Ma Earnshaw put them in the girl's shabby shopping bag.

'Fourpence-ap'ny, dearie,' she said.

The girl dipped her hand in a pocket of her worn black skirt. Her face fell tragically.

'Oh, I been and lost it – I lost it!'

' 'Ave yer now?' said Ma Earnshaw. 'Well, ain't that a shame, dearie?' A lot of them tried that kind of thing on from time to time. 'What yer lorst, yer gold watch?'

'No, the tanner what Mum give me for the veg.' Tears came into the girl's eyes. Sammy turned his back and went deaf. 'It must've dropped out – oh, there's a hole.'

'Fancy that,' said Ma Earnshaw. 'Well, would yer like me to let yer take the veg 'ome and let yer come back tomorrer with the dibs?'

'Oh, would yer let me do that, missus?' pleaded the girl.

'I would if I'd been born yesterday,' said Ma Earn-shaw, her large bosom aggressive. 'You go 'ome now and come back with money what hasn't slipped through a hole in yer pocket, while I mind yer bag of spuds and cabbage.'

'Oh, let me take 'em, won't yer, missus?' said the girl anxiously. 'I did have a tanner, honest I did.'

'Well, yer ain't got it now, 'ave yer?' said Ma Earn-shaw. A body had to harden her heart or they'd be at it all the time. 'No, I'll 'ave to take them veg back, dearie, or sell the rags orf me back to keep meself alive.'

'Oh, I can't go 'ome and say I lost the tanner,' said the girl, and turned to look pleadingly at Sammy. Sammy busied himself rearranging some vases, and wished Bert would turn up. He was late as it was.

'Mister?'

'Roll up,' Sammy called to wandering shoppers, 'roll up. We got plates for fried onions, so don't mind yer bunions, just roll up for bargains and pay us in farthings.'

'Mister?'

Sammy gave her a reluctant look. She was wistful and woebegone. And she was poor. Her black skirt was patched, her white blouse limp with age. Her boots were cracked and her legs bare of either socks or stockings. She might have been twelve, she might have been sixteen. Her elfin face was pale, her eyes hungry. The black ribbon tying her fair, pigtailed hair was cheap and tired-looking. Sammy frowned, for her hungry eyes were blue, bluer than his own, and they were misty with desperation.

'I'm busy,' he said.

The girl gazed up into eyes that seemed angelic. Sammy had made full use of them from the shrewd age of eleven. They had persuaded many a housewife to give him jobs to do, jobs that often did not really need doing. And when appealing for a penny for the guy on November 5th, he had sometimes collected small

51

fortunes in halfpennies and pennies. He had hoarded his gains, and had never been known to spend anything except in an emergency or for family birthdays. Christmas was a terrible drain on his pocket, for Christmas meant buying presents for all the family, and that now included his sister-in-law Emily.

'Mister—'

'Sorry,' said Sammy, wishing she'd take her wistful eyes off him.

'Oh, but couldn't yer loan me, mister, just for the taters an' cabbage? I'll pay yer back tomorrer.'

'Your family's hard up?'

'Terrible 'ard up,' she said, anxiety dark in her eyes.

'So am I,' said Sammy.

'Oh, I just don't know 'ow I'm goin' to tell me mum and dad I lost that tanner.'

Sammy frowned again, at himself.

'D'you have to keep looking at me?' he asked.

'Mister, if yer could loan me, I'll come back and pay yer soon as I can, honest I will,' she said in desperation.

Sammy looked at his watch. He had a family commitment, and needed to be away in not less than five minutes. That Bert was a good-for-nothing at timekeeping.

'Dead honest, are you?' he said.

'Mister, cross my 'eart.'

'And you've had schooling?'

'Course I have, at St John's Church School. I left last year, I'm fifteen now. Oh, mister, could yer—'

'How much is one and tuppence added to fourpence three farthings?' asked Sammy, touched more than he knew he should be by having attended St John's himself.

'One and sixpence three farthings,' she said.

'And if you sold something for sevenpence farthing, how much change would yer give for a florin?'

'One and fourpence three farthings,' said Susie Brown, quick as lightning. 'Mister, are yer goin' to loan me?'

52

'What's eleven times eleven?' asked Sammy. That was always a teaser.

' 'Undred and twenty-one,' said Susie.

'Well, good for you,' said Sammy. 'All right, then, would you like to look after my stall till my partner Bert turns up? Know how to serve a customer, do you?'

'Oh, honest I do, I've 'elped behind stalls lots.'

'Well, I'll give you a tanner. It might only be a few minutes of minding before Bert turns up, but I've said a tanner and a tanner it'll be.' Sammy knew he had just made a hundred per cent profit on a load of brass and copper. He had sources and outlets that Ernie didn't. 'Can I trust yer?'

'Mister, oh, yer can trust me to me dying day,' she said, and her hungry blue eyes shone.

'The prices are marked on the boxes and trays,' said Sammy. They were his starting prices, but he didn't say so. 'Don't let anyone diddle yer.' Sammy knew Ma Earnshaw would keep an eye on her, a sharp eye. 'Hold on, you sure you're fifteen? I don't want the market bobby knockin' me off for employing child labour.'

'Oh, I am fifteen, really I am,' said Susie.

'I believe you. What's your name?'

'Susie Brown.'

'All right, Susie, I'll leave yer to manage things, then. I've got to take a brother of mine to hospital. Here's your tanner.' He extracted the coin from the morning's takings, and pocketed the rest. 'Don't lose it. Put it under that bit of Delft china there.'

'That ain't Delft, that's Birmingham,' said Susie.

'Oh, smart, are you, as well as honest?' said Sammy, then frowned again. 'Stop all this looking at me. Oh, all right, you're hungry. Who ain't? Give her a couple of apples, Ma.'

'They'll cost yer,' said Ma Earnshaw, 'and what's come over yer? Dropped on yer bonce this morning, were yer?'

'See she don't get diddled, Ma,' said Sammy, which

meant keep an eagle eye on the girl. He little knew how Susie's blue eyes followed him as he made his way through shoppers, or how she smiled as he disappeared.

He sat on the bench in the tiled waiting area of the eye hospital. There were several benches and other people. Hospitals always seemed to be full of people waiting. People obviously poor waited patiently. People obviously not so poor waited less patiently. Sammy waited with his mind on how much money this kind of lark was costing him. Still, he had had to come with Boots. Boots visited the hospital every three months for a check on his blinded eyes. Chinese Lady usually accompanied him, but had so much ironing to get through today that she had asked someone else to go. Emily was tied to her job all day, and Tommy was tied to his. Only Sammy with his stall was his own master.

Thinking about what the hospital meant, Sammy just hoped Boots's visits would come to an end one day soon. The whole family knew he carried hope with him on every visit, but Sammy thought, and so did Tommy, that Boots was fighting a lost cause. Few blinded ex-soldiers ever got their sight back. Chinese Lady would never listen to that kind of talk, of course. And Emily had to keep hoping because Boots was her husband and she was the breadwinner, and she didn't want it to be like that all her life. And Lizzy got into a temper if anyone suggested Boots had got to resign himself to permanent blindness. They all knew Lizzy was specially fond of her elder brother.

It had been hard for Emily, though, always having to remember Boots was blind, that he had limitations, and always having to consider she might never be able to leave her job. No one liked that very much. Sammy thought Boots couldn't like it at all. Emily got a little ragged at times, and a little irritable with anonymous eye specialists who never went much beyond sending Boots back home each time with comments like well, you never know, come again in three months.

Sammy picked up a copy of the midday edition of the *Evening News* that someone had left on the bench. He glanced at the front page. There was a rousing bit about the Prince of Wales, who was making a tour of Australia and New Zealand, and getting enthusiastic welcomes. Popular bloke, he was. It was his boyish smile that did it. And there was an item about Joan of Arc. The Pope was making a saint of her at St Peter's in Rome. What a carry-on, thought Sammy. She'd been dead for hundreds of years, she'd been roasted at the stake. It was a bit late making a saint of her now, wasn't it? If they'd made up their minds at the time, she might have roasted in a happier frame of mind.

What was happening with Boots? He'd been in there over half an hour.

Boots appeared then, a nurse with him. Sammy got up and went over.

'He's all yours,' said the nurse, 'but don't let him get drunk on the way home.'

'Believe me,' said Sammy, 'if I got so careless as to let him get drunk, I wouldn't take him home, I'd have to help him walk it off. If I didn't, I'd get me titfer knocked off, and then me head.'

'Stern father?' enquired the nurse, smiling.

'No, high-principled mother,' said Boots. 'So long, Mary.'

'So long,' said the nurse.

'Lead on, Sammy,' said Boots.

When they were outside, Sammy said, 'Same as usual, I suppose? Come again in three months?'

'Sammy old lad,' said Boots, 'I think we could pop in somewhere for a drink, after all.' He tapped the pavement with his white stick, and the tap seemed chirpy.

' 'Ard luck, mate,' said Sammy, 'the pubs are shut. And I've got business to see to, anyway. Half a mo', you got a special reason for suggestin' a drink, the same reason the nurse had for tellin' you not to get drunk?'

'Operation, Sammy. Next week.'

People stopped to look as Sammy took off his trilby hat and threw it into the air in a gesture of extravagant delight. It landed at the feet of a woman. She stared at Sammy, stared at the hat and picked it up. Sammy advanced on her.

'You gorn cuckoo, young man?' she said.

'Right first time, missus, I've just gone right off me chump.' Sammy took the hat from her. 'Ta. I'll remember yer at Christmas.' He popped his hat on jauntily. His blue eyes were bright. The right one winked at her. 'Good luck to yer, love.'

'Saucy,' she said.

Sammy winked again and returned to Boots, clapping him on the shoulder.

'What happened?' asked Boots.

'Me hat blew off,' said Sammy. 'Boots, they're goin' to do it, give yer eyes an operation?'

'With a sixty-forty chance,' said Boots, sounding reborn.

'For or against?'

'For,' said Boots.

'Well, I'll tell yer,' said Sammy, 'you get sixty per cent of yer eyesight back and the drinks are on me.'

'If I get as much as that back,' said Boots, 'I'll stand treat.'

'No, it ought to be my pleasure,' said Sammy. 'Still, if you insist. Holy Joe, wait till Em'ly and Chinese Lady hear the news.'

Around the supper table that evening sat Chinese Lady, Sammy, Tommy, Emily and Boots. The evening sun slanted in through the kitchen's bay windows, and outside the windows dust danced like tiny golden specks. The family couldn't stop talking about the forthcoming operation.

'God's in his heaven, Em'ly,' said Chinese Lady.

'You mean He's been on holiday and forgot Boots till now?' enquired Tommy, who had grown into a handsome young man of twenty.

'We don't want them kind of remarks, thank you,' said Chinese Lady, 'we want a bit of real hope and gratitude.'

'Boots, it's got to be real hope now, hasn't it?' said Emily, who was coming up to twenty-two. She was still peaky-faced but very much the young woman now, and she dressed her auburn hair in stylish magnificence. She and Boots had been married three and a half years, and it hadn't been easy. She didn't know how she could have managed without the help of Chinese Lady, who ran the house and looked after the family without ever a grumble. Emily was just a little tired of her role as breadwinner. It could be wearing with its implication of possible permanency. And Boots's pension wasn't a lot, really, and they never had much money to spare. They paid Chinese Lady rent for the two rooms they had upstairs, and also gave her money for the house-keeping expenses. If Boots did recover his sight enough to help him get some kind of job, her own job would feel less of a responsibility to her. She could enjoy it more. Not that Boots had been difficult to live with, he didn't complain or have aggravating moods. He'd put up with things very well, really. All the same, it had been a bit of a strain. 'The specialist said you'd got a good chance, didn't he?'

'I think I heard the nurse say I might have a good chance of seeing the Derby,' murmured Boots, thinking the waiting period between now and next week was going to feel like a restless year. Weaving baskets by touch was all he was good for at the moment, and he had moments when he soberly reflected on whether or not he'd been fair to Emily in asking her to marry him. It was more than a man ought to have asked of a woman's compassion, and he knew some men of the blind fraternity would not even have suggested it. He also knew Emily had accepted his proposal in a mood of extreme compassion. He felt he had begun to hold her back. Emily had character and a quick intelligence, and could be making much more of her life than she was at present, especially as there was no question of having children.

She had had the sense and foresight during the last year of the war, while still at her factory job, to attend evening classes at a Kennington school and to learn what Chinese Lady called new-fangled typing. She had passed with flying colours, at eighty words a minute. It enabled her, immediately after the war, and when the labour market was in a state of flux, to secure a job as copy typist in the town hall in Walworth Road. It thrilled her, it improved her standing and gave her burgeoning self-confidence an extra lift. She could walk to work in five minutes, and typing kept her hands nice. He knew she was no longer the girl who had breathlessly begged him to help her face up to the perils of shopping in Gamages ladies' wear department. Emily had became a mature young woman.

'Yer know,' mused Sammy, 'I've got a feeling in me bones.'

'Oh, not now, not at a time like this,' said Chinese Lady, mind wholly on Boots's operation, 'and you can't be rheumaticky at your age.'

'Cripple 'is rich future, that would,' said Tommy, who had a job with an engineering company in Bermondsey. It wasn't well paid, but it was steady, and he knew he was lucky to have it when there were so many unemployed ex-servicemen about.

'It ain't that kind of feeling,' said Sammy, 'it's astrerlogical.'

'Sammy, you idiot, you can't have that kind of feeling in your bones,' said Emily. 'Astrer – what you said – is something to do with Old Moore's Almanack.'

'Well, Old Moore's Almanack is telling me Boots's

luck has turned,' said Sammy. 'I'll bet yer a tanner on it. Well, thruppence, say.'

'As much as thruppence?' said Boots, whose eyes never looked blank and sightless, although during his first days back home they were red-rimmed when he awoke in the mornings. 'Sammy, that must be quite a feeling you've got.'

'It's in me bones,' said Sammy, doing his best to help Boots approach the operation with optimism and confidence. He was a believer in self-conviction.

'Well, I 'ope—' Emily stopped. She felt they shouldn't talk on and on about it. They were all trying to make wishful thinking do the work of the operation. Wishful thinking was a bit like inviting trouble. Boots hadn't said too much himself, and she understood that. She guessed that the kind of hope he was experiencing had to be painful.

Chinese Lady came in with what she considered was the only suitable declaration, the only right one.

'We'll all go to church on Sunday and offer up prayers.'

'I'll offer mine up at the stall,' said Sammy. 'Sunday mornings in the market is lucrative.'

'Well, let's 'ope your feelings turn out lucrative too,' said Emily. 'Now,' she said briskly, 'who's going to be a help to Chinese Lady and do the washing-up? You and Tommy, Sammy?'

'I'm willing,' said Tommy, always equable.

'I got work to do on me account books,' said Sammy.

'All right,' said Boots, 'you wash, Tommy, and I'll dry.' He had long since learned to do simple jobs by touch and feel.

'Yes, you're best when you're doing something,' said Emily, and gave his arm a pat.

Sammy called at the stall next morning to check on things, and to give Bert a piece of his mind. Bert took a piece of his mind airily, which made Sammy give him another piece, tart with vinegar.

59

'Keep yer shirt on,' said Bert. 'I'm 'ere day in, day out, an' where are you?'

'I'm always here on me agreed times,' said Sammy. 'Other times I'm mindin' me own business. Your business is just the stall. I paid for the goodwill on be'alf of the partnership, and on the understandin' you'd cough up reg'lar instalments to pay off your share.'

'I've paid yer some,' said Bert.

'I'm informin' you that what you consider reg'lar I consider downright irreg'lar,' said Sammy.

'Yer'll get it all in the end,' said Bert, 'but it ain't exactly what I like, being be'olden to someone only half my age. As fer all that beefin' about yesterday, I had to see me sister, didn't I? So I couldn't 'elp being late back, could I?'

'Couldn't get yourself out of the pub in time, that's what you mean,' said Sammy, not disposed to refrain from speaking his mind because he was only eighteen. He eyed Bert's florid nose disapprovingly. There was just a touch of Chinese Lady about Sammy sometimes. 'Listen, did you see that girl I left in charge yesterday?'

'What got into yer?' asked Bert, tubby, red-faced and blue-suited. Sammy insisted they both wore suits. Suits gave a high-class look to the goods. No chokers or jerseys. People liked to think the goods were high-class, even if the prices were low. 'She said yer give 'er a tanner to mind the stall, and blimey if yer didn't go off and leave 'er to it.'

'You owe me that tanner,' said Sammy. 'I wouldn't have had to make use of her if you'd been back on time. I told yer, didn't I, I had to take me brother to hospital. Did she sell anything?'

Bert, making a display of the day's bargain, a dinner service with a carving knife included gratis, looked up at Sammy.

'Well, I got to admit she did,' he said. ' 'Alf a Windsor

60

tea service, six dinner plates, and cups and saucers outer the job lot. Except she said the tea service wasn't Windsor, cheeky puss.'

'What?'

'Straight up,' said Bert. 'I told 'er it'ud got the castle on it, and she said it still wasn't—'

'Never mind that,' said Sammy. 'What time did you turn up?'

'Say ten past one,' said Bert.

'That means quarter past, I bet,' said Sammy, 'when you should've been back at half twelve. I left at five to one. You telling me she sold half a tea service, six dinner plates and various cups and saucers in twenty minutes, and during Thursday dinnertime?' Sammy enunciated slowly and clearly.

'I checked 'er takings,' said Bert. 'All correct.'

'Well, she earned her tanner,' said Sammy, impressed. 'You got her takings separate?'

'Me? Course I ain't. She's got 'em. Said she 'ad to give 'em special to you.'

'She said what?' Sammy's blue eyes flooded with darkness and pain. 'I've been done, I've been rolled over and skinned.'

'So have I, then,' growled Bert, 'and my loss is comin' outer your pocket, Sammy.'

'Yer gormless haddock,' said Sammy furiously, 'why'd yer do a daft thing like lettin' her mosey off with the takings?'

'I just told yer, didn't I? She said that was what you said. Stone the bleedin' crows, you put 'er in charge, didn't yer? So she skinned yer. So yer ain't as smart as yer like to think, are yer, Sammy?'

'I'll get her,' ground Sammy, 'I'll get her.'

Bert grinned. It wasn't every day that slick young Sammy Adams fell flat on his face.

Ma Earnshaw, listening as she opened up her stall, said, 'I told yer yer got dropped on yer 'ead yesterday, Sammy. Didn't I tell yer? Well, it's a lesson to yer, and

61

yer'll have to grin and bear it. Did yer get yer brother to the 'orspital all right?'

'If it's all the same to you, Ma,' said Sammy, 'I ain't in the mood for solicitous conversation, and I've got business to see to in Camberwell.'

'Hurtin', are yer, Sammy?' said Ma Earnshaw.

'Considerable,' said Sammy, and went off grinding his teeth.

CHAPTER FIVE

On Saturday, the people of Walworth thronged the market. Saturday was a big day for the stallholders, the day when men who had jobs handed out the housekeeping money to their wives, and their wives swarmed into East Street to search for the best prices. Kids lurked about and darted about, picking up specked apples that had been discarded or the odd potato that fell.

On Saturdays, Sammy was always at his stall, using his patter to draw a crowd, and exercising cajolery to draw the money from their purses. By ten-thirty, he was in good voice.

'There you are, ladies and gents, there's a prime example of a fine Worcester tea service. You'll never clap your peepers on better. Still warm from the Potteries, this china is. Ever see a tea service more pretty? You could ask the vicar and his wife to tea if you laid yer tables with this stuff. Look at them roses—'

'You sure it's Worcester?' asked a woman.

'Missus, would I do a diddle on yer? I'm not here today and gone tomorrow. You know me. Here most days and every Saturday unfailing. Why? Because I'm one of yer, and yer don't diddle yer own. Cross my heart if this genuine Worcester tea service, consistin' of over forty pieces, don't represent something you're never going to see the like of, at my price, between now and the time when the good Lord comes to lead yer to the heavenly gates. I know I got a soft heart, but my customers are me friends, and that's what a soft heart's for, to bring quality goods to friends at prices that'll make yer weep with gratitude. Now, I—'

'Get on with it,' said a man.

'Don't give me a headache,' said Sammy, who was standing on an upturned wooden crate, 'or I won't know what I'm doing. I might even give these services away, which at my price I am, anyway. Now I ain't got fifty sets, nor thirty, so I can't oblige all of yer. It's first come first served for what I have got, just a dozen sets. Now what am I asking? No, not twenty pounds—'

'That's it, make me die laughing,' said the man.

'It's no joke, I mean it, I ain't asking twenty, nor even fifteen—'

'Well, yer wouldn't, would yer?' said a keen-eyed woman. 'Yer knows we ain't barmy.'

'I know something,' said Sammy, blue eyes full of winking light, 'I know I'm a mug. I must be, because all I'm asking is twelve pound ten – no, I tell a lie, not even twelve ten. Ten quid. There y'ar, just ten quid. You don't believe me? No, course yer don't, it makes yer think it's Christmas come again.'

'When yer gonner tell us the real price?' asked the woman.

'You're right, lady, ten quid's a dream price,' said Sammy, his smile casting blessings. 'So who's goin' to be the first to speak up? Come on, ten quid for a dream. Listen to that.' He flicked a fingernail against the edge of a tea plate he held. It rang. 'A Bow bell's Sunday chime, that is.'

'Never heard Bow bells,' said the woman. 'Yer can't, not from 'ere. Sounded more like a pudden basin to me, that plate did.'

'You're a hard lot, you are,' said Sammy genially, 'but I won't hold it against yer. All right, here's me final asking. Seven-ten. Now don't rush, you'll break things. Come on, tell me where else you can get a full Worcester tea service for seven-ten and I'll sell yer one of these for four quid.'

'Petticoat Lane,' said the woman.

'Done, missus, yours for four quid,' said Sammy. 'Free box and all. Wrap it up for the lady, Bert.'

'I ain't payin' no four quid.'

'You're a trial to me, missus, you are. But san fairy, seeing it's you, and seeing I can't help liking yer, three pound ten and that's it.'

'I'll 'ave one,' said a man, and that induced a like response in other people. Bert began to hand out full boxes from a pile under the stall. Sammy took a breather when a mug of tea was brought by the market runabout boy. He retired behind the stall, gulping the hot beverage.

'Mister?'

He turned. It was her, the elfin-faced girl with the dark, hungry blue eyes. They still looked hungry. Sammy put his mug down and laid a hand on her shoulder.

'Gotcher,' he said. 'You little Turk, you rolled me over.'

'No, I ain't a little Turk,' she protested, 'I've brought yer the takin's I took.'

'Eh?'

Susie was wearing an old brown coat that reached to her ankles. Sammy recognised it as a grown-up's cast-off. She dipped a hand into the right pocket and brought out a piece of drab linen knotted around coins.

'I sold things for yer, I did,' she said, 'an' I wanted yer to know. I brought the takin's yesterday, only I saw yer weren't here, so I brought 'em now. Mister, you were kind to me, so I couldn't do yer down. I wouldn't, anyway, honest. It's all there, eighteen shillings an' sevenpence.'

Sammy gave her a searching look. He was shrewd, acquisitive, ambitious. At only eighteen, he was already well-known in the markets and warehouses of London, and among wholesalers handling a wide range of goods. He knew the big-hearted Jewish communities that were

65

only too pleased to tip the wink concerning profitable bargains to any Gentile ready to play fair with them. Sammy had quickly learned that people who mattered did not mind if he thought charity began with himself as long as he was fair in a transaction and could keep his word. Being charitable was all right for the rich, they could afford it, but it was a hard life for everyone else. He was, however, very family-minded and would always lend money to his mother or his brothers at minimum interest rates. Deep down he did have a little of his brother Tommy's soft centre, but he guarded that with a ring of steel. He couldn't think why he had dropped his guard a couple of days ago because of hungry and wistful blue eyes. There were eyes like that all over Walworth. In this immediate post-war period, factories no longer required to manufacture the machines of war had laid off hundreds of workers.

It was something to realise this girl hadn't taken advantage of his moment of weakness, after all.

'You sold that much stuff, did you?' he said.

'I did, honest, and the money's all there, mister. I told yer friend—'

'Yes, I know what you told him.' Sammy's frown arrived, because there she was, eyeing him again in elfin wistfulness. 'How long were you at the stall?'

'Twenty minutes,' she said, which was what he had thought. 'Yer friend Bert come then.'

'Well, I won't tell a lie, that was good going, eighteen and sevenpence in twenty minutes,' said Sammy, always less the cockney when he was thoughtful or speculative. He turned, he finished his tea and put the mug down again, avoiding her eyes. 'What did you say your name was?'

'Susie. Susie Brown.' She watched him weighing the linen-wrapped coins in his hand. He hadn't attempted to count them yet. She hoped that was a good sign, that he had trust in her.

'Well, Susie, I'm going to give you another sixpence,'

he said. He paused before adding, 'You earned it.'

'Mister,' she breathed gratefully, 'that'll make a shilling you've give me in all. Oh, I ain't met no one more kind.'

'I said you earned it, didn't I?' Sammy felt slightly disconcerted at being called kind. 'Here, a tanner.' He unknotted the linen, found a silver sixpence, and gave it to her. She received it gladly.

'Mister?' she said tentatively.

'Well?' said Sammy cautiously, deciding to keep his eyes on milling shoppers.

'Mister, could yer give me a job? We got desperation at 'ome, me dad's only got a small pension. Come out of the Army with a crippled leg, he did. Mum keeps 'aving to go on parish relief.'

'I don't want any hard luck stories,' said Sammy. 'I'm a hard luck story meself, so's everyone else.'

'Oh, but could yer, mister? Say a few hours a week on yer stall? If I could earn about five bob it 'ud be a big 'elp to me mum an' dad. Could yer do that, could yer give me a few hours work? I'm good at selling, honest.'

'Stop breakin' my heart,' said Sammy tetchily, and tried to blind himself to her earnest eyes. What did they have to come into his life for, eyes like she'd got? What with them and her long lashes, if she had her eyebrows and her face done up she could get a job being photographed for Yardley's lavender soap.

'I could come any time to suit yer, morning or afternoon an' Saturdays,' she said. 'I listened to yer selling them Worcester tea services, and yer do a grand job, mister.'

'You got something to say about them?' asked Sammy, leaving Bert to see to things for the moment.

'They ain't Worcester, I bet,' said Susie, 'but I wouldn't say they wasn't to no one. You 'ave to make everything sound pretty, like. I could do that if yer'd let me work a bit for yer.'

'Oh, gawd,' said Sammy.

'Yer shouldn't take the Lord's name in vain,' said Susie.

'Eh?' said Sammy.

'Well, yer shouldn't,' she said bravely.

'I'm dreamin',' said Sammy. There she was, pale-faced, hungry and wearing a cast-off coat down to her ankles, with a family in desperate straits, and she believed in God. He wrestled with himself. 'All right, I'll take you on, Susie.'

Her face lit up and her eyes grew bright.

'Oh, yer got my undying gratitude,' she said.

'I'm not askin' for that, only for a selling talent. I'll pay you a penny out of every shilling you take. You sell five quid of stuff a week, and you'll earn yourself – all right, how much? Can yer work that out?'

It took Susie only a few seconds to say, 'Eight bob an' fourpence. Could I come every day all week?'

'Come when yer like,' said Sammy brusquely, 'you're workin' on commission.'

'I bet I could do ten quid a week,' said Susie, flushed and eager. 'Oh, that 'ud be over sixteen bob.'

'Up to you,' said Sammy, and again wished she wouldn't keep lifting her eyes to him. It seemed to interfere with strict business. 'I'll give yer tuppence a day for turning up, as long as yer put in at least four hours. It'll buy yer a hot pie at the pie and mash shop.' If she proved any good, she could take his place on the stall on the occasions when he put in weekday stints himself. That would give him more time for his side-lines. 'I ain't arguing terms with you, now or in the future. I've laid 'em down, and that's it. You take 'em or leave 'em.'

'Oh, I could kiss yer, mister,' gasped Susie in delight.

'You do that, and I'll sack yer before yer start,' said Sammy, who considered girls an interference with ambition.

'Mister, could I stay now, could I 'elp yer with yer

Saturday selling? Yer get lots of people Saturdays. Could I work for yer today?'

'Oh, all right, you're here, I suppose, but I'm not givin' you any tuppence, seeing you've come of your own accord. Only take that coat off. It's horrible, it'll frighten customers into an early grave.'

Susie, far from being offended, looked overjoyed.

'Oh, yer the kindest man I ever met,' she said.

'No, I'm not,' said Sammy, 'I'm a businessman, as yer'll find out.'

'Oh, yer look the part, mister, really yer do,' she said. Sammy was in a grey suit, striped grey shirt, white collar and natty striped tie. She didn't know when she'd seen a smarter stallholder, nor one with such lovely blue eyes. She took off her coat, revealing the same old white blouse and patched skirt. Sammy thought she ought to look a bit better than that. A china and glassware stall wasn't like greengrocery or second-hands. He'd have to think about what she looked like, for the sake of customers. He frowned, knowing it might cost him money to put her into an attractive overall. Blue. Dark blue. Might be an investment. Or he could lend her the money and dock her commission a bit each week until she'd paid him back.

He'd think about it.

Susie ran up the stone stairs to the third floor of Peabody Buildings in Southwark, where the family lived in a flat. It consisted of a living-room, a kitchen, a loo and three small bedrooms. She darted into the kitchen. Her mother was at the sink, washing the Saturday supper dishes, her father drying up. Mrs Lily Brown was a plump woman given to jolliness. But over the years, especially the war years, it had been hard to retain her plumpness and just as hard to keep jolly. Her husband, Jim Brown, had given up his job as a checker at the docks to volunteer in 1915 for Kitchener's Army. He had returned home in August 1918 with a crippled leg and a little pension. He hadn't been able to get his job back, but had been promised a similar one as soon as there was a vacancy. That could mean this year, next year, never. No one would have said the labour bosses at the docks were a caring lot.

It was a threadbare existence, living on his pension, for there were four children, Susie being the eldest at fifteen. She had left school last year at fourteen, but had only managed to get bits and pieces of work, and things weren't getting any better with so many ex-soldiers looking for jobs.

'Mum! Dad! Oh, what d'yer think? I've got a job!' In her excitement, Susie danced around the kitchen table, where they ate all their meals. With its dresser, larder, gas cooker, sink and table, the kitchen was cramped for space, but Susie still found room to dance.

Mr Brown, his once sturdy frame thinned by the privations of war and the strain of his crippled leg, limped a few paces and looked his daughter in the eye. Susie laughed in her bliss.

'We been wondering where you was,' he said, 'goin' out this morning and not comin' back till now, with supper over and all. We wondered what you was up to, it had yer mum worried.'

'I'm not worried now,' said Mrs Brown, 'not if you really got a job, Susie.'

'I 'ave, Mum, honest,' said Susie, 'at the china stall in the Lane.' East Street market was referred to as the Lane. 'It's the one I told yer about, where the gent that runs it give me a tanner to mind it for a little while. Dad, what d'yer think, I worked there today, from eleven till now.' Now was just after eight in the evening. 'Yer'll never believe, but I earned seven shillings and five-pence. I sold four pounds and nine shillingsworth of goods, and 'e give me a penny on every shillingsworth.'

'You earned 'ow much?' said Mr Brown.

'Seven an' fivepence,' said Susie joyfully.

'All that in a day?' gasped Mrs Brown.

'I did, Mum, honest. Ain't it lovely? Dad, yer can treat yerself to a glass of beer tonight. I'll give Mum six bob, shall I? Mum, could I keep one an' fivepence to save up for a frock an' things?'

'Susie, I got six shillings comin' from you?' asked the astonished Mrs Brown.

'There y'ar, Mum.' Susie handed over silver from her coat pocket. 'The young gent said I could work every day, 'e said I could put in an hour tomorrer morning before I go to church. Oh, ain't it like God's blessing?'

'Susie, you love,' said Mrs Brown, and hugged her daughter. 'You're a real good girl, always trying your best to earn a few coppers.'

'Give us a kiss, you little dear,' said Mr Brown, an affectionate and demonstrative father. He had little else to give his family apart from affection and a small pension. As a man who could not adequately provide for his family, he had his sad moments, but kept them to himself. He traded in optimism. At thirty-nine he reckoned there was still time for his luck to change. He only had one ambition, and that was to dress and feed his children decently, and to put a reasonable amount of housekeeping money in his wife's purse. In cockney parlance he called his wife his trouble and strife, but he thought the world of her. 'I can leave the beer, Susie,' he said, 'it ain't important, not at the moment. When yer ma and me can afford to go out and enjoy a drink together, then we will, and it won't be long. Our luck's turning, I reckon. You 'ad something to eat?'

'I 'ad hot pie and mash from the market shop,' said Susie. ' 'E treated me.'

Sammy had actually done so. He had been keeping an eye on her, watching to see how she dealt with customers. He saw her smiling at them, using her long lashes on them, and making regular sales. Her face and her eyes did the trick well enough, but she was so skinny and so badly dressed that she was a discredit

71

to the stall. In fact, a woman customer told him he ought to be locked up for paying starvation wages to a poor young orphan. Sammy said the girl wasn't an orphan, and nor did he pay starvation wages. Well, she looks like an orphan, the woman said loudly, and next door to starvation too. Sammy knew he'd either got to get rid of what was an embarrassment or do something else about it. It had to be something else. He wasn't going to be able to stand what those eyes of hers would look like if he gave her the sack. So at half-past twelve he handed her fourpence and told her to go and feed herself on a pie and mash, with a cup of tea. Susie could hardly believe such largesse and said he was the kindest gent she had ever met. Sammy told her to hoppit down to the pie and mash shop. When she came back, looking less starved, he told her he'd pay her attendance money of threepence instead of tuppence, and that she was to spend it all on hot midday food.

'Oh, yer real gracious, mister,' she said, 'but I only need a penn'orth of milk midday, and I could save the rest.'

'No, yer couldn't,' said Sammy, although he approved thrift himself, 'yer'll spend it all on eats. Or I'll sack yer.'

'Mister, oh, please don't do that, I begs yer.'

'Look,' said Sammy, with Bert away lunching in a pub, 'I don't want customers blamin' me for you being skinny, or I'll get boycotted.'

'Boycotted?' said Susie, a little upset at having him call her skinny.

'Means they'll pass me stall by. So you get some regular food down you. Pie and mash every day. Understand?'

'Yes, mister.'

'Stop lookin' at me,' muttered Sammy.

Mrs Brown, thinking about Susie being treated, looked hard at her daughter. Susie was getting pretty, there was no denying, and she had lovely fair hair. Done up a treat, like it should be, it would look golden.

'Susie, who treated you?' she asked.

'The young gent what runs the stall,' said Susie, 'the one that give me that sixpence. Well, 'e said—' She stopped. She just couldn't tell her fond mum and dad that he had said she was too skinny, that she needed regular food. 'Well, 'e said he was goin' to give me thruppence every day for pie an' mash. It's a rule 'e's got, Mum. I couldn't say no.'

'Course yer couldn't, Susie love,' said Mr Brown.

'Well, you make sure he don't take advantage,' said Mrs Brown, 'I never heard of any rule like that before. Still, he's give you a job, he must have some Christian feelings. How old is he?'

Susie puckered her forehead.

'Oh, about twenty, I'd think,' she said. Sammy, well-grown, and with a maturity acquired from his gregarious, enterprising contacts with all kinds of people, could pass for twenty. 'Mum, he's real swell.'

'He better be,' said Mrs Brown, and smiled. Susie was a good girl, and had sense too. She wouldn't let a treat of pie and mash bring her to grief. 'It's nice you'll be workin' for a swell.'

'I reckon he's fairly makin' sure you get some food into yer, Susie,' said Mr Brown. ' 'Avin' taken yer on, he won't want to see yer disappear by slippin' down a drain. I don't like yer lookin' so thin.'

'I'm not thin,' said Susie, 'I'm just a bit slender, like.'

'Slender's nice,' said Mrs Brown.

'What're the kids doin'?' asked Susie.

'Playing snakes and ladders, and kickin' each other, I shouldn't wonder,' said Mrs Brown. 'Jim, we could have a joint of beef tomorrer, and Yorkshire pudden.'

'We could, thanks to our Susie,' said Mr Brown. 'I'll get one from the market first thing in the mornin'.'

'A good job I took them takin's to 'im like I did,' said Susie, 'it give me the chance to show him I'd minded 'is stall profitable. I mean, I put the money direct into his 'and, instead of givin' it to 'is partner, an' I'm sure

73

it made 'im think more about lettin' me work reg'lar at the stall. Oh, ain't it a boon, Dad? Mum, if I did well, I could bring 'ome a pound a week. A pound, Mum.'

'That's riches, that is, Susie,' said Mrs Brown. 'D'you want something to eat?'

'Is there anything?' asked Susie.

'Course there is,' said Mr Brown, 'yer mum saved yer a slice of the corned beef with some 'ot potatoes.'

'Oh, I'll 'ave it, then,' said Susie. She paused for thought. 'I don't want to get too slender, not too slender, do I, Dad?'

'That yer don't, love,' said Mr Brown. 'I'd like to see yer growin' up into a young pearly queen, that I would, which yer could with your pretty looks.'

CHAPTER SIX

Boots had not seen his wife Emily since his sister Lizzy's wedding in March 1916, when he had been home on leave from France. It was now May, 1920. The war had been over for eighteen months, and had left scars on the country and people, scars visible and invisible. Invisible also were the fruits of victory. And widespread unemployment was a bitter pill. True, a few events had a bright note. Alcock and Brown had flown the Atlantic non-stop, the first men to do so, the Council of the League of Nations had met for the first time in London, and of all things, an American woman, Lady Astor, had been elected to Parliament as MP for Plymouth.

But Boots had not yet seen Emily, not since she had been his wife. And as his wife she had been affectionate and caring. He hated being handicapped, and had never been able to reconcile himself to a lifetime of blindness. He attended a clinic twice a week where he received Braille lessons, and four times a year he visited the eye hospital for check-ups. The Ministry paying his pension requested him once a year to fill in a form relating to his condition of the moment. Chinese Lady said people who made up forms like that should have been made to serve in the trenches themselves. At home he wove baskets by touch. For each basket sold he received a shilling. He averaged one a month, which Emily said was a godsend. Fortunately for Chinese Lady's domestic budget, Tommy brought wages home from his engineering job, and Sammy earned money from his market stall and from ventures mysterious.

The eye operation which doctors had tut-tutted only as a vague possibility had been performed at last. Emily had been emotional on the morning of the day he went into hospital, but Chinese Lady, who accompanied him there, had been briskly encouraging.

'You'll be all right, Boots. Don't you worry. Them pensions people'll see the doctors do a good operation. Well, they're bound to, seeing it'll save them paying you any more money. You know what our Governments are like. They don't mind how much they pay out to retired generals, but they can't hardly bring theirselves to pay anything to wounded soldiers. So they're bound to make the doctors do a good operation, like I said.' And so on. It kept Boots smiling wryly all the way to the hospital.

Chinese Lady was there now, seated beside his bed. His head rested comfortably on pillows, and he had strict instructions to give his eyes a peaceful time by not jerking his head about. The bandages had come off yesterday for thirty minutes, and had been removed for good this morning. He found it difficult to express his feelings at his rediscovery of visual life. Although his left eye offered only a blur, his right eye was a reborn wonder. He could see beds and patients, the brightness of light, windows that looked out on the world, and Wednesday afternoon visitors. A trolley. Nurses. White uniforms immaculate and crisp, and dark-stockinged legs. Imagine that, legs, and uniforms shorter than they had been four years ago. The nurses, two of them, naturally looked beautiful to him, although one was plump and the other angular.

And what else could he see? None other than his indefatigable mother, Chinese Lady. There she sat, very visible. Her almond eyes were quick between dark lashes. She often looked as if she was searching for something. Usually, impudence in her sons, prospects for them, a nice girl for Tommy, a sign of Christian goodness in Sammy, newspaper headlines that might mean an increase in war pensions, and indications of eventful happenings among neighbours. And they lit up whenever they took in the astonishing loveliness of her only daughter, Lizzy, a wife and mother.

Chinese Lady had a pleasant face, if somewhat careworn at times, and although she looked thin she still had an excellent bosom and surprisingly good legs considering she was in her forty-fourth year. Sammy, when he was twelve, had caught her adjusting her slip because it was showing beneath the hem of her skirt.

'Crikey, Chinese Lady's got corkin' legs,' he said to Tommy, and thereby earned himself a resounding box on the ears, for Chinese Lady never missed that kind of aside.

Chinese Lady also had an upright carriage. She always carried herself proudly, which she had a right to, being a highly respectable Christian woman and a watchful conscientious mother. At home she still looked after the comforts of Sammy and Tommy, and she also did many things for Emily and himself. She liked to give them the impression they were still young. She was inclined to say to her sons, 'Wait till you're older, till you're properly grown up, then you won't do silly things like that.' To Emily she would say, 'Now, Em'ly, you're still young, remember, it don't do to do too many things without thinkin' first.' Emily had always been impulsive, but was beginning to calm down now.

Boots listened to Chinese Lady speaking like a woman in awe.

'It's a miracle, Boots, that's what it is, a miracle. I can't hardly get over it. It's no wonder you look as if you can't hardly believe it yourself. The first Sunday you're home, you and Em'ly can go to church, and I'll come with you. It might make the dinner a bit late, but it won't do us no harm to give grateful thanks. The vicar stopped me on my way here, and asked me to give you his blessing and his pietous hopes.' She meant pious. 'When I tell him a miracle's happened, he'll expect to

77

see all of us in church, so Sammy and Tommy had better come too, if I can get that Sammy by his ear.'

'Never mind his ear, old girl, concentrate on getting his soul into a pew,' said Boots.

'What's that?' asked Chinese Lady, hoping patients and visitors hadn't heard her son being facetious when he should be sounding grateful. 'What's that?'

'Just a passing comment,' said Boots.

'I don't like to think you're being flippant when you shouldn't be. You feel all right, though, don't you?' Cautious maternal concern made its entrance. 'You been lying there very quiet mostly. Are your eyes hurting? And don't the nurses tidy your hair for you? It's all over your forehead.'

'My eyes aren't hurting, and I don't think the nurses do any hair-tidying for patients. And I am giving thanks.'

'That's something,' said Chinese Lady. She was wearing a hat, of course. She was still hardly ever without a hat on, even indoors. And mostly a black hat, as a sign of respect for her dead soldier husband. 'Boots, I think you must of done a bit of Christian good sometime in your life for a miracle to happen to you, though I can't think what, you always being a bit above yourself. Which reminds me to tell you to watch what you say to our Em'ly when she comes to see you this evening, after her work. I don't want you being flippant with her too. Em'ly's been a godsend to all of us, bringing money home regular and being such a help and all. Just make sure now you can see again that you let her know you appreciate her.'

'I hope I've never given the impression I've taken her for granted,' said Boots.

'No, course not,' said Chinese Lady, 'but these years have been a trial to her, not being able to live like a more unburdened wife, nor in any position to have – well—'

'To have children,' said Boots.

'It's what marriage is for, Boots.'

'I'll be nice to her,' he said. 'D'you know what a good-looking old thing you are, considering you're almost thirty-five?'

'Thirty-five?' Chinese Lady peered suspiciously at him, the ward alive with the chatter of visitors and patients. 'Now what's got into you? How can I be only thirty-five when you're nearly twenty-four?'

'Could be another miracle, I suppose,' said Boots.

'Sometimes,' she said severely, 'I've wondered if you didn't get more than blinded, my lad, sometimes I've wondered if it didn't curdle your senses. I'm turned forty, you know that, or you should know.'

'Time you got married again, then,' said Boots, 'you're still good for a cuddle.'

Chinese Lady stiffened her back.

'Well, of all the sauce,' she said, 'my own son givin' me that kind of lip. Don't you talk like that about your mother. I had my cuddles with – well, that's not your business.' Her bosom in her white blouse and blue costume was proudly firm in her indignation. 'What your dad would of said if he'd heard you sayin' things like that, I don't know, except he might of wondered, like me, what your operation's done to you besides lettin' you see again.'

'It's made me drunk,' said Boots. Everything was intoxicatingly new and beautiful to him. But he could not help wondering what the future held for his enduring, widowed mother. 'And the fact is, young Mum, you're very eligible. First-class cook, good figure, nice looks, corking legs—'

'Well!' gasped Chinese Lady. She glanced around appalled, sure other visitors must have heard. Fortunately, they were all absorbed in their own conversations, and Boots was in the last bed on the right-hand side of the ward, with no one in the next bed. 'Boots,' she breathed, 'if you weren't lying there helpless, I'd box both your ears, big as you are.'

'I'm drunk all right,' said Boots.

'Yes, you sound like it, you shameless bit of wretchedness. I never heard the like, that I didn't. That's what comes of joinin' the Army when you was too young to know what it would lead to, of mixin' with all them French girls like that mademoiselle from Armentières. I'm not sure you deserve the miracle that's come to pass.'

'You're a lovely old girl,' said Boots.

'You stop callin' me old girl, it's not respectful,' she admonished. 'You might not have come to sore infliction if you'd been more respectful, more reverent. I don't know where you get your insanctity from, not from me or your dad, I can tell you. How Emily's goin' to put up with this drunk mood of yours is a worry to me.'

'Why, isn't she keen on miracles?'

'There you go again,' said Chinese Lady, shaking her head again, but her eyes were bright.

The plump nurse came up.

'Is he chirpy, Mrs Adams?' she asked.

'Delirious, more like,' said Chinese Lady, 'I can't get no sense out of him.'

'Oh, he's been off his chump since he arrived,' said Nurse Plaskett.

'He wasn't like it when I brought him in.'

'He hadn't met his night nurse then. Nurse Saunders. She drives them all to drink. Has he told you she's a raving beauty? No, of course he wouldn't, would he? He hasn't seen her yet.'

'I've had the pleasure of talking to her,' said Boots.

'Well, I don't know, I'm sure,' said Chinese Lady, slightly confused. 'But it's still a miracle what the doctors done for him. What did they do?'

'Scraped him,' said Nurse Plaskett. She patted the pillows and gave Boots a clinical look. 'Don't lark about, don't get out of bed, don't do any jumps, and don't try fox-trotting with Nurse Saunders tonight or I'll bite your head off.'

'He needs telling,' said Chinese Lady. 'Needs his hair combed too. Do you mean they scraped his eyes?'

'Good as,' said Nurse Plaskett. 'His left eye wasn't too happy about it, but his right one is blissful.'

'I think my derriere's flattening out, though,' said Boots, who had been on his back longer than was comfortable.

'Oh, we'll knock that back into shape before you leave,' said Nurse Plaskett.

'I don't know about derriere, whatever that means,' said Chinese Lady, 'but I'm sure he's grateful for his deliv'rance. You mustn't take too much notice of the things he says. He's always had more to say than he should. I expect he'll calm down a bit. His wife's comin' this evening to see him.'

'Then I'll tell Nurse Saunders to comb his hair and make him look pretty,' said Nurse Plaskett.

'Pretty?' said Chinese Lady, not too sure she liked the sound of that.

'Miracles happen all the time in this hospital,' said Nurse Plaskett.

'I'd like to pass on that one,' said Boots.

'Carry on, sailor,' she said, and gave the pillows another pat before moving away.

'You're not a sailor,' said Chinese Lady, 'you're – oh, there's Lizzy.' Her eyes grew warm as Lizzy came through the ward. Lizzy was her pride and joy, for Lizzy was a lady. In her cream raincoat and brimmed hat of brown, she looked like one. As a girl she had been exceptionally pretty. As a young married woman approaching twenty-two, she was quite lovely, with glossy chestnut hair and brown eyes. Her husband Ned was in the select business of the wine trade, his firm supplying West End clubs, City business houses, certain public houses, and London hotels and restaurants. Lizzy loved her house and garden near Denmark Hill. She and Ned were the proud parents of a three-year-old daughter, Annabelle. She had lately made the discovery that she was expecting a second child. Some of her old Walworth friends thought she had turned posh, meaning snobbish. That wasn't Lizzy, however. It was people who disowned their humble beginnings who were snobs. Lizzy was never likely to disown hers. She was proud of her dead soldier dad, and even prouder of Chinese Lady. But she had always dreamed of a little house with its own bathroom. Her garden with its flower beds was an outdoor heaven to her. Ned and Annabelle adored her, and Ned indulged her. He had an artificial leg now, and was as active as he could be.

Lizzy swooped in a rush of cream coat. Arriving at the bedside, she stared down at her brother, her brown eyes searching his.

'Boots?' she said in affectionate hope.

'Hello, Aunt Victoria,' said Boots.

'Oh, Lor',' said Lizzy, forgetting in her anxiety that he was inclined to teasing, 'can't he still not see, Mum? Was the operation no good?'

'It was a miracle, that's what it was,' said Chinese Lady. 'Of course he can see. He's playing up, when he ought to be in solemn gratitude.'

'Hello, Lizzy love,' said Boots, looking up at his sister and taking in exactly what she was like after four years. A picture. 'Ain't yer swell, gel?'

'Oh,' said Lizzy, and sat down on the bedside chair, opposite her mother. Her eyes filled up. She bent her head and fumbled in her handbag. A hankie appeared.

'If you're going to blow your nose, blow mine too,' said Boots, 'I'm under the doctor, with orders to stay still.'

'Oh, yer clown,' said Lizzy, and blew her nose.

'Boots, stop your antics,' said Chinese Lady. 'Try to be thankful your lovin' sister's come to see you.'

'I'd give her a kiss,' he said, 'only I'm told my head might fall off if I move it.'

'Do you good if it did,' said Chinese Lady, 'do us all good.'

'I don't know that Emily's going to like finding me headless, old lady,' he said.

'Oh, yer stand-up comic,' gasped Lizzy, 'you'll be the death of me and Chinese Lady, you will.' But she leaned and kissed him, warmly and affectionately, on his mouth.

'Lizzy!' It was a shocked whisper from Chinese Lady. 'Lizzy, don't you kiss your brother like that. It's – it's incestry. And there's people lookin'.'

'Boots, oh, I'm so happy for you,' said Lizzy, tears brimming. Lizzy was a romantic, and a sentimental one. 'Mum, it's wonderful, isn't it?'

'A miracle, like I said,' nodded Chinese Lady, who was never going to believe it wasn't.

'Em'ly will dance on the ceiling,' said Lizzy.

'It'll make her life more unburdened,' said Chinese Lady.

'There'll be no stoppin' him now,' said Lizzy, 'he'll be knockin' on the front door of Buckingham Palace and invitin' himself to tea.'

'He'll get hisself locked up if he does,' said Chinese Lady.

'Oh, he'd talk his way out of it,' said Lizzy. 'But imagine it, Mum, he can see again. It's a worry lifted from all our shoulders. Ned'll be so glad he'll probably get drunk.'

'I hope not,' said Chinese Lady. She and Lizzy were talking across Boots now. He didn't mind. He was in contented wonder that he could see them. 'It might make Ned act like Boots. We don't want two like Boots in the fam'ly.'

'I feel like I could drink a whole bottle of port meself,' said Lizzy.

'Anyone brought any grapes?' asked Boots mildly.

'I mean, him being cured after four years, Mum,' said Lizzy.

'He's not been cured all over, only his eyes,' said Chinese Lady.

'Still, Em'ly's goin' to be over the moon about his eyes,' said Lizzy.

'She will be if he don't treat her flippant,' said Chinese Lady. 'And they can—' Chinese Lady leaned over the patient. Lizzy leaned from the opposite side. Chinese Lady whispered.

'Oh, yes, they just couldn't before, not with Em'ly havin' to work,' said Lizzy. 'Did you tell him I'm going to have another?'

'Yes, she told me,' interposed Boots, 'and good luck, Lizzy. If you'd brought Annabelle I could have had my first look at her.'

'I expect he'll be able to get a respectable job clerking in a bank now,' said Chinese Lady. 'That'll make things easier for Em'ly.'

'Sammy told me he's thinking of helping Boots,' said Lizzy.

'Well, I don't know I want Boots livin' off Sammy's charity.'

'Sammy's charity?' said Lizzy. 'That's a laugh.'

'If you'd brought my niece Annabelle,' said Boots loudly, 'I could have had—'

'Oh, dearie me,' said Nurse Plaskett, appearing again, 'what are you shouting about, Sergeant Adams?'

'Ex-Sergeant Adams,' said Boots, 'and I'm trying to make myself heard. This is my sister Eliza. She's the mother of Annabelle. I've never seen Annabelle. I've been trying to point out that if Lizzy had brought her—'

'You've been wasting your breath,' said Nurse Plaskett.

'That's not news,' said Boots, 'that's old hat. Perhaps you could speak up for me?'

'I mean no children allowed except on Sunday afternoons. So don't shout at your sister. And watch yourself when Nurse Saunders comes on duty this evening. She says you've been standing her on her head.' And Nurse Plaskett, with a smile for Lizzy and Chinese Lady, went on her plumply busy way again.

'Boots,' said Chinese Lady suspiciously, 'what've

you been up to with the night nurses here?'

'Oh, just groping blindly around,' said Boots, 'but I'm better now.'

Lizzy clapped a hand to her mouth to smother giggles. Chinese Lady's severe look arrived.

'I sometimes wonder if the hospital give me the right baby after you was born, Boots,' she said. 'Your dad would never of believed we could give birth to a comic.'

'Real miracle that would have been,' he said, 'you and Dad giving birth.'

'Don't you have no respect at all?' asked Chinese Lady, and cast a mildly disapproving look at Lizzy, who was using her hankie to smother more giggles. 'I'm surprised at you, Lizzy, sittin' there and lettin' your comedian brother cast unrespectable aspersions.'

'Oh, Mum, let's be joyful,' said Lizzy, and the faintest smile parted Chinese Lady's firm mouth. 'I'll come again on Sunday, Boots, with Ned and Annabelle. That suit yer Lordship?'

'Did anyone bring any grapes?' asked his Lordship.

He came out of a doze later that day. The ward was full of warm evening light. All light was magical. He heard voices, the voices of evening visitors. He heard a well-known voice close by.

'No, can he really see?' Emily's voice, as clear as a bell. 'His mother said he could. But can he see properly?'

'Very properly, Mrs Adams.' That was Nurse Saunders, known to him so far only by voice. 'It's his tongue that's doubtful. What's it like to live with?'

'Pardon?' Emily sounded uncertain.

'Just my fun, Mrs Adams. As far as his eyes are concerned, his left one needs time, his right one's excellent. At least, that's what I've been told. He's been asleep since I came on duty.'

'Is his cure permanent or will he go blind again later on?' asked Emily.

'He'd better not,' said Nurse Saunders. 'We'll kill him if he does. We don't like any of our good work undone.'

'I'll take a look at him,' said Emily. She arrived at the bedside. 'Boots?'

Boots opened his eyes wide. There she was, his Emily, his mainstay and breadwinner. It had seemed dreamlike, laying his eyes on Chinese Lady and Lizzy again. It seemed just as dreamlike, taking in Emily. Pictures played about in the mind when the eyes lived in darkness, and they were always as old as the duration of the darkness. Without any visions of life, of changing fashions, changing lines, changing faces, the pictures were always based on how people looked when one last saw them.

So this was Emily, eighteen when he married her and now not far short of twenty-two. She was wearing a dark green costume, a cream blouse and a green and white hat as a concession to summer. She looked well-dressed. The money she managed to put aside for clothes was spent wisely, on garments that lasted longer, kept their shape better, and made her look less plain than cheap things did. And in the long run good clothes cost no more. Beneath the hat, her dark auburn hair peeped in soft waves. So she still had a thin face, a peaky nose and a pointed chin. But her hair, her swimming green eyes and her good mouth were adequate compensation. And she looked more sure of herself.

'Hello, lovey,' he said, 'good to see you, damn good to be able to see you.'

'Oh, I'm so glad, Boots, so glad for you and me both,' she said, and bent and kissed him.

'I'm drunk myself,' said Boots. 'Take a seat.' She sat down, gazing at him with the deep relief and pleasure of a wife whose husband had come back into her world.

'I don't hardly know what to say, Boots. I mean, we all hoped, and I spent all this afternoon at work wondering if Chinese Lady would come back from 'er visit with good or bad news, like. Then when I got 'ome from work and she said a miracle had been granted, I just didn't know if I could believe it or not. I even had to ask that nurse if it was true.'

'It's true all right, Em. My right eye's perfect. And you're perfect in that outfit, red costume and navy blue hat.'

'What?' Emily stared at him. 'Me costume's dark green, and me hat's green and white.' Boots smiled and his sound eye winked. 'Oh, yer an idiot. Chinese Lady said you'd been playing up. Well, you can stop all those larks, you got to start livin' seriously.' Emily took his hand and pressed it. 'I mean, we can start livin' all over again and be a help to Chinese Lady together. You'll get a job, you see, then I won't have to feel my own job's a worry. And when you get a job, if you want, we can think about a fam'ly.'

'That's a nice thought, Em.'

'Well, we do get on together, don't we?' she said.

'That's worth mentioning,' said Boots. 'So's a job. So's a family.'

'Lizzy's Annabelle is a lovely little girl. You'd like a baby of our own, wouldn't you?'

'I'd like it better than someone else's.'

'Of course not someone else's, you silly,' said Emily.

'No, of course not, one of our own would be much better,' said Boots, still feeling drunk. 'What do we do, then, order it from Doctor McManus?'

'Oh, Chinese Lady was right, you're really playing up,' said Emily.

'All right, to make up for it,' said Boots, 'we'll have one next week, say, as soon as I get home.'

'Now what you saying?'

'A baby, Em. Let's have a girl baby. As soon as I get home. Next week.'

'Just stop it, will you?' said Emily. 'You're not daft enough to believe we can have a baby next week, and say what kind, are yer?'

'How about now, then, while I'm still in hospital? That's where you have 'em, don't you, in hospitals?'

'You're gettin' unbelievable, you are,' said Emily.

Nurse Saunders approached. She was a brisk, good-looking brunette.

'Well, what do you think of him, Mrs Adams?' she asked.

'He can see all right,' said Emily, 'and that's bliss, that is. But his head needs examining now.'

'So the day nurse said,' smiled Nurse Saunders.

'We've decided to have a baby,' said Boots. Emily, her hand still around his, dug her fingernails into his palm.

'I'm thrilled for you,' said Nurse Saunders.

'Not now, of course,' said Boots. 'Later on.'

'I'm relieved it won't be now,' said Nurse Saunders, 'this is an eye hospital.'

'He needs another operation,' said Emily.

'We'll give him one,' said Nurse Saunders briskly. 'We'll cut it off.'

'Pardon?' said Boots.

'Cut what off?' asked Emily uncertainly.

'His tongue. We'll leave everything else. Have a nice baby.'

Emily laughed.

On the day Boots was leaving the hospital, Nurse Saunders, back on day duty, was saying goodbye to him outside the entrance.

'Are there any more like you where you come from?' she asked.

'You wouldn't like to think there were, would you?'

'Oh, I don't know,' she said thoughtfully, 'we all like to have someone we can feel sorry for. Well, kiss me, then, I've been kind to you.'

Boots kissed her. Chinese Lady, emerging, stopped in shock.

'Well, I don't know,' she said.

'I can't smack his face,' said Nurse Saunders, 'not while his condition is still frail.'

'I never brought him up to take advantage of nurses,' said Chinese Lady.

'I forgive him,' said Nurse Saunders sweetly, 'he's an old soldier.'

A man whom Boots once knew, a lodger called Mr Finch, had told him years ago that the simplest woman was always one step ahead of the cleverest man.

CHAPTER SEVEN

Mrs Madge Stevens, assistant supervisor of the clerical staff in the Sanitary Inspector's department at Southwark Town Hall in the Walworth Road, put her head into the office where the copy typists worked. The girls had just arrived at their desks, and Miss Doreen Tompson, in charge of them, was already handing out work.

'Good morning, Doreen,' said Mrs Stevens, 'could I borrow Emily for today?'

'Of course,' said Miss Tompson. The request could not be refused. 'Emily?'

'Yes, Miss Tompson?' said Emily from her desk.

'Mrs Stevens would like you to help her today.'

'Oh, glad to,' said Emily, who liked Mrs Stevens. Madge Stevens was twenty-five and an attractive dark-haired widow with an understanding manner. Her husband had been called up in June 1917, and been killed in March 1918, during the last great German offensive. Fortunately, she had her job at the town hall, and just as fortunately she had no children. Widowhood accordingly did not mean hardship. She was a self-sufficient person, and her devotion to her job was above any feeling that she needed to go in search of another husband. She had been promoted to assistant supervisor on merit. She appreciated that. The merits of female employees did not always guarantee promotion.

In her office, she produced a notice she had carefully put together.

'Do you think, Emily, you could print this out in

capitals, using duplicating ink, transfer it to a jelly and run off three hundred copies? It's not exactly an intellectual challenge, I know, but I'd like it printed neatly and clearly, and I'm asking you because I know you'll do a good job and not take all week.'

'Love to do it, be a nice change from typin',' said Emily, studying the notice. 'Oh, lor', it's about vermin.'

'Yes. It's to be distributed to shops, mainly food shops. Grocers, bakers, butchers, fish and chips, refreshment places and so on – oh, and sweet shops too. It's warning them about the upsurge in vermin since the war, and offering this department's help. I'd like our messenger to get it distributed quickly.'

'I'm all yours, Mrs Stevens, and it's a pleasure,' said Emily.

'My, you are lively these days,' smiled Mrs Stevens, who was fond of Emily, an excellent worker and a rather engaging young lady, even if she couldn't be called beautiful. 'Is this because of your husband?'

Emily's eyes danced.

'He's comin' home today,' she said. 'His mother's goin' to the hospital to make sure he gets home safely. Oh, yer know, Mrs Stevens, I feel like our life is startin' all over again. Our married life, I mean.'

'Well, it's a wonderful thing to have happened, a man regaining his sight,' smiled Mrs Stevens. 'I'm very glad for you, Emily, and I wish you luck. Except—' She smiled again. 'Except I hope we don't lose you.'

The tram rocked over the steel lines on its way down Walworth Road from the Elephant and Castle. Boots observed the passing scene, the scene he knew so well but had been denied sight of for four years. Three-storeyed houses, built in Victorian times, were grey-fronted, but so were most edifices, whatever their original colour. The soot and grime of Southwark were all-pervading. There was some colour, however, in the huge advertisement for Galloway's Cough Syrup painted on one side of a building, and the well-kept lawn fronting the town hall did look beautifully green in the May sunshine. The town hall was the only edifice of architectural renown in the area. It was a proud thing, he supposed, for councillors to command nobility in the place where they pondered and made decisions, but he wondered why ratepayers should subsidise nobility for councillors and their staffs in advance of decent housing for people. It was a question of priorities, perhaps. If Walworth were a virgin wilderness again, with communal life just beginning, he supposed its elected leaders would consider the erection of a council castle the number one priority. Elected leaders did not like their importance to go unnoticed.

It was really no different, Walworth Road. The shops were just the same. Walton, Hazell and Port, the grocers close to Manor Place, still looked as if their window display was a treasure house to the poor.

Boots and Chinese Lady got off at Browning Street, with its working-men's club on the corner. It was on that corner that unemployed men assembled to talk about their prospects or lack of prospects. They usually met at midday, after spending the morning looking for work. Some would resume their search in the afternoon. Among those on the corner now were several wearing the silver-looking medallion signifying they were ex-servicemen. Opposite, on the corner of Manor Place, a barrel-organ was being played by a blind ex-serviceman. Boots grimaced, then stepped off the pavement.

'Where you goin'?' called Chinese Lady, hoping his sound eye wouldn't let him down amid the traffic of horse-drawn carts, new-fangled motor vehicles and the ubiquitous trams.

'Won't be a moment,' he called back, and negotiated the crossing safely. He arrived at the barrel-organ. 'Morning, Nobby,' he said to the man turning the handle.

The handle stopped turning, and the blind man said, 'Who's that?'

Boots saw his eyes were dead and sightless, hopelessly so.

'Only me,' he said.

'Very informative, I must say, but who's me?'

'Bob Adams,' said Boots. 'What happened?'

'Hold on, don't rush me. Bob Adams, you said? I don't remember – 'alf a mo, yes I bleeding do. You mean Sergeant Adams, don't yer?'

'Just thought I'd say hello,' said Boots.

'You and yer stripes,' said ex-Private Nobby Clark. 'All right, put it there, sarge.'

They shook hands.'

'Where'd you cop your packet?' asked Boots.

'I know where you copped yours. Trones Wood. I got mine a few days later. They did for the Major in Trones Wood. Pity. Bit of old English iron, he was.'

'Yes,' said Boots quietly. If he had looked up to any man, it had been Major Harris, a man of bleak, grey granite and an incomparable soldier. 'Like a fag?'

'That I would.'

They both lit up. From the corner of Browning Street, Chinese Lady watched them, her expression set.

'You pensioned?' asked Boots.

'The government says I am. The missus don't think much of it. It keeps the kids in food, it don't do much else.'

'Make anything on this lark?' asked Boots.

'A bob or two. Now an' again. It costs to hire the old joanna, an' yer can't play it where you like. You have to take turns at the best pitches, like up West or Hyde Park Corner. You all right now, sarge?'

'Yes, I'm all right now,' said Boots. 'D'you want a couple more fags to keep you going?'

'You got a job, you workin'?' asked his old West Kents comrade.

'Yes,' said Boots.

'What yer doing here, then, at this time of day?'

'Day off. Sergeant's privilege.'

'Well, seeing you were a bleeding sergeant, I'll take three fags. Just slip 'em into me chest pocket.'

Boots did so.

'There y'ar, Nobby,' he said, 'and so long.'

'Good luck,' said Nobby, and as Boots recrossed the road, the barrel-organ began to play again. The number was 'Pack Up Your Troubles'.

'You give him cigarettes,' said Chinese Lady.

'So I did,' said Boots. 'You can't pass 'em all by, especially not the ones you knew.'

'Not right, a blind soldier havin' to play a barrel-organ,' said Chinese Lady. 'The Government ought to be blown up. We need another Guy Fawkes, that's what.'

They walked down Browning Street, Chinese Lady occasionally glancing at her son in case his sound eye was giving him trouble. The hospital had supplied him with spectacles, the right lens of plain glass, the left lens of black glass. He wasn't wearing them. He was soldiering on without them, adjusting to the blurred vision of his left eye. She was glad he was doing that, she couldn't have borne to see her eldest son wearing glasses. No one knew the affection she had for him, nor the extent of her pride in him. Except perhaps Lizzy, his sister. To Chinese Lady, Boots was like his dad. He was manly. He was a disgrace sometimes, when he tried to be comical instead of serious, but he was still manly.

'It's just the same, Browning Street,' she said. 'Can you see it is?'

Browning Street ran all the way through to Brandon Street, the cockney heart of Walworth, where the scroungers and scavengers rubbed elbows with hard-working housewives who spent their lives striving for respectability. Hope was always present, hope that there was something good just around the corner. They had great-hearted husbands, or boisterous husbands, or husbands who took to drink. And some, a few, took to drink themselves in the end. Many, if they couldn't afford a hat, wore their husbands' flat caps, and put shawls around their shoulders in the cold weather when they stood gossiping at their doors. Chinese Lady occasionally wore a shawl in the house on a winter's day, but always put a coat on when going out. One thing she had never pawned in winter was a coat, her own or any of her children's.

Caulfield Place, off Browning Street, might have looked dingy, with its drug mills at its closed end, and a printing works on the left. But a pride almost ferocious made the housewives keep their doorsteps, their windows and their faded curtains clean. They fought a constant battle against the invading hordes of the enemy, the enemy being the smoking, sooty chimneys of Walworth, where fogs were thick and yellow. Few housewives could bear for a neighbour to step over a grimy stone approach to their doors. There were the slatterns, of course, but they were few and far between. Boots, more widely travelled than any of the family, had never encountered housewives with more pride than the make-do housewives of Walworth, who stood shoulder to shoulder with their husbands against everything life could and did throw at them. Their little Victorian rented houses were their castles, and they kept those castles fit to receive the most critical visitors, even if their cupboards were bare. Boots thought them hopeful, not envious. He thought them courageous, not whining. Their patriotism and their belief in God were unshakeable. St John's Church, Larcom Street, was full most Sundays and packed at Easter and Christmas.

And God help any man who robbed his own kind. Nothing was said about those who picked pockets at Ascot or Epsom, or did over a house in Dulwich, but any petty thief who went to work in East Street market was given short shrift. The local bobbies turned a blind eye to an act of local justice, providing there wasn't too much blood about.

'There, we're home,' said Chinese Lady, opening the door of their house in Caulfield Place by pulling the latchcord depending from the letter-box. 'I'll put the kettle on and we'll have a nice cup of tea. You all right, the light's not been hurtin' your eyes?'

'Not a bit,' said Boots, determined to let his still damaged left eye carry on its fight. He had no intention of wearing a patch. He closed the door and followed his mother through the narrow passage. He saw the enduring hallstand, with its narrow mirror and its pegs. He saw the wallpaper. Bloody old, it was. 'New wallpaper,' he said.

'What's that?'

'New wallpaper.' Boots looked into the parlour, with its Victorian furniture, including the old upright piano. 'New wallpaper.'

'You better talk to the landlord, then.'

'I will, and if necessary, I'll do it myself.'

'Now don't get critical on your first day home,' said Chinese Lady, and they entered the kitchen. Boots smiled. Kitchen equalled home. The range was alight, the coal burning slowly. There was a rice pudding in the oven. The room was warm, old, tidy and welcoming, its covered deal-topped table laid out with cups and saucers, sugar bowl and slops basin. The dresser was crowded with china, and the china had a gleam to it. The dresser shone. 'Me and Em'ly give everything a good polish last night for your homecomin', Boots. We didn't want your first look at things to be umpty.' Umpty to Chinese Lady meant disagreeable. 'Em'ly's a good girl.'

'I do know,' said Boots, and looked around while Chinese Lady went into the scullery to put the kettle on the gas. 'New wallpaper,' he said.

'Don't go on about it, there's a good boy,' said Chinese Lady, and he smiled. She wouldn't accept he was nearly twenty-four.

'And we'll paint all the doors and cupboards white. They've never been anything but a drab old brown. We'll paint 'em white.'

'They won't stay white,' called Chinese Lady.

'You can wash paint down,' said Boots.

'Paint costs money, my lad,' she said, and it wasn't one of her priorities, anyway. 'Kettle'll soon be boiling, it's been warming on the hob. You sit down and stop prowling about like some cat that's lost its kittens. Boots? You there?'

'Just going upstairs,' he called.

'Well, mind how you go. We don't want you rushing about up too many stairs when you're only just learning how to see again.'

'I got you, Chinese Lady, I'll learn carefully.' Boots went up to the bedroom he shared with Emily. On the mantelpiece above the little fireplace was a picture postcard of the Houses of Parliament. On the back of the card was a message from Emily.

'*Welcome home, darling. Love, Emily.*'

He smiled, he looked around.

'New wallpaper,' he said, 'and white paint. And God bless Emily.'

'Boots?' Emily saw him waiting outside her place of work. Delighted, she ran to him and hugged him. 'What're you doing here?'

'Meeting you,' said Boots, and kissed her, and other office workers laughed as they passed by.

'You come to meet me?' said Emily.

'I thought I'd like to. Should I have sent a note?'

'No, course not, silly. It's grand, you being able to meet me and not carrying that white stick of yours any more. You're all right, you don't feel a bit off colour comin' out of hospital today? You look all right, but shouldn't you be resting?' She was happy he'd come to meet her, but she didn't want him to overdo things, not on his first day out.

'I've been resting long enough in that hospital bed,' said Boots, 'and it's given my bottom a wearing time. Emily, I like the fact that seeing's believing. So here I am, seeing you. That's believing.'

Emily was in a light grey costume, white blouse and close-fitting hat. The long jacket buttoned to clasp her waist, and the straight skirt showed her calves. Her good-looking legs were clad in imitation silk stockings.

'Oh, it's goin' to be nice,' she said, walking with her arm through his, 'it's goin' to be a proper life now.'

'We'll skip the improper,' said Boots, 'out of respect for Chinese Lady.'

'All right, go on, be daft,' said Emily, laughing, 'see if I care now you can see again. I still can't hardly believe it, and I didn't expect you to come and meet me on your first day. Was everything all right at home?'

'New wallpaper,' said Boots, as they walked towards Browning Street.

'New what?'

'And white paint.'

'What're you on about?'

'Our home. Needs smartening up. New wallpaper and white paint.'

'But the money,' said Emily.

'We'll drag it out of Sammy,' said Boots, who felt reborn. To have come out of the darkness into light was still intoxicating.

'You'll be lucky. Oh, I don't care, I think we been as lucky already as the man who fell off the top of Big Ben and all that 'appened to him was that he passed the time on the way down.'

Boots laughed.

'That's a funny,' he said, 'where'd you get it from?'

'Mrs Stevens said it to me once, when a bottle of ink fell off her desk and only landed in her wastepaper basket.'

'I think you've mentioned Mrs Stevens before.'

'Yes. She's really nice. I did a job specially for her

today, and she was ever so compliment'ry. She's the assistant supervisor of all the clerical staff. I work under Miss Tompson, actually.' Emily hugged his arm as they turned into Browning Street. 'She's all right, only she don't have any sense of humour, not like Mrs Stevens. Mrs Stevens said she was goin' to think about gettin' me transferred from the typists' office to work d'reckly under her, which I'd really like. Of course, if we start havin' a fam'ly—?'

'Yes, of course,' said Boots.

'Which we'd like to, wouldn't we, soon as you get a job?'

'I'll start looking tomorrow, Em.'

When they reached home, Emily gave Chinese Lady a kiss. It was an affectionate greeting and also to say thank you for having gone to the hospital to see Boots home. Chinese Lady, never demonstrative, allowed the salutation to caress her cheek briefly.

'Well, there you are, the two of you, and Boots a whole man again,' she said.

'He come to meet me, Mum,' said Emily, 'and on his first day home. Ain't it disbelievable, Boots meeting me and not usin' no stick?'

'I hope he didn't upset you,' said Chinese Lady, her hat still on.

'Upset me?'

'Did he talk about turning the house upside-down doing wallpapering and paintin', and fixin' new webbing under the parlour sofa to stop the springs saggin'?'

'He did mention something,' said Emily, 'and it'll be lovely, won't it? It'll make our home look grand, it'll be the best house in the Place.'

'We'll paint the front door as well,' said Boots. 'Just the weather for decorating. Come on, Em, let's go upstairs and decide what kind of wallpaper we'd like in our two rooms.'

Her impulsive streak motivated her ascent of the

stairs. She ran up them, Boots following. In their bedroom they embraced and kissed, Emily warmly responsive.

'Speaking of babies,' said Boots.

'Not now, if you don't mind,' said Emily. 'Did yer see my card?'

'I did. Thank you, Em.'

'Well, I been thinking of you all day, I been thinking about you comin' home and seeing our two rooms for the first time. Well, the first time since we been married. I've kept them nice, well, nice as I could.'

The bedroom looked clean and tidy. The brass of the bedstead shone, the patchwork cover of the bed was colourful, the mahogany wardrobe and dressing-table gleamed with polish, and the floor linoleum was spotless if worn. Only the old wallpaper struck a wrong note.

'Emily love, you're priceless. And don't ever think I take you for granted.'

'No, course you don't,' said Emily, but he supposed there had been times when his fixation with his problems had made her feel he was giving no thought to her own. 'You just had your awful blindness to put up with.'

'While you had to put up with me, your job, the money worries and other things,' said Boots. He put his hand under her pointed chin, lifted her face and kissed her again. 'Well, it's a new start, Em. What d'you say to a light wallpaper in here?'

'With roses?' asked Emily.

'Trailing roses?'

'Lovely,' said Emily, and they went down the landing stairs to their own little sitting-room, once the abode of Chinese Lady's lodger, Mr Finch. It contained a sofa upholstered in worn but still acceptable brown leather, two upright chairs, a small table, a wall cabinet and shelves for books and odds and ends. It was a room they used now and again. They were both against cutting themselves off too regularly from the family.

They made their decision about new wallpaper, then Boots said, 'Speaking about having a family.'

'I told you, not now, silly,' said Emily. 'Kindly refrain, Mister Adams, from talkin' out of turn. Wait till tonight. No, wait till you've got a job.'

'Sounds reasonable,' said Boots.

The front door shook to a loud knock. They heard it open as a hand yanked on the latchcord. A loud voice battered at the air in the passage.

'Mrs Adams, you there, dearie? You there, Maisie? Is Boots come 'ome, is Em'ly 'ere?'

'That's me dear mother,' said Emily, 'she said she'd come and see you the day you got home. I 'ope you won't find her wearing.'

'Well, she's got a good heart,' said Boots, 'and I think I'll survive as long as she doesn't fall on me.'

'Oh, yer comic,' laughed Emily.

CHAPTER EIGHT

There were four at the supper table in the kitchen that evening, Chinese Lady, Emily, Boots and Tommy. Tommy's job with an engineering company near the Old Kent Road was under threat because of falling orders due to the post-war depression. He had said nothing to his family. He knew it would worry his mum, who thought it a disgrace that any government should allow young men and ex-soldiers to be out of work. She felt men only came to proper manhood when they were working and providing. That was what a man was for, to work and provide. What a woman was for was to be the strength and guide of the family, and she could only do that in the way the Lord ordained if her husband was working and providing.

Tommy, sturdy in his teens, had sprouted and was now almost as tall as Boots. Chinese Lady was proud that all her sons were tall, like their dad had been. Tommy was very good-looking too, and an untroublesome son. His nature was equable. He behaved nicely with girls, too nicely for the fast ones. Lily Fuller, who lived in the end house with her parents, had a fancy for him. Lily at seventeen was a corker in Walworth parlance. With her jet black hair, dark flashing eyes and rich colouring, she only needed to put a rose between her teeth to look like Carmen. She worked in a shoe shop near Camberwell Green. She wore smart, shiny black shoes herself, and always with black imitation silk stockings, and skirts Chinese Lady considered disgracefully short. To say nothing of jumpers that showed off her figure.

Chinese Lady did not intend to let Lily get her hands on Tommy. The girl was fast. She was always going out with different boys, boys who plastered their hair with bay rum and dressed flashily. Although Tommy did not show any sign of falling for her smiles and glances, Chinese Lady knew it was best to keep a watchful eye on him. She dropped broad hints about the fact that he was a nice young man who should be looking for a nice girl, a ladylike one. She had one in mind, but did not say so. Chinese Lady favoured ladylike girls. There were always some to be seen, even in Walworth. She was quite sure the United Kingdom was the most civilised nation in the world because it had the most ladies.

She was apt to compress her lips whenever France was mentioned, for it was her opinion that France exported French tartiness. Nothing could shake her conviction that all French girls were on a par with that Armentières mademoiselle mentioned in the wartime song. Tarty. She was sorry Boots had had to go to France to fight in the war, because she couldn't but wonder how many mademoiselles he had come to know. She had fought for years to keep her children respectable and to talk more proper, and she didn't want any of them spoiled by taking up with disrespectable persons. She had had no real trouble with Lizzy, who had a perfect gent of a husband in Ned, and she meant to have no trouble with her sons. Boots was all right now. He not only spoke the nicest of the family, he was also married to Emily, who had grown out of a bad start to become a good, caring and respectable girl. If Boots had been a bit tarnished by his time in France, Emily was rubbing it all off. He still sometimes said things he shouldn't, when Chinese Lady was quick to tell him it was time he cured himself of his French inflictions.

But that Sammy needed watching. He was too smart for his own good. What was more, he treated girls as if they were an interference with what he called his business ventures. What needed to be drummed into his cocky head was the fact that girls grew up to be wives and mothers, that it was wives and mothers who made the world go round, and it would only spin backwards if it was left to men. Men sometimes forgot what God had put them into the world for, to be loving and protective and providing to women. If Boots hadn't been providing to Emily, that was only because of his blindness. He could be very loving and protective, and there wasn't a happier girl than Emily. And Tommy acted very gentlemanly towards girls. But that Sammy, he was regular irreverent to anything except money.

She eyed her two sons and her daughter-in-law with satisfaction. Then she frowned.

'I suppose Sammy won't be home for supper again,' she said. 'I'd like to be behind him sometimes some evenings, to see what he's gettin' up to. At his age he's liable to put his fingers into pies too hot for him.'

'Don't worry, Mum,' said Tommy, whose brown hair and general appearance always had a naturally tidy look, 'Sammy's too sharp to get his fingers burnt.'

'I think we'll get him to pay for the decorating, less what the landlord allows us,' said Boots.

'You'll be lucky,' said Tommy, spooning creamy rice pudding into his mouth. 'He won't fall for no fam'ly hard luck story. It's nice yer got one good mince pie now, Boots, but make sure it don't see any halo on Sammy.'

'Boots won't see what's not there,' said Emily, 'he don't have a head as soft as that.'

'I should hope not,' said Chinese Lady, 'seeing he got his school certif'cate.'

There was a knock on the front door.

'I'll go,' said Emily, on her feet at once. She had boundless energy, and was always the first to react when movement was required. She was a godsend indeed to Chinese Lady around the house, without ever trying to usurp her mother-in-law's role as head of the family.

When she opened the front door, she saw Mrs Milly Pearce smiling at her. Emily stiffened. If there was one person who put her right out of sorts, it was Milly Pearce, a neighbour of a year. Her husband, so she said, was still in the Army, far away in Mesopotamia, where the victorious British were attempting to bring order to Arab countries released from the yoke of Turkey. Lawrence of Arabia had made post-war headlines in the newspapers.

'Oh, hello, Em,' said Milly, twenty-five, round of hips and bosom, and round of face and eyes. She always made Emily grit her teeth, Emily was sure she would aim her roundness at Boots now he could see. She had taken a fancy to him, and had been almost brazen about it.

'Yes?' said Emily haughtily, and Boots would have enjoyed seeing her with her pointed nose high in the air.

'Oh, I've just come to see how Boots is,' said Milly, a Deptford cockney who affected a posh kind of speech. Her smile was sweet with honey. 'I heard he came out grand from his operation. What a blessing he can see again, to be sure. He's a war hero, and I thought I'd come and ask about him.'

'I'll tell him you asked,' said Emily, putting herself stiffly in the way of any attempt by Milly to enter.

'I've brought him some nice flowers,' said Milly, and a bunch of daffodils suddenly materialised from behind her back.

'Flowers?' Emily's teeth ground in disgust. 'Flowers?'

'I took him some in hospital,' said Milly with sugary, smiling malice, 'only they wouldn't let me see him, they said it wasn't visiting time. Still, they took the flowers. I'll give him this bouquet now, shall I?' she pronounced it 'bokie'. 'It's some nice daffs. Does he likes daffs?'

'No. Just roses, cricket and football. And he's having his supper.'

'Oh, I won't stay more than a minute,' said Milly. 'It's just that I'd like him to have something pretty to look at now he can see.'

Emily could have killed her. She knew exactly what the sugary cow meant, that Boots could easily have married someone with better looks. And she was now ready, in that loose blouse, to as good as throw her dumplings at Boots's sound eye.

'He's having his supper.' Emily spoke cuttingly. 'You don't want to put yourself out standin' here waitin' for him to finish, not at your age.' Four years younger than Milly, Emily made it sound as if Milly was well past her best. 'I'll take him your bouquet.' She pronounced it haughtily – 'boo-ket'.

'Oh, if I'm interrupting, I'll put the daffs in water and bring them in the morning,' said Milly, her smile now bitter-sweet.

That's just what she will do, thought Emily, and while I'm at work.

'He's goin' out all day, I'll take them.' Quicksilvery, Emily whisked the bunch from Milly's hand. 'Well, goodnight, I'm sure you want to get back and see to your little girl.' There was a fine edge of sarcasm to Emily's dismissive remark. Milly Pearce had a five-year-old daughter called Rosie, and treated the child as if she didn't like her. Kids could be obstreperous at times, but a good smack could cure most tantrums. It wasn't right, however, to show unkindness to one's own child day in, day out. And little Rosie didn't seem at all obstreperous. Boots had a soft spot for her, even though in his blindness he had never seen her. 'You don't want to leave her alone too long, I'm sure,' said Emily acidly, and closed the door firmly on Milly's obtrusive roundness. She returned to the kitchen, hiding the daffodils against her ribs on her way through to the scullery.

'Who was that, Em'ly?' asked Chinese Lady.

Emily delayed her answer. She opened the back door, stepped into the yard and cast the flowers into the

106

dustbin. Then she took her place again at the supper table. Boots noted her slight flush. His Emily was somewhat put out. It was something very precious, the ability to see again, to take note again of Emily's little characteristics.

'It wasn't nobody much,' she said, spooning her rice pudding.

'Who's nobody much?' asked Tommy.

'Old Mrs Pearce,' said Emily.

'Old who?' asked Tommy.

'Yes, I said nobody much, didn't I?' said Emily, unusually brusque.

'She's not old,' said Tommy.

'Well, she's years older than we are,' said Emily.

Chinese Lady might have asked why Emily was obviously put out, but that was a question to which she knew the answer. Milly Pearce had been making up to Boots since she first saw him, a year ago, never mind that he was blind and married, and that she was married herself. Not that he'd ever looked blind, just himself. He wasn't what people would call a matinee idol, like Owen Nares, but he always seemed as if he had a smile or joke lurking, and Chinese Lady knew more women would fall for him than for his handsome brother Tommy. But he ought to be more serious and more ambitious, specially now he could see again. He ought to think about a little house with a garden for himself and Emily now that they could have children, which Emily had set her heart on. But Emily wasn't ambitious, either. She only ever wanted what Boots wanted. Chinese Lady hoped he realised by now how much he owed his wife. There were some respectable streets off Brixton Hill that had houses with gardens. That was where they ought to bring up a family. Brixton was superior to Walworth. It had a good market, stores like Bon Marché, and a theatre too, with good music-hall turns. Then there was the new cinema, where you could see Charlie Chaplin films almost every week, and it wasn't a fleapit, like the one in Walworth.

'What did she want?' asked Tommy.

'Who?' said Emily.

'Milly Pearce.'

'Nothing,' said Emily. 'I'll clear the table now, Mum, and put the kettle on.'

'No, you been at work all day,' said Chinese Lady. She believed there were things a man should do, and things a woman should do, but she didn't believe any mother or any wife should let a man just sit around. 'Tommy can do that.'

'I thought I'd been at work all day myself,' said Tommy, 'but I suppose I could just've been dreamin' it.'

'But you didn't help get the supper like Em'ly did,' said Chinese Lady, 'and you're not a wife who's just had her husband come home from the war.'

'I thought he'd just come home from hospital,' said Tommy. 'I suppose I've been dreamin' that as well.'

'It's the same as comin' home from the war for Boots,' said Chinese Lady, 'and I hope you're not goin' to start givin' me the kind of remarks I get from someone else I could name.'

'Me?' enquired Boots. 'Or Em'ly?'

'Em'ly don't give me remarks.'

'She gives me some,' said Tommy, 'like mind where you're puttin' your big feet and keep your elbows off the table.'

'Tommy, you be respectful to our Em'ly, there's a good boy,' said Chinese Lady.

'Chinese Lady no long time see me out of short trousers?' said Tommy.

'If this fam'ly's goin' to grow another comedian,' said Chinese Lady, 'we all might as well go and live in a circus.'

'Come on, Tommy,' said Boots, 'let's clear the table and wash up.'

'All right,' said Tommy good-naturedly, and he and

Boots got on with the chore, doing the washing-up in the scullery sink.

'Mum,' said Emily, 'you brought your boys up to be a real help.'

'Only right they should lend a hand,' said Chinese Lady, 'only right they should make useful husbands. Still, they've grown up good boys, really, and if their dad hadn't got hisself carelessly blown up, I'd of liked one more, and another girl as well. Fam'lies, they're what make the world go round, love. If there weren't no fam'lies, there'd just be dogs and cats, and a fine mess they'd make of parks and gardens and St Paul's Cathedral. Who's that comin' in? Is it that Sammy?'

It was. He entered the kitchen, looking natty in his grey suit, striped tie and trilby hat, the hat on the back of his head. Emily thought, not for the first time, what a good job Chinese Lady had made of her three sons. Once they had been put into long trousers they had never been awkward-looking boys, they had immediately acquired a manly appearance. Sammy at eighteen looked like a young man of twenty-one.

'Here I am, Mum, yer one and only perisher,' he said, placing a brown paper carrier on the floor. Its contents clinked. 'Watcher, Em. Hey, watcher out there, Boots, glad about yer new eyeballs. Chinese Lady got yer at the sink already, has she?'

'You Sammy,' said Chinese Lady grimly, 'I've a good mind to make you go out and come back in again, decent and respectable, not like a common hooligan. I don't know why I signed up to let you take on that stall, seeing it's not doing you a bit of good. And take your hat off.' Sammy tipped his hat further back. Chinese Lady fixed him with a stern look. 'Off, I said. Where's your manners?'

Sammy grinned and removed his hat, placing it on the old Singer sewing-machine.

'Me 'umble apologies, Ma—'

'Don't you call me Ma. That's common too. Just

109

because you spend all your time with heathen coster-mongers, don't think I'm goin' to let you get slipshod and unmannered.'

'I got you, Mum,' said Sammy, 'and you can take it as gospel, I ain't goin' to end up common and unmannered, with me feet stuck permanent in a dustbin.'

'Well, your talk's common,' said Chinese Lady. 'You can speak much more proper when you try. Tommy talks very decent, and Boots like he's almost nearly a gentleman, except when he's being a comedian. D'you want anything to eat? There's fried sausages and onions, with new potatoes and butter beans, keepin' warm in the oven for you.' The family was never short of nourishing victuals these days, with everyone contributing something from their wages or from their pensions, like Boots and his mother. Nourishing victuals were Chinese Lady's top priority, although she still never knew quite where the money went. Except there were new curtains in the parlour, and new bedsheets for all beds. And Sunday dinners were almost banquets.

'Fried sausages and onions?' said Sammy, blue eyes lighting up. 'I'll have some of that, old girl.'

'I'm not old yet,' said Chinese Lady, 'so you mind your cheek, my boy. Kindly sit down and I'll bring your supper.'

'I'll get it,' said Emily, and did so, placing the plate of hot food in front of Sammy, who set to with relish.

'Here, Boots,' he called, 'come and talk.'

'In a moment,' said Boots, who was making a pot of tea and rediscovering all the pleasures of being active and operative. He brought the pot to the table, and Emily set out cups and saucers. With the family all seated again, Boots said, 'Let's see, there was something I wanted to say to you, Sammy.'

'Good on yer, mate, you got yer eyes back in place, so me ears is all yours,' said Sammy.

'They'll get boxed, and quick, if you don't talk nicer,' said Chinese Lady.

Emily smiled. They were all cockneys, but Chinese Lady had always striven to make them understand they would never really get on in life unless they improved their speech. Boots had taken readily to improvement at his secondary school. Emily herself was always trying, and her place of work helped her because most of the administrative staff spoke nicely.

'Sammy don't – he doesn't mean to be slipshod, Mum,' she said.

'Me?' said Sammy, and swallowed a mouthful of luscious fried onion. 'I'm not slipshod, I can't afford to be, not as a businessman. Anyway, what I wanted to impart was me announcement that Boots has got to be celebrated, and it's me heartfelt pleasure to be in the chair. I've got bottles of Guinness for him and Tommy and me, and a bottle of port for Chinese Lady and our invaluable fam'ly godsend, otherwise known as our Em'ly. It's me royal contribution to Boots comin' home with new eyesight.'

'Eh?' said Tommy.

'Pardon?' said Boots.

'Guinness *and* port, Sammy?' enquired Chinese Lady, pouring tea.

'You got it, old lady,' said Sammy.

'You're treatin'?' said Tommy.

'It's me regal pleasure,' said Sammy.

'Didn't it hurt when you let go of the dibs?' asked Tommy.

'I shut me eyes,' said Sammy, 'you can stand the pain better that way.'

'Tommy, Sammy can be a gen'rous boy sometimes,' said Chinese Lady.

'I know,' said Tommy amiably, 'about once a year.'

Sammy, always impervious to such comments, said, 'I can't recall no occasion more celebrat'ry, except when Em'ly was joined legally to the fam'ly.'

'Sammy, you're sweet,' said Emily. 'Oh, and Boots 'as marked the occasion himself, he says we're goin' to have new wallpaper and new paint everywhere.'

'Do what?' asked Sammy.

'You got it, Sammy,' said Boots.

'Don't look at me, try the landlord,' said Sammy, pushing his empty plate aside and sitting back with his jacket open. Against his waistcoat the chain of his pocket watch gleamed. Mr Greenberg, the rag and bone merchant, had let him have the watch and chain cheaply two years ago. Real rolled gold, he said it was. It was Sammy's first and last venture into real rolled gold. Still, the chain looked good.

'We won't squeeze more than a few rolls of wallpaper out of the landlord,' said Boots, 'the rest will have to be paid for. We're all happy you're flush, Sammy. We know you won't mind forking out. For wallpaper, paint and so on.'

'I may be overcome with celebrat'ry happenings,' said Sammy, 'but I ain't daft.'

'Thirty bob should cover everything,' said Boots.

'Thirty bob?' Sammy's eyes darkened with pain. 'And you're all lookin' at me?'

'It's not a lot, I know,' said Boots, 'but we'll still be grateful.'

'I'm dying of hysterics, I am,' said Sammy.

'Now, Sammy, we know you can afford it,' said Chinese Lady, 'and the house will look nice done up like Boots says. We won't have no argument about it, there's a good boy. Let's just be grateful for the miracle that's come to pass. We're all goin' to church on Sunday to give thanks, and we won't have no arguments about that, neither. If we don't go, the vicar'll come round lookin' upset.'

'I can't leave me stall,' said Sammy, 'not Sunday mornings.'

'Now, Sammy.'

'But, Ma—'

'Don't call me Ma. Sammy, you haven't been to church since I don't know when. Em'ly's taken Boots now and again, and Boots has let her take him, even if he might of thought bitterly of heaven because of what the war did to his eyes. And look what's happened, he's been granted a miracle. We all know he's not perfect, what with his disrespectful inflictions and saying things that don't make sense sometimes, but at least he's been to church. So all of us are goin' on Sunday.'

'All right,' said Sammy, 'but if it costs me money I ain't goin' to say too many hallelujahs. Anyway, now Boots has got out of hospital alive and kickin', what's he goin' to do? Are yer goin' after a job, Boots?'

'I'll start looking for one tomorrow,' said Boots, and thought about how many unemployed ex-servicemen there were.

'Yes, do that,' said Emily, thinking of Milly Pearce presenting her sugary smile and female roundness to his sound eye. 'You can start out after breakfast.'

'You'll excuse me kindly, Em, I'm sure,' said Sammy, 'but I have to offer the opinion that it ain't right.'

'What's not right?' asked Tommy.

'Boots traipsing around lookin' for work,' said Sammy, 'not after all the money we spent on his middle-class education.'

'Pardon?' said Boots.

'We?' said Chinese Lady.

'Mind you, it was worth it,' said Sammy. 'Made a gent of him, our sacrifices did.'

'Sammy, am I hearing you correct?' asked Chinese Lady with a touch of asperity. She looked very much the head of the family, sitting as always with a straight back and firm front. She wore a white blouse with a high lace collar, a blue cameo brooch, a family present, fixing the collar. She no longer needed to go out to work herself, and was able on her birthdays and at Christmas to buy herself new clothes with extra money given to her by the family. She had not

113

been to 'Uncle', the pawnbroker, for years.

Sammy said, 'Mrs Pullen told me only a couple of days ago what a real gent Boots was, and what a blessing to hear what his operation had done for him. Being in a thinking mood at the time, it occurred to me what a fine shop manager he'd make. Shop managers should be gentlemanly.'

'What's on your mind?' asked Tommy.

'Well,' said Sammy, 'it's my pleasure to inform you I'm opening a shop at Camberwell Green.'

'You're what?' said Tommy.

'A shop?' said Chinese Lady.

'I don't believe it,' said Emily. Running a stall was in keeping with the family's status. Opening a shop was middle-class.

'I am considering Boots being my partner and shop manager,' said Sammy, 'But first I got to get the lease signed. Boots being over twenty-one, he can sign on behalf of Adams Enterprises.'

'Say that again,' said Boots.

'Adams Enterprises,' said Sammy, cool and self-assured. 'That's you and me, Boots, if yer consider it agreeable. I got the money and the brains, you got education and style.'

'I'll let that go, the bit about brains,' said Boots.

'Business brains, I mean,' said Sammy. 'Of course, I'll be a sort of floating partner till I'm twenty-one, but that won't stop me running things, and doing the buying. Savvy?'

'Chop, chop,' said Boots, while Emily beside him was holding her breath as the possibility of a job dawned.

'Sammy, you leading us up the garden?' asked Chinese Lady, keeping to herself her earnest hopes for Boots.

'I already signed Boots's name,' said Sammy, blue eyes angelic.

'That's forgery,' said Chinese Lady in shock. 'That's well, I never thought I'd see the day when my only youngest son would forge his brother's signature.'

'Now, Ma, it wasn't like that,' said Sammy, 'it was only on the letter I got Isaac Moses's daughter to type for me, the letter agreeing to take the lease at a certain rent. Boots being parlous with his operation at the time, I didn't want to obtrude.'

'Intrude?' suggested Boots.

'You got it, Boots,' said Sammy. 'There y'ar, Tommy, ain't I always said Boots has got style and knows all the words?'

'I'm not arguing,' said Tommy, 'I'm just listening speechless.'

'Tommy, I feel like that too,' said Emily. 'Go on, Sammy.'

Sammy went on to say he was forming a private company called Adams Enterprises, but in Boots's name because he was over twenty-one. He himself would finance it and come in legally as senior partner when he came of age. Adams Enterprises would take up the lease on the empty shop he'd had his eye on for months. Well, he didn't want to be just a stallholder all his life. He had useful contacts both sides of the river. He had filled in a form necessary under the Companies' Act, which he'd like Boots to sign tonight, and that would then allow him to sign the lease when it was ready. He hadn't wanted to copy Boots's signature on official documents as he'd been brought up by Chinese Lady to be respectable and law-abiding. He was going to call the shop Sam's Emporium. Did Boots like that?

'Ask me another,' said Boots.

'I like it meself,' said Sammy. 'We'll be selling WD surpluses.'

'Surplices?' said Emily. 'Ain't they – aren't they what a church choir wears?'

'No, surplus stuff,' said Sammy. 'Use yer loaf, Em, Sam's Emporium ain't in holy orders. I'm stocking up with War Departments goods left over from the war. Clothes and footwear and all sorts. Blankets, for instance. Mind, I got to buy in bulk and I got to get finance, and I got to fix that before the lease is signed. I got friends, of course, inclusive of Mr Isaac Moses, referred to by some as Ikey Mo, and is a gentleman. I'm buying in quantity and selling cheap. Ordin'ry wholesale prices don't offer me advantages. There ain't too much unused money about, but you can tempt people with goods brand new and cheap. Boots'll make a good manager for the shop, he's got a way with him and knows how to pleasure people, specially ladies.'

'Pleasure them?' enquired Boots mildly.

'Kindly don't say things like that, Sammy,' said Emily, 'it don't sound decent.'

'I just meant pleasin' to people,' said Sammy.

'All the same,' said Emily, 'he don't have to be specially pleasing to lady customers, just polite to everyone.'

'Well, Em,' said Sammy, 'it's the ladies who mostly got charge of what money there is for shoppin'. Like Chinese Lady. She's got charge of our money. Boots knows how to bow to ladies and how to talk to them. Mind, he don't have to act like Lord Muck as manager, we don't want that, we had it all when he was younger. Personally, I'm highly gratified the Army cured him.'

'You young saucebox, don't you speak of your eldest brother like that,' said Chinese Lady. 'Boots has got his faults, like all men have, but he's never been a disgrace to me or his dad, not like some I could mention. Still I'm glad you've come to be family-minded, and I'm sure Boots will take the job.'

'Course he will,' said Emily, 'but how much you goin' to pay him as a gentleman manager, Sammy?'

'Well, me kind heart is now goin' to astonish yer, Em. If takings come up to scratch, I'm goin' to pay him two quid a week, which is a hundred and four quid a year.'

Emily, who earned twenty-five shillings a week as a copy typist, said, 'You sure that's a manager's wage? A manager in a suit and tie?'

116

Tommy, whose wage was twenty-seven shillings and sixpence, said, 'Two quid don't sound bad, Em.'

'I ain't saying I wouldn't pay someone else thirty bob,' mused Sammy, 'but Boots is me own brother who come out of the war 'eroically blinded. I got to give in to me kind heart.'

'Two ten,' said Boots.

'Did someone say something?' asked Sammy.

'Yes, I think that's more kind-hearted, Sammy, two pounds ten,' said Chinese Lady.

'Someone did say something,' said Sammy, 'and it hurt my ears.'

Emily, controlling the excitement of high hopes, said, 'You know Boots could be a good manager, Sammy, I bet he'd be worth two pounds ten easy.'

'Stone me,' breathed Sammy, 'here I am, ready and willing to set Boots up in a job highly prospective, and I'm listening to me own fam'ly trying to skin me while I'm still alive.'

'Well, there's profits, Sammy,' said Chinese Lady, 'you could afford ten shillings more a week.' She could now definitely see Emily and Boots, and their children, she hoped, in a nice house with a bathroom and garden.

'Here, hold it, Ma,' protested Sammy, 'I ain't a bottomless barrel. I know I'm makin' it a fam'ly business, and I know the war done things in for Boots a bit, but I ain't his fairy godmother nor his Father Christmas, and Boots 'ud be the first to discline charity as a matter of principle.'

'Decline?' said Boots helpfully.

'I knew you'd agree,' said Sammy. 'Lord love yer, Chinese Lady, even bank managers don't ask for something out of the profits on top of their screw.'

'What's screw?' asked Chinese Lady.

'Wages,' said Tommy.

'It's what employees screw out of kind bosses who've given them their jobs,' said Sammy. 'Screw? See, Mum?'

'Now, Sammy dear,' said Chinese Lady, 'what hardworkin' employees earn won't be called screw in this fam'ly. It don't sound nice. And Boots is your partner, you said.'

'Only as a matter of convenient legislation,' said Sammy.

'There, you can talk very proper when you try,' said Chinese Lady.

'As for profits,' said Sammy cautiously, 'I dunno that there'll be any. It's a good managerial salary, yer know, a hundred and four pounds a year.'

'Managerial's middle-class,' said Emily.

'All right, two pounds ten, then,' said Sammy, 'which is the shirt off me back.'

'Boots'll take that,' said Emily, and Chinese Lady regarded Sammy with a light in her eyes that was quite soft. Her youngest son was a good boy, after all. Never mind that he was a bit sharp about money, he was doing something very nice for Boots, who had suffered four years of crippling blindness.

'Anyone 'ud take a salary of ten quid a month,' said Sammy.

'What's wrong with paying him two pounds ten a week, so it comes in nice and steady?' asked Tommy.

'A manager gets paid a monthly salary,' said Sammy. 'At the end of each month,' he added casually. 'It ain't like an ordin'ry worker's wages. Boots being a gent shouldn't be paid common wages.'

'My wages ain't common,' said Tommy, 'they're me life blood.'

'Boots, you ain't said overmuch,' remarked Sammy.

'I'm thinking, Sammy, that I like yer, old sport,' smiled Boots.

'You'll be me shop manager, then?'

'Course he will,' said Emily.

'You're on, Sammy,' said Boots.

'We won't be demandin' about profits,' said Emily.

'For your information, Em'ly, profits is for reinvestment,' said Sammy.

'What's that mean?' asked Chinese Lady, who believed in knowing exactly what any of her family were up to.

'You use profits to expand, you don't scatter 'em about,' said Sammy. 'Boots understands, don't yer, Boots? Good on yer, mate, I like an agreeable partner. We don't want Adams Enterprises to stand still, and maybe we can bring Tommy in later.'

Emily was exultant. She and Boots would be earning three pounds fifteen shillings a week between them. That was riches.

'Oh, ain't it been a happy day?' she said. 'Boots comin' home and able to see, and Sammy opening a fam'ly business?'

'I reckon it's time we drank to our prospects and the miracle operation,' said Sammy. The bottles of Guinness and the bottle of port were opened. Emily sprang up to get glasses. The celebration began. The talk was noisy and cheerful. Tommy said he'd heard a good story at work that day. Chinese Lady said she hoped it wasn't one of them stories. Tommy said she'd like it, and he told it in his amiable way.

'There was this nice lady who comes home from shoppin' without her doorkey. Seeing she'd left her bedroom window open, she borrowed a ladder and climbed up. A kind neighbour passin' by called to her, askin' her what she was doing. "I'm up this ladder trying to get into my bedroom," she said, "and I feel like a fireman." "Well, you pop into your bedroom," said the kind neighbour, "while I pop round to the fire station to see if I can bring you one." '

Sammy roared, Boots laughed and Emily giggled. Chinese Lady looked at Tommy as if she regretted having him.

'Is that supposed to be funny?' she asked.

'Well, ain't it?' countered Tommy.

'The sooner I get you to church on Sunday, the sooner

you'll have a chance to show holy repentance, young man, and there won't be no more stories like that in this house, if you don't mind, specially not in front of Em'ly, who's still young.'

Emily put a hand to her mouth. Boots eyed the ceiling, Sammy coughed and Tommy put on a straight face.

But for all her conservatism, Chinese Lady drank three glasses of port. Emily went one better, such was her gladness about the future. Boots watched her slowly becoming flushed and dreamy with well-being. He took delight in what everyone else took for granted. Vision. The dark fire in Emily's hair, the dreamy green of her eyes, and the kissable quality of her well-shaped mouth.

'What staff will there be in the shop, Sammy?' he asked, and his sudden reversion to business matters made Sammy look as if the question was against the spirit of the occasion.

'Have a heart, Boots, I ain't got unlimited capital, I ain't even fixed me needed financial loan yet.'

'I got you, Sammy,' said Boots, 'I'm to be manager, counterhand, window-dresser, floor-sweeper and general dogsbody?'

'Well, we all know you can do it,' said Sammy, 'we all got faith in you, and thank you kindly for your understanding. I'll look after the real headaches, like paying the rent, doing the cash-buying, and settin' it all up.'

Boots smiled. He knew, as many other people knew, that Sammy could add up. Two pounds ten a week was as much as he intended to fork out for shop staff.

'Where'd you get this port, Sammy?' asked Chinese Lady.

'Off-licence in Walworth Road, Ma.'

'Did you call me Ma again?' Chinese Lady asked the question mellowly.

'Only accidentally,' said Sammy.

'It's nice port,' she said.

'Lovely,' said Emily, lips looking dewy.

'Pleasured, I'm sure,' said Sammy.

There was another knock on the front door.

'Now who could that be at this time of night?' asked Chinese Lady. It was gone half-past nine.

'I'll go,' said Tommy, and did. Emily, for once, had not reacted. Emily was full of wine-induced dreams.

The caller was Lily Fuller, the girl who sometimes made eyes at Tommy. Clad in a tightly knitted beige jumper and brown skirt, her mouth carmine with lipstick, she flashed her smile.

'Oh, good, it's you, Tommy,' she said. 'Can I come in a minute?'

'Help yourself,' said Tommy.

'In private, like,' she said.

Tommy took her into the parlour and put a lighted match to a gas mantle. She hadn't been inside the house too often. Chinese Lady discouraged her. She gave the parlour a brief inspection, and with a slight wrinkle of her powdered nose indicated she thought it screamingly old-fashioned. Her parents were buying modern furniture on the never-never from Drages, the firm that advertised in Sunday newspapers. Her father was an insurance agent, with a bicycle.

'What can I do for you?' asked Tommy, who liked girls but did not yet have any particular fancy.

'I hardly likes to say,' said Lily, 'and I wouldn't say at all if you wasn't a close friend.' But she put her reluctance aside without too much trouble and asked, 'Could yer lend us five bob? I got embarrassing money problems.'

Tommy had lent her money twice before. She hadn't paid any of it back yet. His pocket money was ten bob a week. He gave Chinese Lady the rest of his wages. Out of what he kept he paid his fares to work and put some aside for clothes and other things. Chinese Lady provided him with sandwiches for his lunch.

'Five bob?' he said. Five bob was two-thirds of an errand boy's wage.

'If yer could, I'd be grateful, Tommy,' said Lily, 'and yer could walk me up the park Sunday afternoon.'

'You don't have to do me that favour for a loan,' said Tommy.

'Oh, I wouldn't go out with no one unless I wanted to on account of likin' him,' said Lily, white teeth moistly gleaming between pink lips. 'I could probably pay yer back next week.'

'Well, all right,' said Tommy, not a young man who could be hard-hearted or even remind her she hadn't yet paid back the previous loans. 'But let's see what I've got first.' He fished silver and coppers from his pocket. They amounted to five and tuppence.

'There, yer got just enough. Ta,' said Lily.

'No, you've got to leave me something,' said Tommy.

'All right, I'll try and make do with four bob,' said Lily, and plucked coins from his palm, leaving him with one and tuppence.

'Gen'rous of yer,' said Tommy drily, and she gave him a smile that forgave him for not letting her have all she had asked for.

'Thanks, Tommy, yer saved my life,' she said. 'I could kiss yer.'

And she did, with lips moist and luscious. She was not sparing in her gratitude, she let the kiss linger, and she let her well-filled jumper rest warmly against his chest. 'Nice, Tommy?'

'I'm not complaining,' said Tommy equably. He did not easily lose his head. He saw her out.

'Don't forget I said Sunday afternoon,' she murmured.

'I won't forget you said it,' said Tommy, and closed the door as she whisked away.

'I know who that was,' said Chinese Lady disapprovingly when he was back in the kitchen. 'That there Lily Fuller. It's time her father smacked her

122

bottom.' Which meant Lily Fuller was no more welcome than the *News of the World*.

'Girls won't do anything for yer, Tommy,' remarked Sammy.

'A lot you know, my lad,' said Chinese Lady. 'You'd soon come to grief and perdition if there weren't no girls at all. You wouldn't know which way to turn for comfort and caring, nor even how to wash your socks. It's time you and Tommy both had nice girls to walk out with, though I don't know as either of you would find one as nice as our Em'ly.'

Our Em'ly smiled very dreamily.

CHAPTER NINE

'You wanted me, Mrs Stevens?' said Emily at the town hall next morning.

'Well, I wanted to thank you again for the duplicating job you did so well for me yesterday,' smiled Madge Stevens. 'The notices are all going out this morning. And I also wanted to ask you how your husband is.'

'You'd never believe it, but it's just like all our yesterdays have come again,' said Emily, 'except he keeps lookin' every which way as if he still can't take in that he isn't blind any more.'

'I can imagine his feelings.'

'And can you imagine mine, specially now his brother's goin' to give him a job managing a shop at Camberwell Green? No wonder I drank so much port last night and just swam into bed.'

Madge Stevens laughed. Emily really was very engaging.

'And how much did your husband drink?' she asked.

'Guinness?' smiled Emily, whose lips still seemed to have a dewy look.

'He drank Guinness and you drank port? Was he swimming too?'

'Oh, drink never turns a hair of his head,' said Emily, 'you just see a smile creepin' up all over him.'

'Well, he does have something to smile about now, doesn't he?' Madge Stevens regarded Emily with interest. 'By the way, have you ever thought about learning shorthand?'

'Shorthand?'

'Local government and business houses are beginning to realise shorthand-typists mean more to them then copy typists. Shorthand-typing is going to provide careers for many girls. And it pays more than copy typing, Emily.'

'I'd have to go to evening classes,' said Emily.

'A Pitman's school would be best,' said Madge. 'It's Pitman's shorthand you'd be learning. They have a school near Brixton, which runs day and evening classes. I thought shorthand worth mentioning to you.'

'Well, I—' Emily paused. Having a family was what she and Boots most wanted. She wouldn't be able to go out to work when she started having babies. 'Well, I'll talk to my husband about it, Mrs Stevens, but thanks ever so much for thinking about it for me.'

'You're an intelligent girl, Emily,' said Madge, 'you do have something to offer local government.'

'I'll tell my husband that,' smiled Emily.

He was waiting outside the town hall again that evening.

'Hello, Emily love.'

'Ain't yer nice?' said Emily in her old style. She looked at him, she kissed him, and she looked at him again. 'But I don't know I want to be seen with you when you're lookin' like that.' He didn't have any hat on, and he was wearing an old and dreadful cricket shirt tucked into belted grey flannels just as old if not quite as dreadful. 'Boots, you're a ragbag.'

'I've been stripping wallpaper,' said Boots.

'Still,' said Emily, as town-hall workers passed by, 'I don't want me colleagues to think me husband's a ragbag.'

'I'll write them a note explaining,' said Boots.

'They'll like that,' said Emily. 'Come on.' She slipped her arm through his and they began the short walk home. 'Boots, what d'you think, Mrs Stevens asked me this morning if I'd like to be a shorthand-typist, not just a copy typist.'

'I've heard of shorthand-typists,' said Boots. 'Are they the coming thing?'

'Mrs Stevens said so. I'd have to learn shorthand, of course. What d'you think?'

'Well, we've agreed we can't have a baby tomorrow or even next week,' said Boots, taking in the Walworth Road scene in the dusty May sunshine. The impediment of his foggy left eye was an insignificance compared with his visionary right eye. 'If you want to have a go at shorthand, lovey, you help yourself.'

'It means me goin' to evening classes,' said Emily. 'Mrs Stevens said there's a Pitman's school near Brixton. She said shorthand-typists are better paid. Boots, imagine me a shorthand-typist, don't it sound highfalutin' middle-class?'

'It'll sound ladylike to Chinese Lady,' said Boots.

Chinese Lady, when told, said, 'Well, I don't know, I'm sure. Are you sure, Em'ly love?' She was thinking that when the shop was open, with Boots the manager, the two of them ought to settle down and have a family.

'Well, Mrs Stevens is lettin' me think about it,' said Emily. 'And what d'you think, Boots, she said I was intelligent, would you believe.'

'Bless me soul, well, I never did,' said Boots, 'and here's me and Chinese Lady thinking you were retarded.'

'Oh, yer funny-cuts,' said Emily. 'No, but she said I got something to offer local government.'

'Well, I don't know, I'm sure,' said Chinese Lady again.

'Of course, it all depends,' said Emily.

'Of course,' said Boots. 'Well, I'll go back to stripping the landing wallpaper, which is depending on me to finish it.'

'Yes, you ought to keep yourself active while you're waitin' for Sammy to open the shop,' said Emily briskly.

To please Chinese Lady the whole family went to church on Sunday morning, although Sammy wore the

126

look of a young businessman sure that it was going to cost him money. On Sunday mornings East Street market was crowded with shoppers, and he knew Bert Lomax couldn't tap the pockets of people as well as he could.

During the service, Chinese Lady offered up silent thanks for the miracle operation and sang all the hymns in a voice firm with gratitude. Emily also gave thanks, sang in a clear voice, and thought about the exciting challenge of learning Pitman's shorthand. Beside her, Boots added his baritone, and thought about the necessity of an extra room when he and Emily started a family.

Tommy thought about the engineering firm he worked for and its falling order books. He thought about his lack of prospects if he lost his job. He would have to compete in the labour market with unemployed ex-servicemen. He didn't much fancy that. But he sang the hymns in his usual tuneful way.

Sammy mouthed his way through hymns and prayers, thinking about his business. He had a scrap yard, the prime share of a market stall, and the prospect of opening a shop. He was committed to that now, because of Boots. It would have been better to have got the lease settled and a loan fixed before offering Boots the managership, but he'd lifted his guard again on account of feeling a painful dislike of Boots traipsing around London looking for work after four years in the dark. It wouldn't have been right to let him do that. It would have upset Chinese Lady. Well, that lease had got to be agreed and signed, and a call paid on Mr Isaac Moses to discuss the loan. Mr Moses's daughter Rachel had fixed the meeting for him. He knew Rachel well. She was a helpful ally.

He wondered how Bert was making out on his own at the stall. You needed two on a Sunday morning, when the mood in the market was almost festive. People wore their Sunday best, and stalls selling cockles, mussels, whelks and jellied eels did a roaring trade. It fascinated small boys to see live eels wriggling in wet trays, and to see them still wriggling as they were neatly chopped up.

Sammy had watched them himself as a small boy.

'But ain't it crool, mister?' he once asked a jellied eel stallholder.

'Crool? Nah. Eels is born to be chopped up, young feller-me-lad. They know it, accepts it, and can't wait for it. They likes it. It's their dest'ny.'

'What's their dest'ny, mister?'

'What they're born for, me young cock sparrer. I tell yer, they likes it. Can't yer see 'em fair wriggling for joy as I does it to 'em?'

'Cor, I wouldn't like it,' said Sammy.

'Course yer wouldn't, sonny. Yer been born a boy, not an eel. If yer'd been born an eel, I'd 'ave yer under me knife in a jiffy. I'll show yer.'

Sammy, seven at the time, escaped with a gasp and ran all the way home.

He was eleven years older now and set on making his fortune. Quickly. Then he could set Chinese Lady up in comfort for the rest of her life. Boots and Emily would be starting a family now, that was for sure. And Tommy would get married in a few years, he was the marrying kind. Sammy envisaged a posh house as far out as Streatham's green fields, with Chinese Lady in charge of the servants, and he himself living the uncomplicated life of a bachelor, a business bachelor. Girls only got in the way. And a wife could skin a bloke of his hard-won fortune inside a couple of years.

The market stall was a bread-and-butter business. Steady bread and butter, with a bit over for investment, like. Bert was all right as a stallholder, but he'd never be more than that. He was useful, he knew about china and glass, and he wouldn't cost more than he got out of the partnership now because he didn't have the savvy to contribute more. He couldn't do bookwork of any kind. He could give the right change, but he didn't know the first thing about a profit and loss account. He was never going to be irreplaceable, and he liked his drink too much at times. Still, with his knowledge of the market, he'd provided a useful back on which to climb. That girl, though, Susie Whatsername, she had a bit of good old-fashioned flair in the way she could take hold of a prospective customer's ear and not let go. Good little barker she was, with her line of girlish patter. As for them big blue eyes of hers, if she dolled herself up a bit the customers would fall into them. He'd fallen in himself. Sammy frowned so deeply that the vicar, catching what he thought was a scowl, wondered if his sermon was striking the wrong note with Sammy Adams.

Sammy knew he'd never make a fortune if he let himself go soft. Still, the tanner he'd originally risked on the girl had proved a good investment. But something had to be done about what she looked like, as if he paid her starvation wages. No investment should look like a bad advertisement.

He sloped off to the market as soon as the service was over. He hadn't heard one word of the sermon. Chinese Lady heard every word. It was a good sermon, based on Love Thy Neighbour. Although a Christian woman couldn't argue too much with any of the Ten Commandments, one couldn't accept that Love Thy Neighbour meant Tommy had to love Lily Fuller. A ladylike girl would suit Tommy much better.

Now what ladylike girls did she know?

She pondered on the problem on the way home.

Bert was doing fairly good business at the stall, but there was no crowd around it. He did not have the patter. Sammy could draw them in three or four deep. Shoppers expected some stallholders to entertain them. Checking the takings, Sammy reckoned going to church had cost him real money.

129

'Mister?'

He knew that voice only too well. It was her. He decided not to look at her. She sounded as if she was about to ask a favour.

'Oh, it's you,' he said, reaching under the stall to pull out the wooden crate he used as a rostrum when he was plying his patter. There were forty minutes to go before the market closed, and he was confident he could make profitable use of them.

'Could I do some selling?' asked Susie, who had just come from church herself. Bert, moody because he'd been on his own on a busy morning, had gone off for a Sunday pint, much to Sammy's ire. 'Could I, mister?'

'Well, I said you could whenever you wanted,' muttered Sammy, and Susie at once latched on to potential customers, a middle-aged husband and wife who were looking for a willow pattern gravy boat and meat dish. The wife said she'd got the dinner on and couldn't stand about talking, so was there a boat and a dish, kindly say yes or no.

'Oh, yes, missus,' said Susie, 'we always got everything yer can think of in willow pattern.' She gave Sammy a quick look, for she had no idea if she had been right, but thought it better than saying she didn't know.

'The kerb crate,' said Sammy, and Susie dived under the stall. She reappeared in record time, with a gravy boat and a large meat dish.

'Well, you're a quick one, aren't you?' said the woman, and Sammy glanced at Susie. She was actually wearing clothes that could pass with a push, a dark blue jumper and a dark red skirt. The skirt looked a size too big, and was probably a second-hand gift from a charity, but the jumper wasn't bad. Well, he could do with her now that Bert had gone off.

He mounted the crate. He tipped his hat to the back of his head and clapped his hands. People stopped.

'Now, me lovely ladies and handsome gents, let's get down to some serious business before you all go home to yer roast beef. I'm not gettin' any meself, I'm a victim of social poverty and me mother's in the workhouse. Yer don't believe me, lady? No, I can see yer don't, and yer right. And why are yer right? Because yer know Sammy Adams ain't the kind to let anyone cart his crippled old mother off to the workhouse. Nor the kind that can refuse me customers a special once-and-only bargain. And what's that, yer'll ask, what's that?'

'Yus, what?' asked a burly man in a flat cap. A crowd was already gathering.

'A real genuine imitation Wedgwood tea service,' said Sammy, dark-lashed blue eyes conveying bright benevolence and a fair deal. 'None of yer ungenuine imitations they diddle yer with in Petticoat Lane, but exclusive real genuine. There, clap yer mince pies on this milk jug to start with.' He held one up. 'I tell yer, I inform yer and I advise yer, with a service like this yer could invite the Prince of Wales to Sunday tea, providin' yer give him cucumber sandwiches, which is his special fancy.' He paused for a moment. Susie, dipping her hand into the cardboard box on the stall, brought out a cup and saucer. She took them around, showing them, and letting the sun dance on the cheap glaze. Bert might have thought of doing that, but probably not. Sammy continued his patter, Susie continued to display, and between them they sold eight sets, all that Sammy had managed to acquire from an East End warehouse that was selling surplus stock at giveaway prices. And before the market bobby reached them in his warning stroll through the market, the stroll that was a signal for the stallholders to close down, Susie had sold several other items by the quickness with which she alighted on customers who only needed someone to make up their minds for them.

Her takings for everything she had sold herself amounted to twenty-five shillings and threepence. Sammy gave her her commission. Two bob and one penny. He hesitated, he frowned, then gave her sixpence more for her help in his selling of the imitation Wedgwood. Her eyes lifted in sunlit gratitude to him. Sammy muttered.

'Mister, oh, ain't that something?' she said. 'Two and sevenpence in just that little while? Oh, I ain't never goin' to forget God's blessing in meetin' a young gent as kind as you. And I ain't so bad today, am I? See, I bought these things in the market first thing this mornin', they didn't cost hardly anything, and I went 'ome and put them on for church.' A little shyly she added, 'I saw yer in church, mister, with people. Was they yer fam'ly? They looked ever so nice.'

'The jumper's all right,' said Sammy tersely, 'the skirt don't fit too good. And stop lookin' at me.'

Susie's pale, elfin face flushed a little.

'Mister?'

'I don't like being looked at,' growled Sammy, 'it makes me feel I'm something in the zoo. Oh, all right, don't take it so hard, you've done a good job this morning, and I'm pleased with you.' But he eyed her frowningly, her paleness that of a girl who lived in smoky Walworth and didn't get enough to eat. 'What've you had this morning?'

The crowds were thinning rapidly, the stallholders clearing up, and Susie looked puzzled.

'Had?' she said.

'Grub,' said Sammy, terse again because he was sure he was going soft.

'Oh,' said Susie. 'Well, I 'ad a nice cup of tea for breakfast and a bit of toast.'

'Not enough,' said Sammy, 'so off yer go now to yer dinner and ask yer mum to give yer two helpings of everything, including afters.'

'Oh, yes, we got roast beef and Yorkshire pudden today, honest we 'ave,' said Susie, and Sammy thought – frowningly – that she had an air of eager life that was like Emily's, and he was very fond of Emily. 'Yer

132

see, me earnings yesterday made us feel rich, so Dad come to the market early and bought a big joint. I ain't seen me mum and dad 'appier for ages, and me sister and brothers—'

'Yes, all right, I know, but off yer go.'

'Oh, can't I stay and 'elp clear up?' asked Susie in willingness.

'Clear up?'

'Yes, yer stall and everything. I'd like to 'elp. We don't 'ave Sunday dinner till two. I'll 'elp yer push the stall to its yard.'

Sammy said aloofly, 'I am not aware I require that kind of help. I'm a businessman, not a skivvy. I am not in the habit of tidying up stalls or pushing them anywhere. Kindly don't associate me with them that do.'

'Oh, crikey,' gasped Susie, stricken with awe and admiration. He had laid it on just like she imagined a magistrate would, and he didn't half look the part too, in a pepper-and-salt Sunday suit with a plain brown tie. Except that a magistrate would be a lot older. Fancy him being able to sound middle-class. Sammy, in fact, and Tommy too, could sound like that whenever they cared to. They only needed to imitate Boots. 'Oh, I didn't mean to suggest you was common 'erd, mister, honest.'

'Kindly let it be known I got people to do my running about for me,' said Sammy. 'My assistant Fred will be along any minute now to see to the stall and take it to the yard. Mr Fred Scribbins. He looks after my yard. Now, you go off home.'

'Yes, mister, thank yer.'

'Half a mo, I want you here all day tomorrow, I'm goin' to be busy elsewhere. Bert'll be with you in the afternoon. Monday's not the best day of the week, so if you're alone in the morning, it shouldn't be a strain. Bert'll let you go off early in the afternoon, if you want.'

'Oh, I'll stay all day, really I will,' said Susie.

133

'Then don't forget your hot pie and mash dinnertime,' said Sammy.

'Yer a real kind thoughtful gent, honest,' said Susie, and went home happily, leaving Sammy muttering to himself.

'Now what did I give her that extra tanner for if I ain't gettin' soft?'

He addressed the question to a Chinese vase made in a Plumstead factory. It offered no reply. It may have been a cheap copy of the real thing, but it did convey an Oriental inscrutability, and was no help at all to Sammy.

As a treat, Chinese Lady put on roast pork for Sunday dinner, with crisp crackling and apple sauce. Pork was always a treat considering how much more expensive it was than beef or mutton. But Chinese Lady did not believe in being thrifty when there was something to celebrate. Everyone was still happily conscious of Boots's restored eyesight, and it was the first time for years that he had actually seen a Sunday dinner. The meal was a lively occasion. Sammy talked about what the shop was going to do for his business, and Boots asked mildly pertinent questions like who was going to clean the shop window or sweep the pavement of snow in the winter? Sammy said he appreciated his future shop manager showing keen interest, and that he hoped Boots would likewise appreciate a bit of time was necessary to sort certain things out. Tommy came in with amiable comments. He supposed, he said, that Sam's Emporium would stock an amount of genuine diddles like the stall did. Sammy said everything on the stall was certified genuine by the makers, and that Chinese Lady had brought him up honest. Emily kept saying she could hardly believe what was happening, or that Boots had such comforting prospects. She said Sammy deserved a kiss, only she knew it would put him off his afters, rhubarb pie and custard.

'Oh, I ain't obverse to a kiss from you, Em'ly,' said Sammy.

'Averse?' suggested Boots.

'Yes, she's me sister-in-law,' said Sammy. 'All the same, I got to say I consider kissing is highly dangerous.'

'Mum, don't give him no afters,' said Emily, 'he's being insinuatin', he's saying if I kiss him he'll catch the measles.'

'No, I'm just saying a businessman can't afford kissing,' said Sammy. 'It interrupts yer due thought processes, and it gets in the way as well. And it can transfer measles to yer. Of course, if yer married yer got to do a bit of it or yer wife goes home to her mother, but if yer not married and yer got important things to do, yer leave it strictly alone. If you don't, you get hooked.'

'Hooked?' said Chinese Lady, serving the steaming rhubarb pie. 'Are you speakin' of marriage as ordered by God, Sammy Adams?' She meant ordained.

'No, he's speakin' of one being able to live cheaper than two,' said Tommy.

Emily laughed.

'Oh, yer sweet, really, Sammy,' she said.

'Don't repeat that, Em,' said Boots, 'or he'll be ordered by God to get married.'

'That's it, be irreverent,' said Chinese Lady.

'All right, don't give me any custard on my afters,' said Boots, 'that'll teach me not to say my prayers.'

Chinese Lady's mouth twitched, and Emily laughed so much that tears came. She fished her handkerchief out of the top of a stocking. Tommy caught a glimpse of her shapely legs.

'Scenery's improved round here,' he said.

Chinese Lady knew exactly what he meant, but made no comment. Tommy was a nice, healthy young man. Young men could be saucy, though. She herself had once had a terrible time on the swings at Hampstead Heath Bank Holiday fair. Tommy's father, handsome

135

in his uniform, had the swing going higher, she holding on to the rope for dear life, and her skirt and petticoat going everywhere except where they should, her legs disgracefully uncovered. She gave him a rare ticking-off afterwards for behaving so shamelessly. He gave her the sauciest smile.

'Makes no difference, Maisie, using your tongue like that,' he said, 'it's a downright pleasure for a feller to know his young lady's got fine legs.'

'Daniel, you impudence, you did it on purpose, you did, just to see.'

'Still makes no difference, Maisie. Goin' to marry you, that I am.'

'Well! Cheek! I need to be asked first, I do!'

'And I'm goin' to ask, Maisie, as soon as you've come to love me, which I hope you will, seeing I'm not goin' to let anyone else have you, except over my dead body.'

A reminiscent smile touched Chinese Lady's face as the basin of hot custard circulated.

'Penny for your thoughts, Ma,' said Sammy.

'They're worth more than a penny,' she said, 'and kindly don't call me Ma.'

A little while after dinner, when Tommy and Sammy were doing the washing-up, Boots pointed Chinese Lady towards the parlour, telling her to put her feet up with the *Sunday Dispatch*. On her way through the passage, a knock sounded on the front door. She answered it. Her eyes blinked at the sight of Lily Fuller in a Sunday frock of painfully garish pink.

'Oh, 'ello, Mrs Adams,' said Lily, treating Chinese Lady to a flashing smile. 'Would yer tell Tommy I'm ready?'

Not while I can still draw breath I won't, thought Chinese Lady.

'Ready for what?' she asked discouragingly.

'Oh, didn't 'e tell yer I told 'im he could walk me up the park this afternoon, Mrs Adams?'

'Very kind of you to offer, I'm sure,' said Chinese Lady, 'but he's busy, and he's got a bone in his leg.'

'Eh?' said Lily. 'A what?'

'Something he tripped on at work,' said Chinese Lady, hoping the vicar would understand a Christian woman had to prevaricate sometimes.

' 'As he 'ad embrocation?' asked Lily. It was Sunday, and she knew Tommy, having been paid his wages on Friday, would have money in his pocket.

'He's just had his dinner, he won't want no embrocation,' said Chinese Lady. 'Kind of you to call, I'm sure. Good afternoon.'

She closed the door.

Even if the vicar didn't understand, Mary the mother of Jesus would.

CHAPTER TEN

On Monday morning, Sammy made sure he could confidently leave Susie Whatsername in charge of the stall. Calling her and thinking about her as Susie Whatsername kept the relationship casual.

He gave her advice on how to handle things on her own, which included not turning her back on a customer, especially one on the kerbside. They could disappear like greased lightning from there. Nifty nickers, said Sammy, operated in every London market. Susie nodded, taking in everything Mister Sammy said.

'Right, then, I'll leave you to it,' he said. 'I expect to be back before the morning's over, before Bert gets here dinnertime, but I can't put an exact time to it.'

'Mister, I'm proud yer got faith in me,' said Susie, 'I won't let yer down.'

Sammy eyed her searchingly. Her old blouse had been washed yesterday, it looked like, and her black skirt looked likewise. But the get-up wouldn't do.

'Something's got to be done about your togs,' he said, 'I ain't in favour of you lookin' like you're headin' for the workhouse.'

'Oh,' said Susie, upset, 'but I laundered everything—'

'I can't stop,' said Sammy, 'I'm meeting me brother.'

He met Boots at the empty shop by Camberwell Green. It was opposite the Green's most attractive-looking pub. Trams went by on the way to Ruskin Park, where they bore left for Nunhead. Sammy, having picked up the keys, took Boots into the shop. Boots looked around. The place was quite large.

'H'm,' he said.

'What d'yer think?' asked Sammy. He had not been wholly philanthropic in offering the job to his older brother. Boots did have style. He had common sense too. And he never flapped. Nobody had ever known him to run about like a headless chicken. He could handle events, and he could handle people. Sammy suspected Boots had been a very good sergeant. Old soldiers always said it wasn't the officers, nor even the privates, who made a battalion a good fighting unit. It was the sergeants.

'Plenty of space,' said Boots, 'but it needs paint.'

'Paint?' said Sammy. 'You gone daft on paint?'

'Needs brightening up,' said Boots, 'like the house. And more gas lamps. Three more. On that side. It's just a cavern at the moment.'

'Stop spendin' my money,' said Sammy, but gave the matter some thought. He was always prepared to consider a suggestion, even if it didn't immediately appeal to him, or to his pocket. This was his first shop, and he knew Boots had imagination, and something to offer in the way of ideas. And he wouldn't charge anything. A solicitor only had to say yes or no to a question, and it cost you seven and six. Sammy had had some of that lately. Next time he needed advice he'd go to his friend Ikey Mo, who hung out in Lower Marsh, this side of Waterloo Bridge. Ikey Mo could spot a weakness in every para of a landlord's lease, and charge no more than three bob, plus sixpence for suggested amendments and alterations inserted in his best green ink. Or there was Mr Greenberg, the rag and bone merchant, who knew everybody and everything. Musingly, he said, 'Well, maybe, Boots.' He thought about his own idea of putting Susie Whatsername into a cheerful overall. It coincided with Boots's suggestion for a cheerful shop. Good point, really. Cheerful was welcoming. 'All right,' he said, 'I'll get a bloke to paint it a nice brown—'

'Hold up,' said Boots. 'In case you haven't noticed, it's a nice brown already, a nice dark gloomy brown, like our rooms at home. Let's think about a Cambridge blue for the panels, with the surrounds picked out in Oxford blue.'

'We ain't goin' to row the Boat Race here,' said Sammy, 'but all right, you choose the colours, and I'll get the gas company to fix three more wall burners.'

'With large mantles and pearl shades, Sammy.'

'You'll cost me, you will, Boots.'

Boots inspected a little room at the back of the shop. It had a sink and a gas tap. There was also a stockroom and a lavatory. And a flight of stairs that led to rooms above the shop. All were included in the lease.

'When's opening day?' asked Boots.

'Depends on a satisfact'ry conclusion to me financial arrangements and when the landlord makes up his mind to accept me suggested amendment to what he's askin' for the rent. He's fightin' it, but it won't do him no good. Well, it wouldn't, would it, when we know the place has been empty for months.' Sammy smiled. 'By the way, I'm not sure if yer like the shop name, Sam's Emporium.'

'Your other suggestion was better.'

'What other suggestion?'

'Bargain Bazaar.'

'Eh? I don't remember suggestin' that.'

'Oh, you talked yesterday about everything in the shop being a bargain,' said Boots.

'Boots, you got something there. Bargain Bazaar. Good on yer, mate, I reckon your operation's given yer brains a polish as well as yer eyes. I'll call the shop Sam's Emporium, then underneath *The Bargain Bazaar*. Now, here's what I thought about how we'd dress the window different each week.'

'Carry on,' said Boots, his smile a little detached from window-dressing. He was thinking of Emily, dressing and undressing. She did it all in an absolute dither, for she neither trusted him not to look nor to resist taking advantage. She was quite sure it wasn't decent for a man to see a girl take her drawers off or put them on, even if she was married to him. She was so quaintly Victorian about it all that she could make such moments hilarious. So he teased her, of course, and she ran madly about in their bedroom, the bed cover wrapped around her, begging him to be decent.

'Oh, I'll tell Mum, I will, I'll tell Chinese Lady she give birth to a monster when she 'ad you.'

And she did at least tell Chinese Lady that Boots was a terrible torment.

'Box his ears,' said Chinese Lady.

'Oh, I couldn't do that,' said Emily, 'he's me one and only husband.'

Chinese Lady smiled. She understood. Emily secretly liked it – whatever it was.

Monday morning business in the market was good at some stalls, desultory at others. It was in between for Susie.

'Give us one of them cheap lot cups,' said a woman.

'With a saucer?'

'Now what do I want a saucer for when me 'am-fisted old man only broke a cup, dearie?'

That was typical Monday morning business at a china stall.

But Susie had sold a pair of vases, a china cruet set, a large pudding basin and six eggcups, in addition to odds and ends from cheap lots. By eleven o'clock, she had earned one and tuppence commission. And Ma Earnshaw had given her two apples, both slightly specked, but very eatable. They were friends now.

Two women came to browse over the cheapest dinner plates on offer. Susie helped their discussion along.

One woman said, 'You in charge?'

'Oh, yes, missus,' said Susie proudly.

'Then it's time Sammy Adams give yer a wage decent

141

enough to keep yerself properly fed and clothed, yer pore mite, and yer can tell 'im I said so.'

Upset, Susie said, 'Oh, I've really only just started workin' for him, and 'e pays me a very decent wage, honest.'

A boy in a peaked blue cap and a blue jersey, with patched trousers, who was dark and wiry and looked about fifteen, sidled up on the pavement to eye the best item on the stall. It was a porcelain shepherdess, and the price marked on the box was fifteen shillings. Mr Greenberg had picked it up from an old lady for a bob and let Sammy have it for five and sixpence, seeing Sammy was a friend of his. Its condition was so pristine it looked new. Susie knew if anyone got interested in it, she could bargain down to twelve and six. But it was not something the market shoppers of Walworth bought every day. While Susie successfully negotiated the sale of six plates, despite the customer's suspicion that Sammy Adams was paying starvation wages, the boy lingered, regarding the porcelain figure admiringly. The women left. Ma Earnshaw was serving customers. The boy picked the figure up.

'No, yer shouldn't touch it, please,' said Susie.

'Why not? I'm buying it, ain't I? 'Ere y'ar.' He tossed two coins into a cup and off he went, eeling his way over the pavement behind the stalls.

Susie grabbed the cup and looked in it. Two halfpennies, that was all. Two halfpennies, She shrieked, she dashed. The boy had disappeared. Frantic, she darted about, trying to catch a glimpse of the rotten, dirty thief.

''Ere, don't leave yer stall, ducky, not while I'm busy!' shouted Ma Earnshaw.

Tragedy showed its stricken mask on Susie's face as she returned to the stall. She searched the cup, hoping there might at least be a ten-bob note screwed up with the coins. There wasn't. Panic and despair seized her. Twelve and six, that was the minimum sum due in the cash box for the shepherdess. Mum and Dad had a few bob to spare because of what she'd earned Saturday and Sunday, but they could never find twelve and six.

'Oh.' She wanted to weep.

'What's up, love?' asked Ma Earnshaw, now clear of customers.

'Oh, that rotten little perisher nicked that lovely bit of porcelain, and right from under me nose. On the kerbside. Did yer see 'im, Ma, did yer?'

'The gorblimey little Turk, no, I didn't. Cunning, they are, ducks, I'm telling yer.' Ma Earnshaw eyed the girl a little dubiously then. She could be in it with the thief. Crafty as monkeys some of them were at her age. But the sudden welling tears were real, and Ma Earnshaw took herself silently to task for her suspicions. 'That's 'ow some of 'em do it, love. Watch to see no one's lookin', then make a fast grab and a nifty scarper. And that makes it your word against theirn. 'Ere, don't cry, Susie, it 'appens to all of us. I couldn't count the oranges I've 'ad nicked from under me nose.'

'But it wasn't no orange,' wept Susie, 'it was the best piece on the stall. Oh, I don't 'ardly know what I'm goin' to do, I'll get the sack and be put in prison, and Mister Sammy Adams, 'e's been so kind to me. I been an' let 'im down something awful.'

'Makes a nice change to 'ear Sammy's been kind,' said Ma Earnshaw. ''E's likeable and all, but 'e can drive an 'ard bargain, though I ain't never 'eard he's ever diddled 'is own. 'E's got 'is principles, like, and if 'e's been kind to yer, I daresay 'e could be kind to yer about this.'

'Oh, but yer see, Ma, he told me – he told me – don't let them come at yer from the kerbside when yer servin' at the front, not unless yer make sure yer givin' them no chance of pinchin'. Oh, I done it in proper—' She stopped as a shadow fell across the front of the stall. She looked up. It was the Reverend John Carr, the curate of St John's. He was also the scoutmaster of the

143

26th Southwark Troop. He smiled at Susie. Ma Earnshaw moved back to her greengrocery. Susie's wet eyes blinked.

'Why, you're Susie Brown, aren't you?' said the curate.

'Yes, sir.'

'Have you been crying?'

'No, sir, it's all right.'

'Well, I've called to pick up a box of enamel plates and enamel cocoa mugs for the troop. Sammy – you know Sammy Adams? – ordered them for me.'

'Yes, I'm workin' for him, sir,' said Susie, hardly able to concentrate because there was so much inner despair. 'I didn't know about the – oh, I'll just 'ave a look under the stall.'

She went down on one knee. She saw a cardboard box, sealed. It was marked 'Scouts – fifteen shillings.' It was heavy. She dragged it out, and up over the kerb. The curate came round to help her.

'This seems to be it, Susie. Well done.'

'A pleasure, sir,' said Susie, woebegone.

'Are you sure you're all right?' asked the kindly curate.

'Yes, sir, thank you, sir.'

'Well, here's the money.' He handed her a ten-shilling note and two half-crowns, one new and gleaming.

'Thank you, sir.'

'Glad you've got a job, Susie. Give my regards to your parents.'

Susie's misery expressed itself in a shuddering sob as the curate went off with the box. She stood, the money clutched in her hand. Fifteen bob. She blinked, opened the solid tin cash-box and dropped in the note and silver. One coin rang. The new and gleaming one gave off a dull sound. Oh, no! Oh, please, God, no. She snatched it up, went down on one knee again, and tested the coin on the pavement. God hadn't heard her plea. She'd been landed with a dud, by a man of God.

A half-crown dud, and that on top of letting the shepherdess be nicked. Oh, I must've sinned something awful to be punished like this.

She straightened up, slowly and miserably.

There was another shadow.

'So there you are,' said Sammy, 'I thought you'd done a bunk.'

Susie, pale with despair, showed eyes of dark tragic blue.

Oh, my gawd, thought Sammy, she's doing Hamlet again, she's going to tell me her dad's going to die unless he has an operation, and have I got ten quid I could loan her to tide the family over.

'Oh, mister, I got 'eart-breakin' news—' Susie's voice faltered and died.

'Yes, I can see you have,' said Sammy, 'and this time you're goin' for the shirt off me back, are yer?'

'Oh, I hardly knows how to tell yer,' gasped Susie, the market cries and the questing shoppers meaning nothing to her against the enormity of getting the sack and going to prison. Her brimming eyes begged Sammy's forgiveness in advance, and Sammy thought, what's she trying to do, haunt me?

'I knew it,' he said and came purposefully round to the pavement and fastened his eyes on the bottom button of her weary-looking blouse. 'Your dad's jumped off the top of Peabody's and needs six operations, and your mum's got pneumonia from the shock. And you're all starvin'.'

'Oh, no,' breathed Susie, 'it's – it's—'

'Serve the customer,' said Sammy curtly, and Susie was forced to attend to a lady interested in an imitation cut-glass bowl, the bargain of the day at a bob, or elevenpence if the customer put up a fight. When the sale had been made, Sammy was with Ma Earnshaw, listening to her, and Susie felt the pit of despair yawning at the set look on his face. She heard Ma Earnshaw's final words.

'It's 'appened to all of us, Sammy, you included, smart as you are.'

'It ain't goin' to happen again,' said Sammy, and moved back to his stall. 'So you let a thievin' young cock sparrer skin you,' he said, and his stern look was not unlike that of his mother's. Susie, head drooping, lifted her wet eyes. Sammy growled. 'Didn't I tell you to keep yer peepers peeled?' he said.

'Oh, he just took it and run,' wept Susie.

'Stop crying,' ground Sammy.

'Mister, it's me breakin' 'eart – yer see – oh, yer see, I got landed with a dud 'alf-crown as well.'

'You got what?' Sammy wondered if his guiding star wasn't paying him out for his desertion of his beliefs and principles in the first place. 'You been a Simple Simon as well as a blind O'Reilly?'

'Oh, mister, please don't walk over me dying body,' begged Susie, 'I already got all the agonies. Only yer see, the curate come for the scout things, and he give me a ten-bob note and two 'alf-crowns while I was still drownin' in misery over that rotten little bugger who—'

'Here, none of that,' said Sammy, 'I don't want to hear that kind of language from a girl who's just served a curate. It's not decent.'

Susie, amazed at that, gasped, 'Oh, I'm sorry, I 'ardly ever uses that sort of word, but I got so much misery inside of me—' She stopped as an elderly man inspected good quality glass tumblers.

'Fourpence each,' said Sammy, 'and you won't get quality glass like that at my price even up in heaven.'

'I'll ask when I get there,' said the elderly man, 'but if you'll knock off a ha'penny each for four, I'll recommend you to St Peter.'

'Take the gentleman's money,' said Sammy, and Susie wrapped up four glasses and took the money. She handed it to Sammy. He studied her critically. Her eyes were still wet, her little nose pink, her mouth quivering. 'Well, let's have a look at that dud.'

She extracted the coin from the cash-box. Sammy weighed it in his hand, then bit it. It was counterfeit right enough. But it was a pretty good attempt at the real thing. Highly creditable, in fact.

'Oh, I'm sorry,' said Susie tearfully, 'and because you been so kind to me, you don't know the 'eavy burden of the cross I'm bearing, I'll be weighed down to me dying day.'

'Stop reading the Bible to me,' said Sammy, looking at the dud coin. It occurred to him she need not have confessed to the dud. He might very well not have discovered it until he'd carried the takings home, when he might have conceded someone as young as her wouldn't have suspected a fake, especially as she'd received it from the curate. 'All right, young Whatsername, I don't see I can blame you for this. I'll call in at the vicarage on my way home tonight. Hope we don't find the curate made it himself. But that porcelain piece, well, better not to say anything to Bert – hold on, did yer get a good look at the nabber?'

'Oh, yes.' Susie described the boy in detail. Sammy's eyes narrowed.

'I think I know that little light-fingered perisher,' he said. 'Offspring of a dubious acquaintance.' The son, in fact, of Ernie Cutts, old gaunt-chops, who dealt in scrap metal but couldn't read the market. Ernie had used his son Arthur to get a bit of his own back? Painful bloke, Ernie. 'All right, young Whatsername, leave it to me. Don't say anything to the market rozzers. Nor Bert, or he'll want you out of it. Now, either I get that porcelain back or it'll have to cost yer, and I'll dock something out of your earnings each week, say tuppence.' Tuppence? What was he talking about? Even the wettest employer would have asked for two bob a week. 'Are you listening?' he asked, for Susie was staring at him with eyes enormous. 'Tuppence out of – here, hold off—'

'Oh!' Susie could not help herself, such was her relief

147

and gratitude. Regardless of whatever people were close by, she flung her arms around Sammy and wept on his chest.

'Oh, my gawd,' he said.

'Mister – oh, I thought you might get me sent to prison, I did.'

'I'll get you locked up somewhere, you bet I will, if you don't get off me suit and tie,' said Sammy, quite sure an employee had no right to embarrass her employer. 'Here, Ma, can't you see to her?'

'I'm busy,' said Ma Earnshaw, 'and I got problems of me own without taking on yourn. There y'ar, look, Bert's comin'. Leave yer stall to him, an' take the girl for a nice 'ot cuppa tea. It's been a shock to the pore mite.'

Sammy, appalled at the thought of Bert catching him with the girl weeping on his chest, took hold of her shoulders and pushed her off.

'Now look,' he said, 'dry yer eyes and wipe yer nose. All right, I'll take yer for a cup of tea and a sandwich, and that'll have to do for yer dinnertime eats today instead of pie and mash.'

'Mister, oh, yer the kindest man ever,' gasped Susie, her relief and gratitude boundless, 'yer one of the chosen of the Lord.'

'No, I'm not, I'm a Gentile,' said Sammy, as Bert arrived.

The eating place was called 'Toni's Refreshments'. It was patronised by stallholders and costermongers. A stallholder could send a market boy with a mug, or nip along himself, and get the mug filled with hot tea from a large enamel teapot. The establishment was run by Toni Bessano and his wife Maria. They were middle-aged, portly and amiably Italian. Toni had a five o'clock shadow and Maria had a light moustache. They had tried years ago to introduce pasta dishes to the Walworth cockneys, but the cockneys peered suspiciously at the concoctions, asked what they were, and said no whatever the answer was. Toni and Maria fought a long losing battle cheerfully, accepted defeat philosophically, and gave their customers what they wanted. Cheese sandwiches with pickled onions. Ham sandwiches with mustard. Corned beef sandwiches with tomato. Fried egg sandwiches, fried bacon sandwiches, and fried egg and bacon sandwiches, the latter known as 'the works'.

Sammy and Susie ate fried bacon sandwiches with cups of tea. Susie was almost recovered, but lingering emotions kept making her cast nervous little glances at him. She thought him a nice-looking young man, with dark brown hair and firm features. And he had unfairly thick eyelashes, which did ever so much for his blue eyes. She had no idea just how striking were her own long-lashed blue eyes. And she certainly had no idea that their expressive appeal worried Sammy.

'I'm goin' to buy you dark glasses like some blind people wear,' he said suddenly.

'Dark glasses?' Her lingering nervousness showed. 'But why, mister? I won't 'ardly be able to see.'

'Good,' said Sammy.

'Oh, yer jokin', mister, ain't you?'

'No. Oh, all right, never mind.' Sammy looked unsettled. He had a feeling she was going to be bad luck. Better if he paid her off here and now. But she was so thin and wistful. If only she'd put on some weight and let her face fill out, her eyes wouldn't look so big and hungry. He glanced at the marble-topped counter. 'You'd better have some apple pie.'

'No, honest, mister—'

'Go and ask for two portions,' he said. 'And tell Maria hot custard on mine. You'd better have that, too. Here's the money.'

'But you already paid for the—'

'Don't argue,' growled Sammy.

'No, mister. Thank yer.'

She got the two portions, with hot custard. The pie

was lovely, the custard creamy with cornflour, and she ate with relish. Sammy ate frowningly.

'I want you to wear a smart overall,' he said.

'Overall?' Susie couldn't make him out at all.

'A blue one. We'll get it on the way back to the stall, and then I'll leave you with Bert, hoping you won't get yourself into more trouble.'

'I got to wear an overall at work?'

'A dark blue one.'

'Yes, mister,' she said. Hesitantly, she asked, ' 'Ow much will it cost?'

'I'll pay,' said Sammy.

'Oh, yer lovely and kind.'

'No, I'm not, because I might just dock yer a tanner a week out of yer wages.'

Susie drew a deep breath.

'Mister, oh, yer really goin' to keep me on, then?'

'Wasn't your fault,' conceded Sammy.

She burst into heartfelt speech.

'Oh, yer'll let me say you're more forgivin' than the 'Oly Ghost, won't yer, mister?'

'No, I won't,' said Sammy. Her face dropped. 'Oh, all right, I'm more forgivin' than the Holy Ghost, then.'

'And could yer—' Susie was hesitant again.

'Could I what?' asked Sammy suspiciously.

'Mister, could yer please give me a little smile to show me yer like me a bit?'

'Jesus,' said Sammy, 'do I have to?'

'Only if yer like me a bit,' said Susie, who felt it would be awful to work for someone who'd been such a blessing to her but who didn't like her.

'Look, of course I like yer,' said Sammy, getting to his feet, 'I wouldn't have yer workin' for me if I didn't.'

Susie's grateful smile flowered, and as she left Toni's with Sammy, she looked as if the sun was kissing her face.

CHAPTER ELEVEN

In the afternoon, Sammy had an appointment with Mr Isaac Moses, commonly known as Ikey Mo or Uncle Mo. He owned several pawnshops, and was a blessing to the hard-up, for all his shops would lend money on articles that really had no value whatever except to their owners. Cracked boots, for instance, or a framed family portrait in faded sepia. The pawning of cracked boots was pathetic, for it meant someone in the family had to go about bare-footed, probably, until they were redeemed.

Mr Moses lived with his family in a flat over one of his pawnbroker shops in Lower Marsh, where the market called the Cut was situated. Sammy climbed the stairs of the side entrance and knocked on the landing door. It was opened by a young woman with raven-black hair and dark liquid eyes. She was quite beautiful. Her name was Rachel Goodman, and she was Ikey Mo's married daughter. She helped him with his books, being brilliant at figures. She was only a few weeks younger than Sammy, and had been the only girl he had ever taken out. For a year, almost every Saturday afternoon, from the age of fourteen, she had gone to the Brixton roller-skating rink with him. It had been a concession on Sammy's part, for he could earn money on Saturday afternons, but he did have a passion for roller-skating at the time and, moreover, Rachel had paid their admission fees. She had had a little money of her own as a girl. She had a little more now. Her thirty-year-old husband was a bookie, and she had been married to him for a mere two months. They lived in her widower father's flat. Rachel adored her father and refused to let him live on his own.

Seeing the caller was Sammy, her full mouth parted in a warm, welcoming smile, disclosing beautifully white teeth.

'Watcher, Rachel, you beauty,' he said. He was safe with Rachel. He was a Gentile, she was of the Jewish faith and she was also married. But he had a soft spot for her. She was a lovely, warmhearted girl.

'Still a saucebox, are you, Sammy?' she said.

'I'm glad you're married, straight up, I am,' said Sammy, 'or I wouldn't know what to do about my illicit desires.'

Rachel, white-bloused and dark-skirted, put a hand to her creamy throat and laughed. She had had dreams about Sammy, mournful dreams. It was to her sorrow that he was a Gentile. No one knew about her dreams, not even her father or Sammy himself. But her perceptive father had once said no girl would interest Sammy until he had made his fortune. Sammy, he said, was destined to build an empire.

'Say that again,' she said.

'I'm glad you're married, Rachel, or I wouldn't be safe from my illicit desires, and nor would you.'

'Liar,' said Rachel. She drew him into a square, oak-panelled lobby. The flat above the shop was a home of handsome dignity. Closing the door, she said, 'My, ain't yer grown a lovely man, Sammy, with them fine shoulders and them blue eyes of yourn?' Rachel, Lambeth-born, was as much of a cockney as Sammy, and could talk like one. Her schooling, however, had done for her speech what Boots's schooling had done for his. Reading out loud came under very critical correction from English teachers at better schools.

'Straight up, love, if I hadn't been brought up to be reverent to married ladies, I might just get you yelling

for help here and now,' said Sammy. Actually he felt
very comfortable with married females. They didn't
look at him as if they were wondering how much he
was worth, or as if they wanted him to be a father to
them, like that Susie Whatsername did.

'Sammy, you pet,' said Rachel, 'You're going to give
me a kiss, aren't you? I swear I won't yell.'

'Bless me tender soul,' said Sammy, 'd'you want me
to get chopped by Benjamin?'

Benjamin Goodman was her husband.

Rachel laughed again. She had embraced without
reservation all the Jewish traditions of wifely faithful-
ness, but she would never be able to resist teasing
Sammy. She had had to exercise all the coyness and
beguilement of her young being to get him to kiss her
when she was fourteen, including paying him a penny
to do so. And she had cried her eyes out when, after
a year, Sammy had said no more roller-skating because
he'd acquired a full-time stall job in East Street.
Greengrocery. Rachel thought she might as well die at
being placed second to greengrocery.

'Sammy, your illicit desires are very weak,' she said,
'and it's not me you've come to see, is it? What do you
want from my daddy?'

'Five hundred quid,' said Sammy.

Rachel expelled a warm breath.

'As much as that?' she asked. 'What are you buying,
a country house and a nurse for Boots?'

'Oh, Boots has got his sight back,' said Sammy.
'Successful operation, I'm glad to say.'

'Oh, I'm so pleased,' said Rachel, 'give him my love.
Sammy, why didn't you come to my wedding?'

'Couldn't,' said Sammy. 'Agony, that would have
been, seein' the only girl I ever loved gettin' churched
to someone else in a synagogue.'

'Oh, yer lovely liar,' said Rachel.

'Did you get me weddin' present, though, the silver
spoons?'

'I wrote and thanked you, didn't I? But I think the silver was electro-plated.'

'Well, would yer believe that?' said Sammy, looking hurt. 'I got dished, diddled and done.'

'Not you, Sammy,' smiled Rachel, 'but it's the thought that counts. So, you want a loan from my daddy of five hundred pounds. It's an awful lot.'

'Can I see him?'

'Of course. He's expecting you. But wait a little longer while I speak to him first.' She opened a door in the lobby, entering a corridor. She returned after a few minutes, a smile on her face. 'Go in, Sammy.'

Sammy walked along the corridor and knocked on a door.

'Come in, Sammy.'

He entered the carpeted office. It had a quiet elegance, one wall lined with shelves full of books. Mr Moses, at his desk, came to his feet. He was a tall and distinguished-looking man in a dark grey suit, his hair iron-grey. His lean face broke into a smile and he put out his hand.

'Hello, Sammy, my friend.' He had known Sammy for many years.

'Nice to see you, Mr Moses,' said Sammy, and shook hands firmly.

'Your family?' enquired Mr Moses.

'Fine. Boots has had an operation and can see again.'

'I'm delighted. Sit down.' They both sat. Mr Moses regarded Sammy gravely. 'You've seen Rachel.'

'I have.' Sammy smiled. 'I told her I might have carried her off if she hadn't been a married woman now. I thought, when she opened the door to me, that I was lookin' at the Queen of Sheba. Now I know why King Solomon fell overboard. In a manner of speakin'. And with all respect.'

Mr Moses lost his gravity and laughed gently. It was impossible not to like Sammy Adams, a young man shrewd and ambitious, but frank and open and honest

154

in the way he dealt with his business contacts.

'It's your own fault, Sammy, if Rachel's welcome was a little colourful. You took her roller-skating, much to her joy, and perhaps much against your will.'

'Oh, well, girls, y'know,' said Sammy.

'I suspect,' said Mr Moses, 'that by the time she was fifteen she was already wishing you were of the faith. But that is a story done with, except for my conviction that you made roller-skating a thing of joy to a young girl. But can I believe what she has just told me? You are looking for a loan of five hundred pounds at five per cent? On my life, my young friend, has anyone ever heard of five hundred pounds at five per cent? I have not.'

'Five?' murmured Sammy, who knew he had said nothing to Rachel about the interest.

'Have you come here in the hope of ruining me?' asked Mr Moses.

'Times are terrible hard,' said Sammy. 'What was that figure, five per cent? That's friendship remarkable, Mr Moses.'

'Very remarkable, Sammy,' said Mr Moses, 'and impossible. And promoted, I see now, by Rachel. What can be done with a young wife of Israel whose affection for a Gentile makes her contrive at the ruin of her father?'

'Pray for her and don't tell her husband,' said Sammy. 'Mr Moses, I need five hundred for buying in bulk, and what I'm goin' to buy I reckon I'll sell inside of six months, and I further reckon that when the six months is up, you'll have the loan paid back in full. And I'll offer an extra seventy-five pounds as simple interest of seven and a half per cent. That's fair business, I'd say, and a sign of trusting friendship too.'

'Ah, trusting friendship,' said Mr Moses. 'I see. You are a minor, Sammy, and know I cannot make you any kind of a loan. So it's to be a matter of trusting friendship?'

'Thanking you kindly,' said Sammy.

'Sammy, Sammy, on my life, I am expected to accept your word as your bond?'

'I've three friends who I hope would always accept my word,' said Sammy. 'Mr Greenberg, Mr Solly Eckstein of Whitechapel, and you, Mr Moses.'

'Five hundred pounds, Sammy, and you a minor. Dear oh dear, Sammy.' Mr Moses shook his head and sighed. 'But you have a guarantor.'

'No, I can't say I have.'

'I made a statement, Sammy, I did not ask a question. Alas, that a man of business should have so foolish a daughter. It's a mistake, my young friend, for any woman to have more money in her purse than is enough to buy herself a new dress.'

'Oh, hell,' said Sammy, 'I don't want Rachel—'

'Let us discuss, Sammy, how a man of business may make a loan of five hundred pounds to a minor without bringing his house down around his ears.'

They discussed it.

Later that same afternoon, Sammy had another call to make, but not a prearranged one. He took Fred Scribbins, his faithful lieutenant, with him. To Cardigan Street, Kennington, where Ernie Cutts lived. They stopped on the corner of the street.

'You wait here, Fred,' said Sammy. His trusty dogsbody nodded. Fred looked after Sammy's yard in Walworth, and accepted delivery of scrap metal and much else. He dismantled old iron and melted down all that was saleable. And he helped to load the carts of customers who called to collect requirements. He was a sinewy man of forty, and his loyalty to Sammy, twenty-two years his junior, never wavered. 'If I take my hat off and go in,' continued Sammy, 'you'll know Ernie's missus is alone. I like doing this kind of thing peaceably. After I've gone in, wait three minutes before you come and do your act. Got it, Fred?'

'I got yer,' said Fred.

'Highly recommendable, you are,' said Sammy appreciatively, and walked down the street to Ernie's house. It was the same as all the others in a long terraced row, and not bad for a man always mournfully claiming both his boots were pointing to the workhouse. The Victorians had filled many areas south of the river with compact, solidly built terraced dwellings for the lower classes, while along Kennington Road and all the way to Brixton Hill they had erected large three-storeyed houses for the better off, with basement rooms to accommodate servants. Theatre people lived on Brixton Hill.

Sammy had seen far worse places than Cardigan Street. He had seen the flat-fronted dwellings in parts of the East End that had deteriorated into overcrowded hovels, where ragged and bare-footed urchins played in the gutters. Cardigan Street, like Caulfield Place, showed scrubbed doorsteps, clean stone windowsills and other evidence of house-proud families.

He knocked at number 14. Mrs Cutts opened the door. She was not gaunt and bony like her husband. She was plump and quite comely, a woman in her late thirties. One or two loose hairpins showed. Other than that, she looked a tidy body.

'Well, if it ain't you, Sammy Adams,' she smiled. 'I'm honoured, I'm sure. You come to patch things up with Ernie? If you have, he ain't in.'

'Pity,' said Sammy, blue eyes bestowing friendly sunshine. 'Kids at school?'

'Except Arthur,' she said. Arthur was her eldest son, a boy of fifteen who was dark and wiry, and always sported a peaked blue cap. 'I dunno where that monkey is, but I never do know. You comin' in for a cup of tea?'

'All right, I will now I'm here. I'll write a note and leave it for Ernie.' Sammy took his hat off and stepped in. Mrs Cutts closed the door and led the way into her kitchen.

'I got some tea in the pot,' she said. 'Sit yerself down

157

while I top it up with some boiling water.' She went through to the scullery, to her gas cooker. From there she said loudly, to make sure Sammy heard, 'Yer know, Ernie ain't felt too fond of you just recent. Says yer did him down something chronic considering the stuff he's let yer have since you was fifteen and trying to get yerself started in scrap.'

'There's good times and bad, Belle,' said Sammy, searching the kitchen with sharp eyes. If the porcelain shepherdess was anywhere in the house, it would be in the kitchen, the hub of every cockney family's life. Anyone arriving home went straight through to the kitchen ninety-nine times out of a hundred. Ernie would come straight through to the kitchen. Had his light-fingered son Arthur been home since he lifted the shepherdess? The piece would have fetched twelve and six easy, it was a class piece, and if its loss hurt, so did the fact that Ernie had used his son to make a mug of Sammy Adams. 'Belle, your Arthur been in and out today?' he called.

'Oh, he come in for a bite to eat dinnertime,' said Mrs Cutts from the scullery. 'Won't be a tick, Sammy, kettle's comin' up to the boil. Shame you and Ernie ain't hittin' it orf lately.'

'Oh, ups and downs, Belle,' said Sammy, then murmured to himself as he spotted an object wrapped in brown paper on a shelf of the dresser. Gotcher, he thought. He moved swiftly and silently. He felt the shape of it. But he left it where it was for the moment. He liked to do things subtly, to avoid arguments, quarrels and fights. When Mrs Cutts came in with the teapot moments later, he was sitting at the kitchen table, scribbling a note.

'The trouble with Ernie,' he said, 'is—' He was interrupted by a knock on the front door.

'Now who's that?' said Mrs Cutts a little impatiently. She was looking forward to a second cup of tea, and drinking it with Sammy. Good company, Sammy was.

'Won't be a tick,' she said, and went to the front door. She was back after a minute or so. 'Some bloke collectin' for wounded ex-soldiers, would yer believe. I told him to go and collect from Lloyd George, what was more responsible than me and Ernie for our wounded. Bloody cheek, yer know, comin' here.' She milked two cups. One of them had a chipped lip. She poured the tea. 'There y'ar, Sammy, I don't have no quarrel with yer meself.'

'Much obliged, I'm sure,' said Sammy, noting the chipped lip. That wouldn't have done for Chinese Lady, except perhaps in former days when they were really poor, and even then, never if visitors were present. Mrs Cutts sat down next to him, and so close that her left knee touched his right knee. 'I was goin' to say,' he remarked imperturbably, 'the trouble with Ernie is he don't keep up with market prices, unless they're rising. The war's been over eighteen months, and he still don't know it. I'm leavin' him this note, I've written down the best prices I can give him for brass, copper and mixed scrap. Tell him the prices represent a friendly gesture. And listen, tell him I don't want any lead. I've made a note of that here, and underlined it. He's knockin' it off, Belle. You tell him.'

'I'll tell him, I dunno he'll listen,' said Mrs Cutts, sipping her tea with her elbows on the table and her knee caressing Sammy's. 'He reckons you're gettin' a cocky young perisher. Me, I like yer, Sammy, though at your age it don't seem right you got more goin' for you than Ernie and other men. When Ernie first met yer three years ago, you were cocky then. You got swagger now, and you've grown a man, that you have.'

'Well, you do grow, don't you, as you get older,' said Sammy, not letting her knee bother him. 'Mind, you don't seem any older, Belle, but you're still growing. You look more and more like a fine woman every time I see you.'

'Well, ain't you a one?' smiled Mrs Cutts. 'We can go in the front room and talk, if yer like.'

If Sammy thought girls got in the way of a man of ambition, he was quite sure that letting a married woman cross his path would mean disaster and ruination of an ungodly kind. Accordingly, he treated married women airily and dismissively.

'Sounds comforting, Belle, a talk in your front room,' he said, and consulted his pocket watch. 'Gawd help us, the time and all. Got to see Mr Greenberg in fifteen minutes, and you got your kids comin' home from school. I'll pop in again when I've got another note to leave Ernie, and I'll write it in your front room.'

'He's out most of the day most days,' said Mrs Cutts encouragingly.

'Well, don't get lonely,' said Sammy, and rose from his chair. 'Don't forget to tell Ernie I'm not in the market for swiped lead. Put yer foot down and keep him off church roofs. So long, ta for the tea.'

She saw him out. The brown paper still covered an object on the second shelf of the dresser. The object was compounded of two eggcups, one on top of the other. The porcelain shepherdess was in Sammy's jacket pocket. There would be a row between Ernie and his son Arthur. Arthur would swear he'd brought the porcelain home with him, and Ernie would swear he had flogged it.

'All right, guv?' asked Fred, when Sammy rejoined him on the corner of the street.

'Well, Fred, my nose don't often point me in the wrong direction, and I'm obliged to you for knockin' just at the right moment. Good on yer.'

CHAPTER TWELVE

The landing and passage had been stripped of old wallpaper, and Boots was making good defects in the plaster. Chinese Lady was in the scullery, peeling potatoes for the evening meal. When Emily came home from work in ten minutes, they'd have a nice pot of tea.

Mrs Milly Pearce knocked on the front door. She knocked quickly and loudly, then pulled on the latch-cord. The door opened and she burst into the passage, her round face white, her eyes dilated. She saw Boots.

'Boots! Oh, you've got to come, I'm near out of me mind!'

Boots looked at her. Up to a little while ago, he had only known her by the sound of her voice. He had seen her several times since coming out of hospital. She was a woman who always had an excuse for popping in. Boots had formed his picture of her in his mind, a picture of a girlish-looking young woman, coyly arch. That was what her voice and conversation sounded like. She was neither girlish nor arch at the moment, she was a woman pale and frightened.

Chinese Lady appeared. She frowned when she saw Milly.

'What's up?' asked Boots.

'Oh, you got to come and take a look at my place,' gasped Milly, forsaking her swanky style.

'Why?' asked Chinese Lady tersely.

'There's noises. There's no one there, except me, but there's noises in me front bedroom. Boots, you got to come.'

Chinese Lady exchanged looks with her son. They knew, as many neighbours knew, though Milly did not, that her house had an unpleasant history. Six years ago, in 1914, a murder had been committed, the murder of Mrs Chivers, a malicious widow much disliked. Her daughter Elsie had been arrested, tried and acquitted. The evidence Boots gave on her behalf at the Old Bailey helped the jury to decide she was not guilty.

No one in the neighbourhood had spoken of this to Milly Pearce. Neighbourly kindness prevailed. Besides which, everyone wanted to forget it. It was not a nice thing to have happened in the lives of respectable, hard-working people. The police had charged no one else. They had closed the file.

'D'you want to go and take a look, Boots?' asked Chinese Lady quietly.

'Oh, you got to,' begged Milly.

'All right,' said Boots, and wiped his hands on a cleaning rag. In an old jersey and ancient trousers, he went with Milly to her house. The door was open. She let him precede her to the stairs.

'It's up there, the noises, like whisperings and scratchings,' she breathed. 'Gawd, I'm thankful you got your eyesight back, that you can see where yer goin' and what to look for.'

'That's a point, what to look for,' said Boots, and climbed the stairs. Milly remained below, staring palely up at him as he climbed. He turned on the landing and entered the bedroom. It was in here that Mrs Chivers had been found in her bed with her throat cut. The furniture was plain and simple, Milly's bed against a wall, a cotton nightdress untidily dropped on a pillow. The dressing-table stood in window light, and a large mahogany wardrobe stood in a corner. On the baize-covered mantelpiece were cheap ornaments and a tin clock. The clock was ticking. That was the only sound he could hear. But it had its atmosphere for him, this room, because he knew what had happened there. The summer afternoon, turning into evening, was pleasantly warm, but he grimaced at his imagination for making him feel the room was without warmth at all.

Milly's nervous voice floated up.

'Are you lookin', can you hear anything?'

'I'm looking,' he called. But what was there to look for? A ghost? The unquiet spirit of a murdered woman? He could only stand and listen.

The noises came. Whisperings, scratchings, and tiny rustles. They stopped. They started again. Boots, his spine cold, strained his ears and closed his impaired left eye. The clear vision of his right eye seemed to sharpen his hearing. The tiny sounds were coming from the wardrobe. Silently he crossed to the wardrobe. He hesitated a moment before opening it. He grimaced again. What was he expecting, a body to fall from it? He was tense, nevertheless, as he pulled both wardrobe doors open. Just clothes and shoes, nothing more, but the sounds stopped. He moved the clothes aside. From the bottom of the wardrobe came a tiny rustle and twitter. But he saw nothing except shoes.

He stood back and silently laughed at himself. He knew what it was now. He stooped and slowly pulled open the drawer at the foot of the wardrobe. It was full of magazines, magazines that were chewed and ragged. There was a whisk and flurry of movement. He closed the drawer at once. He eased one end of the wardrobe away from the wall. He saw the spillage of chewed wood on the linoleum. He went out to the landing. Milly peered fretfully up at him from the foot of the stairs, the prettiness of her round face marred by agitation.

'You've got mice, Milly, in your wardrobe drawer, making a meal of *Home Chat* and *Peg's Paper*.'

'Mice? Oh, bleedin' 'orrible,' said Milly, forgetting completely to be archly ladylike.

'Better than a mystery,' said Boots. 'Go and ask Mrs Pullen to lend you her tabby.'

'What? Oh, I get yer. A cat. Yes, all right.' Milly hastened from the house.

Emily was home, taking her hat off in the kitchen.

'Mum, what a mess in the passage, all that plastering stuff,' she said. 'Where's Boots? He didn't come to meet me like he's been doing.'

'He's been makin' the passage walls good, love,' said Chinese Lady.

'Oh, if he must, he must,' said Emily, 'but where is he, then?'

'With Milly Pearce,' said Chinese Lady, and went into the scullery to put the kettle on.

'Who?' Emily followed her mother-in-law into the scullery. 'Who did you say?'

'That woman Milly Pearce. She's—'

'She's after him, the covetous cat!'

'She's been hearing noises, love.'

'I bet she has. Noises like her own hot pantin'.'

'Don't say things like that, Em'ly.'

'She's after him. Well, she's not goin' to get him, I'm goin' in there to scratch her eyes out.'

'Em'ly Adams, you're not goin' to do any such thing.'

'But, Mum, she's got him in her house!'

'Em'ly.' Chinese Lady shook her head at her angry daughter-in-law. 'Em'ly, don't you trust Boots?'

'It's not Boots I don't trust, it's her,' said Emily.

'Same thing, love, if you believe Boots'll fall for nods and winks. He hasn't ever let hisself be caught like that, and he don't need any woman except his own wife. Perhaps he s grown into the kind of man some women get a fancy for—'

'They got no right to fancy him, not when he's married to me.'

'Boots won't lose his head,' said Chinese Lady. 'It's best you trust him, love. He's only with Milly Pearce because she's been hearing noises. I can't say I like the sound of that, knowing what we all know about her house.'

Emily stiffened.

'Oh, Mum,' she breathed, 'you don't mean that woman 'as been telling Boots she's being haunted?'

'Well, noises she said it was, in her front bedroom.'

'But that's where – that's where—'

'Yes, that's where, Em'ly, we all know that,' said Chinese Lady, frowning. The kettle began to steam. 'A body don't like to think that poor woman's soul can't rest, that it's in the bedroom frettin'.'

'I'm goin' to get him,' said Emily firmly.

The door of the house was open. As Emily entered, a little girl in glasses peered at her from around the kitchen door. It was Milly's daughter Rosie, a girl of five years. She hid herself when she saw Emily, for her mother had told her to stay in the kitchen and not get under anyone's feet. Rosie had learned to be a very obedient child.

Emily mounted the stairs. Mrs Pullen's large tabby cat appeared, two mice between its teeth. It shot past Emily. Reaching the landing, she heard Milly's voice in the front bedroom. As usual, it was her fancy voice. She always put it on for Boots.

'Thank goodness you came in, Boots, thank goodness for your wonderful operation, but I think I'm going to faint, like.'

Emily marched in. She saw the sugary cow all too close to Boots. She drew a deep breath and spoke with controlled acidity.

'Well, kindly refrain from faintin' in my husband's arms.'

Milly, startled, stepped back. Boots regarded his flushed wife with a smile.

'Just some mice nesting in Milly's wardrobe,' he said.

'Never mind that,' said Emily, 'come home.'

'Well, you're all right now,' said Boots to Milly.

'Yes, thanks ever so much,' said Milly, disdaining

Emily, 'and I'm still overcome with gladness about your eyes.'

Emily expelled breath in a hiss and walked out. Boots followed her down the stairs and into the street. Her back was very stiff. He caught her up and put an arm around her. She became stiffer.

'What's up, lovey?' he asked.

'Goin' into that house after her, that's what's up,' said Emily. 'You fell for her trick all right. Noises, that's a laugh. She knew they were mice noises, I bet.' They turned into their house. 'She ain't even a decent mother to her little girl, always sendin' her into the street to play, always gettin' her out of the way. Well, if you like runnin' after her that much, don't forget two can play that game. There's fellers at the town hall gives me looks, come-on looks, I can tell you.'

Boots stopped in the passage. Emily gave him a mutinous look.

'Emily love, you've had a trying four years, I know,' he said. 'But don't ever think I need Milly Pearce or any other woman when I've got you. Believe me, I'd yell like hell for you if she caught me. I don't want to die the death.'

Emily's vexation struggled with her sense of humour and lost. A little laugh bubbled.

'Oh, yer daft thing,' she said.

'I can hear you two out there,' called Chinese Lady from the kitchen. 'I don't know what you're doing, but if it's cuddling and kissing, you can stop it right now and come in here. Tea's poured out, and I want to know what's happened.'

Boots told the story of the noisy mice. Chinese Lady was considerably relieved that it was only mice. Emily then imparted the news that Mrs Stevens had asked her to take the place of a man in the enquiries office of the sanitary department while he was on holiday. Miss Tompson, in charge of the copy typists, was a bit huffy about it, but Mrs Stevens just gave her a sweet smile.

166

'Mrs Stevens says she wants me to broaden my knowledge of the whole department, would yer believe.' Emily was in high spirits about that.

'Is that in place of learning shorthand?' asked Boots.

'No, course not, silly, just that when I am a shorthand-typist I'll have a—' Emily thought.

'A broad knowledge?' said Boots.

'Yes, that's it,' said Emily.

'You're goin' to them evening classes, then?' asked Chinese Lady dubiously.

'Oh, not till September, Mum, after their summer break,' said Emily.

'Well, good on yer, Em,' said Boots, 'I'll get back to my chore and broaden my knowledge on plastering.'

He filled in cracks and holes, the front door open to let in the light. Light continued to be a thing of wonder to him. Out of the corner of his sound eye he picked up a shyly hovering figure. He turned. From the doorway little Rosie Pearce ventured a hopeful glance. She was a pretty girl, but wore cheap, grey-rimmed spectacles. The kids called her 'Four-eyes'. Her light brown hair was curly, and although her pinafore dress needed laundering she had a flair, even at her young age, for looking neat. If she was a little shy, there were often a small girl's giggles close to the surface when her mother wasn't around. She liked Emily very much, she liked Boots even more. She had felt sad he was blind, but she also felt wonder that he never seemed blind, or even gloomy about it. Sometimes he sat on his doorstep and let her sit with him, and they had nice talks together. He would tease her and tickle her, much to her delight. She would look into his eyes, the eyes she knew couldn't see her, and feel childish curiosity because they seemed full of all the exciting mysteries and secrets she would only know about when she grew up. But now he wasn't blind any more. He had shown her he wasn't, and it put her in new wonder because his eyes looked just the same.

Boots regarded her with a smile. She responded with a little smile of her own. He thought what a pity about her cheap, ugly spectacles.

'Hello, Rosie.'

'Can you see me?' she asked.

'Well, I saw you yesterday, and on Sunday, I think, and the day before that – or was it the day before the day before? And I'm sure I'm seeing you now.'

A confused little giggle bubbled, followed by a request. 'Could I come in your house with you?' She had a surprisingly precise way of speaking.

'You can come and help me fill in holes,' offered Boots. 'The little ones down below, while I fill in the big ones higher up. We've got a small trowel. There it is. How about it?'

'Oh, yes.' She entered the passage eagerly. 'I'll be ever so good, I won't get under your feet. And could you—' she hesitated.

'Could I what?' asked Boots in cheerful, matey fashion.

'Could you give me some tickles after?'

'Ten at least,' he said.

A woman in a shabby brown dress, a knitted shawl and a cloth cap, entered the town hall at ten o'clock in the morning. She asked for the Sanitary Inspector, and was directed to a door marked ENQUIRIES. She knocked and entered. She saw a counter. Behind it two people sat at desks, leafing through letters of complaint. One was a man of thirty in owlish-looking glasses, the other was a young woman in a white blouse and dark skirt, who got up and came to the counter.

'Good morning,' she said with a smile, 'can we help you?'

'You better 'ad,' said the woman in a cap, her husband's, 'or me and me old man is goin' to get gnawed out've 'ouse and 'ome. Been there nigh on thirty years, we 'ave, and we ain't standin' for being gnawed out.'

'No, of course you're not,' said Emily sympathetically. 'What's happening, then?'

'Rats,' said her seated colleague, Mr Ernest Simmonds.

'Smart, ain't yer?' said the woman, thin and enduring. ' 'Oo's 'e?' she asked Emily.

'That's Mr Simmonds,' said Emily, 'I'm Mrs Adams.'

'Well, pleased to meet yer, I 'ope. I'm Mrs Gurney, and we got rats all right. Only they ain't ourn. Market rats, that's what they are. We live on the corner of King and Queen Street, right next to East Street. Those rats of theirn. They're 'orrible, and shouldn't be allowed. They're comin' in night after night and gnawin' their way through everything. Gnaw us out of bed, that's what they'll do one night, and then where will we be?'

'On the floor,' murmured Mr Simmonds indistinctly.

'Did 'e say something again?' asked Mrs Gurney.

'He said he was sorry, Mrs Gurney,' smiled Emily. 'Could I just take a note of your full name and address?' Mrs Gurney obliged. Emily wrote down the details. 'There's a chair if you'd like to sit down.'

'Obliged, I'm sure,' said Mrs Gurney, and lowered herself gratefully. 'I dunno, all them rats, and bugs in the summer, it ain't 'ardly worth being alive.'

'We're here to—'

'Yer a bit young, ain't yer, for this job? I expected a 'elpful kind of fatherly gent 'oo knows about rats.'

'Oh, we'll send one of that kind round, Mrs Gurney, we're here to do just that.'

'Well, yer nice even if yer are young,' said Mrs Gurney.

'Did you say they were market rats?'

'Rats are rats,' said Mr Simmonds.

'There 'e goes again,' said Mrs Gurney, 'what's 'e keep pokin' 'is nose in for? Course they're market rats. They spend all day under the stalls, gnawing through the rubbish them stall'olders chucks under, then when the

169

market packs up and they ain't got the stalls to 'ide under, they pick on our 'ouse, because it's nearest. It's criminal, that's what it is, and it's drivin' me old man to drink.' Mrs Gurney frowned. 'And me as well,' she said. 'Yes, and 'oo's goin' to pay for what's been gnawed I'd like to know. Come round 'ere a week ago, me old man did, on 'is way to work, and put a note in yer door what 'e'd wrote out careful, and addressed to the Sanit'ry Inspector. And what's come of it? Nothing.'

'I'm sorry,' said Emily, 'I expect—'

'Not your fault, ducky, you got a kind look, not your fault.' Mrs Gurney glanced over at Mr Simmonds. 'More like 'is. Sittin' there lookin' at papers and things. I bet 'e ain't got rats comin' in and gnawin' 'is desk and legs away, but I bet 'e would 'ave if 'e lived next to the market.'

'Well, we'll do something for you quick,' said Emily, not liking to tell the hard-pressed woman that she would have to wait her turn.

'What we need is yer prime ratcatcher. They're as big as cats, some of 'em. I seen the perishers. And could yer do something about the bugs as well? I mean, yer could 'ardly say me and me old man is leadin' a 'appy life.'

'We'll do what we can as soon as we can,' said Emily.

'Yer better make it sooner than that,' said Mrs Gurney, 'or when the ratcatcher does come he mightn't find any 'ouse left.'

'I'll mark it urgent,' said Emily.

'Well, I wish yer would, it's 'orrible,' said Mrs Gurney, rising stiffly to her feet. 'I'll rely on yer kindness.' She left. A moment later a long, thin man with a blue chin and a hard bowler hat came in, making for an inner door.

'Charlie, 'alf a mo,' called Emily.

'No, I ain't got 'alf a mo,' said Mr Charlie Rains, the principal ratcatcher.

'This is urgent,' said Emily, lifting the counter flap

and going after him. She thrust the note into his hand. 'Got to be seen to today. Official, Charlie.'

'Well, if you say so,' said Charlie. He looked at the address. 'I does happen to be going that way this afternoon. All right, then, gel, I bows to this urgency being more urgent, like.'

'Mrs Gurney says the rats come in from the market,' said Emily.

'She probably don't put the lid on her dustbin,' said Charlie. 'Still, all right, I'll take me dog, me bag and me killing powder.' He disappeared.

'You'll get drummed out, Emily,' said Mr Simmonds. 'There's priority rules and there's procedures, y'know.'

'Oh, well, you got to do something for a poor woman like that,' said Emily, feeling exhilarated at having bypassed procedures. She reported to Mrs Stevens later, and Madge smiled.

'You fought the battle of Copenhagen, did you, Emily, with your blind eye to the telescope?'

'Oh, Nelson, you mean,' said Emily, who was good at history.

'A triumph of initiative,' said Madge. 'But don't do it too often. Some rules are made to ensure fairness.'

'Yes, I'm gettin' to know that,' said Emily.

'You're a bright girl.'

Mrs Gurney reappeared the following day with a pound of prime eating apples. She asked Emily kindly to accept them for being helpful. Emily was touched.

'Could count as a promised bribe,' murmured Mr Simmonds.

'What's that 'e said?' asked Mrs Gurney.

'Oh, he talks to himself a lot,' said Emily.

'Well, I don't like the way 'e does it. You tell 'im, ducky.'

Emily laughed. Work in Enquiries was far more challenging and satisfying than in the typists' office.

CHAPTER THIRTEEN

The new wallpaper in the passage looked lovely. So it did in the parlour and kitchen. And Boots was now finishing the downstairs bedroom, his mother's own. He had been busy for nearly two weeks. Stripping off the old paper and making the plaster good took up most of the time. Chinese Lady, who had just put everyone's favourite in the oven, a fruity bread pudding, came in to watch her son. She knew exactly why he was busying himself this way. Emily, Tommy and Sammy went off to their work each day, Saturdays as well, and Boots, while waiting for Sammy to open the shop, was not a man to sit around. Nor would his conscience have let him.

'Paste all over yourself,' she said. 'Still, I won't say you're not makin' everything look nice. When's that Sammy opening the shop?'

'When the landlord stops asking for the kind of rent money Sammy's not prepared to pay. And Sammy's not bluffing. He's got his eye on an alternative shop in Peckham.'

'We don't want no shop in Peckham, Boots. Camberwell Green's far enough.'

'Well, Sammy's not spending any money putting the Camberwell shop right until he's satisfied, old girl,' said Boots, up on a stepladder.

'I'm not old girl,' said Chinese Lady, 'I keep telling you that. I suppose you're gettin' it from these young people they call the Bright Young Things, all gallivantin' about like high-class hooligans and gettin' theirselves

172

arrested and fined, and callin' everyone old dear or old thing. What with that and Sammy callin' me Ma, I don't know sometimes what the war's done to people.'

'I don't know, either,' said Boots, smoothing a strip of wallpaper into place.

'Oh, I just had a nice letter from Lizzy,' said Chinese Lady. 'She and Ned's comin' to tea on Sunday, and bringing Annabelle. Lizzy says their garden's lookin' lovely. I been thinkin' you ought to think about a nice house that's got a garden. There's some respectable streets off Brixton Hill where all the houses have got gardens. Once you're gettin' two pounds ten a week from the shop, you could afford to rent one of them. You don't want to bring your fam'ly up here, Boots.'

'You brought us up here,' said Boots.

'Never mind what I done, just remember how hard-up we was,' said Chinese Lady. 'I don't want you and Em'ly only havin' a back yard all your lives. Em'ly's sure to want something nicer than this when she starts havin' children. There's trees up Brixton Hill, and more fresh air. Your dad always talked about livin' near there when he retired from the Army. He liked the idea of a garden, and you know how hard it is to keep washing clean in our yard.'

'Emily won't go, not without you,' said Boots. 'Nor will I.'

'Don't talk silly now. You got your own lives to live, and I'll be all right lookin' after Sammy and Tommy.'

'But for how long?' said Boots. 'Sammy will want to move soon, he won't run his empire from here. And Tommy will get married.'

'Well, I hope he chooses someone a bit ladylike.'

'Family business, opening shops, shorthand-typists and ladylike wives, we'll all end up middle-class,' mused Boots, pasting a new strip of wallpaper.

'Nothing wrong with people bettering theirselves,' said Chinese Lady, 'but I don't know why everyone has

173

to be put in classes. Everyone works, don't they, except lords and ladies and other suchlike rich people? If Sammy gets rich, though, the first person who says he's not a worker will get the sharp end of my tongue.'

'How about a cup of tea?' suggested Boots.

'Oh, would you like one?' Chinese Lady was never happier than when performing some act of service for any of her family. 'I'll have one too and bring it in, and while you're workin' we can have more nice talk about Brixton.'

'More nice talk, yes, all right,' said Boots, and gave her an affectionate glance. Improved circumstances meant she rarely seemed harassed or careworn these days, and it was easier to see in her something of the attractiveness apparent in the photographs she had of herself as a young woman. 'Time you started walking out again,' he said, as she reached the door.

'Walkin' out?' she said.

'While you're still young,' said Boots.

'Oh, go on with you,' she said. The front door letter-box rattled. 'Who's that?' she murmured, and went to see.

Little Rosie Pearce was on the doorstep in the pinafore dress she wore for St John's, the church school. She peeped up at Chinese Lady, her eyes a bright blue behind her glasses.

'I just come home,' she announced gravely.

'From school?' Chinese Lady could not refrain from giving the child a smile.

'Mummy's not in. Could I come in and help Mister Boots like other times before?' Her precise speech was very unusual for a child of Walworth. But her mother, thought Chinese Lady, had a very fancy put-on kind of talk.

'You'd like to help, Rosie?'

'Could I, please? The other children's calling me names.' Rosie looked a little sad. 'I've got lazy eyes, Mummy says.'

174

Chinese Lady sighed. Children could be cruel to each other.

'Come in, Rosie. Would you like some tea and a piece of cake?'

'Oh, I would, please,' said Rosie with visible pleasure, and Chinese Lady took her to Boots.

'Here's your little daily help, Boots.'

Boots, pasting a strip, put the brush down and turned.

'Hello, Rosie,' he said.

'Hello,' she said.

'Your mum's not in?'

'No, she's out.'

'I'll put the kettle on,' said Chinese Lady, and left them to it.

'I won't get in your way, Mister Boots,' said Rosie, 'I'll be ever so good.'

She was always saying things like that, and it disturbed him a little.

'You won't be in the way, Rosie, don't think that.'

'You don't have bad eyes now, do you?' she said, and he knew she was really referring to her own eyes.

'Well, yes, I do have one bad eye. This one.' He touched his left eye. 'I can't see you out of this one.'

'Oh, we both got bad eyes,' she said. 'Mummy says mine are lazy. Is lazy awful bad?'

'Oh, I don't think so,' he said. 'Lazy eyes always get better as you grow up, and your spectacles are helping. Now, would you like to stand on a chair and help me put paste on the wallpaper? I'll find a brush for you.'

'Yes. It won't make my clothes dirty, will it? I don't want to look naughty.'

When she said such things, it seemed to Boots as if all the naturally extrovert inclinations of a child were struggling to contain themselves. Why did a small girl have to behave like that?

'We'll find you an old apron. We can't send you home looking all pasted up.'

'No, we best not.' Rosie looked worried. She brightened up when he went out and came back with one of Emily's more ancient aprons.

'Here we are,' he said.

'Mister Boots, I can stand on my head,' she said. 'Can I show you, can I do that first?'

'Well, I wouldn't want to miss it,' he said.

'Look.' She bent over, placed her hands on the floor and brought her legs up, planting her feet against the wall. Upside-down, her clothes showered around her face.

'Little marvel, that's what you are,' said Boots, 'but where are you under all those upside-down clothes?'

That made her giggle so much that she tumbled sideways. Her glasses fell off. Boots rescued them. Rosie sat up, looking pleased with herself.

'I did it, didn't I?' she said.

'Good you were, Rosie. Right there first time.' Boots smiled, then noticed the lenses of her spectacles were dusty. Dust clung in Walworth. He cleaned the lenses with a corner of the apron. He looked through them, using his sound eye. Both lenses were plain glass. Startled, he wondered what Milly Pearce was up to, making her small daughter wear quite useless spectacles.

It was an almost unbelievable coincidence. In that house had lived the witchlike Mrs Chivers and her daughter Miss Chivers. Miss Chivers was short-sighted, and her mother went obsessively out of her way to make sure her daughter was never seen without her glasses. Without them, Miss Chivers looked lovely, and Mrs Chivers hated her looking anything but ordinary. People said no wonder an old harridan like that got herself murdered.

Now here was a lovable little girl wearing glasses because her mother said she had lazy eyes. Perhaps they had been, when she was even younger than now. But plain, useless glass lenses? The coincidence of maternal spite was incredible.

'Mister Boots, I best put my glasses on.' Rosie spoke nervously.

'Yes, of course.' He smiled reassuringly. 'But let's do something first.' He picked up a copy of a women's magazine. He showed it to her. 'What's it called?'

Rosie looked at the title without peering or squinting.

'*Home Chat*,' she said, proud that she could already read, and he opened the magazine and showed her words at the top of a page.

'Can you read those?' he asked.

Rosie looked and said, ' "Begin our new—" I don't know the next word.'

'It's "serial",' said Boots.

'Then next it says, "here." '

'So it does,' he said. 'Look, what's that on the yard wall at the end?'

Rosie looked through the window which gave a view of the yard from end to end. She saw what was perched on the top of the far wall.

'It's a cat, Uncle Boots,' she said, and laughed. Then she cast him a look to see if he minded her calling him Uncle Boots.

'Yes, it's a cat all right,' said Boots, sure now that there was nothing at all wrong with the child's eyesight. But he put her glasses back on her, and she gave him a grateful smile. He came to the painful conclusion that for some reason Milly Pearce did not like her young daughter. 'I think tea and cake will be ready now,' he said, 'let's go and have them before we start work, shall we?'

'Then can I stay until Mummy comes home and calls me?' she asked.

'Of course,' he said, and Rosie eyed him in childish speculation.

'Uncle Boots, do you like me?' she asked.

'Why, of course I do, me pet,' said Boots, 'I likes yer

all the way up from your feet to the top of yer curly head.'

It was not until Emily was arriving home that Milly Pearce, back from a day out, raised her voice in an impatient call.

'You Rosie, where are you? Rosie!'

Emily, going in, found Rosie in Chinese Lady's bedroom, helping Boots with the wallpapering.

'Rosie love, your mummy's callin' you – or, Lor, look at you. Boots, how could you let 'er get in such a mess?'

Rosie had paste on her hands and face. Her clothes had escaped, for they were smothered under Emily's old apron. She looked guiltily at her hands. Boots, noting her look, patted her, then smiled at Emily.

'It's only paste, old girl. We're sharing it. Be an angel and clean her up, while I go and talk to her mother.'

Emily did not think much of that. Her eyes flashed a warning.

'Just tell her Rosie'll be along in a minute,' she said. 'Just that. Don't stand about with her.'

'Stand about, no, right,' said Boots. He wiped his hands, ruffled Rosie's hair, and went to talk to her mother. Milly Pearce was at her gate. Iron railings and gates fronted all the terraced houses in Caulfield Place. Milly, looking cross, showed an immediate change of mood as Boots approached. She brought forth a honeyed smile.

'Hello, Boots, come to give me the glad eye, have you?' she said. The street kids were playing outside the drug mills, and showing no interest in grown-ups. Sure of herself, Milly added, 'Bet you like it now that seeing's a treat.' She made a little forward movement behind her gate, and her covered bosom seemed to come gently to rest on the top of it.

'Treats are a welcome change,' said Boots, who

thought Milly a bit soft and sickly compared with Emily, who had a finely moulded body. 'Rosie's been with me since she came home from school. She'll be along in a moment.'

In quick reaction, Milly said, 'I hope she ain't been—' She checked, and her honey returned. Smiling, she said, 'I do hope, I'm sure, that she's not been a nuisance. I got inconveniently detained, like. Has she been good?'

'Good as gold,' said Boots, his mildness masking his suspicions of her maternal qualities. 'What's wrong with her eyes that she has to wear glasses, by the way?'

'The doctor said they were lazy. Never mind, come in and have a nice beer, I've got some bottles of Watney's brown in my larder.'

'Sounds neighbourly,' said Boots, wondering if the bottles were awaiting her husband's homecoming. 'But I'm all behind with my decorating.'

'I'm all in front with mine, to be sure,' said Milly archly, and let her bodice tighten over her plump roundness.

'Very ornamental,' said Boots.

'Dee-lighted you noticed,' said Milly.

'Well, here comes Rosie,' he said. 'I'll get back to my wallpaper.' He smiled at Rosie on his way back. Rosie had her eyes fixed on her waiting mother. She looked worried. Boots's smile became a frown.

Emily had a word with Chinese Lady the following morning before leaving for work.

'Mum, Boots spoke to me in bed last night.'

'Now, Em'ly, I don't want to hear what he says to you in bed.'

'I sometimes don't want to listen myself.' Emily laughed. 'Anyway, we're not movin'. We're not, Mum. Not without you.'

'But, Em'ly—'

179

'I love you,' said Emily, 'and I'm never goin' to leave you.'

'Why, Em'ly.' Chinese Lady looked embarrassed.

'You been kind to me all my life, even when I was nearly past redemption,' said Emily. 'So, I'm never goin' to leave you, never.' And she kissed her mother-in-law and went on her way to the town hall.

CHAPTER FOURTEEN

It was midday, Friday. The market was busy. Summer's soft fruits were on offer on the greengrocery stalls. Strawberries, raspberries, blackcurrants, redcurrants, cherries, gooseberries. There was already a glut of cherries and strawberries, the latter at thruppence a pound on some stalls. Ma Earnshaw's were fourpence, but she always prided herself on selling no spoiled fruit and her customers knew it.

A glut was a boon to the people of Walworth, for the prices meant the finest bargains. One stall was selling cherries alone, a huge gleaming mountain of them from Kent, at thruppence a pound. With the country still suffering from the colossal expense of fighting the war, the government apparently having little idea how to stimulate the economy or to make Britain, in the words of Lloyd George, a land fit for its heroes to live in, poverty was a bitter thing, and so was the sight of so many unemployed ex-servicemen.

Even so, on this bright day, the busy market, with its crowds of shoppers, wore a cheerful air. In any case, despite poverty, cockneys were eternal optimists. Sammy was typically so, looking forward, never back. He had an appointment this afternoon with the owner himself of the Camberwell shop, and he knew that meant a business session of give and take, with a settlement in mind. There was not going to be much giving on his part. Times were hard, and too many shops had had to close down all over London since the end of the war. The Camberwell man had his back to the wall, and Sammy meant to pin him there and secure a twenty per cent reduction in the rent. Time was catching Sammy up a bit, however. The sale of WD surpluses was taking place next Wednesday. He had his loan from Ikey Mo, and with that plus his own capital of three hundred pounds, he could buy in bulk, as was required and as was necessary in order to retail cheaply. He needed that lease to be settled this afternoon, and for Boots to sign it tonight.

The market bobby appeared, treading a stolid and purposeful way through the crowds. He had two boys with him. School truants, who had no doubt been caught pinching apples or the like. He had each of them by the ear, and they were wriggling. He was taking them to their homes in King and Queen Street.

'Honest, mister, we been ill,' protested one.

'I been terrible ill,' said the other. 'Chicken pox, it was.'

'We'll see, me young perishers, we'll see,' said the bobby.

Sammy, taking a breather, watched Susie working on a customer. Bert had gone to the pub.

'I tell yer what, lady,' Susie was saying, 'I'll knock tuppence off them large plates, and thruppence off the dish. My guv'nor'll kill me, but I'll tell 'im he can't expect to make a profit on everything, not everything, and the Lord blesses them that puts kindness and charity before profits. So there y'ar, missus, the plates and the dish for six bob instead of seven and thruppence. And just look, yer can see they're from the Drayton potteries, which make the best willer pattern in England – no, I tell a lie – in the world.'

Sammy smiled. The Whatsername girl was learning fast, although she would probably follow her declaration by silently asking God to forgive her. She was very religious. She looked acceptable to the eye these days in her neat, dark blue overall. And she had a new blue ribbon holding the long tail of her hair in place. He saw her smile winningly at the customer, who smiled back and gave in.

'All right, I'll have 'em, ducky. Put 'em in a box for me.'

When she had completed the sale, Susie put the money in the cash box, and Sammy entered the amount on the slip of paper on which her previous sales for the week had been recorded.

'Mister, I had to let the lady 'ave that lot at the knockdown price, or she'd 'ave gone away,' she said.

'I heard,' said Sammy. 'You got it right, young Whatsername. Don't let any of 'em escape. As soon as you know they want something, don't let 'em go without it.'

'I've sold 'eaps this morning,' said Susie, glowing with pleasure.

'Well, you'll get your earnings for the week this evening,' said Sammy.

'Am I doing all right for yer, mister?'

'I'm not complaining,' said Sammy from the back of the stall.

'Oh, nor me,' said Susie happily.

'Glad to hear it,' said Sammy drily. He hoped Bert would be back on time. He couldn't leave this girl by herself, not on a Friday.

Blissfully, she said, 'Me mum and dad, they can't 'ardly remember being this well off, Dad only gettin' a bit of disabled pension, like, and Mum 'aving to—'

'I don't want to know,' said Sammy, only too relieved her shining blue eyes were on the other side of the stall and not too close to him. 'I told you, we've all got hard luck stories. I've been next door to dying starvation a hundred times myself.' He muttered, knowing Chinese Lady wouldn't have liked hearing him say that. Even when there'd been nothing left in the house to pawn, one good meal a day had always appeared. 'Well, almost next door to dying,' he said.

'Oh, yes, we been like that, too,' said Susie, 'but now

183

I got this job, well, I'll never know how to thank yer for yer godliness.'

'Stop havin' religious mania,' said Sammy, and Susie gave him one of her quick enquiring glances. She was getting to know Mister Sammy Adams a little better each day. She already knew all she wanted to know about Bert Lomax. Bert was florid and hearty, but a bit casual and a bit moody. He gassed a lot to Ma Earnshaw, which meant he sometimes kept a customer waiting, and that often meant a lost customer if she, Susie, was busy herself. Mister Adams never let that sort of thing happen. He treated all customers as if they were his treasured friends, which they were, of course, in a way. And he had the gift of the gab all right when he was dealing with them, and he used his blue eyes to shower the blessings of sunshine on them.

'I have my faults, young Miss Whatsername, and my virtues,' Sammy said in a sermonising way, then stopped to serve a girl with a blue glass vase which she wanted, she informed him, for her ma's birthday. 'All right, penny off to you, love, so you can have it for fivepence, and wish yer dear ma many happy returns from me, which is yours truly, Sammy Adams, here today and here tomorrow.' The amused girl served, he said to Susie, 'And as I was goin' to say, I do not aspire to godliness.'

'Crikey, what a lovely mouthful,' said Susie. 'Mister, after I've had me pie an' mash, I'm goin' to the shop in Walworth Road to buy meself a summer dress before I come back to the stall, but I won't come back late, honest. You can get a dress in that shop by payin' just a bob to start with, then sixpence a week till it's paid off. D'yer think I ought to buy a nice white one as it's for Sundays?'

Sammy thought the question highly suspect. What was she up to? Trying to make him responsible for dressing her, in a manner of speaking?

'Look,' he said, then broke off to let her collar a sale of two glass tumblers to a woman. She was always quick to latch on, and Bert had growled at her more than once, in Sammy's presence, to let her know she wasn't required to butt in unless there was more than one customer to attend to. Susie's eagerness to be of service and to earn money still ran her ahead of the rule sometimes. When Bert was affected, he complained. When Sammy was affected, as now, he was tolerant. He approved of eagerness and initiative in any form of business. When the customer had gone, he said, 'Look, don't ask me what kind of frock you should buy. Ask yer mum. I know I chose that overall, but that's the beginning and end of me interest in yer female clobber.'

'Well, I only—' Susie interrupted herself to pinch another customer. She knew Mister Sammy accepted it was up to her, while at the front of the stall, to use the advantage this gave her. Mister Sammy, in any cases, had worked hard on his crate, standing on it for two hours to bring the customers crowding in, and always with success.

Ma Earnshaw broke into fruity, bawling singsong.

'I got pertaters, bananas, and juicy termaters,

And Jerseys four pound a tanner,

I got strawberries, raspberries an' loverly Kent cherries

And lettuce as big as a joanner.

Come 'an buy, ladies!'

Susie handed Sammy the money for selling a pair of blue Egyptian vases. Well, they were called Egyptian and stamped so on the bottom, but Susie was sure they had been made in Birmingham. People said everything in the world had been made in Birmingham, including the Eiffel Tower in Paris and the Statue of Liberty in New York. Susie had asked Sammy if this was true. Of course, he said, and asked her in turn if she'd ever climbed Mount Everest. Susie said of course she hadn't, and Sammy said that when she did she'd see 'Made in Birmingham' stamped on the top.

'Mister,' she said now, 'about me frock—'

'Leave off,' said Sammy.

'I only thought as yer've been so stern about what I wear, I'd ask yer about the colour. I didn't want to upset yer by gettin' a colour yer didn't like.'

'Kindly explain what you're talkin' about – no, kindly don't bother, just leave it,' said Sammy.

'Yes, all right, mister,' said Susie, 'as long as yer don't go on about what I do buy and take the Lord's name in vain as well.'

'I'm hearing things,' said Sammy to a jug, 'I'm hearing things, that's what I'm doing. I'm standin' here, mindin' my own business and not offendin' anyone, and all I'm gettin' for it is impudence.'

'Oh, but, mister, I was only trying—' Again Susie interrupted herself as a nicely dressed lady appeared beside Sammy at the back of the stall. She leaned to examine an item he had put on sale again after keeping it to himself for over a week. It was the porcelain shepherdess, too expensive for most people of Walworth. But Sammy knew someone would find it irresistible. Susie had asked how he got it back, and Sammy told her what she didn't know she couldn't talk about. The lady picked the porcelain up to inspect it keenly, her interest unmistakable. It keyed Sammy up, but Susie actually beat him to it. 'Lady, can I 'elp you?' she asked, coming round from the front of the stall.

Holy Moses, thought Sammy, she's jumped me, she's going to take me for one and thruppence commission if she sells it at the top price of fifteen bob. The interested lady handled the piece lovingly, turning it to discover it was Sèvres porcelain.

'Well, my word,' she murmured.

Sammy said, 'You won't find—'

'Yes, it's real Sevvers,' said Susie, and encouraged

186

the lady to bring it from the shade of the stall and look at it in the sunlight at the front, thereby divorcing the customer completely from Sammy. His little grin was admiring but brief. 'It's really beautiful, ain't it?' said Susie. 'Don't yer—' She paused. 'Don't yer think so, madam?' Yes, that was it. Madam. Madam sounded just right. 'Yer'll never believe the price.'

'I'll try not to wince,' said the lady, 'if you'll try to break it gently.'

'Well, the guv'nor's very proud of the piece,' said Susie, 'and he'd like it to go to someone appreciative, madam, him regardin' it almost like it was God's 'andiwork. So he's only askin' twenty-one shillings, a guinea, as long as it goes to a good 'ome.'

Jesus, thought Sammy, she's a natural. She's skinny, she's got mania, and a face with great big blue holes in it, but she's a natural.

'How much?' asked the lady, who was not wincing.

'Twenty-one shillings,' repeated Susie, acting on instinct. Fifteen bob had been Sammy's top price, twelve and six bottom.

'I'll take it,' said the lady, 'is there a box for it?'

'Oh, yes, madam, we couldn't let anyone take it away except in its box,' said Susie, 'and I'll put tissue paper in as well. We are kindly obliged to yer, madam, for yer valu'ble custom.'

The lady smiled.

When she had gone, Sammy said sternly, 'I'll sack yer next time yer lay another fancy trick like that on me.'

'Oh, yer wouldn't, yer couldn't,' begged Susie, 'not when I only want to 'elp yer out as much as I could when yer been workin' so 'ard all morning, and not when she paid six bob more than the startin' price.'

'You've caught me for one and nine commission,' said Sammy.

'Oh, yer can pay me just a bob, honest,' pleaded Susie.

'No, I can't. You sold it for a guinea and you'll get one and nine. I'm proud of yer.'

'Proud of me?' Her eyes shone. 'Mister, are yer really?'

'Here's Bert comin',' said Sammy. 'Go and get your pie and mash, then buy the frock. White's nice for Sundays, but not practical, not in Walworth. It won't wash pure white for long. Blue's your best colour.'

'Bless yer, mister, I'll buy a really nice blue one, then.'

She came back with a mid-blue dress that had a band of lacy white around its hem. She tucked the parcel away in a box under the stall, and with Sammy absent, she spent the afternoon helping Bert. It was a long afternoon, as the market stayed open until eight o'clock on Fridays and Saturdays. At ten past seven, when her day had proved lovely and profitable, Sid Mullins turned up. He was seventeen, and his family lived on the fourth floor of Peabody's. He was a gawky youth, not bad-looking, but Susie had gone off him a bit. She had found him too bossy, too possessive. He acted very impertinent sometimes, like he thought he owned her. Susie was not going to be owned by anyone, ever.

Sid hung around the stall, making a nuisance of himself.

'Oh, go away,' she said, 'yer'll get me into trouble if Mister Adams comes and catches yer messin' about here, and Mister Lomax don't like it much, neither. Go away.'

'I ain't doin' no 'arm,' said Sid, 'I'm just waitin' till yer stall packs up, then I'll walk yer 'ome.'

'I can walk meself 'ome,' said Susie, 'so go away.'

Trade was thinning out, Bert was gossiping with Ma Earnshaw, and Sid was getting pestiferous. Susie's big-eyed, elfin prettiness meant she was not short of the company of boys, but she was not serious about any of them, least of all this irritating one. In any case, none of them fitted the image she had girlish dreams about, someone nice and kind and loving, like her dad. She didn't dream about someone rich, just someone nice and kind.

'I'm stayin' an' waitin',' said Sid, picking up a large china pudding basin and putting it on his head for a laugh. 'Suit me, yer reckon, Susie?'

'No, so put it back,' said Susie.

''Ere, you Susie,' called Bert, 'stop all that larkin' about, you ain't at 'ome.'

'It's not me,' protested Susie. She snatched at the basin with both hands. Sid jerked his head, the basin fell to the ground in front of the stall and broke into pieces. Susie, aghast, knew the cost of it, ninepence, would be deducted from her earnings. Furious, she kicked at Sid.

'Now yer done it,' said Bert, 'and it'll cost yer dear, yer stupid girl, and not just its price.'

'There y'ar,' said Sid, a grin on his face, 'now see what yer been an' done, Susie.'

Susie smacked his face, and his grin turned sour. He seized her wrist. Bert arrived at the front of the stall.

''Oppit, you,' he said to Sid. 'You too,' he said to Susie. 'Bleedin' push off, the pair of yer. 'Oppit.'

'But it wasn't my fault,' cried Susie, who suspected Bert was getting a bit jealous of her.

'Scarper,' said Bert to Sid, digging a finger into his chest. 'Shove off, and don't come round 'ere again, savvy?'

Scowling, Sid disappeared. Susie appealed to Bert.

'Please don't send me 'ome,' she said, 'it's not fair.' She was hoping Mister Sammy would turn up, as he usually did about this time on a Friday evening, to pay her her earnings. She didn't regard Bert as her employer, only Mister Sammy. 'I ain't been paid, anyway,' she said. She collected her week's earnings on Fridays, and was paid daily on Saturdays and Sundays.

189

'Never mind about that,' said Bert, 'yer can come an' collect tomorrer morning, and I daresay yer can collect the sack as well. I ain't lettin' yer lark about 'ere with yer 'ooligan friends and break the place up without seeing yer get what yer deserve. Go on, off yer go, you ain't wanted 'ere.'

Susie could have wept, but wouldn't, not in front of Bert. She put her chin up, turned on her heel and left.

Had she stayed to argue for a minute longer, she would have been able to appeal to the one she trusted, her Mister Sammy Adams. Sammy, arriving after she had gone, listened to Bert's complaints about her.

'What d'you mean, you sent her packin'?' said Sammy. 'She's only a kid.'

'Obstreperous, that's what she is,' said Bert, pointing to the smashed basin. 'Broke it, she did, her and her 'ooligan friend between them, and left it for Fred to clear up.'

'Well, I'll tell you, that girl's no lark-about kid,' said Sammy. 'She's got her heart in her work, and I ain't convinced she'd invite anyone to come and mess about around the stall. What she earns here means a lot to her.'

'You gone daft?' said Bert.

'No, I ain't,' said Sammy, 'I can't afford to.' Secretly, he thought he'd been soft as well as daft over Susie Whatsername. But he could recognise a good worker, and a good worker was an asset. 'Did you pay her?'

'No,' said Bert, 'I sent 'er off with a flea in her ear, like she deserved. Told 'er to come an' collect her pay tomorrer, and probably the sack. She don't fit, and she ain't really needed. I'd've given 'er the sack meself, only—'

'Only you don't have any say-so concernin' staff,' said Sammy.

'Staff? Staff?' Bert was caustic. 'You and yer big ideas, we're runnin' a stall 'ere, not a fact'ry.'

'No difference. Principle's the same. The girl's staff,

and her comings and goings are my say-so. You've got a thirty-five per cent interest in the stall, the rest is mine. Do your sums, Bert, and stick to the agreement, there's a good bloke.' Sammy exuded crisp self-confidence. He had had a highly satisfactory meeting with the owner of the shop, and the lease was to be signed on Sammy's terms forthwith. He investigated the cash box, then totted up Susie's commission for the week.

'Yer a cocky young bleeder,' said Bert, 'but yer ain't daft enough, I 'ope, to forget to dock 'er ninepence for the basin. Eh?'

'I heard you, Bert, I got you,' said Sammy. He glimpsed a white carrier bag in a box just under the stall. 'What's this?' He drew it out and looked inside it. It contained a blue frock, neatly folded. 'Is this hers?'

'I dunno,' said Bert. 'She shoved something down there.'

Sammy frowned at himself for worrying about young Whatsername going off so upset she forgot her new dress.

Susie made a dragging and forlorn way home, eyes blinking back tears. She was going to arrive empty-handed, and with the news that she might be getting the sack. Oh, that rotten lout, Sid Mullins. That's what he was, a lout. She'd have to beg and plead with Mister Adams tomorrow, but if Bert stood against her and if Mister Adams was cross with her, specially after she'd let the shepherdess get pinched, she really could lose her job. She wandered in depression around the buildings block before going in and mounting the stone stairs. On the first landing, a figure darted, and a hand grabbed her wrist.

'Gotcher,' said Sid, and the grin on his face was still sour. 'Yer made me look small, yer did, Susie Brown. Yer got to pay for that, with kisses, but I know yer'll like yer punishment.'

Susie may have been thin, but she was no weakling.

Nor did she lack spirit, any more than her mum and dad did. She wrenched her wrist free and kicked Sid on his shin. He hissed with pain, grabbed her arms and pushed her against the tiled wall.

'Let me go!' Susie writhed and kicked. He pressed close, smothering her, and she twisted her head away as he sought to kiss her. 'I'll scream! Let me go!'

'Come on, yer know yer goin' to like it.'

'Get away – oh, yer hurtin' me – get away!' Susie was disgusted and furious, hating the thought of being loutishly kissed.

Someone, observing the scene from the foot of the stairs, ran up at speed. A hand took Sid by the scruff of his neck and yanked him away from Susie.

'I'll knock you bloody senseless!' shouted Sammy. He rarely lost his temper, and he rarely showed anger. It was his nature to communicate profitably with people, and hostility was a loss-making thing. But a man bruising a woman, or a lout bruising a girl, could make him very hostile indeed, as it could Boots and Tommy. Holding Sid Mullins by his collar, Sammy shook him until the gawky youth was jerking like a puppet on its strings. At eighteen, Sammy was only a year older than the lout, but he was already a vigorous man and Sid Mullins still a callow adolescent.

'Never touched 'er,' gasped Sid, 'just teasin', I was – 'ere, don't – lemme go—'

Sammy let him go, giving him a shove in the process. Sid's back thudded against the wall, and he shuddered.

Sammy, eyes icy, said, 'I know your face now, sonny, which means I've got your number, and if I ever catch you hammering any girl again, I'll skin you alive.' He enunciated every word coldly and clearly, and Chinese Lady would have been very approving of his speech, especially in such a worthy cause. 'Take yourself off, face-ache, and fast.'

Sid, pale and shaken, took himself off very fast, hurtling down the stairs and out of the building. Sammy turned to look at Susie. Her eyes were wide open, staring at him in awe, their blue muted in the shadow of the landing. To one side of her, the landing window transmitted the hazy summer twilight of smoky Walworth.

'Oh, Mister Adams,' she breathed, 'yer came like the avengin' angel, like the sword of the Israelites. Oh, yer smote him 'ip and thigh.'

'Hardly touched him,' said Sammy, 'and stop doing Bible readings. Did he hurt you?'

'He just made me awful angry,' said Susie, really in awe at the way Mister Sammy had dealt with the devil in Sid. 'But I'll be forever grateful yer come when yer did, like Saul in 'is chariot of fire. And why did yer come? 'Ave yer seen Bert? Did he tell yer about what 'appened? But it wasn't my fault, really it wasn't, I didn't ask that rotten larker to come to the stall, honest. Yer got to believe me. I'm near dying of misery, thinkin' you're goin' to sack me, specially after I let that other boy pinch the shepherdess. Mister Adams, yer won't do that, give me the sack, will yer?'

Sammy, seeing the moisture in the blue eyes, rushed in with hasty words to prevent the possibility of having her weep on his chest again.

'Now don't you start crying, there's no need for that. I've brought your – hold on.' He went halfway down the stairs, retrieving the white carrier bag he had dropped in order to have both hands free to deal with Susie's tormentor. 'Here, you forgot this, it's yer new frock. Got yourself a nice blue one, I see. And I've also brought your week's earnings. And I'm not goin' to sack you.'

Utterly rapturous relief so affected Susie that she flung her arms around him and kissed him on the cheek.

'Oh, mister, thank yer, mister.' Susie took the carrier bag from him, then her money, in a brown envelope.

'Well, that's it, then,' said Sammy in the brisk, businesslike fashion of a man who felt it highly necessary

to depart. But he stayed to say, 'D'you know how much
you earned Monday to Friday? Twenty-five bob and
sixpence. You sold stuff worth fifteen quid and six
shillings.' He saw her face light up, and he put himself
rapidly out of kissing distance.

'Oh, I'm rich,' she gasped. 'Bless yer, mister.'

'All right, I'm blessed, then,' said Sammy, 'but don't
let's have any more waterworks, nor kisses and cuddles.
That's no way to behave.'

'Oh, but now you're here, Mister Adams,' she said,
'couldn't yer come up and meet me mum and dad, so
they'll know who me kind benefactory is?'

She's not believable, thought Sammy, she's a danger
to my peace of mind. First her starving eyes, then
her religious mania, then buckets of tears, then kisses,
and now an invitation to meet her parents. If he
wasn't careful, she'd get him to become a second
father to her, and make him feel responsible for her
welfare.

'No, young Whatsername, I can't—'

'Oh, I'm Susie, yer know I am.'

'Never mind that. Just don't take too much notice
of Bert. It's me you work for, and I'm keepin' you
on. You know how to talk to customers. And you're
lookin' better now you're gettin' your regular pie
and mash. But I can't come up and meet your parents.
I've got things to do. I'll see you at the stall tomorrow.'

'Yes, and thank yer ever so much,' said Susie, 'I got
to say you're overflowing with goodness.'.

'No, I ain't, so stop hurtin' my ears,' said Sammy, and
escaped.

Susie ran joyfully up to her parents' flat. They were
delighted at how much she had earned, and there would
be more from her work tomorrow and from the time
she put in before and after Sunday morning's church
service. She did not tell them about Sid, she knew it
would upset them. She went and put on her new
frock. Its colour suited her fairness, and her parents

thought it made her look like a princess, particularly as it was the first new dress she had had for years. Parents who existed in the working-class areas always related the look of a pretty daughter in a new dress to that of a princess. Every pretty daughter was a Cinderella who only needed a fairy godmother to effect the transformation. Mr and Mrs Brown took little notice of the cheapness of the cotton material, which would need endless ironing and lose its shape after only a few washes.

'I could buy another one now,' said Susie, 'I could wear this one and buy another one for Sundays. Mister Adams 'as a high regard for nice clothes, and don't like to see me lookin' shabby in case 'is customers think 'e pays me starvation wages.'

'Well, we got to give it to 'im, he don't do that,' said Mr Brown.

'Is he fond of you, Susie?' asked Mrs Brown, thinking perhaps she ought to warn her young daughter of certain pitfalls.

'Fond of me? Oh, no,' said Susie, 'he treats me very kind but very casual, like, and he still can't 'ardly remember what my name is.'

'That's all right, then,' said Mrs Brown.

'What?' said Susie.

'Never mind he can't remember what your name is, love,' said Mrs Brown.

Susie arrived at the stall on Saturday morning in her new dress, and carrying her overall on her arm. Sammy took a brief look at her, saw what the blue frock did for her fairness and her eyes, and turned his own eyes elsewhere.

'Mister?' she said shyly, wanting to know if he approved.

'Unpack that box,' said Sammy. 'It's got six cut-glass cruet sets on silver stands. Put one on display just there.'

'Yes, mister,' she said. 'Mister, do yer like me dress?'

'It'll do,' said Sammy.

'Oh, yer don't like it? Oh, it's not fair. I asked yer what would be best, and yer said blue, and now yer don't like it.'

'Now did I say that? No, I didn't. Just unpack the cruets.' Bert hadn't arrived yet and Sammy was busy with his displays. 'And don't give me any lip.'

'Oh, I wouldn't, I couldn't, not when I owe yer me life itself almost,' said Susie earnestly. Sammy muttered. She undid the box. 'Mister, these ain't cut glass, an' the stands are tinny.'

'Now look here, Miss Whatsername,' said Sammy, 'the people who use this market can't afford genuine cut glass or silver, so we offer 'em imitations. They don't get cheated, not at the prices we ask. Those cruet sets'll be put on offer as genuine imitation cut glass and genuine imitation silver. Got it?'

'Yes, Mister Adams. Oh,' she said admiringly, 'yer couldn't be more honest to the customers than that. But yer like me dress a little bit, don't yer?'

'Yes, all right,' said Sammy, with the first early morning shoppers entering East Street.

'Seeing I been doing so well workin' for yer,' said Susie, putting one cruet on display, 'I'm goin' to buy another one today.'

Sammy took a second look at her frock. It had the advantage of newness, and it did turn her into a very pretty girl, but there were buts.

'It's none of my business,' he said, thinking of Emily's approach to clothes, 'but pay a bit more for your next one. Good cotton's got more body to it.'

Susie, beginning to see her kind but complex employer as a man of invaluable knowledge and opinions, said, 'Oh, I'll pay as much as two bob more, shall I?'

'It's up to you, Susie,' said Sammy in an unguarded response.

'Oh, yer called me Susie,' she said. 'Mister Adams, yer really so nice to me.'

Holy mackerel, thought Sammy, I was right, I'll end up being her second dad if I get too careless. She'll have me forking out a dress allowance, and she'll be expecting something on her birthdays. Save yourself now, Sammy Adams, get rid of her.

'Look, put your overall on,' he said, 'keep your new frock clean.'

'Yes, Mister Adams. Oh, yer so kind and thoughtful.'

Sammy muttered.

CHAPTER FIFTEEN

Over Sunday dinner, Chinese Lady said, 'Oh, I nearly forgot to tell you Uncle Tom and Aunt Victoria's comin' to tea, as well as Lizzy and Ned.'

'Thrilling,' said Tommy.

'I can hardly wait,' said Sammy.

'I can hardly believe it,' said Boots.

'Mum, they're being sarky,' said Emily.

'I heard,' said Chinese Lady, 'I don't know any woman who's got more aggravatin' sons than I have.'

'I like Uncle Tom,' said Emily.

'I like Aunt Victoria,' said Boots.

'Love her,' said Sammy.

'Me too,' said Tommy. 'When she's at 'ome.'

'When you've finished,' said Chinese Lady, 'perhaps we can all be nice about our relatives. Which reminds me,' she added casually, 'I invited your cousin Vi too.'

It was the casual note that made Boots look at her. And it was her aloof look that made his smile slyly appear. He remembered Vi and her parents had visited him in hospital, and that afterwards Chinese Lady, present herself at the time, said what a ladylike girl Vi had grown into.

Chinese Lady presided at tea in the parlour. Aunt Victoria held forth.

'I must say God's grace has done a real kindness to you, Boots. I said to your Uncle Tom, I said, what goes on between heaven and earth you can never tell about. It's something—' She stopped to think what something was.

198

'Awesome?' suggested Boots.

'Yes, I was only saying to a neighbour of mine that things happen you never dream of. It shows we all ought to be believing. Lizzy, Annabelle's not eating her crusts.'

Lizzy and Ned's daughter Annabelle, in her fourth year, had her mother's chestnut hair and brown eyes. High-spirited, she was not in the least shy of her proud and upright grandmother, and she adored her uncles and her Aunt Emily. She was intrigued by the fact that Uncle Boots could now see. She was also puzzled, as much as Rosie was, because she had never been able to understand why he couldn't see.

She was behaving herself at the table, as her parents had taught her to, but she was loath to eat up her bread and butter when the jam tarts and the fruit cake looked so tempting.

'Annabelle, no cake, you know, unless you eat up your bread crusts,' said Lizzy.

'I always made Vi eat hers,' said Aunt Victoria, 'for the good of her teeth. Vi's got lovely teeth now.' Vi, catching Tommy's smile, rolled her eyes. 'Well, we've all been that thankful about Boots, Maisie, it's not as if he's been undeserving or hasn't behaved gentlemanly most of his life.'

'Don't you believe it,' said Emily, thinking of how wicked her husband could be in bed.

'Emily?' said Aunt Victoria in surprise.

'I didn't say nothing,' said Emily. 'Did I?'

'Well, yer could have said more,' murmured Tommy, 'we're all interested.'

'You'll be lucky,' said Emily.

'I don't know, I'm sure,' said Aunt Victoria, slightly disapproving, 'but as I was saying, God's grace don't fall on the undeserving.' Boots was her favourite nephew because he was gentlemanly. 'But I'm that surprised you're going to work in a shop, Boots. Mind you, Maisie, I was even more surprised at Sammy

199

taking a stall in East Street among all them roughs.'

'It's a livin',' said Uncle Tom, 'you got to make a livin'.'

'It's hard for men with all the unemployment,' said Vi, who had a job herself with an insurance company in Holborn.

'A respectable living's best,' said Aunt Victoria.

'What's an unrespectable living?' asked Ned, who could only think of street walkers.

'Sammy don't live unrespectably,' said Chinese Lady, 'I wouldn't let him darken my door if he did.'

'I just like makin' money,' said Sammy, 'which is highly respectable and most desirable.'

Annabelle eyed her Uncle Boots across the table. He winked, he slid a dish of jam tarts towards her.

'I'm watching you, Boots,' said Lizzy, six months happily pregnant.

'Pardon?' said Boots.

'Annabelle's not eaten her bread an' butter yet,' said Lizzy.

'Nor me,' said Tommy.

'Then you're not havin' any jam tarts yet, either,' said Lizzy.

'Oh, poor Uncle Tommy,' said Annabelle.

Tommy wondered how true that might be. His luck had run out. He was beginning a week's notice tomorrow, along with other men at his firm. He had said nothing to his family. He was hoping a promised recommendation would land him a job with another firm.

Boots too had a problem. He had received a letter from the war pensions department of the Ministry, asking him to present himself to a Mr Preedy on Wednesday. Chinese Lady had said trust that lot not to lose any time stopping his pension. It was a wonder, she said, that they'd never asked her to produce her husband's dead bones to prove she was a widow. Still, now that Sammy was definitely going to open the shop and pay Boots two pounds ten a week to manage it, loss of the pension didn't matter too much.

Ned, touching on Sammy's business interests, said, 'Somehow I never saw you as a retailer, Sammy. Can you make a quick fortune in retailing?'

'Investing profits and borrowing against future profits for investment, that's how you turn one shop into two shops, and two into four, and so on,' said Sammy. 'Me market stall's a steppin'-stone, me shop's a bigger one. Of course, you need good managers.'

'That's where Boots comes in, as a good manager of your first shop?' asked Ned.

'I want me managers to have class and style,' said Sammy.

'Boots don't have much class and style when he comes to meet me at the town hall lookin' like a ragbag,' said Emily. 'And with bits of wallpaper stickin' to him. I don't hardly know where to look.' Boots let a grin touch his mouth. Emily wrinkled her nose at him. 'I don't know what me friends at work think.'

'Well, I am surprised,' said Aunt Victoria, 'Boots has always looked very nice to me.'

'You ain't seen him all over wallpaper,' said Sammy.

Vi laughed. She was fair-haired, hazel-eyed and rather nice to look at. But she was, unfortunately, the daughter of an over-protective mother. Aunt Victoria meant to see the right kind of young man was chosen for Vi. For years Vi had existed in the shadow of maternal possessiveness, which had made her quiet and retiring. Lately, however, with the aid of her father, she had begun to stand up to her mother. But Aunt Victoria still kept a close watch on her.

Vi was very fond of her cousins. She had had a crush on Boots in her early teens. She suffered heartache when he was blinded on the Somme, and desolation when he became engaged to Emily. Emily of all girls. She was so plain. But Boots married her all the same, and sensibly Vi cured herself of her crush.

She thought all her cousins were fun. And Emily,

201

well, she was very lively, and when she smiled everything that was nice about her came shining through,
and she didn't look at all plain then, she really didn't.
Vi supposed Boots had seen what other people hadn't,
how nice Emily was underneath.

'Speaking of the town hall,' said Aunt Victoria, 'how
are you getting on there, Emily?'

'Oh, I'm not just doing copy-typing all the time,' said
Emily enthusiastically, 'I'm associating meself with
sanit'ry problems like drains and vermin and—'

'Here, d'you mind,' said Sammy, 'not when me and
Annabelle's workin' our way through Ma's succulent
jam tarts.'

'That boy Sammy, Tom,' said Chinese Lady, 'kindly
overlook him callin' me his ma.'

'Well, you're a good 'un, Maisie, that you are,' said
Uncle Tom, a kind man, 'your boys couldn't 'ave had
a better.'

'I was goin' to say wall fungi too,' said Emily. 'You
see, Aunt Victoria, I'm in the Sanit'ry Inspector's
department – oh, and they want me to think about bein'
a shorthand-typist so that I might end up bein' one of
them workin' for the Inspector 'imself.'

'Eh?' said Uncle Tom.

'It's like this, y'see,' said Tommy, 'in the sanit'ry
department copy typists pass through drains into
shorthand-typin'. After they've had a bath, of course.'

'I don't think I'll have any cake,' said Sammy.

'Try some fungi,' said Boots.

Emily clapped her hand to her mouth and cast a
glance at Chinese Lady. Chinese Lady was looking
severe. But her mouth twitched. Emily burst into
laughter then.

'You'll excuse this fam'ly bein' full of comics, Uncle
Tom, won't yer?' she said.

'Good as the music 'all at times,' said Uncle Tom.

When tea was over, Boots said he and Tommy would
do the washing-up.

'No, you and Ned can relax and enjoy a cigarette with Uncle Tom,' said Emily, 'you been wearin' yourself out doing all this decoratin' ever since you came out of hospital.'

'I think we got favouritism muckin' us about,' said Sammy.

'Yes, you and Tommy can do it, Sammy,' said Emily.

'I'll be obliged if yer wouldn't chuck my name about like that,' said Sammy, 'not when I've got business calculations to work out.'

'None of that, Sammy, if you don't mind,' said Chinese Lady, 'not on a Sunday and not when we got visitors.'

'I'll help,' said Vi, 'I'd be pleased to.'

'All right, you and me, Vi,' said Tommy, who had been thinking what a nice gentle girl she was, and how good-looking she'd grown.

He and Vi did the chore by themselves, with everyone else in the parlour. They exchanged cousinly conversation, Vi enjoying the fact she found him easy to talk to. She said Boots was doing a lovely job with the decorating, and wasn't it wonderful he'd come out of his operation so active?

'Well, he's got a way with him,' said Tommy. 'You don't think it's 'appening to you, then you suddenly realise he's runnin' things, which is what he likes, only he wouldn't admit it.'

'Oh, I think Boots is awfully nice,' said Vi.

'Got a soft spot for him?' asked Tommy, hands in hot water full of soda crystals.

'I used to have,' said Vi, polishing the cake-stand vigorously with the tea towel. 'I mean – well, I don't think of him like that now.'

'Have you got some nice feller in Camberwell, then?'

'Fat chance I have when me mum—' Vi stopped. 'Oh, you know, Tommy.'

'We all know Aunt Victoria fancies the Prince of Wales for yer,' said Tommy. He laughed. 'Still, she 'hasn't spoiled yer, Vi. You're nice. You'll get some well-off bloke for sure.'

'Don't want some well-off bloke,' said Vi, 'just someone I like a lot. I bet you've got girls.'

'I know a few,' said Tommy, 'I wouldn't actually say I've got 'em. But I've got a problem all right. I've just been given a week's notice.'

'Oh, Tommy.' Vi knew how difficult it was for an unemployed man to get a job. 'Tommy, I'm ever so sorry.'

'I'm not complainin',' said Tommy, 'not yet. Don't say anything, I don't want the fam'ly to know, specially as there's a chance with another firm. Me manager's recommendin' me.'

'Then I'll keep my fingers crossed for you,' said Vi. Her own job was safe, which made her feel it wouldn't be right if Tommy had no job at all. She thought that if she had the vote, she would support the Labour Party, which was on the side of working people. Her dad voted Liberal, being an admirer of Lloyd George, but her mum always told him off about it, saying he'd vote for the Conservatives if he had any sense.

'Like to go for a walk when we've finished?' asked Tommy.

'A walk?' Vi looked disbelieving. She knew her cousins regarded her as a bit of a wallflower. She'd been fighting that image lately. 'You and me, Tommy?'

'If you'd like to.'

'Love to,' said Vi.

While Tommy and Vi were out walking, much to Aunt Victoria's surprise, Ned played the paino. His touch wasn't as gifted as Tommy's, but it was passable, and Annabelle loved to listen. She listened now, cuddling up to Sammy on his lap. Sammy could accept cuddles from small girls. Small girls weren't a threat.

Boots, sitting by the window and keeping company with Chinese Lady's glossy aspidistra, spotted Rosie in

204

the street. Two boys were ribbing her, and she was beginning to look upset. Boots got up and went outside, to the front gate. Emily, glancing through the window, saw Rosie and the boys.

'What's he gone out there for?' asked Chinese Lady.

'To talk to his new girl friend,' said Emily.

'What?' asked Lizzy, and took a look for herself.

Outside, the boys were getting at Rosie.

'Yer a crybaby,' said one.

'Yus, a four-eyed crybaby,' said the other.

'I'm not, I'm not!' Rosie was close to tears.

'And yer talk soppy,' said the first.

'I don't!'

Boots called.

'Hey! Jimmy, Frankie!'

The two boys, both nine, turned. Seeing Boots, they looked abashed. There were grown-ups they made faces at behind their backs, and grown-ups for whom they had a fair amount of respect. For Boots, all the kids had a healthy respect. Boots had been a soldier.

'Yer want us, Boots?' asked Jimmy Murphy.

'I want you to remember you're big and Rosie's small,' said Boots, 'and I want you to remember she's a girl. D'you know what that means?'

'Yes, it means she ain't a boy,' said Frankie Willis.

'Which means I'll tan yer both if you come it,' said Boots.

'Only teasin' 'er, Boots, honest,' said Jimmy, and Rosie drew a noisy breath on a contained sob. It was Sunday, but she was still wearing her pinafore dress.

'All right, a free pardon,' said Boots. 'This time.'

'Sorry, Rosie,' said Frankie.

'Rosie?' said Boots, and she scampered up to his gate.

'I been playing,' she said, 'Mummy sent me out after tea.'

'Well, Uncle Ned's playing too. Inside, on the piano. Would you like to come and listen to him?'

'Oh, could I?' she begged, eyes earnest behind the plain glass of her useless spectacles.

'Come on, then,' he said, and opened the gate. He picked her up and carried her into the parlour. Emily shook her head at him. Ned stopped playing. 'This is Rosie,' said Boots, setting her down, 'she's come to join us. Rosie, that's Aunt Victoria, that's Uncle Tom, there's Aunt Lizzy and there's Uncle Ned. Oh, and that's Annabelle, the small lady making up to Uncle Sammy.'

'Hello,' said Rosie shyly, and Annabelle slipped from Sammy's lap.

'Can Rosie and me play together, Mummy?' asked Annabelle.

Lizzy hoped that although Rosie's dress seemed in need of laundering, the girl's tidy look meant a cared-for head of hair. Lizzy had a horror of headlice, which flourished in Walworth.

'Well, don't roll about together,' she said, 'just sit together an' listen to the music.'

They sat on the floor, Annabelle friendly, Rosie a little in awe. But everyone seemed kind, no one told her to behave herself, and Uncle Boots was close by. And the music was lovely.

Ned played 'Alexander's Ragtime Band'. Aunt Victoria was not sure she liked that, not on a Sunday. Annabelle, of course, liked it very much. She got to her feet. Rosie shyly followed. Annabelle looked at her mummy. Lizzy smiled and nodded. The music was catchy. Annabelle took Rosie's hand and the two little girls skipped about in an attempt to dance to the music. Boots got up, took hold of their hands and joined in with them. It was bliss for Rosie.

'Well, I don't know, I'm sure,' said Aunt Victoria.

'That Boots,' murmured Chinese Lady to Emily, 'dancing around on a Sunday.'

'He's gone soft, Mum,' murmured Emily.

'Soft?'

'On Rosie. I've got a rival.' Emily laughed.

* * *

When the visitors had gone, Boots took Rosie home. He knocked on the front door, which was ajar.

'I 'spect Mummy's gone out,' said Rosie, her hand in his.

Boots pushed the door wide.

'Milly?' he called.

'Mummy likes going out,' said Rosie. 'Uncle Boots, could you take me up and put me to bed?'

'If you like. Then will you be all right on your own?'

'Mummy likes going out,' she said again, which told him she was often on her own at bedtime.

'Come on,' he said, and she went happily up the stairs with him to her bedroom. It was sparsely furnished, and there were no children's books such as Lizzy had had when she was a child. With the bed, there was a small chest of drawers, a washstand with a bowl and pitcher, and a bedside chair. The bed was not made.

'Oh, bless me, I forgot to remember,' said Rosie guiltily.

'What did you forget?' asked Boots.

'To make my bed. I think I remember Mummy called me down before I did, and then I forgot. I needn't tell her, should I?'

'Well, I won't if you won't,' said Boots. 'I'll make it while you get undressed.'

He straightened the bottom sheet and smoothed it. He did not think it very clean. He shook the pillows and turned them. He saw her flannel nightie neatly folded. That was not very clean, either. He began to feel angry. But Rosie's welfare was not really his business, nor was her relationship with her mother. He made the bed. Rosie looked up at him. She hadn't undressed. Her expression was wistful.

'Uncle Boots, could you undress me, please?' she asked, and he knew it was fuss and attention she wanted.

'Well, as I'm here, I might as well be useful,' he said. 'Heave-ho, then.' He took her dress off and her other

207

clothes. Her young body was slim, her legs straight. And she was surprisingly clean. There was a bruise on her right arm. He guessed, but made no comment. He helped her into her nightie. 'There now.'

'Oh, I must wash my face and hands, Uncle Boots,' she said, 'and then all over in the morning.'

'All over?'

'In there,' she said, and showed him water in the pitcher.

'You wash all over in cold water every morning, Rosie?'

'I mustn't not, I mustn't be naughty,' she said, and he sighed for her. He removed her spectacles. There was visible delight in her eyes as he carried her to her bed and tucked her in. 'I do like you, Uncle Boots. Could you come and put me to bed other times when Mummy's out?'

How could he say no?

'Well, kitten, you let me know when Mummy's out and you need to be put to bed. But I think, don't you, that it's to be just between you and me?'

'Oh, I won't tell Mummy, really I won't,' she said.

Boots suspected it was something Milly Pearce would inevitably find out, but he was prepared to face the consequences of that, and to do so in a way that would protect Rosie. He was at fault, of course, in not minding his own business, but he had always had a weakness for interfering. In this instance he was indulging an affection for Rosie. In a selfish way? Yes, perhaps.

'Goodnight, Rosie.' He saw sleepiness creeping up on her.

'Goodnight, Uncle Boots.'

He left her in the quiet, empty house, a child alone. He hoped the ghost of the Witch would not disturb her.

When Lizzy and Ned arrived home with Annabelle, Lizzy took her daughter to the bathroom and ran a fine-toothed comb through her hair for several minutes, much to Annabelle's disgust.

'Mummy, it's tugging me.'

'Never mind, it'll make your hair curly, darling,' said Lizzy, who was performing the exercise with Annabelle's head over the washbasin. She did this every time she brought Annabelle back from a visit to the family in Walworth. She had never found any headlice on her daughter, but she always had a feeling she might.

She found none this time and sighed with relief.

CHAPTER SIXTEEN

Mr Preedy, War Pensions, was a thoughtful-looking Civil Servant, with a touch of dignity in his bearing. He was eminently suited to his department, for thoughtfulness and dignity when dealing with individual pension cases was undeniably commendable, especially as these virtues did not mean he would ever let the department down. Mr Preedy weighed up all the pros and cons, as a dutiful servant of the Crown should, but always made his decisions according to the rule book. And the rule book never let the department down.

At his desk, Mr Preedy was studying the hospital report on ex-Sergeant Robert Alfred Adams for the third time.

Boots sat patiently awaiting authority's observations.

'Well,' said Mr Preedy as a beginning.

'Yes, you go first,' said Boots, fixing his sound eye mildly on his dignified adversary. Mr Preedy was in his forties, an age when dignity fitted a man.

'It seems, Mr Adams, that one might say – indeed, one could say – you have arrived at a happier turn in your life.'

'Yes, one could say that,' murmured Boots.

'The return of one's sight is a singularly happy event.'

'One could say that too. In my case, it's been referred to as a miracle.'

'Yes, quite. Quite.' Mr Preedy looked as if he was not too sure about miracles and how they related to regulations. 'However, to put it concisely, Mr Adams, following the operation performed on you under the auspices of the Royal Army Medical Corps, and taking into consideration that the possibilities and probabilities appertaining to a decline in your present condition are of a minimal nature, it is suggested that such disability as you had no longer obtains at the moment and is not likely to recur, although should it do so you would not be excluded from the privilege of asking for your case to be reviewed.'

'That's concise?' said Boots.

'We appreciate the preference pensioners have for exactitude and brevity,' said Mr Preedy. 'You agree you are no longer disabled?'

'I agree that my disability has been halved,' said Boots.

'Halved?'

'I'm one-eyed,' said Boots.

'Dear me,' said Mr Preedy.

'I agree with that too,' said Boots.

'Your pension, you understand, was awarded as a result of your being blinded in action. Fortunately and happily, we are able to say that, according to the hospital report and the form completed by the surgeon, you are no longer blind.'

'Just half-blind,' said Boots.

'Ah, impaired sight as a result of enemy action qualifies as a pensionable disability,' said Mr Preedy, 'but we are of the opinion that there is no impairment in respect of your present visual capacity.'

'Just fifty per cent, that's all,' said Boots, who was not prepared to accept governmental stinginess, whether he needed a reduced pension or not. 'I think you're trying it on.'

'I beg your pardon?' Mr Preedy looked hurt.

'You're trying to save the government a few bob a week,' said Boots mildly, at which point a woman entered the office. She was dressed in a dark grey costume and white blouse. She wore horn-rimmed spectacles, and her smooth brown hair was neatly arranged, with a parting down the middle.

'Mr Preedy – oh, I'm interrupting?' she said, glancing at Boots. He gave her a smile.

'This is ex-Sergeant Adams,' said Mr Preedy. 'We are dealing—'

'Ah, yes,' she said briskly. 'Good morning, Mr Adams.'

'Good morning,' said Boots.

'There are no problems?' she said.

'Oh, we've just reached the point where Mr Preedy is trying it on,' said Boots amiably.

'No, indeed not,' said Mr Preedy. 'We are merely examining the differences between impaired eyesight and the full visual capacity of the repaired eye, Miss Murchison.'

'We're happy you can see again, Mr Adams,' said Miss Murchison.

'How kind,' said Boots. 'But my left eye is totally impaired. It's surrounded by fog.'

'Oh, dear,' said Miss Murchison.

'I'm in permanent danger of being knocked down and mortally wounded by a tram arriving on my foggy side,' said Boots.

Mr Preedy took on a pained look. Miss Murchison showed a slight smile.

'I am proposing to send Mr Adams form 18B for his completion and signature,' said Mr Preedy.

'Is that a form inviting me to disclaim any right to a pension?' asked Boots in his temperate way.

'Send him form 12A, Mr Preedy,' said Miss Murchison briskly. She smiled at Boots. 'That's a claim for a pension in respect of the loss of your left eye. It will initiate a straightforward process and eliminate the complications of adjusting your present pension. Mr Preedy will approve it when you send it. Mr Preedy, let Mr Adams take the form with him.'

'Nice to have met you,' said Boots and stood up

and shook her hand. Mr Preedy looked in dignified disapproval of this outcome.

'Good luck, Mr Adams,' said Miss Murchison.

It was a battle won through the intercession of the fairer sex.

'Now how did you manage that?' asked Chinese Lady. She had never won any battles herself over her war widow's pension.

'A lady clerk arrived. I told her how kind she was.'

'Made up to her, I suppose,' said Chinese Lady. 'You shouldn't be doing that, it leads to adult'ry, which I don't hold with. You could of just been polite to her. Still, it's not as if she lives next door. Was it her give you the new claim form to fill in?'

'Pardon?' said Boots, mixing paste in the scullery. He had one more room to paper, the little sitting-room he and Emily used upstairs.

'I wish you'd listen to your mother talkin' to you. Well, never mind about it. As long as they're still goin' to give you a bit of a pension, we can count our blessings, I suppose. I was goin' to say something to you about Annabelle. Now what was it? Yes, I know. She wanted to go and play in the street with Mrs Pullen's grandson before tea last Sunday. Did you notice Lizzy wouldn't let her?'

Boots, carrying a bucket containing paste into the kitchen, said, 'No, I didn't notice. Has Mrs Pullen's grandson got measles, then?'

'Trust you not to be serious,' said Chinese Lady darkly. 'Lizzy didn't want Annabelle to get her clothes and hands dirty, which all the kids do playing in the street. It's not gettin' any better here, Boots, there's more dust and dirt all the time. I wonder Cousin Vi come here to tea on Sunday, I don't suppose she'll come too often.'

'Oh, just as often as you arrange it, old lady.'

'What's that mean?'

'Only that our Vi's grown up ladylike,' said Boots.
'What's that got to do with it?'

'Good point, that,' said Boots. 'Yes, what?'

'I hope you're not being insinuatin', my lad,' said
Chinese Lady. 'But I'm not sure why you're goin' to all
this trouble papering and paintin' everything when
the dirt comes floatin' in through all the doors and
windows day in, day out the year round.'

'I think you're talking about a little house and garden
again,' said Boots.

'Tommy and Sammy and me, we don't mind it here,
but you ought to be thinking more about Em'ly and the
children you're goin' to have.'

Boots smiled.

'There are rooms above Sammy's shop,' he said, 'all
included in the lease. He's turning one into an office
to make it the hub of his empire. And I think you'll find
he'll use the other rooms to make a flat for himself and
Tommy. He'll charge Tommy rent, of course. Then you
could live with Emily and me, and the children we're
going to have, if we can find a place somewhere off
Brixton Hill, depending on how successful the shop is.
Sammy's opening it Friday week. Friday's a shrewd
opening day. If things go well, Emily and I will start
looking for the right kind of house. How's that, old
darling?'

'Boots, you and Em'ly don't want me always livin'
with you,' said Chinese Lady, but her expression belied
her protest. Boots knew how well she and Emily got
on together. In a new home, Emily would still happily
let Chinese Lady run things. 'No, you and Em'ly
shouldn't have to put up with me, Boots, I'll be all right.'

'Now, now,' said Boots, 'you know the score.'

'Don't you now now your own mother, young man.'

'We shan't move without you.'

'That's very considerate of you, I'm sure, but—'

'Conversation over,' said Boots, moving doorwards.

'Well, it's comin' to something, I must say, when a

son who's only as old as you are starts laying down the law to me.'

'I know, but I can't talk about it now, Chinese Lady, I've got all this work to do.'

He disappeared with his bucket. A little smile flickered briefly on his mother's face.

Mounting the stairs, he heard a child's voice.

'Uncle Boots?'

He stopped, turned and saw Rosie at the open front door.

'Hello, kitten.'

'I'm home from school,' she said. 'Mummy's out. Could I come in and help you like other times?'

'You're just in time,' said Boots. 'All right, come and be my wallpapering mate, but first go and ask my mother for an apron. And a scarf to cover your hair. That'll keep the paste out of it.'

'Then I'll come up, shall I?' Rosie asked eagerly.

'Then come up, curlyhead.'

Rosie had a bubbly, giggly time for a whole two hours before her mother came in search of her. Milly might have sent the child home and stayed to make herself a pleasure to Boots. But Emily came up and said haughtily, 'I'll show you out, Mrs Pearce.' Emily simply did not trust the woman or her provocative roundness. She did not realise that in her light summer costume and white blouse she was a far more attractive figure to Boots than Milly in her boldly revealing jumper.

Now that Boots was definitely going to have the job of running Sammy's shop, Emily enjoyed her own job very much. There was no worry attached to it. And Mrs Stevens continued to be very encouraging, giving her a variety of interesting work to do outside of her copy-typing stints. She called her in on Friday morning.

'There you are, Emily. Good. Look, did you know there's a Pitman's College in the City? It's their original college. If you're keen, you can take a summer shorthand course in the evenings. It's a course run for office girls in the City. Three evenings a week, Tuesdays, Wednesdays and Fridays, from six to eight. You could go straight from here, after work. The Council will subsidise you, I've arranged that. The course starts next Tuesday, and you could go up on Monday to enrol. It runs for six weeks. What do you feel?'

'Oh, Lor',' said Emily, breathless. Madge Stevens smiled. Emily was so natural.

'Not keen?' said Madge.

'Well, yes, I am really, but I'd have to talk to me husband.'

'Yes, of course. Let me know tomorrow morning.'

'Oh, Lor',' said Emily again, excitement high.

Boots met her outside the town hall that evening. He enjoyed the little walk and the stroll home with her, Emily always full of her day's work.

'Boots, what d'yer think, I could start learnin' shorthand next week, at Pitman's in London, and with the Council payin'. Mrs Stevens said I'm gettin' to be a promisin' asset, would yer believe. The course is from six till eight in the evenings, Tuesdays, Wednesdays an' Fridays, for six weeks. I could go straight from work and come straight home from the college. Would yer mind if I went in for it?'

'Not a bit, if you think you'd enjoy it,' said Boots.

'Oh, I'm sure I would, once I'd got over me nerves. Imagine it, me doing bottle-washin' in that first job I 'ad, and now goin' in for bein' a new-fangled shorthand-typist, and with more money. I'd do me very best. Well, you 'ave to when people like Mrs Stevens 'ave got faith an' confidence in yer – oh, and when a husband's bein' so agreeable about it.' Emily hugged his arm. 'You always been very agreeable to me, Boots.'

'It's time you enjoyed yourself,' said Boots, thinking of all the help she had given him during his dark years.

'It's nice you and me get on so well together,' she said.

'Except when I'm all over wallpaper,' said Boots, and she laughed.

When they arrived home, she expressed herself enthusiastically to Chinese Lady. Chinese Lady, strangely, did not seem too enthusiastic herself. And Emily, thinking about things in bed that night, after she and Boots had made love, began to have second thoughts, because Boots had talked to her during the evening about moving to a new house with a garden. Somewhere near Brixton Hill, where the shops and the market would be a real pleasure to her and Chinese Lady.

The prospect took hold of Emily. Lizzy and Ned had such a nice house and garden, and there were trees and everything. There were trees up in Brixton. She and Boots would have to spend time looking and planning. And all the lovemaking they were doing meant she would surely get pregnant any moment. She couldn't think why she wasn't that way already.

A new house and a baby, they could happen together.

She spoke to Mrs Stevens the following morning, feeling a little awkward and embarrassed in case the assistant supervisor thought her ungrateful.

'That's quite all right, Emily, I understand,' said Madge with a reassuring smile. 'Your husband isn't in favour, is that it?'

'Oh, no,' said Emily, 'he don't mind a bit. When I told him this morning, he said I could decide for myself. Only we're thinking of movin', and there's other things – well, it don't seem as if the time's right for me to do the course with our plans as they are. I'd be happy to think about it later on, when things are more settled.' Emily knew that if a baby came along there probably wouldn't be a later on, but she didn't want to close the door. 'I mean, if you think I still could.'

'Of course,' said Madge, 'there's no such thing as a closing date, Emily.'

'Thanks ever so much,' said Emily.

'A pleasure,' said Madge.

The following Friday, Emily took a tram to Camberwell Green during her lunch hour. She chose the open top deck to get the air, such as it was. There weren't too many open trams left. Closed ones were taking over. When the conductor came up she was eating her lunch, a corned beef sandwich laced with Hayward's famed Military Pickle and prepared by Chinese Lady.

''Ello, 'ello,' said the conductor breezily, ''aving a picnic are we, miss?'

'No, just a sandwich,' said Emily, 'and if you don't mind, I'm a Mrs not a miss.'

'Lucky old mister, then, ain't he, yer better 'alf?'

'I'll tell him you said so,' smiled Emily. 'Penny one to Camberwell Green, if you please.'

The conductor clipped a ticket and gave it to her.

'Penny for the ticket, then, young missus,' he said, 'an' tuppence for makin' use of our picnic amenities.'

'You'll be lucky,' said Emily, her light cotton dress deferring to summer's high temperature.

'All right, but don't spread yer crumbs about or yer'll cop it if an inspector gets on.'

'If he's as cheeky as you are,' said Emily, 'I'll ride in me horse and carriage in future.'

'Very good, me lady, and tell yer lordship, yer better 'alf, that I 'opes he appreciates yer,' said the conductor, and returned to the lower deck with a grin on his face. He was on the platform when Emily descended the stairs at Camberwell Green. The breeze lifted the hem of her dress, and he essayed a soft whistle at the gleam of her legs in imitation silk.

'You're lookin',' said Emily.

'All in me day's work if I'm lucky,' he said.

Emily got off laughing. She was over the feeling that she had let herself down by not taking the shorthand course. There was the pleasure of moving to a new house sometime, and the excitement of the shop. Today was opening day, and Boots and Sammy had been there all week getting things ready. She crossed the busy junction. The shop was in Denmark Hill, some fifty yards away. She stopped outside. People were examining the window display. She saw the name above the window.

SAM'S EMPORIUM
The Bargain Bazaar

The window was pasted with notices, boldly executed.

FINEST QUALITY WOOLLEN BLANKETS, 6 for 19/11d.
MEN'S BOOTS, ALL SIZES AND BRAND NEW, Two Bob a Pair
LADIES BROWN SHOES, Todays Best Bargain at 1/6d a Pair. Try before you buy!
MEN'S WOOLLEN COMBINATIONS, Genuine Winter Warms at 2/6d.
LADIES BLOUSES in Sunshine Brown at 1/6d. (Sunshine Brown was Sammy's trade name for khaki.)
MEN'S GREY SOCKS, One Pair for Sixpence, Four Pairs for 1/11d.
LADIES SUNSHINE BROWN STOCKINGS, Three pairs for 1/3d.
KETTLES, SAUCEPANS, DIXIES, ENAMEL PLATES, EVERYDAY CUTLERY – Knockdown Prices.
LADIES SKIRTS, MEN'S TROUSERS AND OVERCOATS – Giveaway Prices!
NO SECONDHANDS, EVERYTHING NEW! NEW! YOU WANT BARGAINS, WE'VE GOT BARGAINS.

The window was laden with goods. Emily went in. She had simply had to come and look. The shop was crammed with stock and crowded with people. She saw Boots and Sammy attending to customers, and she saw a girl, Susie Brown, whom she had met at Sammy's stall in East Street.

People were literally queueing up to buy blankets at six for nineteen shillings and elevenpence, or singly at three and six. There were customers for men's vests and combinations, and for socks, boots and overcoats. Women were after ladies' skirts, stockings and blouses. Everything was ex-Army, either the men's or the women's branch. And it was all new, with durability guaranteed. Sammy had decided to pioneer the retailing of surplus Army supplies. The War Department had been left with huge stocks at the end of the 1914-18 conflict, and these had been made available to interested dealers. Sammy, learning of the sale through Mr Greenberg, had taken the plunge while established dealers were debating exactly what was in it for them. He had invested eight hundred pounds, his total capital, to buy in bulk at mouthwatering prices, prices he could hardly believe. He thought it wiser, however, not to advertise that all the goods had been manufactured for the Army or the Women's Army Auxiliary Corps, since it would give customers the impresion they were being offered Army leftovers. That kind of thing might make the goods look as suspect as so-called bankrupt stocks or items said to have survived a warehouse fire. The public were never wholly taken in by this, and saw the stuff for what it was in the main, second-rate and shoddy. Working people didn't mind not being dressed stylishly as long as what they did buy had a lasting quality.

All the same, Sammy and Boots had to cope with the occasional pained cries from women examining stout brown shoes designed for Waacs.

'Call these shoes? Clod'oppers, more like. Ain't yer got none with pointed toes an' buttons?'

The shoes, tied together by their laces in pairs, were in a large crate on the shop floor, next to a similar crate containing men's Army boots.

Emily could not get near Boots or Sammy. She had never seen a shop packed with so much stuff or so many people, nor had she seen any shop so fresh with new paint, mostly a pale blue with dark blue surrounds. Nearly all shops were a dingy cream or an uninteresting brown. Boots had a dozen customers needing his attention. He was dealing with two of them, two women, both of whom were interested in overcoats for their husbands. Emily heard one woman speak to him.

'But them brass buttons, mister, look at 'em.'

'I agree, madam,' said Boots, just like a shop manager, 'you don't get quality buttons on every overcoat.'

'I dunno about quality, mister, I just don't know as my 'usband'll like brass ones that'll likely turn green.'

'Don't yer 'ave no coats with ordinary buttons?' asked the second woman. 'Me old man ain't partial to anything fancy.'

'Well, while we specialise in the high quality brass buttons,' said Boots, 'we'd turn a blind eye if you snipped them off and sewed on ordinary buttons. We'd also say nothing if you dyed the coats a navy blue. Perhaps you'd like to think about it while I attend to other customers. Take your time, ladies.'

Emily smiled. It sounded to her as if Boots was a born manager.

' 'Old on,' said the first woman. 'I'll have this one, it's me 'usband's size, and yer a 'elpful gent.'

Boots sold coats to both women. He caught Emily's eye. She gave him an excited little wave. He responded with a wink and a smile. Customers clamoured. The sunshine brown stockings and blouses were proving excellent sellers, the blankets of warm thick wool irresistible bargains. People dipped into shabby purses or well-worn pockets.

Susie had her work cut out as an assistant. She had willingly agreed to help in the shop on its opening day, leaving Bert to look after the stall with the assistance of a nephew. Mister Sammy was paying her a whole eight bob for her day's work. Eight bob for just one day. She was eager, thrilled and conscientious, but she

221

managed to spare a moment to speak to the wife of Mister Sammy's brother, who was called by the strange nickname of Boots and was ever so nice.

'D'you want me to tell yer 'usband you're 'ere, Mrs Adams?'

'No, it's all right, Susie, he's seen me and I've only come to see how the shop is doing,' said Emily. 'Goodness gracious me,' she added, feeling this came suitably from the manager's wife, 'has it been like this all morning?'

'Oh, yes,' said Susie. 'Ain't it 'eart-warmin', Mrs Adams? Oh, yer must excuse me, there's ladies requirin' attention.'

Emily thought the girl pretty, though her dress looked cheap. Cheap things weren't a good buy really. It was nice to be pretty, though. Still, Boots never agreed she was plain herself. She saw women shoppers around him, his easy manner with them, and the smiles they gave him. That Sammy, he knew what he was doing when he made Boots his manager.

She caught her husband's eye again.

'I'm goin',' she called, 'I got to get back to work.'

Boots broke free of customers, came over to her and gave her a kiss.

'Glad you looked in, lovey,' he said.

'My pleasure, I'm sure,' said Emily, 'don't get trampled to death.'

At home that evening, the conversation was of a celebratory kind, for the shop takings had exceeded Sammy's most optimistic expectations. Tommy kept the bad news until bedtime, when he informed the family he had lost his job, that he'd spent this last week looking for another. A promised recommendation hadn't come off.

'Oh, Tommy,' said Emily, 'that's awful bad luck, and just when we all thought the fam'ly was doing real swell.'

'Can't be helped,' said Tommy. 'And just temp'rary, I hope.'

Chinese Lady sighed. Tommy was a nice, easy-going young man, and at his age he really ought to be in work so that he could think about a suitable girl and a suitable future. It wasn't much good finding a ladylike girl for a young man who was unemployed. A pity, really, specially as Vi had turned out very ladylike.

'You'll get another job soon, Tommy,' she said, 'you're good at engineering.'

'Well, y'know, Mum,' said Tommy, 'so are a few million other men.'

Sammy frowned. It wouldn't look good, a successful businessman having an unemployed brother. Tommy needed to get another job quick.

'I'll ask around, Tommy,' said Boots.

'I will too, at the town hall,' said Emily.

'Kind of yer both,' smiled Tommy.

As usual, Susie arrived early at the stall the next morning. Unusually, Bert had preceded her, and with him was his seventeen-year-old nephew Herbert. Also present was Mister Sammy, but looking like a man in a hurry.

'You ain't required,' said Bert to Susie.

'Did I say that?' asked Sammy.

'No, I did,' said Bert, his florid heartiness belligerent. 'Herb done a good job 'elping me yesterday, and 'e'll do likewise today.'

Sammy's eyes glinted a little. Bert was beginning to rile him. Sammy didn't like that. He liked friendly voices, even when they were trying to outsmart him.

'Kindly take a walk,' he said to Susie.

Susie, feeling betrayed, cried indignantly, 'Oh, yer givin' me the push, Mister Adams, how could yer!'

'I mean a short walk,' said Sammy. 'Come back in five minutes.' He was not disposed to lay the law down to Bert in front of the girl.

'Oh, I see,' said Susie in rueful apology. He wasn't

going to betray her, to let pimply Herbert take her place. She went for a walk.

'Well, Bert,' said Sammy, 'it's like this. Every time you take it on yerself to sound as if yer speakin' for the firm, yer gettin' up me bleedin' nose. I request yer to kindly desist from laying unfriendly chat on Susie. And since yer don't seem to have heard me before, I'll tell yer again, I decide who's in and who's out. Herb's out. Got it?'

'I don't mind argufying,' said Bert, 'but I ain't takin' orders, specially from someone who ain't cut his back teeth yet.'

'Well, Bert,' said Sammy quietly, for he rarely raised his voice, 'it occurs to me here and now that you ain't yet grown a head yerself. That girl, as I told yer a week ago, has raised our takings twenty per cent. I didn't notice Herb raised any per cent in yesterday's takings.' Herb shuffled his feet and looked vaguely about at stallholders preparing for the day ahead. 'So we won't have any more talk suggestin' he's goin' to have Susie's job. You got it?'

'Don't sling yer weight about,' said Bert, 'I ain't yer errand boy, I'm yer partner.'

'Well, partner, kindly oblige me by doing what I say,' said Sammy.

'Gawd bleedin' blimey,' said Bert, 'why do I let yer give me all this flamin' lip in front of Herb?'

'Because I'm a sixty-five percenter,' said Sammy, 'because you still owe me for most of your thirty-five, and because Herb ain't yet come to be of much account.'

''Ere, fair do's,' protested Bert.

'Well,' said Sammy, 'you've got a chance to show me exactly what kind of a selling partnership you and Herb can make today. It's Saturday, and the stall's all yours. When Susie comes back I'm takin' her to help in me shop again. You Herbert, stop suckin' your teeth and jump about.'

Susie went gladly to the shop with her Mister Sammy. Bert was no fun at all to work with these days.

CHAPTER SEVENTEEN

Within a month, the shop was a runaway success. Sammy's idea of introducing Army surpluses to the poor people of Camberwell and Walworth was based on the knowledge that they could not afford style, that with what money they had they sought to buy things that would last. Things that lasted among children, for instance, could be handed down from older kids to younger kids. People were always particularly in need of clothes that kept them warm in winter. Men's Army shirts, vests and combinations provided a fine basis. So, for women, did Waac blouses and vests and thick stockings. Army greatcoats guaranteed warmth. Housewives dyed them for their husbands. Khaki shirts could also be dyed, and their shapeless length altered to become more wearable. As for the blankets, they were a consistently popular buy.

Sammy had acquired huge stocks, but inside the first month he began to think about new lines. Customers asked about clothes and footwear outside of his WD stocks. He went to see his friend Mr Greenberg, the rag and bone gentleman whose contacts were legion. Mr Greenberg assured him that for a small fee he could put him in touch with the best East End garment factories that would offer the most reasonable discounts and credit facilities.

'I'm a cash customer, I don't write cheques,' said Sammy.

'Ah, my poy, wisdom has arrived early in your

225

head,' said Mr Greenberg. 'May I ask vhat precisely you're after?'

Sammy was after such things as striped flannel shirts, plain collars, jerseys, suits and feminine clothes, all produced at cut-price rates for cash, but expertly stitched.

'Cheap, but no rubbish,' he said.

Mr Greenberg lifted his hands in protest.

'Sammy, Sammy, vould I recommend a maker of rubbish to a friend?'

'Well, yer might, Abraham old cock, if I'd been born yesterday.'

'You grieve me, my poy, you grieve me. Dear, dear. But I vill put aside pain and accommodate you.'

'And what'll you touch me for in respect of contacts that'll give me ten per cent discount?'

Mr Greenberg's expressive hands lifted in horror.

'Ten per cent, Sammy? You vant no middleman *and* ten per cent?'

'For cash on delivery,' said Sammy.

'On delivery? Sammy, Sammy, no vun pays on delivery.'

'I will, for ten per cent discount,' said Sammy.

'My poy,' said Mr Greenberg, 'in my fondness for you and your family, I've let you cut my throat a hundred times. Vould you cut the throats of my friends too, the poor tailors of Shoreditch? Ten per cent would be their death. No, no, Sammy, have a heart. Did not my good friend, Mr Moses, show you the kindest heart, and you a minor?'

'I hope Ikey Mo hasn't broken a confidence,' said Sammy.

'Now vould Isaac do that, Sammy? Vhy, he vould suffer the tortures of Herod vithout opening his mouth. But vun can read signs and events, my poy. Shall ve say five per cent and cash on delivery?'

'For cash on delivery, ten,' said Sammy.

'For vun so young, you make my heart bleed, my poy,'

sighed Mr Greenberg. 'Yet I von't say cash on delivery ain't a sveet carrot. There, I'll see vhat I can do for a small fiver.'

'How about a large pound note?' suggested Sammy.

'A poor joke, Sammy.'

'I could hunt around Shoreditch myself.'

'You are velcome to.'

'All right, two pound ten for the touch,' said Sammy.

'Four golden sovereigns,' said Mr Greenberg. 'Vhat could be fairer?'

'Four pound notes.'

'Done,' said Mr Greenberg.

'But no rubbish,' said Sammy.

'Sammy, Sammy.' Mr Eli Greenberg, cordially known as Abraham, shook his head reproachfully. 'Now vhat good vould it do me, my dear, if I sent you to sveat-shops? Vould that be friendship, or vould it be false pretences?'

'I got you,' said Sammy, 'and I like yer as me friend.'

'My love to your mother, Sammy, who vould have found favour vith Solomon.'

'I appreciate yer sentiments, Abraham, but I don't fancy she'd have found it respectful or reverent to be one out of six hundred concubines.'

Tommy was tramping the streets of Lambeth, Peckham and Vauxhall, looking for a job. He had been out of work for a month, and it was taking its toll of his equability. The government was still in crisis, and Chinese Lady had tartly said she had never known a time when it wasn't. It had organised a victory parade, at which General Foch had shown himself as a Field-Marshal for winning the war, but what good that did for unemployed ex-servicemen she couldn't think. But Lloyd George, the Prime Minister, had at least taken some care of working people by instituting a national insurance stamp paid for jointly by workers and employers, which helped to fund dole payments and enabled the sick to consult their doctors free of charge except for a prescription payment of a shilling. It was called going on the panel, and was a boon to working people.

Tommy talked ruefully about going on the panel for his sore feet and for the ailing condition of the soles of his shoes. He had stopped seeing Vi, he had stopped taking girls out. He couldn't afford the luxury of girl friends. And he had no prospects.

'I'm not havin' it, Chinese Lady,' said Sammy, when he popped home one day to eat a midday snack with her.

'What aren't you havin'?' asked Chinese Lady, proud that her youngest son had become a successful business gentleman.

'I'm not havin' Tommy poundin' hot pavements every day. It don't reflect well on me, y'know, havin' an unemployed brother. But I can't put him in the shop yet. Boots is managing fine by himself, though he gets a bit pushed at times, and I need to keep expenses down till I've cleared me debts. Boots understands he can't have an assistant yet. I'll say this for him, he's got a gen'rous nobility of mind.'

'Did you get that piece of patronising condescension out of some book?'

'No, out of here.' Sammy touched his forehead. 'It's all up here, Ma.'

'Don't call me Ma. It's common.'

'No, all right. But I like to do right by Boots, yer can't talk about him as if he was an Italian organ-grinder, specially now he's a manager. Anyway, I'll work something out for Tommy.'

'Don't put him in your scrap yard,' said Chinese Lady, 'we don't want him comin' home dirty, smoky and sooty.'

'No, I've already put a young apprentice in to help Fred,' said Sammy, 'yer don't have to pay an apprentice much while he's learning. Nor do I want Tommy doing

228

any job that won't pay him more than twenty-five bob a week.'

'Well, your heart's in the right place most of the time,' said Chinese Lady, sharing a corned beef salad with her son. 'But you've not been to church again lately. You shouldn't forget that all you come by, Sammy, is by the grace of the Lord.'

'Oh, Gawd,' muttered Sammy, at which Chinese Lady rapped his knuckles smartly with her fork. He grinned.

'Stop smirkin',' she said.

'You're a one-and-only, you are, Mum,' said Sammy, 'and I reckon Boots is right. It's time you had a gentleman friend. You don't want to go to waste, not when you're only forty or so.'

'Mind your business, saucebox,' said Chinese Lady, bristling as he regarded her musingly. Secretly, of course, she was proud of her slender waist and well-preserved bosom, and now that she could afford good corsetry out of her housekeeping, her bosom looked as firm as it ever had. Sammy's father had been proud of it too, and also very fond of it. And not always in a respectful way. Still, husbands did have entitlements, and it was better for a man to be disrespectfully fond of his wife's bosom than not to take any notice of it.

'I'll make a list,' said Sammy through a mouthful of lettuce and tomato.

'A list?'

'Of eligible gents,' said Sammy.

'I'll box your ears for you, my lad, big as you are.'

'I know yer will,' said Sammy.

The familiar little twitch touched her mouth.

Coming out of the house in the afternoon, Chinese Lady saw Rosie hovering. She knew why. The child had enjoyed fuss and attention from the family. She doted on Boots and Emily, although Emily was not too sure she liked Boots putting the child to bed some nights, when Milly Pearce was out. Rosie loved it, of course.

Oh, that uncaring, gallivanting mother of hers, thought Chinese Lady. Before she could stop herself, she said, 'Would you like to come shoppin' with me, Rosie?'

'Oh, could I, please? Mummy's out.'

Was the woman ever in?

'Come along, then. I'm goin' to the Maypole. And perhaps the sweet shop. Come along.'

Rosie bobbed happily along beside the brisk-walking lady of whom she was in a little awe, but whom she liked very much. Chinese Lady wondered if she was being wise in giving the child this kind of attention, or if Boots wasn't being just a bit foolish in giving her visible affection.

'Emily?' murmured Boots. They were in bed, and she lay with her back to him, a sure sign that she was not in the mood for what she sometimes called lovey-dovey. 'Emily?'

'Oh, never mind,' she said muffledly, and he wondered if she was a little fed-up with house-hunting. They had spent some evenings and some Sundays in the Brixton Hill area and not seen anything for rent that they remotely liked. Those with boards up were all too big, all three-storeyed houses.

'Never mind what?'

'It don't happen, nothing happens.' The worry she had begun to feel came to the surface. 'We're not goin' to have any baby.'

'But it's only been a few months since we—'

'That's long enough to know. Boots, I feel – oh, yer don't think I'm probably a barren woman, do yer?'

He was sure only Emily could have said a thing like that.

'Well, you know, lovey, I don't suppose it does happen when you most want it to. Don't worry about it. You're still young and healthy. I've a feeling that if we don't worry about it, if we just have fun, we can beat the leprechauns.'

Emily turned then and cuddled up to him.

'Boots, I'm near dying at thinkin' I might be a barren woman.'

'Don't die yet, love. Where would I get another Emily from?'

'Shall I go and see Doctor McManus?'

'Ah, well, no, I don't think so,' said Boots. 'It's a bit early for that much pessimism. Let's give it more time. Let's enjoy having each other. You're still fun in bed.'

Emily pressed closer then, and Boots was as nice to her as he could be. A young wife worrying that she was barren after only a few months had to be given love and kindness.

There was a welcome break in the morning's business at the shop, and Boots made himself a cup of Camp coffee in the little room at the back. He brought it out to the long counter. Someone emerged from the fog in front of his left eye and came into the view of his right eye. He saw smart pointed grey shoes and sleek black stockings. His gaze travelled up from a dove-grey skirt to a matching jacket and a white silk blouse buttoned to the neck. Around the collar hung a thin gold chain, from which depended a gold locket. Her creamy face was classically oval, her mouth moist with pink lipstick. Amused grey eyes were framed by dark lashes, and a grey hat with a curved brim sat on the looping curves of dark brown hair. She looked in her mid-twenties.

'Is the shop open?' she asked.

'I'll be for the pot if it's not,' said Boots, 'the proprietor's a ten-foot cannibal with two heads. Madam, what can I do for you?'

'The proprietor's what?' she asked.

'Fairly normal,' said Boots.

'Well, old thing, I liked ten feet tall with two heads best.' The amused look turned into a smile. 'Are we speaking of Mr Samuel Adams, without whose humanitarian generosity St Stephen's Orphanage would not be

231

expecting new blankets at an unbelievable price? That is, according to my adored stepmother. And is that coffee that's taking up your attention, old bean?'

'I don't quite recognise the description of Mr Sammy Adams myself,' said Boots, 'but he's the proprietor, yes. And this is coffee. Camp.'

'Camp? Chicory-flavoured essence? My dear old lad, it's an ancient comfort of mine. And I'm dying of thirst. It's filthy hot outside. An enervating washout, don't you know.'

'Madam may help herself,' said Boots, 'I haven't touched it yet, only stirred it.'

She gave him a long look. Patently, she liked what she saw. She smiled.

'Cut the butler stuff,' she said, 'I'm a miss, not a madam. Polly Simms, old sport. And if you're offering me coffee, I'll make my own. Just point me to the amenities. Oh, and would you be a darling man and put a nosebag on my nag outside?'

'The amenities are there.' Boots pointed to the relevant door. 'But we don't sell nosebags. Or oats.'

Miss Polly Simms laughed.

'It's on the cart, old thing. I find it such a fag, putting it on Rupert myself. I'll make the coffee.'

'Is madam staying for lunch?' asked Boots.

She laughed again, and glided on long legs through the shop. Boots, temperate and obliging, went outside to attend to the nosebag. Her nag was a shining chestnut pony, her cart a shining dark green trap. A couple of kids, a boy and a girl, were admiring the pony. Boots unhitched the nosebag and slipped it around the animal's neck. Its nose dipped in and its ears twitched happily.

'Mister, can I mind it for yer?' asked the boy.

'Can I mind it too, mister?' asked the girl.

'Well, you can mind it for the young lady,' said Boots, 'and if yer don't run off with it, I'll see she gives yer a penny each. You're on your school holidays, are you?'

232

'We been on 'em a week an' more,' said the girl. 'Mum said we could mind 'orses. Well she said be it on yer own 'eads. Ta for lettin' us mind, mister.'

'Good on yer,' said Boots, and went back into the shop. A customer followed him in and bought three pairs of grey socks. Miss Polly Simms came out of the little room carrying a cup of coffee, without a saucer. She put the cup on the counter, hitched her skirt, and sat down on one of the chairs provided for people like old ladies with tired feet. She sipped her coffee, the while observing Boots attending to his customer, a young housewife now debating the merits of the Army footwear on offer.

'They are new, ain't they?' she enquired. 'They ain't just old ones made good?'

'They're virgin new,' said Boots, 'fresh from the factory.'

'Me 'ubby's highly particular, yer know.'

'I know the feeling,' said Boots, 'I'm highly particular myself.'

'They won't make his feet sweat, like?'

'Only in the Sahara,' said Boots, and Miss Polly Simms made an intent examination of her coffee.

'Oh, he won't be goin' there,' said the young housewife, who seemed pleased by the discussion.

'Good idea not to if he doesn't have to,' said Boots, 'and Southend's much nearer.'

'Oh, you been there?' she said, letting him wrap the boots. 'We went hop-pickin' down in Kent last year, but we've never been to Southend. Must be like 'eaven, sittin' in a deckchair on all that beach with the sea and all.'

'I suppose they've beaches in heaven, with very comfortable deckchairs,' said Boots. 'Three and six, madam.'

'Eh? Oh, yes.' She paid for her purchases. 'Well, I best go, I'll tell me 'ubby the boots is fine except in the Sahara, like. Thank you.'

'Our pleasure, madam,' said Boots, and she left, looking as if she had secured bargains and enjoyed a nice little chat as well.

'I say, old thing,' said Miss Polly Simms, 'this isn't your daily grind, is it?'

'Shopkeeping?' said Boots.

'Well, I hope it isn't.'

'What's wrong with it?'

'Dear Jesus,' she said, 'is that a serious question?'

'It's the best I can do,' said Boots, and drank some of the now lukewarm coffee.

'Piffle,' said Miss Simms.

'Pardon?'

'Oh, give over, old sport, you know it's piffle. It's even painful. There are good men and true with not half your style lording it in India. Wouldn't you like to be a major in the Indian Army with weekend polo?'

'It's a fair question, madam, but no, I don't think so.'

'I'll dot you a feeling one in your eye if you call me madam again,' said Miss Simms.

'All right, old thing,' said Boots, 'let's just say I don't fancy Indian mosquitoes.'

'Nor me,' said Miss Simms, looking very amused. 'Or all that ghastly heat and all the frightful colonels' ladies.'

'Excuse me if I sound commercial,' said Boots, 'but are you here to buy something, or did you just pop in for a coffee and a sit-down?'

'But, my dear old lad, I'm here to collect on behalf of my stepmother. Didn't I say so?'

'Collect what?' asked Boots, at which point two women came in, one young, the other middle-aged. Boots gave them a nod and a smile, then addressed the seated Miss Simms again. 'Did you order something?'

'Do serve those ladies first,' she said sweetly, 'I'm in no hurry.'

Boots turned to the ladies.

'Vests, if you please,' said the younger one.

'Men's?' enquired Boots.

234

'Eh?' she said.

'Men's vests?'

'This is my mum, not my dad,' said the young woman, and asked her loudly, 'Mum, you don't wear men's vests, do you?'

'What?' asked her mother.

'Men's vests,' said the young woman more loudly, 'he's asking if you want men's vests.'

'I don't believe it,' said her mother. 'You gone potty, Daisy?'

'There,' said the young woman to Boots, 'she don't want men's vests.'

'That seems sensible,' said Boots. 'We can oblige with ladies' vests, all sizes at a shilling each.'

'A shilling each, Mum,' shouted the young woman.

'What?'

'A shilling. Each.'

'Don't shout, Daisy, I'm not deaf. Ask for the lady assistant, and if I can try one on. I want two.'

'Where's the lady assistant, and can my mother try one on?' asked the young woman.

'Good question, madam,' said Boots, 'but—'

'I'm the lady assistant,' said Miss Simms, and came to her feet looking a picture of elegance. 'Allow me to help you, modom.'

'She's the lady assistant, Mum,' shouted the young woman.

'What's she wearing a hat for, then?' asked her mother.

'Well, I don't know, do I?'

'The vests?' murmured Miss Simms to Boots, whose smile seemed about to spring. He pointed to some open cardboard boxes on a shelf opposite. An elderly man came in as the cool Miss Simms took on the combination of mother and daughter.

'Got any braces cheap?' asked the elderly man of Boots.

'We have.'

'All right, 'ow cheap?'

'Fivepence a pair, three pairs a bob.'

''Ere, three pairs a bob is fourpence each.'

'You get the advantage of quantity buying.'

'Never 'eard of it. I'll just 'ave one pair of them that's three for a bob.' There was a chuckle in the old, throaty voice.

'You crafty old goat,' said Boots.

'Well, what yer don't ask for, yer never gets, do yer?'

'All right, Dad, sell you a pair for fourpence, then.'

'Bless yer cotton socks, son, you put up fer Parliament and I'll vote for yer.'

'I'll think about it. D'you want them wrapped?'

'No, I want 'em fer wearing, me string's on its last legs,' said the elderly character, and took his jacket and waistcoat off. String provided a belt for his trousers. Boots gave him the Army braces and he put them on. 'Much obliged, son.'

'So will I be when I get yer fourpence, Dad,' said Boots.

'I ain't forgot.' The old man dressed himself and fished coins from his trousers pocket. He gave Boots one penny, four half-pennies and four farthings. 'There y'ar, then.'

'All right, Dad, fair do's,' said Boots. Miss Simms was watching, her amusement having established itself as an apparent permanency. Mother and daughter were in the little room. They came out and paid Miss Simms for two vests. Boots let her wrap the items. The ladies left.

'Many thanks,' said Boots to the intrigued Miss Simms.

'Oh, a welcome giggle, old love,' she said, 'but what a frightful waste.'

'Something else on your mind?'

'Yes, you. Look, it's a joke, isn't it? This can't be what you do for a living. You're standing in for some mousy tea-stained shop assistant, aren't you?'

'No, that's me,' said Boots.

'What's you?'

'I'm the mousy tea-stained shop assistant.'

Miss Simms laughed.

'Oh, brother,' she said, 'I thought what a tearing bore this was going to be, collecting blankets for my stepmother's orphans. "Now, now, don't get ratty, Polly," she said, "just go and do your good deed for the day." She said nothing about the answer to a maiden's prayer.'

'Come again?' said Boots.

'You're gorgeous, old sport, and all this really is a frightful waste. Listen – wait, what's your name?'

'Excuse me, Miss Simms, but you're here to collect blankets?'

'But of course. Twenty of them. My stepmother was advised by Mr Samuel Adams, who has supplied the orphanage with odds and ends, that they'd be ready. Percy couldn't come. He was under the car with an oilcan.'

'Who's Percy?'

'The chauffeur. What's your name, old dear?'

Boots was beginning to recognise her for what she was, one of the many young women whose post-war attitude was restless, brittle, extrovert and flamboyant. The country had lost a million men. It had lost the men of Mons, Le Cateau and the Somme, a great army of the nation's finest soldiers, his commanding officer, Major Harris, among them. It had lost the men of France, Flanders, Gallipoli and Mesopotamia, and it had lost thousands of sailors and airmen. Miss Polly Simms and her kind existed in a vacuum empty of the men of their generation. They were haunted, perhaps, by the ghosts of the men they had known and loved.

He had his own ghosts, the fallen men of his battalion of West Kents, particularly Major Harris, a professional soldier who had been riddled with bullets during the first battle of the Somme, a soldier grey and bitter, who had died in contempt of generals who did not know the difference between war and wasteful carnage.

'I sometimes can't remember my name, only my number,' he said.

'What? I say, have I said something, old lad? You look very odd.'

'Sorry. I was thinking. Well, those blankets now. We've plenty, but your order may have been put aside for you.' He went to the stock room. Sammy was often in and out of the shop, or up in the room now furnished as an office. He kept many things close to his chest, but Boots had a vague recollection now that he had mentioned Mr Greenberg had put him in touch with a lady who was opening a new orphanage and had certain requirements. He saw two large cardboard boxes closed and sealed. Each bore a label marked 'Orphanage'. He put his head out. 'They're here, Miss Simms. I'll carry them out to your horse and cart.'

'What a ripping good sort you are, such an improvement on Percy, our chauffeur, who's too toffee-nosed to like running errands.'

Boots carried the first box through the shop. Miss Simms opened the door for him, her smile dazzling. He took the box to the trap. The boy and girl were still there, minding the munching pony.

'He ain't give no trouble, mister, the gee-gee,' said the girl.

'What a blessing for all of us,' said Boots, and brought out the other box. He returned to Miss Simms in the shop. 'They're aboard,' he said. 'Are they paid for?'

'No, but here's the cheque, old sport.' Miss Simms extracted a folded cheque from her handbag and gave it to him. It was drawn on St Stephen's Orphanage to the tune of four pounds. Boots smiled. Sammy's humanitarian generosity had induced him to charge four shillings for each blanket. The shop price for six or more was three and fourpence each. However, they were still cheap at four bob, and Boots didn't suppose the orphans had to pay for them.

'Thank you, madam,' he said.

'Mind your eye, ducky.' Miss Simms did not seem in a hurry to depart. Another customer came in, and she sat down again while Boots sold two pairs of khaki trousers and a pair of braces. When the customer left, Miss Simms said, 'Look, dear man, you still haven't told me your name.'

'Adams.'

'Adam?'

'Adams. I'm Sammy's brother.'

'I see. That accounts for it, but it's still a waste. What's your first name?'

'Robert.'

'Lovely.' Her smile was vivacious. 'Well, Robert old love, close the shop up and help me drive the boxes back home to Dulwich. You can lunch with us.'

'Kind of you,' said Boots, 'but—'

'No buts, old thing. I love meeting people, especially people like you.'

'Sorry, can't shut the shop, not until five-thirty.'

'Don't pee about, sweetie, just shut it up.' Miss Simms, on her feet, exuded bright, brittle self-confidence and irresistibility. 'Whatever you think your takings will be between now and half-past five, just quote me the profit and I'll give you the amount. It's only filthy lucre. God, isn't life commercial? Let's you and me escape it for the rest of the day.'

'You escape,' said Boots. 'I'll stay and face up to it. Good morning, Miss Simms.'

Her eyes flashed.

'Ducky, you're boring,' she said.

'I know, but we can't all be Charlie Chaplin.'

'Very boring,' she said, and glided to the door. Boots opened it for her.

'By the way,' he said, 'I promised those kids you'd give them a penny each for keeping an eye on your pony.'

'My God,' said Miss Simms, 'a penny? How bourgeois can you get?'

239

'I don't know, is it a stomach complaint?' asked Boots with a smile.

'No, a frightful disappointment,' said Miss Simms, and left. She gave the kids a sixpence and brought ecstasy to them. She took the nosebag off the pony, climbed aboard and drove off at a smart trot.

CHAPTER EIGHTEEN

Emily decided to brighten up and stop worrying. After all, as Boots had said, it had only been a few months. It was just that after three and a half years of having to take precautions against conceiving, she had thought it would be simple to reverse the process. She knew Boots wanted a family, but she'd needed to work all the time he'd been blind. It had been wearing while she was still working at the factory, rushing to catch a tram in the mornings, having to fight to get on, and another rush and push and fight to get home in the evenings. And the work became so boring. It was different at the town hall. She'd been there nearly four years, and everyone knew her now. Even the mayor did. And really they were all working for the good of the people of Southwark. The town hall was open to everyone who had the kind of worries the Council could take care of.

Emily's forced brightness became real when Mrs Stevens asked her if she'd do another stint in the 'Enquiries' office. Mr Simmonds's lady assistant was off sick.

'I'll do it with pleasure, I'm sure,' said Emily.

'I thought you would,' said Madge. 'But have you been a little down lately?'

'Well – well, it's been a trial not seein' a suitable house after lookin' at lots,' said Emily. 'And there's other things.'

'What other things?'

Emily didn't think she could confide at this stage.

'Oh, nothing much, Mrs Stevens.'

241

'Can I help you with nothing much?' asked Madge.

'No, it's all right, I'm fine, really.'

'Well, I hope so,' said Madge.

Mr Simmonds accepted Emily's assistance readily. He liked her, he liked her quick tongue and her vitality. And she had her own way of attending to people who came in with odd ideas about the kind of services the Council could provide. Some asked for money to tide them over a bad patch. Some said couldn't the mayor send a man round to see to other people's noisy, hollering kids. And more than one asked for a man to be sent round to fix their gas stoves or sweep their chimneys. Emily dealt tactfully with all of them, leaving Mr Simmonds free to cope with complaints that arrived in the mail. Emily, bringing her typewriter in, typed the replies he wrote out in pencil. She did so in between attending to callers.

She had to see to two very young callers in the afternoon. A bold knock on the door preceded the entrance of a boy, a ragamuffin type of about nine, in a huge cap.

'Boy?' enquired Mr Simmonds, looking up from his desk behind the counter.

'In a minute, mister,' said the boy, holding the door open. 'Now come on, Effel, they ain't goin' to eat yer. It's me sister,' he said, 'she's 'aving a fit of standin' still. Effel, you comin' in or ain't yer, yer daft date?'

His sister edged in. She looked about six. She was wearing someone else's cast-off frock. It was clean enough, but it enveloped her, and its hem scurfed around her cracked boots. Her face was the face of a slightly smudged angel, for her cheeks were dusted with what looked like soot. Her eyes darted, as if she suspected the office harboured things that jumped out on small children. The boy had a snub nose. Not much more than his nose and his mouth could be seen under the huge peak of his cap.

Emily came to the counter. It could be a defensive bulwark against people aggressive with grievances. It was a formidable barrier to the boy, who could only just see over the top of it.

'Good afternoon, young man,' said Emily, 'what can we do for you and your sister?' She spoke in the helpful voice of an employee who was there to please.

'She's Effel,' said the boy. 'I'm 'Orrice. My mum's Mrs Wivvers.'

'Mrs Withers?' suggested Mr Simmonds.

'Yes, I just said so,' said 'Orrice. 'Sent me round 'ere, she did, and of course Effel 'ad to come. I can't go nowhere wivout she don't foller me. All right, now yer 'ere, Effel, say somefink to the lady an' gent.'

'Ain't goin' to,' said Effel, hovering cautiously by the door.

'I dunno why she's like this,' said 'Orrice, 'yer can't stop 'er yappin' most of the time.'

'Nice change, then,' murmured Mr Simmonds in one of his habitual asides.

'It won't last, mister, I can tell yer,' said 'Orrice, his hearing sharp enough to pick up all asides. His eyes appeared as he lifted his head and looked up at Emily. Emily smiled encouragingly. 'Yer got lovely peepers,' he said.

'Ta,' said Emily, 'yours ain't so bad, either. Well, then, what's the problem?'

'It's me dad's drains,' said 'Orrice, at which point Effel crept up and hid herself behind him.

'Your dad's?' said Emily.

'That's what me mum says. She won't 'ave nuffink to do with the drains, them that's under our back yard. Says she's got everyfink else to worry about. Them drains is Dad's, she says. Well, they ain't workin', miss.'

'Mrs Adams,' said Emily.

'Yus, they ain't workin', missus. Nor's the back lav. Come over the top, it does, when yer pull the chain. Dad said 'e ain't 'aving anyfink to do with that lot, 'e didn't build them drains, 'e said, so me mum said to come round and tell yer to send a bloke. So I come.

243

She says if yer don't send no one we'll all have to wear gas masks and ask to use next door's lav. Them drains is all blocked up, me dad said, an' me mum wants to know what you town 'all people've been puttin' down the sewers. She says is it dead 'orses.'

'Live ones won't go down sewers,' said Mr Simmonds.

'They got sense, then, mister,' said 'Orrice. 'I got to tell yer, missus, that Mum says if yer don't come an' unblock the drains she'll sue yer in front of a magistrate.' He wriggled. 'Effel, gedorf.'

'Won't,' said Effel from behind him.

'Well, I don't want to be sued in front of a magistrate,' said Emily. 'Where'd you live?'

'Deacon Street,' said 'Orrice.

'What number?'

'Eleven,' said 'Orrice, 'but yer don't need to know that, yer can tell which 'ouse it is. It's the one beginnin' to pong.'

'Oh, dear,' said Emily.

'That Effel,' said 'Orrice, 'she's climbin' up me back now. Effel, gedorf.'

'Ain't goin' to,' said Effel, trying for a piggy-back.

'You wait, I'll learn yer,' said 'Orrice, struggling to bear his burden. 'Missus, you goin' to send a bloke?'

'Well, it seems to me we'd better, and quick,' said Emily, 'or your drains will spread diseases. We don't want diseases, do we?'

'Me mum'll come round 'erself if there is,' said 'Orrice.

'We'll send a bloke,' said Emily.

' 'Im?' said 'Orrice, nodding at Mr Simmonds.

'No, Mr Simmonds don't go down drains,' said Emily.

'Well, all right, as long as it's someone what does.'

'I promise,' said Emily.

'I'll tell me mum, then. She'll be fankful, I can tell yer. Ta, missus.' 'Orrice moved off. Effel fell to the floor. 'Come on, you,' he said.

'Won't,' said Effel, picking herself up.

'All right, stay standin' still, then,' said 'Orrice, and walked out. Effel screamed ragefully and rushed after him.

'Kids,' said Mr Simmonds.

'But wasn't he lovely, though?' said Emily, filling in an action-required form.

'Fancy the pictures one evening?' asked Mr Simmonds.

'Ever so,' said Emily, 'only I'd have to ask me husband and you'd have to ask yer wife.'

'All these problems on top of drains,' said Mr Simmonds. 'Those kids probably stuffed something down the lav they shouldn't have.'

'We don't know that,' said Emily, 'we just got a duty under the Public 'Ealth Act to clear any blocked drains. Sometimes you sound as if you don't like your job, Mr Simmonds.'

'Rather wake up one morning and find someone's left me a fortune.'

'I like meetin' people,' said Emily, 'specially kids like those two. Well, I'll take this form along to Sanitation and tell 'em it's urgent.' She went, feeling her work was useful and uplifting.

Susie's eyes brightened. Her Mister Adams was there, working his way through the market crowds. He was travelling about such a lot these days that his only regular times at the stall were on Saturdays and Sunday mornings. Bert was putting too much beer into himself in the middle of each day, and looked coarse and bloated in the afternoons. He breathed beer fumes over customers, and some women took offence at that. Susie worked hard to save such customers from going elsewhere. Compared with Bert, Mister Adams was a fine young gentleman, and looked it too in his nice suit and ties. He still acted awful funny at times, muttering like an old man if she gave him a smile or said what a kind gent he was.

Her mum and dad were blissful about her earnings,

her mum ever so generous, letting her keep lots of shillings for herself. She had two new dresses now, two new blouses, and two new skirts, and some thrilling new undies and stockings. After buying her second new dress, that she had paid a bit more for, because Mister Adams told her to, he had said not to go to that dress shop any more, but to the one nearest the market. So she had bought her skirts and blouses there, and shown them to him. He had looked and muttered, then had said well, yes, that's better, its always better to go for quality even if it strains your purse a bit.

Arriving now, he gave her a nod.

' 'Ello, mister,' she said.

'Where's Bert?' asked Sammy, but not unkindly. Business was going well for him, considering. He never forgot to take note of conditions, and conditions in the country were such that even a small business profit induced a thinking man to give thanks. And his profit on his undertakings looked like being healthy, and was taking good care of the interest he was paying Ikey Mo on the loan. And Susie Whatsername was being responsible for some part of the profit. Also, the way she looked now, no one could accuse him of paying her starvation wages. There was colour in her face, a healthy light in her eyes, and a pretty red ribbon in her hair.

'Bert's gone for a cup of tea,' said Susie.

'That's not on,' said Sammy. 'He's got the market boy to call on whenever he wants a cup of tea. What's that?' He pointed to a half-open square of brown paper in a corner of the stall. There was an apple beside it.

'Oh, it's just bread and marge, mister, I was just goin' to eat it, with the apple, for me midday meal.'

'Oh, you were, were you? Is that what I told you to do?'

'No, but—'

'Don't I make you an allowance of thruppence a day for pie and mash, or a hot faggot with pease pudding?'

'Yes, but all that pie and mash, mister, it's been puttin' pounds on me, and so's them faggots,' wailed Susie.

'Good,' said Sammy.

'Oh, yer not goin' to make me grow fat, are yer?'

'Plump and rosy, that's the ticket,' said Sammy.

'Plump?' Susie gazed at him in horror, then was forced by the interest of two shoppers to attend to one of them. Sammy attended to the other. For the first time it occurred to him that the actual business of selling things like penny cups and saucers from a stall should be left to others. While he would never lose the pleasure of satisfying a customer, whether it was for a farthing profit or a lot more, the time had come to leave himself free in respect of the stall. Fred ran his scrap yard, Boots ran his shop, and Bert half-ran the stall. Bert didn't like being committed to a full day every day. Bert had to be bought out. He could force him out by reason of the fact that he was behind in his repayments of the loan made to him for his acquisition of thirty-five per cent of the stall ownership. To waive that and to offer him sixty quid would be money Bert couldn't resist.

The two shoppers departed, and Susie resumed her pleading, for of all things she didn't want to get fat.

'Mister, I'll remember yer in my prayers, honest I will, if yer'll let me off any more pie and mash, or faggots.'

'I don't want to see you lookin' skinny again,' said Sammy, 'it hurts my eyes. All right, you can give pie and mash a rest, but as soon as Bert comes back, go to Toni's and buy yourself a fried bacon sandwich and a portion of apple pie.'

Susie's horror turned her eyes into dark blue saucers.

'Oh, Mister Adams, God forgive yer,' she gasped.

'With custard,' said Sammy. He thought about the food Chinese Lady had put into him and his sister and brothers, even in the desperate times. Mutton stews with huge suet dumplings, mounds of crisp-coated bubble and squeak with cold meat on washing days,

247

Yorkshire pudding moist with gravy, sausage and onion puddings, boiled beef and carrots, rich kippers, fat and nourishing mackerel, and fruity bread puddings once a week. Prunes and custard. Rice puddings, apple puddings. Of course, often it had only been one real meal a day. But there had been the good times, and none of them had ever grown fat when Chinese Lady had provided food to fill their stomachs regularly. Susie Whatsername and her family had obviously not known many good times. She'd got to have something decently filling at midday.

'Look, mister, yer needn't give me any more thruppences,' she pleaded. 'I get a good dinner now in the evenings, and bread an' marge with an apple'll suit me fine midday. And an apple a day keeps the doctor away, don't it?'

'When Bert gets back, I'll go with you to Toni's,' said Sammy remorselessly.

'Oh, 'elp me, God, I don't want apple pie stuffed into me,' said Susie desperately. She had weighed a little under seven stone when she first began working at the stall. She was only four pounds short of eight stone now. She wasn't sixteen yet and her breasts were filling out alarmingly, a terrible sign, she was sure, that in another month she would have a thick waist and a fat belly. Oh, please, God, don't let him turn me into a balloon. If I don't do what he says, he'll have one of his funny moods and sack me.

Bert came back a few minutes after noon and turned morose when Sammy then went off with Susie to Toni's. Sammy sat her down at a corner table. He ordered from Toni. He carried a fried bacon sandwich and a fruit dish back to the table. The dish contained tinned pineapple. Tinned pineapple could be bought from Walworth grocers for tuppence-ha'penny a tin. Some people said it was cubes of turnip in syrup.

Susie stared in dismay at the thick sandwich.

'Oh, Mister Adams, yer been an' turned from a kind man into a hard one,' she said.

'Now look here, young Whatsername,' said Sammy, sitting down, 'the turning's been done by you. Look at yerself. You're a growing girl now, not a scarecrow. You're a credit to me stall. And the sandwich is for me. The fruit's for you. I can't have you pouring misery into me ears on account of your dietary problems. Just make sure you don't get skinny again, that's all.'

'Skinny? I've never been skinny,' protested Susie. 'I just been a bit slender. Oh, but thank yer for the pineapple, yer really very kind under all yer muttering.'

'Kindly repeat that,' said Sammy, 'I don't think I heard it right.'

Susie blushed.

'Oh, I didn't mean to say that,' she said. 'Yer don't think me a wretched girl, mister, do yer?'

'Eat your pineapple,' said Sammy brusquely, and bit into his sandwich. The bread was new and crusty, the fried bacon tasty. Susie spooned pineapple chunks into her mouth. 'Now listen,' said Sammy, 'I know you work at the stall every day, and do a bit of time Sunday mornings as well, but it's all on a please-yerself basis.'

'Please, you ain't goin' to say you don't want me some days, are yer?' said Susie, looking apprehensive.

'Now would I do that when you're a valuable appendix?' said Sammy. He really meant appendage, but that wasn't the sort of word any self-respecting stallholder would use. 'What I'm saying is I'm offering you a proper, permanent job on the stall, not one you come to on a volunt'ry basis.'

'Permanent?' said Susie.

'Yes. It means you've got to be there all day every day, and Sunday mornings. You can go to church Sunday evenings instead of mornings. It means an official job, young Whatsername, with an insurance card and a weekly stamp, which I'll see to. With early closing Wednesdays and Sundays, it's a six-day week, and I'll pay you a wage of twenty-five bob, or you can still work on commission. Seeing you're good at selling, and know how to treat customers, my advice is to go for commission. Well, then, what d'you say? You've got to be there every day, remember, you can't please yourself, but I'll look after you, as much as I can, seeing you're still not much more than a schoolkid. All the same, you're welcome to make up your own mind about it.'

'Oh,' breathed Susie, and bent her head.

'Now what's wrong?' asked Sammy.

'Oh, there ain't nothing wrong,' she said muffledly.

'You're not suffering more misery, are yer?'

'No – no.' Susie lifted her head, and Sammy ground his teeth as her blue eyes regarded him wetly and swimmingly. 'Oh, yer a blessing to me, Mister Adams, yer a saviour of me fam'ly's fortunes.'

'No, I ain't,' said Sammy, 'I'm just doing what's good for business, that's all. Finish your pineapple. Here, blow your nose first.' He passed her his handkerchief. Susie dabbed her eyes and blew her nose.

'No, I got to say it,' she said, 'you been like God's gift to a fam'ly that's been next door to starvation. Yer givin' me a real, permanent, reg'lar job, and I don't know how I'm ever goin' to thank yer. Only what's Bert goin' to say?'

That had been her worry, Bert's attitude, making her feel things wouldn't last.

'Bert will be gone by the end of the week,' said Sammy, who knew his man.

'Gone?'

'Gone. There'll be someone else in charge.' Sammy finished his sandwich. 'Someone you'll get on better with.'

'Oh, who?'

'I hope it'll be a brother of mine.'

'Mister Adams, not Mister Robert, the one in your shop?' Susie had picked up information on names in her own way. 'Oh, he's nice, and ain't his wife sweet?'

250

'I'm talkin' about my other brother, Tommy. D'you want a cup of tea?'

'Oh, I'll get 'em,' said Susie, her state of happiness exhilarating, 'yer'll let me treat yer, won't yer?'

'You can't treat me,' said Sammy, 'I'm your employer. It's familiarity, treatin' your employer.'

'But you been treatin' me at times,' said Susie, 'ain't that familiarity?'

'Kindly don't be impertinent, Miss Whatsername. What I've done is to help you look a credit to me stall, instead of havin' people accuse me of paying yer starvation wages. All right, yer don't want any more pie and mash, but what you have had has made yer look nice and healthy and plump.'

'Oh, Mister Adams, yer puttin' me in despair,' breathed Susie, amid the boisterous noise of the cafe and market. 'I ain't plump, I ain't, I'd fall ill if I was.'

'You fall ill and I'll sack yer,' said Sammy. 'Come on, never mind any tea, I'll buy yer a cornet.' He ordered two cornets of Italian ice cream from Toni's beaming missus, and he and Susie ate them on the way back to the stall. Susie couldn't help thinking how funny he was, because there had to be a lot of familiarity about an employer and employee walking through the market eating ice cream cornets together.

Bert, still morose, went off to a pub as soon as they got back, and two minutes later Susie's mum and dad turned up. Mrs Brown whispered to her that they'd come to meet Mister Adams. They'd been several times before, but he'd been absent each time. Was that him there now, dressed smart?

'Yes, that's him, Mum,' said Susie. 'Mister Adams, here's me mum an' dad, they've come to meet yer official like.'

Sammy's eyes glinted suspiciously. Official like? What did that mean, that she wanted her parents to look him over and decide if he was suitable enough to be accepted as her second dad? Then what? He was to be officially responsible for her welfare and leave her something in his will? Girls. Crikey, they came from a different planet, they did, and brought all their weird ideas with them. This one was only fifteen, but what went on in her mind only another girl would know. There was Lizzy, who'd fallen in love with Ned when she was a mere fourteen, and she'd got him in the end. It had worked out all right, mind, but Ned probably still didn't know what hit him.

'Beg your pardon?' said Sammy from the back of the stall.

'It's me mum an' dad,' said Susie, 'they want to meet yer, Mister Adams.'

'Howjer do, Mister Adams?' said Mr Brown, thin but cheerful.

'Oh, yes, howjer do?' said Mrs Brown, plump and jolly.

Sammy, strictly brought up by Chinese Lady, lifted his hat to Mrs Brown.

'Good afternoon,' he said.

'Mum, he ain't 'alf swell,' said Susie rapturously, 'he's just give me this job permanent. Permanent, Dad.'

'Well, Mister Adams,' said Mr Brown, 'I got to thank you, that I have. I dunno Susie could've found any job to pay 'er as well as this one.'

'You been very good to her, Mister Adams,' said Mrs Brown, feeling sure now that this was a young man who didn't have designs on Susie. Like Susie, he had blue eyes that weren't a bit shifty. His look was very direct. 'My husband and me, we do appreciate you been good to her.'

'Well, she's good herself at her job,' said Sammy.

'An' don't she look well on it too?' said Mr Brown proudly.

'I am pleased to say she has improved considerable,' declared Sammy in solemn fashion.

'Well, we was desperate hard-up for food till you give her this job,' said Mrs Brown gratefully.

'It's my pleasure to know she's lookin' plumper,' said Sammy.

'Oh, I'm not!' Susie, set on owning an elegant figure, was indignant again. 'Mum, I ain't plump, am I?'

'Course not, dear,' said Mrs Brown, who was plump herself and didn't mind a bit. 'Oh, now we're here, your dad and me thought we'd buy some of them cheap cups and saucers you sell. We got so many cracked ones at home.'

Susie at once helped her parents sort out cups and saucers from the ever-present job lot, doing her best to match them up. Mr Brown said it didn't matter, they were only for everyday use. Sammy attended to two lady shoppers.

Mr and Mrs Brown said goodbye to him in the end and went on their way. Biding her time until there was a quiet moment, Susie then spoke up.

'Oh, I can't 'ardly believe you'd say it right out loud in front of me mum and dad. I'm not goin' to eat anything, not anything, for a month. Not pie and mash, nor faggots, nor nothing at home, either, just glasses of water.'

'Oh, we're off again, are we?' said Sammy. 'Did I say something I shouldn't, then?'

'Yes, yer did,' said Susie firmly and bravely. 'Yer said it in front of me mum and dad that I was fat. I'll die, I will, before I get time to go to church and pray for me mortification.'

'Kindly refrain from excessive female exaggerations,' said Sammy. 'I didn't say you were fat, I just said you were lookin' much improved.'

'Plump, you said, and plump's fat.'

'You're not fat. You're just fine.'

'Oh, yer mean that?' said Susie hopefully.

'Yes, and stop gnashing your teeth at me every time I make a passin' comment.'

'Yer really like me like I am now, mister?'

'You'll do,' said Sammy, but without looking at her.

'Oh, yer nice, really, yer know,' said Susie.

'Maybe, maybe,' said Sammy, 'but that don't mean I'm goin' to be a father to you.'

'A father?' said Susie in astonishment. 'But I got a father.'

'Yes. Well. All right. As long as you don't need me for another.'

'Another father?' Susie's giggles were rich. 'Oh, Mister Adams, ain't you funny?'

Sammy muttered.

In a room on the first floor of a Brixton boarding-house that catered for travelling members of the music-hall profession, the creaking bed creaked faster for a few moments, then sighed to a stop. The springs murmured. A man sighed too, and a woman groaned.

Mr Clarence Rainbould, conjurer, was entertaining a close lady friend. He lay comfortably bedded on her naked roundness, breathing contentedly and relaxing slowly.

'Oh, you know how to pleasure a woman, that you do,' said Milly Pearce.

He slid off her.

'Mutual, Milly, mutual. I own modest gifts, dear young lady, you own the architecture of Venus.'

'Oh, very modest, I'm sure,' said Milly, body and forehead slightly damp from heated achievement. 'And you'll use them on some other woman tomorrow, I daresay.'

'Lord take me, dear heart,' said Mr Rainbould, 'a man in love is sweetly blind to all other women.'

'Oh, I'm sure, tra-la, tra-la,' said Milly, who rarely forgot to put on the style.

'I shall depart sadly for Brighton and the Theatre Royal this evening,' sighed Mr Rainbould, 'unless you cast your reservations aside and come with me. It will be Brighton this month, Eastbourne next month, and then on to the boards of theatres at large. There, my hand is on my heart when I declare I'll keep my promise and train you to take Maggie's place. Maggie's thighs, alas, are beginning to bulge in her tights. Yours, my love, are perfect. Since, as you say, you have no responsibilities or commitments, you may flutter and fly as free as a bird, although I shall beg you, of course, to nest only with me. So come with me this evening.'

'Cross your heart and cut your throat that you'll get me on the stage?' said Milly, soft-lidded eyes calculating.

'Be my bird of paradise and consider it done.'

'What time at Victoria station this evening?'

'Seven of the clock.'

'Well, I might put my trust in you, Mr Clarence Rainbould, I just might and all.'

'It will not be misplaced. I am a man of professional integrity.'

They were a fine pair together.

At half-past four in the afternoon, Rosie Pearce was given a slice of bread and butter by her mother and told to go and eat it in the street.

'Yes, Mummy. I won't come in till you call me, shall I?'

'I don't want you under my feet, I'm busy.'

'Yes, Mummy,' said Rosie.

She went out. She sat on the kerb outside the Adams house, eating her bread and butter and watching other kids at play. She felt a little forlorn. Her Uncle Boots wasn't at home during the day any more, he was working in a shop in Camberwell. She missed helping him, although she did see him in the evenings sometimes. And other times, when she was alone, he put her to bed, bringing a book with him to read her a fairy story.

Chinese Lady, entering Caulfield Place from Browning Street, a shopping bag in her hand, walked in the upright fashion of a woman who did not have the sorrows and worries that others did. Her worst days of poverty were behind her, and although Tommy was still out of a job, she refused to be pessimistic. Tommy had good qualities, honesty and frankness and cheerfulness. Some employer would recognise them soon enough.

Seeing Milly Pearce's little girl sitting on the kerb, a half-eaten slice of bread in her hand, her firm mouth compressed in anger. What a wretchedly uncaring mother that woman was.

'Rosie?'

Rosie looked up through her clear spectacles. A smile broke though her melancholy.

'Hello, Mrs Adams.'

'Isn't your mummy in?'

'Yes, but she's busy, and I mustn't get under her feet,' said Rosie.

'Well, would you like to come in and have a fizzy lemonade what's keepin' cool in the scullery?' Chinese Lady had no qualms at this moment about giving the child some affection.

'Oh, could I, please?' said Rosie, scrambling to her feet. 'I don't 'spect Mister Boots is in, is he?'

'No, not yet, and his brother Tommy has gone to see a firm in Aldgate this afternoon. You won't mind it's just me?'

'Oh, no, Mrs Adams, you're awful nice,' said Rosie.

So Chinese Lady took her indoors and gave her a glass of R.White's fizzy lemonade. Rosie, happier, chattered away. It was an hour before her mother called her, when she then gave the child a tea of fried sausages and two more slices of bread. A little later she gave her a bag of sweets and told her to be good.

Then she went out, leaving the child alone.

Emily and Boots took themselves off to Brixton in the evening to look at two houses that were up for sale or renting. They got back a little after nine, having found both houses too big and rents too high. Sammy arrived home at much the same time, and initiated a family conference. It concerned the stall and a job for Tommy, whose excursion to a firm in Aldgate had proved fruitless. Bert Lomax, fed up in any case with Sammy laying down the law, had accepted his offer and was getting out. So how did Tommy feel about taking charge of the stall for two pound a week, with Susie as his full-time help? Tommy said he appreciated the proposition, but running a china and glass stall was a bit different from engineering, and he couldn't guarantee he wouldn't be a dud at it. If he proved a dud, he'd have to suffer getting the sack from his own brother, and his younger brother at that.

'That's no more than I'd suffer if Sammy thought I was costing him money,' said Boots.

'Well, I'll be honest,' said Sammy, 'if you couldn't make a decent go of it, I'd have to sack you, Tommy. Business is business, yer know.'

'It may be,' said Chinese Lady, 'but I won't have you talkin' as if it's more important than your fam'ly. Sackin' your own brother? The very idea. I'll thank you to remember that your share of the stall is in my name, you still being under age.'

'Now, Ma, you know that's just to make it legal, that it's all been my money,' said Sammy.

'I'll make it unlegal if you take Tommy on and then give him the sack, my lad. He'll manage, he's got commonsense, and nice looks and nice ways. He'll make the stall prosperous for you, he only needs to be properly learned.'

'I'll learn him,' said Sammy. 'And did I say I'd give him the sack? No, he said it, and I only said I'd have to think about it if he didn't make a go of the job. I don't know why Boots mentioned suffering something considerably unprobable—'

'Improbable,' said Boots.

'Sammy, you swallered a dictionary?' asked Chinese Lady, not without pride in her youngest son's sudden leap into a higher vocabulary.

'I'm just saying I'm not considerin' givin' Boots the sack, but that if he don't take to the shop he can always resign.'

'Em'ly love, you read books,' said Chinese Lady. 'Is resigning like being given the sack?'

'No,' said Emily, 'resigning means you're leavin' because you got a better job to go to or if you've done something shameful like embezzling and you been found out. You resign quick then before your firm brings the police round.'

Boots coughed and Chinese Lady looked a bit shocked.

'Em'ly? What's embezzling?'

'Well, it's pinchin', really,' said Emily.

'Thieving,' said Boots.

'That's all right, then,' said Chinese Lady, 'there won't be no resigning in this fam'ly, because I didn't bring any of you up to do thievin', specially not now when you'll all soon be nearly grown-up men.'

Her sons looked at each other. Sammy and Tommy were five feet ten, Boots almost six feet.

'Soon, Chinese Lady?' said Boots. 'Nearly?'

'I hope you'll all be grown-up men one day,' said Chinese Lady. Emily smiled. She knew her mother-in-law didn't really want any of her sons to be anything but her boys. 'Tommy'll take your stall on, Sammy, with the help of that nice young girl.' Chinese Lady had gone to take a look at Susie soon after she began working for Sammy, and although she hoped the girl would learn to speak better, she found her quite sweet. 'Tommy?'

'Well, it's a port in a storm,' said Tommy. 'You show me the ropes, Sammy, and I'll get used to china and glass and standin' on me plates of meat all day.'

'Well, ain't that nice, Mum?' said Emily. 'Now we're all one big happy fam'ly again, and Tommy can start goin' out with girls again once he's earnin'.'

'Cousin Vi hasn't been to Sunday tea lately,' mused Boots, at which Chinese Lady gave him a look. 'By the way, Sammy tells me that Mr Greenberg thinks Chinese

258

Lady would have found favour with Solomon. King Solomon.'

'Didn't he have six hundred wives?' asked Tommy.

Boots said, 'I believe Sammy told Mr Greenberg that—'

'That's it, get me hanged,' said Sammy.

'I don't want to hear no more about Solomon,' said Chinese Lady, 'I don't hold with Frenchified insinuations. It's time you all thought about bed.'

'I suppose it was compulsory with Solomon, thinking about bed,' said Boots.

'You'll get marked down for perdition one day, my lad,' said Chinese Lady.

'We'll see him off with a fireworks party, make sure he goes with a bang,' said Emily.

She and Boots were still up at eleven, talking about their future when they finally found the house that suited them. They didn't mention babies, but Emily did say that if she was still working they'd be able to afford lovely new furniture, which Chinese Lady would like.

'Hold on,' said Boots, 'did I hear something?'

It was the sound of the front door being opened by its latchcord. Then came the patter of bare feet over the linoleum floor of the gaslit passage and the opening of the kitchen door. Rosie stood there in her none-too-clean flannel nightdress, her face pale and streaked with the marks of frightened tears. She was not wearing her glasses. Her mouth was trembling. She had put herself to bed because Boots and Emily had been out.

She swallowed.

'Please—' She swallowed again.

'What's wrong, Rosie?' asked Boots, coming to his feet.

'Mister Boots,' she whispered, 'could you come and take care of me, please? I'm frightened. Mummy's not come back.' She tried hard not to sob. 'Could you come and be with me? Someone's there.'

CHAPTER NINETEEN

Boots was in Milly Pearce's house, Rosie with him, her
hand fast in his. The house, eerie in its associations
with the murdered Mrs Chivers, and soulless in its
relationship with an uncaring mother, was a wretched
place. Having lit the gas mantle in the kitchen, he
looked around. He thought it miserably cheerless
compared with Chinese Lady's kitchen. He saw a used
envelope on the mantelpiece, propped against a tin
clock, its reverse side showing, with pencilled words.

*'Her grandparents are Mr and Mrs Tooley. They're my
parents. They live at 4 Warwick Street Deptford.'*

That was all, and it was not even signed.

'Rosie, when your mummy went out, did she say
where she was going?'

'She just went out, she just called to me.'

'What did she call, lovey?'

'She just called be good. Is she coming back?'

'Oh, I expect so, poppet.'

'She wasn't cross with me, she gave me sweets.'

My God, he thought, a parting gift of sweets? It was
a parting gift, almost certainly. That was why she had
left the name and address of her parents. But what
about her husband, Rosie's father?

'Rosie, was Mummy carrying a suitcase when she
went out?'

'I don't know,' said Rosie, 'I was in here. Mummy
just called to me from out there. Could you – could you
take care of me, please?'

'Of course, kitten,' he said.

'It's dark upstairs, awful dark,' she said, and he felt her fingers tighten around his. She whispered, 'There's someone up there. I was frightened.'

'Oh, I think it might be your mummy, don't you?'

'No. I called her. I went to her room. I called her. It was awful dark. Someone was there. Not Mummy. I ran to see you.' Rosie spoke in nervous little spasms.

'Let's have a look, shall we? Or shall you stay down here?'

'I like it best being with you.'

A candle in a holder, something common to every kitchen in Walworth in case the gas ran out for lack of pennies, stood on the dresser. He applied a lighted match to the wick. Holding his hand again, Rosie went bravely up the stairs with him, to her mother's bedroom, the front bedroom, where the Witch had come to her grisly end. Boots thought the darkness and silence of the house must have been a nightmare to the deserted child. Her mother had had a fright several weeks ago, a fright he discovered to be caused by mice. By the light of the candle he surveyed the room. A dark huddle lay on the bed.

Rosie trembled and hid herself against him. He brought the candle lower. Two gleaming eyes stared out of shadows. He relaxed. On the bed was Mrs Pullen's enormous tabby cat. And on the lino, close to the bed, was a dead mouse. He suspected then that what Rosie had heard was the cat playing with the mouse.

'It's only Mrs Pullen's cat, Rosie. There, see?'

Rosie looked.

'Shoo, shoo!' she exclaimed indignantly. The tabby, liking the bed, purred.

'Come on,' said Boots. 'you can sleep in our house tonight.'

'Could I?' she asked.

'That's best,' he said.

'Boots?' Emily called up from the passage. He took Rosie down. Emily had an enamel mug in her hand.

261

'I brought her some cocoa. Is everything all right?'

'Just Mrs Pullen's cat playing about,' said Boots. 'We'll take the cocoa back with us. Rosie's mother isn't here, so let's have her in with us for the night.' He went into the kitchen, turned off the gas lamp and snuffed the candle, then followed Emily and Rosie home. Emily took the girl up to the little sitting-room and put a match to the gas mantle. The light was a welcoming thing to Rosie.

'You can have the sofa, Rosie,' she said.

'I thought in our bed, with us,' said Boots.

Emily, feeling they should not make the child too dependent on their affection, said, 'She'll be fine on the sofa, with some blankets, won't you, Rosie?'

'Oh, yes,' said Rosie, content to be there.

Boots brought a sheet and blankets, and Emily made up a bed on the sofa, with a cushion for a pillow. Rosie got into the bed and Boots tucked her in.

'There, now you're all right,' he said.

'We'll leave the light on till we come up in a little while,' said Emily.

'Yes, thank you, Auntie Emily,' said Rosie. Very content, her lids fell.

Down in the kitchen once more, Boots said, 'I don't think Milly Pearce is coming back.'

'What?'

'She left a note giving the address of her parents, Rosie's grandparents. Just that. It can only mean she expects them to take Rosie and look after her.'

'She's gone off with some man,' said Emily in fierce disgust. 'What's her 'usband goin' to say when he finds out? And him with the Army in that place Mesopotamia too.'

'D'you think so, Em?'

'What d'you mean?'

'Tomorrow I'm going to ask Rosie if she's ever seen her father. She's never mentioned him, never talked about him.'

262

'Boots, oh, Lor,' breathed Emily, 'you don't think that poor little mite's been born out of wedlock, do yer?'

'I'd like to nose around the house and find out if there are any letters or anything else that might relate to a Mr Pearce, or a Private Pearce.'

'There's got to be,' said Emily. 'I mean, she don't go out to work but she's still got money, she's got to have, to pay the rent and keep 'erself and Rosie. Couldn't it be what she gets as a soldier's wife?'

'I suppose,' said Boots.

'It don't bear thinking of, little Rosie bein' illegitimate,' said Emily.

'Tomorrow I'll write to her grandparents,' said Boots. 'Could we take care of her meanwhile?'

'We'd have to ask Chinese Lady,' said Emily, 'she'd 'ave the responsibility daytimes. Shouldn't we tell the police? It's near to being criminal, a mother desertin' her child.'

'Don't let's have the bobbies round, Em. Look, you go into the house tomorrow and take a peek at Milly's wardrobe. You'll know if she's packed a suitcase. If she has, then I'd say she really has done a bunk. There's no more we can do tonight except go to bed.'

'Just mind you don't get too soppy about her,' said Emily on a practical note.

'Soppy?'

'Well, she's a sweet little thing and I'm gettin' a bit soppy about her meself,' said Emily.

There was disbelief at breakfast the next morning. While Emily was getting Rosie ready, Chinese Lady, Sammy and Tommy gave vent to their feelings. No one in Walworth would ever deliberately desert a child, no matter how desperate their straits. Some, because of impossible poverty, might allow their children to be cared for in a council home, but no one would just walk out on a little girl, leaving her alone in an empty house. Chinese Lady expressed herself bitingly. Tommy, who did not like to think too badly of anybody, nevertheless declared Milly Pearce to be a cow. Sammy, who had met all kinds, spoke a few choice words that made Chinese Lady look reprovingly at him. But she then dismissed Milly Pearce as a bad lot and said only Rosie was important. She assured Boots she would see to the child during the day.

When Emily brought the girl into the kitchen for breakfast, there was creamy-looking porridge to be eaten, with warm toast to follow, and some of Chinese Lady's home-made marmalade. Rosie was greeted affectionately, and she minded not at all about the absence of her mother. Chinese Lady was already mothering her. Boots smiled. Chinese Lady was incurably maternal.

Tommy was going with Sammy to the stall, to pick up what tips he could before starting the job on Monday.

'Glad you're feeling conscientious,' said Sammy. 'I'll unload some of me most valuable advice on yer, but of course you don't get paid until you start officially, which will be after Bert's disappeared in a cloud of pub sawdust, which he will when he's finished his last stint on Sunday morning. Got it, Tommy? Good, come on, then. So long, Rosie, if yer can't be good be careful.'

'I'll be awful good,' said Rosie, who seemed in a dream at being at table with the whole family.

'Where's yer glasses?' asked Tommy.

'She left them behind last night,' said Boots, and there were no comments. They all knew she did not need them.

When everyone had gone off to work, leaving Rosie alone with Chinese Lady, Rosie asked if she should go out in the street and play. It was school holidaytime. Chinese Lady said, 'Do you want to go out, child, or stay in and help me?'

And Rosie said she would like to stay in and help, but that she wouldn't get in the way.

* * *

At the stall, Susie said good morning to Sammy and Tommy. Tommy had met her, as all the family had. He liked her for her enthusiasm.

'Mister Tommy,' she said in pleasure, 'yer goin' to take over from Bert Lomax on Monday, Mister Sammy said. That's gladsome news.'

'Don't say it yet,' said Tommy, 'not till Sammy's sure I'm not goin' to be the ruination of his stall.'

'Oh, Mister Sammy won't let yer be that,' said Susie, 'he's give me all kinds of 'elp and advice. He's been a real Christian gent to me and me fam'ly.'

'Oblige me by not committin' these female exaggerations,' said Sammy. 'Get those glass tumblers polished.'

'Yes, Mister Sammy.' Susie began to polish new tumblers taken out of their paper wrappings, while Sammy set up the day's display, with Tommy watching. 'Me parents come and met yer brother, Mister Tommy, and they was very taken with him bein' such a kind, polite gent. Yer fam'ly must be proud of 'im now he's got a shop as well.'

'We're all swelling up with pride,' said Tommy.

Susie giggled. Sammy gave her a severe look.

'Kindly understand, both of you, that I ain't runnin' a circus here,' he said.

'No, Mister Sammy,' said Susie demurely.

'I'm only here meself to be instructed,' said Tommy.

'Well, I'm goin' to impart the best of me hard-won wisdom,' said Sammy. 'Bert's not due till midday, when I'm then goin' to the shop. All right, let me put some sound learnin' into you. I got faith in you, Tommy.'

'Good on yer, mate,' said Tommy. Shoppers were appearing as he began his stint. Susie felt pleased. Mister Tommy was ever so much more agreeable than Bert.

The young lady in a silk apricot dress and feathered blue hat waited outside the shop until it was empty of customers. She had to wait twenty minutes. Then she glided in.

'Good morning, madam,' said the manager.

'Oh, that's a great help, I don't think,' said Miss Polly Simms. 'Look, I'm sorry I got bitchy. Be a sweet man and forgive me. I was passing and simply had to pop in and apologise.'

'Don't distress yourself,' said Boots, 'we pursue the principle that our customers are never in the wrong.'

'Stop being stuffy,' said Polly. 'Look, I know I can be difficult, but the frightful war, you know, and the even more frightful peace, all these darling Tommies out of work. Don't you suffer filthy tempers at times?'

'Not with customers,' said Boots. 'What can I get you?'

'Ye gods, I'm a customer?' said Polly.

'I don't know, are you?' said Boots.

'Not if it's Camp coffee time,' said Polly, wondering again why such an intriguing man was engaged in the humdrum exercise of running a shop, a ghastly shop at that. 'I'd love one.'

Noting people at the window outside, Boots said, 'I think I'd better remain at the ready, madam. But you know where the amenities are.'

'I'm invited to make it myself? I will, ducky, for both of us.' She eyed him speculatively. A free-ranging soul and honest with herself, she was ready to admit he excited her. She thought him twenty-six or twenty-seven. She was just twenty-four herself. She liked his ease of manner and its suggestion that he could not always have been a shopkeeper. Twenty-six? 'Robert dearie,' she said, 'were you in the war?'

Boots looked at her, his sound eye taking in her air of affluence and the moistness of her delicately lipsticked mouth. He smiled.

'D'you want me to be boring, Miss Simms?' he asked. She was likeable, despite her affectations. 'Or d'you want to go and make the coffee?'

'Coffee, darling. Yes, righty-ho.'

She disappeared as shoppers came in. She made the coffee with hot water, boiled in a tin kettle on a gas ring. There was milk in a half-pint pewter can, delivered on the shop doorstep by the milkman. She waited until the customers had gone before she poured the boiling water. Then she brought the cups of coffee out.

'That's very kind,' said Boots. 'Is it sugared?'

'Don't be crummy,' she said, 'you didn't ask for any.'

'Well, I wouldn't, would I?' said Boots. 'I don't take it in coffee.'

Polly's pearly teeth gleamed in a brittle smile.

'You haven't said if you were in the war or not.'

'It's over,' said Boots. More customers came in, which Polly thought very tiresome. Why couldn't he shut the shop for a while and have a chummy, civilised chat with her over the coffee? She was due to lunch at the Cecil in an hour and a half with some very boring people, and she felt she deserved a little entertainment beforehand. Imagine that, looking for entertainment with a shopkeeper in a ghastly shop selling the ghastliest things. He wasn't even very talkative. She knew some people who could make a sentence last for a thousand words. He was a man of verbal brevities. How refreshing.

She sipped her coffee while suffering little bursts of impatience. She watched him dealing with the shoppers of Camberwell. She noticed what other people noticed after a while, that he looked as if something was amusing him. Perhaps it was people, perhaps he found people and their foibles amusing.

'Excuse me, Robert old dear,' she said, when the shop was quiet again, 'but this is all very frustrating.'

'What is?' asked Boots, returning to his coffee.

'All these petty interruptions.'

'Oh, petty interruptions are my bread and butter,' said Boots. 'Now, are you after more stuff for the orphanage?'

'God, you're unbelievable,' said Polly. 'I'm just here, and in all the glory of my newest creation.' The apricot silk rippled over her figure. 'I wanted to apologise for saying you were boring. You're not. Now tell me something, what's wrong with your left eye?'

'Does it look wrong?' asked Boots.

'Yes, ducky, it does, it looks lazy,' said Polly, and Boots thought of what Milly Pearce had said about Rosie's eyes. 'It doesn't move in concert with your right one. It makes you look sometimes as if you have a cast.'

'It's a little blind,' said Boots.

Polly searched his face.

'You were in France,' she said.

'It's no secret.'

'It was to me,' said Polly, 'until now. Oh, dearie me, don't you know how much the Tommies of France and Flanders mean to me? I was an ambulance driver for four years over there.'

There was a change in his expression. If he could not forget the carnage, neither could he forget the indefinable consolations of comradeship, or the men and women who drove the ambulances, who picked up the wounded under fire.

'A Wolseley ambulance, perhaps?' he said.

'A Wolseley,' said Polly.

'Those great square boxes?'

'Some died on me.'

'The Wolseleys?'

'The wounded. I used to howl at first for every Tommy I lost.' Polly grimaced. 'Look, old darling, you probably think me a silly bitch and a pain in the neck. Well, the real me is still over there, in Flanders, with all the Tommies who died on me because I didn't get them to a field station in time. Did you know Armentières and Poperhinge, and the estaminets there?'

'Yes, I knew them,' said Boots. The shop door opened, and a man and a woman entered. He attended to them and made a sale. Polly felt new disgust that he should

268

be a shopkeeper. He had been a Tommy. She had always called them her Tommies. She had sung with them in Belgian or French estaminets, in those little towns behind the lines, where men took their rests from the trenches. At night the estaminets had been foggily blue from the smoke of fags and pipes, and noisy with song and laughter. The dry, earthy or bitter humour of these men was something she would always remember, like their bawdiness and their laughter. Their lives for the most part were in the hands of obtuse generals, and she could see it in their sooty eyes, but they could still crack their jokes and still make an estaminet erupt with laughter.

Three more customers came in. Polly bit her lip and prowled tigerishly about. The shoppers looked at her silk dress and feathered hat, and wondered about her. It seemed an age to her before the place was quiet again.

'This is very boring for you,' said Boots. 'By the way, about ambulance drivers. Did you know one called Lily Cartwright-Forbes?'

Polly's eyes sparkled

'Lunatic Lily?' she said. 'And could you mean Forbes-Cartwright?'

'I could never remember which came first.'

'You knew Lily?'

'For two brief nights.' Boots smiled reminiscently. 'She showed me how. If she was off her head, so was everybody else. I liked her. She was very helpful.'

'Fire and fury,' breathed Polly theatrically, 'she got to you first, and I never got to you at all? I could weep. What was your regiment?'

'West Kents.'

Polly bit her lip. 'Close the shop up,' she said, 'come to town with me.'

'Don't let's go through that again,' said Boots, 'let's part friends.'

'We're not going to part, old sport, believe me,' said Polly. 'Were you a private?'

'In the beginning. A sergeant finally.'

'Now I know why you look as if people amuse you,' said Polly.

'I think I've got more customers,' said Boots. 'So long, Polly.'

'Oh, rats,' said Polly. 'I'm going to come again, you know.'

'There must be better things you could do.'

'I shall arrive with an order so that I can have your undivided attention, darling,' said Polly, and left to go in search of a taxi that would take her to the Strand. Two men who had looked like possible customers to Boots, entered as Polly went out. They were both blue-jacketed.

'GPO, guv,' said one, and showed a buff form.

'What for?' asked Boots.

'Phone installation, guv. Office and shop. Order from Adams Enterprises. You Adams Enterprises? It says Sam's Emporium over yer shop front.'

'That's us,' said Boots.

It was another step in the building of Sammy's empire.

Sammy came in at one o'clock. He checked stocks and gave Boots a hand with afternoon customers. At four, Boots said he'd leave Sammy in charge.

'Eh?' said Sammy, highly pleased that the GPO men had installed the telephones speedily and efficiently. While he liked to do his deals face to face, these were the days of instant communication by telephone.

'I thought I'd take Rosie to the shops to buy some new clothes for her,' said Boots.

'Eh?' said Sammy again.

'I don't think she's got many clothes,' said Boots, 'so if I leave you to take care of things here, I'm sure you won't mind.'

'Now don't come the old acid, Boots, you know I don't run me businesses like that. You go off before closing time and I'll dock yer pay. I'll have to. It's a matter of principle.'

'Are there any overtime principles, Sammy?'

Sammy grinned.

'The Artful Dodger, that's you, Boots. It's them deceivin' ways of yours. You always look and talk as if you're at peace with the world, and all the time you've got something underhand cookin'. Anyway, salaried staff don't qualify for overtime pay. All right, go and treat Rosie to some new clobber, then, but listen, don't get yourself too attached. We've all seen the weakness you've got for her. Just watch out it don't take an unfortunate turn. She's got a father, remember, even if her mother's scarpered, and she's got grandparents as well.'

'Noted,' said Boots briefly, and left, posting a letter to Mr Tooley on his way.

He took Rosie out to shops in Walworth Road and gave her a breathless time buying her two frocks for school, two frocks for Sundays. He also purchased hair ribbons and undies. Rosie could hardly believe it.

'You're awful kind, Uncle Boots.'

'Well, little girls should be treated sometimes,' he said, as they began their walk home, Rosie carrying one parcel and he carrying the others. Thick clouds made the August day a little sultry, and the light lacked colour. 'I expect your daddy gives you treats whenever he comes home, doesn't he?'

'I don't remember him,' said Rosie. She could not recall ever having seen her father. She had asked her mother about him, but only a few times, because the answers told her nothing except that the questions made Mummy very cross. She could only hope that when her father did appear he would be very kind and very nice, like Mister Boots, whom she had begun to call Uncle Boots.

'Rosie, haven't you ever seen your daddy, then? Hasn't he been home on leave from the Army?'

'I can't remember.'

'But he's sent you birthday cards?'

'I don't remember birthdays, Uncle Boots.'

'No cards or birthday tea parties?' he asked.

'No,' she said, a little unhappy at the questions.

Christ, thought Boots, hasn't she even had a card from her mother?

'Do you see your grandparents sometimes?'

'I don't remember,' she said. A pause. 'There's just Mummy.'

Boots's suspicions crystallised into certainty.

'Never mind,' he said. 'Let's see if we can beat Auntie Emily home.'

But Emily had arrived ahead of them, and Chinese Lady had had a little talk with her, telling her to watch what Boots was about with Rosie. Emily said it was difficult not to give the child some affection. Chinese Lady said yes, no one could say affection wasn't nice to a child who obviously hadn't had much, but she hoped Boots didn't have something unsensible on his mind, like taking the girl in for good, as the grandparents might have something to say about that. And the father, when he got to know.

All the same, when Boots and Rosie came in, both Chinese Lady and Emily could not help fussing and exclaiming over the prettiness of the new clothes. Noting the child's happiness and her attachment to Boots and Emily, Chinese Lady sighed. She knew that she herself had shown Rosie unwise affection.

Emily had not been long at her desk the next morning when the door was thumped by a fist and a woman walked in, followed by a young boy and a small girl. The woman wore a black straw hat, a grey blouse and a black skirt of long, pre-war style. Buxom, she advanced aggressively. Mr Simmonds, recognising the signs, kept his head down. Emily got up.

' 'Oo's in charge 'ere?' asked the woman. Behind her,

Effel stood on one leg and 'Orrice stood half-hidden under his huge cap.

'Mr Simmonds is in charge,' said Emily.

'You see to it,' said Mr Simmonds, who liked a quiet life.

'Can I help?' asked Emily, sure that this vexed-looking buxom woman was the mother of 'Orrice and Effel.

'Yer better, or I'll – 'old on, are you the lady me son 'Orrice spoke to two days ago?'

'Yes,' said Emily, 'and I hope—'

'Mum,' complained Effel, ' 'Orrice is pushin' me.'

'Askin' for it, she is,' said 'Orrice, 'standin' there on one leg an' showin' orf.'

'Be'ave yerselves,' said their mother. ' 'Orrice, come 'ere.' 'Orrice appeared. He lifted his head and looked up at Emily reproachfully. 'I'm Mrs Withers, and 'Orrice said yer promised yer'd send someone round to see to the drains. Well, he ain't come. 'E didn't come that day, nor yesterday, and I ain't goin' to 'ave me home drowned in drains water and muck on account of no one 'ere not doin' what they should, I can tell yer.' Mrs Withers thumped the counter with her fist.

'No one's been?' said Emily, her green eyes beginning to spark. 'Mrs Withers, I—'

'I don't want no excuses,' said Mrs Withers, 'I'll go to the police station and sue the lot of yer. 'Orrice, did yer get a promise from this lady or not? I don't want no fibs now, I want yer to—'

'Mrs Withers, I did promise him,' said Emily.

'Well, it didn't do 'im much good, did it? Nor me, nor 'is 'ard-working' dad, nor young Effel, nor me home. All over the yard lav that muck is, and me tap water won't go down me sink. Me home'll be swimmin' in it soon. 'Ow would you like it if yer town 'all was?'

'I wouldn't like it,' said Emily, fire in her eyes, 'and nor do I like it that we let yer down. You listening, Mr Simmonds?'

273

'I'm in pain,' said Mr Simmonds, feeling his morning was ruined.

'Mrs Withers,' said Emily, 'just wait there, please, and I'll do something, just see if I don't.' She swept back to her desk, pulled open a drawer and took out file copies of various forms she had filled in. She extracted the relevant one. Her every action was furious.

'Steady, Emily,' murmured Mr Simmonds.

'That's it, you just sit there,' hissed Emily. As she swept out of the office, 'Orrice spoke in some awe.

'Crikey, Mum, you ain't 'alf made her shirty.'

Emily presented her angry self to a clerk in the Health and Sanitation office, a Mr Boddy, a shrimp of a man to her at this moment. She slammed the copy of the form down on his desk.

'That work ain't been done!'

Mr Boddy examined the copy, then cast a furtive glance at the spike which held several originals.

'If you got a complaint—'

'I got one! This one!' Emily's ladylike approach to her job vanished beneath pure cockney fire. 'Yer been sittin' on it! There's a fam'ly livin' in that 'ouse, which 'as got a blocked drain turnin' it into a pigsty! That form's marked urgent an' double-underlined, and yer ain't taken a bleedin' bit of notice of it!'

'Here, who'd you think you are?'

'I'm Mrs Adams, an' don't you forget it! That form's still on yer spike, yes it is! Well, it's been initialled by Mr Simmonds, so don't you start sayin' it don't 'ave no authority because it come from me!'

'Don't you raise your voice to me, and don't you come in here like—'

'If you think I'm goin' to stand at yer door and bow three times to yer before I come in, you can think again! This office is Public 'Ealth, it is, and yer supposed to be servin' public people that's in need. Well, if you don't see to this lady's 'ouse immediate, I'll go straight to the Inspector 'imself, and don't think I won't!'

'You're upsettin' me,' said Mr Boddy, chewing his lip.

'Well, get up off yer backside, then,' said Emily. 'I've got to go and make excuses to Mrs Withers, I 'ave, I got to apologise, which you ought to do. Only I ain't goin' to make you—'

'Make me?'

'Yes, I ain't goin' to make you because I'm soft, and I couldn't stand for seein' you eaten alive.'

'All right, all right,' said Mr Boddy, 'it just got accidentally overlooked. We're not all perfect, we don't all have six pairs of hands.'

'That's it, make me 'ysterical,' said Emily. 'Now, I'm goin' to tell Mrs Withers yer sendin' someone right away. Right?'

'Yes, you can tell her that,' said the flattened Mr Boddy.

Emily carried the news to Mrs Withers, and profuse apologies with it. She mollified the angry lady. And she gave 'Orrice and Effel a penny each for sweets. 'Orrice called her a toff. Effel blushed.

News of the incident travelled and reached the ears of Madge Stevens. She called Emily in.

'Well done, Emily.'

'I don't know it was,' said Emily, 'I can't hardly bear to think now how I carried on all that spittin' and scratchin'. The whole town hall must've 'eard me.'

'Sometimes, Emily, the whole town hall needs waking up. Sometimes some of us forget what we're here for and what we're paid for.'

'You don't forget, Mrs Stevens,' said Emily, 'you ought to be Supervisor, not just Assistant Supervisor.'

'Oh, the Supervisor will always be a man,' smiled Madge, 'you have to resign yourself to that. Anyway, well done, Emily.' Madge smiled again. 'Only next time close the door.'

CHAPTER TWENTY

Sunday was to provide an enjoyable outing for the family. They were all going to tea with Lizzy and Ned in the afternoon, taking Rosie with them. Lizzy and Ned had invited Vi too. Boots received this news from Chinese Lady with a sly smile, which prompted her to ask him what he was smirking about. Boots replied by asking her if she'd co-opted Lizzy to help with the campaign. Chinese Lady asked what he meant by campaign. A well-planned advance, said Boots, a tactical push. Push? What push?

'Yes, you may well ask,' said Boots.

'I am askin',' said Chinese Lady.

'Well, you've got my best wishes, old girl, it's a good cause.'

'When you've grown up a bit more,' said Chinese Lady tartly, 'you might be able to give your mother sensible answers instead of clever ones.'

Rosie, meanwhile, danced about in her new home, life a wonder to her. No one ever said she was in the way and to take herself off into the street. On Sunday morning she was at the front door, in a new frock, her hair combed and brushed, a pink ribbon in it. A middle-aged man appeared in the street, looking at the house numbers. He stopped outside the Adams house, opened the gate and advanced to the doorstep, where Rosie looked up at him. His bowler hat and dark grey serge suit made him look like a school inspector. He examined Rosie in curiosity.

'Does Mr Adams live 'ere?' he asked, lined face

worried. Rosie could only think of Uncle Boots. Sammy and Tommy were at the stall, Tommy still under instruction, and Rosie was waiting for Boots and Emily to take her to church.

'Yes, sir,' she said shyly.

'And who might you be?' asked the man.

'I'm Rosie.'

'Ah,' he said, 'so you're her, are you, my little one?'

Chinese Lady appeared.

'Are you lookin' for someone?' she asked.

'For Mr Adams,' said the man. 'He wrote to me. I'm Mr Tooley. I reckon you know me daughter Milly, seeing this is 'er little girl Rosie.'

Rosie seemed to wince. She turned, ran through the passage and up the stairs. Boots and Emily turned as she entered their bedroom. She looked a picture in her new frock.

'Uncle Boots, there's a man,' she said anxiously.

'What does he want?' asked Boots.

'He looked at me.'

Boots glanced at Emily, and they went downstairs, Rosie nervously following. In the parlour, Chinese Lady was talking to a man, a bowler hat in his hand, his hair wiry and grizzled.

'This is my son, the one who wrote to you,' said Chinese Lady.

'Howjerdo,' said the man, 'I'm Mr Tooley, Milly's father and the little girl's grandfather. It's a fine old mess, I'm afraid.'

'Well, we'll see,' said Boots. 'Rosie, will you go and sit on the doorstep and wait for us?'

Rosie went, glad to escape. Boots closed the parlour door.

'Mr Tooley, have you come to take Rosie away?' asked Emily.

Mr Tooley sighed. Chinese Lady invited him to sit down. They all sat.

'It's not a very 'appy story,' said Mr Tooley, 'and it's

hard to believe what you said in your letter, Mr Adams, that Milly's gone off and left that little girl.'

'Her father must be told,' said Chinese Lady, going straight to what she considered the most important bearing on the situation.

Mr Tooley sighed again.

'Who knows who Rosie's father is?' he said.

'Oh,' breathed Emily. To be born out of wedlock was as much of a shame among the working classes as the aristocracy. Marriage ordained by God protected a woman from being used as a plaything. 'Oh, the poor little mite.'

'Spoiled Milly's life, it 'as,' said Mr Tooley, 'and her mother's. Mrs Tooley took it 'ard. I'd better tell you, seeing you've been kind enough to take Rosie in.'

He told the unhappy story. Six years ago in the summer of 1914, Milly got engaged to a soldier in the East Surrey Regiment, a sergeant, a fine chap. Mr and Mrs Tooley were highly relieved about that, because Milly seemed to have worrying flighty ways, painful to Mrs Tooley, not a very strong woman. So it was gladdening when Milly met and fell for such a fine chap, because she mended her ways at once and became engaged to him. Then the war broke out and he went with his battalion to join the British Expeditionary Force that was preparing to go to France. Milly, excited like everyone else about British soldiers going off to fight for brave little Belgium, kept going up West to join the crowds who were cheering and waving flags day after day. She and a girl friend were among other girls who fell in with some young Army officers one evening. Milly was a good-looker right enough, so was her friend, and with the other girls they were carried away by the atmosphere, finishing up with the officers in a house in Maida Vale, where a lively party was taking place.

There was strong drink at the party, and too much of it. And too much excitement. Milly did not get home until the morning, when she still seemed the worse for drink. Mr and Mrs Tooley were worried sick when Milly told them about the party and how it had lasted all night. Mrs Tooley insisted on knowing exactly what she had got up to, but Milly laughed and told her not to be an old fusspot.

She did not laugh, however, when later on she found she was pregnant. She was furious. She had put the happenings of the party out of her mind when she fully sobered up, because of her soldier fiancé. But she could not ignore the consequences, and was in a frenzy about the effect on her engagement. Mrs Tooley said the father must be told, so that he could do the right thing by Milly. Milly had to confess then that she did not know the names or even remember the faces of the several officers who had taken advantage of herself and her girl friend. Mrs Tooley came near to fainting from the shame of this. Milly suggested she could have the baby without her sergeant knowing, if the war lasted long enough, and leave it on an orphanage doorstep. Mr Tooley said that was a shocking way to get rid of the problem, while Mrs Tooley was outraged at this proposed deceit of a fine soldier, a man fighting for his country. A terrible row took place between mother and daughter, with Milly saying such bitter things that Mrs Tolley collapsed and the doctor had to be fetched.

The sergeant, wounded in battle, convalesced in Blighty and arrived on the doorstep one Sunday in hospital blues. It was March, 1915, and Milly, seven months gone, was undisguisedly pregnant. The sergeant was shattered, everyone was shattered, and the engagement was broken.

Milly, very bitter, went to live with a man some months after giving birth to the baby. He accepted the child as well as herself. By this time Mrs Tooley, whose heart was not very strong, was seriously ill, and although she had recovered she had been a semi-invalid ever since. Milly reappeared when her baby, called

Rosie, was a year old. She had had a row with her man friend and been turned out. Mr Tooley suspected it was because she was up to her old flighty tricks again. She asked her parents to look after the child while she made a life of her own. Mr Tooley told her it couldn't be done, since Mrs Tooley was never going to be well enough to look after anyone's baby. Milly said she didn't want the brat, it had ruined her life, and she repeated her previous suggestion of leaving the child at the door of an orphanage. Mr Tooley, whose ancient grandmother had recently died and left him all she had, the surprising amount of six hundred and fifty pounds, informed his daughter he would pay her thirty shillings a week for six years if she would do right by the child and be a decent mother to it. He was a park attendant employed by Deptford Council and could therefore afford this allowance out of his grandmother's bequest. Milly accepted the offer, and he paid the money into her Post Office Savings account every month. She would send the book to him, he would get the money credited and post the book back to her. In this way he kept some control on her spending and did not lose contact with her. She moved several times and gave herself a married name, Pearce. Sometimes she mentioned Rosie was well. Most times she did not mention her at all.

It was terrible hard, concluded Mr Tooley, to believe she had now abandoned Rosie. Was Mr Adams sure she wasn't coming back?

'I honestly doubt it,' said Boots.

'She took all her clothes and things,' said Emily, who had made a check.

'It might be hard to believe she's gone for good,' said Chinese Lady, 'but it wasn't too hard for her to do it. She didn't love the child. She's found someone to keep her, or she wouldn't have give up the allowance you made her, Mr Tooley.'

'I'd say, from what you've said, and from what we've

280

seen, that she saw Rosie as the worst mistake of her life,' said Boots. 'I think she always will.' He could have said more, but he felt Mr Tooley was unhappy enough about the shortcomings of his daughter.

'Mrs Tooley only saw the girl as an infant?' enquired Chinese Lady.

'That's right, only as a baby when she was a year old, the time Milly tried to make us take 'er. I'm not saying Rosie 'erself is a shame to me wife, but Milly is, and more so on account of the tempers and unrepentance she showed. Nor would she ever let me come and see Rosie, and Mrs Tooley's never been well enough to, not with all the 'eart trouble she's got. But something's got to be done for the girl, and that's my responsibility, I reckon, nor won't I deny it. I'll 'ave to look around and see if I can't get 'er fostered.'

'Emily?' said Boots.

Emily, knowing the extent of his affections, said, 'Yes, if that's what you'd like.'

'Would you like it?' asked Boots. 'And you, Mum?'

Emily and Chinese Lady looked at each other. Emily nodded, and Chinese Lady said, 'Well, I'm not goin' to say we don't all think the same as you. Mr Tooley, my son and his wife will foster your granddaughter.'

'Eh?' said Mr Tooley, and gave Emily and Boots a searching glance.

'With your approval, of course,' said Boots.

'You sure you mean that?' asked Mr Tooley. 'I'm not saying me and Mrs Tooley wouldn't have the child if Mrs Tooley was up to it, but she's not and nor is she ever goin' to be. It ain't a whim of yours to foster Rosie, Mr Adams, it ain't a ten-minute wonder?'

'My son don't have whims,' said Chinese Lady, 'not that kind he don't.'

'My wife and I are very willing,' said Boots, 'with a lot of help from my mother.'

Chinese Lady nodded. No one would have guessed,

with the die cast, how much she liked the idea of having a child in the house again.

'I'll have to give it serious thought,' said Mr Tooley. 'You can understand that as I only just met you, I ought to think about it. But I'll say this, who else do I know who'd take Rosie in? And the fact is, now I 'ave met you, you all strike me as nice people.'

'We'd be willing to send you regular reports on Rosie's progress,' said Boots.

'You talk like a real gent, Mr Adams.'

'It's his education,' said Chinese Lady, showing a rare glimpse of pride in her eldest son, 'and takin' after his dad like he does.'

'I'll get off home now,' said Mr Tooley, rising to his feet, 'and I'll talk to Mrs Tooley about your kind offer. It put 'er right back in 'ealth, it did, hearing about Milly's latest wrong-doing. I'll write to you, Mr Adams.'

'We'll wait to hear,' said Boots, liking Rosie's grandfather.

'Yes,' said Emily, willing to care for Rosie because Boots was set on it. But she wondered what would happen to his affection for Rosie if they had a child of their own.

'It's been a pleasure meetin' you,' said Mr Tooley, 'and a relief talkin' to you. I won't keep you waitin' too long for a letter, it's only fair to let you know as soon as I can. Thank you for your time and kindness.'

They saw him out. Rosie, at the open front door, had waited patiently and with her usual obedience. She looked up at Boots in a worried way. He smiled and put a light hand on her shoulder. His touch reassured her, and her smile came.

'Goodbye, little Rosie,' said Mr Tooley, wisely making no attempt to convey anything to her. But he did add, 'It's a pleasure to see you're pretty.' He said goodbye to Chinese Lady, Emily and Boots, put his bowler hat on and went on his way.

Rosie at once forgot him.

'Auntie Emily, we'll be late for church,' she said.

'Too late,' said Boots.

'Oh, lor',' said Rosie, taking off Emily.

'Never mind,' said Boots, 'when we get you to Aunt Lizzy's this afternoon, you can play in the garden with Annabelle. How's that?'

'Yes, please,' said Rosie.

CHAPTER TWENTY-ONE

Lizzy was healthily and happily expectant, hoping for a boy this time, whom she would call Robert Ned, after her eldest brother and her husband. The August day was lovely, the family were coming to tea, and so was Vi. Lizzy agreed with her mum that it wouldn't do any harm to give Tommy a push in Vi's direction. Vi was sweet, and just right for Tommy.

The garden looked colourful with the sun shining and so many flowers in bloom. The lawn was dry and they could have tea out there. Ned was being husbandly, making cucumber sandwiches in the kitchen. and Annabelle, standing on a chair, was doing her best to be a help. Lizzy had been despatched to a deckchair in the garden, to take the load off her feet, so Ned had said. Lizzy said don't call it a load, you common thing

She dreamed in the sunshine. Boots and Emily were looking for a house with a garden, and Chinese Lady was to live with them. And Sammy and Tommy were to live bachelor lives in the rooms above the shop. The family were going to spread their wings after all those years in run-down Walworth, where the headlice got at you if you weren't careful. Lizzy shuddered.

In the Sunday afternoon quietness she heard the sound of a distant train, and then the voice of the first arrival, Vi.

'Lizzy dear?' Ned had sent her to join Lizzy in the garden.

'Come and talk,' said Lizzy, and Vi came to seat herself in a canvas deckchair beside her cousin, her distant cousin. Lizzy thought she was getting very attractive. Her lemon-coloured frock was delicately summery, and worn with fine white silk stockings. 'Silk, Vi? You're splashing out.'

'Silk?' said Vi, whose frock was of fine cotton.

'Your stockings,' said Lizzy. 'Ever so rich and fancy. It's nice you're here, the fam'ly shouldn't be long.'

'Don't your garden look lovely?' said Vi. 'Dad keeps ours lookin' nice, but he grows peas and runner beans more than flowers.'

'A garden's heaven,' said Lizzy fervently.

'You all right, Lizzy?' said Vi a little shyly.

'Oh, baby's coming on a treat,' said Lizzy. She laughed. 'Doctor Carter says I'm God's own handiwork. I carry perfect, he says. Vi, the fam'ly's bringing that little girl Rosie with them. Mum wrote saying Milly Pearce went off and left her, so the fam'ly's looking after her. Vi, that's awful, a mother deserting her child.'

'Tommy told me about it when we went for a walk last time Aunt Maisie invited me to Sunday tea. He said Boots has gone a bit daft over Rosie.'

'Boots has? All soppy, you mean?'

'That's what Tommy said. Oh, they're here.'

The family appeared. Ned came out into the garden with them to unfold more deckchairs. Annabelle came out too, with Rosie.

'Mummy, Rosie's come,' she cried excitedly. 'Can I get my dolls so's we can play with them?'

'Yes, darling,' said Lizzy, 'take Rosie with you.'

The little girls went up to Annabelle's room, and Annabelle asked which doll Rosie would like.

There were three dolls and a teddy bear all resting on the pillows of Annabelle's bed. Rosie stared in awe and wonder. She had never had a doll. Or a teddy bear, which looked awfully cuddly.

'Could I play with the teddy bear?' she asked, and Annabelle picked it up and generously deposited it in Rosie's arms.

'Is it as nice as yours?' she asked.

'I don't have one,' said Rosie.

'Goodness,' said three-year-old Annabelle. She often heard her mother speak like that when she had other mothers to afternoon tea. She picked up a golden-haired doll, and went down into the garden again with Rosie. There they selected a spot on the lawn and sat down together, Rosie making a great fuss of the teddy.

The grown-ups, seated in a circle, were talking about her. Boots had described the meeting with Mr Tooley.

'Oh, it's a cruel story,' said Lizzy.

'I'm afraid quite a few girls lost their heads during the war,' said Ned.

'A French infliction it was,' said Chinese Lady. 'I just hope you and Boots didn't ever get to know them kind of girls. And it's a shock to me that some officer, supposed to be a gentleman, could behave like he did to Milly Pearce, even if she was flighty.'

'It's my considered opinion,' said Sammy, 'that girls can be a danger to fellers as well as to themselves.'

'We don't want no opinions like that from you, Sammy, if you don't mind,' said Chinese Lady. 'You just give girls respect and then they won't be in danger and nor will you. Anyway, Boots and Em'ly are goin' to foster Rosie.'

'If her grandparents agree,' said Boots.

'And if they don't?' asked Lizzy.

'It'll mean Mr Tooley's found someone else, perhaps a couple living nearer to him and his wife,' said Ned. 'I think in calling so promptly in answer to Boots's letter he showed he cares about Rosie, even if his wife can't forgive their flighty Milly. And if he's got something left of his nest egg, he'll be prepared to offer financial help to a suitable young couple willing to take Rosie on. You said, Boots, that he wanted to think things over. That might mean he wanted to consider an alternative.

'But he said he didn't know anyone else,' protested Emily.

286

Chinese Lady looked at Boots. He was watching Rosie and Annabelle, who were out of earshot. He had a little frown on his face.

'Boots won't be counting chickens, Ned,' she said.

'Sensible,' said Ned.

'I reckon what's best for Rosie is for Em'ly and Boots to have her,' said Tommy.

'I do too,' said Vi. 'look how happy she is.'

'Well, she won't cost too much to keep,' said Sammy, 'not like wives do.'

'Mum, I'll never know why you didn't drown Sammy years ago,' said Lizzy.

'It's not too late,' said Chinese Lady, 'big as he is.'

'Send us a postcard when it happens,' said Ned, 'we'd all like to be there. Emily, have you and Boots hit on a decent house yet?'

'Oh, lor', we've only had headaches so far,' said Emily, 'but we're keepin' on lookin'. Boots don't feel we need to rush it. Oh, I must tell yer about the palaver at the town hall the other day.' She described the circumstances and the incident, and her lost temper with Mr Boddy.

'Good on yer, Em,' said Sammy, 'I bet yer near led him to a painful death, like yer nearly led me and Tommy when we were only innocent growing boys trying to stay alive. Terrible spittin' and kickin' tyrant, you were.'

'Put me in hospital a dozen times,' said Tommy. 'Well, nearly. I tell yer, Vi, I know what it's like to be at death's door.'

Vi burst into laughter.

'When you've finished bein' dead comical, Tommy Adams,' said Emily.

'Dead's right,' said Sammy.

Emily swooped on him. Her hands reached and her fingers dug, into his ribs. Sammy, always reduced to helplessness by tickling fingers, threshed about. His deckchair collapsed. Annabelle and Rosie came running.

'Oh, corks,' said Annabelle, 'what's Auntie Emily doing to Uncle Sammy?'

'Nothing serious,' said Boots, 'Uncle Sammy's not yet at death's door.'

Rosie had a blissful time. The whole afternoon was a delight to her, and tea eaten on the lawn was like a fairy-tale happening. The sun shone, everyone chattered, and she and Annabelle offered cucumber sandwiches and cake to the doll and teddy bear. Vi and Tommy volunteered to do the washing-up, and no one stood in their way. Everyone was co-operating with Chinese Lady, who was conducting a motherly match-making campaign.

Tommy, unaware that his mother had decided Vi was just the kind of ladylike girl to suit him, merely felt Vi had become rather nice to be with. He had had a shocking time trying to get Lily Fuller to pay him back the money he'd lent her. He hadn't wanted to ask outright for it, but being out of work had emptied his pockets. Lily had actually said she couldn't remember borrowing anything from him except a bob, and she didn't have that, anyway. But oh well, she said, he could kiss her if he liked and call it square. And he could also squeeze her jumper. Tommy reckoned he'd incurred a bad debt. He also reckoned Cousin Vi was a nice improvement on Lily. That opinion would have made Chinese Lady feel Tommy was learning where to look.

When the family was back home that evening, Rosie was put to bed on the sofa in Boots and Emily's little sitting-room. She snuggled down in sleepy content. Boots tucked her in.

'Wasn't it nice Annabelle letting me play with her teddy bear?' she murmured.

'Very nice,' said Boots. 'Would you like one of your own?'

The sleepy eyes opened wide.

'Could I have one? Are they expensive?'

'Not too expensive. I daresay I could bring you one home tomorrow. Can you wait until then?'

'I think so,' said Rosie, 'I'll try my hardest.'

'Good. Here's Auntie Emily to kiss you goodnight.'

In bed, Emily said, 'We ought not to get too fond of her.'

'I'm already very fond of her,' said Boots.

'Well, yes, she's sweet, but you got to consider that Mr Tooley might write and say no.'

'I'll hammer him into the ground.'

'Now don't go daft. And don't get obsessed, like. You might be lettin' yourself in for a bad let-down.'

'Noted, lovey.'

'Lizzy's due next month,' said Emily.

'She looks due any moment, poor girl.'

'I'm not due at all.'

'I'm not worried, Em.'

'But you want some of our own, don't you?'

'Let's be like Chinese Lady,' said Boots, 'let's see what the Lord provides.'

The next day, when Mrs Stevens was talking to her about the possibility of staying indefinitely with 'Enquiries', Emily suddenly said, 'You and your husband never had any children?'

'Well, we married in 1914, just before the war,' said Madge reminiscently. 'I was very much in love, and you're willing to be all things to a man when you're like that. He wanted children, but then the war came. I knew he'd eventually have to go, I knew that might make a widow of me. So I made sure there were no children.'

'Oh, I see,' said Emily.

'It's not always in her best interests for a wife to do what her husband wants.'

'No, I suppose she does have her own life and interests,' said Emily painfully.

* * *

Sammy came into the shop at noon on Tuesday. He informed Boots there was a large order to deliver to St Stephen's Orphanage after early closing on Wednesday. All ex-Army stuff, like Waac bedsheets and any amount of kitchen things. The girl Susie Thingamabob was coming later this afternoon to box it up. Tommy would be all right by himself on the stall for a couple of hours, he was taking to market selling like a duck to water, and was cheerful to customers, which they liked. Boots said he supposed an engineer could make a go of a china and glass stall.

'Now don't start makin' out running a stall's too common for him,' said Sammy. 'It's good honest work. A tradin' market, remember, was the first thing workin' people invented, where they could exchange the goods they produced by the sweat of their brows. Green-grocery, pots, frying pans and so on. Money was invented later.'

'I'm not sure about frying pans,' said Boots, 'I think they came later, with sausages. And markets weren't an invention, they developed.'

'All right, don't show off,' said Sammy, then waited while Boots served a customer. After which he said, 'Now, there's a conveyance comin' tomorrow at one o'clock, your closin' time, to take the stuff. I'd like you to go with it, to see that the stuff's delivered correct. The orphanage lady, who's a valuable contact put in me way by Mr Greenberg, will accept the invoice and give you a cheque. Be a good profit on it, Boots. Well, a fair one,' he added cautiously. 'Listen, you and Em'ly seriously set on movin' if you can find the right house?'

'Seriously, yes,' said Boots, 'but I'd personally prefer to buy, not rent.'

'Good on yer, lad,' said Sammy, 'it's gratifyin' to know I brought you up to have sense. I never heard you talk as wise as that. You've got yer airy-fairy ways, never takin' anything seriously, but when you're speakin' of buyin' and not rentin', you're speakin' real sense. Ned and Lizzy bought their house in 1916, and now, only four years later, I bet it's worth fifty quid more, even in these hard times, specially seeing what they've made of its looks. You sure you want Chinese Lady livin' with you till I've made me fortune?'

'Emily won't move without her.'

'Well, yer know, I like our Em'ly, even if she is a girl,' said Sammy. 'I never thought I'd come out alive when she was a holy terror, I always thought she'd take her dad's chopper to me head one day. Can't help being fond of her now, though. She'll be lovin' to Rosie if Mr Tooley lets you foster her. Well, I'll show you now what we're goin' to put in the window tomorrow. It's a special line for the ladies, and they're being delivered this afternoon. But I've got a couple of samples up in the office.'

Boots's lurking smile showed itself as a broad grin when he saw what the line was.

Tommy and Susie had already become a good team. Bert's departure had seen an end to friction. Tommy and Susie were kindred spirits, Tommy easy-going and equable, Susie bubbly and winning. She called him Mister Tommy, and she called his brother Mister Sammy or Mister Adams.

Her father was still looking for work, and sometimes earned a bob or two cleaning shop windows or standing in for a sick night watchman. What with that and his little pension and Susie's earnings – she had opted for commission – the family were eating good food regularly. Her mother hadn't had to apply for parish relief for ages, which made her look lovely and jolly.

Susie had a new friend, Danny Higgins. He was seventeen and a grocer's errand boy. Susie thought him quite nice, and he was taking her to the pictures once a week. It was only to the fleapit near Hurlocks the drapers in Walworth Road, but you could get in for tuppence and see a three-hour programme, always including an exciting Pearl White serial. Pearl White got into terrible predicaments, being nearly run over by trains, or drowned in the rising waters of a cellar, or blown up while tied to a barrel of gunpowder. She always escaped tragic death in the next instalment, but it still made you hold your breath. There was the same hero in every serial, a tall, dark and handsome man, who appeared and reappeared, and was mainly responsible for Pearl White being rescued in the nick of time. He obviously loved Pearl White, and she obviously loved him, and at the end of every serial they always kissed. But when the next serial began they acted as if they hardly knew each other, which made it awfully fascinating. She wondered if the hero's eyes were blue, like Mister Sammy's. Oh, he could use them on lady customers, and did, with his hat tipped back and the sun on his face.

He had gone to his shop now to see his other brother, Boots, but he had been very approving of Mister Tommy's progress on the stall. He did have funny ways, but he was never grudging, he always spoke his appreciation if she or Mister Tommy had earned it. She was going to the shop herself at three o'clock to do some packing, and he was going to pay her two bob for it. She knew by now that the stallholders considered him cocky, but they also said he wouldn't cut anyone's throat unless he had to. Which meant he was tough but fair. Ma Earnshaw, a tough character herself, who was often at Covent Garden's wholesale market at four o'clock in the morning, liked Mister Sammy, even if she did say that if he gave a kid a penny he'd get at least tuppence back in kind.

At home, Sammy's resilient mother, in sole charge of Rosie while everyone else was at work each day, was finding the girl a companionable little treasure. Rosie enjoyed being a help to the lady she secretly looked upon as 'Grandma', fetching things, doing things and going shopping with her. She thought about her mother not at all.

Sammy was at the stall early the next morning. He was finding the present arrangements highly satisfactory. With Tommy and Susie already running the stall well together, Fred having an apprentice to help in the scrap yard, and Boots managing the shop with typical sang-froid – Sammy had alighted on that word in one of Frank Richards's Greyfriars stories – he had time to go freely out and about in pursuit of new lines, new contacts and new ideas. He had had a gratifying meeting with the owner of a clothing factory in Shoreditch, an establishment at the top of Mr Greenberg's recommended list. He recognised at once that it was a crowded sweatshop, but the seamstresses were first-class, their stitching faultless, the garments available as mouth-watering bargains as long as they were ordered by the gross. When Sammy asked for ten per cent discount for cash on delivery, the owner, Mr Morris, staggered about and called on his Maker in distraught Hebrew to deliver him from pending star-vation. On this encouraging and enjoyable note the bargaining began, Mr Morris emphasising the suicidal nature of giving ten per cent, and Sammy sticking to the advantages of receiving cash on delivery with no invoice required.

'I should weep tears for a year and drown my family?' said the unhappy Mr Morris.

'Oh, I reckon a year'll give you enough time to build a lifeboat,' said Sammy.

'What has my friend Eli done to me, recommending me to do business with a young man already lost to pity? It's a sad day, but very well, seven and a half.'

'Ten,' said Sammy. 'It's a kosher deal, Mr Morris.'

Mr Morris groaned.

The deal was made. Sammy was to receive ladies' and

293

men's wear at a price that would enable him to retail genuine bargains.

Susie thought he looked very pleased with himself this morning.

'So there you are, young Whatsername,' he said, and Susie wrinkled her nose at him.

'Why'd you keep callin' her Whatsername?' asked Tommy.

'I can't remember everyone's name,' said Sammy.

'Susie's name is Brown,' said Tommy. 'Brown.'

'Much obliged, I'm sure,' said Sammy.

'And it's her birthday today,' said Tommy. 'She's sixteen.'

'Happy birthday, then,' said Sammy, and Susie smiled at him, the morning light dancing in her striking blue eyes. Stone me, thought Sammy, it's a cert she'll haunt me with them royal blue saucers. 'Sixteen, are you? Well, you'll soon be startin' to grow up, as long as you eat regular.'

'Oh, that's not fair,' said Susie, 'at sixteen I am grown up.'

'Many happy returns, Susie,' said Tommy, and gave her a birthday card in an envelope and a little packet containing a metal propelling pencil. She had been a great help to him on the stall.

'Oh, yer so kind, Mister Tommy,' said Susie, 'thank yer ever so.'

Sammy muttered.

'Well, you're all right now, Tommy,' he said, 'you got them new Chinese vases on good display. I've got an appointment. I might be back about dinnertime to see how you're doing. So long. Don't stand about, Miss Green—'

'Brown,' said Tommy.

'Yes, all right, but you got your first customers arrivin',' said Sammy, and went.

He was back at noon, having contracted to sell his complete hoard of brass and copper to a firm manufacturing plumbing equipment in Woolwich. He had been buying it at rock-bottom prices for a year, waiting for the depressed market to rise, as he was sure it would. And it had, even if only by eight per cent. He reckoned it would go down again in a fortnight, for he knew other scrap dealers had been hoarding and waiting. But while he had unloaded immediately, they would be waiting in the hope of prices reaching a higher level. One way or another, they would all be unloading within seven days.

'Had a good morning?' he asked.

'Fair, I reckon,' said Tommy.

'No, it's been good,' said Susie, 'Mister Tommy's too modest, like.'

'All right,' said Sammy, 'I've got to go across the river in an hour, but before I do I'll buy you a mixed ice cream at Toni's for part of your meal while Tommy keeps the stall tickin' over. It's your birthday.'

'A mixed ice cream?' Susie's eyes danced.

'Vanilla and strawberry,' said Sammy.

'Oh, yer a good soul, Mister Sammy,' she said, 'yer bound to be graciously mentioned in heaven's good book.'

'Kindly refrain from givin' me fanciful fits,' said Sammy. Tommy grinned. 'Just do me the goodness to accompany me.'

Susie went with him through the crowded street, her tongue at work.

'With all yer kindness, Mister Sammy, yer shouldn't still keep callin' me Whatsername, and then Miss Green, like yer did this morning. Yer shouldn't let Mister Tommy think yer don't have graciousness, after me tellin' him how yer been a blessing to me. Callin' me names that don't belong makes it look as if yer wouldn't care if I dropped dead at me work, as if you'd just bury me corpse under the stall to keep it out of the way of customers, and not even read the Lord's burial service over me. Mister Adams, I blush for yer being so off and in front of yer nice brother.'

'I'm dreaming this,' said Sammy, pushing his way through swarming people. 'That's what I'm doing, I'm havin' a bad dream.'

' 'Ere, mind who yer shovin', you 'ooligan,' said a fat woman as he bumped her hip.

'There, now see what yer done, upsettin' that nice lady,' said Susie reproachfully.

Sammy, breaking clear at the end of the market, gazed upwards at fleecy clouds sailing through the August sky.

'What's happening to me, God?' he asked. 'Would you kindly tell me, God, what I've done that's givin' me a hurtful ringing in me ears?'

'Oh, Mister Adams,' gasped Susie, 'yer can't talk to yer 'oly Maker like that, it's like yer don't 'old Him in proper awe and respect.'

'Gawd help me if I don't put a sack over yer head and keep it there for a week,' said Sammy.

'Oh, Mister Adams, I'd die, I would,' gasped Susie.

'Well, if I could find time to come to yer funeral, I would.'

'Oh, yer 'eartless monster,' cried Susie.

But when, in Toni's, there was a double portion of mixed ice cream in front of her, she consumed it forgivingly, and with all the natural enjoyment of the young. Sammy bought a fried egg sandwich for himself. Susie said she wouldn't go on any more about his heartlessness. Sammy said he'd be highly gratified if she wouldn't go on any more about anything. She asked if he would remember to call her Susie, like his two brothers did, to show he didn't have offhand disdain for her.

'Offhand what?' asked Sammy, perturbed to find he was beginning to like looking at her.

'Off'and disdain,' said Susie, 'it's in books.'

'I don't go in for being in books,' said Sammy, 'or fairy stories.'

'But I'm only saying—'

'Yes, I know,' said Sammy, wondering what he was doing, spending his valuable time with her, 'but I think I've heard it all before. Look, you're a good girl, Susie, and I can't say fairer than that. You go on now, I'll follow.'

Susie left Toni's to make her way back to the stall. Sammy got back a few minutes after her. While Tommy was busy serving, Susie received a white confectionery bag from her employer. It contained a box of Cadbury's King George chocolates. He had bought it with slightly gritted teeth, for it cost a shilling, and that on top of the cost of the double ice cream. The girl was going to inflict his commonsense with a fateful disease if he was as careless as this.

Susie's eyes danced again at the sight of the chocolates, never mind what eating them could do to her development.

'Oh, Mister Sammy,' she said.

'Just a kind thought of mine for yer birthday, said Sammy.

'I'm overwhelmed,' said Susie.

'Me, I'm off to me yard to see Fred before I cross the river,' said Sammy. 'I don't get any sauce from Fred.'

CHAPTER TWENTY-TWO

Lizzy, out shopping, got off the omnibus at Camberwell
Green, the conductor lending her a fatherly hand from
the pavement. Lizzy's advanced pregnancy was very
evident. But she liked to be out. Inactivity made her feel
lumpish. The conductor swung Annabelle from the bus
to the pavement, which made her beam at him.

'Thanks,' said Lizzy.

'Good luck to yer,' said the conductor, getting back
on and ringing the bell.

'Come on, Annabelle,' said Lizzy, 'we'll go and see
Uncle Boots in the shop first, shall we, and tell him
about the house we've seen.'

'I 'spect he'll give me a penny for sweets, don't you?'
said Annabelle. A penny would buy her some sherbert
powder and two liquorice bootlaces.

Camberwell Green, with its little park and its wide
approach to the ascent of Denmark Hill, was not at all
unattractive. The area north of it, all the way to the river
and the bridges of Blackfriars, London and Waterloo,
was a crowded working-class district. To the south, the
neighbourhood took on a superior look, beginning with
the stateliness of King's College Hospital and the
delightful Ruskin Park, then meandering about around
lower middle-class localities. Because they lived off
Denmark Hill, Lizzy and Ned would have been called
lower middle class. If she'd been asked, however, Lizzy
would have said Ned was a working man and she was
a working housewife. In later life, she could never
understand why the term working housewife only

applied to housewives who worked outside the home. A downright blessed cheek, she called it.

She and Annabelle stopped outside Sam's Emporium. She looked at the window display and its bold announcements of bargains. She blinked at a new notice on white cardboard.

LADIES SUNSHINE BROWN BLOOMERS – SHILLING A PAIR, THREE PAIRS FOR 2/6d – BARGAIN OF THE YEAR – ALL SIZES – HIGHLY COMFORTABLE STYLE – GUARANTEED LASTING QUALITY – ELASTIC WAIST AND LEGS – EVERY PAIR NEW – NEW!

Lizzy could hardly believe her eyes. That Sammy, the brazen sauce he'd got. And Boots, he wouldn't be turning a hair, he wouldn't be past discussing the finer points of the garments with any female shameless enough to encourage him.

She took Annabelle into the shop. And there Boots was, at the counter, folding two pairs for a plump and smiling woman. Another woman stood by, a pair in her hand, waiting for service. On a long shelf were open cardboard boxes containing the items designed for members of the Women's Army Auxiliary Corps. Sizes were marked on the boxes. Two women were examining the goods. Boots smiled at Lizzy. Lizzy showed threatening white teeth. The moment the shop was clear, she attacked.

'You cheeky beast,' she said, 'you got a nerve, doing business in ladies' personal wear. It's not decent. That Sammy ought to be thrown off Tower Bridge. Wait till Chinese Lady gets to hear, she'll box his ears and yours till your teeth are rattling.'

'They're very serviceable,' said Boots. 'Can I sell you three pairs for half-a-crown while you're here, Lizzy? Keep you warm in the winter.'

'You're goin' to shock delicate customers into fetchin' a policeman,' said Lizzy. 'Annabelle, take your head out of that box. Where's Sammy? I'm—' she was interrupted by the entrance of a young woman brisk and businesslike.

'Where's these bloomers?' she asked. 'You sure they're new and good quality? I don't want to be sold the sort of stuff you get at them shops that's always running a closing-down sale. I want strong elastic, not perished, I don't want anything that's going to fall down in front of men with big eyeballs.'

Since she was addressing Lizzy, Lizzy answered. Having once worked in the ladies' wear department of Gamages, she slid back effortlessly into the role.

'We are sorry not to be able to oblige you, madam, but they're all sold out, and we shan't be re-stocking.'

'What's these, then?' The young woman, plainly dressed, advanced determinedly on the open boxes, while Annabelle looked on intrigued. 'Here, you call this colour sunshine brown? Where's the sunshine? Looks like khaki gone into dark mourning, if you ask me.'

'It's evening sunshine, madam,' said Boots, 'or twilight bronze. A welcome change from navy blue, the usual colour for serviceable undergarments of this kind.'

Look at him, thought Lizzy. Butter wouldn't have melted in his mouth, and he couldn't have looked more solemn if he'd been an undertaker.

'Here, you don't think I'm potty, do you?' said the brisk young woman. 'Twilight bronze, my Aunt Fanny, they're khaki drawers.' She turned some over. 'Still, what people don't see, I don't worry about.' She picked out a medium-sized pair. 'I'll try these on. I'm not buying for me and my twin sister if I can't try them on.'

'We don't allow that, I'm afraid,' said Boots. Too late. The young woman stepped into the bloomers and pulled them on. The skirt of her dress rushed upwards. Lizzy almost fell over as she glimpsed the curve of bare buttocks. The woman wasn't wearing any underthings. She pulled the bloomers into place and adjusted her dress. She walked about, bold as brass. Boots mildly pointed out that trying on wasn't the thing to do

'You and your piffle,' said the young woman, 'I never buy what might not fit. I bet you wouldn't, either, would you, little lady?' she said to Annabelle, who ducked her head shyly. 'Well, you're lucky, mister, you've got a sale. They feel fine. Good elastic too.' She picked out another pair. 'I'll have four pairs this size and pay you three and fourpence. I won't pay more. Hold on, I'll call my sister.' She opened the shop door and shouted. 'Here, Cecily!' She waved and beckoned. She stepped out of the shop. And she disappeared, fast, wearing one pair and clutching the other.

Boots was out on the pavement in no time. He saw her, to his left, crossing the road at a run and darting in front of a slow-moving tram. The tram immediately hid her, and when it cleared her line of retreat she had melted away.

'Saucy bitch,' said Boots to a lamp-post. He went back into the shop. 'Diddled me.'

'Well, I never saw a carry-on like that before,' said Lizzy, 'the shameless, thievin' hussy. Let that be a lesson to yer.'

'Can't help laughing, though, can yer?' said Boots, visibly amused.

'Goodness, Uncle Boots, goodness,' said Annabelle, totally perplexed by it all. Boots sat her up on the counter and tickled her. Annabelle dissolved into squeals of laughter.

'That Sammy, he's got you selling these things,' said Lizzy, 'and it don't suit you, you got too much style. Annabelle, leave his hair alone. Boots, give her a smack.'

Boots gave the girl a kiss instead. On her soft nose.

'I could eat you,' he said, 'you're pepperminty.'

'You're goin' soppy over kids,' said Lizzy. Seeing a shopper hovering outside, she went on quickly. 'Oh, before I go, there's a nice house empty in our road, and there's a board up for sale or rent. It's worth you and Em'ly taking a look at. It could be just right for you and Em'ly and Chinese Lady.'

'I'll talk to them,' said Boots, and gave Annabelle a penny for sweets as Annabelle had known he would.

It was early-closing day and he shut the shop at one o'clock, the moment when Jimmy Tompkins arrived. Jimmy, the twelve-year-old son of neighbours, was on holiday from school and available for hire. Boots had offered him a whole bob to do a job for him, plus money for the fare back home. Jimmy would have done it for a tanner, Boots being a local hero. He helped to bring loaded boxes from the stock room to the door. At ten past one an old hansom cab pulled up outside. Boots went and spoke to the cabby.

'Yus, that's right, guv, we got orders to take you and yer parcels aboard.'

Boots, who had his suspicions about the source of the orders, asked, 'Who's we?'

'Me an' Fifi,' said the cheerful cabby.

'Who's Fifi?' asked Boots.

'She's me mare, me soulmate,' said the cabby. 'Go every which way together, we does. Well, look silly, wouldn't it, if we went different ways separately, like.'

'You're delivering the boxes to the orphanage?'

'Lord love yer, guv, that I am, after I've dropped yer at the gracious inhabitance of Lady Simms, which is the wife of General Sir 'Enry Simms and the 'igh and noble stepmother of Miss Polly Simms, which is the young lady what give us our orders, and a lump of sugar to Fifi into the bargain. I'll step down, guv, and 'elp yer stow the goods.' He alighted and gave Fifi a pat.

'The house is where?' asked Boots, sure now that the volatile Miss Simms was playing games with him.

'Dulwich, guv. 'Ighly stately.' The cabby walked to the shop door with Boots, whose braces received the glad eye from a passing girl. With his jacket and waistcoat off on this warm August day, he looked pleasantly casual in his grey trousers, white shirt and striped tie. The cabby and Jimmy carried the boxes to the hansom and placed them inside. 'Right, then, guv,' said the cabby, 'if yer'll kindly dress up and put yer titfer on, I'll proceed forthwith to Dulwich with yer.'

'I can't come myself,' said Boots. 'Jimmy's going in my place. This is Jimmy. He'll escort the goods and help to unload them.'

'You betcher,' said Jimmy.

The cabby, looking dubious, took his hard hat off and scratched his head.

'Well, guv, that's as maybe,' he said, 'but I dunno as Miss Polly's goin' to like it. I knows her and her gracious fam'ly well, plying for 'ire like I does at Dulwich station. Very pertic'ler she was about you being dropped off at the fam'ly inhabitance.'

'Oh, Jimmy will do as well as I will,' said Boots. 'Give Miss Simms my apologies. Tell her something's come up. Jimmy, here's your money and enough for your fare home from Dulwich. And in this envelope is an invoice. Miss Simms will give you a cheque in settlement. Don't forget to thank her.'

'Right, I gotcher, Boots,' said Jimmy.

'Well, I dunno she's goin' to like it, I dunno at all,' said the cabby.

Polly didn't like it. When the cabby and Jimmy presented themselves to her in the handsome hall of her parents' Georgian house in leafy, rural Dulwich, and explained that Mr Adams hadn't been able to come, she took the cabby's bowler hat from his hand and placed it carefully on the polished parquet flooring. Hitching her skirts, she relieved her feelings by taking a flying kick at the hat. It sailed through the hall and bounced off a wall.

'You don't mind, Horace, do you?' she enquired of the cabby.

'That I don't, Miss Polly,' he said, 'you 'elp yourself.'

'Ta muchly, sport,' said Polly, and gave the hat another kick. 'There, that's some help.' Jimmy watched open-mouthed as she picked the hat up, dusted it with her hand and returned it to the cabby. 'I'm much obliged, Horace.'

'A pleasure, Miss Polly. Shall I proceed to the orphanage forthwith and himmediate?'

'Yes, hop off,' said Polly, 'you don't need the boy.'

'Thankin' yer kindly, Miss Polly,' said the cabby, and took himself off unscathed.

Polly's stepmother appeared. Handsome and Edwardian, and a woman of action, she took Jimmy over, had a servant fetch him a glass of lemonade, wrote a cheque on behalf of St Stephen's Orphanage, gave it to him, patted his head and sent him happily on his way. Then she asked Polly why Mr Robert Adams, of whom she had heard so much from her stepdaughter, had not turned up.

'Funked it,' said Polly.

'How very wise of him,' said Lady Simms.

Polly laughed. I'll get him, she thought, he's one of my Tommies.

Boots, having watched the hansom depart, went back into the shop. A man, so enormously stout that he looked like a brown-clothed balloon on legs, gave up his window-gazing and followed him in.

'Sorry, we're closed,' said Boots.

'So you are, sonny,' said the balloon in a brown suit, and shut the door. Beneath his straw boater, his fat red face bore a smile, but his beady eyes were hard and cold. Outside the shop another man appeared, tall and broad. He placed his back against the door and stood there, digging at his teeth with a matchstick.

'What d'you want?' asked Boots in his mild way.

'Sammy here, is he?'

'I don't see him,' said Boots.

'In his office, is he?' The voice sounded squeezed by fat.

'Not as far as I know.'

'I think I ought to tell you I like people to be

informative, then I don't get aggravated,' said the man whom Boots could only think of as Fatty. There was a film-star comedian shaped just as bulbously. Arbuckle. Fatty Arbuckle. 'You follow me, sonny?'

If Boots objected to being called sonny, he did not show it. Fatty was about fifty, he thought, and probably considered all younger persons adolescent.

'I'm fairly intelligent,' said Boots.

'Sammy's brother, are you?' wheezed Fatty.

'His eldest brother. Is this a social call?'

'Well, you could say it's sociable,' said Fatty, his button eyes travelling around the shop. 'But you don't look like Sammy, nor talk like him. Still, I'll take your word for it, seeing I heard his brother's running the shop. Sam's Emporium, eh?' He chuckled. It sounded like lard gurgling in a frying-pan. 'Family business, is it?'

'You could say so,' said Boots, hiding his dislike of the man and showing nothing of his mystification.

'But Sammy's got the purse-strings, has he?'

'That information is confidential,' said Boots.

'A reasonable remark, sonny, but a mite aggravating,' said Fatty.

'Also, I don't know you.'

'Not important. Sammy does. Give him a message. Tell him—'

'I'd like to know who you are first,' said Boots, not unaware of the presence of the large man outside the door.

'I think you interrupted me. That's distinctly aggravating.' Fatty shook his head in reproof. His double chins wobbled. 'Don't do it. You tell Sammy that friend Mr Ben Ford – myself – requests the closure of this emporium in a fortnight. No, I tell a lie. A week. Tell him to start his closing-down sale tomorrow.'

'Pardon?' said Boots.

'Now don't say you're hard of hearing.' Fatty took off his boater and fanned his red face. 'Tell Sammy he's costing me money, that at his age he's got no right to be inconveniencing my pocket. A week, tell him.'

'I'll tell him,' said Boots equably. The fat man was not to know how deceptive Boots's manner could be. 'Mr Ben Ford, you say?'

'Myself. You know me now, eh?'

'I know you, Mr Ford. Good afternoon.'

'My kind regards to Sammy.' The legs moved and the brown-clad balloon topped by a straw boater travelled to the glass-panelled door. It was opened by the waiting man. The balloon exited.

On arrival home, Boots changed into working clobber and spent the rest of the afternoon painting Chinese Lady's bedrom door, both sides. Rosie, given a small brush, helped him. She liked being a help around the house when she was not holding one-sided conversations with her new teddy bear. Boots had shown her how to use a paint brush. She dipped it carefully into the pot and applied it just as carefully to the door.

But she was forced to say once, 'Oh, lor', Uncle Boots, I've gone and painted your trousers.'

'Well, they're only old ones, kitten, and I expect they got too close to your brush.'

He took her for a walk at the end of the afternoon, to the town hall, to meet Emily. Emily, when she saw them and joined them, felt part of a family trio. She also felt Boots, in bringing Rosie into the picture like this, was running ahead of things.

'You're in them old disgraceful clothes again,' she said. 'It's – here, what's that on your nose, Rosie?'

'Nothing,' said Rosie. 'Is it?' she asked guiltily.

'Just a spot of white paint,' said Boots.

'Oh, blow,' said Rosie.

'Suits you,' said Boots.

'You're hopeless,' said Emily.

'I painted his trousers, Auntie Emily,' said Rosie, 'they got in the way of my brush.'

Emily laughed, and Rosie walked home between them.

Boots had a private word with Sammy in the parlour that evening, about fat Mr Ben Ford and the message. Sammy blinked, then his jaw tightened.

'The bleeder,' he said, 'what's he up to?'

'Yes, Sammy, what's he up to?'

'Big Ben or Fatty he's called,' said Sammy, 'and he don't mind either. He's got shops always selling stuff supposed to come from firms gone bankrupt, that sort of thing. He started 'em during the war, but they've gone stale on people. He's got one shop near ours, round in Camberwell New Road, and I reckon there's painful suffering goin' on, Boots. On account of losin' customers to us, and further on account of he's heard about Kennington.'

'Kennington?' said Boots.

'I'm givin' due consideration to opening a shop in Kennington,' said Sammy blandly. 'I've seen an Army bloke I met at a surplus sale, a quartermaster, and havin' crossed his palm with a few versions of the King's head, commonly known as pound notes, there won't be any future sale I don't know about well in advance, nor any lot I can't put me name and money on in advance. Business friends such as hard-up quartermasters like being treated with kindness and sympathy, and I don't mind elevatin' their condition.'

'Alleviating,' said Boots. 'I'd appreciate it, by the way, if you'd keep me informed of developments.'

'Well, I just informed yer, didn't I?'

'Much obliged,' said Boots. 'But I think we're under threat from the big fat balloon, laddie. I'll call in at Camberwell police station tomorrow.'

'Now, Boots, don't do that,' said Sammy, 'it'll cause trouble and besmirch me reputation. Big Ben don't go in for rough-houses. Well, he might have something unfriendly in mind, seeing he can read the newspapers pretty good and consequentially knows how unfriendly certain businessmen can get in America. Still, this ain't America. We've got King George, Queen Mary and the Houses of Parliament, and businessmen here ain't brought up to do rough-housing. I'll talk to Fatty tomorrow morning, tell him he can stand a bit of fair competition with what he's got. As well as that, all the bookies' runners on all the street corners of Lambeth belong to him. Perhaps he thinks—' Sammy paused. A little grin showed. 'Perhaps he thinks all the shops in Lambeth are goin' to belong to me. I'd better have an assuring talk with him.'

'Reassuring?' said Boots.

'You got it,' said Sammy.

'Watch him,' said Boots.

'Eh?'

'Watch him.'

'Course I'll watch him. You can't get him out of your eyeballs once you're in the same room as him. Boots, not a word to Chinese Lady or the fam'ly.'

'I can suck eggs, thank you,' said Boots. 'Why'd you think I called you in here? Have you thought about the stall, by the way, and all that china and glass, and Fred pushing it to the yard every night?'

'Now don't go off yer chump, Boots. Fatty don't play rough. Haven't I just told yer that?'

'You've told me. I don't necessarily believe you.'

'Just leave it to your Uncle Sammy.'

In their bedroom that night, Emily said, 'I'm not sure we're being sensible about Rosie.'

'In making so much of her?' said Boots.

'Well, you got to see it'll be hard for her to understand if we have to give her to Mr Tooley,' said Emily. 'She'll think we don't care for her, after all. She'll think we don't want her. Who's goin' to be able to explain so that she does understand?'

'I must admit I thought we'd have heard from

Mr Tooley today,' said Boots, frowning.

'Well, it's still only Wednesday,' said Emily. 'Another thing, d'you need to do all this paintin' of doors and things now we're goin' to move as soon as we find a house?'

'It's brightening up the old place for the people who'll move in after we've gone,' said Boots. 'Which reminds me, Lizzy called at the shop this morning to tell me there's a house in their road up for sale or rent.'

'Their road? Oh, it's just right there.' Emily looked excited. 'Why didn't you tell me hours ago, why didn't you tell Chinese Lady?'

'It slipped my mind.'

'You're gettin' too airy-fairy for your own good,' said Emily.

'We'll go and look at it. Want any help with your nightie, lovey?'

'Hands off,' said Emily, 'I'm not undressed yet. Boots – oh, no yer don't. Leave off, you ain't decent sometimes.'

'Don't tell Chinese Lady that, Em, or she'll start bringing me up again from scratch.'

CHAPTER TWENTY-THREE

Emily, at the corner of the Place at five to six the following evening, was waiting to intercept Boots on his way home from the shop. She spotted him, his jacket over his arm, his hat in his hand.

'Hello, Em, are you off to meet a gentleman friend?' he asked.

'No, I've just come to warn you you're goin' to catch it from Chinese Lady,' said Emily. 'She's downright disgusted with you. Mrs Pullen went and told her you're selling ladies' underwear in the shop. Chinese Lady don't know how she's goin' to hold her head up, and I don't hardly know if I can, either.'

'Be brave, Em. Stick your chest out and let's face the inquisition together. That's it, both of them.'

'It's not funny, yer know, you 'andling ladies' drawers.'

'It sounds funny.'

'Well, just wait till you get home, you won't be smiling then.'

'I'm not smiling now.'

'Yes, you are. I know you. I can tell. Oh, lor', you're really goin' to catch it from Mum.'

Indoors, Chinese Lady had her hat on. Rosie was out of the way, playing with little Lucy Tompkins in Lucy's house.

'So there you are,' said Chinese Lady as her eldest son entered the kitchen with Emily.

'Any tea?' asked Boots.

'Never mind any tea.' Chinese Lady was straight of face. 'I never thought any son of mine would get to be a common and vulgar disgrace to his fam'ly. I near fell to the floor when Mrs Pullen come and told me what you was selling to ladies in that shop of yours. It's downright unmentionable, that's what it is, and I'll carry the shame of it to my grave.'

'Now, now, old lady—'

'Don't you come it familiar with me, you disrespectable young reperbate. What d'you mean by selling intimate undergarments to female persons?'

'Oh, just for the profit, and strictly business, old girl, and with my eyes shut most of the time.'

Emily emitted a strangled cough. Chinese Lady regarded her son darkly.

'You wretched boy—'

'Pardon?' said Boots.

'Don't you pardon me,' said Chinese Lady. 'What with makin' the shop a low, common place and givin' me impudence into the bargain, you're lucky your dad don't rise up from the dead and take his belt to you. I can't hardly believe ladies have to come and ask you about unmentionables.'

'I'm only asked to wrap them,' said Boots, 'and we don't treat them as unmentionables. They're only elastic-waisted bloomers originally made for Army females.'

'Don't give me no lip. It's disgraceful. No wonder our Em'ly's standin' there hanging her head. That Sammy's in it too. Where you and that boy's goin' to end up I don't know, except perdition. It's goin' to be the death of me if all my neighbours find out sons of mine don't have no regard for decency. It's near to criminal vulgarity, and don't think I'll speak up for you if the police come around and arrest you for unlawful behaviour. I just hope you'll get social punishment as well, like the judge refusin' to let Em'ly visit you in prison.'

'Well, Dartmoor's a long way, of course,' said Boots, 'and she'd save the train fares.'

Emily, hand to her mouth, rushed out and up the stairs. She flung herself down on the marital bed, buried her face in the pillows and smothered her hysterical giggles.

'There, now see what it's all done to Em'ly,' said Chinese Lady, 'and her gettin' to be more respectable and ladylike every day. Wait till that Sammy gets home, I'll learn him. I can well believe it was his idea to put ladies' underthings in a man's shop.'

'It's not a man's shop, old girl,' said Boots, 'it's for everyone. You've got to move with the times.'

'You don't have to move in vulgar, shameless ways, my lad. The Army's not done you no good, I can see that, nor has them unpure French. I don't know how I'm goin' to look the vicar in the face when I next see him.'

'Oh, I think you'll come out on top,' said Boots reassuringly. 'His wife came in this morning. We had a comforting little chat and she bought three pairs for half-a-crown. She said she feels the cold in the winter.'

'Three pairs of what?' asked Chinese Lady, palpitating.

'Elastic bloomers,' said Boots. 'Now you can hold your head up and not die a death. Any tea?'

Upstairs, Emily lifted her head at the sound of the unusual.

Downstairs, Chinese Lady was laughing out loud.

Sammy arrived home at twenty to seven, which was early for him. He was a shock to the family when he limped into the kitchen. His face was badly bruised, his bottom lip split, his right eye discoloured. There was dried blood on his collar and buttons were missing from the jacket of his soiled suit. His right knee was swollen and his ribs were painful, but these two hurts were invisible.

'Hell,' said Tommy, 'what's happened to you?'

'Considerable,' said Sammy, and Boots gave him a long look. Sammy's return look was rueful. 'I fell over gettin' off a tram, and the road came up and clouted me. Very unfriendly, it was.'

Boots thought the use of the word unfriendly was significant.

'How much are you hurt, Sammy?' asked Chinese Lady with surprising calm.

'All over, but it's not fatal,' said Sammy, and sat down. 'Sore knee.' He didn't mention his ribs. 'And bruises. Tell you what, Boots, I think I could do with a nip of your whisky.'

Boots kept a half-bottle in the larder. Occasionally he had a nip. He poured a measure for Sammy, who took a couple of sips, then swallowed the rest. It helped. Chinese Lady studied him. She might have been thinking his fall was a punishment for doing what he shouldn't, like stocking his shop with intimate garments exclusive to female persons.

'What number tram was it?' she asked.

'Can't remember,' said Sammy, split lip painful. 'Me head's gone vague. Well, a number 18, I think. But what's that got to do with it?'

'I just asked,' said Chinese Lady. 'And I'm just thinking, Sammy, that you was given a push by the conductor, perhaps. I'm thinking you might of give him some of your cheek, that he gave you a black eye before he pushed you. That's grievin' bodily harm, which is unlegal.'

'I just fell over gettin' off,' said Sammy.

'You sure, Sammy?' said Chinese Lady, almond eyes quizzing him from under the brim of her hat. 'Only I can't see how the road could come up and give you a black eye without hittin' your nose first, and your nose don't look a bit hurt. You sure you and the conductor didn't go at each other like hooligans? Boots was a hooligan once when he was younger, on Peckham Rye, which shamed the fam'ly. I don't want you goin' in for hooliganism. You wasn't brought up to fight with tram conductors.'

313

'I just took a tumble, that's all,' said Sammy.

'Nasty,' said Tommy.

'Messy,' said Boots, a glint in his eye.

'You been to the hospital, Sammy?' asked Chinese Lady.

'I ain't a hospital case,' said Sammy, 'I just had a sit-down and mopped up a bit of blood.'

'I don't like seeing you lookin' painful,' said Chinese Lady, 'you better go and lie down on your bed, and I'll bring your supper up when it's ready. It's some nice cold ham with a salad and fried potatoes, and a fruit pie for afters.'

'Kind of you, Ma,' said Sammy, 'but I'm not fallin' for that. You'll turn me into an invalid.'

'You already look one,' said Tommy.

'All I need is a wash and brush-up,' said Sammy, 'I'll be down for supper.'

'I'll help you get your gammy knee up the stairs,' said Boots.

'I'll manage,' said Sammy.

'Don't take no arguments from him, Boots,' said Chinese Lady, 'you give him a hand. We don't want him falling over again, not on the stairs.'

Sammy shrugged. He knew Boots wanted to talk to him. He limped out, Boots following. Emily was descending the stairs with Rosie, the little girl in a new nightie, her curling hair crisp from brushing. She was coming down to say goodnight to the family.

Emily stared at Sammy.

'Oh, Sammy love, what you done to yourself?' she gasped.

'Fell over gettin' off a tram,' said Sammy.

'A what?' said Emily

'A tram,' said Sammy.

'Blessed thing,' said Rosie.

'Don't you start,' said Sammy, 'just make way for the injured.'

'I'm taking him up to bathe his wounds,' said Boots.

314

'Uncle Boots, can't you kiss them to make them better?' asked Rosie in concern.

'Not without spoiling my supper,' said Boots. Once in the bedroom Sammy shared with Tommy, he spoke his mind. 'Careless, weren't you? I told you to watch him. You didn't watch him.'

'Look, I already got one headache,' said Sammy, 'don't give me another.' He slipped off his jacket and waistcoat, wincing a little. Boots pulled his shirt and vest off for him. The bruises on Sammy's chest and ribs looked ugly.

'Rough, was it?' said Boots. The glint in his right eye was steely.

'Bleeders,' said Sammy, and Boots filled the wash-stand bowl with cold water from the pitcher. Sammy dipped his head and immersed his painful face. He laved the tender spots with his hands. Boots handed him a towel. Sammy dabbed himself. 'All right,' he said, 'so Fatty wasn't reasonable.'

'And Chinese Lady doesn't like it, Sammy. She's going to ask you over supper where it was you said you fell off the tram. She's no fool. You'd better make your story sound good. What happened?'

Sammy recounted. He had seen Big Ben in the morning, at his office in Kennington. He offered to talk reasonably about fair competition. Big Ben said reasonable talk meant close the shop down or sell the lease to him, together with all stock at fifty per cent of the retail price, plus details gratis of all contacts and contracts. Sammy was disgusted. He had no intention of doing any of that. Especially he wasn't going to hand over the name and whereabouts of his obliging Army friend, the quartermaster. He told Big Ben he was being unfriendly, not reasonable. Big Ben said don't be aggravating. He also said he wanted all Sammy's best saleable scrap metal. He required to add it to his own. Other dealers had consented to be sociable, he said. Sammy knew Big Ben was attempting to corner the scrap market in south London. The increased prices were holding steady. Big Ben meant to unload the moment he had the edge. Sammy said he regretted being unable to oblige him, he'd sold all he'd got. Big Ben knew that had been a considerable amount. All his fat turned purple. That, he said, was going to make dealers unload theirs all over, and was accordingly the most aggravating thing he had ever heard. It meant Sammy had got to come to terms over the shop or close it down a week from yesterday, as already requested. Sammy said if Big Ben couldn't stand competition, he'd better retire and grow roses. He was considerably surprised, he said, that a business gentleman of Mr Ford's reputation might think of doing something illegal. Big Ben requested him to depart.

Sammy had spent the rest of the day feeling a little uneasy, justifiably so, for Fatty's gang caught him just after he left his yard in Olney Road that evening. They damaged him, said Sammy, and with malice aforethought, which wasn't at all legal.

'You didn't go to the coppers?' said Boots.

'Give over,' said Sammy.

'No witnesses?'

'Ask me another,' said Sammy.

'Are you going to shut the shop?'

'I didn't mean ask me something daft. It's our shop, the fam'ly's shop, and my money. My money's been hard-earned. I ain't closin' down to please that fat perisher.'

'Good,' said Boots.

When they were all at supper, with Sammy chewing a little painfully, Chinese Lady asked a question of her youngest son.

'Where was it you said you fell off the tram, Sammy?'

Boots smiled.

'Walworth Road,' said Sammy. 'I was gettin' off to go to me yard in Olney Road. A bobby picked me up. He gave me a fatherly warning about not gettin' off a tram till it stopped, or he'd prosecute me for being dangerous and disorderly. Can yer believe that?'

'Some might,' said Chinese Lady.

Sammy turned up at the stall at ten the following morning. With him was an errand boy, whose pushcart contained boxes of new wares. Susie and Tommy were busy serving. The boy unloaded the boxes and placed them on the kerb at the back of the stall. Sammy tipped him and the boy left. Susie, free of customers, looked at Sammy in alarm.

'Mister Sammy, yer face,' she breathed. 'Mister Tommy told me you'd 'ad an accident, but I didn't realise it 'ad injured yer so bad.'

Sammy's facial bruises had turned purple, and his right eye was swollen and half-closed.

'I'm a trifle damaged, Miss Brown, I'll admit, but kindly don't make a song and dance about it,' he said. 'There's some dinner services here you can unpack if yer'd be so good as to stop gawpin' at me.'

'But your poor eye, Mister Sammy,' said Susie, her own matchless optics offering melting sympathy, 'it must be a pain to yer.'

'I can't stand this,' muttered Sammy, 'it's makin' mincemeat of me peace of mind. I might as well find a cemetery where I can just lie down and pass quietly away.'

'Mister Adams, yer shouldn't say things like that,' said Susie reprovingly, 'it's provokin' Providence.'

Tommy, his customer departing, said, 'What are you two talkin' about?'

'I'm just saying how upset I am at Mister Sammy lookin' so injured,' said Susie. 'It must be awful, falling off a tram.'

'I didn't fall off,' said Sammy, 'I fell over after gettin' off. And I am now goin' off.'

'You've only just got here,' said Tommy, 'so what's yer hurry? Where yer goin'?'

'To a peaceful death,' said Sammy, and went.

'Well, I never met anyone who acts as funny as he does,' said Susie.

'He's scared,' said Tommy, grinning.

'He can't be, not Mister Sammy.' Susie remembered a lout, and how heroically Mister Sammy had dealt with him. 'What could 'e be scared of?'

'You,' said Tommy, for whom the penny had just dropped.

'That young Sammy caught a ripe packet, didn't 'e?' called Ma Earnshaw. 'Juicy mince pie he's got. More like a blackcurrant pie, if yer ask me.'

'Fell off a tram,' said Tommy.

'And I'm Mary Pickford,' said Ma Earnshaw.

Susie served a shopper, then said to Tommy, 'Mister Sammy's scared of me?'

'Yer pretty, Susie.'

'Me?' Susie looked pleased.

'And yer got big blue eyes,' said Tommy.

'But he don't even like me very much,' said Susie, 'I don't think he likes any girls.'

'It's not that he don't like them, Susie, it's just that he ain't partial to what they might do to his pocket.'

'I ain't interested in 'is pocket,' said Susie indignantly.

'Sammy is.' Tommy grinned. 'His pocket's his only interest.'

Just before noon, Boots heard the sound of a barrel-organ outside the shop. It struck a reminiscent note. With two customers dipping into boxes, he glanced through the window. The handle of the barrel-organ was being turned by his blind ex-comrade, Nobby Clark. Well, once a comrade, always a comrade. He felt for his cigarettes. Nobby had always been exceptionally fond of a fag. A thought took hold of him. Comrades.

He left the shop when the two customers had gone, locking the door behind him. He walked across the pavement. Nobby's hat, on the kerb, had a few coppers in it. Three urchins were standing by, listening in rapture to wartime songs.

'Nobby?' said Boots.

The sightless eyes turned his way, and a little smile parted Nobby's lips.

'I know yer this time, sarge.'

'Good on yer, then. D'you also know any West Kents who are unemployed?'

'That ain't a question. It's a fact.' Nobby kept playing, and a passing man, elderly, dropped a penny into the hat. Nobby heard it strike the other coins above the sound of the music. 'Thank yer kindly, thank yer. Ain't it a curse, sarge, good men an' true walkin' the streets on a few bob dole money? What's yer interest in 'em?'

'If you'd like a beer and a sandwich at the pub across the road in five minutes, I'll talk to you then. There's some kids here.'

'I know that. Three, ain't there?'

'Right. They'll keep an eye on the joanna. I'll be with you in a few minutes, and take you across to the pub. What d'you say?'

'You're on, sarge. I ain't holdin' yer three stripes against yer.'

Boots went back into the shop and penned the words BACK IN TEN MINUTES on a sheet of paper. He locked the till, just in case, stuck the notice on the front of the shop door, turned the key and rejoined Nobby. He promised the kids tuppence each to look after the barrel-organ, which they thought money for jam, and took Nobby across the road for a pint, a sandwich and a talk in the pub.

He spent the afternoon clearer in his mind about what was to be done to circumvent the covetous and greedy fat man, and how to make known to him that he objected to his youngest brother being maliciously damaged. Nobby had said if he could not round up enough unemployed West Kents, he'd make up the numbers with East Surrey men, plus a couple of Old Contemptibles of Mons. None of them were going to like what had been done to the brother of a casualty of the Somme, even if that casualty had been a sergeant. So said Nobby.

Boots was sure Fatty would take action immediately after his week's notice to Sammy had expired.

The shop stayed open late that night, Friday. Sammy was helping while doing his best to remain agreeable to customers who wanted to know if he'd had an argument with an omnibus. He and Boots went home together. On the tram, Sammy said he'd been giving thought to the problem of Big Ben.

'Leave it,' said Boots.

'Eh?'

'You nurse your wounds, Sammy. I'll see to Fatty.'

'Here, hold it,' said Sammy, 'I ain't in no way inclined to cop for a junior say-so in Adams Enterprises.'

'What you copped for was a heavy load of Fatty's machinery falling on you,' said Boots. 'I don't want Tower Bridge falling on you next time. It'll bury you. Chinese Lady won't like that, she's not fond of family funerals. And I'll get the blame. I've already had some of that. She took the chopper to me over the Army bloomers we're having the indecency to sell to female persons. Don't be surprised if she arrives at the shop one day and sets fire to what we've got left.'

'Ain't she the one and only?' said Sammy admiringly.

'You could say that, Sammy. So no funerals. Leave Fatty to me. Oblige me by doing as I say when the time comes. It'll be next Thursday, if the shop's still open, as it will be.'

'You bleeder,' said Sammy, 'you got yer crafty mitts on the reins of me new-funded empire.'

'New-founded.'

'Funded,' said Sammy, 'and it's my money.'

'Just nurse your wounds, sunshine.'

'Boots, yer takin' liberties,' said Sammy, 'yer nickin' me authority from under me. And I also got that girl—' He lapsed into mutters.

'Girl?' said Boots.

'I didn't say anything,' said Sammy, 'I just got morter rigours on me mind, that's all.'

'As in death?' said Boots.

'Well, we've all got to go sometime,' said Sammy, 'except I ain't partial to goin' just yet.'

'Somehow,' said Boots, 'there's a connection between girls and dying a death.'

'I echo them judicious sentiments,' said Sammy. 'Now tell me what you got in mind concernin' Fatty.'

'I won't bother you with details,' said Boots.

'Thoughtful of yer,' said Sammy. 'By the way, are you still waiting to hear from Rosie's grandfather?'

Boots was. And no letter had arrived today, either. Rosie was waiting for him to say goodnight to her. She lay in her made-up bed on the sofa.

'Not asleep yet?' he said. He stooped and kissed her. Her new teddy bear was in the bed beside her. Rosie looked dreamy. 'Goodnight, kitten.'

'Goodnight, Uncle Boots. You smell ever so nice.'

'Well, that's something I've never been told before.'

Emily, watching them, wondered if she and Boots weren't overdoing things in their affection for the girl. But Rosie was just so lovable.

'Goodnight, Rosie,' she said, and she kissed the girl too.

CHAPTER TWENTY-FOUR

Susie went to the pictures with her new friend, Danny Higgins. On the way he told her he'd spoken to her mum and dad, and they'd said they didn't mind him and her walking out steady together.

Susie thought Danny quite nice, really, but wasn't sure she wanted to go steady. Going steady meant thinking about getting engaged later on, and that wasn't in her mind at all. Going to the pictures once a week with him, and meeting him in a park Sunday afternoons, that was as much as she wanted. And, anyway, he was only a grocer's errand boy at the moment.

She said, 'Oh, we're all right as we are, Danny.'

'Yes, I like goin' steady with yer, Susie,' he said.

'No, just friendly,' said Susie, 'we ain't properly developed yet.' She meant adult, but what she had said made her think of what was happening to her. She had been growning rounder ever since Mister Sammy had put her on pie and mash. And a girl kept on growing until she was twenty-one. She silently begged Jesus not to let her get like Ma Earnshaw, who always looked as if she was going to over-balance into her greengrocery.

'What's proper development?' asked Danny.

'Proper grown up, of course,' said Susie.

'Well, I dunno about that,' said Danny, 'you already look proper grown up to me.'

Oh, lawks, thought Susie, if he's noticed, then I must be getting fat.

'Kindly don't be personal,' she said aloofly. She'd have to tighten her stays and stop eating potatoes.

However, she had a nice time at the pictures with Danny, then he took her home and her mum gave him a cup of cocoa and a slice of cake before he left.

After he'd gone, Mrs Brown said, 'He wants to walk out steady with you, love.'

'But he's not grown up yet,' said Susie.

'Still, he's a nice well-behaved boy,' said Mrs Brown.

'I don't mind meself,' said Mr Brown, 'but it's best to let Susie make up her own mind.'

'Yes, course it is, dear,' said Mrs Brown.

'Honest, I ain't ready to go steady with anyone,' said Susie. 'And Danny don't 'ave a decent job yet, he's just an errand boy.'

'My Aunt Belle walked out steady for six years with my Uncle Fred,' said Mrs Brown. 'She wasn't never set on rushing things, and even on her weddin' day, with me a bridesmaid in rose pink, I heard her say she hoped she wasn't being too impulsive like. Still, it worked out all right, except she still takes a week to make up her mind to spend a penny.'

'Blimey,' said Mr Brown, 'that's a bit of a strain, ain't it, takin' a week to make up 'er mind to do an 'owjerdo?'

Mrs Brown, seeing his larky grin, said, 'You saucy old thing, you know I didn't mean that. Fancy makin' a vulgar joke like that in front of our Susie. Ought to know better, didn't he, love?'

'You're a caution, Dad, you are,' smiled Susie. 'Anyway, I don't want to get married till I'm nineteen or twenty.'

'Course yer don't, Susie,' said Mr Brown. 'You and Danny can just be friends.'

'That's all right, then,' said Susie, who had a preference for the Prince of Wales.

On Sunday evening Boots took Rosie up to bed. She sat up between the sheets while he brushed her hair. Her eyes peeped and giggles bubbled.

'I'm good, aren't I?' she said, and he thought how

unhappy her life with her mother must have been. There was always this thing about being good.

'You're a pickle, Rosie.'

'What's a pickle?'

'An imp.'

'What's an imp?'

'A pickle,' said Boots, which she thought very funny. He kissed her nose and tucked her in. He wondered why Mr Tooley had not kept his promise to write soon. He thought a week a long time.

Emily came in then to join Boots in saying goodnight to the girl.

The blow came by way of the midday post on Monday, by way of a letter from Mr Tooley. Boots and Emily read it when they came home from work. Mr Tooley said he was sorry he hadn't been able to write earlier, but the fact was he felt he'd had to talk to relatives about his granddaughter, and he'd done this, and a nephew of his had asked him not to make a decision for a few days.

'*Last night, Friday*,' wrote Mr Tooley, '*Mick my nephew and his wife Nellie came round to see me and offered Rosie a home with them. They've got a boy of four who'd be company for her, and I suppose it's right she should be with relatives. I felt you'd be happy to give her a home yourselves, which you said you would be and which was heartfelt kind of you, but I couldn't help feeling guilty about you taking on all the burden and responsibility and us not doing anything ourselves. I can't thank you enough for taking Rosie in and looking after her but it's a relief not having to push her on to you for good, which wouldn't have been fair when she's got willing relatives like Mick and Nellie. I'll come and collect her Monday evening, I'll come straight from work and be there about half six or thereabouts.*'

It was now five to six. Boots and Emily had thirty-five minutes to get Rosie's little possessions together and to let her know what was to happen to her. She

324

was in the parlour at the moment, tinkling on the keys of the old upright piano, which fascinated her. Chinese Lady was with her, having wisely taken her there while the letter was being read.

Emily felt numb. Boots looked stricken. They had both come to love the girl. They did not know what to say for the moment, not even to each other. Chinese Lady came in, having told Rosie to stay at the piano for a while. As soon as she saw the faces of Emily and Boots, she knew what the letter meant to them. She had never seen Boots in silent shock before, and there were tears in Emily's eyes.

'So Mr Tooley's goin' to take her?' said Chinese Lady.

'To relatives,' said Emily, a catch in her voice.

'There's nothing any of us can do, Em'ly love.'

'Oh, Mum,' said Emily.

'No, there's nothing,' said Boots.

'It's grievin' you,' said Chinese Lady, feeling for the son who had committed himself so whole-heartedly to the child's welfare.

'It's my own fault,' said Boots flatly, and Emily winced because he had never taken anything as hard as this.

'No, we all let our feelings get the better of us,' said Chinese Lady, 'we should all of made Rosie understand she might only be with us for a little while, instead of makin' her feel it could be for always. I been in fault myself, givin' in like I have to the pleasure of havin' a child in the house again.'

'We all give in to honest pleasure,' said Emily. 'Mum, Mr Tooley's comin' to collect her at half-past six.'

Chinese Lady bit her lip.

'Well, we got to face up to it,' she said, 'but who's goin' to tell her that her grandfather's comin' to take her to a new home?'

Boots was silent. It hurt Emily to see him so lost for once. No one and nothing had ever seemed to catch him on the wrong foot before.

He grimaced and said, 'I think that's my responsibility.'

'We'll both tell her,' said Emily, and went into the parlour with him. Rosie turned on the piano stool.

'Can I come now, Auntie Emily?' she asked.

'Yes, there's things to do, darling,' said Emily, then sighed to herself at letting the endearment slip out. Chinese Lady was right. They had all allowed their feelings for the child to get the better of them.

Boots made his effort.

'Rosie, do you remember the man who called last Sunday when we were getting ready to go to church?'

'Yes,' said Rosie, and at once anxiety showed itself.

'He's your mummy's father,' said Boots, 'your grandfather.'

Rosie looked at Emily, then back again at Boots. The anxiety increased.

'Is he coming again, is he going to take me away?' she asked.

Emily was close to tears. She heard a little sigh from Boots.

'He'll be here soon, Rosie,' he said, 'he's going to take you to live with his nephew, whose wife has a little boy. They're your relatives, cousins of your mummy. Do you see?'

'Yes,' said Rosie, and Boots saw resigned sadness in the child, as if she had felt her time with him and Emily and the family had been too good to last. There were no tears, just this look of quiet resignation. She was a child who had been taught by her mother, perhaps, never to argue.

He could not help saying, 'It isn't that we want you to go, Rosie, only that your relatives have more right to take care of you. Do you understand that?' He desperately wanted her to know he and Emily would have loved to take care of her themselves until she was old enough to make decisions of her own about her life. He wanted her to know that, he did not want her to think he and Emily did not care for her. 'Do you understand, Rosie?'

'Yes,' said Rosie, and slipped from the piano stool to stand looking down at her feet, like a child who had not been very good.

'Are you unhappy, Rosie?' asked Emily gently.

To which Rosie replied, 'Auntie Emily, you won't forget me, will you?'

'No, of course not,' said Emily, 'nor will Uncle Boots.'

'You've been very very good, kitten,' said Boots.

Rosie lifted her head. Her mouth was quivering, but there were still no tears. Just five years old, thought Boots, five years, and she was as brave as they came. She was leaving people she knew, people she had come to trust and care for. Her grandfather was a stranger to her, and her foster parents would be total strangers. But there were no tantrums, no scenes.

Swallowing, she said, 'Could you come and see me sometimes?'

He was not to know the question was put because there was still a tiny hope flickering in her mind. But how could he answer it? He knew he and Emily must make no claim on Rosie's affections once she was living with her foster parents. Neither he nor Emily could intrude on Rosie's relationship with her new guardians, or do anything that might be seen as interference.

All the same, he said, 'We'll see if we can come on your birthdays and bring you a little present.' But when was her birthday? Rosie herself had said she didn't know, that she had never had a birthday card. But her grandfather would know, surely, and they would know round at the school. 'Will that do, Rosie?'

'Yes,' she said, but it was obvious from her wistful expression that she realised he was not offering very much.

'We'd like to come more often,' said Boots, 'but it would depend, you see, on what your new parents thought about it.'

'We'll come when we can,' said Emily, but she knew, as Boots knew, that such visits would do no good, even if they could be arranged.

Rosie said worriedly, 'Do I have to have them as a mummy and daddy?'

'Oh, you can have them just as nice people who want to look after you,' said Boots with forced lightness.

'We got to collect your clothes and things now,' said Emily very gently, 'and find something to put them in. Will you come up with me?'

'Yes,' said Rosie, and went up with Emily. The first thing she did was to hand her teddy bear in silent appeal to Emily, and Emily knew that of all things the teddy must be packed.

Boots sat at the kitchen table, mouth compressed, jaw tight. Chinese Lady gave him the only antidote she could think of, a nice cup of hot tea.

Mr Tooley arrived a little after six-thirty, and with him was Mrs Nellie Nicholls, the wife of his nephew. Twenty-six years old, she was a brisk and cheerful woman, neatly but plainly dressed. She viewed Rosie approvingly, and gave her a brisk, cheerful hug. It elicited no response from Rosie, except for a nervous little twitch.

'There, cheer up, little lovey,' said Nellie Nicholls, 'you'll be all right, I promise yer. You're goin' to get a nice supper at your new home, and jelly too.'

Boots gritted his teeth, feeling Rosie was going to have a brisk, well-organised and no-nonsense life. But since Chinese Lady seemed to be in approval of Mrs Nicholls, he supposed he was not only prejudiced, he was also jealous.

Holding Rosie's hand, Mrs Nicholls chatted away with Chinese Lady and spoke of the new home and little brother the girl was going to enjoy. Quietly, Mr Tooley drew Boots from the parlour into the passage.

'She's a good homely sort, Mick's wife,' he said, 'and Rosie won't lack for kindness or for being properly mothered. I want yer to know Nellie and Mick are – well, genuine about it all. They don't want no financial

328

'elp from me, they just think as relatives that they'd like to have Rosie. I told you last week I didn't know where to turn to find anyone except you and your wife. I didn't think I'd got any right to suggest to any of me relatives that they might be willing, but I did think I ought to tell them about things. Nellie and Mick came up with their offer a few days later. I hopes you feel like I do, it's best for relatives to take the girl on.'

'Emily and I feel we only want what's best for Rosie,' said Boots.

Mr Tooley gave him a keen look.

'Mr Adams, d'you feel you'd've liked things to be left as they were? I'll be straight with you, I been a bit worried about am I doing right by you, considering you and your wife seemed happy havin' Rosie, but as Mick and Nellie offered of their own accord, well, I couldn't say no, of course.'

Boots did not really want to talk about it. He had never thought, in the beginning, that his feelings would run away with his commonsense. He had made a bed of nettles for himself. A neglected little girl had looked at him, talked to him and put on an old apron so that she could help him with the decorating. Even reasonableness was deserting him, because he found himself wishing quite savagely that he had never written to Mr Tooley.

He could only say, 'Emily and I would have fostered Rosie with pleasure. We'll be sorry to lose her.'

'Then let's 'ope that what I've arranged works out right, let's 'ope that the way Milly's behaved don't mean she's messed up Rosie's life as well as 'er own.'

'When's Rosie's birthday?' asked Boots abruptly.

'Eh? Oh. I did send a birthday card once, but Milly sent it back, saying she didn't want no reminders of the day she gave birth to a – a—' Mr Tooley faltered.

'Yes, I know,' said Boots.

'Anyway, her birthday's early May – let's see – yes, the 5th.'

329

'I think we'd like to send her cards—' Boots was interrupted by the arrival home of Tommy. He had been to Manor Place Baths for a hot soak and scrub after leaving the market. He looked fresh-faced and healthy. Seeing Mr Tooley, he checked. He glanced at the little group in the parlour, where Mrs Nicholls was still chatting on. He saw her, a homely-looking woman, holding Rosie's hand, and he saw the sadness on the girl's face and Emily's upset expression. He guessed what it was all about. He nodded to Mr Tooley, whom he had never seen before, and it was a curt nod for a young man as equable as Tommy. Then he strode through to the kitchen. From there he called Boots, who joined him.

'That Mr Tooley?' asked Tommy.

'Yes,' said Boots.

'And is that woman with Chinese Lady goin' to take Rosie?'

'Yes. She's the wife of Mr Tooley's nephew. They're going to foster Rosie.'

'And you're letting 'em?' asked Tommy.

'There's nothing Emily and I can do.'

'That's a fact, is it?' said Tommy. 'Then you ain't the man I thought you were. Anyone can see Rosie's breakin' her heart. Don't yer know she dotes on you and Em'ly?'

'Emily and I have no legal rights,' said Boots harshly, 'that's something you should know.' He went back to the parlour. Rosie was saying goodbye to Chinese Lady.

'You been a sweet child,' said Chinese Lady, and touched the girl's shoulder in the lightest of affectionate gestures.

Rosie swallowed. She turned to Emily.

'Goodbye, Auntie Emily.'

'Rosie – I—' Emily's strength of character deserted her for once and she ran from the room.

'My, my, what's up with her?' asked the surprised Mrs Nicholls.

'It's only natural, Nellie,' said Mr Tooley.

'Goodbye, Rosie,' said Boots, and bent and kissed her. And from under her little round straw hat, Rosie looked at him, into his eyes, and was riven by a suppressed sob. Boots felt utter disgust at the cruelties and perversities that blind fate forced the innocent to endure. 'I'll take her out to the gate while you and Mrs Nicholls say goodbye to my mother, Mr Tooley,' he said.

He took Rosie out to the gate. He thought how very sweet she looked in her little hat and one of her new daytime frocks. But her face was pale now.

'I have to go,' she said.

'Yes, you have to, Rosie.' Unable to help himself, he added, 'But I love you, will you remember that?'

'Yes,' she said, and he thought her sadness made a lonely child of her. 'Will you always love me?'

'Always, Rosie.'

Mr Tooley and Mrs Nicholls came out. They said goodbye to Boots. Mr Tooley shook hands firmly.

'Mr Adams, you got my likin' and my thanks,' he said.

'Goodbye,' said Boots.

Chinese Lady and Tommy came out. With Boots they watched Rosie walking out of their lives, between the man and the woman, the woman holding her hand, the man carrying by its string a large cardboard box containing her clothes, her little possessions and her teddy bear. Rosie did not look back. Mr Tooley and Mrs Nicholls were talking. Rosie was silent, her little hat lightly bobbing. Boots was not sure how he was going to reconcile himself to losing her. He watched until the man, the woman and the child reached the corner of Caulfield Place at its junction with Browning Street. Rosie stopped then, and she turned and looked back. Mr Tooley and Mrs Nicholls halted for a moment. Rosie saw the figures at the gate.

'Goodbye, Rosie love!' called Tommy.

'Goodbye, child!' Chinese Lady lifted her voice.

Emily rushed out and looked and called.

'Rosie, goodbye!'

Only Boots stayed silent. He just looked. And Rosie just looked. He felt guilty in his helplessness. He could imagine her apprehensions, and her bewilderment about what love meant. He wondered exactly what the parting was doing to her. He knew what it was doing to him.

Mrs Nicholls said something to the child and tugged at her hand. Mr Tooley bent his head and spoke to her, and his manner seemed gentle. Rosie went on then with her grandfather and her foster mother.

The little straw hat bobbed and vanished.

'You won't forget me, will you?' she had said to Emily.

But could the memories of a few months, however precious to her now, last for very long in the mind of a child of five? If her new home gave her comfort, and if her foster parents gave her love and understanding, those memories, thought Boots, would begin to fade in six months and be gone in a year.

'Well, I suppose it's all for the best,' said Chinese Lady, sighing.

'Bugger the best,' said Tommy.

'I'll forget I heard you say that, Tommy Adams,' said Chinese Lady. She was suffering for Emily and Boots, and for the child. 'It's been a trying time.'

'Why the hell did Boots let her be taken?' asked Tommy. 'Is fancy talk all he's got?'

Boots said nothing. He was still at the gate, Emily close to him, and Emily gave Tommy an angry look.

Chinese Lady said quietly, 'When you've learned more than you have so far, Tommy, you'll know an only child that's been deserted belongs to its own, not to neighbours, and it don't matter how good the neighbours might of been to it.'

Tommy went back into the house. Boots was away, walking up the street.

'Boots, where you goin'?' called Emily, with street kids watching in curiosity.

'He's got to walk the worst of it off, Em'ly,' said Chinese Lady, 'he's not goin' to be able to sit quiet or even eat his supper. Why don't you go and walk with him, love?'

'I got to,' said Emily, and went after her husband. When she caught up with him in Browning Street, he slowed his striding pace and put an arm around her.

'Emily love, we've lost her,' he said.

'No, we haven't really,' she said, knowing she had got to bring him to his senses. 'She was never ours. We tried to make her ours, but it hasn't worked. Anyway, you still got me, you'll always have me. Don't yer know that?'

CHAPTER TWENTY-FIVE

'There's a new Tom Mix film at the Golden Domes this week,' said Tommy, trying to lighten the conversation at breakfast the next morning. The Golden Domes was a cinema near Camberwell Green.

'Thrilling,' said Sammy, who had been rendered speechless by the news of Rosie's departure when he arrived home late last night.

'Some people hardly ever go to the pictures,' said Chinese Lady. 'That Lily Fuller is always goin'', her mother says. Cousin Vi never does. Well, you all know what Aunt Victoria's like.'

'I'll drop her a line and ask if she'd like to go with me,' said Tommy.

Chinese Lady took on a look of innocence as she poured tea. Boots smiled faintly. Emily was quiet.

At work later, she felt depressed. She was rarely like that, she was far too resilient mentally, far too involved with life, to suffer moods. But she felt very depressed today, not only because of Rosie going, but by the certainty that Boots would now want children more than ever. And she wasn't conceiving. Lizzy had no trouble, she would soon be presenting Ned with their second child.

Emily was short with Mr Simmonds. And she was even short with a caller, a man who came to complain that the roof of his house was letting in the rain because of broken tiles. It was raining today.

'Go and see yer landlord,' said Emily, 'it's his business, not ours.'

'Been to see 'im,' said the man, a market coster-monger. ''Alf a dozen times. 'E says 'e'll see to it, but 'e don't. Now we get a wet ceiling and a wet bedroom every time it rains. It's 'armful to our kids' 'ealth. 'Armful to 'ealth is town 'all's business.'

'Broken tiles aren't,' said Emily brusquely. 'D'you pay yer rent?'

'Course we do.'

'Then stop paying it, that'll make your landlord do something.'

'Yus, it will, it'll make 'im chuck us out.'

'Not if you got a good reason for 'olding back yer rent,' said Emily irritably. 'Go round and tell him you're not paying till he's seen to the tiles. It's between you and him, it's nothing to do with us.'

'Well, seeing yer so 'elpful,' said the costermonger, 'I'll do that, I'll go round and tell 'im, but if it makes 'im chuck us out I'll bring me missus and me kids round 'ere and camp in yer office. Yer get me?'

'You can't do that.' Mr Simmonds spoke up from his desk.

'I'll do it all right, mister, yer can lay to that.' The costermonger departed in a highly dissatisfied state. A girl put her head inside the inner door.

'Emily, Mrs Stevens wants to see you.'

'Yes, all right,' said Emily.

'Having a bad day, Emily?' asked Mr Simmonds sympathetically.

'You're no help,' said Emily, and made her way to Madge Stevens's office. In the corridor she met young Mrs Wade from the typists' office. Mrs Wade was humming a song. 'Glad someone's 'appy,' said Emily.

'Oh, I am,' said Mrs Wade impulsively. 'Emily, I'm going to have a baby.'

Emily stared in almost angry disbelief. Mrs Wade had only been married three months.

'I wish yer luck, then,' she said, and went on with her mouth compressed and her depression acute.

335

Madge Stevens looked up from her desk and smiled when Emily entered, but the smile disappeared as she detected a visible glitter of tears in the green eyes.

'Emily? What's wrong?'

'Everything.'

'Sit down.' Emily sat down, heavily. 'Would you like to tell me about it?'

Emily confided then, and at length.

'So yer see?' she said at the end.

Madge said gently, 'I'm so sorry. You've lost a little girl you and your husband were hoping to foster, and you haven't been able to conceive. And your husband's upset, of course.'

'Well, he set his heart on Rosie, and he's set too on havin' a family of his own.'

Madge reflected, then said, 'And that's landed you with anxieties and worries. It's the way of things, Emily, it's always the woman who has to shoulder the more acute anxieties and worries. I don't know your husband, but I'm sure he's very nice. All the same, you have to understand men are selfish creatures. Some are a little selfish, some moderately selfish and the rest very selfish. It's their wants and wishes that come first with them. Sometimes, Emily, a woman should consider her own preferences. You're feeling very depressed about things, but is this because of what your husband wants rather than what you want? You enjoy your job, don't you?'

'Yes, I do,' said Emily.

'But you'd have to give it up if you had a baby?'

'Well, yes.'

'You were thinking of that when you turned down the summer shorthand course, weren't you?' said Madge, gently positive.

'I had to think of it,' said Emily.

'Well, I'm going to suggest now that you don't worry quite so much about how to keep your husband happy,' said Madge, 'but think a little more about yourself.

You're entitled to happiness too, you know. Well, as much as any of us can expect, life being what it is with its unpleasant surprise packets at times.'

'You don't think I should worry about not havin' babies?' asked Emily, a little confused, a little uncertain, but glad she had someone to confide in.

'I suggest you don't worry as much as I think you do. Emily, you've a secure job here, a job you enjoy, and that's a consideration and a consolation, isn't it? I called you in to tell you it's definite that you can look on your job in Enquiries as permanent until your next move upwards. You're no longer in any way connected with the typists' pool.'

'Oh, I'm that pleased,' said Emily.

'It means a rise of two and sixpence from this week.'

'Oh, now I can't hardly say how pleased I am.'

'Please me by thinking of yourself a little more, Emily,' smiled Madge.

Mrs Rachel Goodman, the young wife of a rising race-course bookmaker, and the beloved daughter of Mr Isaac Moses, knocked on the door of Sammy's office above the shop at Camberwell Green. Boots had directed her up. The office could be reached from the shop or by a side entrance.

'Come in,' called Sammy, engaged in working out the gross profit for the time the shop had been operating.

Rachel entered, her lustrous beauty clad in a shining black mackintosh, and a rain hat on her head. The weather had turned wet.

'Dear to goodness,' she murmured, 'so it's true. A large gentleman did cause some damage.'

Sammy's eye still looked discoloured, although the swelling had subsided.

'Hello,' he said, 'who have we here, may we ask? Let's see, it's – now who is it?' He rose from his desk chair. His office was equipped with solid furniture, and the desk stood on a large square of brown Wilton carpet, acquired by Mr Greenberg from an old gentleman who kept tripping over it and took ten bob for it. Mr Greenberg had sold it to Sammy for fifteen. 'Got it. Lily Langtry.'

'Lily Langtry has got wrinkles,' said Rachel.

'Hold on, half a mo,' said Sammy, 'it's me lost love. Kindly do me the honour of takin' a pew.' He came round and dusted the seat of the visitor's chair with his handkerchief.

'Sammy, Sammy, why are you such fun and so many men no fun at all?' Rachel laughed and sat down. 'Shall you kiss me?'

'I exclude married ladies from my kissing list,' said Sammy, 'they've all got husbands.'

'Give us a kiss, lovey,' said Rachel, dark eyes velvety.

'Stop playing about,' said Sammy, backing off.

'Give yer a penny for one,' said Rachel. She had done that in the old days, given Sammy a penny to kiss her. It was the only way of coercing him, of getting a kiss, she with her eyes squeezed tightly shut, her young ruby lips enduring girlish bliss, and Sammy, fair as always once payment was made, giving her a very generous penny'sworth.

'Listen,' he said, 'I don't want to be unanimously sacrificed at your feast of the Passover and eaten for afters.'

'Unanimously sacrificed?' purred Rachel in sultry joy. ammy, you darling, aincher got just a little kiss for yer devoted skatin' partner?'

'Devoted my eye,' said Sammy, taking up a safe position on his side of the desk and sitting down. 'You're a saucepot. I'm not sure I shouldn't tell my friend Isaac that yer contradictin' the rules of holy Yiddish wedlock.'

'My daddy loves me,' said Rachel. 'He loves you too. More since you've told him you're going to repay the loan in full by the end of September with the promised interest. Now, take me to lunch and tell me all about your

338

quarrel with the large gentleman who's also very fat.'

'Look, we eat dinner here, not upper-class lunch,' said Sammy. 'Kindly go away. I'm considerable busy.' His telephone rang. He lifted it off the hook. He spoke in a high-class voice. 'Good morning, Adams Enterprises here. Ah, just a moment, sir, I'll see if I can disturb him for you.' He put the receiver against his chest for a few seconds, then took it to his ear again. 'Sammy Adams speaking,' he said into the mouthpiece.

Rachel put a gloved hand to her lips to stifle laughter. She had a rich sense of humour, and the only fun she could have with Sammy now that she was married was to tease him. She listened as he carried on a business conversation that ended with him thanking the caller for his order.

'My life, Sammy, very impressive,' said Rachel. 'But, darling, this trouble between you and the King of Fat, look at you. Thank God you're still alive.'

'You heard, did you?'

'Mr Greenberg heard, so my daddy heard, and so I heard. What are you doing about it?'

'Nothing,' said Sammy, 'but I'm considerable perturbed.'

'Nothing?' said Rachel. 'That's not my Sammy.'

'I am speakin' on a note of personal mortification,' said Sammy, 'havin' been treacherously undermined by a certain crafty gent whose monicker shall remain nameless. This geezer is dealing with what I'm perturbed about. For example, my injured left mince pie and my bent ribs and what caused the damage. But I am requested to nurse my wounds, which is takin' a liberty with my status, but which I'm forced to submit to because of my close association with said geezer and his craftiness.'

'Oh, dear,' murmured Rachel, 'Boots is putting on the elder brother act?'

'Oh, yer cunning female,' said Sammy, 'you been puttin' your ear to keyholes.'

'Sammy, Sammy, you've just told me. Who else but Boots would make you and could make you sit tight, and leave things to him?'

'I didn't say anything, Mrs Goodman. Don't tell me you've got second sight or you'll turn me into a bag of nerves.'

'No second sight, lovey,' smiled Rachel. 'You simply gave me a perfect description of a younger brother taking orders from his elder. And I know Boots. I'm relieved he's seeing to things. My daddy and I don't want you to suffer assault and battery again. Will you take me to lunch now? I told Benjamin you might treat me, and Benjamin said that'll be the day.'

'Nice husband you've got,' said Sammy, 'but a bit careless with his wordage. Y'know, I been thinking lately that some girl's goin' to cripple me business prospects. I never thought it might be a married woman. Still, you can't be after my money, so I'll take you over to the pub and you can have a ham sandwich.'

'Tck, tck, Sammy.'

'Apologies,' said Sammy, 'no ham, of course not. Cheese, then, or cold beef, though I can't promise it'll be kosher. With a Guinness. You sure Benjamin won't mind?'

'Only if you run off with me.' Rachel's smile was sweetly lush and very teasing. 'I'll accept what the pub has to offer. With a light ale. Guinness is fattening.'

'All right, come if you must,' said Sammy. 'By the way, who's paying?'

Rachel's laugh was rich with amusement.

Lizzy was waiting for Chinese Lady to arrive for an afternoon cup of tea and a family chat. Although heavy with child, Lizzy felt life was being very good to her. She loved her house. Her front room, bright with light, its armchairs and sofa cosy, provided a view of the avenue and the houses opposite. There were flowering trees from one end of the avenue to the other, and the wild cherry right outside the front gate was a profusion of blossom in the spring. Most of the houses were bordered by green privet hedges. Lizzy liked the suburban atmosphere, despised though it was by Bloomsbury intellectuals who referred to the growing number of suburbanites as Britain's boring bourgeoisie. Chinese Lady, coming across a pertinent quotation in her daily newspaper, had to ask Boots what it meant. Boots said it meant people who liked being respectable, planting their own daffodil bulbs and minding their own business. Chinese Lady couldn't see what was boring about having your own daffodil bulbs come up or being respectable instead of going in for hooliganism. Did them arty-crafty people actually think it was wrong for people to be respectable?

Boots said yes. Chinese Lady asked if that was a joke. Boots said it was no joke, that Russian Bolsheviks who liked shooting the bourgeoisie were currently all the rage with arty-crafty people. Chinese Lady said kindly don't mention them bloodthirsty Bolsheviks in her house, it was bad enough knowing some of them were lurking about in London, waiting to throw bombs at King George and Queen Mary. It was a pity they couldn't take to being respectable, then there'd be a bit more peace in the world. Boots said Chinese Lady ought to be Prime Minister. Chinese Lady asked if that was another joke. Boots said it was the most serious declaration of his life.

Lizzy, of course, hadn't the slightest idea Bloomsbury people wrote unkind things about her. It was simply a pleasure and a treat, after years in a Walworth back street, to live in a road with trees and to actually have a bathroom. The houses had been built by enterprising pioneers of suburban development before the war, when working people were beginning to better their way of living and to be able to afford to rent such places. Ned and Lizzy's neighbours were nearly all people who had managed to escape the smoke and grime of inner

341

London, and they'd done wonders with their gardens considering they hadn't known the first thing about the cultivation of flowers and vegetables.

Not far along the avenue was the empty house Lizzy had mentioned to Boots. He and Emily were going to take a look at it. Lizzy hoped they'd have it, as it would be nice with them and Chinese Lady living only a dozen doors from her and Ned. And winter fogs here weren't quite as thick and yellow as in Walworth.

After Chinese Lady arrived, she and Lizzy began to enjoy a gossipy chat over tea and biscuits. Annabelle was upstairs, playing with a friend from next door. It had been a very rainy morning, and the garden was wet, the afternoon humid. Chinese Lady told Lizzy exactly what had befallen the little girl Rosie.

'I did say it could be for the best, but Boots has took it hard, I can tell you. He's not been a bit conversable, he's been spending his time paintin' more cupboards and doors, though I don't know what for if we're goin' to move. Mind you, Lizzy, there's something to be thankful for, he's not givin' me too much of his comic stuff. He went out to see some old Army friends last night, he said. Em'ly couldn't have liked it very much, but she never said anything. Well, I suppose he does have some good points, and no one could say people complain about him. He's not always acting Frenchified.'

'Oh, I expect Em'ly enjoys his Frenchified ways,' said Lizzy, tongue in cheek.

'What?' asked Chinese Lady.

'It's a shame about Rosie, though,' said Lizzy, 'Boots was real gone on her. I was sure he and Em'ly would adopt her.'

'No, Lizzy love, they couldn't of done that, you have to get the consent of the parents, and who can lay their hands on them, I'd like to know. Where Rosie's wretched mother is, or her father, is a mystery.' Chinese Lady fortified herself with several sips of tea before divulging, in low tones, the next piece of news. 'It's hard to say so, Lizzy, and don't let it go no further for the poor child's sake, but Mr Tooley told us his daughter wasn't married, that she didn't know exactly who the father was, she'd had unlawful relations with – with – well, never mind about that, it don't bear thinking of, let along talkin' about.'

'She was a tart you mean, Mum,' said Lizzy. 'That poor little girl. It's all the more reason why Boots and Em'ly should have been allowed to keep her. It wouldn't have worried Boots, and I bet with Sammy's help he'd have handled everything just right, I bet they'd have wangled a birth certificate to make it look right too. Boots don't care much for the do's and don'ts of civil service regulations.'

'I don't think you should talk like that, Lizzy, I didn't bring any of you up to perform unlegal acts.'

'Oh, wangling don't count, Mum, not when it's done with a good heart for a good cause. Still, it won't happen now Rosie's been taken away. Em'ly's probably – well, d'you know if she's clicked yet?'

'Clicked?' asked Chinese Lady suspiciously.

'Yes, you know, has she clicked yet for her first baby? Only that would make up for losing Rosie.'

'Lizzy, it's nice you turnin' out ladylike and all, but I don't know it's ladylike to say clicked when you're talkin' about something that comes from the blessing of God. You mean is Em'ly expectin'. Well, she hasn't said anything to me. Yes, I'll have another cup, love, then I think I'll just go and look at that house that's up for renting. Of course, I don't want to make up Boots's mind for him, not when he's nearly reachin' full-grown manhood.'

'I thought he'd reached it,' smiled Lizzy, 'during the war, like, him and Ned both.'

'Lizzy, how can you say such a thing? Boots was hardly old enough to be out of school when he joined Kitchener's Army. No wonder he did it behind my back,

343

he knew if I'd caught him volunteering at his age, I'd of boxed his silly ears till he'd come to his senses. Still, he did win some medals.' Chinese Lady mused. Lizzy smiled. Chinese Lady always relished talking about her only oldest son, hiding her affection for him under prim maternal carping. 'I expect your dad would of been proud of him, though I can't say medals ever did anyone any good. Anyway, I'll go and look at that house.'

'I'll come with you,' said Lizzy, 'we both ought to help Boots make up his mind, you know how airy-fairy he is.'

'Em'ly'll make up both their minds if she likes it enough, Lizzy. But I don't think you ought to come, not the way you are.'

'Oh, little walks do me good,' said Lizzy, 'even if I do have to carry all before me.'

Chinese Lady, remembering Lizzy's first had been premature, was really not too sure she should allow it, but Lizzy insisted she'd like a little outing. She called Annabelle and her friend down to join the walk, being quite against leaving small children alone in a house, even for five minutes. Someone would be bound to have an accident, or set the place on fire.

'Lizzy, you're not goin' like that, are you?' questioned Chinese Lady when everyone was ready. 'Not with nothing on, are you?'

'Nothing on?' said Lizzy, bulky in a loose dress.

'You ought to wear a coat.'

'A coat won't hide it, Mum, and it's too hot, anyway. Come on, it's only down the road.'

The two small girls scampered ahead. Certainly, it was not very far, but Chinese Lady was sure they would meet someone, and an expectant mother advertising her advanced condition was hardly the most decent thing.

The house was detached, with a central door and bay windows up and down. There was a path of crazy paving, a little front garden, a wrought-iron gate and a privet hedge lately neglected and in need of a trim.

Chinese Lady, inspecting the look of the house, thought it would suit Emily and Boots very nicely, and it was for sale or rent. Of course, they couldn't buy it, it was probably over three hundred pounds, but the rent shouldn't be more than a pound a week. She paid fourteen shillings for the Walworth house.

'It's nice, Lizzy.'

'Yes, they ought to take it,' said Lizzy, and Chinese Lady felt pleased her daughter and Ned wanted Boots and Emily to live near them. Most relatives got on better living as far apart as possible. Relatives could get very touchy with each other. But Boots and Emily were Lizzy and Ned's best friends.

Chinese Lady thought there couldn't be anything more suitable in Brixton. Annabelle and her friend peeped at the house through the wrought-iron gate. And Lizzy was suddenly biting her lip.

'Mum,' she said, a little agitated, 'I think we'd best go back.'

'Oh, my,' said Chinese Lady, and linked her arm with her daughter's.

'I think I'm goin' to have to telephone the doctor. It's a blessing Ned had us put on the phone when he did.'

'Yes, all right, Lizzy love. Don't worry now. It's not far, you can hold on, I know you can. Don't hurry, walk nice and steady on my arm. That's it. The children are following. You'll manage. You gettin' any contractions?'

'Twinges, Mum, and a feeling. And after the doctor said I was a good carrier too. I believe he only said that so's I wouldn't worry. Oh, lor', ain't I a silly girl?'

'Of course you're not, love, but oh my, you are a one for wantin' your babies to come early, aren't you?'

Earlier that afternoon, at five minutes to one, when Boots was about to shut the shop for early closing, a young woman came in.

'Hello, old sport,' said Miss Polly Simms, fashionably

clad in a mauve dress and a close-fitting hat of maroon. She smiled forgivingly. Her mouth was delicately shaped with lipstick, her teeth were white, her eyes soft with amusement.

'Ah,' said Boots.

'We meet again, you devious beast,' said Polly. 'You diddled me last time. You sent a boy instead of coming yourself. What a stinker. My father said I could have you shot, for cowardice.'

'Your father's a general, I was told,' said Boots.

'Oh, not one of those, darling, I assure you. He was nearly executed at dawn once or twice himself. By Haig. For raising fiery hell about attritional warfare. You'd like him. Of course, you'd have to serve up exceptional apologies for giving me the raspberry. But I think you'd end up friends.'

'What can I get you?' asked Boots, not in the mood for a frivolous dialogue. He still had Rosie on his mind. It was bad enough to have lost her. It was worse to have seen her go in such quiet sadness. 'You've got a minute to make up your mind. Then I'm closing.'

'I say, are we a teeny bit grumpy today?' asked Polly. 'Just so-so.'

Polly looked for some sign of his usual good humour. But he was almost po-faced. That did not lessen her interest in him. Far from it.

'What's up, old thing?' she asked.

'Some days aren't as good as other days,' said Boots.

'God, don't I know it,' she said. 'Can I help?'

'I don't actually need a Wolseley ambulance,' said Boots.

'Bloody hell,' said Polly, 'what do I have to do to get you to like me?'

'Nothing,' said Boots, 'I do like you. I like all ambulance drivers, past and present. Now kindly state what you're after. A pair of braces?'

'Yuk to braces,' said Polly, 'my French pretties are self-supporting.' She glided. 'Robert old dear, what are these?'

346

'A new line just in. Ready-to-wear suits.'

Polly stared at serge suits in dark blue and dark grey on hangers.

'People actually do wear them?' she asked.

'For twenty-one shillings.'

'Ghastly, even at that price.'

'Not to our customers,' said Boots.

'Don't, you're breaking my heart,' said Polly. 'Oh, that my most droll Tommy should have sunk so low. And what are these?'

'Another new line. Flannel shirts. One and nine-pence, with two free collars.'

'A shirt is a shirt is a shirt,' said Polly, taking off Gertrude Stein, the post-war novelist and verbal eccentric. 'Except these. They're unspeakable. Oh, my God, and look at these. You swine, you're selling khaki bloomers.'

'Hoppit,' said Boots.

'Stop being filthy to me. Actually, these things are old friends of mine. I wore two pairs at a time in the French winters. Listen, would you mind not walking about as if I'm not here? I've come to sweeten you. Stepmother Mama was so delighted with the quality of the blankets and other stuff that she's decided to have new bedding altogether, and to chuck out the second-hand junk. The orphanage is opening next month, for forty orphans, and I've a list of what she wants you to supply for four dormitories, including mattresses and bolsters. You'd never believe what's there now. It wasn't donated, it was dumped on Mama. But she's been using her wiles to get cheques out of plutocratic war profiteers, so the orphanage is in funds and she's set on providing the orphans with first-class dormitory comfort. Now you will deal with me, won't you? I don't think I want you having too much to do with Mama in case she takes you up as a good cause. She's dotty on good causes. Are you with me? Do say something.'

'D'you need me to?' said Boots. 'You're doing very well by yourself.'

'Oh, dear,' said Polly, 'am I offending you in trying to bring a little business to you?'

'Is it genuine or larky?' asked Boots.

'Look, I might lark about with everyone else – well, you can't take this mess of a post-war Arcadia seriously, can you? – but never with my Tommies. Here's Mama's list of requirements. Sheets, blankets, mattresses, everything. Do let me know if and when you can supply, old love. My phone number's included.'

Boots took a sheet of notepaper from her and scanned it. Polly examined him with renewed interest. He was different, of course. That was an old chestnut, someone who was different. But he was quite unlike any of her noisy, extrovert friends who chased about in search of the bright new world that was to make up for the monstrosities of the war. She chased about with them, frequently looking for Utopia in London's night clubs. She did not think this man would go to night clubs in search of something that would tell him the war had been worthwhile. If he was in a more serious mood today, he was still very natural and unaffected, with none of the flamboyance her friends used to draw attention to themselves. He was a survivor of the trenches. That made him special. So many of her Tommies had been special. They had made a comrade of her, and she had felt privileged. Who this man's parents were, and what his background was like, she did not know. Nor did she know if he was married or not. She did not want to know. The merest mention of a wife could discourage the building of a beautiful friendship. He really ought to put this ghastly shop behind him. She could help him in that. With the assistance of influential friends she could turn him from a shopkeeper into a captain of commerce or industry.

He looked up from the list. The light seemed to creep lazily into his left eye.

'I'll speak to my brother,' he said, 'he knows the sources of supply.'

'Jolly good,' said Polly. 'Are you pleased with me now?'

'I'm much obliged,' said Boots.

'Ugh,' said Polly.

'It'll cost a tidy sum of money.'

'Don't be disgusting, I hate talking about money.'

'Yes, well, I might hate it myself if I had sackfuls of it,' said Boots, 'but I haven't, so I don't.'

'Never mind, ducky, you've got sackfuls of everything that's adorable. Must dash now, I've a friend to meet in town. Don't forget to ring me about supply and delivery.'

'Of course.'

Polly smiled. She was quite prepared to take her time to make him fall in love with her.

'Toodle-oo, old dear,' she said.

CHAPTER TWENTY-SIX

Boots left the shop ten minutes later. He had to go to Shoreditch, Sammy being engaged elsewhere. There was a new order and cash for a previous order to hand to the owner of a tailoring sweatshop. The owner did not like cheques. They disturbed his peace of mind, he said. Banknotes had a more tranquil effect. Boots thought about Rosie during the journey, and also about the fat man. The week's notice was up today. If the shop opened tomorrow, trouble could be expected. Boots had accordingly laid his plans.

He did not think much of the sweatshop, a small factory in which the seamstresses, girls and women, worked in crowded and unhygienic conditions. They were typical of the people of the East End, whose lives were scarred by poverty and privation. Hungry and dark of eye, skin taut over cheekbones, the seamstresses did indeed sweat at their machines in order to take a few shillings home to their families. Yet they had not lost all their natural cockney ebullience, which was evident in the way they greeted Boots as he walked through the muggy factory with the proprietor, Mr Morris.

'Oh, ain't yer loverly, ducks?'

'Oi, mister, can yer give our Gladys five minutes? 'Ere she is.'

'Go on, Glad, drop 'em for the nice gent.'

'Yer, come on, mister, we'll 'old 'er dahn for yer.'

'Glad ain't 'ad no bliss since 'er old man fall orf a ladder 'an bent 'is owjerdo. 'Ave yer, Glad?'

Boots kept a straight face. Mr Morris shook his head warningly, but no one had stopped working while the comments were being flung. No one could afford to.

When Boots left the factory, it was in his mind to tell Sammy that this kind of sweatshop should not be encouraged. But he knew what Sammy would say, that though those women and girls didn't have much of a job, it was better than no job at all these days.

The streets of Shoreditch appeared grimy and dusty in the light of the humid afternoon, the flat-fronted dwellings characterless, but even here some doorsteps looked as if brooms and scrubbing-brushes were used on them. The street kids in the main were more ragged than those of Walworth, and there was a starved, urchinlike look about them that Dickens would have recognised. Women stood gossiping at open front doors, and eyed Boots a little suspiciously as he passed by. He was not only recognisable as a stranger, he was also respectably dressed. Kids emitted catcalls because of his collar and tie. One, more opportunistic than derisory, ran after him.

'Mister, giss a penny, would yer, mister?'

Boots knew that if he gave the little ragamuffin anything at all, a whole horde of kids would be on his tail. But he was not able to squash summarily what he knew was a constant hope of the deprived, a little bit of sunshine on one more drab day.

'I suppose your name's Albert, is it?' he said, keeping to his long stride.

The boy, scampering beside him, said, 'No, course it ain't, mister. Albert's back there.'

'Well, I knew there was an Albert somewhere,' said Boots, approaching the corner of the street, 'there always is.'

'Watcher talkin' about, mister? You got somefink for Albert? Could yer find somefink for me too? An 'a'penny'll do, or a farving.'

Boots turned the corner, the boy with him. Out of

351

sight of the other kids, Boots stopped and fished coins from his pocket. He sorted out coppers. The boy's eyes lit up in his dirty face. Boots saw the predatory gleam, a gleam kindled by the glint of silver among the copper coins. He became deliberate in his actions, waiting for the boy to attempt a snatch. If he did, he would get nothing. The temptation was there, there were no rozzers about, and he was on his home ground. He gave Boots a quick upward glance. A sound right eye met his furtive peepers. He grimaced, wrinkled his snub nose and essayed a grin.

'I ain't goin' to nick from yer, mister, honest.'

'Then I ain't goin' to have to knock yer bonce off, am I?' said Boots, and gave the boy what coppers he had, three pennies and five half-pennies.

'Crikey, yer a toff, you are, mister.'

'All right, sunshine, now buzz off,' said Boots, and went on his way at a fast stride. He caught a tram that took him to the north-east edge of the West End, and walked from there to the Embankment to catch a tram home. Going down Surrey Street, he became aware of an altercation. A group of kerbside musicians, all ex-servicemen, were being requested by a policeman to move on. Two young women were protesting, vigorously. So vigorously that the bobby was reaching for his notebook. With a sweeping gesture of further protest, one young lady knocked it from his hand as soon as it appeared, and Boots had no doubt she would claim it was accidental. A little knot of people looked on in amusement, while the ex-servicemen, with gestures of their own, signalled to both young ladies to make themselves scarce.

The bobby laid an arresting hand on the arm of Miss Polly Simms. Boots recognised her. The other young lady pushed indignantly at the constable, and Polly knocked his helmet off. He lunged after it. Polly stuck out a well-shod foot and he fell over. The other young lady made a dash, and the ex-servicemen opened ranks to let her through. Boots arrived fast. The bobby, on the ground, produced his whistle and blew it. Boots grabbed Polly's wrist.

'I think we'd better get you home, Miss Lloyd George,' he shouted, and yanked her along with him, going back the way he had come, towards the Strand. Polly gasped as she was forced to move at a run. When she overcame her astonishment, her run became delighted flight. The police whistle sounded again.

'Eureka! It's you, you darling man!'

'Never mind that *Girls' Friend* stuff.' *Girls' Friend* was the female equivalent of the *Magnet*, of Harry Wharton and Billy Bunter fame. 'Just run. But walk as soon as we hit the Strand.'

'Yes, dear old darling, whatever—'

'Shut up,' said Boots, pulling her along at speed. There was a third blast on the whistle. Polly, far more exultant than worried, ran fast. They turned the corner and slowed to a walk. Boots let go of her wrist. Polly slipped her arm through his. The moment they reached the restaurant at the beginning of Fleet Street, he took her in. A number of people were being served with tea, but there were several vacant tables, and Boots chose one that could not be seen from the door. They sat down, Polly exhaling triumphant breath.

'Darling, what a lovely meeting of kindred spirits,' she said, her face flushed, her eyes bright. 'Do you know, this is the first time in my life I've been rescued from drowning. You dear, delightful old sport. But I can't say I was too thrilled being mistaken in the first place for Lloyd George's daughter Megan. Is she a love of yours?'

'Kindly be your age,' said Boots.

'Oh, I say, after being Sir Lancelot, you're not going to be grumpy again, are you?'

'I called you Miss Lloyd George to give the bobby a red herring to chase. God knows what the Prime Minister's going to say when constables arrive at

Downing Street to ask for an interview with his daughter.'

Polly's eyes filled with laughter.

'Oh, you clever old sweetie,' she said.

'I hope it works, I don't—' Boots stopped as a waitress came up and asked for their order.

'Champagne,' said Polly.

'Pardon?' said the waitress.

'She means a pot of tea,' said Boots. 'For two.'

'I'll bring a strong pot,' said the waitress, departing in earnest.

'You were saying?' enquired Polly, utterly tickled by the circumstances of the meeting.

'Nothing very much,' said Boots, 'except you need your bottom smacked.'

'Oh, come on, old thing, that's well below your usual standard. And look, I'm never going to pass by on the other side of the street when the hairy arm of the law is applying the order of the hobnailed boot to ex-Tommies trying to earn a few musical pennies.'

'You haven't helped those men by making a fool of the bobby in front of them.'

'Whose side are you on?' asked Polly.

'Theirs.'

'Well, I'm their guardian angel, and as their guardian angel I've been arrested and fined more than once, you know.'

'Silly girl,' said Boots.

'Steady,' said Polly, 'I'm a raw woman under this get-up.' The tea arrived and she poured. 'Some of us have got to stand up and let the public know what a lousy deal old soldiers are getting from the government. The last time I was arrested was for inciting revolution at Speakers Corner in Hyde Park. The magistrate told me I could address people on the supposed benefits of revolution, but not incite it by calling them to march on the House of Commons armed with bricks. He fined me twenty quid. Twenty quid. I nearly told him to take a jump off Nelson's Column, the pompous old bugger. But what good could I do if I opted for Holloway? Darling, you really did rescue me from drowning because he said he'd give me a prison sentence without any option next time.'

'What does your father, the general, think of all this?'

'Loves it,' said Polly, 'can't wait for each episode.'

'Silly old general, then,' said Boots, making the most of the refreshing tea.

'I'll tell him that, I think he'd like you,' said Polly, regarding him affectionately. He was so unflappable, yet a man of instant action. She had experienced total exhilaration when he appeared out of nowhere to set her running from the arms of the law. 'Robert, old love, do you mind that I'm fond of you?' she asked.

'You're fond of something that's over. The war. Go home and forget it.'

'Can you forget it?' she countered. 'I bet you can't. No one who was in it can.'

'I try not to carry it about with me,' said Boots. 'Polly, join the Salvation Army. I'm off now. You stay here and lie low.'

'Certainly not,' said Polly, 'I fight from the front. I'll come with you. But first, is there a ladies' room where I can repair the ravages?' She spoke to a passing waitress, who directed her. 'Shan't be a tick, old scout.'

'Take your time,' said Boots, and left the moment she disappeared. He paid the small bill on the way out.

Discovering his defection when she reappeared, Polly might have shown considerable vexation. Instead she silently laughed. If he had to run away he must be weakening.

Boots got off the tram and walked down Browning Street in a reflective mood. The August heat dragged at Walworth. A street cleaner mopped his brow with his shirt sleeve. An empty dustcart, its horse plodding, exuded the stale odour common to all such vehicles. A boy with patched shorts called after the driver.

'Oi, Mister Pong, yer don't arf smell of sweet violets.'

In Caulfield Place, boys and girls were playing hop-scotch on the pavement, and despite everything their mothers had done to keep them clean, the inescapable grime was winning the battle as usual.

It was time to leave. The house, the Place, the Walworth Road shops, the East Street market and the church all had their memories for the family, memories that were not unhappy, but it was time to go, to give Emily and Chinese Lady a chance to breathe cleaner air, and to relieve Chinese Lady of her daily round of drudgery. It was drudgery, the constant fight a house-proud woman fought against the smoke and dust of Walworth. It depressed her sometimes, but she never gave up.

He and Emily must go and look over the house near Lizzy and Ned. Emily, he knew, would almost certainly say yes to it, if only because it would put her in close touch with Lizzy, her lifelong friend. Emily's decision would be deserving of support.

The front door, that he wanted to paint cream, looked a dour, melancholy brown, as if it was grimly and sadly resigned to its discouraging colour. That made him think again of little Rosie's sadness.

Entering the kitchen, he knew at once that Chinese Lady was not at home. It was rare to find her absent, and her absence was always a tangible thing. It could be felt. She was the arbiter and protector of family life, fussy, maternal, critical, funny, caring and providing. Yes, it was time for her to have a little garden to sit in on summer days, and to hang out her Monday washing in air less sooty than Walworth's. She was probably sitting in Lizzy's garden now, prolonging her visit. He wondered if there was any point in doing any more painting.

Whether there was or wasn't, he was rubbing down

the door of the bedroom he shared with Emily a few minutes later.

Emily, coming in from work, found Boots busy upstairs. He was hardly decent. It was hot all right, but to have stripped down to just his short underpants was a bit much. Even his feet were bare.

'Well, I don't know,' she said, 'if someone comes and sees you like that, they'll have fits.'

'I've been hoping Gladys Cooper might turn up and take advantage of me.'

'You'll be lucky,' said Emily. 'Look, what you doin' that door for? It's a waste of time. Or ain't we goin' to move?'

'We're going to move, Em. No harm, though, in leaving our bedroom door looking pretty, and it's something to do. How about a pot of tea? Chinese Lady's not back from Lizzy's yet.'

'You make it if you want it,' said Emily, 'I just finished a hard day's work.'

'I have made a few pots in this house, Em, about ten thousand. Has it been a bad day at the town hall, lovey, as well as a hard one?'

'It's not that,' said Emily. 'You're so airy-fairy. You could've come to meet me, it would've been nice walkin' home together. Or better still, you could've gone from the shop to look at that house in Lizzy's road.'

'I thought we ought to look at it together.' Boots gave her an enquiring look. Emily, straight-faced, stood up to it. He tried a smile. 'Well, we're together now, with the house to ourselves. Would you like a little fun?'

'No, I wouldn't. And it's not fun any more, anyway.'

Boots looked astonished.

'Emily?'

'Well, it's not, not for me. It's all right for you, but every time we do it I'm left worrying about if – well, if we've made a baby. And now Rosie's gone, I've got

357

all the worries and anxieties of feeling responsible for givin' you a fam'ly.'

'Giving me a family? Worries and anxieties?' His astonishment took on a perturbed note. 'Emily, for heaven's sake, where did you get that from? I don't want you to look at our life like that, I don't want to cause you worries and anxieties. You're my Emily—'

'But you want us to have a fam'ly, don't you?'

Boots looked as if he was worried now, badly.

'Emily, isn't that what you want too?'

'Boots, honest, it's been nice since your operation, seeing you not dependent on no one but yerself, and enjoying being manager at the shop. It's made me able to enjoy me own job. But trying like we keep doing to start a fam'ly, it's depressing me.'

'Depressing you?'

'Yes.' Emily was making a stand, Mrs Stevens's words of advice still fresh in her mind.

'Jesus,' said Boots.

'You got to consider my feelings.'

'I honestly had no idea your feelings were all worries and anxieties, lovey. We'll give it a rest, shall we?'

'Give what a rest?'

'Love-making. Trying to make babies. Trying to start a family. We'll give it a month's rest, shall we? Or longer, if you like.'

'Boots, that's really nice of you. But—' Emily paused. He woke up sometimes, when they were warm and dreamy and close, and she in her dreaminess was willing. 'Well, it'll be – well, it won't be easy for you.'

'Jesus,' said Boots again, realising she actually favoured abstention from love-making, that he was a worry to her in bed, and no longer a pleasure. 'You have my promise, Emily. We'll give it a long rest.' His forced smile was a wry grimace. His natural male ego had taken an unexpected hammering.

'Oh, it's only till I get over me silly feelings,' she said, 'really it is.' But she was thinking she could take an autumn shorthand course at Pitman's in London. She knew Mrs Stevens would be pleased if she did. And her job was such a satisfying part of her life now. 'Boots, you mustn't mind too much about me feelings, except I like yer for being so nice and considerate.'

'Worries and anxieties,' said Boots in stunned disbelief. 'Jesus Christ.'

'Oh, don't take it like that,' said Emily.

'I'll put some trousers on and make some tea,' he said, 'and would you like to go and look at that house this evening? We shan't be able to get the keys, but we can see what it looks like from the outside.'

'I'd love to,' said Emily, and gave him a kiss to show there were no hard feelings.

A little absently, he said, 'Where's Chinese Lady got to, I wonder?'

Chinese Lady did not get home until twenty to seven. Tommy was in, Sammy not yet back from a long day out on business.

'Oh, thank goodness,' said Emily, 'we been gettin' downright worried, Mum.'

'Lizzy had a turn,' said Chinese Lady. 'We were out, lookin' at that empty house, and Lizzy thought the baby had started. Well, Annabelle was a month early, remember, and we both thought this one was goin' to be three weeks. Still,' she said proudly, 'Lizzy didn't get into no panic, she came back to her house with me good as gold, and telephoned the doctor. I'd of done it myself if I'd had to, even though them contraptions frighten me to death. They're not natural. Lizzy kept havin' twinges, and fits and starts, but by the time the doctor come I'd got to feeling they were all false alarms, which they were, he said. He said she was carrying very nice this time, but he thought not more than another week. Boots, is there salt in the potatoes, and did you put mint in the peas, Em'ly?'

'All done,' said Boots, turning plump sausages in the frying-pan. 'How is Lizzy now?'

'Feeling a bit unsettled, I bet,' said Tommy.

'No, she's all right now,' said Chinese Lady, 'the doctor put her mind at rest, and the district nurse will be poppin' in regular. I stayed with her till Ned come home, and you should of seen him, fussin' about like some old hen, which made Lizzy laugh and perked her up no end.'

'Emily and I will look in on her this evening,' said Boots in sober vein, 'we're going out after supper to see what that house is like. If we fancy it, Emily will get the keys from the agents on Saturday afternoon and see what it's like inside.'

'Yes, you ought to make up your minds about it,' said Chinese Lady, 'it looks very nice from the outside. It won't take long for Em'ly to make up her mind, I'm sure. She's not as airy-fairy as you are, Boots.'

'Still, Boots is very considerate,' said Emily.

When they returned from their excursion, Sammy was home. They reported that they liked the house very much, and that Lizzy was fine. Boots said he'd leave the decision to Emily after she had inspected the interior on Saturday afternoon.

Boots spoke privately to Sammy later, giving him the list of requirements for the orphanage dormitories.

'Can you get everything?'

'If I can't, my name ain't Sammy Adams. Good on yer, Boots, you've done a good job with yer charm on the orphanage lady's daughter. Look, about tomorrow—'

'Just keep out of the way,' said Boots brusquely.

'All right, keep yer shirt on,' said Sammy, 'you've put me out considerable as it is by handin' me the junior-ship. You sure you know what you're doing concerning Big Ben? His lot ain't goin' to be weaklings.'

'Nor are my lot,' said Boots.

He lay awake for some time beside Emily that night.

The next day was an uncomfortable one for Susie. Mister Sammy made a brief appearance at the stall a little after ten, and said only a casual good morning to her before going off again. Whenever he was like that, Susie thought it was to do with some failing of hers. Then there were several men who kept appearing and reappearing. She spoke to Mister Tommy about them. They kept coming and looking, she said, as if they had ideas about pinching everything off the stall.

Tommy had been told by Boots there might be developments. If so, he was to do nothing, he was to keep out of the way. Tommy knew it all concerned Sammy's health, so he asked no questions. He gave Susie a reassuring smile.

'Don't worry,' he said, 'they're probably men from the Ministry of Markets.'

'I never 'eard of no Ministry of Markets,' said Susie.

'You sure?' said Tommy.

'Course I'm sure,' said Susie, 'I can read and write, yer know.'

'Then I'm glad for yer, Susie, and it's no wonder Sammy thinks the world of yer.'

'No, 'e don't,' said Susie.

Sammy turned up again in the afternoon, Boots refusing to let him hang about in the shop or use his office, while Fred Scribbins had politely requested him to take himself off from the yard as per instructions from his eldest brother.

'I asks yer, guv, with all due respect, and without h'intimatin' I 'as less obedience to you than yer eldest brother. It's just that it's for yer own sake, like.'

Boots had also put the stall out of bounds to Sammy, but Sammy, feeling restless and also certain that not being in direct contact with any of his ventures was costing him money, wandered into the market again. He asked Tommy how he was doing.

'Reasonable,' said Tommy, 'reasonable. But since you're not supposed to be here, you'd better push off. Susie's seeing faces.'

'Well, she would, wouldn't she, with the eyes she's got,' said Sammy.

'Yes, pretty blue, ain't they?' said Tommy artfully. 'Like cornflowers or forget-me-nots.'

Susie, dealing with shoppers, heard none of these murmured words, but she was very aware of Mister Sammy's presence. Seeing her customers off with a smile, she gave him a tentative look.

'Well, I can't stop, Tommy,' he said, 'so long.' Nothing had been mentioned about possible happenings.

'Excuse me,' said Susie, 'but I'm 'ere too, Mister Sammy, in case yer 'aven't noticed.'

'Yes, good afternoon, Miss Brown,' said Sammy, and went restlessly off again.

'Oh, would yer believe 'e could treat me so scurvy!' exclaimed Susie.

'Scurfy?' said Tommy.

'Scurvy,' said Susie. 'It means without Christian kindness.'

'Susie, you got him scared down to his socks,' said Tommy.

Which was a great puzzle to Susie.

Boots answered the shop telephone at twenty to five.

'Sarge? Mitch 'ere. In me uncle's Kennington fish shop. They're on their way, we reckon. A mob of 'em.'

'All right, Mitch. You can go in now.'

'Right, very good, sarge. Prisoner to be 'eld in custody, under armed guard, like you said.'

'What're you armed with, you Turk, sandbags?'

'Elbows and 'obnails, sarge.'

'I'll expect his own sets of hobnails about closing time. I thought that might be the moment.'

'Reckon you thought right. Well, we'll look forward to seeing yer, sarge. At your convenience.'

362

* * *

Just before the shop was due to close, four men in caps and mufflers walked in. There was only Boots. They locked the door from the inside.

'Come in,' said Boots.

'Don't get in the way, cully,' said the leader, 'then yer won't 'ave to get yer bones fixed. All right, lads, start work.'

'Just a moment,' said Boots and whistled. The door of the stock room opened and eight men filed out. They all bore wooden cudgels. An ex-corporal of the East Surreys gave the order.

'Right, advance in line, East Surreys. Objective dead ahead. No prisoners.'

The East Surreys charged. The shop was strangely clear of stock at its centre, and it was at the centre that Big Ben's hirelings were beaten flat to the floor. Caps fell off, bare heads were thumped. Blood flowed.

'Would yer believe it,' panted one East Surrey, 'this one's bloody bleedin' and we ain't hardly started yet.'

The mob of four fought and cursed amid the flailing cudgels. Boots, standing by, called a halt.

'Dusty,' he said to the ex-corporal, 'get their names and addresses. Then let 'em go. Lock the door when you leave, and give the keys back to me later, in the pub.'

'Names and addresses, right, sarge. Lock up, right. Report to you in the pub. Right, sarge.'

They were hard, lean-muscled and enduring, these men who had once belonged to a battalion of the East Surrey Regiment, and they would do for an ex-comrade of the West Kents what they wouldn't do for most other people. They knew why he wanted the names and addresses of the roughnecks. Not to give the details to the police, but to know where to find them and their families. Which would give them food for thought. Sergeants were sergeants because they knew all the questions and all the answers too. And

363

they knew how to deal with emergencies.

A similar pattern of events followed at the scrap yard. Nothing happened to the stall, but when Fred pushed it from the market to the yard, two men emerged from the street that lay next to Olney Road and followed at a distance. And four other men, those whom Susie had glimpsed from time to time in the market, and who had followed Fred all the way, kept their own distance in the rear. Fred turned into Olney Road. The yard was a little way down, its large spiked wooden gates closed, but not padlocked. He called to his apprentice to open up. The first two men hurried, and as the apprentice pulled the gates open, two more men came at a run from Draco Street, almost opposite the yard, mufflers around their faces as a disguise. Fred suddenly found himself being bruisingly harassed at the moment when he was pushing the stall into the yard. Four men, all with their faces covered, had arrived to smash up the yard, the stall and the china and glass. Fred, of course, had been expecting them. One man shoved the apprentice aside and made to close the gates. But the entrance was suddenly blocked by four more men, the men who had kept protective eyes on the stall all day in the market. They had served during the war with the West Kents.

'All right, you buggers, we'll close the gates,' said the man in charge. 'You watch your backs. You've got a platoon of East Surreys comin' at your rear with fixed bayonets.'

From the large, brick-built yard hut emerged several more men, men who had also kept watch all day. There were no bayonets, however, just wooden cudgels.

The gates were quietly closed, and the men of the trenches went into action. It was child's play compared with going over the top.

Mr Ben Ford, known as Big Ben or Fatty, and called King of the Fat by Rachel, the only girl friend Sammy had ever had, owned a dour-looking building in one of Kennington's drabber streets near Upper Marsh. But his office on the first floor, fully carpeted, was quite sumptuous. He liked an atmosphere of plush comfort. Immediately below, on the ground floor, was a plain little office exclusive to the tall, broad man whom Boots had noticed on the occasion when Fatty had called with a message for Sammy. He was Fatty's personal factotum.

At this present moment he was sitting in his chair and bound to it, a gag in his mouth, an ex-serviceman taking care of him and advising any callers that Mr Ford was out. Mr Ford was very much in, his huge bulk encased by his vast desk chair. Three of Boots's old comrades had kept him confined there since a little before five to await the arrival of ex-Sergeant Adams. Boots, there now, was talking to him.

'So you see, it's all led to more damage, Mr Ford. There's blood all over your hired labourers. It's messy.'

'Get on with it, sonny,' wheezed the fat man, beady eyes suffused.

'In my family,' said Boots, 'we don't like any of us coming home looking damaged. I particularly don't like damage being done to my youngest brother. Even more particularly, my mother doesn't like it. Hooliganism upsets her. Kindly don't do it again.' Boots seemed in pleasant, reasonable voice, but his eyes were icy, the left one discerning the fat man as a foggy lump. 'If you do, you'll suffer damage yourself. My friends will wrap you in a coil of barbed wire and roll you all the way down Brixton Hill. At night. Do you understand?'

'I'm beginning not to like you,' said the gross Mr Ford, looking as if he was having trouble drawing breath, 'and I'd appreciate it if you'd get yourself run over by a train.'

'Do you understand, Mr Ford?' asked Boots again.

'I'm not deaf. All right, so Sammy can get you to call up the Army, but tell him I'll undercut his shop and his scrap until he's crying his eyes out. You tell him that, sonny.'

'I'll tell him,' said Boots, 'he'll accept that as allowable competition.'

'And tell him you're more bloody aggravating than he is.'

'Dear oh lor',' said the man called Mitch, an ex-corporal, 'shall I cop 'im one, sarge? I don't like to hear 'im talkin' to you like that.'

'Leave him,' said Boots, 'let's go and meet the others.'

They all met in a pub at the Elephant and Castle, where Boots received the shop keys and two lists containing names and addresses for future reference, if required. Nobby Clark, the blind ex-serviceman, had produced for Boots twenty-one men formerly of the West Kents and East Surreys. Some of them were unemployed, and some had given up a day's wages. Boots bought a pint of beer for each man, including Nobby, and he talked about what he owed them. Two quid apiece, plus reimbursement for those who had lost wages.

'Just the lost wages,' said Mitch.

'Don't talk like that,' said Boots.

'No one's asked for anything.'

'I've not asked them to ask. I laid down the terms with Nobby, so don't give me any rhubarb, corporal. It wasn't a romantic reunion, with everyone having to bring their own sandwiches. You did a job. You get paid. Two quid for each man, plus any lost wages. Nobby agreed.'

'He's right, it's fair do's,' said Nobby.

'Bleedin' sergeants,' said Mitch, 'I never met one that didn't want the last word, like some old woman. No offence, sarge, that's not personal. All right, fair do's then.'

'Much obliged,' said Boots, 'and don't have any hard feelings if I say thanks very much.'

'Sorry I missed it all,' said Nobby, 'but that's the trouble when yer can't see.'

Boots paid him too.

CHAPTER TWENTY-SEVEN

When Boots finally arrived home, he had a disappointment for Emily. The house near Lizzy and Ned had already been spoken for. He had telephoned the agents from the shop to ask about picking up the keys, and they had informed him there was no point. Emily's face fell, but she at once bucked up and said they'd soon find somewhere else now they'd really made up their minds.

'Ought to have gone after the place quicker,' said Chinese Lady, also disappointed. 'But what's made you so late home, Boots?'

'Oh, business,' said Boots.

'You been up to something,' said Chinese Lady. Sammy and Tommy kept quiet. No one was going to tell her about the fat man. She'd raise the roof.

'Just looking after the interests of the shop, old girl,' said Boots. Emily took that unsuspectingly. Chinese Lady did not.

'What's that mean?' she asked. She could read all her sons.

'Oh, and I did run into some Army friends,' said Boots by way of a disarming answer.

Chinese Lady, whose pleasant looks became progressively more pleasant as money worries progressively receded, took on a thoughtful air. The interests of the shop. Old Army friends. That was the second mention of them in a few days. Then there was Sammy's injurious condition.

'Robert Alfred Adams,' she said magisterially, 'have you been up to hooliganism?'

'Pardon?' said Boots.

'Yer can't mean Boots, Chinese Lady,' said Tommy.

'Not after we paid for him to be educated, Ma,' said Sammy, 'and turned him into a gent.'

'I was askin' Boots, not you,' said Chinese Lady. 'I wouldn't like to think our Em'ly had to put up with a husband who was a hooligan as well as irreverent.'

'Mum, Boots would never be a disgrace like that,' said Emily, feeling loving towards her husband because he'd been so considerate of her feelings. 'And I don't mind his irreverence.'

'Well, I just like to know what's goin' on in this fam'ly,' said Chinese Lady, 'specially when Tommy and Sammy is sittin' there lookin' like I don't know what.'

'I give you my word, Chinese Lady, that in looking after the interests of the shop, I haven't raised a finger in anger,' said Boots quite truthfully.

'You and your old Army friends,' said Chinese Lady, which was as good a shot as she could have fired.

Boots spoke to Sammy and Tommy later.

'Well, I got to say it, you did a highly professional bit of work,' said Sammy, 'and I don't mind Big Ben trying his hand at price-cuttin'.'

'You got some helpful Army friends, Boots,' said Tommy.

'Cheap at the price, Tommy,' said Boots.

'What price?' asked Sammy.

'Fifty-three quid in all,' said Boots.

'It cost yer that much?' said Sammy, aghast.

'Not me, you bonehead. The shop till.'

'Oh, yer conniving bleeder,' gasped Sammy, 'that's gross profit for a week.'

'Nett,' said Boots.

Cousin Vi wrote in answer to Tommy's letter, saying she'd love to meet him at the Golden Domes cinema on Saturday evening. She didn't say her mother had been dubious about her going out with someone who was only a cousin and ran a stall. Vi, with the help of her dad, had overcome that objection.

Chinese Lady said what a nice surprise it was to hear Tommy was taking Vi to the pictures. Boots said it was a surprise to him that it was a surprise to her. Chinese Lady said kindly don't talk in comical riddles.

'Emily, you're looking pleased with yourself,' said Madge Stevens. 'No more problems?'

'Oh, I had a talk with my husband,' said Emily impulsively.

'Good,' said Madge. 'You look as if you won the argument.'

'Oh, there wasn't no argument, not really,' said Emily. Her worries had been lifted. Boots was being very understanding, he wasn't making any advances to her in bed, advances that led to the act that put her on edge about its hoped-for consequences. He was keeping his promise. It was such a relief, except that once or twice she'd felt uncomfortable, as if she was the one who was being selfish and not Boots. 'He was very considerate of my feelings.'

'That's a welcome change, a considerate husband,' said Madge, whose job made her blissfully independent of men. 'But was he shocked to find you could stand up for yourself?'

'No, he just seemed surprised about me havin' me own wishes and feelings,' said Emily.

'I'm sure,' said Madge, 'not many of them think we have feelings of our own, or even minds of our own.'

'Mrs Stevens, you don't think I'm being a bit mean, do you, talkin' about my husband like this with you?' Emily was suddenly troubled by the feeling that it was mean.

'I think it's a great relief for a young wife to be able to talk to someone.'

'Well, yes, it is, really,' said Emily. She had overlooked

Chinese Lady, who would have given her far better advice than Madge Stevens. Madge, consciously or unconsciously, was driving a wedge between husband and wife. 'I been thinking, Mrs Stevens, about could I go in for an autumn shorthand course.'

'Why not? At Pitman's in London?'

'Yes,' said Emily.

'That won't be any problem, Emily,' smiled Madge, and gently patted her arm.

Tommy had a very friendly time with Vi at the cinema. They bought fish and chips afterwards, and ate them out of the newspaper wrapping while Tommy walked Vi home. He thought Vi really quite sweet, and a whole lot nicer than girls like Lily Fuller. Aunt Victoria thanked him for bringing her daughter home, but didn't invite him to stay for a cup of tea, as Chinese Lady would have done.

Sammy came home one day with a large cardboard box, from which he unloaded a gramophone and a trumpet.

'What's that?' asked Chinese Lady, coming in from the scullery.

'A gramophone,' said Sammy, fixing the trumpet and fitting the handle.

'I can see that. I mean, what's it doing on the table when we're just servin' supper? Take it off, and take your hat off too.'

Sammy placed his hat and the gramophone on the closed top of the sewing-machine.

'There's a record,' he said, extracting one from its paper sleeve. 'His Master's Voice. I'll treat you to some supper music, this being a highly distinguished music fam'ly.'

'Leave that contraption and sit down, if your hands are clean,' said Chinese Lady. 'We don't want none of that tinny jangling over supper. Supper's for talkin' together, not for playing contraptions.'

370

'Oh, let's give it one go, Ma,' said Sammy. 'What d'yer say, Em'ly?'

'Well,' said Emily, who rarely went against Chinese Lady. 'Well, just one side of the record, couldn't we, Mum?'

'What with them unnatural telephones and these tinny contraptions,' said Chinese Lady, ladling crisp-looking sliced runner beans onto plates from a steaming colander, 'we'll end up upsettin' our Maker, I shouldn't wonder. Still, you can play one side for Em'ly, Sammy, and could you all kindly sit down while your supper's still hot?'

Sammy put the record on, wound the handle, released the turntable catch and placed the steel needle in the groove. The record began to emit the strains of the popular song, 'I'm Forever Blowing Bubbles'. Sammy sat down with the others, a businessman's satisfied smile on his face.

'How about that, Boots?' he said.

Boots, tackling his mutton chop, looked slightly bleak. The sound of a gramophone always took him back to the trenches. Nearly every dugout had its gramophone, on which the same records were played over and over again to relieve the monotony of waiting periods. His bleakness had its extra edge. He was affected, acutely, by the change in Emily's attitude towards their more intimate relationship. He knew she liked her job. He was beginning to suspect she liked it more than the prospect of having children. He could not relate such a change to his old Emily, his eager, loving Emily.

'You dreamin', Boots?' said Tommy.

'Oh, the gramophone,' said Boots. 'Yes, it's a fairly familiar thing to me.'

The record played on.

They fly so high, nearly reach the sky,
Then like my dreams, they fade and die . . .'

Chinese Lady, resolute in her loyalty to the family piano, said, 'Sounds like empty cocoa tins jangling about.'

'I'm forever blowing bubbles, pretty bubbles in the air . . .'

Sammy, eating healthily, said, 'What d'you think of them for the shop, Boots? And I might put a few on the stall, Tommy.'

'Gramophones?' said Tommy.

'Bought two hundred and fifty,' said Sammy. 'Fred's taken delivery of 'em at the yard this afternoon. I made the desirable purchase of same at a surplus sale on Friday. Supposed to have been for officers' wartime messes. My helpful friend, the quartermaster, had the admiring gumption to—'

'Admirable,' said Boots, and Emily put a hand on his knee under the table and squeezed it, to show she liked the fact he was still being his own self. Usually, such a loving little gesture would make him put his hand on her own knees, under her skirt, and do things to send her legs wild. There was no response this time.

'Admirable, all right,' said Sammy. 'Anyway, he advised me to put me name down for the lot, by which kind piece of helpful wordage I got a pre-sale arrangement of a highly valuable nature. Tell you what, Boots, we'll have one playing in the shop. That'll bring the customers in, or me name's not what it is.'

'What your name is, Sammy William Adams, is what me and your dad give you,' said Chinese Lady, 'so don't mix it up with unmusical machines invented by somebody whose hearing couldn't of been right.'

'Fortune's always smiling, I've looked everywhere . . .'

Sammy said, 'No, I got you, old lady.' The record came to an end and he got up and switched off the turntable. Emily said she didn't think people had a lot of money to spend on gramophones. 'Well, that's true, Em, very true, I'm glad yer got thinking powers.'

'Sarky tonight, are we?' said Emily.

'Of course, Em'ly knows and I know she's talkin' about the painful amount of dibs people have to fork out for gramophones sold in stores,' said Sammy. 'I don't propose to charge our customers them kind of criminal prices myself. We'll knock 'em for six in the Old Kent Road at what we'll ask. Nineteen bob.'

'A gramophone for nineteen bob?' gasped Emily. 'Trumpet included?'

'You got it, Em,' said Sammy. 'Nineteen and eleven-pence to be exact, which'll sound like nineteen bob to the customers. Buying two hundred and fifty was a risk, mind you, but at these WD sales there's some lots they won't split. It's all or nothing. Still, I reckon we'll sell 'em all by October or November. If not, then by Christmas. I'll lay me best shirt on it.'

'Better if you sold pianos or violins,' said Chinese Lady, 'instead of unnatural inventions.'

'Oh, gramophones can be quite catchy, Mum,' said Emily.

Chinese Lady excused her daughter-in-law's lack of judgement by saying soothingly, 'There, you're still young, Em'ly love.'

'Ain't our Em'ly out of nappies yet, then? I thought she was,' said Tommy, and received from Chinese Lady what this called for, a tart reference to the desirability of growing up without turning into a comic, like some-one else she could name.

Emily, half-waking in the night, turned and cuddled up to Boots, murmured dreamily and went contentedly to sleep again.

Once more heavy morning rain had come and gone, leaving the market looking shiny-wet as the sun broke through parting clouds. Discarded cabbage and lettuce leaves lay soaking in running gutters. A boy darted through puddles and bent under a greengrocery stall. Ma Earnshaw, for all her bulk, stooped swiftly and seized him by the seat of his ragged shorts.

'Gotcher,' she said, 'What yer swipin,' eh, what yer swipin'?'

'Only yer rotten apples, honest,' said the urchin.

'Wha'dyer mean, rotten?' In a crate under the stall were a few apples Ma Earnshaw had had to discard since opening up. The urchins of Walworth, the poorest ones, came hunting for such rejects, making quick dives under stalls to grab what they could before darting away. Ma Earnshaw had caught Sammy at it when he was an urchin himself, his family chronically poor. He had struck an immediate bargain with her, offering a penny for every four pounds of specked fruit she wouldn't sell, anyway. One look into his angelic blue eyes, and Ma Earnshaw was done for. She agreed the bargain on a regular basis. She looked now into wary brown eyes. 'I'll 'ave you know there ain't no rotten apples on my stall,' she said.

'I mean them under yer stall, missus, them yer don't want,' said the wriggling boy.

'They still ain't rotten, not yet they ain't, and nor ain't they there for you to nick.'

'Missus, you ain't nabbin' me, are yer?' begged the urchin. 'You ain't goin' to call the dicks?'

'Now look 'ere, young Charlie Peace, I don't like pinchin' and thieving,' said Ma Earnshaw. 'Come at me closin'-down time, and ask perlite. Just ask, see? Then I might give yer some to take 'ome with yer. And when yer ask say please. You got that?'

'Yus, I got yer, missus, and God bless yer.'

'All right, 'oppit, yer saucebox and come back later, like I said.'

The grateful urchin disappeared.

'Ma, you got a warm Christian bosom,' said Susie from her stall. Mister Tommy had gone to Toni's for a bite to eat, and she was temporarily in charge. The pouring rain had kept shoppers at home, but they were appearing now. She served two customers, then took an apple from a paper bag and bit into it. At which point Mister Sammy arrived.

Spruce in a light grey suit, he said good morning to

374

Ma Earnshaw, looked at Susie's apple, gave the display an approving examination, glanced under the stall and said, 'It's wet down there.'

'It's been wet up 'ere too,' said Susie, 'and I'd like to say I still work 'ere, yer know. I'm not up in the sky or sittin' in the park. Yer could say good morning to me.'

'Now don't let's have a carry-on,' said Sammy, hoping she wasn't going to get worked up and grow big misty eyes. 'You know I appreciate all you do.'

'Oh, excuse me, I'm sure,' said Susie, 'I'm only saying you ought to say good morning to a faithful servant.'

'All right, good morning, faithful servant,' said Sammy.

'I don't like to feel unregarded,' said Susie.

'Now, Susie, I regard you highly,' said Sammy. He could have said he tried to pay her as little attention as possible for the sake of his peace of mind.

'There, it didn't hurt yer to say that, did it, Mister Sammy?' she said, and smiled at him. The strengthening sun danced in her eyes and put gold into her fair hair, tied today with a ribbon of black velvet. Sammy gazed helplessly. Was that lipstick faintly tinting her mouth with pink? What had turned a skinny female ragamuffin into a pretty picture?

'Well, you're a genuine credit to the business now you're growing pretty.' The words were out before he could stop them.

'Crikey,' said Susie in astonishment, 'was it you just said that, Mister Sammy?'

'Never mind that,' said Sammy hastily. 'The point is you're an investment.' He looked under the stall again. The bottom of a large cardboard box containing a gramophone was soaking up the wet.

'What's an investment?' asked Susie, business still patchy at the moment.

'Something that costs money,' said Sammy, 'but gives a fair return if it don't turn out a dud. Bert was a dud. You're not. I'm not saying I'm makin' a rapturous profit

375

out of you, seeing I'm still paying you a penny out of every bob you take, but I'm gettin' a reasonable return. So it's only fair to say your value to the business is highly gratifying.'

Susie's eyes grew big with pleasure. Sammy at once transferred his attention to the top of her head.

'Mister Adams,' she said, 'I got to perjure meself of unChristian resentments which rise up in me each time you upset me.'

'Upset you? Me? I don't go in for upsettin' anyone, it's not good business.'

'Oh, yer don't mean to be upsettin', I'm sure,' said Susie, 'yer a good kind soul underneath, Mister Sammy, yer one of the Lord's true shepherds and yer look after yer flock very Christianlike.'

'Kindly do me a favour of not talkin' like the Archbishop of Walworth,' said Sammy.

'Mister Sammy, there's no Archbishop of Walworth.'

'There wasn't, no, not till you were consecrated,' said Sammy. 'Try and get yourself unfrocked. Now, before I push off to attend to more pressin' business, there's a gramophone in that box that's gettin' a wet bottom—'

'Oh, yes,' said Susie eagerly, 'Mister Tommy told me. Imagine selling gramophones on the stall.'

'And His Master's Voice records too, if me nose can point me to the right warehouse,' said Sammy. 'Tell Tommy to unpack this gramophone and find space on the stall for it. I want him to play it to see what it does to draw customers. That there is a record I've just brought. See it don't get broken. You and Tommy can take orders, but make sure you get a deposit. Half-a-crown, say. Tommy's told you the price, I suppose. Nineteen and eleven. Start at twenty-two and six.'

'Mister Adams, I'll strain me every endeavour at twenty-two and six,' said Susie with enthusiasm, 'and I know Mister Tommy won't fail yer with 'is endeavours.' Susie thought Mister Tommy had learned fast, except he was different from Mister Sammy. Mister Sammy joked with people and exchanged comical remarks with them, and used his eyes on all the ladies. Mister Tommy had a kind of friendly patter, he seemed to pass the time of day with the people, and arrived at the bargain prices with the smile of a generous friend. With Mister Sammy, it was more like a circus act. They both got results.

'Well, I'll leave you to talk to Tommy,' said Sammy, and let her serve a customer before going on. All customers had priority. 'By the way,' he said, 'is your dad still out of work?'

'Yes,' said Susie a little dolefully, 'and Mum says it's mortal 'eart-breakin' for a man like Dad not to be able to provide proper for 'is fam'ly.'

'Well, I've nearly been put in me grave by mortal heart-breaks of me own in me time,' said Sammy. 'Notwithstandin' such, I can give your dad a little regular work, if he's not too proud to use a broom. He can go to the shop at eight each morning to tidy it up and sweep the floor, and give the windows a clean from time to time. It'll be an hour or so's work each morning before the shop opens up, then he can go to the scrap yard and do some tidying up for Fred, say for a couple of hours each day, only he's got to tidy up to Fred's likin'. Will his gammy leg stand up to it?'

'Yes, oh, yes,' Susie's eyes shone. 'Mister Adams, I think yer—'

'No, we don't want any psalms, Miss Brown, and you've got another customer.' Sammy watched her attend to an elderly woman and her husband. He noted her smiling willingness to help them get the best buy in brown glazed teapots for the little money they could afford. She was a natural at relating to customers. The elderly couple went away happy. 'Now I can't give your dad any sittin'-down job, just cleanin' and tidying-up, and using a broom. Fred's got his apprentice, but they're both too busy to do a proper job of keepin' the yard tidy. And my brother Boots, commonly known as the Lord Mayor of High Falutin'—'

377

'Oh, Mister Sammy, your brother's nice.'

'Well, the nice Lord Mayor of High Falutin' is handing me ultimatums about a cleaner. Which means he's screwing me down. So there you are, it's work for your dad, if he wants it.'

'Oh, the Lord bless yer, Mister Sammy.'

'Yes, we've had all that,' said Sammy. 'Tell yer dad I'll pay him ninepence an hour.'

'Oh, if it's three hours a day except Sundays, Dad'll earn thirteen an' six a week,' gasped Susie in bliss. 'Mister Sammy, don't God work in mysterious ways wondrous to be'old? The day you give me a tanner to mind yer stall, that was like a wondrous workin' of God's mysterious 'and, don't yer think so?'

'I'm gettin' out of here,' said Sammy, 'it's too much like a Palm Sunday church service, with me standin' in for the Holy Ghost.'

He left at speed.

'What yer been an' said to 'im?' asked Ma Earnshaw. 'I never seen Sammy Adams depart as quick as that.'

'Ma, ain't he droll, though?' said Susie.

Boots was pleased to close up at the end of a busy Thursday. The new lines Sammy was stocking were attracting new custom. Gramophones at nineteen and eleven each were proving mesmerising to slightly more affluent shoppers, those from the Denmark Hill area. Sammy had obtained the gramophones at a cost of a little over nine shillings each.

With the shop set to do consistently well because of Sammy's astute buying, Boots thought how easily he and Emily could afford to move. They were still looking, but were making comparisons between everything they saw and the house they had lost. They felt that was the one they would have really liked, the one close to Lizzy and Ned's. Emily was quite happy to continue looking. She rose resiliently above all disappointments. She was very happy with life, very sweet to him because he was understanding of her feelings, which were just a bit mixed-up at the moment, she said. All the same, he found it difficult himself to adjust to an Emily who did not want him to make love to her.

He wondered about Rosie, if she was finding happiness with her foster parents. He would have given much to visit her, even though he knew it would not be wise. Leaving the shop, he locked the door. A waiting man stepped forward to speak to him.

'Good evening.'

Boots turned. He stared in astonishment.

'Jesus Christ,' he said.

'No, myself, dear old Boots,' said Mr Finch, the family's erstwhile lodger. 'How very glad I am to see you.'

CHAPTER TWENTY-EIGHT

Mr Finch, now a man of forty-seven, with an air of vigorous masculine maturity, had lodged with the Adams family for several years until 1916. Chinese Lady always considered him a kind and untroublesome gentleman. He became a close friend of the family without ever indulging in familiarities. He developed a special rapport with Boots, who appreciated his whimsical paternalism and his little gems of wisdom, but could never quite make out why a man who had sailed the seven seas and was a river pilot with the Port of London, seemed content to exist in Walworth as a lodger.

Mr Finch declared himself very content. He had a great respect and admiration for Chinese Lady, and was particularly addicted to her Sunday teas in the parlour, to which he was invited whenever Miss Elsie Chivers was present. Miss Chivers was the long-suffering daughter of Mrs Chivers, a sour-tempered widow destined to be murdered in her bed.

The family thought the only way Miss Chivers could escape her cage was for Mr Finch to fall in love with her and carry her off to Gretna Green. Boots had a secret feeling Miss Chivers would not object to this, but Mr Finch was never anything but polite to her, and she was the same to him.

The murder, when it happened in 1914, was terribly trying to everyone in the Place, especially as there was the war to worry about as well. It was more trying to Miss Chivers than anyone, for she was charged with the murder. Various neighbours were called as witnesses, either by the defence or the prosecution. Chinese Lady was an upright defence witness, Mr Finch a calm and convincing one, but it was Boots who turned the scales in favour of Miss Chivers.

In 1916, Mr Finch quietly disappeared, and so did Miss Chivers, a clerk with the Admiralty. Boots alone knew why. Mr Finch returned to the house very late one night when Boots, blinded on the Somme, was sleepless in the parlour. He did not see Mr Finch, but he heard him, and Mr Finch wryly confessed he was a German spy. British Naval Intelligence had uncovered him, and Miss Chivers too, who had thrown in her lot with him. He had come back to the house to retrieve her carving knife, which he had had from the day of the murder. This seemed to suggest it was Mr Finch who had cut the victim's throat. Boots had never believed this. He suspected it was Miss Chivers herself.

What had happened to her and Mr Finch after they disappeared, he did not know. What he did know was that he was looking at Mr Finch now, and that there was still the same whimsical twinkle in his eye. He was four years older, and he not only seemed fit and healthy, he also seemed untroubled. His smile was that of a man who had nothing on his conscience whatever. There was only one man in Boots's life whom he had admired and looked up to without reserve. His commanding officer, Major Harris, killed on the Somme. There was also a man he had never ceased to like, irrespective of his history and his secrets. Mr Finch.

'Are you real?' he asked.

'Boots, old chap, of course I'm real.' Mr Finch spoke English like a native, with not the slightest trace of a German accent. And in a tweed suit and cap, he looked English. He still had the weathered appearance of a seaman and river pilot. His smile widened as he realised Boots was for once off balance. Chinese Lady's eldest son was very much a man now. When a boy at school, a boy enquiring and amusing, Mr Finch had felt a fatherly fondness for him. He said, 'I'm not only real, I'm a British citizen.'

'Jesus lend me strength,' said Boots, 'I thought you'd have been hanged by now.'

'Hanged?' Mr Finch seemed surprised. 'For what, Boots?'

'This, that and the other,' said Boots.

'You were always imaginative,' smiled Mr Finch. 'You're going to take a tram home, I suppose. Shall we walk part of the way, unless you're in a desperate hurry?'

'Is that an invitation to hear you talk?' asked Boots.

'I'd like to talk, yes,' said Mr Finch, and they began walking amid the going-home citizens. It was early September, and the leaves of the trees in Camberwell Green Park were crisp and dry. 'You know, Boots, I spoke to you more than once about the conflict that can arise between loyalties and affections. My affections for your family and your country proved stronger than my loyalties to Germany.'

'Not during the war,' said Boots. 'You and Miss Chivers were responsible for passing on the information that helped to sink the *Hampshire*, weren't you?'

'And Lord Kitchener was lost. Water under the bridge of war, Boots.'

'Murky water,' said Boots.

'Yes,' said Mr Finch equably, 'but I was speaking of my subsequent feelings when I got back to Germany.' They crossed the junction and entered Camberwell Road. Mr Finch went on to say he had eluded British Naval Intelligence and crossed the Channel in the uniform of a British Army Officer. Miss Chivers was with him, disguised as a Red Cross nursing sister. They reached Germany via Switzerland in different disguises, where they were cordially received by German Intelligence. It took Mr Finch very little time, however, to realise he had spent too many years away from Germany and too many years in England. His patriotism had taken a hard knock when war came about in 1914. He had collected and despatched all kinds of information on British naval matters during his many years in England, but was decidedly unhappy about the outbreak of war. He felt it was Germany's backing of Austria's vainglorious ultimatum to Serbia that was responsible for the spread of the conflict.

He could not settle down in Germany. He had no family, his parents were dead, and he did not feel German any more. He had become an Anglophile. He cast aside all ethics and principles, and in January 1918, while acting for German Intelligence in Austria, he slipped into Switzerland and then into France. From there he returned to Britain, where he delivered himself up to British Intelligence and offered extremely valuable information in return for immunity. His case was considered, and he was granted provisional immunity while they tested the credibility of such information as he was prepared to give at this stage. Satisfied, they asked him to come up with something that was of really priceless value. He told them General Ludendorff was preparing a massive offensive that was to be mainly directed at the British 5th Army. This was received with scepticism, for British Army Intelligence insisted the Germans were no longer in a position to fight anything but a defensive war. Further, there were no signs of a German build-up in any sector opposite the British front. But when Ludendorff did launch his mighty assault a week later, with devastating results, there were no more doubts about Erich Moeller's worth to the British. Erich Moeller was Mr Finch's German name.

'Just a moment,' said Boots, fascinated, 'you've said nothing about how Miss Chivers featured in all this, except that she arrived in Germany with you. Didn't she come back here with you?'

'Ah,' said Mr Finch, and looked wry. 'No,' he said.

'You left her in Germany?' enquired Boots. They were walking slowly, and Mr Finch, despite looking a country gentleman in his tweed suit, seemed very much at home in the working-class environment of Camberwell. 'Why?'

'A charming and very affectionate lady,' said Mr Finch, 'but there was too much between us for us to marry.'

Highly likely, thought Boots. Without doubt, one of them had put paid to Mrs Chivers, and it had proved too much for the other to live with. Boots had a surer feeling now that the guilty one was Elsie Chivers. He did not think Mr Finch would have come back, had it been him.

'You're talking about the murder, aren't you?'

'I never talk about it, Boots. Much too painful.'

'It can't be more painful than being indirectly responsible for the deaths of all the men who went down with the *Hampshire*.'

'Can't it? That was a legitimate act of war, Boots. As legitimate as the act of any British agent that resulted in the loss of German lives. If I have sorrows and regrets, they aren't those of a guilty man.'

'If you left Miss Chivers in Germany,' said Boots, 'what kind of a life is she having there?'

'Oh, quite comfortable,' said Mr Finch, eyeing with a smile a costermonger wheeling a barrow of fruit home. 'She's the wife of a Bavarian landowner, whom she met in Munich. She married him in the summer of 1917, she and I having parted earlier, by mutual consent. Why, Boots, do you still have a crush on her?'

'Oh, I grew up in the end,' said Boots.

'Forget her, old chap. I know you're married to Emily, a girl with the warmest heart in London, and London has a great heart. I know you had a successful operation, that Lizzy and Ned have a little girl, and I know about Tommy and Sammy, and Sammy's penchant for making money. You'll understand I've a talent for collecting information, and in the end I could not resist finding out all I could about the Adams family. You have no idea how much you've all been in my thoughts. Am I an embarrassment to you?'

'The war's over,' said Boots, 'and I can't say I'm not pleased to see you again. You were good to us when we were young, and generous to my mother. But am I to believe you really are a British citizen now?'

Mr Finch said it had been impossible not to become attached to Britain, its people, its institutions and its traditions. The most likeable and most natural people he had ever met, he said, were Boots and his family. His happiest days were those he had spent among them, watching them grow up, watching Lizzy fall in love, watching Emily from next door creating havoc, and watching Boots's mother fighting her resolute fight against poverty. There was, he said, no woman quite like her.

'Carry on,' said Boots, walking the dusty pavements with the man who had come back.

Mr Finch said he made discreet enquiries through his friends in the British Secret Service about the possibility of becoming a naturalised subject. Among those friends was the chief of Army Intelligence. He heard nothing for some months, and was then told to make his application. He was granted citizenship in March, five months ago. He had a British passport in the name of Edwin William Finch. He wondered now if Boots had told his family of their conversation in the dead of night four years ago.

'No,' said Boots, 'I thought it better to keep it all to myself.'

'Why?' asked Mr Finch, watching horse-drawn traffic competing with noisy, motorised vehicles.

'It would have done no good,' said Boots.

'You're a very civilised young man, Boots. You were particularly civilised on that occasion, when you might have been brutally hostile, and bitter too, for you'd been blinded in a Somme battle. And so, you've kept our conversation to yourself? Does that mean if I called to see your family, they would not turn their backs on me?'

'I don't think so,' said Boots. 'I suppose they all have their own opinions about your disappearance. Emily thought you and Miss Chivers had simply eloped.'

'Ah, Emily,' smiled Mr Finch, 'Emily who had a girlish longing to belong to you, and had so many frustrations because she thought she would never be pretty enough to belong to anybody.'

'Emily,' said Boots, 'is a beautiful girl.'

'Yes, it's all there, isn't it, Boots, the girl that Emily really is.'

'What are you doing now?' asked Boots.

'Oh, cypher work, I think you'd call it,' said Mr Finch.

'Well, come to tea on Sunday.'

'Boots, I should be delighted. I can hardly wait to see you all again.' Mr Finch consulted his pocket watch. 'Shall we say until Sunday, then?'

They shook hands. Then Boots continued walking, and Mr Finch went his own way.

Chinese Lady was astonished.

'Mr Finch?' she said.

'Mr Finch,' said Boots.

'Mr Finch?' said Emily, open-mouthed.

'Mr Finch,' repeated Boots, this time with gravity.

'Not Mr Finch,' said Chinese Lady, a little flush on her face.

'What's this, a Mutt and Jeff act?' said Boots. Mutt and Jeff were a pair of daft eccentrics, dreamt up by an American comic artist.

'What did he say to you?' asked Chinese Lady, and Boots recounted as much of the conversation as was tactful. 'Am I hearing you correct, young man?'

'You are, old girl.'

'Yes, but you might be having us on,' said Emily. 'We know what you're like sometimes, don't we, Mum?'

'Boots, you look me in the eye now,' said Chinese Lady, 'and you tell me did you really see Mr Finch and talk with him like that, and hear him say he don't know where Miss Chivers ever got to after they left?'

Boots, feeling that Mr Finch should tell the family all the facts himself, if he wished to, said, 'He's coming to tea on Sunday.'

'Oh,' said Chinese Lady, and sat down at the kitchen table as if her knees had given way. She had only the warmest and most respectful memories of her former lodger. If she had felt uncomfortable about the way he had departed, just going without a word to anyone, she had long forgotten it. Boots saw her little flush deepen, and he suspected she was unusually pleased about Mr Finch turning up again and wanting to come to Sunday tea. 'Boots, you sure he's comin'?'

'Quite sure.'

'Oh, ain't that nice?' said Emily. 'I always liked Mr Finch. He kissed me once, at Christmas, when we played Postman's Knock. I told him he didn't have to, me being a wretched handful at the time, but he said he was goin' to. I wasn't incurable, he said.'

Boots thought there speaks the old Emily.

'Well, surprise him on Sunday,' he said, 'show him you're still not cured.'

'Yes, I am,' protested Emily, 'I'm a lovin' angel now, I am.'

'Agreed,' said Boots, and Emily coloured a little and bit her lip. She wondered if she was doing him wrong. And she hadn't yet told him she was going to start her shorthand class in three weeks. She had an uneasy feeling he would think it was to do with putting off having a baby. Oh, blow it, she thought, now I'm going to start worrying again.

'Boots,' she said, 'why did Mr Finch and Miss Chivers go away like they did? Was it because they eloped and didn't want anyone makin' a song and dance about them being romantic together?'

Boots knew something had to be said.

'Well, there was so much talk, Em, especially as the police had never charged anyone else with the murder. Mr Finch said they thought it best to quietly depart. They intended to get married, but Mr Finch was called to do government work of a special kind, and Miss Chivers married someone else.'

'Oh, I see,' said Emily. She smiled at Boots, trying to let him know she still thought him lovely. 'It was the war and everything, I suppose.'

'You really sure he's comin', Boots?' asked Chinese Lady for the second time.

'Let's start this conversation all over again,' said Boots, 'let's decide our certainties. If we don't, I'll get confused and expect Charlie Chaplin.'

Emily laughed, sure she had the most understanding and entertaining husband ever. She must tell Mrs Stevens how nice he was. Mrs Stevens sometimes spoke as if there was no such thing as a nice husband.

Lizzy had gone the full nine months, after all, and was delivered of her second child in the comfort of the maternity wing of King's College Hospital. It arrived in the evening. Lizzy, perspiring, her teeth clenched, suddenly felt herself eased of strain, pain and body weight. A moment later, she heard a lusty yell.

'It's a boy,' she said faintly.

'Yes, how did you know?' asked the attendant nurse.

Relaxing, Lizzy murmured happily, 'Boys always make more noise and fuss than girls. I got three brothers.'

Everyone was delighted for Lizzy when Ned brought the news, although Emily had to struggle to contain other feelings. She wondered, in her own typical fashion, if her failure to conceive was because God was punishing her and Boots for stopping babies happening during the years he was blind. It made her feel she just had to give herself breathing space.

388

'Boots,' said Chinese Lady last thing on Saturday night, 'I want to talk to you.' Sammy and Tommy were in bed, and Emily had just gone up.

'Fire away,' said Boots. There was no reason for him to hurry up after Emily. Emily at that moment was descending the stairs in her stockinged feet. She had forgotten her handbag. She always took it up with her. She checked on the stairs as she heard Chinese Lady say something. The kitchen door was half-open.

'Boots, what's goin' on between you and Emily?'

'Going on?' Boots sounded taken aback.

'There's something which I'm not sure I like,' said Chinese Lady. 'It's not my business, of course, but I hope you're not mistreatin' her.'

'I'm not mistreating her.' Boots now sounded casual.

'Well, it seems to me you two aren't like you always have been to each other.'

'Aren't we?'

'I can tell,' said Chinese Lady. 'Boots, you're my only oldest son, and I wouldn't like to think Em'ly's caught you playing about. It's something I never thought you would do, but you might be.'

'Playing about with another woman, you mean? Perish the thought, old lady.'

'That's a relief,' said Chinese Lady, 'but I still feel you and Em'ly don't act the same together. Boots, you got to remember it was hard for her, all them years you were blind, and if the strain's caught up a bit with her, you ought to be understandin'.'

There was a pause before Boots said, 'Yes, she did have to put up with the strain of it, and I think it has caught up with her.'

'You don't get vexed with her about it, do you?' Chinese Lady sounded concerned. 'Em'ly's been a good and lovin' wife to you, Boots.'

'Well, if I did get vexed with her, I hope she'd thump me,' said Boots.

'Just give her time,' said Chinese Lady. 'She don't mind still goin' out to work, and it's helpin' both of you save, and she's got more likin' for the job now you're earning too. And they must think something of her, givin' her that half-crown rise.'

'I'm not discouraging her,' said Boots.

Emily stole quietly back up the stairs, feeling emotional. She also felt very relieved that Chinese Lady was on her side, that she understood about strain and worry.

Boots asked his mother if there was anything else on her mind.

'Well, you've not said what you feel about Mr Finch. Tommy and Sammy said they just feel that whatever him and Miss Chivers got up to when they went off together, it's a pleasure to know he's come back to London.'

'What should I feel about him myself?' asked Boots.

'You know what I mean,' said Chinese Lady, 'the way he disappeared and them two stern gentlemen I told you come lookin' for him. I'd put it out of my mind, but I can't help wondering now.'

'Oh, we can let sleeping dogs lie,' said Boots.

'Some sleepin' dogs get up and bite,' said Chinese Lady.

'Not this one,' said Boots. He knew his mother had associated Mr Finch's disappearance with something uncomfortably secretive, but never with the murder. Nor would she ever have believed Miss Chivers could have done it. Miss Chivers was a lady, Mr Finch a gentleman. She would only allow that Mr Finch might have his secrets. 'Don't worry, old girl.'

'You and your old girl,' said Chinese Lady, but she felt better for Boots's reassurance. She had more faith in her eldest son's sense than she would ever admit. 'Still, if you say we don't need to have no worries about Mr Finch, that's all right, then. It's nice we can be happy about havin' him to tea tomorrow. Oh, I wrote invitin' Vi. She hardly ever goes out to Sunday tea.'

'Shame,' said Boots, 'when she's so ladylike. By the

390

way, wear your best bonnet and one of your best blouses with a lace collar. And the silk stockings Emily gave you last Christmas. In honour of Mr Finch, your best features ought to be highlighted.'

'Well,' said Chinese Lady in shock, 'I can't hardly believe your impudence.'

'I know,' said Boots, 'but I'm still proud of you, me old darling, and yer queenly figure.'

'That don't entitle you to be disrespectful to your own mother,' said Chinese Lady, a born Victorian. 'We won't have no more Frenchified insinuations, thank you. But at least it was nice you goin' to see Lizzy and her new baby this afternoon while Sammy looked after the shop. It shows you got some commendable ways. My, that infant, eight pounds, would you believe.'

'Yes,' said Boots soberly, 'a brother for Annabelle.'

'Yes.' Chinese Lady hesitated. 'Boots, you shouldn't still be thinking about little Rosie.'

'Oh, she comes to mind now and again,' said Boots.

'I know,' said Chinese Lady, and gave him one of her light pats on her way to her bedroom. 'Just think about a nice house and garden for Em'ly.'

She hoped that as well as a nice house and garden, Emily would also have her first child.

Boots, smiling wryly, thought about 'another woman'. Polly had visited the shop at midday. With Sammy there, helping out, Boots had been collared by the irrepressible Miss Simms, who implored him to have lunch with her. He requested her to find a hungry tram conductor who was off duty. Polly made faces and asked what about her mother's large list of orphanage requirements? He told her all would be provided, he would let her know when. Polly said he was turning into a mean old ratbag. He said one mean old ratbag would smack her bottom if she didn't make herself scarce. Polly said she'd call again, when there were no customers, and he could try it on then. She departed laughing.

CHAPTER TWENTY-NINE

It was Boots who opened the door to Mr Finch on Sunday afternoon. With a minimum of well-chosen words, he let Mr Finch know that his most personal secrets were still his own.

'Ours, I think, Boots,' murmured Mr Finch with a smile, 'yours and mine, and I could not have shared them with a finer friend.'

Boots took him into the parlour, where the old durable mahogany table was laid for tea. Mr Finch noted new wallpaper and new paint, paint that brightened the room. Apart from Lizzy and Ned, the family were all there, and all on their feet to receive him. With them was Vi. She knew Mr Finch from the old days. His eyes alighted on Chinese Lady, still the undisputed head of the family. She had decided hats were not worn for Sunday tea, however gentlemanly the visitor. But she was wearing her best blouse of ivory-cream broderie anglaise on fine cambric, with a high collar. It gave her an Edwardian look, which she favoured. But her brown skirt was post-war length, showing her silken-clad calves. Her smooth dark brown hair was fixed with a cheap tortoiseshell comb that nevertheless looked attractive, and her almond eyes were unweary.

Mr Finch placed a huge bouquet of red roses in her arms.

'My dear Mrs Adams, you have no idea how pleased I am to be here.'

Chinese Lady stared at the bouquet, and was lost for words. Mr Finch tactfully busied himself renewing acquaintance with Emily, Sammy, Tommy and Vi. Emily delighted him in an apple-green Sunday dress, her auburn hair magnificent, her eyes swimming with pleasure as he took both her hands and kissed her on the cheek.

'Oh, Mr Finch, it's so nice to see you again,' she said in her quicker voice, her impulsive voice. 'Would yer ever 'ave believed you'd come back and find me married to Boots? Me, would yer believe, that wretched urchin girl.'

Boots felt a twinge of painful love. That was his Emily, his endearing Emily. The other Emily was not believable. The real Emily loved a cuddle, a kiss and a teasing.

'Emily,' said Mr Finch, 'you look to me as if Boots has got the nicer bargain.'

'Especially as she's cured,' said Boots.

'Cured?' asked Mr Finch, smiling.

'Well, she ain't broke any legs lately,' said Sammy, 'she's just aimed a kick or two.'

'She's half-cured at least,' said Tommy, 'yes, you could say that.'

'Oh, yer rotten pair of heathens,' said Emily. 'I don't know what me and Chinese Lady are ever goin' to make of you.' She wrinkled her pointed nose then. 'Oh, blow, now look what you made me say.' It was an unwritten rule that their mother was never referred to as Chinese Lady except within the family.

'Pardon granted,' said Sammy.

'Still,' said Tommy, 'you can see she's near to being cured all over, Mr Finch.'

Chinese Lady, her bosom smothered by the bouquet, found her tongue.

'Mr Finch,' she said, 'I don't know how I come to have such disgraceful sons. Em'ly's been a godsend to all of us, and well they know it. But of course, Boots picked up Frenchified ways in France, Sammy's been mixin' with all kinds, and Tommy keeps forgettin' his upbringing. I'm just grateful their Cousin Vi's grown up so ladylike. And pretty too.'

Vi turned pink. Mr Finch regarded her with a smile, his twinkle visible.

'Well, I think Cousin Vi and Emily are lovely compensations, Mrs Adams,' he said, 'and there's always the hope Tommy and Sammy will improve.' He was already at home among them, his pleasure obvious as he exchanged conversation with them. Tommy and Sammy were tall young men now. He thought Tommy good-natured and likeable, Sammy sharp, loquacious and funny. He thought Boots was himself, a family member with a difference, a kind of mild, quirky sophistication. But he also thought Boots could show steel if the occasion called for it. Emily was really quite fascinating, her love of life still a vivacious thing, her plainness so much offset by her beautiful hair and her quick green eyes. Vi had a gentle charm, and was far more talkative than when she had been a young girl. As for Mrs Adams, Mr Finch was aware that she had lost her careworn look, that in four years she seemed to have become younger. She must be over forty, since Boots would be twenty-four now.

When tea was on the table, Chinese Lady presided in her usual way, treating her family as if they still needed to mind their manners when there were guests present. She sat with her back straight, the inspiration behind traditional Sunday tea, the large teapot close at hand. Mr Finch was in frank enjoyment of the tradition, common to every home in the country, and very much a part of every cockney's Sunday. The cockneys of Walworth favoured shrimps and winkles, fishpastes and celery, watercress or mustard-and-cress, bread and marge and jam (bread and butter for visitors, if the purse could run to it), home-made rockcakes and fruit cake, toasted muffins from the muffin-man in the winter, and endless cups of tea. Each family made its choice of such items according to means, and if means were very low there was usually only bread and marge and jam, with rockcakes, the cheapest form of home-made confectionery. But it was still an occasion, and everyone sat formally down to every Sunday tea, with mother presiding over the teapot.

To Chinese Lady, it seemed as if Mr Finch had never been away. It seemed just like the old days, when he'd been such a help to the family, always paying his rent promptly and a week in advance, always giving every-one Christmas presents, but never intruding or inter-fering. And he hadn't hardly changed at all, he looked just the same, his light brown hair thick but tidy as always, with no sign of grey. She knew what his age was, it had come out when he'd been a defence witness at the trial of Miss Chivers. She knew he was now forty-seven, and it amazed her that he'd never had a wife. There must have been lots of women only too glad to have been asked. He could still make some woman a good husband. He was mature, that's what he was. Being mature suited a man. Men took a long time to stop being boys. It was no wonder young women gave Boots the eye the moment they got to know him, like that nurse at the hospital. Boots had stopped being a boy in France. When he'd come home on leave to give Lizzy away at her wedding, he was only nineteen but already a man. It wouldn't have done to have told him so, he might have won more medals by having both legs blown off because of feeling that was what a man should do.

Chinese Lady hoped very much that there was nothing serious spoiling Boots's relationship with Emily. Only he was quieter with her. He wasn't getting up to his teasing larks with her. There were no squeals from upstairs when they got home from work, and she hadn't heard Emily yelling, 'Oh, yer wicked devil!' for weeks. And there was no Emily flying down the stairs and bursting into the kitchen to gasp, 'Mum, that son of yours, I don't know how you ever let him be born.' Not that one wanted to encourage them kind of ways, but it was better them than none at all.

Like Boots, Mr Finch wasn't a matinee idol. He was manly. To Chinese Lady, that was what a woman mostly liked a man to be. It was a pity Lizzy and Ned couldn't be here. Lizzy had been a favourite with Mr Finch, and she'd once said what a nice dad he would make. Still, he was enjoying seeing Emily and Vi again. One had to be proud of Emily, she dressed ever so well these days considering what a terrible mess she'd always looked when she was a girl. She went off to work looking very smart. She said lots of the men in the town hall gave her the eye, would you believe.

Chinese Lady had a sudden unhappy thought then. Was it Emily and not Boots? Had some man at the town hall turned her head?

She sat very upright.

'More tea, Mr Finch?'

'Dare I ask for a third cup?' said Mr Finch. 'Well, why not? After listening to Sammy's account of a prospering family business, I think I could manage a third.'

'Prospering, well, I don't know,' said Sammy cautiously. 'Makin' a bit of a livin' is more like. You can't get rich overnight, yer know, and havin' to pay out highly lucrative wages to Tommy, and a painful, demandin' salary to Boots, that gives the takin's a hurtful hiding, which holds back me prosperity.'

'Everyone get their hankies out,' said Tommy, 'and we'll all have a good cry for Sammy. Come on, Em, come on, Vi, hankies out.'

'Not goin' to,' said Vi, 'not while you're sittin' next to me.'

'Bless me,' said Sammy, 'does Vi keep her hankies in the same place as our Em'ly?'

'Oh, stop him, someone,' said Vi.

'Sammy, I'll kick you,' said Emily.

'There, told yer, Mr Finch,' said Tommy, 'told yer Em'ly was only half-cured.'

Sammy came in with his own interpretation of some music-hall doggerel, in a singing voice.

'*Oh, ain't it terrible, awful shocking,*
 Vi keepin' hankies in the top of her stocking?'

Vi shrieked, Emily clapped a hand to her mouth, Tommy roared, Boots smiled and Mr Finch laughed. Chinese Lady was alone in her disapproval.

'That's right,' she said, 'let Mr Finch and Vi see what comes of you mixin' with them vulgar costermongers.'

'What's wrong with stockings, Ma?' asked Sammy. 'We all know that's where Em'ly keeps—'

'Sammy Adams, you're at Sunday tea,' said Chinese Lady sternly.

'Yes, Ma. I merely had a passin' thought concerning Vi's hankies, that's all.'

'Visionary?' suggested Boots.

'Is that the same as a flash of lightning?' asked Tommy.

'Well, a quick glimpse, like,' said Sammy.

Vi laughed. She never had more fun than when she was with her cousins. Mr Finch solemnly helped himself to a slice of fruit cake, the stand passed to him by Tommy.

'Mum, I don't believe it,' gasped Emily, 'look at them all, did yer ever see innocence like they can put on? And it's all underhand talk about our legs.'

'On a Sunday too,' said Boots. 'At the tea table and all.'

'Auntie Maisie,' said Vi, 'could I please saw Boots's head off with the cake knife?'

Laughter erupted.

'Good on yer, Vi,' said Sammy, 'yer made a funny.'

'Mr Finch,' said Chinese Lady, 'it's my hopeful wish you'll excuse all my sons growin' up to be comedians. What their dad would of thought grieves me.'

'What can I say?' asked Mr Finch.

'Yes, come on, Mr Finch, what can you say?' said Emily.

'Believe me,' said Mr Finch, 'this fruit cake is delicious.'

'They're all wicked,' said Vi.

'Very sad,' said Mr Finch.

'Lovely,' said Vi.

'More tea, Em'ly?' enquired Chinese Lady, looking directly at her daughter-in-law. Emily smiled in affection, her green eyes swimming with the clear light of a young wife who had nothing on her conscience.

'Please, Mum,' she said.

'All this tea,' said Sammy. 'Next thing you know there'll be a lot of running goin' on for the – well, no, I'd better not mention that, not at the Sunday tea table.'

'Hit him, Mr Finch, you're nearest,' said Emily.

Mr Finch looked as if he had entered a magic circle.

He stayed until eight o'clock, sitting with the family in the parlour. Tommy played the piano for an hour, at Vi's request. She loved the atmosphere when Tommy was performing. She thought he ought to be a professional pianist and play at cinemas. Her mother would think that much more acceptable than running a stall.

Subsequently and inevitably, Sammy asked Mr Finch exactly why he had gone off like he did four years ago. Was it because he and Miss Chivers wanted a quiet life? Mr Finch said much the same as Boots had, that he and Miss Chivers felt they needed to get away from Walworth for a while, and their decision to go coincided with the government making demands on his services. (Boots thought he phrased that well). He was given no time to say formal goodbyes. He and Miss Chivers might have married if his commitments hadn't separated him from her. As it was, she eventually married someone else. Now he was on full-time government work. Chinese Lady said well, she hoped Miss Chivers was now living in happy married obscutery. She meant obscurity. Emily said it would be nice if she was, after all she'd gone through. Mr Finch agreed.

398

Boots said nothing, but his little smile was lurking.

When Mr Finch was about to leave, Chinese Lady remembered the roses, now a profusion of scarlet blooms in a vase. She made a little speech of thanks, and said the family would be pleased to see him whenever he cared to call. Mr Finch said he had to go to Belgium for a month or two, but would get in touch on his return. He thanked her for a magnificent tea and for having such an entertaining family.

'He's still an awf'lly nice man,' said Emily after he had gone.

'Yes, isn't he?' said Vi.

'A gentleman,' said Chinese Lady, 'which is more than I can say for some people I know.'

Sammy said, 'Am I to draw the unhappy conclusion, Ma, that all the money we spent on Boots's education has gone to waste?'

'You Sammy,' said Emily, 'I'll box your ears if you say things like that about my managerial husband.'

'And I'll box them till his head comes off if he calls me Ma again,' said Chinese Lady.

'Women,' said Sammy.

A young boy and a small girl entered the Enquiries office of the Sanitary Inspector's department. Emily got up from her desk and went to the counter. She smiled and shook her head.

'Not you two again,' she said. It was 'Orrice and his sister Effel. That was how she thought of them. 'Orrice looked up at her from under the peak of his outsized cap.

'Mum don't feel well,' he said. 'Does she, Effel?'

'Ain't saying,' said Effel, hiding behind him.

'This isn't the doctor's surgery,' said Emily.

'We been there,' said 'Orrice. 'The doctor said 'e'd go an' see 'er soon as 'e could. Dad said to come and tell yer 'e still ain't – what was it 'e said, Effel?'

'Dunno,' said Effel.

'She's in one of 'er moods again,' said 'Orrice. 'I know, Dad said 'e still ain't partial to the drains. Mum ain't, neither. She said they're makin' the tap water taste funny.'

'Funny?' said Emily, alerting, and Mr Simmonds joined her at the counter. He peered searchingly down into 'Orrice's earnest face.

'Are you sure?' he asked.

'Well, it does taste funny,' said 'Orrice. 'Don't it, Effel?'

'It ain't my fault,' said Effel, still hiding herself.

'Dad said it's like 'orse's wee-wee,' 'Orrice was slightly accusing in his survey of Mr Simmonds. ''E don't want us drinkin' it. And 'e don't feel too good 'isself. But 'e's gorn off to his work, 'e won't get paid if 'e don't.'

'Listen,' said Mr Simmonds, 'is it upset stomachs?'

'I dunno what that is,' said 'Orrice, who would have understood if Mr Simmonds had said bellyache. 'I just know Mum keeps on 'avin' to go to the lav.'

'But you're all right, you and your sister?' said Emily.

'Yes, are you?' asked Mr Simmonds.

'Effel was sick last night,' said 'Orrice. 'Wasn't you, Effel?'

'Ain't saying,' muttered Effel.

Mrs Stevens entered through the inner door. She looked at the shabby boy and girl.

'What are they doing here?' she asked.

'Their parents sent them,' said Mr Simmonds. 'Something about their tap water, after trouble with their drains.' He and Emily suspected contamination.

'You shouldn't be dealing with children,' said Madge Stevens, 'not unless they're accompanied by a responsible adult.' The arrow was aimed at Mr Simmonds, not Emily. To 'Orrice she said, 'Go and tell your father to come.'

'No, I ain't goin' to,' said 'Orrice bravely, 'Dad's at work and Mum's chronic.'

400

Madge eyed him with faint distaste.

'See to him, Emily,' she said, 'and then will you come and see me?'

'Yes, all right,' said Emily, a little perturbed at this lack of sympathy. When the assistant supervisor had disappeared, she said to 'Orrice, 'Don't worry, we'll send someone.'

'Yer a lady toff, missus,' said 'Orrice. 'Ain't she, Effel?'

'Ain't talkin',' said Effel.

'Make sure the doctor comes,' said Mr Simmonds.

'I'll go round again if 'e don't,' said 'Orrice. 'Come on, Effel, or I'll wallop yer.' But he put an arm around her shoulders as they left.

'The poor kids,' said Emily.

'Action form, Emily,' said Mr Simmonds.

'Mrs Stevens thought—'

'Never mind her,' said Mr Simmonds, 'I don't like the sound of things. I'm not too keen on her, either.'

'But she's nice,' said Emily.

'So's my Aunt Alice – from a distance. Fill the form in, Emily, I'm going to see the public health factotum.'

Emily filled the form in, marked it urgent and underlined it. She left it for Mr Simmonds to initial. When he came back she gave it to him and went to see Mrs Stevens.

'Did you get rid of those urchins, Emily?' asked Madge.

'Poor little devils,' said Emily, 'Mr Simmonds thinks they might 'ave contaminated tap water.'

'He's not taking their word for it, is he?'

'Mrs Stevens, I honestly think—'

'The man's an idiot, Emily. I'd like to see you in his job in time.'

'Mrs Stevens, I don't want his job, he's got a wife and fam'ly.'

'You're a kindness to him.' Madge waved a hand, dismissing the subject of Mr Simmonds. 'Look, I've got you enrolled for the shorthand course beginning the fourth week of this month. I do hope you won't let that husband of yours change your mind for you again.'

The scales began to fall from Emily's eyes. She prickled a little.

'Excuse me, Mrs Stevens, he's not that husband of mine, he's my husband and the best one I could have.'

Madge smiled placatingly.

'I'm sure he is,' she said, 'and some of them do have their little human moments, don't they?'

There was something so patronising about this remark that Emily thought it quite disagreeable. It occurred to her then that although Mrs Stevens had never met Boots, she had made up her mind she did not like him.

'Thank you, Mrs Stevens, about the shorthand course,' she said, and walked out. Mr Simmonds looked up on her return.

'All right, Emily?'

'Yes, thank you.'

'I've insisted on action.'

'I'm glad. Mr Simmonds?'

'What's up?' he asked.

'I just want you to know I like you for supportin' them kids,' said Emily, 'and that I like workin' for you.'

'Excelsior,' said Mr Simmonds, his glasses making his smile owlish.

Sammy was using the telephone in the office of Mr Morris's factory, by kind permission of the owner.

At the other end of the line, Polly Simms said, 'Who did you say you were?'

'Mr Sammy Adams, proprietor of Sam's Emporium.'

'Ugh,' said Polly.

'Pardon?' said Sammy.

'Ugh to Sam's Emporium, old sport. And I don't know why I'm hearing from you about these items when I'm dealing exclusively with your brother Robert.'

'No difference, I assure you, Miss Simms,' said Sammy, quite capable of putting on the style if he thought it necessary. 'We're partners, except I'm senior.'

'Listen, ducky,' said Polly, 'I've met both of you. I'm sorry, old thing, but you're not in his class. Oh, you're a sweet boy in your way, but it's Robert I'm dealing with on behalf of the dear old orphanage – well, new orphanage, actually. Tell him to ring me. Or I'll get the order cancelled. So long, old top.'

'Hold on,' said Sammy, but the line went dead. He waited a few moments, then got on to the operator and requested her to call the number again. Connected, he asked the butler, or whoever it was the answering voice belonged to, to put him through to Lady Simms.

'Might Hi enquire who is speaking, sir?'

'Mr Adams.'

'Kindly hold the line, Mr Adams.'

Lady Simms arrived at the other end, and Sammy, who did not suffer from any sense of inferiority, breezily informed her he was now in a position to supply her with everything that had been listed for the dormitories.

'Oh, my stepdaughter's dealing with that, Mr Adams,' said the energetic Lady Simms. 'I am dealing with the lives and well-being of the unfortunate children, whom I have now decided to put into uniform.'

'They're going to wear specially designed St Stephen's uniforms?' enquired Sammy, business acumen clicking.

'St Stephen's, yes, what an excellent thought,' said Lady Simms. 'Uniforms of an attractive kind, not cast-off clothing. Really, the ideas some people have about dressing orphans are quite pitiful.'

'Your ladyship,' said Sammy, 'have you been quoted for the manufacture of selfsame garments?'

'I've only come to the decision this weekend. I shall make enquiries, Mr Adams.'

'I think I should come and see you,' said Sammy, in

403

the fashion of a kind businessman ready to do her a favour. 'You give me the details, Lady Simms, and it will be my pleasure to quote you for high quality uniforms from high quality manufacturers. You would want two uniforms for each orphan, of course. Yes, I can see that. And hats for the girls and caps for the boys.'

'I also require warm winter mackintoshes and galoshes,' said Lady Simms, who never wasted words and never dithered. 'Come and see me Thursday morning at ten o'clock. Punctual arrival, please, Mr Adams. As for the dormitory items, although I'd want to see your quotation and to have your guarantee of durability, please deal with my stepdaughter Polly.'

'The reputation of Adams Enterprises has been built on guaranteed goods, your ladyship.' Sammy sounded commendably well-spoken. He kept his market-style cajolery for his stall customers, who believed a picturesque harangue was what they were entitled to.

'Oh, I can recognise rubbish, Mr Adams,' said Lady Simms. 'However, Mr Greenberg, a most helpful gentleman, has assured me several times you could be relied on. Thursday morning, then, at ten, and I hope delivery of the uniforms won't take too long, although I understand it would be impossible to get them until after opening day.'

'I might be able to pleasantly surprise you,' said Sammy, and made a mental note to have a word with Mr Morris.

'Really? How promising. Goodbye and thank you.'

Sammy spoke to Boots at supper that evening.

'Telephone Miss Simms first thing tomorrow, Boots. Tell her we can supply this week and give her the total cost. First thing. Don't forget.'

'Sammy,' said Chinese Lady, 'kindly don't give Boots orders. He's older than you and don't get up to things I don't know about. And who's Miss Simms?'

'Young lady Boots is doing business with over stuff for an orphanage,' said Sammy. 'She desires his exclusive attention.'

'Oh, she does, does she?' said Emily, whose working day had been one of intermittent self-examination. 'Well, she's not gettin' it.'

'Now, Em'ly love, if it's business, Boots has got to be obliging,' said Chinese Lady.

'Not exclusive he hasn't,' said Emily.

'Yes, and how obliging has he got to be, Em?' asked Tommy. 'That's the dauntin' question.'

'We won't have no uncalled-for insinuation, Tommy,' said Chinese Lady, unfailing in the watch she kept on her sons' talk and behaviour.

'What's she like?' Emily asked of Boots.

'Oh, reasonably female,' said Boots.

'Never heard of reasonable females,' said Sammy misguidedly, 'didn't know there were any.'

Chinese Lady sat up straight and asked, 'Am I hearing you correct, Sammy Adams?'

'Well, Ma, I got to admit it,' said Sammy, 'I just committed an error of highly 'orrendous multitude.'

'Magnitude,' said Boots.

'Hand on me 'eart, Chinese Lady,' declared Sammy, 'I never made a more grievous error in me life. I consider you and Em'ly to be highly reasonable females, gratifyin' to your fam'ly.'

'I don't know, words fly about in this house like weddin' confetti,' said Tommy.

'Sammy, don't you call me a female,' said Emily, 'I'm a married wife.'

'Married wife,' murmured Boots, 'yes, that sounds reasonable.'

'Anyway, you're not goin' to be exclusive to that Miss Simms,' said Emily, doubts about her recent wifely attitude assailing her, 'I'm just not havin' it.'

'More and more reasonable,' said Boots, 'a married husband should only be exclusive to his married wife.'

'Are you teasin' our Em'ly?' asked Chinese Lady, hoping he was. He hadn't been doing too much of it these last weeks. It had a special meaning to her. She saw it as love-teasing, however much she upbraided him about it.

'Only pointing out what married men owe to their married wives,' said Boots.

Emily laughed. Chinese Lady looked pleased.

Boots woke up. It was two o'clock in the morning. Emily was snuggling and cuddling. He felt the warmth of firm bare breasts against his chest. Her face was buried in the pillows close to his. She was awake, her arms around him, her shapely body inducing arousal in his.

'Emily?'

'I can't get to sleep.' Her voice was faint and muffled.

'What's the matter?'

'You. No, me. Boots, oh, I been so silly, I been thinking me job could take the place of a baby.' He felt her shudder as if she was racked. 'Now I'm scared.'

'Scared?'

'In case I've made you stop wantin' to love me.'

'You and your worries,' murmured Boots in affection, 'I can't stop wanting that. It's just that we agreed to give it a long rest—'

'Oh, don't bring that up. That's what I've been so silly about. Love me, love me now.'

'Emily, you sure?'

Her arms tightened around him, her face turned and she whispered, 'You're the best husband a girl could have. You got to love me or I'll never never get to sleep.'

He loved her. She was intensely passionate. He was very affected to find she wept a little afterwards.

'Emily, has that made you cry?'

'Oh, yes. It was lovely, wasn't it? Wasn't it?'

'Yes, Em, very lovely.'

CHAPTER THIRTY

Boots, a much happier man the following morning, telephoned Polly at nine-thirty.

'You stinker,' she said, 'I'm having my breakfast.'

'I'm surprised you're out of bed,' said Boots. 'Or perhaps you're not. I won't keep you, I just want to say yes.'

'Yes? Yes what? That you'll make love to me?'

'No, I won't say that,' said Boots.

'That's it, make my day a thing of bliss.'

'Now, Polly, be your age.'

'I'll break your leg,' said Polly.

'I believe you. However, we can arrange to deliver all the stuff this coming Thursday.'

'Well, aren't you a clever old scout? What time?'

Boots had the answer ready, knowing Sammy was seeing Lady Simms at ten o'clock.

'Say about eleven at the orphanage, madam.'

'Rats to madam.'

'Well, the customer's always right,' said Boots.

'This customer is a tiger,' said Polly. 'I'll meet you there, at the orphanage. You can come on your delivery van, I'll drive you back to your shop after we've had lunch here. That's an order, Robert. Well, pleasure should mix with business on auspicious occasions, don't you think so?'

'I like the sound of auspicious,' said Boots. 'Will the Royal family be there?'

'No, me. I'm auspicious.'

'Good morning, Miss Simms, enjoy your porridge.'

* * *

In order not to give Sammy any time to make enquiring telephone calls, Boots did not tell him about delivery arrangements until Wednesday evening.

'Carter Paterson's are picking all the stuff up from the warehouse, Sammy, and will deliver it at the orphanage about eleven tomorrow morning. You're required to meet Miss Simms there at that time. You can go from the house, of course. She wants a responsible partner of Adams Enterprises on the spot, so that she can chuck any faulty items back at you. You're the more responsible partner.'

'I'll go,' said Sammy. 'Be a pleasure after I've collared this new order for uniforms and etceteras from her gracious mum. But don't talk about faulty items, Boots, it sounds like you don't have confidence in the business. Talk like that might get about, and we don't want our foundations to sound as if they're comin' apart before the cement's had a chance to set. So oblige me by watching what comes out of your airy-fairy north-and-south.'

Hearing that, Emily marched from the scullery into the kitchen.

'Sammy Adams,' she said, 'kindly don't speak to my one-and-only husband like he was a skivvy from nowhere, and you was the High Lord of everywhere. Boots is head of the fam'ly after Mum, and you ain't come of age yet.'

'I'm beginnin' to really like you, Em,' said Sammy, 'you're takin' after our Chinese Lady.'

That was a compliment as far as Emily was concerned, so she gave him a pat after the fashion of Chinese Lady, and said, 'Good, it's nice to 'ear you soundin' human, Sammy.'

'My pleasure,' said Sammy. 'Where's Tommy?'

'Gone to Aunt Victoria's,' said Chinese Lady from the scullery, where she was frying liver and bacon and onions.

'What for, has she ordered a dinner service from the stall?' asked Sammy.

'He's goin' to the pictures,' called Chinese Lady.

'With Aunt Victoria?' said Sammy, choosing to be a bit simple.

'With Vi,' said Boots, reading about the threat of another coal strike in the daily paper, 'and without a push.'

'What's that you said, Boots?' asked Chinese Lady.

'Nothing very much,' said Boots.

'Em'ly love,' said Chinese Lady, 'I don't know any other nice girl who'd of taken on that flippant son of mine like you did. Him and that upside-down tongue of his, it must make you feel sometimes you don't know if he's comin' or goin'.'

'Well, he can be a desp'rate handful, Mum,' said Emily, 'he really can. I do my best to fight the devil that's in him, but he nearly always finishes up on top.'

'Pardon?' said Boots.

'Could yer repeat that, Em?' asked Sammy.

'Oh, me gawd.' Emily turned pink. 'I didn't mean – I wasn't talkin' about – oh, 'elp.' She rushed back into the scullery, to the sanctuary of Chinese Lady's understanding. The funny side of things caught her, and she giggled. The frying-pan fumes caught Chinese Lady, and she coughed.

Miss Polly Simms found it almost impossible to believe herself the victim of another piece of trickery by the man currently occupying most of her thoughts. It was his brother Sammy who arrived at the orphanage a few minutes before the horse-drawn Carter Paterson van turned up. Polly had been at the orphanage since ten, exercising much the same kind of energy as her stepmother in getting the four dormitories cleared of everything categorised as junk. When she realised Robert Adams wasn't going to present himself, Polly showed her teeth in a fixed, glittering smile of wicked-minded frustration. It might have intimidated anyone other than Sammy. Then, because she was what she was, a free and irrepressible young woman, with a highly developed sense of humour, she shrieked with laughter. It made Sammy wonder if she was all there. It did not worry him. The orphanage and its chief patron, Lady Simms, were all that counted. Lady Simms had just approved the prices quoted for the dormitory supplies, and he had enjoyed a very promising conversation with her concerning uniforms, mackintoshes and galoshes, in respect of which he had already found sources of manufacture and supply. He had in mind a sixty per cent profit, and was beginning to like his growing connection with the rag trade.

He coped blithely with the idiosyncrasies of Polly, whose comments on the stuff brought in by the Carter Paterson men had to be heard to be believed. She did not invite him to have lunch with her at her parents' house. She only asked him, just before he left, to give a message to his brother Robert.

'My pleasure,' said Sammy.

'Tell him I'm devising a painful death for him, slow burning by fire.'

'I trust, Miss Simms, my junior partner hasn't upset you in any way,' said Sammy in well-spoken business style.

'Sammy,' said Polly, 'don't pain me in my pinny by referring to him as your junior. It's not on, old lad. You're coming along nicely, and I know some schoolgirls who'd be willing to share an ice-cream cornet with you, but you're still out of Robert's class.'

'He's a little older, I'll say that much, but doesn't have my business experience,' said Sammy.

'Dear boy, who's talking about business experience?'

'I am, Miss Simms.'

'Ugh to business experience, old bean, and don't call me Miss Simms. Just tell Robert he's going to die an excruciating death.'

It did not occur to Sammy that Polly Simms had set

410

her cap at Boots. He rarely thought about things like that. They got in the way of business.

A little after six o'clock that day, Chinese Lady, placing a freshly-made pot of tea on the kitchen table, heard sounds from upstairs. Emily and Boots were up there, having not long been in from work.

'Boots! Oh, yer swine! I'll kick yer silly if yer don't let go!' Emily was yelling, but there was laughter in her voice.

'Never seen any as pretty as these, Em.' That was Boots, teasing.

'I'll give yer pretty when they've just been ironed – oh no you don't, yer wicked devil.'

Chinese Lady smiled to herself. She had been ironing during the day and had left a neat heap of underwear on Emily's side of the bed. Boots was like his dad. Well, some men took a very wicked interest in a wife's underwear.

Emily sounded hysterical with laughter.

Chinese Lady smiled again. Whatever had been wrong with those two, they were just like they always had been now.

'Where's the girl?' asked Sammy when he arrived at the stall last thing Friday evening.

Tommy, packing up to get the stall ready for Fred to take away, said with heavy sarcasm, 'I presume it's Miss Susie Brown you're kindly askin' after?'

Sammy, who could ride any kind of sarcasm, said, 'Yes, where is she? She don't usually go off on Fridays without her dibs.'

'I sent her home this morning,' said Tommy, grateful that it was almost time to go home himself. He'd had a busy day on his own, and a trying one too, with people coming up to inspect the gramophone on display, and to ask for a sample listen to 'I'm Forever Blowing Bubbles'. If only Susie had been there they could have

411

taken more orders than he'd had time to manage. But Susie had obviously been very unwell when she arrived, and he'd simply had to send her home.

'On a Friday?' said Sammy, frowning. 'Not being well on a Friday is considerable inconvenient. What's she got, a summer cold and a runny nose?'

'No, mumps,' said Tommy, 'and mumps is painful.'

'Mumps?'

'So her father said. He came along this afternoon. Susie went to the doctor's on her way home. Her mum put her to bed. Her dad asked if we wanted a doctor's certificate. I said no, seeing a doctor's certificate would cost her a bob. Her dad asked if her job would be all right. I said yes. I'd have liked it, by the way, if you'd put in an appearance for a change.'

'Hold it,' said Sammy, 'I don't want to hear you gripin' like Bert did. Bert knew the arrangements, so do you. You're in charge of the stall, and you got Susie as assistant, and you're both highly remunerated. Me, I've got a hundred and one other things to do.'

'Don't get saucy,' said Tommy.

'Just pointin' you at the do's and don'ts, Tommy, that's all. But all right, I'll give yer a hand tomorrow if Susie's still off sick.'

'Well, it'll help you not to lose money,' said Tommy.

Susie's mother, Mrs Brown, opened the door of her flat the next morning to find Sammy there. He lifted his hat to her, out of respect for what Chinese Lady would have expected of him.

'Oh, you're Mister Adams,' said Mrs Brown.

'Right first time,' said Sammy, 'and top of the morning to you, Mrs Brown. How's your unwell daughter, may I ask?'

'Well, a bit hot and flushed, like, but the medicine's done her good, and thank you for askin'.'

'I'd better say hello to her,' said Sammy. 'I don't want her thinking I don't have no regard for unwell employees.'

'But she's got mumps,' said Mrs Brown.

'Dear me, poor child,' said Sammy, 'but I've had mumps, measles, chicken pox and whoopin' cough myself, and am accordingly immune.'

'Goodness, would you believe,' said Mrs Brown, impressed.

'And even if immunity had passed me by,' said Sammy, 'my reputation as a considerate employer wouldn't allow me not to come and give me sympathy to your misfortunate daughter, Mrs Brown.'

'Well, my word, I never did,' said the overwhelmed Mrs Brown. A wrapped sheaf of roses came to her eye, as did two bulging brown paper bags in a cardboard box.

'I come bearing solicitous gifts for yer daughter that's laid low,' said Sammy.

'How kind,' said Mrs Brown. 'You best step in, Mister Adams, while I go an' tell her you're here, like.'

Susie, in the double bed she shared with her small sister, was flushed and aching. She let out an anguished wail when told she had a solicitous visitor and who he was.

'Mum, no, yer can't let 'im in, not with me face like this, all swoll up. I'll die.'

'Course you won't, love. You just gone a bit red and lumpy, that's all.'

Susie wailed again. 'Mum, I'll die, I tell yer,' she cried, 'I'll just pass away if Mister Sammy sees me lookin' like I been boiled.'

'Now why would you die, you silly?' said Mrs Brown soothingly.

'Because I would, that's why,' said Susie, who felt all the horror a girl of sixteen could feel at the thought of a healthy young man discovering she was hideous with mumps. 'Mum, tell 'im I'm goin' to me death or something, that visitors is fatal to me complaint.'

'He's come to see you very consid'rate, like,' said Mrs Brown, 'and I think he's brought you some nice flowers—'

413

'Well, when he's gone,' said Susie despairingly, 'put them on me grave as a wreath.'

'Well, dear, I don't think I can't not let him see you. I'll just ask him in to say hello to you.'

Susie, fraught, gulped as her mother disappeared. She tugged frantically at the covering sheet. When Sammy came in she was lying with the bedclothes pulled up to her chin and part of the sheet hiding all of her face except her eyes, which gazed up at him in enormous dark blue horror.

Holy bananas, thought Sammy, why am I doing this? I might have known she wouldn't be anything but great round saucers. Look at them. If I don't watch myself, I'll end up as her second dad, her first uncle, her daft grandfather and her fairy godmother as well. I might even leave her something in my will. There ought to be a law against eyes like she's got.

He muttered. Susie, body hot and prickly from mumps, face red and lumpy under the sheet, prayed for Jesus to take her up to heaven and save her from torturing mortification.

'H'm,' said Sammy, 'I can't say you gettin' the mumps is convenient, Miss Brown.'

'Oh, how can yer be so unfeeling?' moaned the suffering patient.

'Now, Susie, I've come to give you me condolent sympathy, which is only right,' said Sammy. 'I suppose that is you, is it, under that sheet?'

'I wish it wasn't,' croaked Susie, 'and I'll only be a dying corpse soon, I'm near to death already.'

'Don't talk like that,' said Sammy, 'how'd you think Tommy's goin' to run the stall without you?' The huge eyes became a dark and more distraught blue. 'Look, cover your eyes up as well if the light's hurtin' them.'

A suffering moan came from behind the sheet.

'Oh, I never endured more dread mortification than this.' For all that she had had only an elementary education, Susie often showed a gift for words. Sammy wondered again why he had let himself in for this, especially as he had pressing business to attend to as a Saturday help to Tommy.

'Now, Susie, it ain't as bad as that,' he said, and Susie stared in terrible dismay as he sat down on the bedside chair. Oh, he wasn't going to stay, was he? He wasn't going to sit there and watch her slowly die? Horror became chronic. 'Mumps is nothing to worry about, not now you're a growing girl. After a couple of days all yer lumps, bumps and aches will hardly bother yer.' Susie moaned again. 'I don't want to hear any dispiritin' sounds,' said Sammy. 'Come on, sit up, and I'll peel you an apple. Fruit's good for mumps.'

'Sit up, sit up?' The covering sheet turned moist against her mouth. 'Oh, may the Lord forgive yer, Mister Adams.'

'I'll ask Him to remember me compassion,' said Sammy. 'Look, I've brought you apples and pears, and Ma Earnshaw sent you some grapes. Oh, and there's a few roses your mum is puttin' in a vase for you. They'll cheer you up.' Sammy thought the little bedroom cheering itself. It looked as if Mrs Brown kept it so. Many Walworth women were like that, never mind how poor they were. As for the roses, Sammy had lifted half a dozen from a vase at home when Chinese Lady wasn't looking. Mr Finch's huge bouquet was still in acceptable condition. 'Susie, you listening to me? You goin' to sit up and let me peel an apple for you?'

'Oh, Mister Adams, yer could kill a girl with that sort of kindness,' gasped Susie. 'But I got to thank you for the roses, only I don't mind if yer want to go now, seeing you must be terrible busy.'

'Well, I can't stay here gassin', and that's a fact,' said Sammy. 'Tommy needs me on the stall. Your mum's got your earnings for the week, and your dad's doing a good job at the shop and yard.' He came to his feet and picked up his hat from the foot of the bed. Her fearful eyes followed his every movement. 'Now don't

415

forget to take your medicine, and come back to the stall when you're feeling better. Is your sweetheart comin' to see you?'

'He's not me sweetheart,' mumbled Susie wetly, 'he's just me friend.'

'Well, perhaps he'll come and sit with you this evening and cheer you up.'

'I'll be dead by then, that's what I'll be, and 'e'll 'ave to sit with me corpse,' cried Susie as passionately as she could against the moist sheet.

'That's it, you're sounding livelier already,' said Sammy, and escaped the outraged blue eyes by leaving.

The unkind fates that had deprived Emily and Boots of Rosie, and given Emily her own kind of worries, relented a little. They received a letter from Ned, telling them the empty house was back on the market. They went to look over it. They liked it very much, its living-room and kitchen overlooking a garden that actually boasted an apple tree – a wonder to Emily – and its four bedrooms all a good size. And it had a bathroom, just like Lizzy and Ned's house did. When they returned the keys and asked for details of rent and what the freehold price was, the agents said they would write to them.

Susie fretted. She'd been off work a week and two days, and the doctor said she wasn't to go back until he gave his permission. She began to have thoughts about getting the sack. What with that worry, and not earning any money, and not being allowed out of her room if her sister and brothers were around, Susie felt life was giving her an awful pasting. Mumps of all things, imagine catching mumps at her advanced age. Kids caught mumps, not grown-up girls of sixteen. Oh, the humiliation of being told by the doctor she was contagious. Her young sister had had to sleep on a mattress in her brothers' room. Eight-year-old Sally thought that screaming fun. Not so her brothers, William and Freddy. Sally was a terror at starting pillow fights. It all went on, the yells and the shrieks, while Susie had to stay by herself in her bedroom. It was like being a leper. Unclean. She said so to her father when he brought her in a cup of tea and rockcake hot and fresh from the oven one afternoon.

'I never heard you talk silly before, Susie,' said Mr Brown. 'Course you're not unclean, lovey.'

'Well, I feel it,' said Susie. 'I bet when I do go back to work, people won't come near the stall. I bet I'll be all spots and rashes and peeling skin. I'll 'ave to go into a leprous institution and never come out. Dad, you best ask the vicar to come round and give me a last blessing from the doorway.'

'No, I don't think I'll do that, me angel, not when you ain't got a single spot or rash, and nor can I see no peeling skin. You're just a mite pale, that's all, but still pretty as a picture. Well, p'raps yer gone a bit thin—'

'Oh, no,' wailed Susie, 'Mister Adams'll ask Mum to stuff me up with steak-and-kidney puddings. Oh, yer done it now, Dad, telling me I've gone thin.'

'Well, not all that thin, just a bit peaky, like,' said Mr Brown.

'I'll have to beseech the Lord in me prayers tonight, I just know I will.'

Mr Brown nodded sympathetically.

'Well, praying never does no 'arm,' he said.

'I also got to pray I don't get the push for being off work so long,' said Susie mournfully.

It was exactly two weeks before she did go back to work, arriving anxiously early on a Friday morning. To her horror, a woman of about thirty was there. Mister Tommy hadn't come yet. The woman was arranging the day's display. Susie said hello.

'Oh, you're Susie Brown, are yer? Glad to meet yer. I'm Mrs Walker.'

417

'Mrs Walker, you been taken on by Mister Sammy Adams?'

'Well,' said Mrs Walker cheerfully, 'I been spendin' time helping, and yesterday Sammy give me the job permanent. I was in china and glass down the Cut for years, so I 'ad experience to offer.'

'Oh,' said Susie, feeling she had been dealt a mortal blow.

'Watcher, Susie,' called Ma Earnshaw, polishing apples. 'Better now, are yer, ducky?'

'Yes, thank you,' said Susie, who had never felt iller, such was the wounding nature of being replaced.

'That's good,' said Ma Earnshaw. 'Yer look a bit suffering, but at least them mumps didn't take yer fatally.'

Susie thought fatal mumps wouldn't have mattered now, except her mum and dad would have been upset.

'Well, there you are, Susie,' said a friendly voice. Turning, she saw Mister Tommy. And Mister Sammy was with him. Tommy looked stalwart and comforting, Sammy looked lean and businesslike. 'Nice to see yer, Susie,' said Tommy, a welcoming smile on his face. 'Feeling better?'

'I was,' said Susie in pointed bitterness, and gave Sammy a disgusted look.

'Morning to you,' said Sammy, who could take disgusted looks by the dozen, but suffered traumatic weakness whenever Susie's eyes got the better of him. 'We're gratified you're on your feet again. Let's take a look at you.' He took a look, Susie clean and neat in a blouse and skirt, her working overall folded over her arm. 'You've lost weight,' he said accusingly.

'Oh, you'd 'ave liked me to rise up from me sickbed like a suet dumpling, I suppose!' whispered Susie fiercely.

'Sammy, you want me to display some of this Delft china?' enquired Mrs Walker. There was a stout cardboard box on the stall. On it was stencilled DELFT CHINA in bold capitals. In between those two words, and in much smaller letters, was stencilled STYLE.

'What's that?' asked Sammy, concerned, much against his will, by Susie's peaky look.

'These Delft pieces,' said Mrs Walker, 'd'you want—'

'They're not Delft,' said Susie bitterly.

'Leave 'em till I come back,' said Sammy, 'I'll be about thirty minutes. Now, kindly come with me,' he said to Susie.

Suspecting he was going to give her the sack in private, Susie compressed her lips. She glanced at Tommy. He gave her a cheerful smile.

'What 'ave I got to come for?' she asked Sammy.

'For the good of yer health,' said Sammy.

She went stiffly with him, walking between the rows of stalls preparing to open up. Her small nose was in the air, her young bosom as proud as Chinese Lady's could be.

'Where you takin' me?' she asked.

'Had any breakfast, have you?'

'Yes, thank you,' she said, 'a cup of tea and some toast, but if I'd known I'd lost me job I'd 'ave asked me mum to give me 'emlock. I didn't think you'd take on someone else when I was in me sickbed. When I think of how I've praised yer to the Lord, Mister Adams, I wonder at me simple-mindedness.'

'Kind of yer to give me a mention,' said Sammy, 'but you can put yer Bible away and duly consider the benefits of a mug of hot Bovril at Toni's.'

'I don't want nothing, nothing. I'd choke to death.'

'I'll come to yer funeral,' said Sammy.

'Oh, yer 'eartless monster!' breathed Susie.

'While you're choking, we'll have a little talk,' said Sammy, and ushered her into Toni's. Costermongers who had been up since dawn were breakfasting. Susie was quivering as she sat down. Toni supplied Sammy with a mug of hot Bovril and a steaming cup of tea.

Sammy placed the mug in front of Susie and sat down opposite her.

The aroma of the Bovril was something to be savoured, and Susie said, 'It's kind of yer, Mister Adams, but I 'ope yer won't mind me saying it feels like yer givin' me the condemned felon's last meal.'

'Well, I do mind, Miss Brown, because I'm not,' said Sammy. 'I just don't want you startin' your new job lookin' sorry for yerself. I'm considerable pleased Jesus didn't take you up to heaven, not at your age, but—'

'Mister Sammy, what d'yer mean, new job?' Susie came to life. 'What new job.'

'I'm transferring you,' said Sammy, 'so drink that Bovril.'

Susie experienced the bliss of a reprieve as he talked to her. He'd been thinking things over, he said, while she'd been hiding her mumps under the bedclothes. The stall was good bread-and-butter business, but it wouldn't make anyone a fortune. There was more important work Susie could do. The shop was doing well considering there wasn't much money about. The trouble with the country was that governments didn't know the first thing about using money to make more, they just gave most of it to civil servants. If all the politicians were chucked out of Parliament, and fifty sharp businessmen and fifty sensible women like his mother were given the job of running things, the country would benefit accordingly.

The reason why the shop was doing well was because it specialised in bargains. Men's suits were selling good, and he was thinking of stocking ladies' costumes. People said you couldn't sell clothes for both sexes in a shop, but you could in a store, and Sam's Emporium was going to be advertised as a store. Boots was in need of an assistant, and he'd have to have one when ladies' wear became an important part of stocks. A female one. Boots had agreed Susie could do the job, even if she was a bit young. She'd not have to face the freezing cold of the market in winter. Anyone who caught mumps out of doors in summer was liable to catch pneumonia in the winter, specially a female girl who'd gone a bit skinny again.

There was plenty of space at the back of the shop, where a small fitting-room could easily be knocked up. Susie wouldn't have to work on Sundays, so she could start going to the morning services again, but he hoped that wouldn't mean she'd bombard him with more Bible talk. He'd pay her a wage of twelve and six a week, plus five per cent commission on all her own sales. If she was smart enough she could earn unlimited dibs. Did she fancy the job?

Susie was eyeing him like a girl who'd been rescued from an overturned lifeboat in a stormy sea. She had drunk her Bovril in dreamlike fashion while listening to what she thought was a wondrous recitation. It had come like poetry to her ears.

'Mister Adams,' she said, and her eyes were big and melting, which made Sammy transfer his interest to his teacup. 'Mister Adams, I'm never goin' to call you hard names again, specially after misjudging yer like I did when I thought—'

'Yes, all right, never mind that,' said Sammy. 'It's just a matter of good business.' Which he considered it was. He'd recognised her selling ability ages ago, and whatever commission she earned in the shop would mean she also earned profits for him. 'I'm considering opening an exclusive ladies' shop later on, and if you proved really smart in me emporium, I might think about havin' you run the ladies' establishment for me. I'm only saying I might, now, and only when you're a bit older.'

'Oh, Mister Sammy.' Susie gazed at him with her soul in her eyes. Sammy had a shocking feeling he was falling into them. He muttered. 'I can't 'ardly tell yer just how pleasured I am,' she said earnestly.

'Well, if you'd stop lookin' at me as if I'm the twelve

disciples, that would be something,' said Sammy. 'Listen, there's all kind of businessmen. There's the ones that give charity and accordingly don't last, the ones that just keep goin' and always have headaches, the ones that make steady profits by not takin' any risks, and the ones that make fortunes by being as hard as iron. Well, I'm as hard as iron.'

'Mister Sammy, course you're not,' said Susie. 'I know I miscalled yer, much to me shame, but yer see, the mumps brought me spirits dreadful low. I'm never goin' to believe you're as hard as iron, or that you grind the faces of the poor and 'umble, not when I know you're kind and lovin' really.'

'Eh?' Sammy felt appalled. Loving was plain suicidal. Blind O'Reilly, she really would get him in the end, she'd make him her guardian and benefactor. It cost a fortune to be a benefactor, specially to a female. 'Now look, cut that out, there's no lovin' goin' on.'

'Oh, I meant Christian lovin',' said Susie hastily, 'like the Good Samaritan showed. Or fatherly, like.'

That's it, thought Sammy, that's really it. She's come right out with it.

'Once and for all, I ain't the Good Samaritan,' he said, 'I don't go in for personal ruination. And I'm not yer father. Got it?'

'Yes, Mister Sammy.'

'So don't let's have any more of it.'

'No, Mister Sammy.'

'Right. You can start work at the shop on Monday. Or if you feel up to it, you can start today and do a full day tomorrow. That'll earn you a few bob by tomorrow night, you're probably skint after being off for two weeks.'

'Oh, I'd love to start now,' said Susie in gladness. 'Mister Sammy, yer so—'

'Leave off,' said Sammy. 'Boots'll look after you at the shop, but I recommend you don't keep on about his Christian soul, he ain't too partial to overdoses of the New Testament, likin' it only in moderation.'

'Yes, Mister Sammy,' said Susie, 'but I 'ope yer won't mind me saying it's been a pleasure workin' for Mister Tommy, and that it's goin' to be a pleasure workin' for Mister Boots. You got two awf'lly nice brothers.'

'Yes, all right,' said Sammy tersely, 'just as long as you remember I can't afford to be nice myself. I got to stick to being businesslike.'

'Yes, course you have, Mister Sammy, you got to try being as hard as iron.'

Sammy, not sure if that was a piece of young female sauce, peered suspiciously at her.

'I trust, Miss Brown, you ain't trying to hand me a lemon,' he said.

'Oh, no,' said Susie. 'I want yer to know that from this day forth I'm goin' to cast out me sins of resentment and give yer respect.'

Sammy struggled to repress an involuntary grin. He failed. The grin arrived and spread. The next moment he was laughing. Other diners looked. Susie looked. She smiled.

That Mister Sammy was so droll.

CHAPTER THIRTY-ONE

'Two pounds?' said Chinese Lady, bristling.

'That's what the landlord's agent says in this letter,' said Emily.

'Two pounds a week rent?' said Chinese Lady.

'Or three hundred and eighty-five pounds freehold,' said Boots.

'It being in a 'ighly desirable residence area, the letter says,' remarked Emily, looking as if the fates had been unkind again.

'What's freehold?' asked Chinese Lady.

'Ownership of the property,' said Boots.

'Blackmail, that's what two pounds a week rent is,' said Chinese Lady, 'scandalisin' blackmail to try and make you buy it. No wonder it come up for sale again. Well, you can't find all that money, it's a fortune, and you can't pay that much rent, not out of your two pounds ten a week. I know there's Em'ly's wages too, but I hope no son of mine is goin' to expect his wife to go out to work all her life. A wife's got a home to build, and a husband's got to provide, like ordered by God. That landlord, well, I never heard of anyone more graspin'.'

'Boots would like to buy, really,' said Emily, 'like Lizzy and Ned did.'

'Glad to hear you speak up, Em,' said Sammy, interrupting his thoughts on what a profit-making contact Lady Simms was, and highly valuable too in the way her requirements had taken him deeper into the realms of the garment-manufacturing industry, commonly called the rag trade. 'You and Boots don't want to pay

424

rent, in any case. It's a game for mugs and for poor blighters stricken by poverty. Poverty gets yer trapped, and I ain't keen on anyone in this fam'ly gettin' trapped. We been through it all with Chinese Lady, which is our reverent ma—'

'Revered?' suggested Boots.

'There he goes again, that Sammy Adams, calling me Ma,' said Chinese Lady.

'Humble apologies, old girl,' said Sammy. 'But none of us don't want to get dragged under again by paying rent to graspers and Scrooges. You finish up not owning anything. Don't you pay two quid a week rent to any of 'em, Boots.'

'He's not goin' to,' said Emily, 'but it's awful disappointing.'

'Still,' said Tommy, thinking of his future, 'you got to consider paying rent to start with. Well, you got to in most cases.' Taking Vi regularly to the pictures had given him thoughts about what it would be like to marry a really nice girl, and Vi was a good example of just how nice some girls could be. Tarty girls had their place in the lives of some blokes, but most fellers steered clear of marrying one.

'Boots could buy our house if he got a loan,' said Sammy. 'The landlord couldn't ask more than two hundred for it.'

'Boots and Em'ly don't want this house,' said Chinese Lady firmly, and went into the scullery to look at the potatoes, boiling on the gas cooker. The steam rose as she lifted the lid, and she coughed.

'I'm havin' the rooms over the shop done up,' said Sammy, 'so that me and Tommy can move in sometime, which means you don't need to worry about us, Boots.'

'Oh, I get lumps in me throat thinking of the fam'ly breakin' up,' said Emily.

'Em'ly, you don't want us under your feet all your lives,' said Sammy, 'it wouldn't be right or fair. Besides which, Tommy's courtin' Cousin Vi.'

'Eh?' said Tommy, and only then did it occur to him that he didn't, after all, know a nicer girl than Vi. 'Jigger me,' he said. Then, 'Mind yer business.'

'Fam'ly business, that is, you and Vi,' said Sammy, 'and Chinese Lady's got a very fond regard for her.'

'I heard that,' called Chinese Lady, opening the oven door to discover the sausage toad-in-the-hole had risen to brown perfection.

'Good on yer for hearing, old lady,' said Boots, 'we all share your fond regard.'

'Boots, none of your clever remarks,' she said, 'come and help me dish up.'

Boots joined his mother in the scullery. She was mashing the boiled King Edward potatoes, adding margarine, pepper and a little milk to them. He took the sausage toad out of the oven.

'Well?' he said, as he began to divide it up.

In a low voice Chinese Lady said, 'I just want to say don't you let none of the fam'ly make you stay here, in this house. We've had our time here, Boots, we've had trying times and fam'ly times, but now we've come to movin' time. You can still get a house cheap to rent near Brixton Hill if them near Lizzy and Ned is too expensive. You could rent for fifteen shillings a week, and still have a garden. I'm not saying being near Lizzy and Ned wouldn't be nice, I can't think of nowhere nicer, but—' She coughed again, a little raspingly.

'Don't worry, Emily and I will work something out,' said Boots. 'And you go and see Doctor McManus about that cough.'

'No need for that,' she said, 'it's only a chest cold.'

The telephone rang at the back of the shop. Boots answered it, leaving Susie to deal with customers.

'Is that Stinker Adams?' enquired Polly Simms.

'Sam's Bargain Bazaar,' said Boots, 'you've got the wrong number, madam.'

'No, I haven't, that's you all right, you coward. When

426

I popped in last week it was to murder you for doing me in the eye again.' Her visit had been fruitless and frustrating. There had been too many customers, as well as an obtrusive girl assistant. She disliked her at once. Far too beguiling a creature. 'Oh, well, I've reached the stage of almost forgiving you.'

'Very decent of you,' said Boots, 'but I'm a bit too busy to deal with almost. Send me a postcard when I'm fully forgiven.'

He heard gurgling laughter at the other end of the line.

'Darling, do stop fighting Polly,' she said.

'Are we fighting?'

'I'm not. You are.' She laughed again. But she was beginning to be alarmed for herself. Fancying a man was one thing. The suspicion that she was actually falling in love was another. She enjoyed men being in love with her, but she was sure her spirit of independence would not let her enjoy being in love herself. She had let Tommies make love to her, as other women ambulance drivers had, in an emotional desire to give them pleasure before they became part of the rising mountains of dead. But she had escaped the chains that possessive love for a man would put around her. Further, it would be hell to fall in love with a man who was married, as she suspected Robert Adams was. It had been fun in the beginning to go after him. Now she was in serious pursuit, something she had never contemplated before. Always it had been the other way about. 'No, really, old thing, you're fully forgiven, and my father would like to meet you.'

'The general?' said Boots. 'Hard to believe he would, but if it's true, tell him to come to the shop and I'll sell him some ex-Army braces. Or socks. Or both.' He might have told Polly to push off, but her stepmother was a valued customer. 'Well, a pleasure to talk to you, Miss Simms. Good morning.'

'I'll give you Miss Simms, you ratbag. How would you

like me to chuck a brick through your shop window?'

'It might be worth watching,' said Boots, 'but it wouldn't be a great help to business.'

'Then just say when you can come to lunch and meet my father.'

'I'll give it serious thought and telephone you.'

'You'd better. Ask of Polly anything you desire and you shall receive.'

'Three hundred and eighty-five pounds?' said Boots.

'What?'

'Well, three hundred would do.'

'Is this phone deceiving my ears?' asked Polly. 'Are you talking about filthy lucre again? Stepmother Mama doesn't owe you all that, does she?'

'I hope not. It's bad business to sue valued customers. Must go now. So long, Polly.'

'You're a lovely man. See you, darling.'

Boots replaced the phone. Susie called.

'Mister Manager, I just sold a suit.'

'To a lady?' smiled Boots. Susie was an engaging young girl.

'Well, she said she just wanted to look, to see if one would do for her 'usband, but people who just look don't always come back, do they? So I asked about 'is size, and showed 'er one that would probably fit, and said if it didn't she could bring it back and we'd change it. Did I do right?'

'I think we could say, Susie, that you turned a might-have-been into a customer.'

'Oh, yer nice to work for,' said Susie. She thought Boots ever so distinguished-looking, considering he was only in his mid-twenties, which Tommy had said he was. Women customers sometimes couldn't hardly tear themselves away from him, because he treated them very gentlemanly, like, yet with a little bit of the devil about him, exciting to some ladies. Lots of the lady customers chatted to him about everything they could lay their tongues to.

A young woman, entering at this moment, made straight for him. Susie knew she had been in before. She looked about twenty-three, and wore a cheap brown costume and a cheap brooch on the neck of her blouse. But you could see she did what she could to keep her costume from looking shabby.

Boots was really nice to her, selling her two men's handkerchiefs – another new line – for sixpence, and letting her talk to him about her problems. Susie smiled when she even asked him if he knew what kind of baby's dummy was best to buy for her little son, coming up to a year old. Boots, looking as grave as a sympathetic shop manager could look, told her that from his experiences as an infant himself, he'd recommend no dummy at all. His mother, he said, had made him see the wisdom of not sticking a germ-laden dummy into his north-and-south.

'Oh, yer mum talked to yer like that when you was only one?' said the young mother, fascinated.

'From when I was a day old,' said Boots, 'and I became a good listener.'

'Fancy, well, fancy that.' Confidingly, she said, 'But if I don't give little Alfie a dummy, I'm never goin' to wean him, he's that persistent.'

'Fill him up with bread and milk,' said Boots, 'but don't give him a dummy. As well as other things, it'll make his bottom lip pendulous.'

'Oh, my goodness, gawd 'elp the little mite, he won't want that. What's pendjerlous, Mr Adams?'

'Awful,' said Boots. 'Fat-lipped.'

'Oh, a boy don't want no fat lip,' said the young mother, 'and yer a good sort sparing me yer kind advice. Me neighbours keep telling me to buy a dummy and dip it in sugar and water.'

'Tck, tck,' said Boots, and Susie smothered giggles.

'I think I'll do what yer suggest,' said the young mother, 'and feed little Alfie lots of bread and milk. He won't take a bottle, Mr Adams, he's too fond of what

429

comes more natural, but I got to wean 'im, 'aven't I? Little devil for me bosom, he is.'

'Well, there's a consolation and a blessing in that,' said Boots. 'Knowing he's got good taste. But I agree with you, you can't encourage him to be greedy.'

Susie, sweet sixteen, emitted a strangled sputter and made a dreadfully urgent dash for the lavatory, which was at the end of a passage whose stairs led up to Mister Sammy's office. Once behind the locked door, the alarm proved false, but she had to stay for a couple of minutes to let her hysterical giggles come forth.

The young mother told Boots she'd pop in again some time, and let him know if his welcome advice had worked.

Susie was already aware that Boots was invaluable to business. So many lady customers came back regularly just to be attended to by him. And the shop kept increasing its lines as a result of Mister Sammy going out and about all over London, especially the East End. Mr Greenberg sometimes came in to see him, and to look around and say, 'Oh, very good, very nice, Sammy my poy. My life, should I still be pushing a barrow vhen you're buildin' castles?'

Sammy never bought any line he could not promote at bargain prices. He ordered small items by the gross, not the dozen, to secure top discount, and earned the best terms going by always paying cash. He knew there were three essentials people had to have, a roof over their heads, food and clothes. They especially needed clothes in the winter. There was knitwear in the shop now, like jumpers, though only two colours at the moment, yellow and brown. They were stupendously cheap considering their quality. Susie bought one for herself, Boots giving her an employee's discount.

Sammy arrived in the shop one afternoon when Susie was wearing her new jumper. A pristine leather attache case swung in his jaunty hand. He saw Susie. She was interesting a lady customer in the jumpers. He placed his case on the counter and opened it. He fished out sample socks, a tie and a lady's scarf.

'What d'you think of that for a silk scarf at a giveaway price, Boots?' he asked.

'Imitation silk,' said Boots.

'Yes, but like some of me best china, genuine imitation,' said Sammy.

'Oh, well, genuine imitation should fool some of the customers some of the time,' said Boots.

'All right, don't be airy-fairy, just keep all of 'em happy all the time,' said Sammy. 'And look, as well as the tie and the socks, here's a gent's woollen scarf and a cloth cap. All samples.' He turned the items out onto the counter. 'Let me know what you think, old lad, you got a good eye for saleable lines. What's Susie doing in that brown jumper?'

'Wearing it,' said Boots. Two women came in for blankets. There were always blankets. They were best sellers.

Boots attended to the new customers, and Susie sold two jumpers to her lady. Sammy, going to his office, asked her to follow him. In his office he spoke to her.

'That jumper,' he said.

'Yes, Mister Adams?' Susie was cautious.

'Don't suit you,' said Sammy, 'take it off.'

'Oh, yer jokin',' said Susie.

'It's one of ours.'

'Yes, but I bought it. Yesterday. It fits me perfect.'

'Wrong colour,' said Sammy brusquely.

'But it matches me skirt,' said Susie, looking hurt.

'It don't suit yer mince pies,' said Sammy. 'You can't wear brown jumpers or brown frocks. It wouldn't matter if yer eyes were pink or purple, but they're not. Is the jumper marked or anything?'

'Oh, Mister Adams, how can yer say a thing like that when yer know I don't ever go spilling tea or cocoa down meself. I'm a clean girl, I am.'

'I only asked. Just take the jumper off—'

431

'No, I ain't goin' to, I've never took any of me clothes off in front of a man, and I'm not goin' to now.' Susie was indignant.

'I don't mean here,' said Sammy. 'Get yourself one of the yellow jumpers, hide yourself where you like, remove that brown one, smooth it out, fold it up nice and put it back in one of the boxes. I'll give you two minutes, then you can present your new self to me, and no sauce.'

'Yes, Mister Adams,' said Susie, but left his office a little haughtily. She reappeared fifteen minutes later. Sammy was at his desk. All his office furniture had been supplied by Mr Greenberg, who had acquired it, mainly piece by piece, on his rag-and-bone rounds. It was old, heavy and handsome. Sammy liked it. It gave the office a look of old, enduring Victorian respectability.

He looked up as Susie came in. The yellow jumper clung to her, as the brown one had. But the bright yellow showed defining shadows. The curves of her young breasts were enhanced. Sensitive about that, because she was sure her present development threatened future plumpness, she was quite pink.

'I thought I said two minutes,' observed Sammy.

'But there were customers when I went down,' protested Susie. 'Oh, Mister Adams, you're goin' to really upset me with all yer vexations.'

'Me?' said Sammy. 'I'm vexatious?'

'Yes, and I can't bear it, not when yer mostly so kind to me.'

'Look,' said Sammy, 'all I want is for you to look a credit to yourself and the shop. You're not bad-lookin', considering you've hardly left school—'

'I been left two years, yes, I 'ave.'

'Yes, all right, you're comin' on, and you're buying clothes that fit you and don't look as if they're goin' to drop off. But make sure you get your colours right. Now that's not vexating, is it?'

'No, Mister Adams.'

432

'Colour, cut and fit, Susie, can give you style. Take Boots's wife, Em'ly. She don't have the looks of Gladys Cooper or Marie Lloyd, but she does have style and a good figure, so you never notice she's a bit plain. I've seen fellers turn their 'eads when Em'ly's walked by.'

'Oh, yes, I've met Mrs Adams a few times,' said Susie, 'and she's ever so attractive. Ain't she got a lovely smile and wondrous eyes to be'old?'

'Oh, eyes,' muttered Sammy, who was never going to admit that this little dialogue was all about Susie's blue eyes. He frowned at papers on his desk. 'Well, you'll get style, I expect, which'll be something I'll want to see in yer when I open a ladies' shop exclusive and put you in as manageress. Well, off you go, Susie, or there'll be a mob of women crowdin' Boots down there and eating his shirt buttons.'

'Yes, Mister Adams. And yer really like me in this jumper?'

'It shows you're growing up, it makes you a good advertisement for all them new jumpers.'

Susie, blushing, fled. She thought being a good advertisement was hardly decent, it meant advertising her bosom. Oh, supposing it really did keep on getting rounder until she was twenty-one? Please, Lord, don't let me grow fat ones like Ma Earnshaw, or Mister Sammy won't ever make me a shop manager, and I might only get a husband like Mr Earnshaw.

Mr Earnshaw, who had appeared at his wife's stall sometimes, was a thin, weedy man who looked as if he lived a squeezed life.

Susie didn't have that kind of a husband in mind at all. She fancied the Prince of Wales most. He had a lovely smile, and looked ever so kind. But she didn't suppose she would ever be his Cinderella.

CHAPTER THIRTY-TWO

The summer had gone and chilly autumn winds were taking the leaves from the trees in Ruskin Park. Boots and Emily had offered twenty-five shillings rent for the house near Lizzy and Ned. It was still empty. The owner, sticking to his demand of two pounds a week, showed he preferred to sell.

Chinese Lady went about with little spots of colour in her cheeks, and a persistent cough. Boots kept on to her about it, and when she visited Lizzy to see how the baby was getting on, Lizzy said it was time she went and saw her doctor. Chinese Lady said she would.

She had felt a little depressed lately. She envied Lizzy, for Lizzy had a lively child about the house and a baby to look after as well. It was such a pity Mr Tooley's relatives had taken Rosie. Rosie had made her days more fulfilling. Chinese Lady thought there was nothing more appealing to a woman's domestic instincts than the sight and sound of a child in one's home.

Chinese Lady had not really wanted her sons to grow up. The three of them had been a handful at times, especially as she had had no husband to help and support her, but she would not have said her trying moments were less worthwhile than her better ones. Critical as she was about her sons, she was proud of what they were making of their lives. Tommy was running the stall to Sammy's satisfaction, and without fuss. Tommy never fussed or made mountains out of molehills. That Sammy, of course, was cocky. But people couldn't help liking him, even if he was almost sinfully covetous about money. Still, he made up for it by being family-minded. He talked about his business a lot, and regularly mentioned it was a family business. And Boots, well, he never changed, he'd always treated life as if it was pleasing, never a worry. He was that casual he probably never knew if it was summer or winter outside. Except he hadn't been casual about Rosie. He hadn't even been commonsensical.

She wished her sons could have stayed in their teens and been her young rapscallions for ever. She would lose Tommy and Sammy soon. But she would still have Boots and Emily.

She felt unlike her usual busy self. She even felt a little lonely. She thought about all her years as a widow. Thirteen years in all. Her husband had been a good man, a fine soldier, a corporal. She still had her memories of him, but memories were really only like shadows, and not the same at all as someone living, breathing and strong, someone whose companionship was comforting.

She sat on her bed the following day, feeling just a little frightened now. An awful weakness had seized her, and she had just coughed up discoloured phlegm. For a fortnight her phlegm had been pink-tinged. The pink was deeper now, and her hankie looked a dreadful mess. And just when she was about to go and see Dr McManus. Her hat and coat were on, but her legs felt as if they weren't going to carry her. She made an effort, she stood up and managed to reach her chest of drawers to get herself a clean hankie. She knew she simply must get out of the house and take herself to the surgery in Walworth Road.

Outside, a London taxi pulled up and Mr Finch, bearing a bouquet, stepped out into the gloom of an October afternoon that was slightly foggy and distinctly chill. He asked the driver to wait a moment, in case there was no one at home. He had made the journey on impulse. He knocked on the door. There was no immediate answer. He stopped and looked through the letter-box. The familiar gas lamp in the passage was alight. He knocked again. He heard someone then, someone who took a long time to reach the door and open it.

He saw Mrs Adams, her face pale beneath her hat, her cheeks tinted by bright spots of colour.

'Mr Finch? Mr Finch – I–' Her voice was faint. She swayed. He dropped the bouquet and she collapsed into his arms.

Dr McManus came out of his surgery into the waiting room. He beckoned to Mr Finch, whom he knew, and drew him outside.

'Mr Finch, thank you for bringing Mrs Adams. I've telephoned for an ambulance.'

Mr Finch showed intense concern.

'How ill is she?' he asked.

No less concerned himself, Dr McManus said, 'I'm certain it's tuberculosis, which people here call consumption.'

'God Almighty,' said Mr Finch in shock. He pulled himself together and said firmly, 'Forgive me, doctor, but she must go to that hospital in Brompton, where they specialise. Could you possibly arrange that? Might I use your telephone? I know Dr Josef Uberst, a consultant there. He came over from Germany many years ago.' Again he asked, 'Might I use your telephone?'

'I've heard of Dr Uberst,' said Dr McManus. 'Come with me, Mr Finch.'

Emily was the first one home. The house was silent and empty. There was a note on the mat. She picked it up and read it. It was from Dr McManus, and was addressed to Boots. It informed him his mother was ill and had been taken by ambulance to Brompton Hospital. Dr McManus requested Boots to come and see him. Emily, who loved Chinese Lady, ran from the house. She ran all the way to the tram stop in Walworth Road. She boarded a tram for Camberwell Green. It was Friday, when the shop was open late.

'TB?' said Boots to Dr McManus.

'Oh, that's consumption, doctor,' said Emily in distress.

'Brompton will let us know if my diagnosis is correct,' said Dr McManus gently. 'It may not be.' He was sure, however, he had made no mistake. He had seen too many cases during his time here. He was fifty-one and had practised in Walworth for twenty-three years. 'And even assuming the worst, we may have taken it in time. How long has she had a cough?'

'Two months at least,' said Boots, sick with self-disgust that he had not taken his mother to the surgery himself weeks ago.

'Have you ever noticed her cough into her handkerchief?'

'No,' said Boots, 'but I've noticed her get up and go to her room, and give no reason for going.'

'Doctor, it can't be terrible bad, can it?' said Emily worriedly. 'We'd 'ave noticed something a bit chronic, wouldn't we?'

'Not if she was able to hide it from you. Did you notice, perhaps, if she used a lot of handkerchiefs, if there were a lot on her Monday washing-line?'

'No,' said Boots, 'and we should have.'

'Oh, don't take blame, Boots,' said Emily, her voice unsteady, 'none of us really noticed. But we did keep saying to her, doctor, that she ought to let you give her some medicine for her cough.'

'She was flushed sometimes, and there were pink spots,' said Boots, swearing at himself for accepting Chinese Lady's persistent declaration that it was only a cold on her chest. She had never liked going to the doctor, never liked showing a weakness to her family.

437

'Well,' said Dr McManus, 'let's be grateful that your friend Mr Finch arrived at your house at that particular moment. I've told you how he brought her here, by taxi. I can also tell you he accompanied her to Brompton, after he and I both spoke on the telephone to a specialist, Dr Uberst. Mr Finch will call on you tomorrow morning at eight, to see you before you both go to work. You'll want to see her, of course, but that won't be possible until Dr Uberst has conducted a prolonged examination, and carried out the necessary tests. However, you could telephone the hospital tomorrow afternoon, say, and find out when you can visit. Emily, don't be too upset.' Emily was dabbing at tears. 'Our patient is a very resilient lady, a born fighter.'

Dr Josef Uberst, German-born but a naturalised British subject, like Mr Finch, wasted no time in applying himself to the case of Mrs Maisie Adams. He gave her a protracted examination, carrying out tests and having X-rays taken. He diagnosed that her left lung was sound, her right lung badly infected. The treatment known as AP (Artificial Pneumothorax) was decided on. It meant a local anaesthetic and the insertion of a long needle to collapse the lung, this to be repeated once a week at first, then every ten days, for three months in all. It kept Chinese Lady strictly confined to her hospital bed. She remarked to Dr Uberst that if he thought he was going to make her bedridden for the rest of her life, he had better think again. When could she get up? In time, said Dr Uberst. In time? What time? We'll see, he said. She was ill, of course, and she knew it. Since she hated any kind of weakness, she fought her condition, which was all Dr Uberst asked of her. A Jew, and a brilliant physician, he was a wry listener on the several occasions when Mr Finch threatened to have him sent back to Germany if he failed to save a lady dear to her family and friends.

Members of the family visited her on Sundays, taking

turns to sit with her. She had good days and bad days. It was not in her nature to welcome any of her family on her bad days, for she disliked intensely any situation or circumstance that put her at what she considered a disadvantage. The worst kind of disadvantage was that of being ill in the presence of her family. She treasured her maternal role, and could not abide any ailment that made a weak vessel of her in the eyes of her nearest and dearest. So if any Sunday was a bad day, she allowed family members only five minutes each with her.

Mr Finch appeared frequently, but he avoided Sundays, which he felt belonged to the family. The ward nurses thought him an arresting man, yet somehow a lonely figure.

The family endured feelings of crisis. No one wanted to discuss what was in every mind, the possibility that Chinese Lady would not recover. No one spoke about what life would be like without her. She had come to be regarded by her sons and daughter as indestructible, a figurehead destined to be always there. That was how Ned and Emily saw her too. Sammy and Tommy took a harder look at Boots these days, but without finding him wanting. He seemed to accept Chinese Lady's bad times soberly and calmly, he made decisions for the family, and provided a willing shoulder for the tears Emily could not help shedding on occasions.

'Well, I suppose he's always had his good points,' said Sammy to Ned one day, 'but we did think, Tommy and me, that his airy-fairy style might've let him down at a time like this.'

'Airy-fairy my arse,' said Ned, 'are you telling me you don't know your own brother as well as I do? There was never any chance of Boots letting the family down, or himself.'

The one member of the family critical of Boots was Lizzy, even though she had always been closest to him. Lizzy knew, as everyone knew, that there was one

439

certain thing to be done if Chinese Lady pulled through. She would still have to go to a sanatorium for months, but when she finally left she could not come back to Walworth. She could not come back to smoke and grime and deadly yellow fog, she had to live where the air was cleaner, where washing on the line did not gather soot. Lizzy was passionate about that, and had a bitter moment with Boots, telling him he'd been far too casual and don't-care about moving at all. Almost it was on the tip of her tongue to say Chinese Lady wouldn't be where she was, and in the condition she was, if Boots had taken that house for rent back in August. But she caught a warning glance from Ned, and Emily's look of distress, so she bit on her tongue. Boots did not argue a case for himself. He said he knew he was in the wrong.

Emily took on Chinese Lady's domestic role willingly. Boots, Tommy and Sammy all gave a hand. That was how they'd been brought up, to give a hand. Emily, however, would have given up the role even more willingly than she had taken it on if only Chinese Lady were to come home. Emily did not merely love her mother-in-law, she adored her. She had a daughterly affection for her mother, loud and blowsy though she was, but it was Chinese Lady who was precious to her.

Aunt Victoria turned up trumps. She came regularly to the house, bringing things like steak-and-kidney puddings, apple pies and blancmanges to save Emily cooking every evening when she got home from work. One day she went all through the house, cleaning it from top to bottom. When she got home quite late, and Uncle Tom learned what she had been up to, he made her sit down, he prepared an evening meal himself, and said, when they went to bed, he'd take her to Margate for a second honeymoon next year. Aunt Victoria said if she'd known what she was letting herself in for, she'd have cleaned Cousin Maisie's house well before now.

Vi spent every Sunday with her cousins, and went

to the hospital with them. Tommy thought her an angel.

The family, with Chinese Lady still worryingly sick, could not work up a great deal of interest in Christmas, just over a week away. But Boots made one seasonal decision, although he did not know if it was the right one. Emily said she didn't know if he was doing right, either, but to go ahead. So he sent Rosie a Christmas card with a postal order, addressing it care of Mr Tooley. He posted it on leaving the shop. It was Wednesday, half-day. Emily was with him, having asked for the afternoon off from her work. They went to Brompton by train, to see Chinese Lady. Arriving at the hospital on a grey, cold day, they were told by the ward sister they could go in. Some patients were up, but most lay in bed. The ward was airy, the windows casting the limited light of the December afternoon. Chinese Lady lay with her head and shoulders propped high on four white pillows. Her eyes were closed and she looked thin. But her hair did not lack lustre, and illness had not introduced any grey. Emily and Boots sat down at the bedside, opposite each other. Emily swallowed, and she saw that Boots's lips were tightly compressed.

'P'raps we'd best not wake her, darling,' she whispered, 'I don't mind just sittin' with her.'

A woman patient in a dressing-gown came up. She looked at Emily, then at Boots. She did not seem like a TB patient, for her face was quite rosy. She offered a smile.

'Excuse me, are you Mrs Adams's son?' she asked Boots.

'Yes,' he said.

'Could you be the one she calls Boots?'

'Yes.'

The woman smiled again.

'Then you're the family comic, are you?' she said.

'The disreputable one?' said Boots, while Emily

441

thought it very out of place for the woman to be so cheerful when Chinese Lady was obviously so ill.

'Oh, we talk,' said the woman. 'She'll be glad to see you.' And she went on her way.

Chinese Lady opened her eyes, their almond brightness a little dimmed, her expression vague and wondering. She saw Boots.

'Dan?' she said, slightly husky. 'Where did you come from? Dan?'

Dan was short for Daniel, her long-dead husband. Emily stiffened and looked anguished.

'Mum, it's Boots, it's Boots and me,' she said.

'He's goin' to be saucy like you, Dan, that boy Boots. Still, he's not a bad boy, really. Dan, where's your uniform?'

Boots felt crucified. His mother closed her eyes again.

'Oh, hell,' he said.

'Boots, she's not – she's not – they'd have said—' Emily was incoherent in her distress.

The sister came in.

'Dr Uberst is here,' she said. 'He'd like to see you.'

They followed her, Boots silent, Emily tremulous. Dr Uberst, waiting for them in a consulting room, rose from the desk as they entered.

'Mrs Adams? Good afternoon. Mr Adams? Please sit down.' Unlike Mr Finch, whose English was faultless in every respect, Dr Uberst still had a little German thickness in his speech.

'Is my mother having one of her bad days, particularly bad?' asked Boots.

'Is she? I did not think so,' said Dr Uberst, a man of fifty with a five o'clock shadow. He gave the matter some thought. He smiled. 'Ah, so?' he said. 'She was awake most of last night, I was told. Asking for the glasses of water, we are to believe. What is it you say? Ah, yes, as lively as a cricket. Do you see?'

'Not quite,' said Boots, nerves on edge.

'Glasses of water. Very good. The night nurse gave

442

her a sleeping draught eventually, Mr Adams. I am afraid the effect has made the day sleepy for her, and given her dreams. You found her – what shall we say – languid?'

'Doctor, she was delirious, like,' said Emily agitatedly, 'she mistook my husband for his father. Doctor, she ain't – she's not recessing, is she?'

'Recessing?' Dr Uberst looked puzzled. But he had heard much of this family from Mr Finch, and had sufficient command of English to realise, after a moment, that this young lady with extraordinary green eyes and magnificent auburn hair, meant regressing. 'No, Mrs Adams, I am sure she is not. No, no. On the contrary. If she mistook you for your father, Mr Adams, ah, well, shall we say it was the imagination of dreams? Was she awake when Sister Jones asked you to come and see me?'

'No, not really,' said Boots.

'It follows, it follows,' said Dr Uberst. 'Now, ah, yes, I have seven X-rays here, three taken during her first week, the rest at intervals, the last one two days ago. Would you care to see them?'

'What will they show us?' asked Boots.

Dr Uberst opened a large folder. He carried it to the window. Boots and Emily followed. He held up each negative in turn, and in chronological order, drawing attention to what was entirely detectable to him, but was foggy to Boots and Emily.

'The spots on the right lung, do you see? Very worrying in their persistence until – there, do you see? The last two X-rays. Do you see what perhaps to you are blurred edges in this one, and a more definite blur in this, the last?'

'Recessing, Emily,' said Boots with the faintest of smiles.

'Ah?' Dr Uberst's smile was not in the least faint. 'Recessing, yes, that is good enough. Or receding. What does it matter? English is the language of adjectives and

443

alternatives, of great poets. One always has a choice.'

'Doctor, d'you mean – oh, do them X-rays mean Mrs Adams is gettin' better?' asked Emily, eyes wet with emotion. 'Is she, doctor, is she?'

Dr Uberst clasped the folder of X-rays to his black jacket, grey waistcoat and gold watch-chain. His clasp seemed almost affectionate.

'These tell us the condition of the patient has improved. So, one can say she is better, yes. I am of the opinion that betterment will continue – ah, there is an English noun for you, betterment. Pulmonary tuberculosis is quite curable, if taken in time and the patient does not – ah – feel too sorry for herself. Or himself. I was informed by her doctor that our patient is a lady of resilience. It would be foolish to say we have no more worries, but I am willing to stand by my optimism.'

'I'd like to stand by it too,' said Boots.

'I think your mother will help us,' said Dr Uberst.

'Oh, bless you, doctor,' said Emily earnestly, 'and I do 'ope you have a lovely Christmas because you've made it so that we can look forward to a much happier one than—' She stopped, blushing with embarrassment at forgetting Dr Uberst was Jewish.

Noting her confusion, he smiled.

'Mrs Adams, every religion enjoys a festival of rejoicing, every religion has its own kind of Christmas. I celebrate our Passover. I am able to appreciate the spirit of your Christmas.'

'That's ever such a nice thing to say,' said Emily.

'Is it so? Good. You both understand, I'm sure, that continued improvement still means Mrs Adams won't be able to leave hospital for the Frimley convalescent sanatorium for some weeks. And convalescence? Three months, say?'

'That's understood,' said Boots. 'Dr Uberst, thank you. We'll go and take another look at her now.'

* * *

That evening, Lizzy was having her first real quarrel with Ned.

'I don't care, it is Boots's fault, it is!' she stormed. 'He could've taken that house, he could've afforded the rent easy, with Em'ly working. They must rake in four pounds a week at least between them. My suffering mother could've been livin' near us before the first week in August was up, instead of havin' to breathe in all that Walworth soot.'

'Give it a rest, Eliza,' said Ned, 'you're not being fair.'

'Oh, that's very husbandly, that is, I don't think,' said Lizzy. 'You're always on Boots's side, never mind I'm your wife and let you give me babies and nine months of carrying them. It's a wonder you didn't marry Boots instead of me – that would have been a tale of fairies all right! And I suppose you'd have been happier with him than me.'

'Well, he'd be better company than you at the moment,' said Ned.

'Oh, yer beast, I hate yer! Go away, go and get a divorce, if that's what you want!'

'Eliza—'

'Don't you touch me, Ned Somers, don't you lay a single finger on me! Nor don't come into my bed tonight!'

'Your bed?'

'Yes, mine!'

'You're off your chump,' said Ned.

'Am I? Well, no wonder, with my husband against me and my mum dying!'

'Eliza, for God's sake—'

The telephone rang. Lizzy sped tigerishly into the little hall and answered the call tigerishly.

'Yes, who's that, who is it?'

'Me,' said Boots, after pressing the button marked A of the public phone.

'Oh, you,' said Lizzy, flushed and furious. 'What d'you want?'

445

'Lizzy love, I've just got back from Brompton with Emily. There's an improvement. Chinese Lady could be winning. She was a bit muzzy from a late sleeping draught when we arrived, but later, after we'd had the good news from Dr Uberst, she came to and put us through our paces. She wanted to know if the house, windows and doorstep were being kept clean, and if not, why not, seeing we all had two hands and hadn't been brought up to be helpless. She also wanted to know if any of us had done anything to disgrace her, and if Tommy was treating Vi proper, which meant was he respecting her ladylike virtues. And she said wasn't it time she heard how much weight your baby had put on this month. Lizzy love, she is better. I thought I'd let you know. Tommy's gone to take the news to Aunt Victoria, and to put some cheer into Vi. Lizzy, are you there?'

'Yes, I'm here,' said Lizzy in a small and subdued voice.

'I think Chinese Lady's fighting the good fight. Emily sends her love, and you can powder your infant's pink bum for me. Oh, and Emily and I are going to settle things on that house immediately after Christmas. We'll pay the rent the owner's asking for. So long, Lizzy old girl, regards to Ned, love to Annabelle.'

'Boots? Boots?'

But Boots had rung off. Lizzy stared at the receiver, then put it back on the hook.

'Eliza?' called Ned.

'She's better, me mum's better,' said Lizzy emotionally.

'Then I feel better too,' said Ned. 'Can we be friends now, Eliza?'

'Oh!' Lizzy rushed back into the kitchen, and she rushed at Ned, flinging penitent arms around him. Ned, his artificial leg unprepared for the emotional onslaught, fell over. Lizzy fell on top of him.

'Sod this,' he said, 'I'll sue you, Mrs Somers, for assault and battery.'

446

'I didn't mean all them things, I didn't.' Lizzy, unhappy with herself, came up on her knees. Ned stayed grounded. 'I'm sorry, honest, I said rotten things to yer. I didn't mean them.'

'I know you didn't.'

'Oh, don't lie there. Ned – oh, lor', you're not hurt, are you? Oh, I'm sorry.' Lizzy began to cry. Ned sat up and put his arms around her. She sobbed against his shoulder. 'I never been so awful to anyone.'

'All over, darling. Just think how good it is, knowing your mother's better with Christmas coming up. Was that Boots on the phone?'

'Yes. Oh, I feel so ashamed, I been rotten to him for weeks.'

'Well, I think he felt he was in some fault, that he should have made your mother see the doctor long ago. But the tide's turning, so how about a glass of the firm's sherry, and then some dinner? And I'll play you crib later, penny a game. No, let's go the whole hog. Tuppence. How about that, Eliza?'

Lizzy kissed him with penitent fervour.

'Oh, goodness, Mummy.' Annabelle, now four, had come down from minding baby Bobby in his cot. The baptismal name of Robert had already become Bobby. 'Mummy, you're kissing. Bobby's awake. He's crying. I think he's hungry. You better come, 'cos I can't do anything with him. Mummy, why are you on the floor with Daddy?'

'We're saving wear and tear on the kitchen chairs,' said Ned.

CHAPTER THIRTY-THREE

Emily had taken and finished her Pitman's shorthand course. In her quickness she was a natural, and received a certificate stating she had passed at eighty words a minute. Boots had raised no objections. He had encouraged her.

'But I don't have the town hall in mind,' he had said, and went on to point out Sammy was going to reach the stage of requiring office assistance in the shape of a shorthand-typist. What did she think of joining the family firm? Emily thought it would be lovely.

Mrs Madge Stevens expressed herself happy for Emily, but did not come up with any offer of shorthand work. She was a little cool, for Emily had made it clear she did not like discussing her husband with her.

Then there was the day when the Sanitary Inspector himself, Mr Woodhurst, who had letters after his name, walked through Enquiries, turned at the door and said, 'Mr Simmonds, there are too many forms marked urgent coming from this office.'

'Sir?' said Mr Simmonds.

'You'll give urgency a bad name,' said the Inspector.

'Sir, I don't mark any urgent that's not urgent,' said Emily, quite prepared to defend her judgements, which were always backed up by Mr Simmonds.

'I've been shown a large batch that make urgency seem normal,' said Mr Woodhurst. 'Try to remember our limited resources. It means applying a certain amount of brutality, Mr Simmonds.'

Mr Simmonds said, 'I'm not sure how we—'

'That's all,' said Mr Woodhurst, and the door closed behind him.

Mr Simmonds grimaced and said, 'Someone doesn't like us, Emily.'

'I don't care,' said Emily, 'if something's urgent it's urgent. I ain't goin' to be brutal. He can take that responsibility, or he should. It's not 'im that gets shouted at when people come in about something that's not been done.' She knew she and Mr Simmonds had scored some notable triumphs. A doctor had come in to say thanks to whoever had caused prompt action to be taken in respect of contaminated tap water in a certain house. Delay might have resulted in some typhoid cases.

'All the same, we'll have to examine every complaint more carefully,' said Mr Simmonds.

'Urgent is urgent,' said Emily, 'we got to agree on that.' But she had her mind now on a job in the family business. If no babies came along. 'Well, good morning,' she smiled as two old friends entered, 'Orrice with boyish aplomb, and Effel with her usual air of uncertainty. 'Orrice placed a little cardboard box on the counter.

'Dad sent 'em,' he said. 'Fer Christmas.'

Emily lifted the lid of the box. Inside were four fancy boxes of stoned Tunisian dates. 'Why, thank you, 'Orrice,' she said. And 'Orrice smiled at her, and Emily wished, emotionally, that she could have a son just like him.

Mr Finch, who had a small flat in Chelsea and whose address was now known to the family, received a letter from Emily on Saturday morning.

'*Dear Mr Finch, I don't know what you'll think, me writing to you like this, but the family all agreed about it, though we expect you've already made arrangements, only if you haven't would you like to come and spend Christmas Day with us like you did in the old days, we'd*

449

be pleasured to have you, we can't forget what you did for our loved mother in the nick of time. It was like a kind of revered happening, and I said so to Boots, and he said he couldn't think of any happening more revered. He said it in that way of his, but I think he meant it.

'He said you probably might know our loving mother has turned the corner, well we think she has, Dr Uberst being very pleased with her, so Christmas is going to be happier for us than we thought, even if she can't be with us her own self. Lizzy and Ned, and Annabelle and the baby are coming too, and Vi, she's going to be there as well, and Sammy of all people said could we play Postman's Knock like we used to, he said he's going to find out what numbers I'm given so he could treat me to smackers, he said it in front of Boots, would you believe. Well, you know what Sammy is, he never used to like kissing at all, specially kissing me. Boots told me he's got the urge now because he'll feel safe with me, and with Vi. I asked safe from what? Boots said unattached girls, but I never know what that husband of mine's talking about sometimes.

'Well, they all said I should write and ask you, they all said I was the one to, and Boots said most letters are instant forgettable or something like that, except not my letters, which I know means he was having me on as I can't really write for toffee, but my fruit cakes keep turning out better all the time. If you can't come, never mind, we'll just think of you and what you did for our loved mother, and I'm enclosing our Christmas card to you which is from all of us and signed accordingly with love specially from me. Yours respectfully, Emily Adams, Mrs.'

Mr Finch, having read the letter, put it away as a thing to treasure and replied to say he would be delighted to come. He would arrive, he said, in the fond hope that Postman's Knock would indeed be played.

On Saturday night, Emily said, 'We're all going to church tomorrow.'

'Eh?' said Sammy. 'The Sunday before Christmas, with the market crowded with customers and cash?' He was not very often at the stall these days, but Christmas was different. 'You got a hope.'

'It ain't – it's not a question of hope,' said Emily, 'we're all goin' to church, and that's it.'

'Am I hearing you correct, Em'ly Adams?' asked Tommy, taking off Chinese Lady.

'You are, Tommy Adams,' said Emily, doing likewise because she thought she should. 'Vi will look after the dinner, so she's excused. You're not, nor Sammy, nor Boots. We got to go, you know we 'ave. It's only right. We got to pray to God to bless our fam'ly with another miracle, and we got to give thanks in 'umble anticipation and gratitude. And we got to pray Chinese Lady will come back to our bosom by Easter at least.'

Boots coughed and looked at the ceiling. Sammy grinned and Tommy spoke with an air of innocence.

'I dunno I quite got that, Em. Come back to what?'

Emily, resolute in her role, said, 'To the fam'ly bosom.'

'A kind of set of warm chests?' said Boots.

'One with knobs on?' suggested Sammy.

'Oh, you Sammy, don't you use vulgarities to me,' said Emily, 'it's disgraceful disrespect to our faithful mother. And don't you sit there lookin' innocent, Tommy, and what're you staring at the ceiling for, Boots? I know you, you always look at ceilings or out of windows when you've got something wicked on your tongue. Well, I don't want this fam'ly saying or doing what it shouldn't just because Chinese Lady's not here to keep her eye on you. We're all goin' to church to pray for another miracle, and I don't want no arguments. And don't you go using vulgarities that ain't nice in a fam'ly gathering, Sammy.'

The three brothers looked at each other.

'What d'you think, Tommy?' asked Boots.

'What d'you think, Sammy?' asked Tommy.

451

'What d'you think, Boots?' asked Sammy.

'I think we've got another Chinese Lady here,' said Boots, 'I think we're all going to church.'

'There, I knew you'd come round,' said Emily, and gave his arm a pat. 'You got your wicked ways, but you got virtues too. You're all good boys, really.'

Boots got a bone in his throat, Tommy had slight hysterics and Sammy spoke up.

'Holy Moses, ain't she a perisher?' he said. It was half-past nine, but he took a walk a few minutes later to Peabody Buildings. Susie was just home from a visit to the church's evening Christmas bazaar at St John's Institute. Her friend Danny had been with her. She was drinking hot cocoa when Sammy knocked. Mr Brown answered the door and Sammy asked if he could see Susie on a matter of business. Mr Brown gave him the use of the little living-room for his talk with Susie. She came in, and Sammy asked her if she would help Mrs Walker on the stall tomorrow morning, on account of Tommy and himself having to go to church.

Susie said she couldn't ever say no to him, specially at Christmastime, and that she was so glad his mother was better. She said she could see his mother's illness had been paining his kind heart and making his brother Boots lose his winning smile. Would Mister Sammy like a cup of hot cocoa as it was such a cold night outside?

'Kind of you,' said Sammy, 'but cocoa's not my cup of tea. Well, you're a good girl for promising to help out tomorrow morning, and I'll remember yer in me will.'

'What?' asked Susie, startled. Like Emily, she took many things literally.

'Did I say something?' asked Sammy, feeling sickeningly sure he had.

Susie, worried, said, 'Oh, you ain't got a fateful disease, Mister Sammy, 'ave you? You ain't goin' to pass away, are you?'

'Pass away?' said Sammy.

'Well, makin' yer will and leavin' me something in it.'

452

'Gawd help me,' he muttered, 'I knew it 'ud come to that, I knew it.'

Susie went quite pale.

'Mister Adams, oh, yer can't know, yer can't, yer still a young man,' she gasped, 'yer can't be in a fateful condition, yor look so healthy. Oh, you ain't caught that misfortunate consumption from your mum, 'ave you? And even if you 'ave, if she's goin' to get better, you might too. I begs yer won't give up hope, I'll pray for yer night and day, and at Evensong tomorrer evening. Oh, yer mustn't talk about makin' yer will, and I don't want anything.' Her blue eyes beseeched him not to give in, but to have faith in God's wondrous works. 'It's Christmastime, it's when our Lord Jesus was born under the 'oly star of Bethlehem, yer got to be 'opeful—'

'Kindly shut up,' said Sammy.

'Oh, Mister Adams!'

'Listen, Miss Brown, I don't have consumption, I'm not fateful and I'm not goin' to pass away. I'm not ready to, I got me fortune to make.'

'Oh, 'eaven be praised,' breathed Susie, 'but yer shouldn't 'ave give me a fright like that, saying it 'ud come to you 'aving to make yer will. The kindly light would go out of me world if I thought you was dying.'

'Oh, my aching head,' said Sammy, 'I don't know what I'm goin' to do with all this holy gospel you keep givin' me. All I did was come and ask you if you'd help on the stall tomorrow, and look what's happened, I've had a Christian burial service read to me.'

'But, Mister Adams,' protested Susie, 'you said—'

'Look, I spoke unconscious, like,' said Sammy, wishing her eyes would go away and come back looking nondescript.

'Unconscious?' said Susie.

'When I said I'd remember you in my will. And whose fault is it that I spoke unconscious? Yours.'

'Mine?' Susie sometimes couldn't make head or tail of Mister Sammy, he was that puzzling. 'Mine?'

'Yes. Don't ask me why. It's probably me kindly soul worrying about the welfare of me employees in these hard times. Still, you've come on reasonable healthy since yer mumps, and I hear the customers like yer. Just don't get me confused, that's all.'

'But I ain't done nothing, Mister Sammy,' said Susie, eyes dark with mystification.

'No, well, all right,' said Sammy.

'I just don't understand about you speakin' unconscious and me gettin' you confused.'

'I don't understand it myself,' said Sammy, 'except I hope it don't interfere with me business prospects. Anyway, thanks for standin' in tomorrow, you're a good girl. Goodnight.'

That Mister Sammy, thought Susie, he was getting more droll all the time.

The overnight misty fog had gone, and with it the wintry chill. Sunday dawned clear, and the morning became fine and unseasonably mild, the temperature taking a dramatic rise to nearly sixty. The country awoke to Christmas week and fell out of its bed into sunshine. People said kinder things about Lloyd George and the government, and old soldiers said a better time had to be coming. The original Bright Young Things, the pioneers, emerging from country houses, cried 'Tally-ho!' and dashed into the sunshine in their silk pyjamas.

Vi arrived early, and because she dearly wanted to go to church with everyone else, it was agreed the joint and the potatoes for roasting could be put in the oven, and everything else left until they came back.

Tommy answered a knock on the front door at quarter-past ten. He came back into the kitchen looking perturbed.

'Boots? You got a visitor. It's Mr Tooley. He'd like to see yer. In private, he said. I've left him in the parlour.'

'Mr Tooley?' Boots was perceptibly affected. He thought about the Christmas card and the postal order he and Emily had sent to Rosie care of the girl's grandfather. Had that caused ructions?

'What's he want?' asked Emily, tense.

'I'll see,' said Boots, and went to the parlour. Emily took her apron off.

'I got to go and be with Boots,' she said quietly.

Mr Tooley, bowler hat in his hand, gave her a nervous little nod as she entered the parlour to stand beside her husband.

'Good morning to you, Mrs Adams,' he said, 'best I speak to both of you.'

'Sit down,' said Boots, and scarcely recognised his own voice, so taut were his nerves.

Mr Tooley placed his hat carefully on the mahogany table and sat down.

'To tell the truth, I 'ardly know where to begin,' he said, 'or how to, and if you conclude I'm none too happy at havin' to come here, you'd be right. But I felt I had to see you today when tomorrow I'll be at work. It's like this, y'see—' He paused and rubbed his forehead worriedly. 'It's Rosie, y'see.'

'What about Rosie?' asked Boots, suppressing an inclination to tell Mr Tooley to get on with it. Emily, glancing at her husband, had a feeling the child had never been out of his mind.

'Well, the fact is,' said Mr Tooley, looking frankly worried, 'the fact is, Rosie's never goin' to be mutual with my nephew and his wife. It's not that she's played 'em up, you couldn't have a more obedient child, or better behaved. But she's not been happy since the day Nellie collected her. She's so quiet, y'know, she just don't make conversation or chatter like young kids do.' Mr Tooley sighed, and Boots thought how little conversation Rosie had been encouraged to have with her mother. Had she reverted? 'She only talks when she's spoken to or when she's expected to answer, like. She goes out into the street a lot, and sits somewhere with that teddy bear of hers. The only real talkin' she does is to that teddy, though she's a kind playmate to Nellie's little boy, when Nellie asks her to be. Nellie can't get no real response from her, and it's the same with me nephew Mick, who ain't a difficult man. She says her pleases and thank-you's, she does everything she's told, but she's not happy, Mr Adams, she don't smile. Oh, she does if you ask her. "Give us a smile, Rosie," you say to her, and she gives you one, like she feels it's polite to. But it's not a real smile, if you know what I mean. I been goin' regular to visit her, feeling it's only right I should, but it's best Mrs Tooley's kept peaceful of mind by not being told too much about her. She gets agitated, y'see. Her mind and health got wrecked by everything our daughter Milly got up to, and I know I can't ever have Rosie livin' with us, partic'ly as Mrs Tooley wouldn't be up to it, anyway.' Mr Tooley's homely face creased in regret. 'I said to Rosie, "Don't you love your new mum and dad?" I said it to her only three days ago, when I took her that card you and your lady wife sent. Now I don't want you to think I'm trying to play on your kindness, or trying to get you to do something you don't want to, specially now you're probably settled in your minds, but I got to tell you Rosie said she loved her Uncle Boots and Auntie Em'ly. Is that you Mr Adams, the one she calls Uncle Boots?'

'Yes, that's me, Mr Tooley,' said Boots.

'When I give her the card you sent, and the postal order, which was kind of you both, she looked at the card and read it, and she looked at me and thanked me, but didn't say anything else. I asked her what she was goin' to buy with the postal order. She didn't say anything for a little while, she just put the postal order inside the card and kept a tight hold of it. Then she asked me if she could please keep it. I said it was to buy herself something for Christmas. She just said she wanted to keep it. I tell yer, Mr Adams – Mrs Adams

456

– she's been carrying that card with the postal order ever since she first took 'old, accordin' to Nellie. She carries it about with her teddy. That's not right in a little girl, it's a sadness to my way of thinking. I got to ask you, d'you still want to have her, d'you still want to take care of her? Why I'm askin' is because, well, Nellie came round last night, bringing Rosie and her belongings. She said she'd tried, but it was no good. She'd tried all these months but hadn't got no more heart for it. She said it wasn't fair to anyone, the way things were, and nor was it fair to Rosie herself. "Rosie likes you more than she likes us," Nellie said to me, "so I'm handin' her to you to do what you can for her, she won't enjoy her Christmas with us." That left me with a terrible problem, which is what made me come this morning to see you soon as I could, and I 'ope you won't have ho hard feelings about it, whatever you decide. Do you want Rosie? Don't think I won't understand if you say no. I mean, there's water gone under the bridge these last months.'

Emily, knowing what Boots wanted, said, 'We love her. Where is she?' She felt Boots's hand take hers and squeeze it. It told her he loved her.

'Well, to tell the truth,' said Mr Tooley, 'I brought her with me, but not to your door. I felt that wouldn't be fair on yer, I felt it might look as if I was using her to force things with you. And I had to think of Rosie. If I'd brought her right to your door, she'd have had hopes and wishes, and expectations, like, never mind what I'd told her, which was that we were just goin' to see some friends of mine, that we might stay the night. When we got off the tram, I told her I had someone private to see for a few minutes, and she was to stay there, by the tram stop, till I got back. She'll be as good as gold there, and not have the expectations she might have had if I'd brought her to your home with me. She won't move, she'll wait for me. I got to tell you I brought her case with all her things in it, just in the 'ope you

457

still felt the same about havin' her. She don't know that all her belongings are packed, I didn't want her askin' questions I couldn't hardly answer. Look, you mustn't think Nellie's been unkind to her. Nellie's a good woman, but a bit businesslike, and maybe – well, it don't matter, it all comes down to your feelings about things.'

'Mr Tooley,' said Boots, 'Emily and I will walk to the tram stop with you and collect Rosie.' He checked the time. It was nearly twenty to eleven. 'We'll take her on to church with us.' He smiled at Emily. 'We're all obliged to go this morning. Perhaps you'd bring her case back here, Mr Tooley, would you? Then I rather think you'd like to get back home to your wife.'

'I would that,' said Mr Tooley, 'it'll be a real relief this time to tell her you've lifted our worries. I don't know how to even start thanking yer. It's my belief that with you, Rosie'll start being happy again. I'm sorry I didn't use my commonsense and let her stay with you in the first place.'

'We'll have Rosie, Mr Tooley,' said Boots, 'and I'll only ask you to write us a letter officially approving us as her foster parents.'

'I'll do that,' said Mr Tooley, 'and I'll get it done legal, like. I'll bring Rosie's case back here, and I want you to know I don't feel you're strangers to me, I feel Rosie's goin' to be in the care of friends, if you don't mind me callin' you that.'

'We like you, Mr Tooley,' said Boots. 'Emily, would you put your hat and coat on while I tell the others what's happening?'

'Yes, darling,' said Emily, and gave him a glance that was loving and wholly supportive.

Rosie was sitting on the doorstep of the working-men's club at the corner of Browning Street, watching trams and people go by in the sunshine. The case containing her belongings was close by. She wore a dark blue winter coat and had a red ribbon in her hair. Her little boots were polished. Her teddy bear was cradled in her right arm. In her left hand she held a Christmas card. Her teddy bear she called Shoe. It was the nearest she could get to associating it with her Uncle Boots, who had given it to her.

Her grandfather may have kept certain things from her this morning, but she knew where she was, and she knew she was close to where Boots and Emily lived. There was a small ache in her heart, and wistfulness in the eyes that dreamed in the sunshine. Ringing church bells sounded far away.

Her grandfather, returning, smiled down at her.

'Rosie, look who's come to take you to church with them,' he said, and Rosie glanced up and saw Emily and Boots. Perhaps she had cherished hope, perhaps she had guessed who her grandfather was going to see, for hope sprang with misty brightness and her mouth quivered.

'Hello, kitten,' said Boots, 'would you like to come to church with us, and then come home with us?'

'And stay with us?' said Emily. 'Would you like to, darling?'

She came to her feet. She looked up at her grandfather. He smiled again, and nodded. She looked up at Boots and Emily, rapture a flushed shyness. Boots could not resist her. He took her up into his arms, and her teddy bear and her Christmas card were held secure against his chest as she wound her arms around his neck, pressed her cheek to his and clung in bliss. She gulped.

'We love you, puss,' said Boots.

Rosie gulped again and whispered, 'Uncle Boots, could you – could you—'

'Could we what?'

'Could you and Auntie Emily be my mummy and daddy?'

Boots was not a man who had ever demanded a great

deal from life, and he thought at this moment that he had been given as much as he could ask for. Life had given him his sight back, given him back the miracle of being able to see the people he loved. It had given him his own inimitable Emily, it had given him hopeful news of his mother, and now it had given him Rosie.

'Yes, kitten,' he said.

And so after dinner, eaten early, Rosie went with the family on the train to see Chinese Lady, and on the way she was a child of eager life, full of chatter, although she constantly glanced at her new mummy and daddy as if to reassure herself they were real, she was real, and the moment was real.

CHAPTER THIRTY-FOUR

On Christmas Eve the shop was doing heady business.
Sammy had stocked up with highly suitable lines purchased direct from manufacturers. He had exhausted
his cash reserves, but if he had grumbled in his younger
days about taking pennies from his savings to buy
Christmas or birthday presents, he did not hesitate in
business to use all he had in pursuit of what he
considered profitable investments. For the shop, he had
invested in no items that would not continue to sell
after Christmas. Ties, socks. Ladies' stockings. Plimsolls
that were a very cheap alternative for kids whose
parents couldn't afford shoes or boots, and, among
other things, imitation silk knickers with lace hems,
each pair in a white cardboard presentation box. He
had pounced on this fancy feminine line a month ago,
when Mr Greenberg, for the small fee of a pound note,
informed him how to get an advance look at bankrupt
stock that was going on sale to wholesalers. The
information helped Sammy to beat Mr Ben Ford, the
fat man, to the bankrupt bargain of the year, five gross
of the prettiest ladies' undergarments he had ever seen.
The prettiest he had seen up until then had been
Rachel's girlish drawers, when she had been bowled
over on the skating rink and practically stood on her
head. All dainty white lace and little pink bows, they
were. He had picked her up, dusted her down and been
severe with her, telling her he wasn't teaching her to
skate so that she could make an exhibition of herself.
Rachel had asked didn't he like them, then? Not on the

461

floor of a skating rink, said Sammy, so don't do it again.

Women liked fancy under-pinnings, there was no doubt about it. The five gross of lacy knickers became available to him when he placed ten bob into a receptive hand, and the price he paid meant each pair had cost him just under a shilling, including box.

Just prior to the Christmas rush, Sammy called Susie up to his office and showed her a pair in rose pink with black lace hemming the legs.

'Pretty, don't you think?' he said.

Susie, blushing, said, 'Mister Adams, you shouldn't, they're intimate.'

'They're business, good business, I hope,' said Sammy. 'Look, hold them up against you and let me see if me imagination will work.'

'Oh, I couldn't do that,' said Susie, going pinker.

'They won't bite you,' said Sammy, 'they're delicate longeray, and I'd just like to see if they'll do something special for ladies, being silk.'

'They ain't silk, they're imitation,' said Susie, 'and I'm not goin' to 'old them up against me. Mister Adams, it's not decent, and I don't know 'ow yer can ask such an unseemly thing of a girl.'

'All right, Susie, I didn't mean to upset you,' said Sammy, who knew far more about buying and selling than he did about girls. What he did know about Susie was that it was getting to the stage where he couldn't stand her looking upset or unhappy. 'Well, just tell me what you think of 'em, you being a feminine young female. I mean, to start with, they're pretty, don't yer think?'

'Oh, you're makin' me blush fit to fall down,' said Susie, 'but if you must know, Mister Adams, it's not being pretty that counts, it's being too fancy and expensive for our customers. What little money they've got they spend on things plain and cheap. Poor people can't afford to dress romantic.'

'Romantic, eh?' said Sammy. 'You made some good

points there, Susie. But suppose we price 'em at just one and elevenpence three-farthings, includin' the high-class box?'

'One and eleven-three?' gasped Susie.

'Tempting, you reckon?' said Sammy, a gleam in his eye at the thought of a hundred per cent gross profit. Susie looked wide-eyed at him. He shifted his gaze.

'Oh, I'd buy a pair for—' She stopped and turned pink again.

'For yourself?' said Sammy. 'Glad to give you a gen'rous discount, Susie, seeing they'd look highly swish and romantic on you.'

'Oh, yer shouldn't talk so intimate,' blushed Susie, eyes reproaching him. Sammy shifted his gaze again. 'Mister Adams, excuse me, but don't you like the way I do me hair? Is there something wrong with the way it looks on top? Only you're always givin' it frowning glances.'

'Such glances are unconscious,' said Sammy stiffly.

'Me dad says yer can't trust men that don't look ladies in the eye. Oh, not you, Mister Adams, I didn't mean you. I'd trust you with me life, really I would, and I'm sure there's a good reason why yer always lookin' at me hair and not at me.'

'I happen to be highly experienced in matters relating to hair,' said Sammy loftily. 'Now, to continue—'

'What's 'ighly experienced?' asked Susie.

'Would you mind not turnin' this business discussion into a gossip, Miss Brown?'

'But I only—'

'I'll excuse yer,' said Sammy, 'and I'm pleased you agree these luxurious knickers in exclusive boxes mean good business. If we happen to have some left over by the time we close on Christmas Eve, I'll get you and Boots to put 'em in our New Year sale.'

'Oh, what sale price would yer want us to charge instead of one and eleven-three?' enquired Susie with interest.

'Two and a penny-three,' said Sammy.

'Mister Adams, that's not Christian.'

'I won't make me fortune if I'm too Christian,' said Sammy. 'All right, off you go, Susie, and I appreciate yer valued contribution to our discussion.'

'Thank yer, Mister Adams,' said Susie, 'and I won't make no charge.'

'Cheeky puss,' muttered Sammy as she went out.

Now it was Christmas Eve, and customers with Christmas club money were buying up bargains. Sammy never purchased any line he couldn't offer as a genuine bargain. Nor did he stock anything he suspected might hang fire. He had hired two temporary woman assistants to help with the Christmas week rush. This gave standing to the shop, a manager and three assistants. Business was first-class. Susie's selling ability paid dividends, and Boots got crowded by women who were new or regular customers. Sammy was quite aware his eldest brother had an effect on females without really trying. He supposed Boots had been faithful to Emily. Well, Chinese Lady would have known by instinct if he hadn't, and performed a verbal massacre job. Anything that escaped her eyes or her ears she picked up by instinct.

Several of Sammy's business acquaintances, mostly of the Jewish fraternity, came in to drink a glass of port with him in his office. Dark, smiling and expansive men, they had an admiration for his business acumen. Sammy asked Boots to come up each time. Boots refused the port and took a small nip of whisky instead. Whisky frequently reminded him of Major Harris, who had introduced him to its beneficial effects in the trenches. He could take numerous nips without acquiring more than a sense of warm well-being. On Christmas Eve, this gave a totally disarming look to his smile, and Susie thought once or twice that some of the known lady customers looked as if they wished they'd brought mistletoe with them.

Rachel, the daughter of Isaac Moses, came into the shop in the early afternoon. She had a little chat with Boots, whom she knew well, and then went up to Sammy's office. Sammy, a forest of papers on his desk, came to his feet as she knocked and entered. She was a lush and vivid picture in a warm red coat and a black fur hat, her healthy skin glowing from the tingling cold of the day.

'Bless me soul,' said Sammy, 'what brings you into my Christmas Eve?'

Rachel, affecting a Mayfair accent, said, 'I was passing by, don't you know, dear boy.'

'Welcome,' said Sammy, who had a soft spot for this beautiful young woman. 'What can I do for Your Sumptuous Highness?'

'Well, yer can kiss me, lovey, for a start,' said Rachel, who never disowned her cockney background.

'I was speakin' serious,' said Sammy .

'So was I,' said Rachel, 'it's Christmas.'

'Not yours,' said Sammy. 'Still, have a glass of port.' He poured one for her. Rachel unbuttoned her coat, hitched her dress, and sat down. Sammy refrained from dwelling on legs clad in black silk stockings.

'Don't be coy,' smiled Rachel, 'you know they're worth a look.'

'Come again?' said Sammy, who liked to avoid distractions.

'Legs, Sammy, legs,' said Rachel, and sipped her port.

'I trust you ain't one over,' said Sammy.

'No, I'm not, nor am I likely to be. This is very cheap port, Sammy.'

'Christmas present from a business friend.'

'Port like this you should only get from an enemy. By the way, my daddy heard Boots did a quietly thunderous job on King of the Fat.'

'Took a liberty, Boots did, usurpin' me authority,' said Sammy. 'Still, I won't say he didn't come up with some highly impressive wallop. But speakin' of your lovin' daddy, who always arrives handsome in me ears, I'm thinking of doing myself the honour of callin' on him again after Christmas.'

'Why?' asked Rachel.

'I need a new loan.'

'Well, he was delighted you paid off the old one so promptly, but you can't need another, Sammy dear. Everyone knows you're already a success.'

'I'm not saying I've got problems, but I'd still like a new loan.'

'Three cash businesses, all doing well, and you need another loan?'

'It's for Boots,' said Sammy.

'Boots?' purred Rachel. 'My life, there's another lovely Adams. Is it fair that your mother's sons are all Gentiles? What does my beautiful Boots want a loan for?'

'To buy a house. I ain't in favour of havin' him rent it.'

'Hard luck, darling, my daddy doesn't loan on house property.' Rachel paused for thought. 'How much does Boots want?'

'Three hundred quid,' said Sammy. 'Well, I'm doing his thinking for him. The house is three eighty-five, but it's my guess he can find the balance. He and Em'ly have been savin' hard. He's in needful consideration of our mother requiring to leave Walworth and live with him and Em'ly near Lizzy and Ned when she's finished convalescing. Which reminds me to record me appreciative thanks for the card of condolence you kindly sent.' Rachel had sent the family a card as soon as she heard Mrs Adams was in hospital. She always interested herself in the activities of Sammy and his family. It was compulsive. They had all been good to her when she had been Sammy's one and only girl friend. 'Have you heard she's on the mend?' he asked.

'Yes, Sammy love, and I'm so glad. So Boots and Emily are going to move and take your mother with

466

them. But if Boots wants to buy and not rent, why doesn't he go to a building society?'

'I am strictly uninclined to let him do that,' said Sammy. 'They ask old-fashioned questions, examine your prospects, inspect your wallet and look inside your shirt. And there's all that inconvenient interest. I thought your lovin' daddy might offer a simple interest loan again, seeing our fam'ly used to be the best customers at his Walworth Road pawnshop.'

'Why can't you lend him the money yourself?' asked Rachel. 'You must have three hundred pounds available.'

'It's all tied up with Adams Enterprises,' said Sammy. 'Besides which I am proud to remark I have strictly non-alterable business principles, which include never loanin' real money to a relative, specially a close relative.'

'You could make Boots a gift,' said Rachel.

Sammy got up and tottered about, hand to his forehead, horror on his face.

'A gift of three hundred nicker?' he breathed. 'I'd suffer dying ruination just when I'd got one foot on me fortune's ladder. Have a heart, Rachel.'

'Well, Sammy darling, I like your mother,' said Rachel 'and I adore Boots. I'll advance him. I've money of my own. He can have a loan of three hundred pounds at ten per cent simple interest, providing it's all paid up by the end of three years.'

Sammy stared at her.

'Yer don't mean that,' he said.

'Yes, I do.' Rachel smiled. 'Sammy, you taught me how to roller-skate, you picked me up each time I fell over, brushed me down, told me I'd got two left feet but pretty legs, and kissed me for a penny. You treated me as if I were as good as any Christian girl, you invited me to Sunday teas with your family, and they treated me just the same.'

'Why shouldn't you be treated the same as anyone else?' asked Sammy. 'All right, don't answer that. I know. But this loan, it's not what I had in mind, borrowing from you, and it's not what I like. Money of your own you ought to keep, Rachel.'

'I'm investing it in the Adams family,' said Rachel.

'Look,' said Sammy, 'I do have feelings outside of business feelings, and I just don't feel partial to takin' money from you. And simple interest of ten per cent will only give you a return of thirty quid.'

'Sammy love, you gave me the happiest year of my life. I know I'll never have fun like that again.'

'I'm still considerable dubious,' said Sammy. But a reminiscent grin appeared. 'Yes, fun all right. You and your legs up in the air.'

'And penny kisses?' said Rachel.

'Couldn't have been worth that much.'

'They were to me,' said Rachel, 'and you can think about the loan on behalf of Boots.'

'Yes, I'll have to,' said Sammy, 'but that don't mean I'm not in appreciation of yer warm heart. Three hundred quid, paid back at two quid a week, plus the simple interest.' He frowned. 'Holy Jericho, Boots'll be askin' for a rise. That makes it serious.'

Rachel laughed.

'Sammy, you're lovely,' she said.

'Not if it interferes with business, I'm not,' said Sammy.

Rachel came to her feet.

'Special friends, Sammy? Always?'

'You always been special, Rachel, you and your daddy.'

'Shalom, lovey.'

'Shalom, Rachel.'

The postman delivered a small package to the shop, addressed to Mr Robert Adams. It carried a French stamp. Boots, opening it while taking a short break for a cup of tea, discovered six French silk handkerchiefs, with his initials RA embroidered in dark blue. There was also a letter, from Polly, to whom he'd given short shrift during his mother's illness.

'Dear old thing, I'm doing my duty, keeping Pa and Stepma company in balmy Cannes. Dearest Stepma, exhausted from her orphanage travails, is escaping Christmas fog with good old Pa. We've been here nearly three weeks, we aren't returning until the New Year, and I'm bored, old love. Everyone is either frightfully old or frightfully adenoidal, and there are Russian Grand Dukes wearing scent. I assume in my decent way that it's to keep Bolsheviks at bay. There's no one here remotely like you, no one to excite me and amuse me. Do you mind that I miss you more than is good for me? How is that ghastly shop, stacked to the ceiling with Yuletide bloomers and flannel vests? How can you endure it? Never mind, old sport, you're to come and meet my father quite definitely in the New Year, and I shan't let you dodge the column this time. Pa has a friend who is looking for someone like you to run a company of his. Meanwhile, here is a small token of my affection for you, and my merry Christmas greetings. Much love, Polly.'

Boots put the handkerchiefs in a drawer and forgot them. He disposed of the letter. It was as well Chinese Lady knew nothing of this matter, or she would have come home and boxed Polly's ears. In absentia, of course.

'Merry Christmas, Mrs Stevens,' said Emily, putting her head round the door of the assistant supervisor's office. Madge Stevens, in animated conversation with a new typist, a pretty girl of eighteen, broke off to glance at Emily.

'Merry Christmas to you too, Emily,' she said, and looked at her wall clock. It was fourteen minutes to five. 'Are you going now?'

'Well, it's been quiet all afternoon,' said Emily, 'and Mr Simmonds suggested I could go a bit early as it's Christmas Eve.'

'How kind of him,' said Madge.

'It's all right with you, Mrs Stevens?' said Emily. 'I don't want to take no time off if I shouldn't.'

'Oh, you've got your hat and coat on, I see, so off you go.'

'Goodnight, then, merry Christmas again. Merry Christmas, Amelia.'

'Merry Christmas,' said the new girl.

Leaving the town hall, Emily thought Mrs Stevens was a bit of a funny woman, really. She don't like me much any more. She likes having favourites, and she's got a new one, Amelia Green. I'm not getting any shorthand practice, it's all a waste. I just hope I can go into the family business, like Boots said. Oh, but there's Rosie. We can't expect Mrs Pullen to look after her all the time while Chinese Lady's away.

Mrs Pullen, in kind neighbourly fashion, had gladly taken on the job of looking after Rosie during the hours Emily and Boots were at work. But they couldn't ask her to do it indefinitely.

'One of them gramophones, please,' said a voice in Tommy's ear. He turned and looked into Vi's hazel eyes, brightly reflecting the light of the flaring stall lamp.

'Jigger me, where did you spring from?' he asked, and in pleasure put an arm around her and gave her a cousinly squeeze. He left customers to Mrs Walker for the moment. It was always nice to see Vi.

'We all got off early from the office,' said Vi, 'so I stopped on me way home to come and buy a gramophone as a Christmas present for Mum and Dad. Gosh, isn't the place crowded?'

East Street market was a seething mass of shoppers, and Ma Earnshaw's stall was abundant with holly and sprigs of mistletoe, as well as blood-red Christmas oranges. Pink-nosed kids were darting and scrounging, acetylene lamps feeding greedily on frosty oxygen, stallholders declaiming never-to-be-repeated Christmas bargains.

'Give yer a discount, Vi, seeing yer our favourite cousin,' said Tommy, 'and seeing we've only got two left. And I'll bring it up on the tram after I've finished here. Might not be till about ten o'clock, though.'

'Oh, would yer do that for me really?' asked Vi, and Tommy thought she looked glowing in a plum-coloured winter coat that reminded him of one Lizzy used to wear, and a close-fitting black hat with cherry blossom decorating it.

'Pleasure, Vi,' he said.

'I won't be in bed,' said Vi.

'Just get yourself under the mistletoe,' said Tommy.

'Oh, you makin' a promise?' said Vi.

'I'm makin' a promise to bring the gramophone,' said Tommy, 'you make a promise to be under the mistletoe when I get there.'

'Tommy, oh, you are fun,' said Vi, which was what Rachel thought about Sammy, and what Emily had always thought about Boots.

Vi bought a sprig of mistletoe from Ma Earnshaw before she went on her way.

Sammy left his office at half-past four and went to the yard to pay Fred and his apprentice their wages. He gave Fred a Christmas box of two pounds. Fred had always been a good investment. The apprentice received an extra half-crown. Then he went to the market to see how Tommy and Mrs Walker were doing. Business was booming, the market bursting with people, Ma Earnshaw's Christmas oranges, a traditional item for Christmas stockings, selling at a penny each or seven for sixpence. Boxes of crackers were on offer at a shilling, twelve crackers to a box. Chestnuts for roasting were tuppence a pound, and a pound of mixed walnuts, brazils, almonds and cobs cost sixpence.

Sammy paid Mrs Walker her wages and presented

her with three half-crowns as her Christmas box. Mrs Walker was competent but not irreplaceable. He intended to give Susie six half-crowns. He was tickled to hear from Tommy that Vi had bought a gramophone for her parents.

'Uncle Tom'll love it,' he said, 'Aunt Victoria'll have a fit.'

He got back to the shop at five past six. That was where the real money was entering the till. Emily and Rosie had just arrived. Boots was going to take them shopping. Most shops would stay open late. Emily was in a sentimental mood. It was the first Christmas since their marriage that Boots had been able to see. He was taking the evening off, and Sammy had offered to lend Susie and the two temporaries a hand.

Off they went, Emily and Boots, Rosie between them, she in a ferment of excitement, her new little world a rapture to her. Everyone had given her pocket money so that she could buy presents. And for the first time on a Christmas Eve she was to hang a stocking on a chair so that Santa Claus could fill it with gifts when he came down the chimney during the night.

They went in and out of shops in Walworth Road, Emily and Boots helping her to select presents, but letting her go into a confectionery and tobacco shop on her own, so that she could buy something for them in secret. She was perfectly self-possessed, an engaging delight to the shopkeeper, who assisted her in choosing a shilling pipe for Boots and a shilling box of chocolates for Emily. All her money had been spent now, except for a copper or two, and Boots asked her if she would like to cash the postal order she still had.

'No, thank you, Daddy,' she said, as they walked amid the festive atmosphere of decorated shop windows.

'Aren't you goin' to change it for money, darling?' asked Emily. 'The post office is closed, but Daddy will give you the five shillings.'

'Could I just keep it, please?' asked Rosie.

'Course you can, Rosie, as long as you want,' said Emily, 'it'll be like savings.'

But Rosie meant to keep it, with the Christmas card and her teddy, for ever and ever.

'Let's buy a bottle of port for Mrs Pullen,' said Boots.

'Oh, yes, she deserves something for lookin' after Rosie,' said Emily.

So Mrs Pullen received a bottle of Sandeman's port, which she clasped happily to her floury apron. She was making her Christmas pudding.

With so much to do at home, Emily made a pot of tea and some sandwiches for supper, and afterwards Rosie had her Christmas Eve bath, in front of the glowing kitchen range. Boots popped her into the warm soapy water in the old galvanised tin bath, and she laughed in bliss as, down on his knees, he gave her a thorough sponging. She kicked and splashed, and at the end Emily said there was more water on the floor than in the bath.

Rosie now had her own little bed in the upstairs room. Mr Greenberg had brought it on his cart two evenings ago, delivering it with a little speech.

'Ah, Boots my poy, and Em'ly my dear, hearing as I did from Sammy that you had come into valued possession of a small child of God, and on a day vhen I myself come into happy possession of a child's bed, should a man even as poor as I am not end up at your door? Do me the honour of acceptin' the bed, nor von't I even charge you cartage.'

'How about a whisky, then?' asked Boots.

'Ah, my friend, such a fine fam'ly you are, even though in dealing with Sammy I am gettin' poorer and poorer. There is a friend for you, ain't it, Em'ly my dear?'

When, after her bath, she was taken up to bed, Rosie was given on old sock by Emily to hang over a chair.

'Mummy, will Santa Claus really come?' she asked.

'Course he will,' said Emily, 'he comes for all little girls and boys who hang a stocking up.'

'Crumbs,' said Rosie, 'he must get awful busy.'

They tucked her in and kissed her goodnight, and the lids of a tired but happy child drooped.

'That's it, then, kitten,' said Boots, 'it'll be Christmas Day when you wake up.'

The drowsy child murmured, 'Daddy spilt all that water. Naughty Daddy.' She fell asleep.

Down in the kitchen again, Emily said, 'Boots, it's a happy Christmas, don't you think? You're happy, ain't you, with Chinese Lady being better, and us havin' Rosie and the shop and everything?' She wanted to hear him say he was happy, that it didn't matter about her being a barren woman, as she was sure she was, sadly.

'Emily, old girl—'

'Don't call me old girl.'

'Emily love, do you know what you are?'

'I'm not old, I know that much.'

'You're a godsend,' said Boots.

She hugged him. He cuddled her. And Emily felt nothing mattered except the family and having Chinese Lady come home one day.

It was gone half-past nine and the shop had just closed. Sammy paid off the two temporary assistants, gave them each an extra half-crown, emptied the till into a money bag and took it up to his office, calling to Susie to come and receive her wages and commission. The latter he worked out with the speed of a natural financier. It came to an intoxicating amount, and Susie expressed her thanks giddily, her shining blue eyes making Sammy feel mesmerised. He couldn't think why it kept happening. There were other females with blue eyes. Blue eyes happened all over the place in Walworth. He dragged his gaze off Susie's saucers and regarded a heap of half-crowns.

'And you got a Christmas box comin' to you,' he said, taking up a handful of the handsome silver coins.

'Oh, crikey,' gasped Susie, and stared in wonder as

he began to hand her the coins one by one. Looking up at her, he fell into her saucers again as he made the transfer from his hand to hers. 'Mister Sammy, ten half-crowns, ten? Twenty-five shillings?' Susie was breathless.

Sammy came to. Now what had she made him do? Fifteen bob, that was the amount he'd intended, but he'd simply given her all the coins he'd picked up from the heap. There was nothing he could say except, 'Well, you deserve it.' Actually she did. She was a considerable asset, especially as she was only sixteen, and he frankly didn't want her to go off and work for someone else. 'Boots said you've been a marvel at shifting our ladies' things.'

'Oh, if Boots – Mister Manager, I mean – if he says so, I'm that 'appy, Mister Sammy. Ain't 'e just a girl's dream?'

'Pardon?' said Sammy, and gritted his teeth at finding he wasn't too keen on that remark of hers.

'Oh, I didn't mean – I mean, him being married and all.' Susie was confused. She did have a little crush on Boots. But so she did on all three sons of Mrs Adams. She thought Sammy electric and droll, Tommy handsome and nice, Boots manly and fascinating. 'It's just that he's been so kind to me.'

'I hope, Miss Brown, that that don't mean I've had me hobnailed boot on yer neck by comparison,' said Sammy stiffly.

'Oh, no, course not,' protested Susie. 'You been our fam'ly's saviour, givin' me this job and givin' Dad his little job. And now this lovely Christmas box, an extra blessing. Why, Mister Sammy, 'ow could yer think I'd think you really was as hard as iron and wore 'obnailed boots? You been swell to me, and I 'opes you have a lovely Christmas. I best be off now.'

Sammy cleared his throat. 'I'd better see you home,' he said, 'just give me a few minutes.'

'Mister Sammy, you don't need to do that.'

'It's late for a young girl hardly left school to go home alone, Miss Brown.'

'Stop callin' me Miss Brown,' said Susie.

'Eh?'

'It's Christmas, and peace and goodwill to all,' said Susie, 'and it's not peace and goodwill to call me Miss Brown. And I'm not hardly left school, you keep saying things like that. Shame on yer, Mister Sammy.'

'I'm havin' one of me dreaming fits again, I am,' said Sammy, 'and it's givin' me earache. Was it you said them unsolicited things, or was it a passin' saucebox?'

'Mister Sammy, I can get 'ome by meself, really I can,' said Susie. A little smile appeared. 'Mister Sammy, yer so funny.'

'I ain't gen'rally considered so,' said Sammy, 'And I'm goin' the same way home as you, so don't argue.'

'No, Mister Sammy.' Susie really felt very sweet towards him, the wondrous Christmas box on top of everything else could hardly make a girl feel otherwise.

Sammy took her home, riding on the tram with her down to Browning Street, he with his leather attache case full of money, Susie full of bliss at all she had earned and been given. She walked down Browning Street with him, the night frosty, the windows of houses showing the glow of gas mantles. Outside the pub on the corner of King and Queen Street, boozy men and women were singing 'Knees Up, Mother Brown,' and suiting their actions to their words, the women with skirts and petticoats hitched high.

'Ain't Christmas fun?' said Susie. 'Mum and Dad are goin' to give us a real swell party this year, seeing 'ow much better off we are, we're goin' to 'ave a real fam'ly treat. I think you got a nice fam'ly, Mister Sammy, like we 'ave. People can stand their 'ard-up days better when they belong to a nice fam'ly, don't yer think so? Me mum and dad still made jokes even when we was near to being destituted. When Mum said we was probably 'eading for the workhouse, Dad said with a bit of luck it might fall down before we get there. Wasn't that – oh, look, yer can see the frost on that lamp-post. Don't yer think a frosty Christmas Eve night is kind of haunting in an 'oly way, Mister Sammy?'

'I'm against being haunted in any kind of way,' said Sammy, 'but I get inflicted sometimes.'

'Oh, what by?' asked Susie, as they entered Brandon Street.

'Things that interfere with me peace of mind,' said Sammy, 'and they don't do my business much good, either.'

'What things?' asked Susie.

'You may well ask,' said Sammy, taking her into Peabody's and up to the door of her parents' flat. 'There, you're all right now. Hold on, I almost forgot.' He opened his attache case and took out a wrapped thin square box. 'A little present for you.'

'But you been so good to me already,' said Susie. 'Oh, I almost forgot too.' She rummaged in her handbag and brought out a little packet wrapped in white paper. It contained a Woolworth's gold-coloured tiepin in a small box. She had already given one to Boots, and Boots was taking one home to Tommy. 'A happy Christmas, Mister Sammy, and I'll never know how to thank you for all yer Christian goodness to me.'

What came over him, Sammy did not know, unless it was her eyes again, darkly blue in the dim light of the landing lamp. He kissed her on her mouth He kissed her quite positively, and found her lips tingling from the cold and very sweet. Susie quivered, the pleasure of the unexpected kiss startling her, even disturbing her.

Sammy, in shock at himself, said, 'There, a merry Christmas, then.'

'Mister Sammy, you kissed me,' she said in astonishment.

477

'Well, have a nice time,' said Sammy, and disappeared at unseemly speed.

Later, in her bedroom, with her little sister fast asleep, Susie opened Sammy's gift to her. She blushed crimson. It was a pair of those boxed knickers, the colour pastel blue, the lacy legs dark blue. Hastily, she rewrapped them. What was he thinking of, giving her such an intimate present? Her mum and dad would never let her accept underwear from a man, specially underwear so fancy. She'd have to give them back, she'd have to.

CHAPTER THIRTY-FIVE

Christmas morning at Brompton was cold but bright, the air crisp and clear. Chinese Lady had taken a walk to the bathroom by herself. It was the third time she had done so since yesterday, much to the satisfaction of the staff, and Dr Uberst was contemplating sending her to the Frimley sanatorium towards the end of January, when she would have been hospitalised for fifteen weeks. She was improving daily at the moment, a slow but steady improvement. By the time she reached the sanatorium, he was sure its more vigorous atmosphere would accelerate her recovery. Convalescing patients did much for themselves. A doughty fighter such as Mrs Adams would relish a routine that encouraged a generous amount of freedom and allowed one to be a help to oneself.

A little weak, but quite triumphant, Chinese Lady seated herself in her bedside wheelchair. Warmly wrapped in her dressing-gown, she exchanged seasonal talk with other patients, the ward cheerful with Christmas decorations.

'Well, you've made a fine start to Christmas Day, Mrs Adams,' smiled Sister Jones, stopping to talk.

'Kind of you, I'm sure,' said Chinese Lady, glad that breathing was no longer so troublesome. 'I don't want my fam'ly to think I'm goin' to have to keep lying down for the rest of my days. It was nice they remembered me.' She had opened Christmas cards from her family, relatives and friends, and unwrapped presents brought by Emily and Boots on their last visit. 'Mind, it's not the same as Christmas Day at home, where there's a new little girl to bless the place.' She meant Rosie. She was very happy about Rosie. 'Lord knows how they're managing, though. I dread to think what might happen to the roast beef, which my daughter-in-law Em'ly told me they're havin'. Em'ly's a godsend, but a big rib of beef might be a bit much for her. They might of got Christmas chicken for once, I'd of thought, except it's expensive. Not that they couldn't of afforded it, with everyone workin'. But I didn't want to make interfering suggestions, seeing I'm not there. I just hope my eldest son won't take it into his head to act the comedian when Em'ly starts preparing the beef for the oven. He's had a good education, so he ought to be more serious-minded than he is.'

'Oh, I like men who aren't serious-minded,' said Sister Jones.

'Well, I don't know about that,' said Chinese Lady, but did not look too displeased. 'I just hope I don't hear their Christmas dinner wasn't put on the table when it should of been, with the roast beef ready to melt in their mouths. I don't want to have to speak to them when they come tomorrow.' They were all visiting on Boxing Day. 'Christmas Day's special, and a fam'ly should pay proper reverence to it and see everything's done as it should be, Sister, like in Dickens. I've tried to bring my fam'ly up reverent, but you know how it is these days, so many people not being as sanctified about God as they should, on account of what the war done. Nor don't I like them suffragettes still encouraging women to take jobs men should have. If a man can't be the breadwinner, Sister Wilkins, like ordered by God, that man is as good as nothing. A man's for providin' and protectin', like I've often said, and a woman's for home-makin' and keepin' the peace.' Chinese Lady paused for breath, feeling her lungs were a bit reluctant to keep up with her.

'I'll get Nurse Rees to bring you your hot Bovril,'

smiled Sister Jones. Mrs Adams was already recognised as a character. Nurse Rees entered the ward then, carrying a wrapped sheaf of Christmas roses. She spoke in a whisper to Sister Jones, who said, 'Yes, of course, why not? Some regulations can be broken on Christmas Day.'

Nurse Rees came up to Chinese Lady.

'Mrs Adams, these are for you,' she said, and handed her the sheaf.

'Oh, my gracious,' said Chinese Lady. There was a card bearing best Christmas wishes from Mr Finch. She coloured faintly. 'Oh,' she said.

'Mrs Adams,' said Nurse Rees, 'do you feel up to another little walk, just a short one? You have a visitor, the gentleman who brought the roses.'

'Oh, mercy me,' said Chinese Lady, 'on Christmas Day?'

'It's not allowed, of course,' said Sister Jones, 'but if you would like to see him—?'

'Oh, I can't hardly say no if he's come all this way,' said Chinese Lady. She reached for her hand mirror on the bedside cabinet, and looked at herself. She was pale, That was to be expected. She fluffed up her hair a little and rose from her chair. She tidied her dressing-gown, and Nurse Rees took her to a small waiting-room. There Mr Finch, hat in hand, grey overcoat on a chair, received her with a warm smile, and Nurse Rees withdrew, closing the door behind her.

'I'm very glad to see you on your feet, Mrs Adams,' said Mr Finch, 'very pleased you are up with other patients on Christmas Day. Do sit down.'

'Yes. Oh, dear,' said Chinese Lady, in an unusual flutter. She sat down, knees a little weak at the unexpectedness of the occasion. And with Mr Finch so healthy-looking, she felt again dislike of being ill. 'The roses – I don't know what to say – all that expense of bringing them all the way here yourself—'

'I came to talk to you as much as to bring flowers,' said Mr Finch.

'To talk to me?' Chinese Lady wondered if it was right to have a gentleman like Mr Finch talk to her while she was in her nightdress and dressing-gown and alone in this room with him. In her Victorianism, she favoured the propriety of being fully dressed in the presence of a man. She had an extraordinary shy feeling now that without stays or corset, her bosom was vulnerable. 'Mr Finch, do you mean talk about something special? Oh, it's not any of my fam'ly is it? Sammy hasn't got hisself into trouble?'

'No, Mrs Adams, it's not any of your family,' said Mr Finch, 'and I don't imagine Sammy will ever get himself into any kind of trouble that he can't get out of. But it is special, very special. To me. I'm not sure of the best way of going about it, except that I think I should be brief but not abrupt. I am extremely fond of your family, Mrs Adams.'

'I'm pleasured, Mr Finch.'

'And of you.'

'Oh,' she said, and the faint colour touched her again.

'Let me just say I'm forty-seven, still a bachelor and still wondering if I'll come to the end of my life without knowing the pleasure and comforts of companionship with a woman. I have known women – do you understand that, dear Mrs Adams?'

'I know most men can't be sellerbut all their lives,' she said. She meant celibate. 'I can't think how the Pope and his priests get on, and I don't know as God specially ordered that, which don't seem natural to me. Mr Finch, you being a pleasing gentleman, I don't see you couldn't easily find a nice woman who'd be pleasured to marry you, if you wanted.'

Mr Finch, still on his feet, eyed her whimsically.

'You, Mrs Adams, are a very nice woman, and more than that. Would you marry me?'

Chinese Lady stared up at him, almond eyes dizzy with incomprehension.

'Mr Finch?' she said faintly. 'I don't think I heard you proper.'

'Mrs Adams, I've known you since Sammy was a young boy. I watched you face up to all the hardships of poverty. Poverty reduces some people to despair and hopelessness, and they end up as bundles of rags in London's gutters, or as bodies in the Thames. I have never once seen you in any kind of despair. You never stopped fighting to do everything possible for your family, and to bring your daughter and your sons up to fight too. And see what you've made of them. Lizzy bloomed as a lovely flower in the heart of grey Walworth, and if there is a finer or more likeable man than Boots in the country, I haven't met him. I heard you in your determination to make Lizzy speak more proper.' Mr Finch paused and smiled. 'You helped her become a lady and realise the dream of a little house with a garden. I am longing to see her again, which I shall do later, for I'm going from here to your house to spend the rest of the day with your family. At their invitation.'

Breathless, confused, Chinese Lady said, 'I only did for my children what their father would of done. He had his dreams for them and me, once he finished his time in the Army.'

'What you did alone has stayed in my mind since I left Walworth,' said Mr Finch. 'If I were asked which woman I admired most, I'd name you. If I were also asked which woman I'd like as a companion for the rest of my life, it would be you. Mrs Adams, am I making it clear I care a great deal for you?' He might also have said he wanted to take great care of her, but knowing her as he did, he was not going to make the mistake of suggesting she might never be as strong as she had been.

Chinese Lady thought herself dreaming. She did not have wild moments. Even if she had, not in her wildest moments would she have envisaged receiving what had actually sounded like a marriage proposal from a gentleman like Mr Finch.

'Mr Finch, I – I – did you ask me to marry you?'

'I did.'

'Oh, you can't hardly be serious,' she said, 'you're a travelled gentleman, and I'm only ordin'ry.'

'Ordinary?' Mr Finch smiled. 'You're far from ordinary. Dear Mrs Adams, am I embarrassing you? I hope not. Nor am I going to press you, only ask you to spend time thinking about whether you'd consider marrying me or not.' Knowing how reserved she was, he added, 'I'd ask only for companionship, only for the pleasure of being with you and standing with you against all the trials and tribulations most women have to endure. I've taken you by surprise, I know, but not with the intention of making you feel at a disadvantage.'

'No, I don't feel that,' said Chinese Lady, colour high, 'I just feel I've had all my breath taken. And there's – there's—'

He knew she wanted to say her illness.

'There's nothing, Mrs Adams, nothing, that makes you any less to me than you've always been. I think I should leave now, not only to make sure I arrive at your house in time, but also to let you get your breath back. I'm not going to press you in any way. You may have all the time you want to think things over, and if you say no in the end, I shan't attempt to force a change of mind. So have no worries.'

'Mr Finch, you've spoken very understandin', very gentle,' she said, 'but I don't know I'll be able to do any thinking without my head spinning and turning, I really don't.'

'Have no worries,' said Mr Finch again, 'and I shall say nothing to your family. Goodbye, Mrs Adams, and a very happy Christmas to you.'

A hand lightly touched hers, and a moment later he was gone. She sat there in bewilderment, her heart in fluttering agitation. Marry Mr Finch? What would her family say if they knew he'd proposed? What would Boots say? Oh, that son of hers, he'd give her his sly look, his sly smile, and make remarks with a hundred and one meanings.

Marry Mr Finch? How could she, the way she was now? If she couldn't do the Monday washing or the housework, she couldn't be any man's wife.

But why wouldn't she be able to do these things, why wouldn't she? She wasn't ill. She had been. She wasn't now. She was just a little weak, that's all. There were lots of people far worse off than she was, like men who'd lost both legs in the war, and women who'd had awful accidents in munition factories and were still crippled.

I'm not ill, I'm getting better every day. If I can't do the things a woman should, my name's not Maisie Agnes Adams.

She came to her feet. She walked to the door and opened it. She walked back to the ward.

'Mrs Adams?' Nurse Rees arrived beside her. 'Why, you're looking pleased with yourself.'

'Yes, I just had something in the way of a very nice Christmas present,' said Chinese Lady, and glanced round as a patient entered, a young woman tight of mouth and poker-faced, due to go convalescent. 'Happy Christmas, Amy.'

'Sod Christmas,' said Amy, striding by.

Poor young thing, thought Chinese Lady, she's in one of her depressed moods. It was like that with some of the younger ones. It was a bitter blow to them to find themselves consumptive at their age.

'Nurse,' she said, 'if it won't be no bother to anyone, I think I'd like to get dressed for the hospital's Christmas dinner.'

The streets of Walworth took on a silent and empty look after the morning market closed, and the pubs shut their doors until Boxing Day. An occasional vehicle appeared, and along the Old Kent Road a horse-drawn cart carried singing pearly kings and queens home from an Elephant and Castle pub. Everyone who had been out went home, when the silence of the streets became indicative of the fact that all were about to sit down to Christmas dinner. If the tables in some homes showed a minimum amount of Christmas fare, this did not mean an air of festivity was absent. Only the direst poverty reduced the spirits on Christmas Day, and it would have been hard to find any home where children had not made and hung coloured paper chains. And the church, in a gesture of practical Christianity, had had food parcels made up and delivered by the local Boy Scouts into the grateful hands of the poorest families. The vicar asked people to be devout, but he had never expected them to exist on devotion alone.

In a few homes, as was often the way, housewives rained blows on the heads of husbands coming home tipsy and noisy from pubs, bringing them back to a sober state before allowing them to sit down to dinner. Sons and daughters who had mothers capable of giving erring fathers a good hiding, were proud of them.

'My mum don't 'arf pack a wallop.'

'My mum don't, she gives us cuddles.'

'I don't mean she wallops us, yer loony-bin, I mean me dad.'

Susie and her family sat down to a Christmas dinner the like of which they hadn't known for years. With his little job and his little pension, and with Susie's handsome earnings, Mr Brown had persuaded Mrs Brown to put on a feast. Susie had been to church to give thanks for God's goodness, and to ask Him to forgive Master Sammy his wrong-doing. To have presented her with shockingly intimate fancy underwear had not been other than an act of wrong-doing in her mind. But she was sure the Lord would forgive him, because he was very Christianlike in many ways, and she promised the Lord she would hand the gift

486

back and help Mister Sammy to repent.

If the streets were silent and empty, houses were noisy and full. They echoed to the music of Christmas, the music of excited voices, the laughter of kids, the gurgle of bottles pouring beer or fizzy kola water, and the clatter of busy knives and forks. Uncles and aunts and cousins contributed to the merriment.

In the Adams house, dinner proved a triumph of family co-operation under the supervision of Emily, who laid down the law as admonishingly as Chinese Lady and caused Sammy to remark he might leave home after he'd had his roast beef.

Mr Finch had received a rousing welcome from all, and his reunion with Lizzy and Ned brought him a loving hug and a warm kiss from Lizzy. He soon became acquainted with Annabelle and Rosie, and was touched by the story of how Rosie came to belong to the family. He said nothing of his visit to the sanatorium, only mentioning how pleased he was to know the patient had begun to win the fight.

Rosie and Annabelle, fast friends, sat together at the table, bibs tucked into the necks of their frocks, and chattered endlessly, to each other and to everyone else. Rosie was in wonder at so many people and at none of them telling her to be quiet. The old deal-topped table had had to be unwound and the leaf inserted, because there were twelve at dinner. Aunt Victoria and Uncle Tom had come, as well as Vi. When Vi told Tommy a few days previously that she really ought to eat Christmas dinner with her parents and come on later, Tommy at once said the family would gladly have them. Aunt Victoria and Uncle Tom accepted, Uncle Tom noting that his wife seemed quite pleased. She said they ought to go to make up for poor Cousin Maisie not being there.

After the meal, Ned, Tommy, Sammy and Mr Finch attended to the huge pile of washing-up, and when that was done everyone repaired to the parlour. Boots said either the parlour had grown smaller or they had grown larger. Ned sat on the floor with Annabelle and Rosie to help them put together a big cardboard doll's house given to Annabelle by Emily and Boots. Each girl had a new doll, but Rosie's teddy was still close by. In Chinese Lady's room, three-month-old Bobby slept soundly as the conversation ran freely and optimistically on the prospects of the patient. Mr Finch cut in gently by saying he supposed the family realised their mother would probably not be home until the spring.

'Well, who's goin' to complain?' asked Tommy. 'She'll be better off at Frimley while we've still got winter here.'

'Yes, and she can't come back here to live, anyway,' said Lizzy, 'she'll get consumptive again.'

'Lizzy and I will have her with us until Boots and Emily get themselves fixed up,' said Ned, using scissors to cut out a wall of the doll's house.

'We're fixing up my doll's house, aren't we, Daddy?' said Annabelle.

'I'm helping,' said Rosie, who was experiencing the magic of Christmas for the first time. She had woken up to find Santa Claus had actually been. He'd filled the old sock with little presents, including an orange and a new penny. And there'd been more presents at breakfast. She gave out those she'd bought, and one each to her Uncle Ned and Auntie Lizzy when they arrived. And it pleased her to see her new daddy with the pipe between his teeth. Boots, a cigarette smoker, became a convert.

'I don't suppose Granny Lady could have my doll's house to live in when it's finished, could she?' said Annabelle. Granny Lady was her own name for her maternal grandmother.

'She'd need to grow down a bit, like Alice in Wonderland,' said Boots, 'but she won't have to do that. Emily and I are taking the house near yours, Ned, at the asking rent. I did say so when I spoke to Lizzy on the phone last Wednesday.'

'Yes, I know,' said Ned, 'but two pounds a week.'

'Daylight robbery,' said Sammy, 'and I hope I can trust yer, Boots, not to do anything as daft as that.'

'It's not daft to do anything for the good of our mum,' said Lizzy.

'I'm sure Boots has thought about that,' said Aunt Victoria, a quite handsome woman who was inclined to look and speak as if she dwelt on higher planes than most other people.

'Look,' said Sammy, 'our mum would have fifty different fits if Boots chucked his money away like that. After five years he'd have paid out five hundred quid and still not own a single brick. I don't know what the thought of that does to the rest of you, but it makes me feel ill.'

'I agree,' said Ned. 'If you're going to fork out two quid a week, Boots, it might as well be in repayment of a mortgage.'

'True,' said Mr Finch, who did not want to say too much about what was solely a family matter. He was simply interested in what they had in mind concerning their mother's future welfare, since he had a feeling she would turn his proposal down.

'Well, Boots and me, we told the landlord's agent we'll pay the rent,' said Emily. 'Just so we can make sure we get the house. We don't mind two pounds a week really.'

'Well, I mind,' said Sammy, who felt it wouldn't look too good if his eldest brother failed to see money should be invested.

'We'll be getting in touch with a building society after Christmas to find out about a mortgage,' said Boots.

'You'll end up paying double what you borrow,' said Sammy. 'A simple loan's best, paid off as quick as you can.'

'Never heard of a simple loan,' said Tommy.

'Nor me,' said Uncle Tom, 'except loanin' five bob to a 'ard-up friend.'

'You're a soft touch, you are,' said Aunt Victoria.

'No, Dad's just kind-heared, Mum,' said Vi.

'I ain't talkin' about Boots goin' to moneylenders,' said Sammy. 'They'll nail him for his last farthing, then for the shirt off his back, and then probably for Em'ly's Sunday vest as well. I don't want them goin' about feeling draughty as well as stony broke.'

'Kindly don't be personal, Sammy Adams,' said Emily.

'I ain't meanin' to be,' said Sammy, 'I'm just saying paying rent or gettin' a mortgage ain't my idea of what's best.'

'Sammy, don't keep saying ain't,' protested Lizzy. 'It'll be something else next, and I don't want Annabelle pickin' up what she shouldn't, I want her to speak a bit nice, like our mum always wanted us to.'

The cardboard doll's house collapsed as Annabelle and Rosie put the shaped, cut-out roof on.

'Oh, Rosie,' said Annabelle, 'oh, the bleeding thing.'

'Oh, crumbs,' said Rosie.

Lizzy wailed. Aunt Victoria looked shocked. Tommy grinned. Sammy kept a straight face. Boots said, 'Did someone speak?'

'Annabelle, Annabelle,' said Lizzy, 'don't you ever say words like that again, you hear?'

'Yes, Mummy,' said Annabelle, not sure what she had said.

Sammy, thinking about Rachel's generous offer, put aside his doubts. If Rachel looked at it as a friendly investment, well, perhaps interest of thirty quid over three years wasn't too bad, although no professional moneylender would think so.

'Tell you what, Boots,' he said, 'I might be able to get you a friendly loan at ten per cent simple interest. A three-year loan, say. You'd have to pay back at the rate of two quid a week, plus four bob a week interest.'

'Sammy,' said Lizzy, 'you talkin' about makin' the loan yourself?'

'Now, Lizzy,' said Sammy, 'I know it's Christmas, but me strictest business rule, like I told someone else, is not to loan real money to me brothers, me sister, me sister-in-law, me brother-in-law, and me nieces Annabelle and Rosie. No, I got a certain acquaintance in mind. So don't start paying rent or gettin' a mortgage, Boots, till I've spoken me piece to selfsame acquaintance.'

'Give you a week,' said Boots.

'I know you'll do what's right to make sure of things, Boots,' said Lizzy, which was her way of saying she was sorry for being a bit rotten to him.

They all enjoyed a pot of tea then, and a slice of Emily's Christmas cake, after which Lizzy asked if they were going to play some party games.

Mr Finch smiled and said, 'There was some talk of Postman's Knock, I believe.'

'What's Postman's Knock?' asked Rosie.

'Kissing in the passage,' said Boots.

'Oh, I'll play, could I?' said Rosie.

'And me, me,' cried Annabelle.

'Oh, everybody has to play Postman's Knock,' said Boots.

'Even Sammy,' said Emily.

'And Aunt Victoria,' said Boots.

'Oh, I really don't know,' said Aunt Victoria.

'Lead me to it,' said Sammy, feeling on safe ground, 'or at least lead me to Em'ly and Vi, Rosie and Annabelle, and Aunt Victoria.'

'We won't have none of your wangling, Sammy Adams,' said Emily, 'nor any of your tickling larks, not when we got exalted visitors, if yer don't mind.'

'Tickling's not in Postman's Knock,' said Vi.

'In this house, it's crept in accidental over the years,' said Tommy.

'Well, I really don't know,' said Aunt Victoria.

'What you should know, Aunt Victoria,' said Boots, 'is that if you get Sammy he'll charge you sixpence to kiss you and sixpence not to tickle you.'

'Oh, Uncle Sammy can tickle me,' said Rosie.

'He'd better not try it on with me,' said Aunt Victoria.

'I'll box his ears if he does,' said Emily.

'Our Em'ly, ain't she a perisher?' said Sammy admiringly.

The curtains were drawn, the parlour cosy with fug, the games riotous. Rosie and Annabelle romped ecstatically through them all, Postman's Knock, Blind Man's Buff, Hunt the Slipper, Mrs O'Grady and Straight Face. Then Forfeits. Boots conducted this. Mr Finch roared, and Aunt Victoria actually laughed until her tears ran. But Lizzy eventually yelled at her brother.

'Oh, yer devious devil, Boots, all the forfeits for me and Em'ly and Vi make us show our legs! I'm complaining, I am.'

'I'm not,' said Tommy. 'You complaining, Sammy?'

'Not me,' said Sammy. 'You complaining, Uncle Tom?'

'Me?' said Uncle Tom. 'Not likely. You complaining, Ned?'

'Not from where I'm sitting,' said Ned. 'You complaining, Mr Finch?'

'One shouldn't complain at a Christmas party,' said Mr Finch. 'What about you, Boots?'

'I'm impartial,' said Boots.

'No, you're not,' said Vi, 'you're wicked.'

'I don't know where our mum got 'im from,' said Emily.

'Rosie,' said Boots, 'have you ever done a knees-up?'

'No, Daddy,' said Rosie, and giggled as she received a wink from him.

'Or you, Annabelle?'

'No, Uncle Boots,' said Annabelle.

'Well, we can't have that,' said Boots, 'no little girls

can go through a Christmas party in Walworth without doing a knees-up. Kindly place your bottom on the piano stool, Tommy. Rosie, Annabelle, hold my hands and we'll do it with your mummies.'

'Don't you wake my baby,' said Lizzy.

'Oh, baby can join in too,' said Boots, 'it's never too early to learn "Mother Brown".'

Oh, that husband of mine, thought Emily, no one can say no to him, and don't he like running things? Wait till I get him in bed tonight, I'll bite him all over.

'Come on, everyone in,' she cried, laughter in her eyes, and in her quick, vivacious way, for she could never wholly repress the madcap in her, she went around pulling everybody to their feet, even Ned, who remarked he was only a one-knee-upper. 'Oh, yer can perform with Lizzy and me, Ned lovey, and together we'll do a five-knees-up. Come on, Uncle Tom, you too.'

'I'm willing and able,' said Uncle Tom, 'I ain't had a knees-up since your weddin', Em.'

Tommy played and the knees-up began, in the parlour, and the house rang to the sounds of active legs and singing voices. Mr Finch might have excused himself, but did not. Cockney life had always fascinated him. It was born of warm hearts, big hearts, extrovert tongues, family loyalties and unfailing optimism. He formed an arm-in-arm trio with Vi and Sammy. Vi was exhilarated, the more so because her mother was actually participating hand in hand with her father. Lizzy, she thought, Lizzy and Ned, Emily and Boots, and Tommy and Sammy, there weren't any people who were more fun to be with.

Emily laughed at the antics of Rosie and Annabelle, who thought knees-up meant jumping. And Lizzy gave Ned a hug because he was performing so gamely. She wished Chinese Lady could be here, sitting by the fire watching us. She thought, I've got to tell Boots he's a love about that house, I know he'll get it all furnished and new decorated by the time our mum comes home.

She spoke to him when supper was being put on the table in the kitchen, and she was alone in the scullery with him for a moment. Boots gave her a squeeze.

'Well, I did hang about a bit, Lizzy, I know.'

'Yes, but I got – oh, it don't matter now, just as long as I'm still yer favourite sister. And I'm glad for you about Rosie, you've got a sweet girl there, Boots.'

Over supper, Annabelle fell asleep at the table, so Ned put her to bed in Chinese Lady's room, where he and Lizzy were to stay for the night. Infant Bobby woke up, and Lizzy had to interrupt her supper to feed him. Rosie tried to stay awake, but her eyes kept drooping, so one more little girl was put to bed. Boots carried her up. In bed she made another struggle, this time to say her prayers, as Emily had been teaching her to. She won this struggle.

'God bless Jesus, God bless Mummy, God bless Daddy, and God bless me.' Then, very drowsily, 'Ain't Christmas nice, Daddy?'

She fell asleep, tired out. Well, thought Boots, there are so many 'ain'ts' flying about in our house that she's bound to think she's entitled to a few.

Aunt Victoria, Uncle Tom and Vi left after supper to walk home, for there were no trams running. A taxi called for Mr Finch at eleven o'clock. He thanked the family for giving him such an enjoyable Christmas Day. Emily asked if he was sure he had enjoyed himself. She thought he had one or two quiet moments. He said he wanted them to know that whenever he was among them he could never fail to enjoy himself. He asked them to give his affectionate regards to their mother when they visited her tomorrow.

By midnight, only Emily and Boots were up. Boots sank into a fireside chair, to enjoy a cigarette after sucking his new pipe all day. Rosie had overlooked the fact that a pipe needed tobacco. Emily let her husband have a couple of puffs, then took the cigarette from him and put it in the ash tray. Then she sat on his lap.

'You're after something,' said Boots.

'Just a cuddle,' said Emily. He gave her one. She snuggled. 'We missed our mum, I know,' she said, 'but it's been a really good Christmas Day, don't yer think so? Everyone had a lovely time, I'm sure they did.'

'Well, I did,' said Boots, and kissed her. 'What else?' he asked.

'Well, Rosie. We can't ask Mrs Pullen to have her all the time. Then when she goes back to school, we won't like her comin' home to an empty house, Boots, will we? I got to give up my job.'

'Which you don't want to?' asked Boots.

'Not as much as I might 'ave,' said Emily, and ran a hand through his hair to ruffle it. 'Only we won't have much to live on once you start paying out rent or mortgage. And then there's the five bob a week for the Lady Almoner at Brompton.'

'Oh, I told Sammy twenty minutes ago I'd need a rise.'

'Oh, yer did?' Emily combed his hair back into place with her fingers. 'What did he say?'

'Fell over. Then tottered up to bed with ruination on his mind.'

'He won't be able to say no,' said Emily. 'I'll give the town hall a week's notice after Christmas. You see, Rosie's got to come first, we got to give her a proper home life, she's got to know there's always you or me, or both of us, in the house, and you got to be our breadwinner. But when Chinese Lady's home and Rosie's at school, p'raps – oh, you know.'

'You'd like to work during the hours Rosie's at school?' asked Boots.

'If I could get a part-time job, yes, I would,' said Emily.

'I'll speak to Sammy. About you being our part-time office girl. Part-time office shorthand-typist girl and filing clerk.'

'Oh, I'd like that, and the money would be useful,

495

wouldn't it?' Emily hugged him. 'Sammy would pay me something, wouldn't he?'

'It's usual, even in a family business,' said Boots, cuddling her knees. 'But I'll mention it in an unimportant way.'

'What's an unimportant way, yer daft darling?' asked Emily.

'A way that won't make him fall over again, lovey. He might not get up next time.'

Emily laughed and wound her arms around his neck.

'Oh, yer a laugh a minute sometimes, ain't yer?' she said, and her green eyes were swimming with affection. 'Would yer like a treat when we go to bed? You can undress me, if you like.'

'That'll make it my turn to fall over,' said Boots. His Emily was extraordinarily modest about her body except within the security and cover of their bed.

'No, but I'll let you – all over – everything—'

'Everything, Em?'

'Yes, but only in the dark,' murmured Emily.

CHAPTER THIRTY-SIX

The family were delighted to see that Chinese Lady was up when they arrived at the hospital on Boxing Day, Vi with them. Wrapped in her dressing-gown, Chinese Lady was waiting for them in the corridor leading to her ward. She did not want them in the ward, asking questions about the vase of Christmas roses. Most of all she did not want Boots asking sly questions. She did not want to talk about Mr Finch in any way until she had made up her mind about his proposal. A woman's mind that was not made up would get into a proper dither if she had a son like Boots asking questions. Mind, not many women did have sons like Boots. That little conclusion made her feel quite proud.

In the room where Mr Finch had proposed yesterday, she accepted greetings, and pecks on the cheek. They studied her. She looked a little fragile, but the dark-eyed shadows of illness were much lighter, her expression that of a woman who had no quarrel with her condition. Boots felt she was having a very good day and would accordingly put all of them through their paces. If she seemed pleased to seat herself, that was to be expected. He noted the light in Emily's eyes, the gladness in her smile, and he knew she loved Chinese Lady as much as any of them did. It was as much for Chinese Lady as for anyone that she wanted to move to greener fields and cleaner air.

Chinese Lady elected first to tell them that Dr Uberst was going to send her to Frimley the last week in

January. To convalesce. That brought happy exclamations from Lizzy, Vi and Emily.

'Yes, well, we'll see,' she said, 'though I don't want to be there all the months God sends. God knows what you'll all be gettin' up to. Lizzy, is that another new coat? It looks dreadful expensive. You and Ned want to put some money away for a rainy day, it's always best to have some savings.' Chinese Lady had never been known to have savings herself. 'Still, it's Christmas, Ned, and I daresay Lizzy deserves something new, seeing she's give you two lovely babies.' Little Bobby was cradled in Lizzy's arms. 'Lizzy, you sure that baby isn't a bit peaky?'

'Mum, of course he's not,' said Lizzy.

'You don't want him gettin' peaky at only four months. See if he's got a cold nose.'

'I got a pink one, Granny Lady,' said Annabelle, 'Daddy said so.'

'It looks a nice nose to me,' said Chinese Lady. 'My, my, you're growin' pretty, Annabelle.'

'Yes, me and Mummy's awful pretty,' said Annabelle.

'There's a pet,' said Chinese Lady, a white shawl, crocheted by Lizzy as a Christmas present, around her neck and tucked inside her dressing-gown. It gave her a soft look. 'Sammy, stop fidgeting.'

'Kindly observe, Ma, I was merely crossin' my legs in the approved fashion of a City business gent travelling first-class to London Bridge,' said Sammy.

'Sammy's pickin' up verbosity,' said Vi.

'It's all over the place in our house,' said Tommy. 'Boots started it when he was at school, Lizzy caught it later on, Sammy's pickin' it up now, and I got a worrying feeling I'm goin' to catch it meself.'

'I don't know about Sammy's verbosity,' said Chinese Lady, 'but I know I don't want him pickin' up fidgeting when he already gets up to things I don't get told about. And Sammy, don't use that common word Ma to me, specially not now.'

'Why specially not now?' asked Boots.

'Did you say something?' asked Chinese Lady.

'Yes. Why specially not now?'

'We don't want enquiring remarks from you, Boots, thank you. I'm just pleased to see you all. Rosie, did you have a nice Christmas Day?'

'Oh, yes,' said Rosie, 'I like Christmas, Nana.' Emily had suggested that was what Rosie should call Chinese Lady, because Granny Lady ought to be just for Annabelle, who thought it up herself. Rosie went on to say a little shyly, 'Santa Claus came and put presents in my stocking when I was asleep.'

'He put some in mine too,' said Annabelle.

'And did you both have a nice Christmas dinner?' asked Chinese Lady, showing a smile. 'Well, I hope everyone did, and that it come on the table without the rib of beef being overdone on account of certain people larkin' about instead of being a help to Em'ly. I didn't like thinking that with Aunt Victoria and Uncle Tom there, and our Vi as well, the dinner wasn't what it should of been.'

'Well, we missed your touch, old girl,' said Ned, 'but I can tell you the whole dinner was perfect.'

'The Yorkshire pudden and horseradish sauce was noble,' said Tommy.

'Lovely, really it was, Aunt Maisie,' said Vi.

'Mr Finch was also there,' said Boots.

'I'm pleased everything come up so good,' said Chinese Lady, 'which I hoped our Em'ly was thanked for.'

'Of course, it wasn't really as good as you could've done, Mum,' said Emily, to whom love and loyalty meant far more than being considered equal to Chinese Lady as a cook. 'Aunt Victoria was very compliment'ry, and so was Mr Finch, so I didn't feel I'd done too bad, and the boys helped.'

'What boys?' asked Sammy. 'I didn't notice any boys. Did you, Tommy?'

'Don't ask me,' said Tommy, 'I wasn't lookin'. Did you see any boys around when you arrived, Ned?'

'Short ones?' said Ned. 'About so big? No, can't say I did.'

'Oh, very comical,' said Lizzy.

'We're here to talk to our mum,' said Emily, 'not to have 'ysterics. Don't take no notice, mum, they'll only get worse. I suppose it's Boots's fault, really, he's turned them all into comedians. By the way, Mr Finch was so sorry you couldn't be with us, and he sent you his kind regards.'

'His affectionate regards,' said Boots.

'Yes, well, I had a nice boiled egg for breakfast this morning, and Christmas dinner yesterday was very nice,' said Chinese Lady, and this piece of irrelevance made Boots take a thoughtful look at her. Chinese Lady ignored it. 'Vi, that's a pretty hat you're wearing, I must say. I don't know any girl who looks more ladylike in a hat than you do.'

'Thank you, Aunt Maisie,' said Vi, a new hat of sleek brown velvet nestling around her hair.

'And I like Tommy's new suit,' said Lizzy, tongue in cheek.

'Yes, it's all very promising,' mused Boots.

'What is?' asked Vi.

'Yes, what is?' asked Tommy, not yet aware that Chinese Lady had decided Vi was the right one for him.

'Just a passing thought,' said Boots, 'and it's gone now.'

'Still, it's a nice suit, Tommy,' said Chinese Lady, 'but your tie's not straight and your jacket's undone. I never seen you look nearly slipshod before, you've always looked tidy, and you've always been better behaved than Sammy and Boots, Sammy gettin' up to every trick the devil puts into boys, and Boots comin' out of the Army with hardly no respect to speak of.'

'Your Granny Lady thinks Uncle Boots is headin' for

perdition,' murmured Lizzy to her now wide-awake baby. She put her little finger into the infant's mouth, and the infant sucked at it without giving any indication it was being cheated.

'We could all come to perdition at Em'ly's hands, Mum,' said Tommy.

'So we could,' said Sammy. 'It's me painful duty, Ma, to inform you our Em'ly's been boxin' ears left, right and centre. In a manner of speakin'.'

'Sammy, just wait till I get you 'ome,' said Emily. 'Mum, don't you believe a word of it, I just been havin' to put me foot down sometimes, that's all.'

'Em'ly,' said Chinese Lady fondly, 'I'd be glad any time to hear you've boxed a few ears, it'll help them be more commonsensical when they're grown-up men. Still, Boots is showing more promise lately, makin' up his mind about the new house and managing the shop like he is.'

'Yes, he's been a good boy lately,' said Emily.

'Did we mention Mr Finch sent you his affectionate regards?' asked Boots, and Chinese Lady gave him a Victorian look, one that implied boys should be seen, not heard. Her only oldest son smiled.

'I'm not sure I like that smile of yours,' she said.

'Mummy, is Uncle Boots naughty?' asked Annabelle in a stage whisper.

It was Rosie who answered up.

'Oh, no,' she said, 'my daddy's never naughty.'

'My daddy is,' said Annabelle, 'my mummy says so.'

'Oh, well, my daddy's a little bit naughty sometimes,' confessed Rosie, 'my mummy says so too.'

'I think that's taken care of you and me, Boots,' said Ned.

Chinese Lady smiled. Emily's eyes danced. Vi had a little giggle. Boots looked up at the ceiling.

'Now, Sammy,' said Chinese Lady, 'I think I'd like to hear what you been gettin' up to in your business Christmas week.'

Sammy faced blithely up to the inquisition.

The day after Boxing Day was not a busy one at the shop, and when Sammy came in at noon, Susie was able to spare time to follow him up to his office, a brown paper carrier bag in her hand.

'Could I see yer a minute, Mister Sammy?' she asked.

'You might have to take your turn when I've been knighted for me services to the country,' said Sammy, 'but there's no queue now. Enjoy your Christmas?'

'Oh, yes.' Susie glowed. 'We 'ad a lovely time, and roast chestnuts round the fire as well. I 'ope you did too. Ain't it a blessing your mother's better all the time? Boots – Mister Manager – told me she was in fine form yesterday.'

'I can confirm suchlike was so,' said Sammy. 'Now, what's on your mind?'

'It's the present you give me on Christmas Eve,' said Susie. 'I begs yer won't think me ungrateful, like, but – well, they're too intimate.'

'What, them unprecedented fancy knickers?' said Sammy.

'I just can't accept them,' said Susie, pinking, 'I'd feel like a fast and common girl. Mister Sammy, I couldn't 'ardly sleep thinking of yer wrong-doing.'

'My what?' asked Sammy, hanging up his hat and coat.

'Mister Sammy, it was very wrong of yer to give a girl a present like them. Me mum and dad would've been awful shocked if they'd known. When I went to church Christmas morning, I asked the Lord to forgive you yer little sin. You being so kind gen'rally, I know yer'll repent graciously, specially as yer gave me a kind Christmas kiss.'

'Here, mind what you're saying.' Sammy put himself at a distance. 'I don't remember any kiss, and what's all this religious rhubarb about me sinning on account of presentin' yer with a deserved gift?'

'Oh, Mister Sammy, yer know it was wrong,' said Susie. 'I was that embarrassed I near died, knowing men only give girls intimate things when they've got forbidden designs on them. Oh, I'm sure yer didn't mean it that way yerself, but people would think you did, so yer must take them back.' She placed the carrier bag on his desk. 'I won't say no more about it, honest, I'll just pray the Lord accepts your repentance.'

'Well, I don't know I'm believin' my own ears,' said Sammy, 'I never heard such a carry-on. Praying, kissin', repenting and forbidden designs, I'm walkin' on the ceiling, I am, only I know I can't. So kindly pay attention, Susie Brown. I've got plans for you, providin' you don't catch religious influenza every time I say something or give you something. You've got nice manners and welcoming ways when you're talkin' to customers, and you've got good business understandin' concerning how much money people have got in their pockets or their purses, and how to make 'em spend it in our shop. Being a female girl who's goin' to be a female woman in time, you're bound to know what I know, that it's mostly women who've got charge of spending dibs. Which means shops exclusive to women always do better than shops exclusive to men. Which means I'm goin' to open a women's shop, and when I do there'll be intimate female garments all over the place, and you'll maybe have to dress wax dummies in corsets and fancy knickers as well as in frocks and skirts and blouses. I'll likely take you with me to warehouses and factories when I'm buying, so as to get your female opinions and so on. Accordingly, I'm kindly requestin' you to stop your churchified sermonising, which is hurtin' my ears considerable. I don't want you praying for me, it might just persuade the Lord to render me so soft and daft that I'll give up all me businesses and go off as a missionary to darkest Africa with me best white collar turned back to front. Or I might carry on makin' me fortune in order to give it all away to orphanages or homes for unfortunate females. Now, have you got all that, Susie?'

'Oh, Mister Adams, I'm just overcome,' breathed Susie, 'you can speechify as good as John the Baptist addressin' the multitude, you lifted me up into dreams of a wondrous future, you did.'

'I think I'm gettin' a headache,' said Sammy.

'Oh, d'yer want a headache powder? I'll get yer one.'

'Kindly don't bother, I'll just take me head off and put it down somewhere quiet.'

'Oh, yer so droll, Mister Sammy. Would it 'elp if I—' Susie hesitated. 'I mean, if I kept yer pretty Christmas present—'

'Just put 'em back in stock,' said Sammy.

'No, I couldn't be that ungrateful, not now I know yer got such praiseworthy intentions for me future,' said Susie earnestly. 'I'll keep them in 'appy memory of me best Christmas ever, but not wear them till I'm more worldly, like. I'll do that, shall I, Mister Sammy?'

Sammy looked for the hundredth time into wide blue eyes, searching them for signs she was having him on. But there was only the clear light of the young and innocent. A little smile peeped, however, by which Chinese Lady could have told him Susie was beginning to understand why he sometimes shifted his gaze to mutter and growl.

'All right, off you go,' he muttered, and Susie's smile danced.

'Yes, Mister Sammy,' she said, and took the carrier bag with her.

Sammy hoped she was going to be more of an asset than a problem to him. He'd had a problem when he was only fifteen, when he'd hardly been able to believe what young Rachel Moses could do to his feelings. She was a beauty even at her age. It had been almost a relief getting a fulltime Saturday job in the market that knocked roller skating on its head. Rachel had cried when he told her, she had wept enough tears to float an ark, and he had had to pat her, jolly her, cuddle her and even kiss her for nothing. And Rachel had said, 'But you'll still love me, won't you?' And he had said, ' 'Course I will, it's just that a feller's got to start makin' his fortune sometime.'

He'd got to get in touch with her this week, to take advantage of her generosity and arrange that loan for Boots. Boots had agreed three hundred pounds would be enough.

It was on New Year's Eve, in the afternoon, when Sammy came into the shop after being absent for three hours. He had a cheque with him. It had cost him the price of a lunch and a single kiss. And a promise never to stop being friends.

He asked Boots to come up to his office. There he handed him the cheque for three hundred pounds.

'You're all clear now to buy that house, Boots, you're all clear to give Em'ly and Chinese Lady a clean washing line and a garden.'

Boots looked at the cheque. It was signed by Rachel Moses.

'Rachel?' he said. Rachel was well-known to the family as Sammy's erstwhile girl friend, his one and only girl friend. 'You got Rachel to make the loan? At ten per cent simple interest? That's more like a gift than a loan. And Rachel Moses? I thought she was married.'

'She is,' said Sammy, 'but she's got money of her own and one or two little interests, and uses her maiden name. It's a friendly gesture. You got to have that house, and get it furnished and ready. You might not get a mortgage that easy, anyway. Building societies don't take any notice of a wife's earnings, not when wives have to give up work on account of this, that, or the other. All you got to do with this loan is pay off three hundred and thirty quid over three years, which is precisely approximate two quid four bob a week repayment, which means yer goin' to screw the till for the rise yer want in yer salary, yer bleeder.'

'Nicely put, Sammy. Say a quid for starters.'

'A quid?' Sammy went slightly hoarse. 'A quid a week rise?'

'What did you have in mind, then?' asked Boots mildly. 'Two?'

'I don't hear very good when someone's makin' unfunny jokes,' said Sammy. 'Listen, you got Em'ly's earnings—'

'Emily's giving notice,' said Boots. 'There's Rosie to look after.'

'Ah,' said Sammy. Approvingly, he said, 'Now yer talkin' different. That's good. Rosie needs a lovin' mother. And a lovin' father.'

'Glad you agree.' Boots smiled. 'All right, split the difference.'

'Hold it, hold it,' said Sammy, 'what difference?'

'What you had in mind, two quid, and what I suggested, one quid. Shall we settle for a thirty bob rise?'

'Oh, yer bugger,' said Sammy.

'This loan,' said Boots, 'is there an agreement to sign?'

'Wait a minute, let me get over me faintin' fit,' said Sammy. He flopped into his desk chair, took out his wallet and extracted a folded sheet of paper. 'Here y'ar, hand-writ by Rachel, but all legal. Sign it, get a witness, and let me have it back. Listen, I got to up your money to four quid a week?'

'Not you, Sammy. Adams Enterprises. Rosie, Emily and self would all like to eat, so would Chinese Lady when she's out of convalescence. Give Rachel my love for her friendly gesture.'

'Well, she likes our fam'ly,' said Sammy. 'All right, we'll go home later and tell Em'ly you're goin' to buy the house, and we'll all have a New Year drink.'

'Good on yer, old cock,' said Boots.

Tommy took Vi to the pictures that evening. Vi

wondered if Tommy would ever ask her to walk out steady with him. Tommy wondered if Vi might consider walking out steady with him once he was twenty-one.

At the end of February, Chinese Lady wrote a letter to Mr Finch from the Frimley sanatorium.

'Dear Mr Finch, I am in good health considering and the doctors seem pleased. Being improved as I am I have been giving attention to your kind proposal which I am sure was a compliment I never dreamed of and more unexpected than I ever thought, specially coming on Christmas Day and all. I don't know I'd ever be up to a gentleman like you, although I can't say it's right you shouldn't have a desired companion as we aren't made to live alone all our lives. I've looked after my children all these years and now they're grown up and making their own way in the world which I'm naturally proud of but regretful about in a way. There's Tommy and Sammy going to live over the shop soon, Lizzy a wife and mother, and Boots and Emily and Rosie in their new house. I am pleased of course that they've invited me to live with them which is very tempting as I'm as fond of Emily as if she was my own and Boots having been a soldier like his dad.

'But after all these years as a widow I can't say it wouldn't be nice to have a husband to look after and turn to, but I would only be wishful of such blessings if I'm up to doing all the things a wife should. I'm doing things here for myself like we have to but I don't know how long it might be before I can do everything I want to. I thought it was only fair you should hear from me by now about how I'm getting on and to say perhaps it would be best not to give you an answer until I've been home a while, and I should be home by the middle of May according to Dr Uberst. Then later on in the summer I'll be more sure about if I'm going to be myself again, only I wouldn't want to live too far from my family in any case and miss seeing Rosie and Annabelle grow up and little Bobby too. A woman can't put her children and grandchildren out of her mind, although if I did marry again I wouldn't put my husband second best as that wouldn't be right. I know you haven't been to see me since Christmas because of letting me think things over by myself which was kind of you, but if you like you can come about the middle of March and we can have a talk. I do hope you are keeping well, Yours truly Maisie Adams.'

Mr Finch, on receipt of this letter, took a philosophical view of its cautious note. He knew she was very attached to all her family, and that attachment could well be the governing factor in her eventual decision. He thought the one thing that would make her decide to continue living with Emily and Boots would be Emily having a child. She would not easily give up the pleasure of being a direct part of that child's life.

Miss Polly Simms, meanwhile, had been made to understand by Boots that the war was over. In January he had told her, among other things, that what she was looking for she would never find. It was gone, buried beneath a million white crosses in France and Flanders, and no one was going to start another world war for her.

'We've all got our ghosts,' he said, not for the first time. 'Not only you, but the women whose men didn't come back, the men who did, and thousands of other people. But stop carrying yours about with you, Polly. Find something useful to do, only be a good girl and leave me out. I'm married, with a wife and daughter.'

'Bloody hell, did you have to tell me?' said Polly. 'I care for you, you know. What am I expected to do, turn myself into a nurse or a schoolteacher?'

'You might make a passable nurse,' said Boots, 'you'd never make a schoolteacher.'

'Wouldn't I? Why wouldn't I? I like kids. If you can

run a shop, for God's sake, I can teach kids. And I will. I'll show you.'

Hell having no fury and so on, Polly was now at a teacher's training college, her teeth gritted. She opted for the challenge out of sheer frustration and bravado. She had an excess of bravado, and in its most admirable form it had made a courageous ambulance driver of her. But it was by virtue of different gifts that she was destined to become a good schoolteacher, the while nursing an obsessive determination not to lose touch with Robert Adams. She set her sights on the school attended by his daughter Rosie, whom she had met in the shop one day. Not knowing the true relationship, she thought the girl a captivating reflection of Robert's irresistible appeal.

On a crisp morning in March, Emily came out of the doctor's surgery wanting to dance in her exhilaration. She had done it. Boots had done it. They had both done it. Together. She wasn't a barren woman. She was pregnant.

When Chinese Lady received the news she thought all was as well with her own little world as it could possibly be.

THE END

KING OF CAMBERWELL

CHAPTER ONE

'Mister Sammy?'

Sammy Adams, a young man of initiative and enterprise, looked up from his examination of a proposed lease on a Kennington shop. He met, as he feared he would, the deep blue eyes of Susie Brown, assistant in his shop below his office at Camberwell Green, South London. Invaluable, the girl was, but he wished her blue saucers would not always have the effect of making him feel he was going to say yes when his every instinct cautioned him to say no.

'What is it, may I ask?' he enquired.

'Boots said—' Susie hesitated. Boots was his eldest brother and the manager of the shop. 'Boots said you and Mister Tommy's goin' to move out of your house next month to live in the rooms here.'

'You have been informed correct, Miss Brown. Them selfsame rooms is presently being made ready for our desired occupation.'

Susie wrinkled her nose. She knew Mister Sammy was always on his guard when he called her Miss Brown and spoke to her in careful prose.

'Well, you see,' she said, 'Mum and Dad, well, what with Dad's bit of pension for his gammy leg, and what he earns doing odd jobs for you, and me earnin' my bit too, owing to your kind generosity, we'd like to move out of Peabody's and 'ave—' Susie stopped in recognition of her dropped aitch. Working in the shop with Boots, who spoke ever so educated, had brought about an instinctive improvement in her own speech. 'Well, we'd like to have a nice little house like the one your fam'ly's lived in so long. Mister Sammy, could you speak for us to your landlord, could you put in a word for us?'

'Eh?' Sammy sat back and rolled his fountain pen between his fingers. 'Are you makin' known a desire to take our old house over, Miss Brown?'

'We've got a likin' to, so could you speak for us?' Susie knew Caulfield Place in Walworth. It was off Browning Street, near Browning Hall and its clinic. At the clinic, kids could be treated for conjunctivitis, an eye condition not unknown among the poverty-stricken families of Walworth. Caulfield Place was one of the streets clustering around St John's Church and its school. The church was the centre and fount of social activities, and the little terraced houses in those streets, with their modest rents, were always well sought after, and none of them ever stood empty. Susie couldn't think of any house her family would rather have than the one that had known Mister Sammy's family. She was sure they had made a happy home of it. Her mum and dad said that when you moved into a new home you could always tell what sort of people the previous tenants had been. People always left something of themselves behind. 'Mum and Dad would be ever so grateful, Mister Sammy.'

Sammy, practical though he was, could not help being touched by the request. He said, 'In consideration of you being a credit to me business, Miss Brown, I am happy to inform you I'll use me highly regarded influence on your behalf.'

'Oh, I thank you considerable, Mister Sammy,' said Susie, who had learned how to respond in kind to Sammy's verbal indulgencies.

6

'Now, if you don't mind, I'll continue examining me business affairs,' said Sammy, his dark brown hair thick and well-brushed, his features pleasantly masculine, and his own blue eyes capable of wheedling glances.

'Yes, Mister Sammy,' said Susie. In her seventeenth year, she was fair-haired, slim and pretty, and acquiring an improving dress sense. She returned to the shop below in a state of high hope. Mister Sammy had given his word, and he never broke it once he gave it. He had funny ways, and was very droll sometimes, but he had good principles.

The following day, when Mr Eli Greenberg, a valuable business go-between, called to see Sammy, Sammy mentioned the house in Caulfield Place. It was occupied at the moment only by himself and his brother Tommy. Boots and his wife Emily had moved out two months ago, in January. And Sammy's mother was convalescing from TB in a Frimley sanatorium. She would live with Boots and Emily when she came out.

'In respect of same,' said Sammy, 'I am requestin' your kind co-operation, Eli old cock.'

Mr Greenberg, son of a Latvian father and a Russian mother who had escaped Tsarist pogroms when he was a child, put on a wise look. Wisdom was priceless, and added considerably to the value of co-operation.

'Vould you say it's goin' to be my pleasure, Sammy?'

'A trifling act of friendship is all I'm askin',' said Sammy. 'Kindly do the needful by seeing Susie Brown and her fam'ly get first option.'

'Ah,' said Mr Greenberg. He lifted his ancient black hat and resettled it until it roundly crowned his dark, majestic features.

'No ahs, Eli,' said Sammy. 'Kindly speak to the landlord, Mr Small, an old friend of yours.' There were few businessmen in South London who weren't old friends of Mr Greenberg.

7

'For you, my poy, I ain't averse, but there's a little matter of a vaiting list.'

'A waiting list? In this day and age?' Sammy looked disgusted. 'And in Walworth? It beats me, Eli, the way you can talk like that without hardly movin' yer lips.'

'Come, come, Sammy, such desirable residences,' said Mr Greenberg.

'Don't make me choke to death,' said Sammy. 'Kindly arrange for the Browns to go top of the list.'

'My life, should I do such a thing?' Mr Greenberg looked shocked. 'Could I do such a thing? The poor vaitin' families, Sammy, should they vait longer?'

'That's it, make me die laughin',' said Sammy. 'Listen, it's me that's kindly requestin', not some geezer you've only just met.'

'Sammy my dear, ain't I alvays treated you like my own son?' protested Mr Greenberg.

'It's been highly mutual and given me cause to love yer, Dad,' said Sammy, 'so you see Susie's fam'ly get the house.'

'Sammy, there is only vun Jesus, my poy. Should I be expected to valk on vater vhen I am only me? But I ain't saying a vhite vun von't help.'

'Hold on,' said Sammy, 'I don't think I'm hearing you right. You didn't mention a fiver in passin', did you?'

'It costs to climb a vaitin' list, Sammy, and love is vorth a little vhite vun, ain't it?'

'No such thing as a little white one,' said Sammy. 'They're all worth five nicker apiece. Wait a minute, what d'you mean, love?'

Mr Greenberg looked wisely knowing.

'Such a pretty smile, my poy, such sveet blue eyes. My vord, ain't such eyes the light of a young man's life? Vell, say four pounds, Sammy, and I'll see vhat I can do for her family.'

'Oblige me by leavin' off,' said Sammy. 'You're

hurtin' my ears and strainin' me pocket. Also, I ain't in love, I just happen to have a kind heart.'

'Vhy, Sammy, there ain't a kinder heart in the kingdom,' said Mr Greenberg generously, 'but—'

'All right, I'll slip yer five bob,' said Sammy.

'Sammy, Sammy.' Mr Greenberg showed pain. 'Say three pounds ten, my poy.'

'Thirty bob,' said Sammy, 'which offer means I'm off me chump.'

'Done at two pounds, my friend.'

'Some friend,' said Sammy, 'and I still got to get it back from Susie.'

'I should believe that?' said Mr Greenberg.

'I ain't a benefact'ry institution,' said Sammy. 'I'm kind, but I ain't daft. Also, this ain't the year of plenty, it's the year of the locusts.' It was 1921, and the Exchequer coffers were bare, according to the Chancellor.

'In such hard times, Sammy, friendship is dear to me. Ah, should I collect now?'

'Fair do's, if I can tell Susie it's on.'

'Vell, vhy not, Sammy, vhy not?' said Mr Greenberg, and Sammy handed over two pound notes.

'I'll tell her she can go round to the landlord at the end of the week, right?' said Sammy.

'Right it is, Sammy,' said Mr Greenberg. Going through the shop on his way out, he smiled at Susie.

'Good morning, Susie,' he said.

'Good morning, Mr Greenberg,' said Susie.

'Vould even the prettiest daughter of Abraham have such blue eyes?' said Mr Greenberg, and departed chuckling.

Susie was called up to Sammy's office later.

'Yes, what is it, Miss Brown?' he asked.

'Well, I like that,' said Susie protestingly. 'You called me.'

'Did I? Me mind's unconsciously occupied – oh, half

9

a mo', I remember now. The house, Miss Brown.'

'Yes, Mister Adams?'

'Tell your parents to go and fix things up with the landlord at the end of the week. I suppose they know the rent's fifteen bob?'

'Oh, Mister Sammy, ain't you a love?' said Susie rapturously.

'No, I ain't,' said Sammy, 'I'm yer employer.'

'But you did it, you spoke for us. Thank you, Mister Sammy, and we can afford the rent. I got to say it, you been a shinin' light to me fam'ly.'

'Shinin' lights come expensive,' said Sammy.

'Expensive?' said Susie. 'What d'you mean?'

'I mean—' Sammy saw her blue eyes flicker anxiously. He dropped his gaze and frowned at his blotter. 'I mean it's goin' to cost yer.'

'But if it's the rent, I just said we can afford that.'

'All the same.' Sammy cleared his throat. Miss Susie Brown, invaluable assistant, was getting worryingly pretty. 'You sure you can?'

'We got near to two pounds ten a week comin' in these days, Mister Sammy, really we have.'

Sammy said, 'Well, the donkey's been fed a carrot and you got to pay for it.'

'Oh, we don't have no donkey, Mister Sammy,' said Susie. 'What would we do with a donkey, and nowhere to put him, either? Mister Sammy, ain't you funny sometimes?'

Sammy sighed. It was no good. He couldn't do it.

'Well, all right,' he said, 'you can go back to your work, Miss Brown.'

'Yes, Mister Sammy.' Susie hesitated. 'Mister Sammy, you all right? Only you look a bit woebegone, like.'

'I'll get over it,' he said. Two quid, he thought, two quid, and I don't have the strength to even mention it, let alone ask for it. It's me who's the perishing donkey, and I've got a horrendous feeling it ain't going to get better. It had been like that for nearly a year, ever since he had taken her on. It was crucifying what she could do to his pocket, and at her age too. Those mince-pies of hers, supposing a feller had to live with them day and night, including week-ends? He'd walk about mesmerised, and his business would go to rack and ruin. He'd been in business on his own since he was seventeen, and he'd reckoned to be a self-made man by the time he was twenty-one. He'd miss it by years if he didn't cure his weaknesses. 'I am not proposing to fall ill, Miss Brown.'

'Oh, we'd all miss you dreadful if you was took queer, Mister Sammy,' said Susie, who often wondered why little intermissions with him always made her leave his office singing to herself.

'Should I pass away at me desk, Miss Brown, be so good as to inform Boots me eldest brother to let Mr Greenberg see to the funeral arrangements on account of Mr Greenberg knowing which undertakers will give the fam'ly the best discount.'

'Yes, Mister Sammy, I'll tell Boots that if it happens,' said Susie demurely, 'but I do hope it won't happen this week, like. We'd all be prostrated.'

'Hoppit, yer saucebox,' said Sammy.

'Yes, Mister Adams.' Susie went to the door, her neat blue frock a tribute to her improving taste. She turned and said, 'I just got to say it's heavenly thinkin' about leavin' Peabody's and movin' into your fam'ly's house.'

'I can't afford heavenly thoughts meself, not now I can't,' said Sammy. 'I just committed an act near to financial suicide.'

'Mister Sammy, don't you go jumpin' out of no high windows,' said Susie, and was singing to herself as she went down to the shop.

11

CHAPTER TWO

It was moving day for Sammy and Tommy Adams, a crisp cold March day. It was also early closing day for shops and the East Street market. Sammy arrived from his Camberwell Green shop at half-past one. Tommy, who looked after Sammy's china and glassware stall in the market, was already there. Sammy was not quite nineteen, but in his smart suit and his air of self-assurance, he looked a good twenty-one. Tommy, coming up to twenty-one, was the handsomest of the brothers, but was easy-going where Sammy was demanding and Boots cryptic. It was Sammy the youngest who was the family live wire, however, an engine of perpetual motion that constituted the driving force of Adams Enterprises, the family business.

Tommy quietly surveyed the kitchen, the place that had been the hub of family life. The glowing range had kept it warm in winter, its thick Victorian walls cool in summer. All the furniture was there, except for the old sewing-machine. That was the only thing Boots and Emily had taken from the kitchen when they moved to their new home near Denmark Hill. They had taken it because Boots's mother, Chinese Lady, was attached to it. Her family called her Chinese Lady because she had almond eyes and had once taken in washing to augment her meagre income.

'We only want some crockery, cutlery and a few odds

12

and ends out of here,' said Sammy.

'Let's take the dresser and coal scuttle,' said Tommy. He looked on the ancient dresser and the wooden coal scuttle as family heirlooms. The flat he and Sammy were to live in above the shop at Camberwell Green consisted of two bedrooms and a living-room with kitchen facilities.

'The dresser's a bit big,' said Sammy.

'Not too big,' said Tommy, 'and we got to have somewhere to put things. Besides, it's an old fam'ly piece.'

'It's only a dresser,' said Sammy, regarding the move in a more practical way than Tommy. 'Well, all right, we'll take it.'

'Oi, oi, you there, Sammy my poy?' called a voice from the open front door. Mr Greenberg had arrived. The rag and bone man, known all over South London and in some areas north of the river, had contracted to do the removal job, as he had for Emily and Boots. He was not only willing to cart what furniture Sammy and Tommy wanted for their flat, but also to buy what they didn't want. Two pounds was his price for the removal job, which included five bob each for two sturdy Jewish lads who were to do the humping.

Sammy and Tommy went outside. Mr Greenberg had brought a horse and open cart. Sammy eyed the ancient cart dubiously.

'You sure that unsalubr'ous vehicle ain't going to fall to pieces under the weight?' he asked.

Mr Greenberg's pained look arrived.

'Now, Sammy, vould I hire a cart that vould deposit your furniture in the Valvorth Road? Vhat good vould that do to my business and your furniture? No, no, all shall be delivered safe, ain't it? Of course. Ah, but it's a sad day, Tommy, you and Sammy leaving your home as the last of your kind family, and I veep tears over it. But time is still money, so show me vhat you require to be

13

carted to your new home, and vhat you vould like me to take off your hands, for vhich service I von't charge you, no, not a penny.'

'Half a mo',' said Sammy. 'Eli, I'm frequent not hearing you too good these days. Just make a fair offer for what me and Tommy don't require, as was formally agreed, and then I won't have no further ear trouble.'

'Vell, you got a point, Sammy, and business between friends ain't like other business,' said Mr Greenberg, and began the task of discovering, in company with the brothers, what was to be loaded first, the unwanted stuff. Tommy was a little restrained, Sammy brisk and forthright. The sturdy Jewish lads, Russian Hebrew constantly alternating with South London cockney English, carried the relevant items of furniture out to the cart, Mr Greenberg making a pencilled note of each piece in his pocket book. When it came to moving the wanted items, Tommy began to wander about in the house. It seemed to him that his old home was being bruisingly dismantled. The kitchen, empty and bare eventually, was like a hollow ghost of its former self. And the parlour, once so alive on Sundays, seemed to become devoid of all life except for faint, lingering echoes. The smiling Jewish lads humped, hefted and carried, and the removal of each piece took a little more from the heart of the house.

'I don't know I've had a more depressin' time,' Tommy said to Sammy.

'Fair comment,' said Sammy, 'but when you got to go, you got to go.'

'Boots and Em'ly wouldn't like it like it is now,' said Tommy.

'Well, they're on their way to Frimley, to see Chinese Lady,' said Sammy. 'Cheer up, mate, it's not the end of the world. I'm pleased to remind yer that Chinese Lady her very own self said it was time we all moved.'

14

'I'm only trying to say it's been a good home to us,' said Tommy. 'I suppose you got some feelings outside of yer wallet, ain't you?'

'I got fam'ly feelings which I ain't ever goin' to let go of, and that's gospel,' said Sammy.

Booted feet clumped, and dismantled iron bedsteads were carried out. Finally, the house stood empty, although curtains still hung at windows. Tommy and Sammy were leaving them for Susie's family, as well as gas fittings and gas globes.

'Remember Sundays in the parlour?' said Tommy, he and Sammy now in the passage. His voice rang hollowly. 'And the Christmases?'

'Cost me money, Christmases did,' said Sammy. 'Still, they were good. So were Chinese Lady's Christmas puddings, all of us gettin' a stir for luck when she was mixin' them Christmas Eve. Look, we're movin' out, Tommy, but we got our memories to take. You can't leave memories behind. We've got 'em for life. And there's Susie and her fam'ly comin' in after us, they'll fill the place up again. They're a lively bunch and the old home'll take 'em happy to its bosom. Come on, we'll ride to Camberwell on the cart and save the tram fares.'

'You go,' said Tommy. 'I got Mr Greenberg to leave a broom and dustpan. I'll tidy the place up. Can't leave bits and pieces, or corner dust. Susie wouldn't think much of that, nor would Chinese Lady. I'll follow later.'

'Ah, my young friends.' Mr Greenberg entered the passage. 'All loaded up, all lashed. Now, for vhat you vish me to take off your hands, let me see.' He licked the end of his pencil and totted up figures in his notebook. 'Vell, you're my friends, and friends ain't the same as people. So I von't offer five bob, vhich I vould to people, it being a fair price, but ten bob, vhich is a friendly

15

price. Vill I lose on the deal? I vill, seeing most of it is only good for firevood, but vhat's a small loss vhen it's for the sake of friendship?'

'Don't make me fall over, I might never get up,' said Sammy. 'Heart failure can kill yer, Eli, don't yer know that? We'll talk about it on the way to Camberwell.'

'Vell, I don't mind being hurt a little, Sammy,' said Mr Greenberg, 'but at my age could I stand the pain of havin' you empty all my pockets before we reach Cambervell?'

'I'll just bargain with yer,' said Sammy, who was never going to be able to resist the challenge of fighting for an extra bob or two, however affluent he became. Mr Greenberg smiled in pleasure. To bargain with Sammy Adams was to make a day worthwhile for any man who appreciated the subtleties of wheedling financial dialogue. Sammy, giving Tommy a pat on the shoulder, walked out to the cart with Mr Greenberg. The humpers were already aboard, comfortably ensconced with the furniture. There were only little kids about, their elders all at school, but some women who had been watching from their front doors came over to the cart. There were old friends and neighbours among them, including Mrs Pullen, Mrs Blake and Mrs Higgins.

'Afternoon, Mr Greenberg,' said Mrs Blake, wife of a coalman, and Mr Greenberg lifted his black hat to her and smiled. 'Yer orf for good now, Sammy?'

'Not precisely for good if yer mean really for good,' said Sammy. 'As you know, my fam'ly and me has a high regard for all you ladies that's been our kind neighbours for years. Movin' elsewhere from here don't mean forgettin' you or yer fam'lies or yer kindnesses, which is what really for good would mean. We'll be with yer in spirit, don't you worry.' Sammy never minded making a speech. It didn't cost anything, except a few minutes of his time, and people liked it. 'Me fam'ly wishes you to know it ain't goodbye, just so long, and any time I'm passin' I'll knock one of yer up for a cup of tea.'

'I'll be waitin' and willing, Sammy love,' said Mrs Higgins.

'You sure you said that right?' asked Mrs Pullen.

'I am referrin' to me kettle and teapot,' said Mrs Higgins.

'Appreciated,' said Sammy. 'On behalf of all me fam'ly, I want yer to know all good turns done by yer gen'rous selves during times hard and grievous is also appreciated. If me brother Boots was here he'd deliver educated talk about what yer neighbourliness has meant to us, but as he ain't, I hope yer'll accept my simple wordage in the spirit in which it's given.'

'Lor' love yer, Sammy, you got the gift yerself,' said Mrs Pullen, 'but I can't say I ever noticed you was simple; yer done me for more pennyworths of rotten apples turned good side up than I like to think about. Still, it ain't goin' to be the same round 'ere without you and yer mum and the rest of you. You make sure you give yer mum me best wishes for her consumption when you next see 'er.'

'Bless yer, Sammy,' said Mrs Blake, 'I ain't 'ad a dry eye since Boots and Em'ly moved in January, knowin' you and Tommy was goin' too, and yer mum. They don't make many like yer mum these days, nor like Boots.'

Sammy offered up a knowing smile. Boots was always bound to get a special mention from a female woman.

'Time we was off, Sammy,' said Mr Greenberg from the seat of the cart. 'Vould you kindly bring your fond farevells to a close?'

'Comin',' said Sammy. 'Now don't fret, ladies, you

17

got a nice fam'ly takin' our place next week. Being a thoughtful bloke concernin' old friends and neighbours, I took it upon meself to make sure our house, which is sacred to our much improved mum, wasn't taken over by some of them dubious geezers from the East End.'

'Well, God bless yer for that, Sammy,' said Mrs Higgins. 'We don't want none of them East End people in Caulfield Place, they don't have no manners nor any respectability, and their kids is all little tea leafs.'

'I give yer me word, yer goin' to have a real nice genuine Walworth fam'ly move in,' said Sammy. 'So long now, and may yer washing lines never collapse on a foggy Monday.'

'It's grievous to lose yer all, Sammy,' said Mrs Pullen, and wiped a tear from her eye with a corner of her apron.

Sammy climbed up beside Mr Greenberg, who lifted his hat again to the ladies and said, 'My dears, I concur vith my friend Sammy's vordage, who vouldn't?' He set the horse in motion and Tommy, from the door, watched the cart move off. Sammy turned his head, and Tommy thought that for a moment his younger brother showed human weakness by taking a last look at the house where they had all grown up together. There was even a little wave. Tommy acknowledged it, then went back into the house. He took up the broom and set about sweeping the floor of every room. He knew Chinese Lady would expect this to be done. He was quite willing. He felt the house deserved to be left clean and tidy. Boots had done a good job painting the doors and woodwork six months ago, as well as hanging new wallpaper. It was only right the floors should be cleaned up. He worked conscientiously. It did not surprise him, the amount of dirt and dust the broom found in some places, the places one could never normally get

18

at because of things like wardrobes and chests of drawers. Walworth grime was like that. It crept in invisibly and found places where it could stay invisible. He emptied panfuls of sweepings into the dustbin in the yard. When he had finished, he washed his hands under the sink tap in the scullery. It was time to go then. There was no more to be done. He thought of Chinese Lady. He spoke to her.

'Well, what d'you think, old girl, will it pass with a push?'

She would want to hold her head up about the state of the empty house. He thought she would be able to. The paintwork and wallpaper still looked new, the lino-covered floors looked clean. He began to say a silent goodbye to his old home, going back into every room to do so and to indulge a last, final look. He could not help himself. Tommy had a softer streak than anyone else in the family, even Lizzy.

This was where they had all grown up under the watchful eye and quick tongue of Chinese Lady, where in some miraculous way she had kept the worst effects of poverty at bay, and taught them that of all things in life family values were the most important.

In the bedroom he had shared with Sammy, Tommy looked out over the street. If the house was not the same in its emptiness, the street was as it always had been. Little kids not yet of school age were watching a man fitting a nosebag to the horse of a collecting van outside the printing works. There were always kids out there. The street was a place of homes, hard-working parents, and kids. In the summer it was a cul-de-sac playground.

Ghosts of the past intruded on his reflections. Chinese Lady coming down the street with her shopping bag and her upright walk. Chinese Lady at her sewing-machine, patching shorts or turning up the hem on a frock bought second-hand for Lizzy. Chinese Lady at

19

the kitchen fireside, darning socks. She darned socks the moment they showed holes, and she tubbed her family every Friday night, making sure they scrubbed themselves free of Walworth grime. Sammy. Sammy with a gleam in his eye, counting his savings, his farthings, his ha'pennies and his pennies, earned by running errands or doing any kind of job. Sammy getting his ears boxed for careless language. Lizzy in the old pinafore dress she wore for school, playing forbidden street cricket with the boys and clouting the ball in reckless disregard of fragile window panes. Ernie Jones yelling in frustration because he couldn't bowl her out. Ernie Jones, killed in France at the age of nineteen during the victorious advance of the Allies in 1918.

Lizzy. Lizzy steel-combing her hair with the ferociousness of a girl determined not to suffer headlice. Lizzy beginning to sound her aitches at fifteen because she was in love and because she wanted to be a lady. Boots strolling home from his secondary school in his casual, lordly fashion, and consequently having the street kids call out, ' 'Ere comes Lord Muck,' and Boots not turning a hair. Boots the gent of the family, with Chinese Lady getting after him sometimes in case he got above himself. Chinese Lady again, going off to the pawnbroker, her shopping bag containing some article or other on which she hoped 'Uncle' would lend her a bob, but walking as if she was on her way to Buckingham Palace.

And Emily, Emily from next door, a living, breathing terror when she was a schoolkid. Skinny, scruffy and never standing still, coming into the house with a rush, her eyes darting quick, flickering glances, and mostly at Boots. No one realised she was more of a terror to Boots than anyone else simply because she craved his attention. Emily at thirteen, stringy as a bean, pointed of nose, auburn hair tangled and unwashed, who would have thought she could have turned herself into a well-dressed young lady and become a godsend to the family?

Tommy wondered where all the years had gone. The family had been poor, yes, bleeding poor, but they'd still been good years, the house warm to come home to in winter, the kitchen range welcoming and the spicy aroma of a hot, fruity bread pudding mouth-watering. They'd gone, all those years, and not one single day could be pulled out of all of them to be lived again.

In the parlour, there were marks on the lino where the old upright piano had stood. It was now standing in the new home of Emily and Boots, because Emily had begged to have it, as well as the round mahogany table. The piano and table represented to her all that she had enjoyed most about Sundays, tea in the parlour and music after tea.

Tommy thought of cousin Vi then. Vi had enjoyed coming to Sunday tea as much as Chinese Lady had enjoyed always having a guest or two at the table. Vi was just about the nicest girl he knew, but he hadn't seen much of her since Christmas. The fact was that in running the market stall for Sammy, he didn't have much to offer a girl like Vi. Her mother, Aunt Victoria, was quite certain about that. She also thought stall-holders were common. For his part, he was glad to have the job, even if he did feel it was going to pull him into a rut. Still, it would be nice to see Vi again, just as a friend. Vi had no side herself. He ought to look her up, she was a pleasure to be with.

He took a last look at the kitchen. Endless chatter, that was what the kitchen had known. Perhaps it was glad to enjoy some silence. Sammy had pulled his weight last night by cleaning the range and emptying the ashcan. The grate, the hearth and the range itself couldn't be faulted.

The chimney sighed to a sudden draught of wind, and a little soot fell. Tommy cleaned it up and used the dustbin for the last time. In the yard the clothes line drooped in a neglected way. He was lingering uselessly, reluctant to make the final break. He walked through to the passage. He thought the house itself was sighing, as if it did not like being empty. Did bricks and mortar have feelings? He grimaced at his imaginings. Still, Susie and her family would soon be moving in, and he thought Chinese Lady wouldn't mind handing the old place over to them.

He opened the front door. He turned, looking back through the passage that had known endless comings and goings. He closed the door quietly as he left. The latchcord was still hanging from the letter-box. Well, the dustmen would want to get in tomorrow, to get to the dustbin. He went on his way, up towards Browning Street. At the corner he stopped to take a last look back, as Sammy had done. He knew he was in a right old state then, because as he looked back he thought he heard laughter, just like the clear bright laughter of his sister Lizzy as a young girl.

CHAPTER THREE

That evening, Aunt Victoria answered a knock on the door of her house in Foreign Street, near Coldharbour Lane, Camberwell. Tommy was on her doorstep, the collar of his overcoat turned up against the chill of March. He lifted his hat. Well, I'll say this much, thought Aunt Victoria, he's got polite ways. But he ought to be doing something better than running a stall.

'Evening, Aunt Victoria,' said Tommy, and smiled at her.

Aunt Victoria, a handsome woman in her early forties, said, 'Why, it's you, Tommy.'

'Right first time,' said Tommy. 'Is Vi in?'

'Vi?'

'Your daughter,' said Tommy amiably. 'You must remember her. She's this high, with two feet and all her teeth.'

'Oh, you and your jokes,' said Aunt Victoria. 'No, she's not in. Did you want her for something special?' The question was asked a little discouragingly.

'Just to know if she'd like to come to the pictures on a convenient evening,' said Tommy.

'I don't know about that,' said Aunt Victoria. 'She's out with her young man just now.'

'Is that a fact?' asked Tommy, and looked rueful. Something like that was bound to happen. Vi was getting very attractive.

Uncle Tom appeared in the gaslit passage. He was a kind man and mild of nature, electing mostly for peace and quiet instead of argument. ' 'Ello, Tommy,' he said. He liked Tommy. 'Glad to see yer, but don't stand on the doorstep, come in.' He glanced at Aunt Victoria. He knew Tommy's mother wouldn't keep a relative standing on the doorstep, especially on a cold evening. 'Come on, Tommy, yer can probably do with a hot cup of tea.'

'He hasn't come for a cup of tea, he's come to ask after Vi,' said Aunt Victoria. 'Still, if he feels like one —?'

'It's all right, I've got things to do,' said Tommy. 'Sammy and me moved into the flat above the shop this afternoon. I thought I'd take a rest from me labours of gettin' straight, and walk round and see Vi. Thanks all the same for yer offer, Uncle Tom. Well, give Vi my regards.' He walked to the gate. Uncle Tom called to him.

'How's yer mother, Tommy, when's she comin' 'ome?'

'Some time in May,' said Tommy, 'and she's doing fine. So long.'

'Vi'll be sorry she missed yer,' said Uncle Tom. 'Drop in any time yer like, Tommy, now that you're livin' much nearer, you're very welcome.'

'Thanks,' said Tommy, and went on his way.

Uncle Tom closed the door. Aunt Victoria attacked.

'I wish you wouldn't go against me,' she said. 'You know I don't want anyone encouraging him to come after our Vi.'

Uncle Tom decided to stand up to her.

'That's up to Vi,' he said, 'it's not up to you, it's not up to neither of us. It's Vi's business who she wants to go out with. And why not Tommy? I don't know a nicer young bloke meself.'

'He's common,' said Aunt Victoria. 'Vi don't have to

24

go out with anyone common, she's good enough to take her pick of respectable young men, she is.'

'Tommy ain't any more common than I am, or you are,' said Uncle Tom.

'You mind your tongue!' snapped Aunt Victoria furiously.

'All right, I'll mind me tongue, and I recommend you mind yer business,' said Uncle Tom, at which Aunt Victoria launched herself into a new offensive. 'I'm not listenin',' he said, and went and shut himself up in the parlour.

'That's it, have a sulk!' she shouted at the door. 'Go on, sit in there and freeze yourself to death!'

He was still there an hour later. Biting her lip, she went and rattled the door handle. He had locked himself in. At which point a key slipped into the front door lock. The door opened and Vi came in, warmly wrapped in a winter coat, with a close-fitting hat snug on her head. Her brisk walk from the tram stop had put a glow on her face.

'Mum?' she said.

'It's your silly father,' said Aunt Victoria, 'he's sittin' and sulkin' in the parlour, and gettin' 'imself—' She stopped, biting her lip angrily at dropping an aitch. She had long since taught herself to speak in what she called a respectable way. 'Yes, getting himself frozen stiff, I shouldn't wonder.'

'Course he isn't, Dad's not as silly as that.' Vi knocked on the locked door. 'Dad? It's me, Vi.'

Uncle Tom called, 'Comin', Vi.' He unlocked and opened the door. The room was warm. He had the fire going, something Aunt Victoria never allowed except on a Sunday. He had his *Evening News* in his left hand, his pipe in his right. He had even been smoking in there.

'Dad, what you up to?' asked Vi. She caught a wink from him. She smiled. 'You cheeky thing, you've lit the fire.'

'What d'you think you're doing, playing me up like this?' stormed Aunt Victoria.

'Just gettin' a bit of peace and quiet,' said Uncle Tom.

Vi smiled again. She took her hat off and pushed at her compressed hair. It fluffed into wavy softness. Uncle Tom felt a pride in her looks and her niceness. No one could say his warm-natured daughter hadn't grown up attractive, and it was good that she'd stopped hiding her light under a bushel.

'Mum,' she said, 'you two have got to stop gettin' at each other.'

'Oh, yer mum's all right, love,' said Uncle Tom, 'it's just that we don't always agree. By the way, Tommy called to see yer about an hour ago.'

'Tommy?' Vi quickened, then said casually, 'Well, it's nice to know he remembered where we live.' She unbuttoned her coat. 'What did he want?'

'Nothing special,' said Aunt Victoria, fiddling with her brooch.

'What's nothing special?' asked Vi.

'Well, he wanted to know if you'd like to go to the pictures with him some time,' said Aunt Victoria, sounding a bit ratty. 'I told him you were out with your young man.'

'Mum, you didn't have no right to say that,' said Vi quietly. 'He's not my young man, just a friend from the offices, and we only spent a bit of time at Lyons Corner House together.'

'Still, being in insurance makes him a nice, respectable young man with a safe job.'

'That still doesn't make him my young man,' said Vi.

'I'm sure he'd like to be,' said Aunt Victoria. 'Next time you go out with him, bring him home after, so I can meet him.'

'Just you?' said Vi. 'Not Dad as well?'

'Your father don't understand these things like I do.'

Vi looked at her dad. He gave her another wink.

'I don't know about bringing him home, Mum,' she said, 'he don't have very much conversation. Not like Boots and Sammy and Tommy. Dad, would you like a cup of tea if I put the kettle on?'

'You needn't ask me twice, Vi,' said Uncle Tom, and smiled because Vi, once so much under her mother's thumb, had found her feet.

Tommy received a brief letter from Vi on Friday.

'Dear Tommy, Dad said you called last night while I was out. We were all relieved to know you were still alive, not having seen anything of you lately. Mum said you asked about taking me to the pictures, which was very gracious of you. I'm giving it consideration. Yours truly, Vi.'

Jesus, thought Tommy, that's the kind of letter that's a bit hard to take.

Vi, on her way home from her Saturday morning's work in Holborn, got off the tram at East Street, off the Walworth Road. She entered the crowded market. The day was fiercely frosty but brilliantly white, and even the drabbest roofs of Walworth were sparkling and glittering, except around the smoking chimney pots. The smoke smudged the sky, but did not reduce the clarity of the light, which, combined with the cold crispness, had an exhilarating effect. The light and the cold touched the faces of people, and faces tingled, and the light sharpened the faded colours of women's shabby coats. The voices of stallholders declaiming their Saturday bargains cut briskly into the market hubbub.

Vi made her way along the pavement behind stalls until she reached the one run by Tommy. His display of china and glassware was mountainous. He was there. He was always there on Saturdays, from nine in the

morning until seven or eight in the evening. He had a
mug of hot Bovril on the back of the stall, together with
a half-eaten sandwich. His assistant, Mrs Walker, was
serving customers at the front of the stall. Tommy was
saying cheerio to one he had just served himself. Vi,
sneaking up behind him, said, 'Got any cracked cups,
mister? If yer have, why don't yer mend 'em?'

Tommy turned. Vi's smile changed into a challenging look. Her red winter coat and her black
astrakhan hat, picked up cheap in a Soho market one
lunchtime, gave her a picture postcard look. Help,
thought Tommy, she knows how to make herself look
good.

'Is that you, Vi?' he asked.

'Yes, you may well ask,' said Vi, courage fortifying
her.

'Ask what?'

'Is it me. I mean, I don't suppose I'm hardly recognisable to you these days.'

'Good to see you, Vi, and I'd know you anywhere.'

'I bet,' said Vi.

A woman, brushing Vi's elbow, leaned over the stall
and searched the display.

'Got any brown china teapots?' she asked. 'Ours got
broke. Me old man, as usual. Got 'ands like two left
feet. Still, you can't say nothink. Navvying with a pick
and shovel all day don't make a man dainty. Well, come
on, where's a brown teapot?'

'You're lookin' at one,' said Tommy.

'Call that brown? I call it anaemic. Me sister's
anaemic, 'ardly got no colour at all, and she eats her
fried liver nearly raw, would yer believe. Don't you
have brown?'

'That's brown, lady,' said Tommy, 'light brown.'

'Oyster, that's what that is. Oyster won't go with me
brown milk jug, me brown slop basin, and me brown

28

sugar bowl. Come on, you surely got a brown teapot in all this lot. You look as if you know what brown is, you don't look as if yer mum dropped you on yer 'ead when you was little.'

'Oyster brown's very fashionable,' said Tommy, with Vi looking quite fascinated.

'Listen to that,' said the woman to Vi. 'I don't know you can even get sense out of grown-up men these days. It must of been the war. I mean, did I say I wanted a fashionable teapot? We don't get any visits from the Duke of Connaught, yer know.'

'Tell you what you can get out of me,' said Tommy in his amiable way, 'and that's an oyster brown teapot, milk jug, slop basin and sugar bowl. All genuine imitation Stoke pottery.' That little touch he had got from Sammy. It made a silent laugh spring to Vi's hazel eyes. 'I can't make more sense than that, even in front of me female cousin, Lady Vi.'

The woman, casting a glance at Vi, said, 'Well, you're a nice improvement on 'is teapots, I must say. Can yer credit it, not a brown one in sight? There's nothink looks nicer on a table than a good, old-fashioned brown teapot.'

'I like that oyster colour myself,' said Vi, 'it's sort of delicate.'

Mrs Walker, attending to customers on the other side of the stall, looked up, a slightly anxious expression on her face. A homely widow in her early thirties, she needed her job with Tommy. She hoped he wasn't thinking of replacing her with that attractive young lady. Tommy, catching her anxiety, gave her a reassuring smile. The woman in search of a brown teapot was taking a new look at the light brown one.

'Well, I suppose you could say it's more delicate, like,' she said. 'Except I'd 'ave to keep me old man out of its way, and I'd 'ave to 'ave the jug, basin and bowl as well. 'Ow much, then?'

'Ninepence the teapot, sixpence the jug, fivepence the bowl and fourpence the basin,' said Tommy cheerfully. 'And I'll do yer a favour, let you have the four pieces for two bob. Me lady cousin's me witness.'

'All right,' said the woman, 'seeing you're doing me a deal, I'll 'ave 'em.'

When she had gone, Vi said, 'Tommy, you crook, two bob wasn't a favour.'

'Never mind, she's gone off happy,' said Tommy, 'and I did put the stuff in a dec'rative box for her. And she's still got a bargain. Nice you were a help, Vi. Anyway, what're you doing down this way? Meetin' your young man?'

'Don't you start, I've had all that from Mum,' said Vi. 'I don't know why people want to push me where I don't want to go. And didn't you ask if I'd like to go to the pictures with you?'

'I got your letter about considering it,' said Tommy, leaving things to Mrs Walker for the moment.

'Yes, well, I was considering if you wanted me to fill in for someone else,' said Vi, an unusually crisp bite to her voice. 'Seeing you've been socialising with other girls, I suppose I'm being graciously required as first reserve, or second, perhaps.'

'Eh?' said Tommy, flabbergasted.

'I mean, have all your other girls got flu?'

'Hold on,' said Tommy, 'that's not you talkin', is it, Vi?'

'Oh, I do talk sometimes,' said Vi. 'Well, I've got to get home now, I really only came to make sure you hadn't fallen down dead.'

'Ouch,' said Tommy.

'See you at Christmas, perhaps,' said Vi.

'Hold on,' said Tommy. He spoke across the stall to

Mrs Walker. 'Daisy, can you manage by yourself for ten minutes while I see me lady cousin to the tram stop?'

'Be pleased to,' said Mrs Walker, and Tommy began to walk with Vi through the market.

'You don't have to,' said Vi. 'I can see myself to the tram stop.'

'I don't know you can,' said Tommy. 'The way you've been goin' on at a certain innocent party you're more likely to go up in fire and smoke before you reach Walworth Road. Your mum and dad wouldn't like that, and nor would I.'

'You probably wouldn't even notice,' said Vi.

'My eye,' said Tommy, 'I didn't know you could get ratty.'

'Well, I didn't know you were goin' to act as if you'd passed away,' said Vi. 'I thought we were gettin' to be really nice friends together, I didn't know I was only goin' to be asked out when it suited you.'

'Look, I know I haven't seen much of you since Christmas, but what with Em'ly and Boots movin', then Sammy and me, and our mum away convalescing, things ain't been exactly like I'd like, and you get a bit low just running a stall.'

'Oh, that's silly,' said Vi. 'I mean, all the people you must meet, specially people like that woman who wanted a brown teapot.'

'Well, yes, you get characters,' said Tommy, 'but a feller's got to think about lookin' ahead.'

'He don't have to think silly,' said Vi, who thought the atmosphere of the market stimulating.

Tommy smiled. Vi was turning into a character herself.

'Anyway, have you been goin' out with someone else?' he asked, as they manoeuvred a way through shoppers.

Vi said, 'Well, I do happen to be acquainted with insurance men.'

31

'That's fair, I suppose,' said Tommy, 'seeing your office building must be full of them. Can't say I like the sound of them, though.' He stopped as they emerged from the market. 'You're me favourite cousin, Vi, and that's a fact.'

Vi made a little face.

'That's an old record,' she said. 'Are you goin' to take me to the pictures or not?'

'Tonight?' suggested Tommy.

'Golden Domes cinema, eight o'clock?' offered Vi.

'I'll be there, I'll leave the stall early,' said Tommy.

'Well, I'll be there too,' said Vi, and went home feeling she'd won a little battle.

Aunt Victoria expressed displeasure.

'Well, I don't know, I should've thought you could have found someone better than Tommy,' she said. 'I'm not saying anything against him—'

'Yes, you are,' said Vi.

'Well, workin' in a market won't do much for him, Vi.'

'What you work at don't mean as much as what you are,' said Uncle Tom.

'I wish you'd keep out of it,' said Aunt Victoria.

'Wish away,' said Uncle Tom.

'Dad's got rights too, you know,' said Vi.

'I don't like him speaking out of turn,' said Aunt Victoria.

'He don't speak out of turn,' said Vi, 'he works hard and he likes a bit of peace and quiet when he comes 'ome.' She dropped the aitch deliberately. She was like her cousins. They could all sound their aitches and moderate their cockney when they chose to. They had come to speak 'more proper' because of Aunt Maisie sternly persisting with them.

Chinese Lady, although a Kennington cockney herself, had always tried not to murder the English language, which was what she thought the broadest cockney did to it. She was proud of her country and its language, and she was proud too of the way her late husband had risen above his Old Kent Road beginnings to self-educate himself by comprehensive reading. He had always carried books in his kitbag, and during the Boer War had read any amount of Dickens.

Aunt Victoria, shocked by her daughter's attitude, said, 'And what d'you think I do all week? Not sitting around, I can tell you. Making beds, doing the washing and ironing, cleaning up, suffering headaches and goodness knows what else. It's all right for him—'

'Who's him?' asked Vi.

'Your father, of course.'

'Well, you ought to say that, not just "him",' said Vi. 'Saying "him" like that's demeanin'.'

'Now, Vi,' said Uncle Tom placatingly.

'Well, it is,' said Vi.

'What's come over her?' Aunt Victoria put the question accusingly to her husband.

'She's all right,' said Uncle Tom.

'No, she's not, you heard how she spoke to me. What's come over you, Vi?'

'Mum, do leave off,' said Vi.

'Well!' Aunt Victoria fumed. It was true she thought the world of her daughter, but only as long as Vi was placidly obedient. 'I'm not havin' that. Go to your room.'

'Mum, don't be silly,' said Vi, 'I'm twenty years old.'

'Well, you're not actin' like it,' said Aunt Victoria, 'you're actin' like you've spent too much time in Walworth with your Aunt Maisie's family. Going there all those Sundays last year hasn't done you any good, I can see that, it's made you pick up too many of their common ways.'

'That's talkin' daft,' said Uncle Tom, 'so stop it. I never heard such a carry-on just because Vi's goin' to the pictures with Tommy.'

'I don't want any lip from you,' said Aunt Victoria.

'Mum, I don't like you calling Aunt Maisie's family common,' said Vi. 'All the boys are lovely, and so's Emily, and so's Lizzy and Ned, and so's Aunt Maisie. And nor do they have carry-ons like we do in this house.'

'Well, I don't know, I just don't,' said Aunt Victoria, 'speakin' to your own mother like that. I won't stand for it, nor any of them ideas you've got in your silly head.'

'Vi, don't have a silly head,' said Uncle Tom. 'Vi, go and put your 'at and coat away.'

'Yes, all right,' said Vi, and gave him an encouraging look as she left the kitchen.

'Now,' said Uncle Tom, and thereupon got his face smacked by his angry wife. 'That's done it,' he said, and took hold of her. Only then did she realise just how strong her husband was. Uncle Tom was a man who dug up roads and pavements, and laid gas conduits. He had whipcord muscles. He made a puny thing of his furious, struggling wife. Aunt Victoria choked back every outraged yell as she found herself face down over his knees. She refused to shriek, she refused to let Vi hear a single sound from her as Uncle Tom delivered a single hard smack on her bottom. Then he let her go and she fell from his knees in a collapsing heap. 'Victoria, that was to show yer what I could've give yer, but what I can't give yer, because I don't 'old with bruisin' a woman, and if I can't bruise a woman, even more I can't bruise me wife. But just don't go on at Vi any more. You got a good daughter, a sweet girl who's never give either of us no trouble, and it's time you let 'er live 'er own life, it's time you stopped livin' it for 'er.'

Aunt Victoria sat up, face flushed with fury, eyes glittering.

'You disgustin' brute!' she cried.

Uncle Tom slipped from the chair and sat on the floor beside her.

'Come on, old girl,' he said, putting an arm around her, 'we've lasted twenty years and more, we can last another twenty without makin' a misery of ourselves, can't we? You've got yer funny ways, but I'm still fond of yer or I'd 'ave walked out long ago. When you're in yer 'andsome moods, there's nothing Vi and me wouldn't do for yer. If Vi's sweet on Tommy, which I reckon she is, that ain't so bad, yer know. Yer won't find too many as nice as he is, and they're not close blood relations. Yer know he's nice really, don't yer, love?'

Aunt Victoria put her face in his shoulder and cried.

When Tommy brought Vi home from the pictures that night, Aunt Victoria said, 'Stay for a cup of tea, Tommy, and I've made some nice sandwiches too.'

At which, Vi gave her mum a kiss.

Mr and Mrs Brown and their family moved into the house in Caulfield Place the following Monday. Mr Greenberg did the removal job for them, quoting a highly favourable all-in price of thirty bob on account of Susie being dear to Sammy's heart. So he said to Sammy. Sammy, alarmed, repudiated what he termed a slanderous accusation, and did so with some choice verbiage. It put a twinkle into Mr Greenberg's knowing eyes.

Susie asked if she could have Monday afternoon off. Boots said of course. Sammy said she wouldn't get paid. Susie said she didn't expect to be, not for time off. All right, then, said Sammy.

At the end of the afternoon, with the job finished and the gas lamp alight in the passage, Susie sat on the top of the stairs in the family's new home. Her mum and dad were in the kitchen, her mum preparing a large pot of tea. With them were William, Sally and Freddy. William was fourteen, Sally nine, and Freddy seven.

Susie sat dreaming. She'd been right. You could tell the Adams family had made this a happy house, a warm house. They'd left something of themselves behind. It was so easy to imagine Boots and Sammy and Tommy and Lizzy all growing up here, and growing up in a lovely boisterous family fashion. If you closed your eyes and really listened, you'd be able to hear the echoes of their voices. If you wanted to. Those kind of echoes were always left behind in a house that had been a warm and happy home to a family. It was nice knowing that family so well, and knowing too that the mother, Mrs Adams, was recovering from her illness in a convalescent home. She'd brought them up all by herself most of their lives, and could be proud of what she'd made of them.

They'd left the house looking ever so clean, and all the paintwork and wallpaper was just like new. Mum had said you could have eaten a meal off the kitchen floor. Imagine that in Walworth.

The echoes were there, floating up from the passage like faint whispers of laughter, she was sure. They made her feel dreamily happy.

'Susie?' Mrs Brown, plump and equable, came out of the kitchen and called. 'Susie?'

'I'm up here, Mum.'

Mrs Brown appeared at the foot of the stairs and looked up at her eldest child, the apple of her dad's eye.

'What you doing, Susie, sittin' up there on the stairs?'

'Oh, just thinking. Ain't it grand, Mum, movin' out of Peabody's into a house all to ourselves?'

'Your dad's that pleased with himself he's said I can have a new hat an' coat. But the tea's ready, love, and you don't want to stay sittin' up there. You'll get cold.'

'No, it's not cold here, Mum, nor anywhere. It's a warm house, don't yer think so? It's the way Mister Sammy and his fam'ly made it and left it. We're goin' to be ever so happy here, and it's goin' to be so nice for you and Dad, havin' lots more room and everything.'

'Well, the kitchen's really nice just now, Susie, your dad's lit the stove fire, so come on down and have your tea.'

'Yes, Mum.'

CHAPTER FOUR

Rosie, the foster-daughter of Boots and Emily, was six. For her birthday party, they had bought her a new frock. Boots and Emily were the sunshine of her life. Her natural mother, having conceived her out of wedlock, resented her, disliked her, and had done her best to reduce the child to a negative being before finally deserting her. With the approval of Rosie's grandparents, Boots and Emily had agreed to foster her.

She had a rapturous birthday party on 5 May 1921. All the family were there, except Chinese Lady, whom she called Nana and who did not forget to send her a birthday card and a postal order from the Frimley sanatorium. Rosie had been to see her lots of times, in company with Boots and Emily, and the awe in which she held Chinese Lady was turning to shy affection. She adored all the family, Uncle Sammy, Uncle Tommy, Uncle Ned and Aunt Lizzy included. And she was also very attached to Annabelle, the bonny-looking daughter of Lizzy and Ned.

Boots thought Rosie the sweetest and most affectionate child ever. Lizzy told him he was soppy about her.

'Is that good or bad?' he asked.

'What a question,' said Lizzy, a vital and colourful mother of two.

'I only asked because Ned's soppy about you,' said Boots.

'Well, I'm special,' said Lizzy.

'So's Rosie,' said Boots.

'And Em'ly?' said Lizzy.

'And Emily,' said Boots. Emily was expecting their first child.

'Pleased with yourself, are you?' said Lizzy.

'So-so,' said Boots.

'Mum'll be home soon,' said Lizzy.

'I'll buy a red carpet,' said Boots.

'You do that and she'll box your ears,' said Lizzy.

Mrs Maisie Adams, otherwise known as Chinese Lady to her family, left the sanatorium during the third week in May. In her forty-fifth year, she was a pleasant-looking woman who still owned a firm bosom and straight legs, and who carried herself in proud upright fashion. Illness had taken its toll during her time in hospital, but she had fought the weakness of a badly infected lung with the resolution of a woman who had always been enduring. She emerged from four months' convalescence entirely to the satisfaction of her physician, and to not a little satisfaction of her own. Emily and Boots, arriving at the sanatorium to take her home, saw that the shadows of illness were gone, and that her colour was healthy. She had spent as much time as possible out of doors.

When she reached Emily and Boots's new home in an avenue off Red Post Hill, near Denmark Hill, she expressed pleasure on discovering how bright and airy the house was, and how nice the garden looked. There were four bedrooms, and the one Boots and Emily had chosen for her overlooked the garden. And in addition to a large front room and adequate kitchen, there was actually a room specially for eating meals. It was a dining-room. Imagine that. With Lizzy and Ned having one too, the family was coming up in the world.

Still, she would never mind eating in the kitchen herself. Kitchens were cosier.

'Well, we always do eat in the kitchen, Mum,' said Emily, 'unless we got company for dinner.'

'My goodness, Em'ly Adams,' said Chinese Lady, 'you invite company in for midday dinner?'

'It's called lunch south of Camberwell Green,' said Boots, 'and the evening meal's called dinner.'

'Well, I never thought I'd hear you and Em'ly had taken to livin' upside-down,' said Chinese Lady. 'Still, everything's getting new-fangled since the war. I don't hardly know what's round the next corner these days. Still, you got a nice bright kitchen.'

The kitchen faced the garden, and was very airy, but Chinese Lady couldn't think how Emily managed without a scullery. Fancy having the mangle in the garden shed. But it wasn't for Chinese Lady to say so, specially as she'd wanted them to have the house. Boots said he'd been putting in some work on the lawn and flower beds. Chinese Lady asked if there were any roses. Everyone with a garden ought to have roses, she said. Boots said there were rose bushes and took her out through the back door to look at them. He'd pruned them in March, and he showed her the new shoots. He had acquired a gardening book, and also a second-hand mower, the latter having been sold to him by Mr Greenberg for seven and six. He had cut the lawn for the first time in April.

'Well, it's made the grass look nice,' said Chinese Lady, breathing the fresh air. 'I always hoped you'd come to be a proper grown man one day, with a proper consideration of your responsibilities.'

'I expect one day might arrive eventually,' said Boots.

'Is that one of your comic remarks?' asked Chinese Lady.

'Oh, he don't change his spots very often,' said Emily,

arriving in the garden with Rosie. 'He still makes porridge sound like mashed potatoes, if you know what I mean, Mum.'

'But he's not naughty, Nana,' said Rosie, 'we don't have to be too cross with him.'

'Well, it never did him much good, lovey,' said Chinese Lady, putting a light hand on the child's shoulder.

'I'll make a pot of tea,' said Emily, 'and you can come in and sit down as soon as it's ready to pour.'

'Em'ly, all that sittin' down I've done on the train home,' said Chinese Lady, 'I don't need more sittin' down now. Still, I must say you've got nice kitchen furniture.'

'Well, except for what we brought with us, like your pianner, parlour table and sewing-machine, we got everything else from Mr Greenberg,' said Emily.

'At knockdown prices,' said Boots, 'and probably allowing ten per cent for Sammy, who was in on the deal.'

'That boy, makin' money at the expense of his own fam'ly,' said Chinese Lady, 'he'll aggravate me into an early grave, I shouldn't wonder.' They all returned to the kitchen, where she sat down, her hat still on. 'Still, now Boots has shown he's got good points, I dare say Sammy will show he's got some too. Em'ly, you comin' along all right?' That was a reference to Emily's expectant condition.

'I'm fine, Mum,' said Emily, warming the teapot, 'and the doctor says so as well.'

'Nana,' said Rosie in sudden excitement, 'did you know the doctor's going to bring us a baby?'

'Yes, I know, lovey,' said Chinese Lady.

'A real one, Nana, a real one,' said Rosie.

'It had better be,' said Boots. 'If it's not, we'll send it back.'

'Yes, we don't want one that doesn't work, do we,

Daddy?' said Rosie. 'Will the doctor bring it himself?'

'You bet,' said Boots, 'he's responsible for delivery. I'll remind him we want a real one.'

'Mummy, when's the doctor bringing it?' asked Rosie.

'In a few months,' said Emily, milking cups.

'Can't we have it tomorrow?' asked Rosie, blue eyes earnest. 'Daddy, can't we?'

'That's a question only mummies can answer,' said Boots. 'Daddies can't do much about it, except walk about, bite their nails and fall ill.'

'Oh, crikey,' breathed Rosie in alarm, 'isn't that awful, Mummy?'

'It would be,' said Emily, pouring tea, 'if it wasn't a big laugh.'

In the evening, Sammy, Tommy, Lizzy and Ned arrived to pay their respects to Chinese Lady and to welcome her home. Lizzy sat with her eight-month-old son Bobby on her lap, while her daughter Annabelle played with Rosie up in Rosie's bedroom. The two little girls were already forging a faithful friendship.

Chinese Lady regarded her family with the satisfaction of a woman who knew herself home again, even if the home was a different one. Her affection for Ned, her son-in-law, stemmed from her pleasure in his qualities as a good husband and provider. Her fondness for Emily, her daughter-in-law, was constant. Emily had been a godsend to Boots, especially during the four years he had been a blinded war casualty. He still couldn't see properly out of his left eye, and it looked lazy sometimes.

They all seemed to be talking at once. Except Boots, of course. He sat with that sly smile of his showing from time to time, and making only occasional remarks.

'Yes, well,' she said, 'it's nice you're all here on my

first day back and my first day living with Em'ly and Boots. I kept thinking in the sanitorum about how you were all gettin' on, and what Sammy was up to, and if Ned was takin' proper care of hisself. I didn't like what you said in your last letter, Lizzy, that he'd been climbing ladders with that wooden leg of his.'

'It's not wooden, Mum, it's artificial metal,' said Lizzy. Sammy grinned, Ned smiled, Tommy coughed and Boots looked at the ceiling. 'Have I said something?' asked Lizzy haughtily. 'Pardon me, I'm sure.'

'Climbing ladders with a leg like that,' went on Chinese Lady, 'I thought the next thing I'd hear was that he'd fell off. I don't know it would do any husband any good to fall off a ladder, nor his wife, either. Still, I won't say a husband shouldn't do decoratin'. Boots did our Walworth house up very fetching, which was a nice surprise to me, seeing how airy-fairy he's always been. Who'd of thought it, I asked myself, my only oldest son pastin' up new wallpaper and paintin' all the doors like he'd suddenly turned serious-minded. Is that one of them smiles of yours on your face, Boots?'

'Just a passing one,' said Boots.

'I'm only saying you get to thinking of worrying things when you're in hospital,' said Chinese Lady. 'I feel better now I'm out and can keep more of an eye on all of you. You're all still young yet.' Ned coughed. Chinese Lady gave him a look. 'First Tommy coughing, now you, Ned. Have you got a cold?'

'Just a tickle in my throat,' said Ned, a good-humoured man of twenty-six, who made light of his artificial leg, but was presently having a job to keep his face straight.

'Where was I?' asked Chinese Lady.

'Keepin' an eye on all of us,' said Sammy, who thought she was already in fine form.

'It'll be my death the day I don't keep a special eye on

43

you, my lad. I been hearing you're up to all kinds of tricks, includin' consorting with people in Shoreditch, which is full of foreigners and suchlike.'

'Well, Ma, if you must know—'

'There you go, calling me Ma as if I'd brought you up common,' said Chinese Lady. 'And you're fidgetin'. I noticed you'd picked up fidgetin' habits when you visited me at Christmas. That's what comes of spendin' all your time at business and going to foreign places like Shoreditch instead of takin' up with a nice ladylike girl who'd make you a good wife later on, when you're old enough.'

'Here, watch it, old lady,' said Sammy, 'I'm not goin' to be old enough for that kind of caper till I've made me fortune and can settle down to take care of it.'

'Count it, you mean,' said Tommy.

'Sammy Adams, don't you call marriage a kind of caper,' said Chinese Lady. 'Marriage is holy wedlock, as ordered by God, not a dance round a Maypole. And while you're makin' your fortune, just remember a good wife's worth a lot more than money.'

'Well, I won't mind a good wife as long as she spends her own money and not mine,' said Sammy. 'Not now, of course, Ma. Later on.'

Lizzy rolled her brown eyes. In her twenty-third year, she was a vivid brunette of picturesque looks who always seemed richly fulfilled.

'Em'ly, that Sammy,' she said, 'can you hardly believe he's real? I mean, when you're listening to him, don't it make you feel he's come from somewhere dubious?'

'Madame Twoswords?' suggested Emily.

'Chamber of Horrors?' said Lizzy.

'That's dubious,' said Ned.

'I tell most people I don't know him,' said Emily, 'then I don't get funny looks.'

44

'Don't mind me,' said Sammy, who didn't mind himself. He was immune to this kind of repartee, which had followed him about since the days when he had lent Chinese Lady money out of his savings at exorbitant interest rates.

'Tommy,' said Chinese Lady, 'are you and Sammy set up proper in that flat over the shop?'

'Fairly proper,' said Tommy, liking the way she was going on in her old style. He knew she wasn't going to say a word about her illness, nor allow anyone to suggest she wasn't as able as she'd always been.

'I think I'd best come round and have a look at the place,' she said. 'I hope I don't find the two of you livin' in a mess. I didn't bring none of you up to live in a mess.'

'It's no mess, Mum,' said Sammy, 'except Tommy could improve his cookin'.'

'I heard that,' said Tommy, who had been missing his mother's spotted dog and all other forms of roly-poly puddings. 'D'you mind me pointin' out you can't cook at all?'

'I got other talents,' said Sammy, 'which Ned has complimented me on, I'm honoured to say. Ned don't have aggravatin' turns of speech like me sister Lizzy.'

'Well,' said Ned, 'I did once say that if Sammy got marooned on a Pacific island, he'd be selling the natives their own coconuts by the end of his first week.'

'Can't no one do anything about Sammy?' asked Lizzy. 'Can't you, Boots? You're our oldest brother.'

'There's room for him in our garden shed,' said Boots. 'If we took the mangle out.'

'What's wrong with putting him through it?' asked Tommy.

'Oh, I like that, Tommy,' said Emily, green eyes joyful, 'he'd come out flat and we could hang him on the line.'

'Very comical,' said Sammy.

45

'Could we have some sensible talk?' asked Chinese Lady.

'Speak your piece, old girl,' said Boots, who thought there was something more on her mind than a need to deliver typical little homilies. She gave him one of her suspicious looks. He gave her one of his disarming smiles.

'Tommy,' she said, 'where's Vi?'

'She'll be here any moment,' said Tommy. 'She said she'd pop in to see you.'

'That girl's so thoughtful,' said Chinese Lady, 'and she's grown up as nice as Lizzy and Em'ly.'

At which point Vi arrived on cue. Boots let her in, helped her off with her raincoat, and brought her into the front room. The family greeted her exuberantly, and she traded kisses all round before swooping on Chinese Lady, seated in a fireside chair.

'Aunt Maisie, oh, it's really lovely to see you,' she said, and kissed her. 'Don't you look wonderful? Almost like you've been on holiday, you've got such a good colour. Mum's goin' to pop in tomorrow afternoon to have a nice chat with you, and Dad's goin' to call in on his way home from work. They won't hardly believe how well you look. Don't she look well, everyone?'

'Is that our Vi?' murmured Sammy. 'Our Vi on stage?'

'I've had a few surprises meself lately,' said Tommy.

'Nice you've come, Vi,' said Chinese Lady, 'let's look at you. Well, I never seen you more ladylike, I couldn't be more proud of you.' If Vi wasn't quite the beauty Lizzy was, she had a soft, fair attractiveness that Tommy found very appealing. 'Sit down, Vi.'

'Love to,' said Vi, who always enjoyed being among the family. Tommy made room for her on the sofa.

'I been havin' a talk with everyone,' said Chinese Lady, 'just to make sure the ones in trousers haven't been actin' up while I've been away.'

'Oh, I think they've all been good boys, Aunt Maisie,' said Vi.

'Did Vi say that?' asked Sammy. 'Was it her again?'

'Was it?' asked Ned.

'Her lips moved,' said Boots.

'Was it something funny that came out?' asked Tommy.

'I don't understand women,' said Sammy, 'they don't make sense to me. That's excludin' you, Ma. And Rosie and Annabelle. Those two angels ain't women yet, for which I'm gladly thankful. And gratified as well.'

Little Bobby woke up, yawned, gazed up at Lizzy, yawned again and fell asleep again.

'Little pet,' said Chinese Lady. 'Well, with the summer comin' on, I don't want anyone to think I won't be gettin' out and about, which I will be regular.' Boots looked at the ceiling. 'I happen to have a gentleman friend.'

'A whatter?' asked Tommy, sitting up.

Lizzy, delight in her eyes, said, 'I bet I know who.'

'I don't,' said Sammy, whose mind was nearly always on business. 'Who is the geezer, Ma?'

'Sammy Adams, kindly don't give me no costermonger talk,' said Chinese Lady, and went on to inform her family that Mr Finch, once her lodger, had been taking a kind interest in her well-being, and now she was home he felt she should enjoy regular country air. Accordingly, he was arranging to take her out in a hired motorcar once a week to the Surrey Hills, and would provide a picnic hamper.

'I don't know what's happening to me facilities,' said Sammy, 'but just recent I keep havin' days when I don't hear so good.'

'Faculties,' said Boots, a smile surfacing.

'No difference,' said Sammy. 'I mean, I didn't hear

casual talk about motorcars and picnics and Mr Finch, did I?'

'Mum, you talkin' about wedding bells?' asked Lizzy.

'Yes, are you, Mum?' asked Emily.

'I don't recall mentioning wedding bells,' said Chinese Lady, who had no intention at this point of telling her family that Mr Finch had proposed to her at Christmas. They would make the kind of comments she didn't want to hear, particularly as she hadn't yet made up her mind whether to say yes or no. 'Mr Finch has done me the compliment of being a gracious friend, and I thought I'd best let you all know. I don't want Boots comin' out with clever remarks no one understands except hisself.'

'Box Hill, that's the place,' said Boots.

'Box Hill?' said Emily. 'What d'you mean, Box Hill?'

'It's near Dorking,' said Boots. 'Beauty spot. Lovely views. Highly romantic. You go up single. You come down nearly married.'

Emily smothered a giggle. Ned coughed.

'I knew it,' said Chinese Lady. 'Ever since that oldest son of mine learned to talk he's been makin' clever remarks. I wouldn't know where this Box Hill was myself, so can anyone tell me what he means when he says you go up single and come down nearly married?'

'He means something it's best not to listen to,' said Emily.

'I've heard of Box Hill,' said Tommy, 'I don't know what happens when you get to the top of it.'

'It's high up,' said Ned.

'Is that why Boots said it was highly romantic?' asked Vi.

'Intoxicating,' said Ned. 'Rarefied oxygen.'

'What's rarefied oxygen?' asked Lizzy.

'Heady,' said Ned, and Emily smothered another giggle.

'Now I know,' said Lizzy. 'That Uncle Boots of yours,' she said to her sleepy, dribbling infant, 'he'll finish up in purgat'ry, he will.'

'Go up single, come down nearly married?' said Sammy. 'Well, good luck to you, Ma old sport, but I beg to inform everyone I'm seriously uninclined to go up singular with any female woman meself. I can't afford to get intoxicated, not yet I can't.'

Chinese Lady regarded her family aloofly.

'If I'd known I was comin' home to a circus,' she said, 'I'd of stayed where I was. It makes me wonder if you've all been goin' regular to church. I don't want any of my fam'ly gettin' clever and disreligious by not goin' to church. You all need some religion. It learns humility, and Sammy and Boots specially could do with a lot more humility than they've got at present. Well, I think that's all. I just want everyone to know Mr Finch is goin' to keep me company at times. Perhaps we could have a pot of tea now, which I'll be pleasured to make.'

'I'll do it,' said Emily, always alive with nervous energy. 'You sit there, Mum, you don't need to—' She halted, then gave Chinese Lady an understanding smile. 'All right, you make it, Mum. By the way, Mr Finch has been here a few times. Boots and me have been invitin' him.'

'Just to help the cause along,' said Boots.

'What cause?' asked Chinese Lady.

'The cause of kind and gracious friendship,' said Boots.

'Anything else to say, my lad?' she asked.

'Not at the moment,' said Boots.

'I'm sure we're all grateful for that,' she said.

Lizzy laughed.

'Mum, it's lovely having you home again,' she said.

CHAPTER FIVE

Mr Edwin Finch, a man of vigorous, worldly maturity, whose affection for Chinese Lady was born of his admiration for the way she had brought her family up in the face of grinding poverty, called for her at ten on Sunday morning. He arrived in a hired motorcar, which Rosie thought awesome. The day being fine, Chinese Lady had elected to wear a brown costume and a brown hat. Boots suggested she took a coat with her, just in case.

'Just in case of what?' she asked.

'Well, a snowstorm, perhaps?'

'A snowstorm in May?' she said.

'Just in case,' said Boots, and she gave him a faint smile. She knew he and Emily were going to regard her as something of an invalid for the time being.

'You're fussin',' she said.

'I think I agree with Boots,' said Mr Finch. He and Boots had a rapport. 'A coat just in case.'

'Well, if you think so,' said Chinese Lady, and fetched a coat. 'By the way,' she said with a forthrightness that was for the benefit of her eldest son, 'I don't want to go up Box Hill.'

'Box Hill?' said Mr Finch. Emily hid a smile.

'It's too rarefied.'

'I wasn't thinking of Box Hill,' said Mr Finch, 'but a place that would offer us a pleasant walk and a pleasant picnic spot.'

'Sounds very attractive,' said Boots. 'Enjoy yourselves.'

When they had gone, Emily said, 'Did you notice how she fell in with his advice about takin' a coat? I wonder, d'you think it could lead to weddin' bells? D'you think they'd suit each other, seeing there's differences?'

'Different worlds, you mean?' asked Boots.

'Well, different class, really,' said Emily. 'We're all working class, and Mr Finch is 'ardly that, is he?'

'I don't believe in these labels, Em, and I don't think Mr Finch does, either,' said Boots. 'I'm against any labels being stuck on us because of what we work at, or what our fathers worked at, or where we live. It's behaviour that casts you as to what kind of a person you are, and I couldn't fault Chinese Lady's behaviour, could you? Further, not many of us stick labels on ourselves, they're stuck on for us, mostly by people with axes to grind, political axes usually, by fatheaded Conservatives, granny-minded Liberals, and class-conscious Socialists. Have nothing to do with it, lovey, it's something they use for their own purposes. Don't go around saying you're working class and proud of it, when we all know we'd rather be filthy rich. I know we've been poor, perishing poor, but it was never a virtue, it was a condition. Sammy saw that before he was ten, when he began to fight his way out of it. He knew that to improve things for yourself, you don't rely on a political party, you roll up your own sleeves. Witness his advancement. All his own work, Em. And it wasn't any political party that took us out of Walworth and put us into a house with a garden and a bathroom. It was you and me.'

'Help,' said Emily in astonishment, 'you just made a serious speech, you just give me a serious talk for the first time ever.'

'As a married woman, you've got a vote,' said Boots. 'Who did you give it to at the last election?'

'Not telling you. I didn't tell you then, I'm not telling you now. It's not your business. But you didn't vote at all. That's criminal backslidin'. Still, it's a change to hear you talk like this, all serious for once.'

'Don't you like me being serious?'

'Well, yes, in a way,' said Emily. 'But don't be like it all the time, will yer, because—' She stopped, and smiled.

'Because?' enquired Boots.

'It sounds as if it could be a bit boring,' said Emily. 'Me Dad always said keep politics in the back of your head and don't let 'em get out. He said people liked talkin' about other people best.'

'You had a good old dad,' said Boots.

'Liked his beer, he did,' said Emily, 'and he liked you. Ain't it a rotten shame he's not around to see we've got a house and garden and each other? And wouldn't he have been glad about Rosie, and me havin' our own baby?'

'Oh, I expect the angels are keeping him informed.'

'You get to sound more like Lord Muck all the time, d'you know that?' Emily gave him a little dig with her rolling-pin. 'Love me, do yer?'

'Love yer, Em. What's for Sunday dinner?'

'Men,' said Emily in disgust.

'I don't know I fancy a joint of roast men,' said Boots.

'Oh, very funny. Peel the potatoes for me.'

Rosie danced into the kitchen.

'Daddy, can you come and play in the garden?' she asked.

'Not yet, kitten. I'm on cookhouse fatigues. How about giving me a hand and helping me peel potatoes?'

'Oh, could we have lots of water for splashing?' asked Rosie.

'A bucketful,' said Boots.

'That's it, flood me kitchen,' said Emily. 'I don't know

52

what I'm goin' to do with you two sometimes, you're a daft pair together, both of you.'

'Oh, crikey,' whispered Rosie, one of the family, 'does Mummy mean you and me's potty, Daddy?' Boots said yes, and Rosie looked quite proud. 'I don't suppose everyone's potty,' she said.

'No, just you two in this fam'ly,' said Emily.

Chinese Lady went on her Sunday outings with Mr Finch, without saying much more about them than that she'd had a very nice time. On other days she went shopping with Emily or out by herself. She called frequently on Lizzy, who was close by. She took bus rides down to Camberwell Green to visit the family shop, now called the Bargain Bazaar, where she spoke her mind to Sammy about his improper practice of stocking ladies' female garments along with men's garments. She was quite sure, she said, that it was unlegal, and that he'd have a policeman come in one day and ask him uncomfortable questions. Didn't lady customers get embarrassed? Sammy said not to his knowledge, not as long as they could get Boots to serve them. Further, he said, it was a good way of doing business, because some ladies buying things for themselves alighted on unresistible bargains for their husbands.

She inspected the flat above the shop more than once, drawn compulsively to the habitation of her younger sons. It was adequate, she thought, but not her idea of a home. It had hardly any atmosphere. She did not, in any case, like this new-fangled notion of men having what were called bachelor flats. Men had no right to live shut off like that. It was against God's human designs. It was unnatural and selfish. There were hundreds of thousands of women robbed of marriage by the war. Men shouldn't set up as bachelors, specially not when so many of these women wanted affection,

53

marriage and a family. God hadn't put men on earth to live like hermits, but to be responsible husbands and fathers. Not on any account was she going to let Tommy and Sammy live in that flat for longer than was decent and right. She'd set it on fire first.

Still, she did cook them suppers on a few occasions. She also visited her old hunting ground, the East Street market, to see Tommy while he was working at the stall. Among other questions, she asked him one day if he was walking out formal with Vi.

'I can't talk to you personal here, Mum,' he said, 'not with Mrs Walker around.'

'She's not listening, she's servin' a customer. Not that I know why you get the customers you do, it's all Birmingham stuff, I'll be bound. And what's that mean, "Genuine Imitation Worcester China"? I never saw such a silly thing as genuine imitation.'

'It's a bright idea of Sammy's,' confided Tommy. 'It tells the truth, but makes people feel it's superior to ordinary imitation.'

'They want their brains testin', then,' said Chinese Lady. 'That Sammy, he's got more hoodwinkin' ideas than that man the police took to court for selling the Houses of Parliament to a Persian gentleman. I wouldn't put it past Sammy to try that sort of thing hisself, and next thing we'd hear would be he'd sold Tower Bridge to Lord Rockinfeller.'

'He's an American, Mum, not a lord.'

'Makes no difference, you know how smart Sammy is.' Chinese Lady let a flicker of pride show. 'Anyway, I asked you about Vi.'

'Vi's fine.'

'It's not my business, of course, but I shouldn't wonder if a nice girl like Vi don't get attention from young men she meets at her work.'

'I shouldn't wonder, either,' said Tommy.

'Well, you've got to think about your future.'

'I just run a stall,' said Tommy. 'That's my future.'

'What's that mean?'

'It means you got to offer a superior girl like Vi a bit more than I can.'

In high dudgeon, Chinese Lady said, 'I'll box your ears if you talk like that. I don't want to hear any of my fam'ly puttin' theirselves down. You're makin' an honest and steady livin', which is more than some men are. All this unemployment still about. Criminal, I call it. All them men who fought in the trenches should have jobs. Now, that flat you and Sammy's livin' in. It's all right, but it's not a proper home, it don't have a woman's touch, and I don't want you and Sammy thinking it's more than temp'ry. Well, you've got some customers lookin' things over now, so I won't stay longer. Just remember what I've said.'

'I'm not sure what you want me to remember,' said Tommy.

'I don't know why I've got three sons all more argufying than your Aunt Victoria,' said Chinese Lady, and went briskly on her way.

'Sammy, it won't be long before you're twenty.'

'Quite correct, Ma,' said Sammy. Chinese Lady had him cornered in his office.

'Time you found a nice girl to walk out with.'

'Not at my age,' said Sammy. 'It ain't decent, not at my age. I'm not matured. If I was I wouldn't keep saying yes when I ought to say no.'

'Yes what? And who to?'

Sammy decided to ignore that. 'I got business brains, I grant yer, Ma, and they're currently pointing me to a new shop in Kennington, not at any young female woman. I ain't ready for that yet.'

'I'm not askin' you to get married.' Chinese Lady,

sitting opposite her youngest son, gave him a firm look across his desk. 'I'm just saying it's time you thought about how to get on with girls. I shouldn't like to think you was afraid of them.'

'Well, I am,' said Sammy, 'they've got horrendous ways of weakening a bloke and turnin' him upside-down in a manner of speakin'. I ain't partial to ending up lookin' as if I don't know which way up I am, it's bad for me business reputation. I know yer got romantic ideas for all yer fam'ly, which is natural and also kindly thoughtful, but like I've said before, Ma, I think I'll wait till I'm forty and matured before I start takin' up with skirts.'

'What your dad would of thought of a son of his makin' remarks like that, I can't hardly think,' said Chinese Lady. 'He wasn't afraid of girls, he was very sociable when he wasn't soldiering, though I had to put a stop to that, of course, when we began walkin' out formal. I'm not havin' you shut yourself up in that flat doing your business books and gettin' seclusive. I didn't bring you up to be a hermit. You've got to learn to be sociable, otherwise you'll never know how to treat girls.'

'I ain't desperate to treat any of them,' said Sammy. 'I need all the money I've got to capitalise me ventures.'

'I don't mean that kind of treatin',' said Chinese Lady patiently, 'I mean how to treat them kind and gracious. Girls like young men to be kind and gracious. I was thinking, that's a very nice girl who's assistant to Boots in the shop.'

'Oh, gawd,' breathed Sammy.

'Pardon?' said Chinese Lady.

'I got some telephone calls to make.'

'Never mind them. That nice girl, her name's Susie Brown, isn't it?'

'Something like that,' said Sammy.

56

'Well, she's very cordial and pleasing, except she could learn to speak a bit more proper. I noticed her when I first saw her last year, workin' on the stall for you, and I thought then, now there's a nice-lookin' girl with nice mannerly ways. Sammy, is something hurtin' you?'

'Just me ears,' said Sammy. 'I been gettin' every kind of ear complaint for a year now.' Susie had been working a year for him.

'You better see the doctor,' said Chinese Lady, 'you don't want to go deaf at your age. Now I don't want to interfere in your life, I just want to see you and Tommy set up like Lizzy and Boots, with nice homes and fam'lies. You've got your good points, Sammy, you only need to remember what God give you life for.'

'Yes, to make me fortune and not to get married till I know how to take care of me fatal weaknesses,' said Sammy.

'Say in a few years,' said Chinese Lady, and gave him a pat as she left.

She spent a fair amount of time thinking about things, and eventually decided all her sons had grown up and become independent of her. They were all living their own lives and developing their own ideas. Tommy had certain ideas about Vi, and Chinese Lady could only hope he wouldn't be silly about his own self. Sammy had his business, and she didn't think he was going to be distracted from it, not until he realised it wasn't natural for a man not to have a wife. And Boots was absorbed in his life with Emily and Rosie, with a baby to look forward to.

As for Lizzy, her only daughter, well, her life was just what she'd always wanted it to be. She and Ned were always going to be right for each other, specially now they had two children, and specially now Lizzy knew how to manage Ned, just as Emily knew how to manage

Boots. That was always the best way in a marriage. Women being more sensible than men, they were the ones who knew how to hold a marriage together. All they needed first of all was to learn how to manage their husbands. Sometimes it depended on who had the stronger will, of course. Lizzy had a very strong will. Emily had a very sharp mind, which was as good as a strong will, and she didn't let Boots give her any trouble. Those two marriages would be all right.

Well, she thought, seeing my family don't really have too much need of me these days, which is a bit sad but can't be helped, and seeing I feel fine, I don't think I need to wait any longer to give Edwin an answer.

CHAPTER SIX

It was no real surprise to the family when Chinese Lady announced she was going to marry Mr Finch. They happily accepted the expected, although Emily was a little regretful that she was no longer going to have her supportive mother-in-law living with her and Boots. Lizzy, however, made no bones about the fact that she was delighted for her mum. She had felt years ago that she would like Mr Finch as a father.

The wedding took place in the church on Denmark Hill, on a Wednesday afternoon in July, when the shops and market were shut, and Boots, Tommy and Sammy were free. Ned took the day off, and Vi was allowed to leave her work at noon. Many of Chinese Lady's old friends and neighbours from Walworth attended. So did Emily's large, hearty and florid mother, who managed to fortify herself with a glass of rich, nourishing stout on her way to the church.

Also present were Susie Brown and Mrs Rachel Goodman. Susie, hearing about the wedding, asked Sammy if she could come to the church. Sammy said as she knew all the family, she could come to the house as well, Boots's house.

'Mister Sammy, oh, I didn't mean—'

'You're invited, Susie, and you can help hand round the sandwiches and suchlike.'

'Oh, if I can be a help, I'll be overwhelmed with pleasure,' said Susie.

'Very good, Miss Brown, consider yourself overwhelmed, and me family'll be pleasured themselves to have you.'

That same day, Mrs Rachel Goodman telephoned Sammy. She was a young woman of the Jewish faith, married to Benjamin Goodman, a rising course bookie. She knew all of Sammy's family extremely well, having enjoyed Sunday teas with them during the time when she had been Sammy's only girl friend. As a schoolgirl, she had given her heart to him, and he still had a large part of it.

'Sammy, I should believe your darling mother is to be married? Is this what I hear?'

'You've heard correct, Rachel.'

'Sammy love, how delicious. Ah, such a good mother to all of you. So?'

'So what?' asked Sammy.

'I have not had my invitation.'

'Well, it don't happen to be my weddin'.'

'My life, I should want to come to your wedding? Have a heart. But to see your mother married, that I could enjoy when she was so good to me, a shy little Jewish girl.'

'Shy?'

'Is it right, Sammy, that you should keep your only sweetheart from your mother's wedding?'

'There's something wrong with this line,' said Sammy, 'it's handin' me peculiar wordage.'

A little laugh escaped Rachel and travelled vibrantly to Sammy's ears.

'Sammy, you're so funny, and I'm only pulling your leg, I'm only phoning to ask you to give your mother my loving regards and my very best wishes.'

'Come and give 'em to her personally. Come and join

the fam'ly. Boots'll be pleased to give yer a grateful smacker for the loan yer made him on his house.'

'A smacker from Boots? Yer temptin' a girl, Sammy.' The cockney in Rachel surfaced. 'Yer invitin' me official?'

'Official nothing. You're a fam'ly friend and welcome.'

'I should be proud?' said Rachel. 'Well, I am. Shall you take me to lunch this week?'

'I'm a bit short of lunch dibs,' said Sammy. 'Besides which, I ain't disposed to make a habit of lunching with married wives, as yer well know.'

'A habit? Last time was February, five months ago.'

'That's it, like I've just said. It's gettin' a habit. People'll start talkin', and Benjamin'll send his runners round to smash me shop window.'

'Say Thursday, lovey. I'll be at your office at noon.'

'At noon on Thursday I'll be ill in bed,' said Sammy.

'No, you won't. Sammy, it's only for company and a talk. My life, don't be such a skinflint with your affections.'

'My affections for you, Rachel, are considerable. Ain't they always been?'

'I like to think so, lovey,' said Rachel.

Emily had asked Chinese Lady what she was going to wear. Not white, said Chinese Lady, a woman should only go once to the altar in white. Sammy spoke to Mr Greenberg about a new costume, and Mr Greenberg turned up with a swatch of sample materials. Lizzy and Emily helped Chinese Lady to select a dove grey. Mr Greenberg, delighted about the wedding, returned a few days later with the made-up costume at a fitting stage. Only one alteration was required, to the sleeves. When the versatile rag and bone man brought it back two days later, it fitted perfectly. It gave Chinese Lady elegance.

'Lord,' she said a little breathlessly, 'I daren't hardly ask how expensive it is, but you'd best speak up, Mr Greenberg.'

'Vell, Mrs Adams, I ain't saying fetching and carrying don't come a bit costly,' said Mr Greenberg, black hat held to his chest, 'there being vear and tear on my horse and cart. Vill a bob be acceptable?'

'A bob?' said Emily.

'I can't make sense of that,' said Chinese Lady.

'Speak up, Eli,' said Boots with a smile.

'Vell, seeing times is still hard, I'll take ninepence,' said Mr Greenberg.

'Mr Greenberg, ninepence for what?' asked Emily, seven months gone.

'For fetching and carrying,' said Mr Greenberg, 'all else being friendship, vhich is a precious thing to my people and ain't to be found in every country. From Russia my father and mother came, and vith nothing except a hope and a vish to live in peace. Vhy, I have seen my old mother in tears because here the police protect us, vhich vas an astonishing thing to her. Don't I have more gentile friends than Jewish? I vish to charge only for the fetching and carrying. All else is a privilege of friendship. Vhat more can I say?'

'Have a whisky,' said Boots.

'If you vill join me, my poy, that vill be a pleasure.'

'You must come to the wedding,' said Chinese Lady.

'Vhy, Mrs Adams—'

'Of course you must,' said Emily, 'and to the house afterwards.'

'An honour,' said Mr Greenberg, and blew his nose.

Uncle Tom gave the bride away. Aunt Victoria seemed genuinely pleased about that. She looked mellowly handsome on the day. Uncle Tom looked rugged and homely. He was losing half a day's pay, but it was worth that and a bit more to officiate, for he was very fond of his cousin Maisie.

In the church, Mr Greenberg followed the ceremony solemnly. Susie was entranced. Emily and Lizzy were moist-eyed because Chinese Lady not only looked lady-like in her new costume and matching hat, she also looked visibly pleased with herself. Mr Finch in dark grey stood square-shouldered beside her, with Boots as his best man. Chinese Lady made her responses quietly but firmly, believing in what they meant. Mr Finch's responses were just as firm. Rosie and Annabelle were in wide-eyed wonder as Uncle Tom gave the bride away, Rosie's hand clinging tightly to Emily's. Vi sat between Tommy and Sammy, thinking how moving all the family weddings had been.

Mr Finch gave Chinese Lady a gentle kiss at the end. It signified his understanding of their new relationship. Their marriage was to be one of companionship, which Chinese Lady considered entirely suitable for people their age. He was forty-seven, she nearly forty-five. She saw companionship as mutually satisfying, and liked the thought of it when they were both old. It was best for a woman to grow old with a man and not to be a burden on her children. She was not a woman who could live alone, with no one to talk to, and to have a husband again was something she reflected on with pleasure, particularly as she knew she and Mr Finch had affection for each other. Her late husband Daniel, a soldier, she had loved. She still had love and respect for his memory. He had been killed on the Northwest Frontier years before the Great War. She always said it had been very careless of him to get himself blown up like that.

The reception at the house of Emily and Boots was a crowded crush. So many people swarmed in, all jostling to pay their respects to the bride and groom. Old friends and neighbours were amazed at how posh everything looked compared with Walworth homes, and at there actually being a bathroom as well as a garden. And electric lights. My, that Boots and Emily, hadn't they come up in the world? Mrs Pullen asked Lizzy if electric lights were dangerous, and Lizzy said well, Emily and Boots hadn't been electrocuted yet.

Aunt Victoria paid handsome respects to the newly-weds. Vi paid affectionate respects. Susie paid shy respects. Rachel's tribute was warm and sincere, and it delighted her that Chinese Lady remembered her so well.

'Nice you've come to my weddin', Rachel. My, you've grown up lovely, but then you always was a lovely girl. That Sammy of mine, a pity he gave you up on account of always wantin' to make his fortune. Still, I suppose – well, you know, I'm sure.'

'Yes, I know,' smiled Rachel, well aware she could never have married outside her faith. She could not resist adding, 'And I suppose you know you've brought up the three loveliest young men south of the Thames?'

'Rachel,' said Mr Finch, who had known her before he left Walworth, 'I couldn't agree more.'

Chinese Lady allowed herself a faint smile of pride.

Susie and Vi helped Emily and Lizzy distribute food to guests in the house and garden, the afternoon being warm and sunny. Boots, Ned, Tommy and Sammy saw to the supplying of drinks. There was some first-class Spanish sherry contributed by Ned. Sammy carried a gramophone into the garden and put on a record, 'If You Were the Only Girl in the World'. The Walworth guests began to dance and sing. A loud voice sounded from the garden next door.

'Here, what's goin' on? Hampstead Heath on a Bank Holiday?'

'Come and join us, Mr Mitchell,' called Boots.

'Eh? Well, don't mind if I do.'

'Bring the missus,' called Boots.

Chinese Lady and Mr Finch, snatching a few moments to themselves at last, turned to each other.

'You're not tired, Maisie?' he said.

'My fam'ly fuss,' she said. 'I hope you're not goin' to.'

'Oh, I'll fuss,' he said, 'I'm looking forward to that. Do you know, by the way, how well you look, what a nice-looking woman you are?'

'You already want to borrow something when we've only been married five minutes?' she said.

He laughed.

They left shortly afterwards, to drive to Cromer in a hired motorcar, where Chinese Lady could expect to enjoy the ozone of the East Coast for a fortnight. The farewells were many and prolonged. Chinese Lady had a last word for Boots just before she entered the car.

'Boots, you mustn't think your dad would of minded.'

'I don't think that,' said Boots, 'I think our dad loved you. We all love you. Good on yer, young lady, enjoy yourself.'

'You've not grown up a bad boy,' said Chinese Lady.

Mr Greenberg lifted his hat to the departing motorcar and its trailing old boot.

'A fine lady, my poy,' he said warmly, 'and a fine gentleman, ain't it? Vhich reminds me of your own fine lady vife Em'ly. Such a mangle she has.'

'Inherited from the previous owners,' said Boots, watching the car disappear.

'Should any vife in her happy condition have such a big mangle in such a little shed? I vill bring a smaller vun, as good as new, vith rollers to squeeze tears from the finest silk sheets. Vould you say five bob for such a mangle and to take the other off your hands, Poots?'

'Done,' said Boots.

'Such a beautiful day, my young friend, ain't it?'

* * *

The hotel at Cromer was grandly Victorian, and accordingly spacious. The journey there had given Chinese Lady time to reflect on her wedding vows, and on a marriage of companionship. In her old-fashioned way she had felt that at their respective ages, passion would be undignified and also make her unfaithful to her long-dead Daniel. There were separate rooms for them at the hotel. Adjoining, but still separate. They would have separate rooms in their house on the outskirts of Dulwich. That was not being married, that was not being man and wife. What would people say if they knew? She and Edwin had taken vows as man and wife. To have separate rooms, not to be properly man and wife, couldn't be right in the eyes of God.

She braced herself and spoke to her husband after they had finished dinner in the grandest dining-room she had ever seen. She had drunk wine for the first time. It gave her a heady courage. So she spoke to Edwin.

She woke up early the next morning, and actually blushed at what had happened. Edwin was beside her, still sleeping. She did not disturb him. She lay in quiet thought. It all came down to one thing, really.

She and Edwin were man and wife, as ordered by God.

After Cromer, they set up home together, their surroundings a great improvement on the crowded and sooty neighbourhood of Walworth. Mr Finch kept a watchful eye on her, accompanying her once a month to Brompton Hospital for a check-up. His work with a Government department allowed him generous flexibility, and it was a pleasure to Chinese Lady to realise she was now more important to him than the department. She did the cooking, the housework and the Monday washing, all with the pleasure of a woman who prided herself on knowing what was the role of a wife and what was the role of a husband. There was also the pleasure of finding herself perfectly able.

If she missed close contact with her family, she did not say so. She knew where they all were and visited them regularly. And they all came to see her from time to time. That Sammy, though, he was no sooner in the house than saying he had pressing business to see to.

It was a little after half-past three on a September afternoon that Emily gave birth to a son in King's College Hospital. A nurse took the waiting father to see the baby at a few minutes after four. The mother was being given time to relax, to have her perspiring face and neck washed, to have her hair tidied and to be lightly made up. Emily insisted. She felt wonderful at being relieved of a dragging, painful and obstinate weight, and was dying to see Boots, but not before another nurse had helped her to look presentable. She knew she always had to make the most of her good features, her hair, eyes and mouth. It was her peaky nose, her thin cheeks and her pointed chin that were unkind to her.

The first nurse regarded Boots with a smile.

'Well, say something,' she said.

Boots, not an unsophisticated man, gazed in curiosity at the crinkly face and screwed-up eyes of the infant child.

'That's a baby?' he said.

'It's not a turnip,' said the nurse.

The baby's mouth wriggled and bubbled.

'It's talking,' said Boots, 'it's a miracle.'

'A seven-and-a-half-pound one, Mr Adams.'

'Bless you, Nurse Nightingale.'

'I'm Nurse Caldwell.'

'You'll always be Florence Nightingale to me. Where's my wife, the miracle performer?'

'Just a moment, I'll get my lamp and see if she's ready to receive you.'

Emily was quite ready. Boots came in. She had pillows piled under her head. Her face was a little pale under her light make-up, the shadows of strain beneath her eyes faintly visible, her auburn hair brushed and her nose powdered. He leaned and kissed her. She smelt of face powder and disinfectant. She put her arms around his neck. It was a moment of wonder for the two of them, the wonder of two having become three. Boots reflected on precisely what a woman experienced in conceiving, carrying and giving birth. Apart from the moment of conception, which she would not even be aware of, he could only associate the life-forming process with a long period of discomfort, and the birth itself with inescapable pain. And in giving birth, a woman divided herself to become two separate living bodies. It had to be considered some kind of a miracle. No man could ever know precisely what it all meant, what it entailed, and what it all did to a woman.

'Pleased with me?' murmured Emily.

'You're a living wonder, Em. And I've just seen the other one.'

'It's a boy, would you believe.' Emily relaxed on the heaped pillows, her eyes looking large and dewy. She felt dreamily loving towards him. If there had been moments, a few moments, when she had wished him to be as vigorously active as Sammy and not so airy-fairy, such moments had not lingered. It was his airy-fairy nature that made him so likeable. Strangely, although she was closest to him as his wife, Emily had never noticed the little gleam of steel in her husband. Mr Finch was aware of it, so was Sammy, and so was a certain Mr Ben Ford, who had once clashed with Boots to his cost. 'It was no trouble, Boots, not really. It tried to play up, but I wasn't havin' that. We've got a son, darling. You and me.'

'All your own work, lovey, and I mean the work.'

68

'And you're really pleased with me?'

'You're my one and only,' said Boots.

Nurse Caldwell brought the infant in and placed it in Emily's arms. Emily held it with all the sensitive tenderness of a mother in wonder at her first-born. It opened its eyes. It opened its mouth.

It yelled.

'There, it knows us already,' said Emily.

'Does it?' said Boots. 'What's all the noise about, then? Has it decided it doesn't like us?'

'That's not noise,' said Emily, softly cuddling the bawling mite, 'that's it talking to us.'

'That's not the kind of talking I heard when I first saw it,' said Boots. 'What's your opinion, Nurse Nightingale?'

'New babies are loudly talkative,' said Nurse Caldwell.

'Well, my wife and I wouldn't want an old one, of course, but I hope our new one won't be as loud as this when he arrives home.'

Nurse Caldwell laughed. Emily smiled. Infant babies always yelled when they found their world was no longer dark, warm and cosy, she knew that.

The baby stopped yelling. It nuzzled.

'Oh, lor',' said Emily with a distinct blush, 'it can't, not already.'

'I'll go and look for Rosie,' said Boots tactfully. 'Lizzy said she'd bring her here from school.'

Rosie, after her first look at it, thought the baby wonderful, although not quite the colour she had imagined.

'Mummy, fancy the doctor bringing us a red one,' she said.

'Better than a striped one,' said Boots.

'Oh, yes,' said Rosie, 'and it is real, isn't it?'

Emily asked for her son to be called Timothy, her father's second name.

CHAPTER SEVEN

Vi put the cover on her typewriter at the end of her day's work. Miss Anderson, in charge of the typists, liked every girl to leave her machine neatly covered and her desk clear. She also liked the girls themselves to look tidy and fully covered, preferably in dark grey dresses with white cuffs and collars, a distinctly pre-war office fashion that did not find much favour with the post-war girls, especially as their supervisor expected such attire to be ankle-length. Miss Anderson looked askance at typists who arrived for work showing their calves.

Vi had defied conventions today by wearing a light summer dress of azure blue. Miss Anderson, quivering with shock, suggested its look and its length were not at all appropriate. Vi respectfully suggested it was the only thing she could think of for a hot tenth of September. At which point a departmental manager came in to speak to Miss Anderson. Noticing Vi, he said, 'Charming.' Miss Anderson was defeated.

Ready now to go home, Vi was not in her brightest mood. She could think of nothing more dull and boring than to be a typist all her life. Emily had been a typist. She wasn't now. She had her own home, she had Boots and Rosie, and now a baby boy. And Lizzy was just as well off. Typing, ugh.

She could hardly believe her eyes when, emerging from the building with other girls, the first person she saw was Tommy. She didn't know anyone she liked being with more than Tommy. She had been out with three other young men who had shown interest in her, all of them in the insurance company. One had been impossible, gawky, inarticulate, and no fun at all. As for the other two, one had actually been disgusting enough to put his hand up her clothes in the cinema, he had actually tried to push it between her legs. The other had been quite nice, quite good-looking, but was so serious it was painful. Vi could not help always comparing young men with Aunt Maisie's sons. Boots and Tommy and Sammy, oh, they were such fun, and Vi had an instinctive feeling that one couldn't make a go of marriage unless a sense of humour was always lurking about. She did go out fairly regularly with Tommy, but he was really never definite in his attitude, and he had no idea how much she wanted him to be. Tommy was not only fun, he didn't grope and he didn't have hot hands. Aunt Maisie hadn't brought any of her boys up to have hot hands, she was sure.

Her eyes brightened. Tommy was just the tonic she needed, never mind why he happened to be here. He didn't half look handsome. She detached herself quickly from the other girls in case any of them got competitive ideas. Prospects for any girls of twenty-one and over were hardly wonderful. A million men whose average age would have been about twenty-eight now had gone. In a park on a Sunday, in the streets of the West End any evening, or at Hampstead Heath on a Bank Holiday, one saw young women by the dozens and so few men of the right age. Boys, yes, but not men. And the young women were lonely. Vi, who had found her feet, but still did not have too much self-confidence, prayed that she would not be lonely when she was twenty-four or twenty-five.

Tommy came towards her. It was Wednesday, the

East Street market closed for the afternoon, and he had had plenty of time to call on Aunt Victoria and get to Holborn by five o'clock. He picked Vi out very easily. She looked so colourful in her light blue dress and little dark blue hat. And Chinese Lady would have approved her very ladylike white gloves. Just as well he'd put his best suit on. Just as well he had a best suit. Not every feller did.

'I think you're my cousin Vi,' he said, and Vi liked it that he could greet a girl without being loud and brash. Boots had always been like that, and Tommy and Sammy both knew how to take him off. 'I don't mind a bit that you've kept me waitin'.'

'Well, I like that,' protested Vi, 'I didn't know you'd be here, and, anyway, I've come out at my usual time. Tommy, what're you doing here?'

'Lookin' at you,' said Tommy, 'and you look like Sunday on Wednesday. I'll tell you something, but keep it under your pretty titfer.' They stood on the edge of the pavement, away from the swirling rush of office workers hurrying for tube stations or railway stations or trams, or for the growing option of open-top omnibuses run by the London General Omnibus Company, now making a name for itself. Most workers always hurried in an attempt to avoid what usually proved unavoidable, scrambles and crushes at pick-up points.

'Nice you think my hat's pretty,' said Vi, 'and all right, tell me something that you want me to keep under it.'

'I've formed a guard unit,' said Tommy solemnly.

'A whatter?' asked Vi. 'A guards' unit?'

'Guard,' said Tommy. 'Guard singular.'

'Guard singular?' Vi laughed. 'Yer showing off.'

'I get it from Boots, he's been showing off his vernacular since he first opened his mouth. Well, I'm the unit, just me. For special duties. Like the constabulary specials.'

'I didn't know you could say that,' said Vi. 'I couldn't. What duties you talkin' about?'

'Protective.'

'Protectin' what?' asked Vi, happy to linger and talk.

'You,' said Tommy.

'Me? Me?' Vi looked as if the boredom of her day had come to a sudden end. 'What from?'

'Insurance men,' said Tommy.

'You said that before, that day I came to your stall.'

'It's serious now,' said Tommy. 'I said to your mum this afternoon, I said Vi's gettin' too pretty for her own good. I'll go and protect her from all those insurance men she works with, I said, or one of them might sell her a policy that'll bind her hand and foot. I don't want her gettin' tied up like that, I said.'

'Yes, I can hear you talkin' to my mum like that, I don't think,' said Vi.

'I said to her, I'll go and carry her off.'

'I don't know I can hardly wait,' said Vi. 'Where to?'

'Well,' said Tommy, 'I thought a Lyons teashop first, for tea and toasted tea-cakes or suchlike, and then two-bob seats at a theatre, or a ride to Hyde Park, where there's a band playing this evening.'

'What?' said Vi in delight.

'Your lovin' mum said it was all right, she said she was near worn out takin' care of you all yer life up till now, and wasn't goin' to mind a bit if I took up a share of the burden.'

'She didn't say that, I bet she didn't,' declared Vi.

'Well, something like it,' said Tommy, 'so here I am, your protective guard unit.'

'Oh, you idiot.' Vi laughed. 'But go on, then, carry me off to a Lyons and then to Hyde Park. A band concert'll be lovely on an evening like this. Better than

73

a hot theatre. Did you really come all this way to treat me to a nice evening?'

'I like treatin' my favourite cousin.'

'There, I was just thinking you were fun, and then you come out with that boring old bit about me being your favourite cousin.'

'I meant favourite girl. Come on, let's walk to Lyons.' They began to walk, Vi's light dress fluttering a little. Holborn and High Holborn never seemed to be affected by the depression, its shops and offices always appeared to reflect prosperity. 'I've been thinking, Vi.'

'What about?' asked Vi. Tommy took her gloved hand. She gave it to him willingly. His clasp wasn't hot and sticky, it was cool and firm.

'About you,' said Tommy.

'Me?' A little nervous beat momentarily disturbed Vi's pulse rate. 'Tommy, did you really go and see Mum this afternoon?'

'I thought I'd better let her know I was comin' to meet you out of work, so she wouldn't worry if you didn't get home at your usual time. Highly charitable, she was, as Sammy would say. Gave me a cup of tea and a slice of cake.'

'Oh, I'm so glad,' said Vi in a soft little rush.

'Here we are,' said Tommy, and took her into Lyons. There were a number of young people at tables. Girls met their boy friends here after work. Tommy and Vi sat down. A plump waitress appeared. Tommy said hello. She gave him a tired smile.

'Wish I was you,' she said to Vi.

'Why?' asked Vi guardedly.

'I could be where you are, sittin' down. Me feet's killing me. Never believe it, you wouldn't, but I took this job to get me weight down, and all it's doing is wearing me legs out. What can I get you?'

'Toast and toasted tea-cakes, Vi?' suggested Tommy.

'Lovely,' said Vi.

'Don't want to wear you down to your knees,' said Tommy to the waitress, 'but could you make that for two, and a pot of tea for two?'

'Be glad to,' said the waitress, 'if you could lend me your feet when I finish at six.'

'Be a pleasure,' said Tommy, 'only I'm using them meself this evening.'

'It's not my lucky day,' said the waitress, and limped away.

'I was saying,' said Tommy.

'That you'd been thinking,' said Vi.

'You're a lovely girl, y'know.'

'How much d'you want to borrow?' asked Vi.

'It's not much of a job I've got, runnin' the stall.'

'Why'd you say that?'

'Well,' said Tommy.

'Yes?' said Vi, on edge now.

'I've been thinking,' said Tommy.

'I'll hit you,' said Vi.

'No, it's a fact, Vi, runnin' a stall's not much to offer.'

'Tommy Adams, why're you goin' round in daft circles?' asked Vi.

'Dunno,' said Tommy with a wry grin, 'I don't usually come all over serious nerves. It's being in love, I suppose. Gives me a headache as well.'

Vi took a deep breath.

'Who you in love with?' she asked.

'That ain't a serious enquiry, is it?' asked Tommy.

'Tommy?' Vi was suddenly misty-eyed.

'Best girl I know, you are,' said Tommy. 'I've been thinking that if you happen to have fairly affectionate feelings for me, and it don't worry you too much that I'm only runnin' a stall—'

The pot of tea and the rounds of toast arrived, and the waitress said, 'Bring you the tea-cakes in a minute, if I can last out. Or was you thinking of eating them first and the toast second?'

'You got it the right way round, love,' said Tommy.

'Makes a change,' said the waitress, and left them alone again. Vi, a little flushed, jerkily tugged her gloves off.

'I was saying something,' said Tommy.

'Tea?' said Vi.

'No, not about tea.'

'I mean, shall I pour?' asked Vi, hiding her flutters.

'Yes, you pour, Vi. You all right? I mean, have you been following me?'

'Yes, and I'm very happy, thank you.'

'That's encouragin'. Well, then—'

'Could you wait till we get to Hyde Park and the band's playing?'

'Come again?' said Tommy.

'I'll like it better in the park, with music and everything.'

'It?'

'It won't sound right while you're eatin' toast,' said Vi.

Tommy laughed. People looked.

'You'd like music with it?' he asked.

'Yes, if it means you're goin' to propose to me.'

'Well, I'd like to,' said Tommy.

'In the park,' said Vi, and Tommy enjoyed his toast hugely then, and the tea-cake that followed. Vi, trying to cope with emotion, wasn't sure what she was eating.

The evening air in Hyde Park was balmy, and any amount of people had come to listen to the military band. The outward signs of the economic depression never seemed to touch Hyde Park, any more than it did parts of the City and West End. Seated in deckchairs at threepence a time, Vi and Tommy listened to 'Soldiers of the Queen', a great favourite with Chinese Lady. The music was stirring to Tommy, romantic to Vi. He proposed midway through a Sousa march. Vi heard it. No one else did. She squeezed his hand tightly.

'Does that mean yes?' he asked.

'It's been yes for a whole year,' said Vi, and thought the rest of the programme was made up of the most exhilarating music she had ever heard. Tommy thought that if he'd been unemployed, it would have made him join the Army.

They had the top deck of a tram to themselves on the way home. Tommy said he thought two years would be about right.

'Two years?' said Vi. 'Two years engaged? Tommy Adams, I'm twenty-one, as you well know, and I'm not waitin' two years.'

'I was thinking I need time to give me a chance to add to me savings, so we could furnish a rented house. And me prospects might be better by then.'

'I'm not waitin' two years.' Vi was surprisingly firm in defence of her rights and her expectations. 'I've got a job, you know. We could get rooms to start with, and save together.'

'I don't fancy goin' into lodgings, not with you, Vi. Nor would my mother like it. She'd read me the riot act. It's got to be something better than lodgings. I'll get to work on it.'

'You'd better,' said Vi, sounding even firmer. She felt so heady she could have taken on the Prime Minister. 'You'd better, because I'm goin' to ask my vicar to read the banns.'

'When for?'

'Six weeks,' said Vi.

'A weddin' in six weeks?' said Tommy.

'There, you said that quite nice,' smiled Vi, the tram gliding smoothly over the lines on the straight run of

Walworth Road. 'I never heard anything more silly than two years.'

'I wasn't saying that six weeks—'

'The last Saturday in October would be just right,' said Vi. 'It might turn out one of them really nice autumn days. I think you're awf'lly sweet, not arguing about it.'

'I could argue, I could say where're we goin' to live, then?'

'We'll find somewhere. A nice little flat, not too expensive, say between Camberwell Green and Brockwell Park, so that we'd be able to save for something better.'

'I think I'll ask Sammy to mention it to Mr Greenberg. If anybody ever wants anything special, Eli's the feller. He's a walkin' notebook.'

But it was Aunt Victoria who came up with the answer. Not only did she accept the news of the engagement with handsome good grace, she also gave practical thought to the problem of suitable accommodation. She spoke to Uncle Tom about it. In times past she would not have bothered to consult him. Uncle Tom agreed with her suggestion, he being delighted about the engagement and very willing to help them all he could. When Tommy came round the following evening, Aunt Victoria talked to him and Vi. She agreed with Tommy, she said, that they mustn't start their married lives in common lodgings, that sort of thing soon turned dispiriting for young married couples. So she and Uncle Tom were willing to make a flat for them of their upstairs rooms. She and Uncle Tom would live downstairs, turning the back room into a bedroom. The three rooms upstairs would provide a bedroom and a little living-room, and the third could be turned into a kitchen. Vi and Tommy could live separate from her and Uncle Tom, and not be interfered with, but perhaps they could all have family dinner together on Sundays. Now, what did they think about it?

Vi looked at her father. Uncle Tom smiled and nodded.

'But it's up to the two of you,' he said. 'Mother and me ain't goin' to force yer.'

'Oh, it's so good of you and Mum,' said Vi, and looked at Tommy. Tommy was giving it thought. 'Tommy, what d'you think?'

'It's gen'rous of your mum and dad, and that's a fact,' said Tommy soberly, and Aunt Victoria thought then that he was going to turn the suggestion down, that she wasn't going to enjoy the pleasure of still having Vi under her roof.

'Emily and Boots lived with your mother, Tommy,' she said, 'and it seemed to work fine.'

'Well, Em'ly and Boots like a good old fam'ly atmosphere,' said Tommy, and smiled. 'So do I, and at Sunday dinner especially. You sure you don't mind splittin' your house in half?'

'We don't mind a bit, partic'larly for you and Vi,' said Uncle Tom.

'And you needn't pay any rent,' said Aunt Victoria, 'and that'll help you save more for your own proper place later on.'

'I think we should pay rent,' said Tommy.

'Yes, Mum, we ought to pay something,' said Vi. 'Oh, it really is good of you and Dad.'

'I see yer point about rent,' said Uncle Tom. 'Five bob a week suit yer, Tommy?'

'That's not very much for the whole of the upstairs,' said Tommy.

'Well, what d'you think, then?' asked Uncle Tom.

'Seven and six would be fairer,' said Tommy, wisely not wanting to be too beholden.

'All right,' said Uncle Tom, 'but we won't mind

knockin' it down to six bob if Vi stops workin'.'

Which meant if a baby came along, of course. Vi, not worldly, coloured a little as she drew the inference, then she laughed and hugged her father, and then her mother.

Aunt Victoria let the young couple have the parlour to themselves afterwards, where they talked and made plans, Vi in excited fits and starts, Tommy in his thoughtful and agreeable way. And for the first time they cuddled, kissed and caressed like lovers. Tommy discovered Vi had exciting legs and a warm, loving mouth, and Vi discovered Tommy was a healthy pleasure to her. All the same, she had to make some protest. It was only proper to.

'Tommy, you cheeky devil – well, I don't know!'

'What's up?' murmured Tommy.

'My dress.'

'Can't think how that happened,' said Tommy. 'Still, can't be helped, and it's all in a good cause.'

'What good cause?'

'Mine,' said Tommy.

Chinese Lady could hardly disguise her pleasure when Tommy called on a Wednesday afternoon to have a cup of tea with her and give her the news that he and Vi were going to be married.

'Well, I never, imagine that,' she said. 'You and our Vi, who'd of thought it?'

'You would,' said Tommy, 'you thought of it when I was one year old and Vi was still in nappies.'

'Don't you start soundin' like Boots,' said Chinese Lady, 'I get enough clever remarks from him. Still, you got sense, Tommy. Best for young men to marry lady-like girls with all them flighty ones about since the war. Our Vi'll be a nice wife. Always been a sweet girl, she has.'

'Tell you what,' said Tommy, letting his mother refill his cup, 'this fam'ly's gettin' the best collection of legs that ever knocked 'em in the Old Kent Road. Lizzy's always had corkers, Em'ly's grown two unbeatable ones, Vi's got sparklers, and I 'ad it on good authority from Sammy once that you got—'

'I'll box your ears!' said Chinese Lady.

'Help yerself, Mum. Still, you can't argue with what's fact. Makes you feel proud what this fam'ly could show the world when Vi joins up.'

'If I thought you was goin' to turn vulgar, Tommy Adams—' Chinese Lady stopped. Her mouth twitched. 'You better finish up that cake and tell me about the wedding and everything.'

She had her own news to impart, but kept it to herself for the time being. Edwin had been very thoughtful, very observant, and had come to know how much she missed being near her family. She had been fretting lately about how Emily was coping with her first baby. She'd have liked to keep a daily watch on the infant.

Mr Finch knew this. He suspected it was because it was Boots's first child. She had never shown favouritism, but he knew, as Lizzy knew, that she had special feelings for Boots, her own first child. He also knew that her sons and her daughter were an indivisible part of her life. So he had recently had a long conversation with Boots and Emily, both of whom had been entirely responsive. Accordingly, they were now looking for a large house, one that could accommodate all of them, but without getting in each other's way. Boots knew his mother would protest at the arrangement, but welcome it, and Emily could hardly wait. An only child, Emily craved a home full of family sounds.

A month after Vi and Tommy were married, the move

took place, to a very commodious house near North Dulwich railway station. Chinese Lady could not have been more contented. She had a husband, a son, a daughter-in-law and a grandson to keep an eye on. And she also had Rosie, for whom she had a special affection.

CHAPTER EIGHT

In 1923, when Susie was nineteen, Sammy opened a ladies' wear shop in Brixton and put her in charge as manageress, thus keeping a promise he had made to her. He was fully acquainted with her talents and her acquired self-confidence. He was sure she could do the job, with the help of an assistant. Susie quickly proved herself. Sammy kept the shop stocked with every kind of ladies' wear, including coats. Most items emanated from a Shoreditch sweatshop at prices the owner, Mr Reuben Morris, swore would bankrupt him. Talk like that bounced airily off Sammy, who didn't believe it, anyway.

After a successful first year, he added a lingerie department and engaged a second assistant for Susie. He called in once a week to see how things were going, to check takings and stock, and to pay the wages. He never failed to compliment Susie, conducting his dialogues with her with the ease of a man who had freed himself of distractions. Apart from his weekly visits, Susie and her mesmerising blue eyes were out of the way in Brixton, and he carried on unhindered in Camberwell.

He was making money. His three shops – he had a third in Kennington – were renowned for offering bargains. The Kennington and Camberwell shops dealt in clothing, household linen and household goods, mostly

WD surplus. The ladies' wear shop at Brixton offered up-to-date styles of very passable quality and excellent stitching at prices that were irresistible. His mark-up was low, but it ensured an increasing turnover and a reasonable profit. He was building steadily on that.

However, during the second year as manageress at Brixton, Susie began to feel the challenge was losing its flavour. She felt she was actually out of things, that everything exciting about the progress of Adams Enterprises was happening in Camberwell, not Brixton. She felt something was missing from her life.

There was another young girl in the house in Caulfield Place where Rosie had once lived. Nine-year-old Daisy was the daughter of Mr and Mrs Cook. She had black hair and eyes as bright as polished brown buttons. She was a little plump and the street kids called her Pudden.

On his way home from school one day, ten-year-old Freddy Brown, Susie's younger brother, saw Daisy in the middle of a group of street kids. Charlie Higgins, eleven, and the leader of the kids, had Daisy's woollen hat on. It had two pom-poms. He was holding Daisy off as she tried to snatch her hat back. The other kids were laughing. Freddy liked Daisy. She was a newcomer but a sport. She had spirit too, and was showing it now in her attempts to kick Charlie. Her teeth were gritted in determination.

There was no great harm in the general antics of street kids. Dads walloped erring offspring who went too far, or the local bobbies tweaked their ears and spoke magisterially to them about the terrors of Dartmoor. It was a fact that boys sometimes picked on easy targets, and they all liked to tease girls.

Freddy stepped off the pavement, pushed inside the group and whipped Daisy's hat off Charlie's head.

' 'Ere, whadyerdo that for?' asked Charlie, peeved.

'It don't suit yer, Charlie,' said Freddy, 'not unless yer wear a frock with it.'

'I'll bleedin' spiflicate yer,' said Charlie.

'What for? Was yer actually thinkin' of buyin' a frock, then?' asked Freddy, who was as tall as Charlie and a lot more cheerful.

'That's done it,' said Charlie amid the guffaws of other kids. He spat on his hands. 'I'm goin' to bash both yer mince pies to the back of yer bonce so's yer won't know if yer comin' or goin'.'

'Nasty, that sounds,' said Freddy. Charlie balled his right fist and began to wind his arm up. 'Charlie, yer showing off.'

'Watch yer conk,' said Charlie, 'it's in me way.'

'You Charlie!' Mrs Higgins called from an upper window. Her head was out of it. 'What you doing?'

'Nuffink, Ma,' said Charlie. 'Yet,' he muttered.

'What's that?'

'He's talkin' about buying a frock, Mrs Higgins,' called Freddy, and Daisy, standing beside him, hat back on her head, giggled.

' 'E's talkin' about what?' yelled Mrs Higgins.

'It's to go with a pom-pom hat,' called Freddy.

'Oh, yer bleedin' monkey,' hissed Charlie. The other kids were all huge grins.

'What's that?' shouted Mrs Higgins. 'I'll give 'im pom-pom 'ats. Charlie, you come indoors so I can find out what you're up to out there.'

'Me?' said Charlie. 'Me? I'm just standin' 'ere, Ma, that's all I'm doing, just standin' 'ere.'

'Well, all right. But don't let me see yer 'elping yerself to young Daisy's 'at, if that's what it's all about. You treat girls nice, you 'ear?'

'Yus, Ma,' growled Charlie.

'Just jokin', he was, Mrs Higgins,' said Freddy. 'Come on, Daisy, I'll treat yer to one of me mum's jam tarts.'

'Oh, ta and fanks,' said Daisy, and went with her champion.

'Then yer can 'elp me with me Meccano,' said Freddy generously.

'I'm good at Meccano,' said Daisy. She thought. 'I fink.'

She enjoyed two jam tarts under the motherly eye of Mrs Brown, then helped Freddy finish the building of a Meccano crane.

In January 1924, the poor people of London danced in the streets. So did some Russian exiles, to celebrate the death of Lenin, and in ignorance of the fact that the cold mercilessness of Lenin was to be replaced by the savage butchery practised by Stalin.

The poor people danced because a Labour Government, under the Premiership of Mr Ramsay MacDonald, had been elected for the very first time. There was great hope at last of a better deal for the poor. The Labour Party had made firm promises. Ex-suffragettes also celebrated, for among the promises was a better deal for women. Ellen Wilkinson, a member of Mr MacDonald's cabinet, was a fiery redhead and a champion of women's rights.

Everything pointed to an improvement in the lives of the oppressed. Emily said a Labour Government certainly couldn't be worse than a Liberal or Conservative one. Chinese Lady said she'd wait and see what Labour did for the war widows, the war disabled and the unemployed ex-servicemen before giving any opinions. She didn't trust any politicians, she said. If she favoured any of them at all, it was the Conservatives, simply because she secretly felt they were the most respectable. She did say she didn't think there were any good Parliaments anywhere. Mr Finch said he thought the British Parliament was an improvement on most others. Boots said Sammy had bought a new overcoat of herring-bone grey. Chinese Lady said she'd given up hoping the day would come when her only oldest son might start talking sense. What, she asked, was Sammy's new over-coat to do with a new Labour Government? Boots said not very much, but he just thought she'd like to know Sammy looked a prosperous businessman in it. Chinese Lady said she was gratified to hear it, but it still didn't make sense to her. Emily said Boots never took much interest in politics, and hadn't bothered to go and vote again, which was a backsliding act. Mr Finch said it was a privilege to have a vote, and that not to exercise it was an expression of democratic freedom. Emily insisted it was backsliding, and that if too many people backslided you could lose that freedom. Boots said he hadn't come across the word backslided before. Chinese Lady said nor had she, but it sounded all right to her and made sense, which was more than he did. Mr Finch said that not making sense could be very enter-taining. Chinese Lady at once said she hoped he wasn't going to go the same way as her comedian son.

The Labour Party, the voice of the people, probably had the shrewdness to realise that conversations expressing both hope and doubt were going on all over the country, for they committed themselves enthusias-tically to their manifold tasks. They had an excellent Chancellor of the Exchequer in Philip Snowden, but almost at once he came up against the same economic problems that had bedevilled previous Governments. But he persisted, and so did his Party.

Alas, the first Labour Government did not last long. It fell in November. The Conservatives returned to power, with Mr Stanley Baldwin as Prime Minister. Emily said it was a crying shame. Chinese Lady said it was more trying than crying, that people ought to know by now politicians all made promises they knew they couldn't keep or weren't going to keep. Rosie, now nine, said everything was awful confusing to girls her age. Mr Finch said it was just as confusing to men his age. Emily said she hoped the Labour Party would get another chance, she thought they were at least more honest than the Conservatives or Liberals. Chinese Lady said honesty was all right, but not much good if they were mental deficient. Emily said, oh Mum you can't really say that about the Labour people. Chinese Lady said she was saying it. Mr Finch said he thought it was ministerial inexperience due to the fact that the Labour Party had never governed the country before. Same thing, said Chinese Lady. Boots said Vi was giving up her job. What, asked Chinese Lady, was that to do with Labour's minist'ral inexperience? Wait a moment, she said, giving up her job? Our Vi? Boots said Tommy had called at the shop to give him the news. Mr Finch asked if that meant a happy event was expected. Boots said Tommy hadn't mentioned happy event, only that Vi was nicely in the family way. Chinese Lady, delighted, nevertheless said don't be common. Rosie asked what the family way was. Emily said the doctor was going to bring Uncle Tommy and Auntie Vi a baby later on.

Emily had a part-time job herself, with the Camberwell Green estate agents, from nine until one o'clock. Chinese Lady was not too sure she approved, but all the same she happily looked after three-year-old Timothy while Emily was at work. Emily said she had prospects with the firm. Chinese Lady spoke to Boots. She said she was afraid Emily was forgetting she was a wife and mother, and the time might have to come when he'd have to put his foot down, which was what a husband should do when his wife talked about prospects outside her home and family. Weren't they going to have any more children? Two wasn't much, especially as only Timmy was their own. Boots said he was hoping for others, and had been during the last year or so. Look at Lizzy and Ned, said Chinese Lady, they've got four now, Annabelle, Bobby, Emma and Edward. Yes, lovely, said Boots. I don't know what's coming over our Em'ly, said Chinese Lady. She likes having a job, said Boots. That's all very well, said Chinese Lady, but there's wives whose husbands don't have any job at all, and half the time she's not here being a mother to little Tim.

Boots thought about it and spoke to Emily, without mentioning his mother's opinions. Emily sprang to her own defence and would have quarrelled with him, except that Boots wouldn't let her. He simply told her to take it easy, and that if what she was doing was what she really wanted to do, to carry on doing it. Did she want to work for the firm some time, by the way? Emily said she thought she liked it better being on her own, like, it was more of a challenge.

Boots said it was a pity there had been no more children. Emily said well, they had Rosie and Tim, they couldn't grumble.

Vi gave birth to a baby girl in May 1925. She and Tommy called her Alice. Aunt Victoria lost her head and acted as if she was the only woman who had ever been a grandmother. She frequently called on Chinese Lady and regaled her with minute accounts of the baby's amazing activities. Chinese Lady did what she could to fill Aunt Victoria's mouth with home-made cake and to get in a few words of her own, every one of which sailed over the top of Aunt Victoria's head. Uncle Tom's feelings were expressed less verbally. His beaming smile told all.

Vi was entirely happy with Tommy and her infant daughter in the flat she and her husband had fashioned for themselves in her parents' house. Tommy, however, had his mind on a house of their own. Things, perhaps, were a little better than they'd been in 1921, unemployment a little less acute, and business in the market quite brisk. All markets did consistent business, for every market offered people the lowest prices they could get. Tommy thought a great deal of Vi. She had a very warm and affectionate nature, and if she had learned to stand up for herself, she did so with him in an unquarrelsome way. Tommy, who was like Boots in that he did not ask for the moon, nevertheless wanted something better for Vi than a flat in her parents' house. Lizzy and Ned had a house with a garden. Boots and Emily lived with Mr Finch and Chinese Lady in a house with a garden. Tommy thought he ought to work to provide Vi with no less. He told Sammy he was keeping his eye open for an engineering job with prospects. Sammy almost fell down.

'Not on your Nelly,' he said, recovering.

'Did you say that for a laugh?' asked Tommy.

'Did I hell,' said Sammy. 'Let me inform you, mate, I owe me advance to a limited company to me rigid inclination never to say anything for laughs.' Adams Enterprises had become a limited company late in 1924, Sammy the managing director and major shareholder, Boots the chairman. 'Kindly let it be known my reliance on you as manager of the market stall is one of fam'ly faith. All right, I'll give yer a rise. Five bob. From this week. How's that?'

'Bloody enormous,' said Tommy, 'and I'll still be keepin' my eyes open.'

'You'll upset me considerable with that kind of language and that kind of ingratitude,' said Sammy, 'and you a husband and father too. Yer know I was brought up respecting these things. I might be a husband and father meself one day. If I can find the time.'

'It'll cost yer,' said Tommy.

'Jesus,' said Sammy, 'you've already given me a nasty turn, don't give me a gorblimey headache as well.'

' 'Strewth,' said Tommy, 'I never heard anyone carry on like you do about the 'orrors of affordin' a wife. Yer missin' out, cock, and yer don't know it. It's me honest opinion you're running scared. You got Susie out of yer way by sendin' her to Brixton, didn't you?'

'Susie?' said Sammy. 'What Susie? Oh, Susie Brown. Good business move that was, Tommy, makin' her the manageress. She's a natural. I ain't askin' to be complimented on me business savvy, but I'd be obliged if you'd make yer conversation more cultural.'

'You're killing me,' said Tommy.

'It's a furnished room,' said Mrs Stubbs of Westmoreland Road. Her caller was obviously a widow, for she wore a black coat, a black hat and a black veil.

'Furnished?' It was a soft-spoken enquiry.

'I only let furnished. It's five shillings a week.'

'How kind. Thank you.'

'I don't know about kind,' said Mrs Stubbs. 'I couldn't ask less, and I'm not askin' more. D'you want to see it?'

'Thank you.' The veiled woman murmured to herself. 'Yes, may I see it?'

She speaks very nice, thought Mrs Stubbs, she must have come down in the world to be looking for lodgings.

'Come in. I'll show you the way.' Mrs Stubbs led the woman up the stairs to the back room. It was adequately furnished and looked clean and tidy. A companion set stood in the hearth, but there was no fire laid. The room was cold on this late autumnal day. 'I can order some coal for you, it's a nice cosy room when the fire's goin', and there's a gas ring in the corner.'

'How kind.' The woman's soft voice was not much more than a murmur. 'Yes, thank you, I'll take it.' She looked down at the suitcase she was carrying. She placed it on the floor with a sigh of relief.

'All right,' said Mrs Stubbs, who preferred gentleman lodgers on the whole. But she felt sympathetically disposed to a woman obviously recently widowed. 'Come down and I'll make a pot of tea. I expect you'd like a cup of tea, carrying that heavy suitcase and all. Then I'll make out a rent book. The rent's in advance, of course, y'know. Could I 'ave the pleasure of knowing your name?'

'Yes. Thank you.'

'Mrs—?'

'Pardon?'

'You're Mrs—?'

'Oh, yes, my name.' The woman smiled beneath her veil. 'Mrs Smith.'

'I'm Mrs Stubbs, and pleased to know you, Mrs Smith.'

'Such a problem, you know.'

'What?' asked Mrs Stubbs.

'A cup of tea will be so nice. Thank you.'

There was hardly anything to be got out of the woman over the tea. She offered no information about herself, and answered questions only in a vague way, but Mrs Stubbs thought her a nice, gentle person.

The woman went out the following day. She was dressed in a dark blue coat, a matching hat and a blue veil. She descended from the tram at Manor Place and stood in the road, looking about her. The tram went off, and the driver of a corporation water cart brought his pair of horses to a sudden stop. The pair reared and plunged He bawled at the woman.

'Don't stand there waitin' for Christmas, missus! Gedoudavit!'

The woman neither answered nor looked at him. She crossed the tramlines heedless of the traffic and was bawled at again, by the driver of a fruit wholesaler's van. She took no notice. She reached the pavement and proceeded down Browning Street in a leisurely and almost dreamy way. She passed Caulfield Place. She stopped, seeming unsure of where she was. She retraced her steps and entered Caulfield Place. She halted midway, her heavy veil masking her face and her expression of uncertainty. Mrs Higgins, cleaning her front bedroom, raised the window and put her head out.

'Who yer lookin' for, love?'

The woman, startled, turned about and walked back to Browning Street. She turned left. She walked to St John's Church. She went in. It was empty. She sat down in a pew.

Her lips moved, as if she was praying.

CHAPTER NINE

On a morning in November 1925, Miss Polly Simms, teacher at St Luke's Church School, which lay to the west of Ruskin Park in South-East London, stood at the entrance and peered through the fog. She picked out the vague shapes of children coming in through the gates. They could be better heard than seen, but even the clarity of their young voices was muted by the blanket of yellow.

' 'Ere comes old Beaver,' said the voice of a boy invisible.

Poor Mr Stokes. Due to retire soon, his beard had always provoked sly cheekiness behind his back. This time, however, the miscreant had been heard.

'Stay in after school, Potts,' said Mr Stokes, headmaster.

Polly heard Potts say in shocked innocence, 'What, me, sir?'

'Stay in after school. Report to me.'

'Me, sir?'

'Yes, you, sir.'

'Whaffor, sir?'

'Impertinence.'

'Crikey, I ain't done nothink.'

'Impertinence is not nothing, Potts. Impertinence is punishable by death.'

The dialogue sounded hollow in the fog hanging

thickly over the school playground. Mr Stokes emerged from the yellowness. He was coated and hatted, and wore a woollen muffler around his neck. He gave Polly a nod and a smile.

'Good morning, Miss Simms. This is going to last all day.'

'I hope not,' said Polly, twenty-nine and quite the most attractive teacher growing boys could ever get a crush on. The frontal points of her bobbed dark hair curved in the fashion of film star Colleen Moore. Mr Stokes entered the school. Polly looked at her watch. Seven minutes to nine. She heard other voices, girls' voices, then Potts again.

'Lummy, 'ere's our Lady Mucks. Didn't yer get lorst, then?'

'Ugh, it's spotty Potty,' said ten-year-old Rosie Adams.

'Blessed urchin,' said Annabelle Somers, almost nine.

'Gertcher,' said Potts, a shifting figure in the fog.

'Rosie? Rosie Adams?' called Polly, who had taken up teaching in a spirit of defiant challenge. Her father, a general, had helped her secure a position at St Luke's two years ago. St Luke's, because it taught children of working-class and lower middle-class parents, was another challenge, and it was also in the right spot. It kept her in touch with the father of one of the pupils. She was a first-class teacher and it exhilarated her to know it.

Rosie appeared, Annabelle beside her. Both girls were in warm winter coats. Rosie's honey-coloured hair, showing two pigtails tied with dark blue ribbons, was crowned with a straw boater. Annabelle wore a beige tam-o'-shanter over her chestnut hair. Rosie was extraordinarily pretty, her blue eyes already long-lashed. Annabelle was round of face, brown-eyed and bubbly. She and Rosie were fast friends and destined to be so all their lives.

'Good morning, Miss Simms,' said Rosie in her precise little way. 'Isn't the fog just awful? Annabelle and me – oh, lor', Annabelle, where's Bobby?'

Bobby was Annabelle's five-year-old brother, and this was his first term at St Luke's.

'You Bobby!' called Annabelle. 'Where are you?'

'Here,' called a young boy's voice. Then, 'Girls, don't they fuss, Olly?'

'That boy,' said Annabelle, 'I don't know what we're going to do with him sometimes.'

'Yes, we both had to hold his hands when we left the bus, Miss Simms,' said Rosie, earnestly informative. 'It simply crawled, the bus. Daddy came to the school gates with us—'

'Is he there?' asked Polly.

'Oh, no, he's gone on to his work, Miss Simms, and Mummy left earlier. I hope he doesn't get lost, he can only see out of one eye, you know. He said the pea soup was so thick you could eat it, if you had a knife and fork, and I said you need a spoon for soup. Daddy said no, you can slice it into chunks when it's as thick as this, and Annabelle said ugh. It's not quite as bad as this at home, thank goodness for our grandmother, who used to be consumptive, you know, but is much better now. Did you want specially to see me, Miss Simms?'

Polly smiled. Words always poured from Rosie.

'Only to ask if your father is coming to see me this afternoon, Rosie.'

'Oh, yes, Miss Simms, I asked him last night and he said he would, he said how could he refuse? He said he'd take time off from his work, and was there going to be a cup of tea for him in the teachers' room which wasn't stewed like one you gave him before. I told him it wasn't very nice to say something like that, and he said fathers had to face facts in the teachers' room. Nana – my grandmother – said to tell you to try and

96

excuse him, that he'd been a comedian all his life, and she'd never been able to do anything with him.'

'Nor have I,' said Polly.

'Not with my Uncle Boots?' asked Annabelle in innocence.

Polly wrinkled her nose. She thought a nickname like Boots for a man like Robert Adams a disastrous family accident.

'Oh, some fathers are more comical than others, Annabelle,' she said. 'So are some uncles, of course.' She laughed to cover emotions she showed to no one. She had an effervescent personality that struck a responsive chord in her pupils. She shed her vocationary role at week-ends, when she participated with the Bright Young Things in extrovert activities. There was still something of the madcap in Polly Simms, an ambulance driver during four years of war. But she had a warm, enduring affection for the men who had fought in the trenches, and she regarded Boots as very special.

'Daddy's really quite nice,' said Rosie, which was an understatement of her true feelings for her foster-father.

'Why, of course, Rosie,' said Polly. She checked the time again, and began to ring the bell. The girls and boys still in the foggy playground started to troop in. St Luke's was a good school, offering a sound primary education, including reading out loud in class in an attempt to make the young cockney pupils cure themselves of gabbling. The brightest pupil by far in Polly's estimation was Rosie Adams, and Mr Stokes considered her a natural scholar. Since the beginning of 1925, Rosie had achieved top marks in every end-of-term exam.

Other things had happened in 1925. Oxford sank in the Boat Race. Mr Winston Churchill, Chancellor of the Exchequer, took sixpence off income tax, much to the disgust of the Labour Party. But Mr Churchill said it would provide more spending money and stimulate the economy. Old-age pensions at sixty-five and widows' pensions were introduced. Madame Tussaud's waxworks exhibition took fire and burned down. Legislation to increase summertime was passed. It entailed putting clocks forward an hour in April, and putting them back in October. People who thought God had invented clocks said the Bill was sacrilegious. Hindenberg was elected President of Germany. That did not stop a political firebrand called Adolf Hitler being an irritation to him. Amundsen of Norway flew over the North Pole. Charlie Chaplin and Pearl White established a new ascendancy in the cinema. A peculiar type of aeroplane made a vertical take-off at Farnborough, Hampshire. This eccentric flying machine impressed nobody of importance. By way of a minor happening, Adams Enterprises Ltd acquired the scrap metal business of a certain Mr Ben Ford, and an East End sweatshop at the beginning of November.

In the kitchen of the Browns' house in Caulfield Place, Walworth, Susie Brown buttoned her dark red winter coat. A navy blue cloche hat hugged her shingled hair.

'I'm off now, Mum,' she said. 'I've got to meet Mister Sammy at his new fact'ry in Shoreditch, the one he's just bought.'

'What's he want you to go there for?' asked Mrs Brown, a plump and jolly woman. 'And who's managin' your Brixton shop?'

'I shan't know what he wants till I get there,' said Susie. 'I don't see him often enough or long enough to be told anything much. The assistants are lookin' after the shop.'

'Well, he must have your good at heart, love, seeing you're still manageress at Brixton and bringing home two pound a week. I hope the fog don't hold you up. Oh, and when you see Mister Sammy, tell him we're still very 'appy in his fam'ly's old house.'

'Yes, Mum,' said Susie, pulling on fine kid gloves. She was able to buy all her clothes and accessories at trade price.

'You look ever so chick, love,' said Mrs Brown. She meant chic.

'Yer mean posh,' said thirteen-year-old Sally, still eating her breakfast porridge. Her brother Freddy, eleven, had just departed for school, and her elder brother, eighteen-year-old William, was in the Army, having been accepted as a drummer boy when he was fifteen.

Susie had a well-dressed look. Mrs Brown thought her a picture. Her prettiness as a girl was now the loveliness of a young woman. Why at twenty-one she wasn't married, Mrs Brown couldn't think. She had had any amount of boy friends, all ever so keen on her. And last year a nice young man she had met in Brixton had started to call on her. Susie lost interest after only a few months.

'So long, then,' she said, and Sally took a peek at her sister's legs as she walked to the door. Susie's coat, an inch longer than her skirt, was no more than three inches below her knees. Hemlines had become progressively higher, and some people said the limit had been reached.

'Crikey, Mum,' said Sally, 'Mister Adams'll lose 'is eyesight when Susie gets close. Can't I wear silk stockings?'

'No, you can't,' said Mrs Brown, 'and they're imitation silk, anyway.'

'Ta-ta, Mum,' said Susie. 'Toodle-ooh, pudding-face,' she said to her sister, and left.

'She's gettin' posh,' said Sally.

'Course she's not,' said Mrs Brown, 'she just looks nice, like you will when you're twenty-one.'

'It ain't fair,' said Sally, as if her sister had no right to be grown up when she herself was only thirteen and boys called her Shorty.

'Finish your porridge, lovey, and get off to school,' said Mrs Brown. 'Freddy's already gone.'

'Gone off, that's what 'e's gone,' said Sally.

'You pickle,' said Mrs Brown, and smiled her jolly smile.

The fog crept into the house.

Sammy looked pointedly at his pocket watch when Susie arrived in the office of the garment factory in Shoreditch. Susie did not miss the look. It was a quarter to ten, and he had asked her to be there at half-past nine.

'I'm sorry,' she said, 'but the fog was terrible. The buses stopped running, and I had to come on the Underground from Kennington Oval.'

'Have I said anything?' asked Sammy.

'You looked at your watch,' said Susie.

'I happen,' said Sammy, 'to own a real rolled gold watch to which I refer constant and out of habitual habit, it being my firm belief that time costs money, which is hard to come by.'

'Yes, it is, for most of us,' said Susie. Sammy glanced at her. Whatever the cold foggy weather was doing to other people, it had given Susie a glow and made her look a young lady tingling and alive. What a problem she was to him, even out of the way at Brixton. He doubted if he would have the strength to endure one more year without something drastic happening. There had been a change in her during these last few months. Very cool and quiet, she was. Not that it didn't suit her. It gave her the kind of ladylike air his mother liked best in a girl. All the same, he thought he preferred the old Susie, hiding nothing of her feelings and declaiming her faith in the goodness of God and His wondrous works. She had turned the Brixton shop into a small gold mine, and he had asked her two months ago to spend a few days at his new shop in Peckham Rye, to find out why it was more like a lead mine. Susie consented, but in very straight-faced fashion, and took only a short time to make the shop a going concern, simply by rearranging the displays and teaching the manageress and assistant how not to make customers feel inferior to them. Sammy thought about sacking the manageress. Susie reacted quite coldly to that, telling him if he did sack the woman then he ought to sack himself too, because he was responsible for giving her the job in the first place. Sammy, shocked, said he'd be obliged if she'd kindly remember not to give him that sort of advice. But he kept the woman on, and she was doing a much better job in the Peckham Rye shop now.

He interrupted his reflections to ask, 'Is something wrong?'

'I don't know, is there?' said Susie.

'I'm suffering a discomfortable feeling you've got problems.'

'Really?' Susie's speech had improved considerably during her time at Brixton. She could put a very lady-like inflexion into the word really. Of course she had problems, and if he of all men didn't know what they were, she was always going to be stuck out there in the wilderness of Brixton. 'Please don't concern yourself, Mister Adams. Kindly have the goodness to explain what you require of me now I'm here.'

Sammy, not for the first time lately, could hardly believe what came out of her mouth sometimes, nor the way it was said.

'I'll excuse that piece of peculiar wordage, Miss

Brown. It's my pleasure to explain this fact'ry represents the advantage of manufacturing for ourselves. Profit not being come by easy, we're eliminatin' paying someone else for makin' our garments, so we've got rid of his hurtful profit by buying him up.'

'We?' enquired Susie.

'It's my pleasure to consider you inclusive.'

'Inclusive of extra profit?'

'Eh?' said Sammy.

'Or did me last Christmas bonus of three pounds make me inclusive, Mister Adams?'

Astonished, Sammy said, 'Is my ears deceivin' me? You sounded like a disbelievable little ingrate.'

'I'm not little, Mister Adams, and you got no right to call me an ingrate.'

Sammy shifted his feet and muttered. She'd got him off balance, like she had umpteen times before. All right, so she wasn't little, not at five feet seven, but it was still painful to hear her talking like this.

'Well, maybe I spoke a bit hasty,' he said.

'You spoke very hurtful,' said Susie, her heart a sensitive ache. For nearly a year now she had felt detached from the firm. She felt detached from him, and from Boots and Tommy, both of whom she had worked for in the past. For all the challenge of her job in the Brixton shop, she felt out of things. She hankered after Camberwell and Walworth, Walworth being where the market stall and the scrap metal business were. She eyed Sammy in her direct way, thinking how tall and manly he was at twenty-three. He wasn't burly or thickset, his activity and energy kept him lean. He dressed distinguished too, nearly always in light grey in summer, and charcoal grey in winter, with plain ties instead of the natty ones he had favoured when running the stall in East Street market. Oh, happy days, she thought. He used to smile a lot then, in between his funny muttering moments. He was too busy to smile these days, and was always rottenly businesslike with her each time he visited the Brixton shop. But she could not forget how he had virtually picked her out of the gutter, employed her, forgiven her her mistakes, and kept his promise to make her a manageress. It had induced in her a loyalty she thought would never change. A hugely round man called Ben Ford, known as Fatty or Fat Man, with business interests all over South London, had several times offered her a job at a better wage than Sammy paid her. She had always refused, but it made her wonder what her actual worth was.

'If we could refer to business,' said Sammy, 'I'd like to begin by saying this place wants puttin' in order.'

'Yes,' she said.

'I can't stand this,' he muttered, 'it's like talkin' to nobody. It's upsettin' me, Susie. I've done something I shouldn't. All right, what is it?'

Susie could have said it was simply that he made her feel she was only another cog in the wheel of his business, that he took her for granted and never held a sociable conversation with her.

'You haven't done nothing, Mister Adams,' she said, and there was a world of meaning in that. It passed right over his head, of course.

'Well, all right,' he said, but uncertainly, and he hated to feel uncertain about anything. 'Anyway, what d'you think about this place?'

Susie looked around the office, such as it was. It was indescribably mucky, it looked as if it had never known a broom or a duster. The plain, distempered walls were a dirty brown. There were files, papers, garment oddments, discarded samples, overflowing cardboard boxes and other things everywhere. On top of a filing cabinet was a jumbled mess of stuff, and the desk was crowded with yellowing papers stuck on spikes with cork bases.

'It's disgustin',' she said.

'It don't look too promising, I grant you,' said Sammy, 'and when you see the workshop itself you'll find there's room for improvement there too. Anyway, to start with, I'd be much obliged if you'd knock this office into shape. Mr Morris said he'd lend a hand.' Mr Morris was the previous owner.

'If Mr Morris is responsible for this disgustin' mess,' said Susie fiercely, 'I don't want his help, thank you.'

'Now calm down,' said Sammy. 'Just say if you can put this office to rights, and then we'll talk about—'

'I will say! I'll say no, I won't!' It all came to a head then, everything, including the heartache. The words burst from her. 'It's a job for a navvy, and I'm a young lady, I am, come of age, which I don't suppose means anything to you, oh, no. I've give you the best years of me life, I have, and what's it done except make you think all I'm good for is clearing up someone else's filthy mess? A bloody cheek you've got! You find someone else to do it, and you find someone else to run the Brixton shop and put other shops right. Keep all your rotten jobs, I don't want any of them no more, and may God forgive you for what you've done to me!'

Sammy could not believe it. Nor could he believe her rushing act of disappearance. By the time he had come to she was well on her way, but his ears were still ringing.

'Susie?' said Mrs Brown, as her daughter came into the kitchen. 'What you come back home for?'

'Nothing,' said Susie.

Mrs Brown gave her a long look, noting the flush on her face, the fierce set of her mouth, and the glitter in her eyes.

'There's something wrong, Susie. You'd better sit down.'

Susie sat down at the table, the yellow fog hanging against the bay window and blotting out the yard. The range fire was glowing. She stared into the hot coals.

'It's nothing,' she said.

'Now, Susie, don't tell me no fairy stories,' said Mrs Brown.

'Oh, if you must know, I fell out with Mister Sammy.' The words were wrenched from Susie. 'I've given up my job. I'm not goin' to be walked on nor treated as if I was just a bit useful now and again.'

'Susie, oh, lawks.' Mrs Brown was aghast. 'Susie, you can't give up your job, think of all the people who don't have one. You can't bring no wages home. And Mister Sammy's been good to you—'

'He hasn't.' Susie was bitter. 'He's been rotten to me, he hasn't got a ha'porth of ordinary human affection for anyone or anything except his business.'

'Now, Susie,' said Mrs Brown gently, 'you know that's not true. You shouldn't say unforgivin' things like that. Why, I remember the time you had mumps cruelly bad and he come round right away to see you.'

'Yes, to see what a sight I was, he did that all right. Well, if he comes round again and goes down on his bended knees beggin' me to go back, I won't. I can get another job easy, with a man called Ben Ford. He's offered more than once. I'll go and work for him, I will.'

'Susie love, don't talk like that,' said Mrs Brown in concern. 'Mister Sammy can't have been roaring and bellowing at you, can 'e? He wouldn't, not Mister Sammy. He treats your dad very good down at the scrap metal yard.' Mr Brown had full-time work at the yard now. 'Susie, Mister Sammy hasn't got cross, he hasn't shouted at you, has 'e?'

'I wish he had, it might have meant he cared a bit, then, it might—' Susie stopped and turned her eyes on the fire again.

'Susie?' Mrs Brown was maternally enquiring. 'Susie?'

Susie got up.

'I'm goin' out again,' she said. 'I'm goin' to walk to Kennington and see Mr Ford. He'll give me a job on the spot, I know he will, and at more than that Sammy Adams pays me.'

'No, don't do that—'

'I'm goin' to,' said Susie, and left the house with her bitterness still fierce. She walked through the fog, the fog that was choking Walworth and muffling every familiar sound.

Four minutes later, the worried Mrs Brown answered a knock on her front door. Sammy stood there, in a trilby hat and a grey herring-bone overcoat. He had left the factory as soon as he had recovered his wits. His first clear thought had appalled him. It told him he couldn't do without Susie.

'Morning, Mrs Brown, is Susie home?' he asked, and Mrs Brown thought he looked as worried as she felt.

'Mister Adams, go an' catch her before she does what she shouldn't. She's walkin' to Kennington to get a job with a man called Ford. She'll go up through Manor Place, she's awful upset about things – Mr Adams?'

Sammy was gone, striding recklessly fast through the fog.

He caught her up just as she turned the corner of Penton Place into Kennington Park Road. He considered himself lucky. Visibility was chronic, and he heard her before he saw her. He heard the click of her patent leather shoes on the pavement. He came up beside her. She gave a startled little gasp, but continued walking, mouth shut tight, chin up and nose high in the fog.

Sammy spoke penitently. 'Susie, I upset you. I'm sorry. I'd be grateful if you'd let me take you back home and talk to you.'

'Go away,' said Susie.

'I can't do that, Susie, I've got to talk to you.'

'Then I'll call a policeman, the first one I see, and complain you're molestin' me.'

'Look, if I did yer wrong, I'm in Christian repentance, on the Bible I am.'

'Kindly don't make me laugh, I'm not in the mood,' said Susie. 'I decline to speak to you, Mister Adams, I am declining to speak to you ever again. That kind gentleman Mr Ford has offered me a job more than once, and I'm goin' to take it.'

'The Fat Man ain't kind, nor a gentleman,' said Sammy, 'and you're not takin' any job he offers.'

'Who's goin' to stop me, may I ask?'

'I am,' said Sammy.

'Is that another joke?' asked Susie.

'It's no joke,' said Sammy. 'I mean it, even if it costs me two broken legs and a hole in me head.'

'Have a nice time in hospital.'

'Susie, is that a nice thing to say? I never thought I'd hear you talk so uncaring.'

Susie, walking stiffly through the fog, said, 'Yes, you still think I'm a Sunday School kid that wouldn't speak ill of anyone. Well, I'm pleased to inform you, Mister Adams, that I'm considerably grown up.' While growing up, Susie had learned to confound Sammy with his own kind of vernacular. 'I am now a grown woman and don't wear rose-tinted spectacles any more, but that don't mean I've given up believing in the Christian faith, only that I can see certain people for what they are.'

'Oh, my suffering head,' said Sammy, 'I never heard such obstreperous wordage. Look, Susie love—'

'Susie what?' She stopped then, much to his relief. Trying to talk to her while blundering through the fog, with other pedestrians a menace, was hardly promising. He faced her. They became two static figures shrouded in yellow. 'I hope you ain't – I hope you're not being familiar, Mister Adams.'

'Now what've I said?' Sammy cleared his throat. Susie's eyes searched him. He cleared his throat again. 'All right, I've got to say it, you've grown up very creditable, you look as good as Pearl White, and I'm proud of you.'

'I've heard all that before, thank you,' she said, but she was thinking he must care a bit, he must, or he would never have come after her like this.

'Now, Susie—'

'Oh! Don't say that! I won't be condescended to!' Susie actually stamped a foot.

'Now, Susie—'

'Oh, you done it again, I'll hit you!' cried Susie, and was mortified then as a figure came out of the fog, bumped into them and made known it had heard what she said.

' 'Ere, yer'd better cart yerselves orf 'ome an' do yer wallopin' there, 'cos I'm tellin' yer, yer dangerous hobstructions to innocent walkers while yer standin' there an' not showin' no fog lamps.' And it went grumbling on its way.

'Never mind that prime specimen of how not to make friends in the dark,' said Sammy. 'Here, Susie, where you goin'? Oh, me gawd.'

Susie, still too proud to encourage reconciliation, had stepped off the kerb into the fog that blanketed the road. He heard the heavy sound of a slow-moving vehicle. He rushed, flung both arms around her from behind, lifted her and plunged back on to the pavement as pale fog lamps loomed up. A corporation watercart

108

passed by. Susie turned in his arms and for a moment he felt her warm body alarmingly close to his. There was even a calamitous urge to pull her closer. Susie broke free, her breathing a little quick and noisy.

'If you don't mind,' she said, but there was a catch in her voice.

'Susie, don't you ever do that again, don't you ever step off a kerb like that in fog like this.'

'Can I help it I'm upset?'

'You're not the only one,' said Sammy. 'How d'you think I feel about all this carry-on?'

'It's nice to know you've got feelings,' said Susie. 'I didn't think you had, seeing you've kept me locked away in Brixton all these years.'

'Locked away?' Sammy's astonished breath escaped. It steamed into the fog.

'That's what it felt like,' said Susie.

'Well,' said Sammy helplessly, 'I just don't know what I'm goin' to do with you, Susie Brown. Didn't I keep my promise to make you manageress of my first ladies' wear shop?'

'I didn't know I was goin' to be eternally banished.'

'Eternally banished? I'm goin' to fall unconscious in a minute from all this ringing in me ears.'

'Someone will pick you up, I'm sure,' said Susie, experiencing little leaps of exhilaration because he was so obviously on the rack. 'I can't stop here talkin', Mister Adams, I have to proceed on my way to the offices of Mr Ford, the gentleman mentioned previous.'

'Nothing doing,' said Sammy, 'you'll get run over for sure next time. Besides which, the mentioned gentleman is a dubious geezer who's not goin' to be your employer except over my dead body. And would you do me the favour of not talkin' about being banished?' Sammy was having a terrible time fighting the ruinous urge to give in. And Susie was watching him, watching

109

his eyes trying to avoid hers. 'Look, if I was displeasing to you this morning, I'm sorry, specially as I had a proposition to put to you after we'd worked things out at the fact'ry. It so happens I'm up to my eyeballs in work at the office, and I need a personal assistant, someone who looks highly creditable and has got considerable mental engineering works. Which is you, Susie. I'd be more than gratified if you'd come back to Camberwell as me private secretary and personal assistant, which is a necessary appendix to any businessman of reputable standing. I can get another manageress for the Brixton shop. There's smart women lining up for that kind of job. Well, what d'you say, Susie?' Sammy had given in. He knew what it would do to him, bringing her back into his daily business life.

Susie's blue eyes turned misty. Sammy sighed. Calamity was in the offing, he could feel it. Sooner or later he was going to chuck away all the benefits of remaining a bachelor businessman.

'Mister Sammy?' she said, a little husky. 'Do you mean that?'

'I never make unmeaningful business propositions,' said Sammy. 'Would twelve pounds a month suit you?'

'Twelve pounds? Three pounds a week?' Susie knew few young ladies of twenty-one earned that amount. But it was not the money alone that mattered, it was something else, something far more necessary to her.

'I'd like you to go to evening classes and learn typing, of course,' remarked Sammy.

'Yes,' said Susie and drew a breath. 'Mister Sammy, I'm sorry I said all those awful things about you, and you mustn't ever think I didn't know how good you were givin' me the job as manageress. Only – only I don't want Brixton for always, I'd love to come back to Camberwell. I did get upset at the fact'ry, thinking you didn't have any regard for me—'

110

'Susie, my regard for you is highly affectionate,' said Sammy.

'Oh,' said Susie, eyes mistier.

'Which, of course, don't mean I'll make improper advances,' said Sammy, stepping hastily back from the brink.

'Why, Mister Sammy, as if you would,' said Susie, wondering what he thought an improper advance was, and wondering too what it would do to her. 'I'm sure any girl could trust you to advance very proper on her.'

'Well,' said Sammy vaguely and helplessly, 'well, yes, I hope so, Miss Brown.'

Silent laughter welled up inside Susie then. He was so funny, just like he had always been. He looked mature, he really did, but he didn't know a thing about girls. He had no idea that during the last year she had been longing to get back to Camberwell. His regard for her was highly affectionate? He was still so droll.

With her tongue in her cheek, she said, 'Twelve pounds a month is wondrous gratifying, Mister Sammy, specially as it won't come with improper advances.'

Sammy coughed.

'Fog in me throat,' he said. 'Well, I'm glad you've accepted.'

'When do I start?'

'Tomorrow.'

'Utter bliss,' said Susie. 'I'll come back to Shoreditch with you now, if you like, on the Tube. We can talk about the office and fact'ry when we get there.'

'We'll do that tomorrow, I've got other calls to make now, includin' one on an unemployed female manageress I happen to know, concerning takin' over the Brixton shop. You meet me at the fact'ry same time tomorrow and we'll sort things out. I'd like the fact'ry to look a bit better than a sweatshop, it's a principle of mine not to have any part of Adams Enterprises lookin' discreditable. All right, Susie, you've had an upset morning, so take the rest of the day off. I won't dock yer wages. You go home and enjoy a mug of hot revivin' Bovril.'

'Yes, Mister Sammy, thank you.'

'My pleasure,' said Sammy, and they parted, he conscious his future was doomladen and Susie utterly and blissfully sure he cared for her.

The woman wore a black coat and hat on this day, with a heavy black veil. She wandered along Walworth Road, murmuring to herself. She went into Maypole's, the grocers. A counter assistant, sympathetic about her widow's weeds, asked her in kindness if he could serve her. She shook her head in a startled negative and left the shop. Reaching Browning Street, she turned into it, hurrying her step. At Caulfield Place she stopped. Her veil moved to her murmuring voice. A passer-by looked at her. She went quickly on, to Walcorde Avenue, and from there to the church.

The vicar found her there twenty minutes later, seated in a pew, her veiled face bent. He did not interrupt her. She left when she became aware of his presence.

She wandered murmuring through the fog.

CHAPTER TEN

At three o'clock that afternoon, Boots entered Sammy's office. Sammy had just returned from making a number of business calls. He had always believed in the benefits of personal contacts. The telephone on his desk was a useful piece of equipment. Once installed, it could not be done without. But it was not the same as being face to face with people, shaking hands with them and showing them an honest countenance.

Boots placed a slip of paper on the desk.

'Plonk your peepers on that, Sammy.'

'I'm plonking,' said Sammy, 'but why do I have to?'

'We're spending a small fortune on collection and delivery charges. Look at the amount we've paid Carter Paterson for the first six months of the current financial year.'

'What?' Sammy studied pencilled figures.

'Wake up, Kruger.'

'I ain't aware I'm asleep.'

'We need a van.'

'Pardon?'

'A van. For collecting and delivering, and serving all our shops. A motor van, not a horse and cart.'

'Cost a fortune,' said Sammy.

'That's a fortune in those figures,' said Boots, 'and it's increasing every year. Don't muck about, sonny, get a van.'

'Capital expenditure, that is,' said Sammy.

'It hurts, of course, but you can get treatment.'

'And a van needs a driver.'

'That'll make a steady job for a deserving ex-soldier,' said Boots, 'and we'll still save money.'

'Hold up,' said Sammy, 'I ain't running parish relief for your old mates in khaki.'

'My old mates saved you from being swallowed up by Kaiser Bill. Shake yourself, Sammy. A delivery van's a must.'

Sammy, who knew Boots never offered unprofitable ideas, said, 'All right, I'll see what Susie says.'

'Pardon?' said Boots.

'What did I say?' asked Sammy, opening a desk drawer and rummaging uselessly through it.

'I think you mentioned the manageress of the Brixton shop.'

'Oh, young Susie Whatsername, you mean,' said Sammy, keeping his head down.

'Not that old chestnut,' said Boots, and noted the obvious fact that Sammy wasn't his usual self. 'All right, out with it.'

'I happen to need an assistant,' said Sammy, closing the drawer. 'Look at me overloaded in-tray, and me overburdened business day. I'm totally disinclined to die from being overloaded and overburdened. So I'm takin' Susie on as me private secretary and personal assistant.'

'I see. Giving in at last, are you, Sammy?'

'I don't consider that an appropriate remark,' said Sammy. 'Well, a van and a driver. I'll give it me serious attention as soon as I've got time.'

'No need for that,' said Boots, 'just show the figures to your new private secretary and personal assistant. She'll make sense out of them. And tell her I know a bloke she can offer the driver's job to.'

114

'Would you be so good as to inform me who you think's in charge here?'

'I think it's going to be Susie,' said Boots. 'Smart piece of work, Sammy. Susie's a bright girl. She'll help you live a lot longer.'

'I like some of your jokes,' said Sammy, 'I don't like 'em all.'

'Buy a van, Sammy. I'm off now, I've got to see one of Rosie's teachers. Love to Susie.'

Boots walked through the afternoon fog to the school. Lights of crawling vehicles and the lamps of horse-drawn carts peered through the gloom. He thought about the family. Emily was more energetic than ever at twenty-seven, dashing off to her part-time job in the mornings, spending the afternoons doing things around the house, giving time to Chinese Lady and to four-year-old Tim in between, and participating in every evening activity. She adored Tim, of course, and indulged her delight in him by taking ages to put him to bed at night. She romped with him in his room. Chinese Lady wasn't too sure it was a good thing to get a child all lively at bedtime, but didn't interfere.

Emily enjoyed having Chinese Lady and Mr Finch living with them. Mr Finch had sold his previous house and bought a large one at the south end of Red Post Hill, close to North Dulwich station, some fifteen minutes' walk from Lizzy and Ned's house. At the same time, Boots and Emily sold their house, and Chinese Lady showed guarded pleasure when they all moved into the new house, a well-built Victorian residence. There were four bedrooms on the first floor, with a bathroom and a huge airing cupboard, to accommodate Boots, Emily, Rosie and Tim. Chinese Lady and Mr Finch lived downstairs, where there were five rooms, including a large kitchen. There was also a scullery, which Chinese Lady thought right, proper and wholly necessary. She and Mr Finch had their bedroom and their own cosy sitting-room, plus a study for Mr Finch. The remaining room, spacious, was used by Boots and Emily as a living-room, and on frequent occasions everyone gathered there. One end of the room was set aside as a dining area, and they all had tea there on Sundays. Most other meals they ate together in the handsome kitchen. Emily handed over control of the kitchen to Chinese Lady as soon as they moved in, and Chinese Lady happily took up the role she cherished. She was the natural guardian of family life and the dispenser of provender. She was happy to be a wife again, and if there was one other factor that also gave her pleasure, it was having two children around, Rosie and Tim.

Boots knew his mother was very happy that she had a whole family around her, including a husband. She and Mr Finch got on remarkably well, although they were completely different. She was a woman of elementary education and old-fashioned attitudes, and with a fixed belief in what was right and proper. Mr Finch had attended university, been an agent for German Intelligence up to 1918 and become a British citizen in 1920, having crossed to the British side before the war ended. Only Boots knew these things about him. Chinese Lady admired and respected him because she considered him a gentleman, and he admired and respected her because he thought her remarkable.

The house was a palace to her and Emily because of its huge bathroom, three toilets, large hall and magnificent garden. The arrangement might not have worked, but Emily willingly deferred to Chinese Lady in all things domestic, and Chinese Lady had too much commonsense to let her opinions, always frank, sound too much like interference. Emily was currently working on her in a wheedling way, for Emily still wanted her job to be a full-time one, and she needed Chinese Lady to look after Tim all day until he went to school. Boots knew Chinese Lady would be resistant to that, not because it would be too much for her, but because she had decided ideas about who should be the family breadwinner and who should be the home-builder. She still thought it wrong and unnecessary for Emily to be out at work at all, but did not say so to her.

Boots rode on the bus with his Rosie every morning, and Annabelle and Bobby boarded it on the way. All three children got off at the school stop, and Boots stayed on until Camberwell Green was reached.

Lizzy and Ned now had four children, Annabelle, Bobby, three-year-old Emma and one-year-old Edward. Lizzy lived in singular content. Ned's job with the wine merchants of Great Tower Street was now a very well-paid one. He and the children made Lizzy the hub of their existence, and ups and downs were taken in their stride. Lizzy made her family go regularly to church, and here Ned saw a little of her mother in her. Chinese Lady believed people experienced a sense of humility in church, and Lizzy was apt to say that a bit of religious humility was good for everyone. It stopped them thinking they didn't owe anything to their Creator.

Tommy and Vi were the delighted parents of six-months-old Alice, but couldn't afford to rent a house of their own. Vi was not too concerned about this and neither was Aunt Victoria. Tommy, despite his own equability, very much wanted something better for Vi than the flat they had in her parents' house. He had come across two engineering jobs, but neither offered as much as the wages of two pounds five shillings that

Sammy paid him for running the stall. He and Vi could have afforded to rent a house in Walworth, but they both preferred an area farther south.

Boots came out of his reveries as he arrived at the school. It was cloaked by the fog, the classroom lights a dim glow. He went in, made for the teachers' rest room and knocked on the door.

'Come in.'

He entered. Polly, standing, smiled at him, her bobbed dark brown hair shining, her eyes bright. Her yellow jumper and dark brown skirt were the last word in simplicity. The skirt, short, revealed slim legs clad in silk stockings. She only ever wore silk, refusing to grace her legs with anything else. Her teacher's pay was pocket money to her, for she enjoyed a generous allowance from her father, General Simms. She had met Boots five years ago and fallen for him, but she had had nothing from him except friendship, friendship of a provoking airy-fairy kind on his part. It was still difficult for her to settle just for that. Through his daughter Rosie she maintained contact with him. And his son Tim would be attending the school next year. She had met his wife Emily and thought her lively but plain. She could not think how on earth a plain woman had netted him.

'Hello,' said Boots. 'Any tea?'

'Stewed, like before?' said Polly. 'I'll give you stewed, you cheap comic. No, of course there's some, just made.' She took the cosy off the pot and poured two cups. She handed him one.

'Much obliged,' said Boots, and she looked him over in a wry way. His hat was on a chair, his overcoat hanging unbuttoned over his long frame, his sound right eye clear, his blind one looking lazy. She did not know any man who handled himself in easier fashion. Her father, one of the school governors, had met him once. A lengthy conversation ensued, and her father said to her later, 'Damned hard luck, Polly, but shouldn't have let him slip you.' 'How the hell could I help it when I didn't get to meet him until it was too late?' retorted Polly. 'Bad organisation, Polly. Get the feller compromised. Your only chance, y'know, divorce.' 'You heinous old ratbag,' said Polly, 'but what a thrilling idea.'

She smiled at Boots again. 'Kiss?' she said.

Boots sipped his tea. She was always playing that kind of game with him.

'Christmas?' he said.

'Mistletoe stuff?' said Polly, wrinkling her nose. 'You're stingy even then. I hope your wife hates you.'

'She will if I go to bed with you.'

'I'll risk divorce if you will,' said Polly.

'Messy,' said Boots, 'and it'll be my divorce, not yours.'

'Yes, darling, I know, but you'd get me as a lovely compensation, and we could have some kids of our own. You like kids, I know you do. So do I. I'd like to have yours.'

'Sounds tempting,' said Boots. 'Why am I here?'

'Because I adore you. Why can't you adore me?'

'It's a mystery to me. You look the part and sound the part.'

'Couldn't you make love to me just once?' asked Polly.

'Easily. But I might get to like you. Can we stop playing games?'

'I don't play games, not with you.'

'Well, shall we be serious, then?'

'Oh, hell,' said Polly, 'seriously, then, and about Rosie. Mr Stokes has let me have the privilege of discussing her education with you.'

'Is it a privilege?'

119

'Of course,' said Polly. 'Don't you know how sweet and gifted your own daughter is?'

His own daughter? Boots had given Rosie his name, and she was entered in the school register as Rosie Adams, implying she was adopted. Boots and Emily had known it was impossible to pass her off as their natural daughter. The school authorities accepted she was adopted. Rosie herself never mentioned she was either fostered or adopted. To her, Boots and Emily were her natural parents, because they loved her.

'Polly, you know, of course, that—'

'I know she's yours,' said Polly, her back to the fire that kept the teachers' room warm on winter days. 'You've made her yours, and she adores you for it. Rosie's your very own.'

Boots looked at her. Polly made a face, as if she had been guilty of exchanging commonsense for sentiment.

'Polly, that's very sweet of you,' he said.

'Well, you see, darling, it really isn't a game,' she said. 'I wish I were yours too. But listen, Rosie is very gifted. She's too much of a natural scholar not to be given more than an elementary education. In fact, all children of talent should have the chance of higher schooling. Between now and Easter, 1927, when Rosie will be in her twelfth year, we have time to help her. As you know, I've been teaching her French out of school, and you've helped in that too. And Mr Stokes is willing to cram her in English Literature. Further, old thing, the school has been given the opportunity to offer one girl a chance to sit an examination in London for a scholarship to St Mary's College near Brighton. She would be sitting the exam with other girls, and she does need to have a sound basic knowledge of French. There are four scholarship places, and thirty-two girls will be competing for them in January 1927. I'm going to ask you to allow Mr Stokes and me to give Rosie the extra tuition and homework necessary to help her qualify for the exam. If she were among the four successful girls, it would mean being at St Mary's for five years.'

'Is St Mary's a boarding school?' asked Boots.

'Yes,' said Polly, 'but you'd only have to pay for little extras, everything else would be found. It's a very generous bursary.'

'I'll speak to Emily,' said Boots.

'Yes, I suppose so,' said Polly, who was never going to make Emily her best friend. She had a fanciful conviction that that green-eyed woman had swiped Boots when her back was turned. The fact that she had not known him then did not alter her conviction. 'But how do you feel about it yourself?'

Boots thought. It meant the family parting with Rosie for five years. But there would be the holidays, of course, and how could they deny her the chance of such a good education?

'Let's see what Rosie says, Polly. Can you call her from class?'

Polly fetched her. Rosie came in looking intrigued. Boots spoke to her about the scholarship exam, the tuition she would need, and the education she would receive at a school called St Mary's if she secured a place there. He did not say it was a boarding school, but he did say it was in Sussex.

'What d'you think, kitten, would you like to do a year's cramming and try for one of the scholarships?'

'Would you like me to, Daddy?' asked Rosie, his wish counting most.

'Yes, if you'd like it too.'

Rosie gave no thought to how far away the school was, or to the possibility of separation. She thought only of pleasing him.

'Then I'll try my hardest, really I will,' she said

121

earnestly. 'Of course, you're not to think it's no sooner said than done. I mean, with thirty-two girls at the exam and only four scholarships, I'd have to be pretty spiffing, you know.'

Boots smiled. No wonder some of the pupils here called her Lady Muck. He had been called Lord Muck himself by the street kids. Rosie's favourite adjectives were ripping and spiffing. She was a devourer of the school stories written by Frank Richards about Harry Wharton, Bob Cherry and Billy Bunter.

'All right,' he said, 'I won't think it's no sooner said than done.'

'Yes, it's best to be sensible,' said Rosie, 'and it's a good thing you can be.'

'Kind of you to say so,' said Boots, and Polly thought how attached these two were to each other. A bell rang. Classes were over.

'You can get your hat and coat now, Rosie,' said Polly, 'and go with your father.'

'Oh, we must wait for Annabelle and Bobby, Miss Simms,' said Rosie. 'Mustn't we, Daddy? I don't know what Annabelle would say if we didn't, except what a rotten swizz. I'd better go and find them.' She went.

'Isn't she adorable?' said Polly. 'Aren't you a lucky old daddy?'

'So-so,' said Boots.

The buses were running again, and Annabelle and Bobby were with Boots and Rosie when they boarded one. Annabelle hung back so that she could sit with her uncle. Rosie made no protest. She knew she did not have to fight for her father's attentions. She knew instinctively she was special to him.

That evening at the supper table in the kitchen, Chinese Lady said, 'Well, I don't know, I'm sure. It's a lot to ask of Rosie.'

'Oh, I want to try, Nana,' said Rosie.

'And you should, Rosie,' said Mr Finch.

'Them kind of exams don't bear thinking about for little girls,' said Chinese Lady.

'But, Nana, I'm a big girl now,' protested Rosie. 'I used to be little when I hadn't grown much, but I've put on years since then. Tim, sit up,' she said to her brother beside her. 'Mummy, just look at that boy, he's nearly got his nose in his plate. I don't know sometimes what we're going to do with him, do you, Grandpa?'

'Don't want nothing done with me,' said four-year-old Tim. 'Do I, Grandpa?'

'Something could be done about the gravy on your nose,' said Mr Finch, a man happy to have acquired a ready-made family.

'Yes, you've got a nice nose for a boy,' said Rosie graciously, 'you oughtn't to put it in your gravy.'

'I didn't,' said Tim, and got on with his dinner, which Chinese Lady still called supper. Emily, on his other side, wiped the spot of gravy off his nose. Tim looked at her. Emily gave him a smile and a wink. He offered her a little grin. 'There wasn't no gravy, was there?' he said.

'Any,' said Boots.

'See?' said Tim to Rosie. 'Daddy said there wasn't as well.'

'There isn't, not now,' said Rosie. 'Eat your dinner up, there's a good boy. Nana, I told Daddy and Miss Simms I could only try about the exam.'

'Well, I just hope it don't get to be a strain,' said Chinese Lady, presiding in as upright a fashion as ever.

'I think Rosie's up to it,' said Mr Finch.

'I don't know I'm too keen on that Miss Simms,' said Emily.

'Oh, but she's awf'lly nice,' said Rosie, 'and she likes

123

Daddy lots, she's always asking after his health. "How is your father, Rosie?" she says. "Is he well?" "Oh, he's vital with health," I say.'

'Bless us, that child,' said Chinese Lady, 'what's vital with health?'

'Vigorous?' suggested Mr Finch.

'Lor', the words she uses,' said Chinese Lady, and glanced at Boots.

Emily, who also had her eyes on him, said, 'I can't say he talks vigorous, just airy-fairy like he always does, and not tellin' you much.'

Chinese Lady said, 'I think I'd like to come and meet Miss Simms, Rosie.'

'Oh, she'd be thrilled, Nana,' said Rosie. 'I've told her lots about you, how you brought up Daddy and Uncle Sammy and Uncle Tommy and Auntie Lizzy, and made them a credit to you except Daddy, who turned out only fit for the music hall. I told her I expect you wondered sometimes what you were going to do with him.'

Mr Finch smiled. Rosie, only ten, was already capable of teasing her father deliciously.

'I wonder myself what I'm going to do with you, young lady,' said Boots.

'But, Daddy, I only said what I've heard Nana say lots of times,' protested Rosie, 'and Mummy and I don't mind about you only being fit for the music hall, and Miss Simms said it was a good thing some people were different from others or life would be awful boring. Honest, we don't mind a bit if you've been an aggravation at times. It's better than being awful boring, isn't it, Mummy?'

'Can't no one stop her talking?' asked Tim.

'I'm still not too keen on Miss Simms,' said Emily pointedly. She thought Rosie's favourite teacher had all kinds of false mannerisms.

'Good teacher, harmless female,' said Boots.

'Yes, I think I'd better come and meet her some time,' said Chinese Lady, suspicious of any lady teacher uncommonly interested in the health of Boots.

In their house in Walworth, Mr Brown said to Mrs Brown, 'Our Susie's feeling better, she's been down in the dumps lately and worrying me.'

'She was nearly down for good this morning, I can tell you,' said Mrs Brown. 'She fell out with Mister Sammy.'

'Yer jokin',' said Mr Brown.

'It wasn't no joke, love. Real cut up, she was, and told him she was leavin' her job. But he came after her, and she said they had a talk and that he's took her on as his personal assistant. Our Susie, would you believe. She won't have to go all the way to Brixton no more. I never seen her more happy.'

'Well, who'd 'ave thought it, Bessie, Mister Sammy promotin' our Susie like that. All the same, I get worried she ain't being courted. She's gone twenty-one, she don't want to be a workin' woman all her life.'

'Here, what d'you think I am, then?' said Mrs Brown, giving him a cheerful dig in his ribs. 'I'm a workin' woman, y'know.'

'Course you are, me old Dutch,' said Mr Brown. He put an arm around his amiable trouble-and-strife and squeezed her cuddlesome plumpness. 'What I meant was, ain't it time she was married?'

'She's only waitin' to be asked, Jim.'

'Eh? Who by?'

'Best I don't name any names, in case I'm wrong,' said Mrs Brown. 'Here, I had some woman call this afternoon, askin' after Mr Finch.'

'What, 'im that used to lodge 'ere years ago?'

'Well, there wasn't no other gent by that name, was there?'

'What, 'im that's now Mister Sammy's stepfather?'

'I s'pose that's who she meant, that woman. Peculiar, she was. I said he'd gone away years ago. Well, I didn't think I'd tell her about him and where he was livin'.' Mrs Brown spoke firmly. Walworth people were instinctively cautious when strangers came enquiring. Strangers might mean trouble, they might be debt collectors or arms of the law or dubious people. 'Very peculiar, she was, kept saying where was he and not takin' any notice of me saying he hadn't lived here for years. It was like she wasn't hearing what I kept saying. She tried to push her way in, would you believe. I wasn't havin' that, I pushed her out and shut the door on her.'

'Yer did right, Bessie,' said Jim. 'It don't do to be informin' to people like that. It's like openin' up the cupboard door and lettin' a skeleton out.'

'Oh, you don't reckon Mr Finch has got skeletons, do you?' said Mrs Brown. 'Susie said he's a nice distinguished gentleman. She met him at the weddin' four years ago.'

'You did right, old girl,' said Jim again.

That night Daisy Cook woke up. She slept in the room that had once been the bedroom of Miss Elsie Chivers, daughter of the murdered Mrs Chivers. She did not know that, nor did her family.

A woman was there, a dark figure of the night. She seemed to be drifting slowly around and she seemed to be sighing. Daisy uttered a frightened little squeal and rushed the sheets up over her head, burying herself. She heard a long-drawn sigh and the whisper of quick-moving clothes. When she uncovered herself minutes later, the dark figure was gone. She felt it had been a bad little dream, and when she went back to sleep the sheets were over her head again. Covering up kept bad dreams away.

Her mother, Mrs Cook, found the front door open when she came down in the morning. She simply thought someone in the family had been careless. One of her two growing sons, probably. She picked up the pewter can of milk from the doorstep, closed the door and thought no more about it. Open doors in Walworth worried no one, except that they let the fog in and the draughts.

CHAPTER ELEVEN

It was merely misty the following morning. The fog, relenting, had stolen guiltily away after two days of punishing the bronchial tubes of old and young people alike. At Sandringham, Queen Alexandra, the graceful and elegant widow of Edward VII, had just died. Loved by all the people, she had slipped quietly away in her eighty-second year. Many of London's workingmen wore black armbands on this misty morning, such was the affection in which she had been held.

Susie, nevertheless, arrived at the Shoreditch factory with a spring in her step. She entered the office in a mood of fervent loyalty, ready to help in the work of putting it to rights. Faintly she heard the hum and clatter of sewing-machines in the workshop. Astonished, she regarded the office. There was no sign of that disgusting clutter of yesterday. Everything objectionable to the eye had gone. There was a woman down on her hands and knees, scrubbing the worn linoleum with a well-soaped brush. A pail of dirty-brown suds was beside her, a large flannel hanging over the lip of the pail.

'Good morning,' said Susie, who had a carrier bag with her. It contained an old dress and an apron, plus a scarf to protect her hair from dust.

The charring lady, wearing a scarf of her own over her head, looked up.

'Mornin', miss. Watch yer feet, ducky. Floor's slippery, like. Lor', lucky yer didn't come sooner. Dunno I ever seen any office more of a mess, and I seen a few, that I 'ave. George Robey could of sung a song about this one, I tell yer. All gorn now, though. Daft Dick's burnin' the lot in the yard. 'E ain't the brightest bloke this side of London Bridge, but 'e knows 'ow to build a bonny.' She meant bonfire. 'Likes a good bonny, does Daft Dick, and it ain't wise to let 'im get too near a ware'ouse if 'e's got matches in 'is 'andy-pandies.' The woman applied the flannel to the soapy floor. 'Yer want someone, dearie?'

'Yes,' said Susie, 'Mr Adams.'

The woman sat back on her heels, an apron of sacking enveloping her thin body, her worn face lined but good-humoured.

'My, yer a pretty young lady, aincher?' she said. She grimaced and adjusted her posture. 'That's me chilblains catchin' me. You got chilblains, ducky?'

'Not yet,' said Susie, looking around. The dust had gone as well as all the junk. The top of the desk was clear and clean, so was the top of the wooden filing cabinet.

'Crool, they are, chilblains. Mister Adams is in the shop – no, 'e ain't, 'e's 'ere.'

Sammy entered from the passage that led into the factory workshop. His overcoat was over his arm, his hat tipped forward, giving him the jaunty look of a man who had made a cheerfully satisfying start to his day. He placed his coat on the desk, lifted his hat to Susie and smiled at her. Watch him, she said to herself, he's got something up his sleeve.

'Morning, Susie. You've met our invaluable char, Mrs Turner? She's goin' to perform regularly for us at dusting and sweeping. But don't call her Mrs Turner, she's made known she only answers to Ma. Like Ma Earnshaw, the female greengrocery woman in East

Street market, you remember.' Sammy had nothing up his sleeve. His brisk and cheerful approach was simply that of a man accepting defeat bravely. If he had lost his battle by bringing Susie and her mesmerising blue eyes back to Camberwell, it was not in his nature to go about with a long face. True, he had thought last night he might still be· saved, that some acceptable bloke of Susie's acquaintance might pop the question to her and that she might say yes. Unfortunately, that thought was immediately superseded by an imaginative picture of Susie as Mr X's bride. It made him feel horrendously ill. 'Nice to see you, Susie.'

'Nice you haven't consulted your watch, Mister Sammy,' said Susie with cool flair.

'Eh? Oh, that. But slightly cheeky, Miss Brown. Ma, you finished here yet?'

'I almost nearly 'ave, Mister Adams,' said Ma Turner. 'I been held up a bit by me chilblains. They're something chronic this mornin'.'

'Wear woollen socks under your stockings,' said Sammy.

'Lor' luvaduck, Mister Adams, if I do that what chance 'ave I got of gettin' me shoes on? I asks yer, what chance?'

'Wear larger shoes, Ma,' said Sammy. 'I'll bring yer a pair from me Camberwell shop at trade price. Can't say fairer, and I don't want chronic chilblains crippling yer, it'd pain me Christian compassion, which Miss Susie Brown knows is a weakness of mine. Susie, you all right this morning?'

'Fine, Mister Sammy, specially as I don't have chilblains.'

'Pleased to hear it,' said Sammy, who thought she'd acquired style during her time as a manageress. *I'm a drowning man. But I could still be saved. When I get to the stage of final surrender, she might turn me down.* A frown injured his cheerful look.

'Something hurtin' you, Mister Sammy?' asked Susie almost demurely.

'Just a passin' thought,' said Sammy.

'Ain't she a pretty picture on a winter mornin', Mister Adams?' said Ma Turner, scrubbing again. 'Come trippin' in lookin' just like the Lord Mayor's fairy queen, she did.'

Susie laughed.

'Well, it's got to be said,' remarked Sammy, 'you do look as if you only need a coach and six white horses. Ma, look lively.'

'Now yer can't rush a good cleanin' job, or corners don't get done,' said Ma Turner. 'But there y'ar, all done.' On her knees, she wrung water from the enormous flannel into the bucket.

'Fine,' said Sammy, approving the results. 'Now be a good old girl and start the other job, the fact'ry floor. Get it swept and see that Charley Harry collects and burns the rubbish.'

'Yer mean Daft Dick,' said Ma Turner, climbing stiffly to her feet.

'That's him,' said Sammy, and she gathered up her flannel, brush and pail.

'Do a good job for yer, I will,' she said, 'seeing yer makin' it reg'lar work.'

'First cobweb I see I'll sack yer,' said Sammy.

'That ain't Christian, Mister Adams,' said Ma, 'that could be 'ard on a widder woman, that could.'

'Just don't cost me unwarranted money, Ma, that's all,' said Sammy, who always made it clear to newcomers that he expected a fair return for what he paid them.

'We'll get on, Mister Adams, you an' me,' said Ma, 'I likes yer.' She went into the workshop, limping a little on her chilblains. Susie heard a yell of greeting from one of the women machinists.

131

'Oi, watcher, Ma, how is yer, yer old scrubber?'

'She'll do,' said Sammy. 'Now, Susie—'

'Now, Mister Sammy.'

Sammy, suffering helplessness, said, 'Look, when I say now, Susie, it's just an uncomplainin' way of requestin' your undivided attention.'

'Yes, Mister Sammy, I understand,' said Susie, her smile forgiving, 'only could you excuse me requestin' you not to say it as if you're goin' to start learning me the ABC?'

'Oh, my achin' ears,' muttered Sammy.

'Pardon?' said Susie, and Sammy pulled himself together.

'As is no doubt visible to you, Miss Brown, this office has been cleared out and cleaned up. I telephoned Mr Morris yesterday afternoon, and he got a Charley Harry odd-jobber and charwoman Ma to go to work first thing this morning, which was to make up for your unfortunate sufferings of yesterday morning. I've had everything chucked out except the company books, which now repose in that cabinet. We are now in the highly advantageous position of being able to start from scratch, so I'd be much obliged to have you originate a system for keepin' advice notes, delivery notes, invoices and suchlike in a way that won't make it needful to turn the office inside-out to find them. There's the machinists' daily worksheets too. There's empty files in the cabinet for your use, writing paper, pens and ink in the drawer – oh, and on Fridays add up each machinist's worksheet and earnings, put their wages into envelopes and mark them accordin'. You'll be provided with the necessary cash by me. I am enquiring into—'

'Mister Adams, pardon me, I'm sure,' said Susie, 'but I am not agreeable to being banished again, specially not to Shoreditch. It's not what you said.'

'I don't find that word harmonious, Susie. Now why should I want to banish you?'

132

'Yes,' said Susie sweetly, 'why should you?'

'Perish the thought,' said Sammy. 'You'll be workin' in Camberwell, as promised. I just require you to travel to this office on Friday afternoons, check the worksheets, add up the earnings and make up the wages. I am enquiring into the needful necessity of findin' a strong-minded geezer to manage the place, which includes managing the machinists, which are women of vulgarity, impudence, blasphemy and shockin' language into the bargain. Mind, I don't mean they don't do first-class cuttin' and stitching.'

'Mister Sammy, regarding the filing systems and the other work you spoke of,' said Susie, 'kindly inform me why a manager can't do these things himself. I mean, he's goin' to be able to read and write, isn't he? He won't want me comin' in on Fridays to do the wages, which he could do himself if he could add up, which a decent manager ought to, besides lookin' after the machinists and their machines.'

'Ah,' said Sammy thoughtfully. 'Susie, your wordage is like you've been highly educated, and has had the desirable effect of givin' me a helpful idea concerning one of my close relatives. Good on yer, Susie love, you've come on a rare treat—' He coughed to clear his throat. Susie smiled. 'Yes, well, it's something to think about. Meanwhile, you'd better see what the work-shop's all about.'

'Yes, I'd like to,' said Susie. He took her through. The place was very basic with its bare walls and its lack of all but the practical essentials. Susie saw Ma Turner at work with a broom, and long benches running from end to end. At the benches sat the seamstresses, women of all ages from twenty to fifty. Each had her sewing-machine and each was working away. They were all on piece-work. Shawls or scarves covered heads to keep hair out of the way, a few making do with a multitude of hairpins. They all looked thin and half-starved to Susie. There were at least forty of them, some rising above their depressing conditions to keep up a constant flow of chatter and gossip without ever once stopping their work. The windows were filthy enough to kill the better part of daylight, and the floor, littered with scraps of material, was of cold stone. A coal-burning stove in the middle of the workshop offered only a miserable amount of heat. But the machines hummed, whined and clattered, thin fingers pushing feverishly.

At the entrance of Sammy and Susie, several of the women actually stopped work to stare at Susie. Susie, a South London cockney girl in the process of bettering herself, looked to the seamstresses as if she was very much removed from the world of the working-class.

' 'Ello again, Mister Adams, Yer Lordship, 'oo's 'Er Ladyship?' asked one woman.

And two women sang, ' *'Ello, 'ello, who's yer lady friend, who's the little girlie by yer side? I've seen you, with a girl or two, oh, oh, oh, I am surprised at you. 'Ello, 'ello, what's yer little game, don't yer think—*'

'Shut up!' Sammy raised his voice. 'You're all sacked, the lot of you.'

All machines stopped and there was a shocked silence until the first woman spoke again.

'Gawd 'elp us, what for?'

'For impudence and downright disrespect,' said Sammy, given to establishing firm control of employees.

'Oh, yer can't do it, what about our 'ungry kids?'

'We've all got problems,' said Sammy.

'Oh, yer bleedin' 'angman,' gasped the woman.

Susie, shocked herself by Sammy's cruelty, saw a little grin flicker on his face.

'All right, Gertie, all right,' he said, 'kindly spare me a carry-on, it's your lucky day, you're all reinstated. But mind yer manners in future, and mind them in partic'lar when the Lord Mayor's daughter happens to be with me. Kindly accord her due respect.'

Every seamstress breathed with relief, every eye stared at Susie. Susie smiled.

'Oh, pleased to meet yer, me lady,' said a young woman, pale with anaemia.

' 'Owjerdo, madam,' said the woman called Gertie, thirty-five and the senior seamstress. 'It's a pleasure yer come among us.'

'Would yer give me regards to yer dad, 'Is Lordship?' offered a venturesome seamstress.

'Never mind all that,' said Sammy. 'Kindly listen. I'm requiring instructional information which will help me concernin' your welfare.' Mouths dropped open and gaped with incomprehension. 'Inform me first, Gertie, if you get breakdowns.'

'On these 'ere machines what come out of the Ark?' enquired Gertie, thin but resilient. 'Course we get breakdowns.'

'Have you got spare machines?' asked Sammy.

'Three,' said Gertie, 'and it's a sod—'

'Hold up,' said Sammy, son of Chinese Lady, a woman who thought it desecrating for bad language to sit on the tongue of a female, 'Miss Brown heard that.'

'Oh, beggin' yer pardon, Yer Ladyship, I'm sure,' said Gertie, 'but breakdowns is bleedin' inconvenient, to put it more acceptable, like.'

'Oh, I've known bleedin' inconveniences myself,' said Susie sweetly.

'Yer got a kind 'eart,' said Gertie, 'but it's crool, I tell yer, Mister Adams. With the breakdowns we get, we could do with a dozen spare machines. No machine, no work, yer know. No work, no pay.'

'Who repairs the machines that break down?' asked Sammy.

'Some geezer Mister Morris calls in, only Mister Morris ain't 'ere no more. Them three spare machines is being used now. I tell yer, Mister Adams, the 'ole bleedin' lot of machines needs doin' up proper, or yer'll lose money and so will we.'

'I don't like losin' money,' said Sammy frankly, 'it's unhealthy.'

'Starvation don't do our kids much good, neither,' said Gertie. 'Mister Adams, we're losin' bread money now.'

'I am takin' due note of that,' said Sammy, 'and will make it up to yer accordin'. This repairing gent, how long does he take to get here when he's required?'

'Now and again in a couple of hours,' said Gertie, 'but mostly 'e arrives termorrer.'

'I got you,' said Sammy. 'What about the cutting machines?' There were three cutting machines against a side wall.

'They don't give no trouble,' said Gertie.

'Right,' said Sammy. 'Now, kindly listen some more. I know what yer work's like. This fact'ry's been supplying my shops for five years, and yer stitching's earned you me heartfelt admiration. I do also know what yer average turnover is, highly satisfying. I'll make a deal with you. I'll see yer machines are kept in running order day in, day out, and you see you give me a turnover consistent with highly satisfying, and you'll all get a weekly bonus of half a crown. I can't say fairer—'

'Whadjer mean?' asked a woman suspiciously. 'What's a bonus?'

'It's extra,' said Sammy. 'It comes on top of your piece-work earnings and is related to being good girls and conscientiously efficient.'

'Extra?'

'What's 'e saying?'

'I dunno, it sounds Chinese to me.'

'Artful, they are, them Chinese.'

136

The seamstresses gabbled to each other.

Gertie said, 'Whadjer mean, bonus extra, Mister Adams? I ain't never 'eard of that round 'ere.'

'Well,' said Sammy patiently, 'if you earn ten bob for your week's piece-work, which represents a highly satisfact'ry endeavour, you'll get an extra half a crown, makin' twelve and sixpence in all.'

The shabby women of the sweatshop stared at him. Six full days a week they worked, from eight in the morning until six in the evening, and by dint of flying fingers and pedalling feet they managed to take home a wage of ten bob or so. An extra half a crown for no more work astonished them.

'Yer jokin', Mister Adams,' said Gertie.

'I never joke at business and suchlike,' said Sammy. He was not being philanthropic. He was always shrewd and calculating about what his employees and their efficiency meant to him. He knew how skilled these Shoreditch women were, and how important to the trade was first-class stitching. Just as important was the necessity of getting the garments into his shops at low production costs. There was also the question of reliability in respect of delivery, something Morris had fallen down on from time to time. Sammy knew he could get reliability from employees who had something extra to look forward to each week, and whose machines weren't always breaking down. Some sweatshops achieved reliability and low production costs merely by cracking the whip and keeping seamstresses in constant fear of losing their jobs. For all his obsessive need to make his fortune, Sammy had never operated in this way. He did not like keeping employees on the breadline. He did not shower gold on any of them, but he did pay them fair wages, and in return he expected and received a fair effort. He had his opinions about sweated labour. He kept them to himself, but he was

137

well aware these seamstresses were glad of any kind of job. He had grown up in Walworth, where conditions might have been a little better than they were in the East End, but where a job was still something to hang on to, however poor the pay. Handing out a little extra to Gertie and her thin-bodied colleagues would guarantee a mite more happiness and a more willing effort in respect of urgent orders. It might even make some of them smile a bit. They could joke, they could joke in caustic fashion, and they could fling vulgarities that would arouse screeching laughter, but they rarely smiled in the way of women who were enjoying their work. The work pressurised them, their fingers raced and their teeth grated with effort. In the summer they sweated and their hungry faces grew wet and shiny. Sammy often wondered what Chinese Lady would say if she knew how Adams Enterprises had been profiting indirectly from sweated labour and was now going to profit directly from same. Once she knew the factory was his, she was quite likely to take a tram across the river and see it for herself. If conditions for the women were as they were now, she would dismantle him piece by piece. He'd better do something about brightening it up and adding an amenity or two. All the women had now was a sink and a cold water tap, and a gas ring for boiling water for tea during their brief midday break. Their lav was a lean-to outside.

They were still staring at him. Susie had a little smile on her face.

'Mister Adams, yer really means it?' said Gertie. 'We're goin' to get an extra two an' six a week pervidin' we does yer proud with our rate?'

'You got my word,' he said, and Susie noted he said nothing about how it could ruin him. 'But listen, keep it to yourselves. If you don't, if you boot it about like a football and everyone gets to know, I'll likely be hacked to a fatal death by the geezers who run other fact'ries. I wouldn't like that, it'll hurt considerable. I don't mind yer feeling gratified, but I don't want any of you advertisin' it. I might be consequentially forced to cancel it. You all got that?'

'We got yer, Mister Adams,' said Gertie.

'Yer a gent,' said a young woman, 'and we'll do yer proud, yer won't have no fact'ry turnin' out better stuff than we will.'

'You get the orders, Mister Adams, you keep us goin' and we'll keep yer 'appy.'

'Bonuses start this week,' said Sammy, 'you'll get 'em with your Friday wages. Furthermore and so on, I'm puttin' in a manager in place of Mr Morris, presently defunct in a manner of speakin'. He'll treat yer right, he'll cop yer if yer don't treat him right, and he'll keep all yer machines in first-class order. You got a Charley Harry to do odd jobs for you, which is namely Daft Dick, I'm told, and you got Ma Turner who's goin' to keep yer clean and tidy. I don't like seeing an untidy workshop, it don't reflect well on me business, nor on me. Also, tea and biscuits will be provided morning and afternoon at my expense. I am beknown for suchlike Christian gestures, something highly appreciated by the Lord Mayor's daughter, this young lady here, who is Miss Susie Brown and my personal assistant.'

Susie did not know how she kept her face straight. She only knew what she had always known, that Sammy had his own way of talking to people. He now had these hard-working seamstresses in the palm of his hand, and he would get his pound of flesh without using a knife. It was ridiculous, of course, that he thought it a weakness to care for someone.

'Mister Adams,' said Gertie, 'you treatin' us to tea mornin' and afternoon, and with free biscuits too? You doin' that, Mister Adams?'

'Just see you don't diddle me when you hand the expense chits to the manager,' said Sammy. 'You diddle me and you'll all be on dry bread and cold water at your own expense.'

'We ain't goin' to diddle yer,' said Gertie, an efficient chargehand. 'When's the manager comin'?'

'Next Monday, probably.'

' 'E ain't a growler, is 'e?'

'He's recommendable as a gentlemanly geezer who'll keep your machines in order and treat you with love and kindness,' said Sammy.

' 'Ere, Glad'll like that,' said Gertie, 'she don't get much lovin', do yer, Glad?'

'Me old man's got a chronic back,' said Gladys.

'All right,' said Sammy, 'you can all get on with your work.'

They got on with it. Outside in the factory yard, smoke rose from a burning stack of piled rubbish. Ma Turner was still creating other piles with her broom.

'Mister Adams,' said Gertie, 'if the managin' gent ain't goin' to be 'ere till Monday, could I speak to yer about what orders we're d'reckly finishing and when yer gettin' Carter Paterson to call?'

'Mister Adams!' Ma bawled from the door leading to the office. 'Yer got a lady askin' to see someone.'

'Susie, would yer kindly see who she is?' said Sammy. 'If she wants a job, take her name and address.'

'Very good, Mister Adams,' said Susie. She found a woman in the office. She was dark, close to thirty, and with the hungry face and eyes common among many people in the East End. Her hat and coat were cheap, but she wore them with style, and her cracked shoes still shod her feet neatly. Under her arm she carried a large, cardboard-backed folio. 'Good morning,' said Susie, 'can I help you?'

'Good morning,' said the woman, 'is Mr Morris around?'

'Well, no,' said Susie, 'he's sold the business to Adams Enterprises Ltd.'

'Never heard of 'em. Who are they?'

'The Adams fam'ly, prominent in South London,' said Susie. 'The managin' director's Mister Sammy Adams.'

'Don't know him,' said the woman. 'Still, it's not my week. Wasn't last week, either. My life, I could drop dead and there'd still be a million people I'd never met. What's he like, this managing director?'

'Well, he's not started to eat people yet,' said Susie.

'Sounds promising. D'you think I could see him?'

'What about, a job?' asked Susie.

'Fashions.'

'Pardon?'

'All right, I know this isn't a fashion house, but you've got outlets for your own designs, I suppose.'

'I don't know Mister Adams has ever had his own designs,' said Susie.

'Well, I'm a designer.' The woman smiled a little bleakly. 'Well, I think I am, only most don't. Most of the London houses, I mean, and most of the manufacturers. Trouble is, we're ten a penny, and you've got to be a French poof to stand any real chance. If you're not, if you're just another female amateur, all you can do is hope and pray. I fall back on being a dressmaker, running up party frocks for small girls. About one a month, which hardly pays the rent. Is this Adams gent around?'

'He's busy at the moment,' said Susie. 'I'm his personal assistant.'

'Are you influential? I mean, would you like to see my sketches and ideas, and recommend me to him if they take your fancy? Is he adventurous, not afraid of taking chances? I think I'd have found Reuben Morris a bit

141

conservative, but I thought I'd come and have a go at him, since I believe he has the potential with forty and more machinists here. Does your Mister Adams have panache?'

Susie had to guess what panache meant. She guessed that somehow it fitted Sammy. She said, 'Show me.' She was intrigued by being face to face with a fashion designer, even if she wasn't a French poof.

'I'm Lilian Hyams,' said the woman, and Susie placed her among Mr Greenberg's warmhearted fraternity. Times must be exceptionally hard if the Jewish rag trade men were closing ranks against their own. Or perhaps they discouraged enterprise in a Jewish woman.

'Don't the rag trade just copy French designs?' she asked, as Lilian Hyams placed her portfolio on the desk.

'Under licence, of course, or in a naughty way,' said Lilian, and opened the portfolio. Susie studied sketches in water colours as each page was turned, thinking the woman an artist as well as a designer. She studied some sketches at length, the water colours laid on over lightly pencilled outlines. Spring coats and summer coats alternated with summer dresses. Susie thought them very appealing, very stylish. Lilian gave a little commentary on each design. Susie noted neatly written details of materials. Silk, of course, and marocain, printed cottons, shantung and crêpe de Chine. Some of the colours were brilliant. A few Paris designers had been inspired by the magnificent colourfulness of the Tutankhamen discoveries. Susie saw that Lilian had used rich orange reds and golden yellows in some sketches.

Then a purple red dress leapt to her eye. Purple red? And terribly short? The hemline was two inches above the knees. And long strings of beads reached almost to the waist. Lilian waited for a comment.

'Well,' breathed Susie. To the right of the design,

hanging on the white of the drawing paper, were two matching purple garters, neatly sketched.

'Decorative accessories, to be seen if desired,' said Lilian.

'It's so short,' said Susie.

'Wait till the New Year fashion shows in Paris,' said Lilian. 'It's my guess they've decided to aim for the limit. This length.'

'Someone's told you that?' asked Susie.

'I should be so lucky. No, it's my own feelings. Should I gamble on my own feelings if I had the capital? I would. Would your boss?'

Fashions were already short, as short as most people thought they would go. Flappers among the Bright Young Things never wore anything longer than two inches below the knees. Susie's own hemlines were short. But two inches above the knees? That was blush-making.

'Crikey,' she said, the cockney surfacing, 'd'yer think Paris really will go the limit like that?'

'Something like that will be out by the spring,' said Lilian, 'I'd bet ten quid on it if I had ten quid. You're not sure yourself, are you? But at least you're more interested than anyone else I've shown it to. I've had horse laughs spilled over that design. But if your boss would risk it and put money into it, he could beat the Paris fashion houses themselves into the shops over here, he could be the first in the shops with this design and similar ones, and that would be at just the right time, after the Paris shows have all the flappers jumping about in excitement over the new lengths. That's the market to aim for, you know, the flappers' market. And they don't buy new fashions just one at a time. You didn't say, is your boss conservative, is he cautious?'

'No, he's not,' said Susie, and Lilian showed her sketches of similarly short designs. Beads and bangles were prominent. Colours were radiant. 'You sure about the red purple? You're using it a lot,' said Susie.

'Outrageous, d'you think?' said Lilian. 'Flappers like the outrageous. They'll like the garters. They'll go with the Charleston. That's going to be all the rage in the New Year. What's your name?'

'Susie Brown.'

'Well, Susie Brown, you're the first personal assistant to a boss who's taken the time to look all through my portfolio. D'you think I could now see the boss himself? Is he fat, does he chew cigars, is he rude, middle-aged and bald, would a woman dress designer make him laugh his head off? Adams, you said? Could this be a Gentile firm now?'

'You don't mind, do you?' asked Susie, who had taken to the woman.

'I'll put up a fight,' said Lilian, and Sammy came in then, having discussed with the astonished Gertie how to brighten up the workshop and make things a bit more comfortable for the machinists.

'Mister Adams,' said Susie, 'I'm pleased to present to you someone who could be our own French fashion designer. Madame Lilian Dupont.'

'Come again?' said Sammy, and Lilian cast a smiling glance at Susie in appreciation of her quick turn of thought. Then she took a long look at Sammy. Her eyes opened wide. Tall, lean, and with a determined mouth and direct blue eyes, he was far from what she had imagined. He was even young. No more than twenty-four, surely. Young. Alive. Acute interest dawned and hope quickened. She was down on her uppers, she was broke and hungry. But Susie had given her the hope, and the sight of this young man fanned it. Perhaps with his air of alertness, he also had nerve and imagination. He had to have sufficient of those qualities if he consented to gamble on her instincts and intuition.

Susie explained. Sammy listened. He sat down at the desk and went through the portfolio, Lilian providing a commentary. Arriving at the first example of audacity, the purple red design, he showed a little smile and his eyes glinted. He looked up at Lilian.

'You're who?' he asked.

'Madame Lilian Dupont,' said Susie.

'I think you're havin' me on, Miss Brown,' said Sammy.

Lilian gave him her correct name and added, 'I think your personal assistant thought a French monicker might help.'

'Susie's a bright girl,' said Sammy, 'it wouldn't surprise me if she married one of those Russian Grand Dukes that's floatin' about in Paris, I hear.'

'Don't let's have any comical stuff, Mister Adams,' said Susie.

'Kindly continue,' said Sammy to Lilian, and Lilian talked about the January fashion shows in Paris, about the feelings she had concerning hemlines, colours and accessories, and about stealing a march on the French designers. She'd been to London fashion houses, she said, and to manufacturers, without arousing a glimmer of interest. That, she said, was because she wasn't a French poof. One fashion house had advised her to go to Paris and study the art of true fashion. Imagine English fashion houses having no faith in native designers except in respect of tweeds. Would Mister Adams care to comment on her portfolio? Did any of her designs interest him?

'Considerable,' said Sammy, slowly leafing through more pages.

'Considerable?'

'The previous gent in ownership of this business left behind a multitude of unusable articles, all of which my personal assistant referred to as demolishable junk,'

145

said Sammy, 'and which included catalogues of designs
dating back, in my opinion, to the time when fig leaves
were popular. These selfsame catalogues are presently
goin' up in smoke, with all the other articles ancient
to behold, much to the pleasure of Miss Susie Brown.
There's some designs, fairly reasonable, still in our
workshop and coincidin' with orders my staff of seamstresses is workin' on. I was about to make known to Miss
Brown the needful necessity of acquiring up-to-date
designs from sources common to the trade, which task I
am sure she would have performed with considerable
flair and taste, being, as you can see, a young female
woman of style and remarkability.' Sammy paused.
Lilian was looking mesmerised, and Susie hardly knew
how to contain herself. 'However, Madame Dupont,
who needs designs from common sources when here
in front of me admiring mince pies is an exclusive
collection?'

'Mister Adams?' said Lilian, who had not met many
like Sammy.

'I am speakin' of exclusive, I trust, if we take you on?'
enquired Sammy.

'I should come to you and offer you designs not exclusive to you?' said Lilian.

'It's not what I'd like,' said Sammy.

'It's not what I'd do,' said Lilian. 'Mister Adams, am I
reading you right? Are you actually offering to take me
on as your designer?'

'I've seen designs, all sorts,' said Sammy. 'I don't recollect seeing any like these, which I would specifically class
as superior. Adams Enterprises, however, have shops in
Camberwell, Brixton, Peckham and Kennington.'

'I could adapt most designs to cheaper materials,' said
Lilian, 'but with your own label you could aim to open
up an outlet for dearer garments in West End shops and
stores, couldn't you?'

146

'That thought is just crossin' my mind,' said Sammy, 'but I don't know about stealing a march on the French.'

'In respect of my shorter lengths?' said Lilian. 'There wouldn't be any point in trying to if you didn't believe in my ideas. A half-hearted commitment wouldn't work.'

'I don't go in for being half-hearted,' said Sammy, and made another study of the purple red creation. Susie knew he was taken with the portfolio and intrigued by Lilian's audacity. Looking up at the woman, he noted a wedding ring. 'You're married?' he said.

'I was,' said Lilian. 'My husband Jacob was killed in the war. On the Somme.'

'I'm sorry,' said Sammy, and thought about Boots, blinded on the Somme. The Somme had been horrendous. He looked at the design again, then at Susie, still in her hat and coat. The coat was three inches below her knees. Her shapely legs shone in rayon stockings. 'Susie—'

'Oh, no you don't,' said Susie.

'Don't what?'

'I'm not doing any leg show,' said Susie.

'Susie's religious,' said Sammy to Lilian, and Lilian smiled. 'I was merely thinking, Miss Brown, that if you removed your coat I could use my imagination concerning this partic'lar design.'

'That's all you could use,' said Lilian, 'until you had a sample made up. I could do that, if you're interested, and you should be interested in anticipating the French.'

'Well, Lily—'

'It's Lilian.'

'Yes, Hyams you said. Fine old fam'ly name, that, but I think for business reasons I'd prefer Dupont,

147

specially as it was offered up by Susie. Well, Lily, I tell you what, you make up a sample here. Today, if you don't happen to be otherwise engaged. Can you use a cutting machine?'

'Of course,' said Lilian, 'and a sewing-machine.'

'And have you got a pattern?'

'The patterns of all those designs are in the back of the portfolio.'

'I like a self-organised woman,' said Sammy. 'Select a material from our stocks. When you've done the cutting – wait, have you got a sewing-machine at home?'

'Yes,' said Lilian, impressed by the decisive nature of this personable young businessman.

'Then make the sample up there,' said Sammy. 'We don't want too many people knowing you've got certain ideas about the 1926 hemlines. This trade is thick with dubious geezers.'

'Mister Adams, you weren't born yesterday, and that's a fact,' said Lilian. 'Shall I make the sample up to Susie's size?'

'On behalf of my personal assistant,' said Sammy, 'I accept that convenient suggestion.'

'Mister Adams,' said Susie, 'I hope that don't mean I'm goin' to be turned into a clothes horse.'

'My ideas for your future don't include makin' a mannequin of you,' said Sammy, dropping his guard in another weak moment because Susie looked like a picture postcard in her red coat and navy blue cloche hat. He coughed. Susie felt a little spasm of delight. He just couldn't meet her eyes, he couldn't. 'Yes, well, if you could temp'rarily oblige so that we could see what the sample looks like on you, I'd be gratified.'

'Oh, lor',' said Susie, 'all those inches above the knee?'

'Kind of you, Miss Brown,' said Sammy, and gave Lilian another look. She seemed very happy about things, but he noted her aquiline features and her hollow eyes, the all-too-common signs of a person down on her luck. She was fighting for survival, like too many others in the crowded jungle of the East End. And it was a harder fight for a woman. 'It occurs to me that before you select a material and cut it to pattern, Lily, we ought to consider some reviving refreshment. I'll take you both round the corner to Joe's eatin' place, and we'll try for some hot tea and a fried egg sandwich.'

'But it's nowhere near dinnertime yet,' said Susie.

'It's reviving time,' said Sammy. Lilian was perceptibly tempted by the thought of food. 'Afterwards, we'll make some detailed notes concerning how the firm is goin' to adjust to this new prospect, Susie, leaving Lily to go off home with her material.'

'Mister Adams,' said Lilian, 'I think I'm going to like working for you.'

'If I like what you turn out from that pattern,' said Sammy, 'I'll take you on definite and permanent. Our own label. Lily Dupont of Paris. How does that strike you?'

'It strikes me I'll love it,' said Lilian.

'Good. We'll meet you here tomorrow morning.' Sammy, coming to his feet, eyed her again. Jewish, of course. Well, he liked the fraternity. 'You don't mind I'm a Gentile?'

'I don't mind if you're Goliath the Philistine, you take me on permanently and pay me a fair salary, and you won't see me running off if Solly Bergmann makes me an offer. I like it that you liked my collection, I like it that you and Susie both took the time and trouble to consider it. Mister Adams, I also like you, both of you. I hope you'll both like me.'

Susie smiled. Sammy had made another Jewish friend, and had taken another step on his way up, she was sure.

CHAPTER TWELVE

The school playground of St Luke's was ringing with
the noise of boys and girls. Rosie and Annabelle were
seated on a bench eating their dinnertime sandwiches.
It was too far for them to go home for a meal, as a
number of other pupils did. Twelve-year-old Alfred
Grimes approached, a grin on his face.

'Give us a bite, Rosie,' he said.

'I'll save you the crusts,' said Rosie.

'Don't want yer crusts,' said Grimes, 'give us a kiss
instead.' He plonked himself down next to Rosie, slipped an arm around her waist and tried for a kiss. Rosie
stuffed her half-eaten sandwich into his mouth. At the
same time fingers took hold of his right ear. He gurgled
a yell around the sandwich. He lifted his head and
looked up into the face of Miss Simms.

'Depart,' said Polly, 'or I'll wallop you.'

He disgorged the sandwich into his hand.

'Me?' he said. That was the standard response of all
boys affecting to suffer the injury of being misjudged.
'Me, Miss Simms?'

'You,' said Polly. 'Six of the best.'

'Blow me,' said Grimes, 'it don't bear finking of
what can be done to yer when yer ain't done anyfink
yerself.'

'Dear me, oh dear dear me,' said Polly, 'go and write
out the word think fifty times, and then you and I will

150

go through its correct pronunciation fifty times immediately after classes. Go now, go, go, go.'

'Stone the bleedin' crows,' muttered Grimes, as he went on his way, 'yer try an' treat a girl to a decent kiss and this is what yer get. I ain't 'anding out none to that Rosie no more.'

Polly, who would have protected Rosie with her life, said to her, 'As soon as you and Annabelle have finished your sandwiches, will you both come into the hall for some rehearsal?' The school was to perform a Nativity play at Christmas, the play written by Polly herself. Annabelle was in the role of Mary, and Rosie was playing the innkeeper's wife.

'Yes, Miss Simms,' said Rosie. An upright-looking woman entered through the school gates.

'Oh, there's Granny Lady,' cried Annabelle.

'Miss Simms, it's our grandmother,' said Rosie, and both girls got up and ran to meet Chinese Lady, dressed in a brown coat and brown hat. She had stopped wearing black hats after her marriage to Mr Finch, thinking it only right and proper that respect for her late husband shouldn't be inflicted on her new husband.

'There you are, the pair of you,' she said, and gave each girl a pat.

'Nana, we're having our sandwiches,' said Rosie. 'Have you come to see us about something?'

Polly came up.

'I was just passin',' said Chinese Lady.

'Good morning,' said Polly. She had never met Boots's mother, but had heard much about her. She thought her pleasant-looking, but with a very firm mouth that seemed to suggest a no-nonsense approach to her family and to life. 'May I help you?'

'I was just passin',' said Chinese Lady again, shopping-bag with her. 'I thought I'd look in. I'm Mrs Finch, these are my granddaughters.'

'I'm Miss Simms,' said Polly, 'and happy to meet you, Mrs Finch.'

'It's nice to see what my granddaughters' school looks like. Goodness, what a racket them children are kickin' up.'

'We can escape that,' said Polly. 'I can take you round the hall and classrooms, if you'd like to see them. I'm having a little rehearsal of our Nativity play in ten minutes, but there's time to show you round.'

'Very kind,' said Chinese Lady. She gave Rosie and Annabelle another pat each, and went into the school with Polly. 'I hear you're goin' to give Rosie special lessons.'

'Yes.' Polly stopped at the door to the hall. 'She's such a talented girl.'

'Her father said it's all about a scholarship.'

'Yes, I did speak to Mr Adams about it,' said Polly.

'He's my only oldest son,' said Chinese Lady, examining a child's drawing pinned to a wall.

'Your only – ?'

'My oldest. Not that you'd think it sometimes.' Chinese Lady turned from the drawing and accompanied Polly into the assembly hall. The subdued light of the misty day seemed to linger outside the windows, as if reluctant to enter. The hall appeared to be stoically resigned to winter. 'Just like St John's,' murmured Chinese Lady.

'St John's?' enquired Polly.

'The Walworth school my children went to.'

'I see.' Polly, not realising she was under scrutiny, said cheerfully, 'Why wouldn't I sometimes think Mr Adams wasn't your oldest son?'

'He don't always look serious enough at life, and when he was younger, well, he had all the airy-fairy answers to everything you could think of.'

'Oh, he's still like that,' said Polly with the unguarded

frankness of a woman responsive to men of that kind. Clear almond eyes gave her a direct look.

'You've met him, of course,' said Chinese Lady.

'A few times,' said Polly, suddenly cautious.

Chinese Lady, looking around the hall, thought well, I can't say she's not polite and nice-speaking. She sounds almost like she's upper-class. But there's a minx trying to get out somewhere, and it's halfway showing in that short skirt of hers. I just don't know what sociability's coming to, girls and young women flaunting their legs outrageous. I'll never hold with lady teachers flaunting theirs, nor married women. There's Emily going off to work each morning in skirts and dresses nearly up to her knees. And that Sammy selling them in his shops to innocent young working girls. Well, they can't go any higher, it just wouldn't be decent, but I'd have something to say to Sammy if they did.

'Still, his wife takes things more serious, thank goodness,' she said.

'Mrs Adams? Yes, I've met her too, of course,' said Polly, who had been astounded at what she considered the plainness of Boots's wife, even if she did have enviable auburn hair. 'She's serious about everything?'

'Some things,' said Chinese Lady. 'Like her home and her marriage. Well, it's a nice large hall, and I'd best be going now, I'm partakin' with my daughter.'

'Wouldn't you like to see the classrooms?' asked Polly.

'Not now, Miss Simms, thank you, I've got to be at my daughter's by one. It's nice you're being a help to Rosie.'

When she had gone, Polly wondered why she had come at all.

People were pushing a bit in the East Street market in Walworth. It was often swelled by an influx of workers using their dinnertime break to look for bargains. Tommy, in charge of Sammy's glass and china stall,

153

was by himself for the moment. His assistant, Mrs Walker, was giving her feet a rest in Toni's refreshment shop, while taking in a cup of tea and a sandwich. Sammy and Susie appeared at the stall.

'How's business?' asked Sammy.

'What can I show you, guv'nor?' asked Tommy. 'Tea service? Or some other fashionable weddin' present?'

Sammy quivered.

'Leave off,' he said.

Tommy simulated a peer of recognition.

'Oh, it's you,' he said. 'Ain't seen you down here for years. Couldn't think who you were for a moment. Hello, Susie, recognise you anytime, anywhere. Peachy, you are.'

'I like you too,' smiled Susie.

'Real treat to me optic nerves,' said Tommy. 'What's me young brother doing in this strange spot?'

'He's come to see you,' said Susie.

'I'm honoured,' said Tommy.

'How's your little girl?' asked Susie.

'Fat,' said Tommy. 'I'm told that means she's well-fed and healthy. I hope it don't mean it's permanent. A girl's a girl. A dumpling's a dumpling.'

'I like dumplings,' said Sammy.

'Yes, you tried to turn me into one when I was workin' on the stall for you,' said Susie.

Ma Earnshaw at her greengrocery stall called to Susie.

'Watcher, Susie me love, 'ardly recognised yer. My, aincher growed? 'Ow is yerself, eh?'

'All the better for seeing yer, Ma,' said Susie in old-fashioned cockney parlance.

'Real young lady, aincher? And that Sammy there, look at 'im, ain't 'e lordly?'

'Now, Ma, don't get fancified,' said Sammy, 'just keep the fog off yer cauliflowers.'

'There's ain't no fog got at my cauliflowers,' said Ma Earnsaw, 'pure lily-white, they are.'

Mrs Walker, arriving back from Toni's, said hello to everyone. Sammy asked her to hold the fort while he and Tommy and Susie partook of some needful refreshment themselves. They began a walk through the market, with Tommy asking if this was some form of reunion.

'Give over,' said Sammy, 'I don't go in for fam'ly cross-talk when I got serious business on me mind. Referring to present business, kindly meet my new private secretary and personal assistant, Miss Susie Brown.'

'Is that a fact?' asked Tommy. 'If so, I'm pleased for yer, Susie.'

'I'm pleased for myself,' said Susie.

'About time he rescued you from the wilds of Brixton,' said Tommy.

'Yes, it's been very trying,' said Susie.

'You take one step at a time,' said Sammy, 'not two. Or you fall over yerself.'

'Yes, Mister Sammy,' said Susie, and Tommy glanced at her as they forged a way through the crowds. He thought she looked stunning. She'd come a long way from her starved, ragamuffin look of five years ago.

'We'll have a talk at Toni's,' said Sammy, 'and a small amount of refreshments.'

'I'll just eat a cup of tea,' said Susie. 'I was, you recollect, considerably filled up with the reviving refreshments we had in Shoreditch.'

Tommy grinned. Susie had learned to match the verbiage Sammy indulged in at times.

'Now we've got a prolonged afternoon of business in front of us, Susie,' said Sammy, 'callin' at all our shops to talk to the manageresses about the future concernin' our own label, and I don't want you faintin' from lack

155

of nourishment. We'll all have fried eggs and bacon, and you can say grace, if you like, to show we appreciate the blessings of being able to afford what lots of other people can't. That'll make you feel you can tuck in nice and religious.'

Susie smiled. Sammy had always fussed over what he considered was her tendency not to eat enough. He seemed to think she was still a hungry waif with bony knees and skinny ribs. Wait till he arrived at the moment when he would discover she had a lovely body. She was going to marry him, never mind if the thought of taking a wife turned him hoarse with fright at what it would do to his pocket. She just hoped she wouldn't have to do the proposing herself.

It was after one and there was only one spare table at Toni's. Sammy ordered at the counter, then they all sat down. Sammy at once addressed Tommy briskly.

'It's time you came off the stall, Tommy,' he said, 'it's time you had a manager's job. It don't look good, me with a brother still running a stall, and we got to re-arrange you and stop you talkin' about gettin' a job outside the firm. That don't look good, either. Now, how would you like to manage the garment fact'ry we've lately acquired? Managing includes makin' use of your engineering talents, seeing there's nearly fifty sewing-machines of various intricacy which require overhauling and keepin' in permanent running order, which they ain't been up to now.'

'That's not engineering,' said Tommy, but his eyes gleamed. Any kind of machine was interesting to him. He liked to know how any machine worked, how to dismantle it and put it together again. However, he added, 'And it don't hardly sound like a manager's job.'

'But it is, Tommy,' said Susie earnestly, 'you'll be in charge of everything.'

'Right,' said Sammy. 'You'll be in charge of all

machines, all the machinists and the office. You've got a tidy mind, you can read and write and add up, and you keep things in good order. Further, you won't have to work Saturday afternoons or Sunday mornings any more, which is going to please Vi considerable. It's my opinion that a tidy fact'ry's a more efficient one, as well as more of a credit to Adams Enterprises. Limited. Also further, you'll have desirable company in the shape of a French lady, our fashion designer.'

'Now, Mister Sammy,' chided Susie.

'All right, so she ain't precisely French, except we're calling her Madame Dupont,' said Sammy. 'I'll get a temp'rary to help Mrs Walker on the stall tomorrow so's you can come to Shoreditch with me and Susie and take a look at things. It's my pleasure to inform you that Miss Brown gave me the idea that pointed me at you, which is the sort of help I require from me personal assistant, and for which I duly credit her. Well, what d'you say, Tommy?'

'You talk a lot, but I like most of it,' said Tommy, 'and Vi's a consideration, as you mentioned.'

'I appreciate same,' said Sammy, 'even if the opinions of female women don't always make good business sense. Present company excepted, of course,' he added hastily.

'You said that just in time,' murmured Susie. Her foot touched his under the table. Sammy quivered and sat up straight. Susie smiled.

'Eggs-a bacon! Who's-a for eggs-a bacon?' Toni called from the counter.

Tommy and Sammy got up to fetch the plates, with knives and forks. Susie accepted hers, after all, because the aroma was irresistible, and because she had a lovely feeling Sammy was in a corner and she had put him there.

She kept looking at him while he enlarged on things

157

with Tommy. She liked his face very much, especially his firm mouth and his frank blue eyes, which always looked directly at people, even if they did shift about to avoid looking at her. She knew why he did that. He was afraid of loving her, he was afraid that loving her would interfere with his business career. How silly he was not to know that as his wife she would give him all the support he needed.

Tommy was saying, 'You won't mind if I ask about a manager's salary?'

'You're expected to ask,' said Sammy, 'that's good business sense.' He put his knife down and fished a slip of paper from his pocket. He handed it to Tommy. Tommy examined it. Sammy was offering him three pounds a week, plus an extra month's salary at Christmas. Tommy knew Vi would like to see him in a better job, and that Aunt Victoria would certainly like to see him off the stall.

'What prospects, Sammy?' he asked.

'Well, I'll tell yer, old cock,' said Sammy. 'Unlimited. We're going to market ladies' garments for our usual kind of trade and West End trade, all garments with our own label. I'm satisfied, and so is Susie, that in Madame Dupont we have acquired a fashion designer of remarkable forethinking.'

'Don't hand me left-over marmalade,' said Tommy. 'I may be dead ignorant about fashion, but I'm not mug enough to believe a notable fashion designer is goin' to work for any manufacturer who's never been heard of, specially not heard of in the West End. Come on, who is she?'

'I'll grant yer she ain't yet acquired notability,' said Sammy, 'but she will with us.'

'She's actually Mrs Lilian Hyams of Shoreditch,' said Susie.

'Battersea, actually,' said Sammy. 'She wrote her

partic'lars down for me.' Finishing his food, he called for a pot of tea for three. Toni called back.

'Pot? What-a you ask for? A pot, Mister Adams? Is-a a hotel I got here?'

'All right, three cups of tea,' said Sammy. 'Fresh.'

'What-a you doing, Mister Adams?' Toni waved his arms about in Italian fashion. 'First you ask for what-a I don't do, now you insult me. You hear that, Maria?'

Costermongers grinned, Toni's plump wife Maria smiled, shrugged, poured out three cups of tea from a large enamel teapot, and took them to Sammy's table. Sammy gave her bottom a pat, and Maria, giggling, returned to safety behind her counter. Susie gave Sammy a cool look.

'I don't think it becomes the managing director of Adams Enterprises to do things like that,' she said.

'I didn't do anything,' said Sammy. 'Tommy, I have to record it was Miss Brown who came up with a French monicker for our designer.'

'Duly noted,' said Tommy. 'All right, I'll come and take a look at things tomorrow.'

'Tommy, that's lovely, and you'll make a good manager, I know you will,' said Susie, 'and I'm sure Madame Dupont's goin' to be a boon to your fam'ly's future prosperity. Your nice mother'll be so pleased Mister Sammy's recognised your worthiness at last.'

'My what?' said Tommy.

'At last?' said Sammy, looking shocked. 'Kindly understand, Miss Brown, it's been shirts off me back to get where I have got. I have not been in no position to hand out advantageous prospects until now. It is not like handin' out cards at *Beat Yer Neighbour*.'

'No, Mister Sammy, I was only saying, like,' said Susie.

Sammy frowned at her. She smiled. He drank some tea. After they had parted from Tommy and were on their way to the Kennington shop, Sammy asked how she was liking her new position as his assistant.

'Bliss,' said Susie. The bliss came from being with him after two long years in the desert. 'I'm so glad you did what you did do for Tommy.'

'Well, like I said, it don't look good, a brother of mine only running a stall.'

'Can I say something personal?' asked Susie.

'How personal?' asked Sammy cautiously.

'Oh, only that yer lovely, really,' said Susie, 'yer got a real Christian soul inside yer, Mister Sammy.'

'Oh, gawd,' said Sammy.

Susie laughed out loud.

'If it works out all right,' said Tommy at home that evening, 'we can think about givin' your house back to you, Aunt Victoria.'

'Oh, you don't need to think about that yet,' said Aunt Victoria.

'Still, Mum, you want to call the place your own again sometime,' said Vi, who was lovingly happy for Tommy. He was such a good husband, so easy-going, and a pleasure to her whenever they made love. But she had known running the stall had long lost any appeal for him, if it had ever had any real appeal at all.

'You an' Tommy go ahead an' make what plans you want,' said Uncle Tom.

'Now they mustn't rush things,' said Aunt Victoria. 'Tommy having such a respectable job now, he can take a respectable amount of time to find a nice house. We don't want our neighbours thinking we're in unseemly haste to get rid of them. If they took their time, Alice would be grown more. Young parents don't want to move house when a child is only a mite.'

Vi caught Tommy's eye. He winked. They both knew her mother did not want them to move at all.

'We'll take our time, Aunt Victoria,' said Tommy, 'we cert'nly won't go next week. Nor won't we go till we've found just the right place and arranged a mortgage. Vi and me want to buy, like Boots and Ned, we don't want to rent.'

'Sensible,' said Uncle Tom.

'Well, all right,' said Aunt Victoria. 'Tommy, don't you think you should start calling us Mum and Dad?'

'All right, Mum,' said Tommy cheerfully, 'all right, Dad.'

Aunt Victoria looked flustered at that immediate response. Then she smiled. Aunt Victoria, obviously, had come to realise she hadn't lost a daughter, she had gained a son.

CHAPTER THIRTEEN

Susie, with Sammy regarding her as if she had just come out of a Christmas cracker, wasn't sure she was quite decent. Her knees, her legs. Lilian had chosen a dark red crepon, the most suitable material she could find among the factory stocks, and had made it up to near perfection. Waistless, it draped Susie's figure in stylish looseness, its pointed scalloped hem flirting above her knees. Her legs shone in black rayon stockings. Long strings of beads, bought by Lilian from a market, hung low.

'Oh, lor',' breathed Susie, who was certainly sure the effect of the design was not less than audacious, 'I don't know I could go to summer church in this.'

'We should gamble the flappers will?' said Lilian. 'We should. Susie, it looks a dream on you, you have perfect legs for such a style. Mister Adams, say something, even if only throw it away.'

Sammy inspected the short, sleeveless dress with new interest.

'You're lookin',' said Susie.

'Well, I am,' said Sammy, 'and that's a fact.'

'Oh, don't mind me,' said Susie.

'How does it feel on you, the dress?' asked Sammy. 'Short.'

'Kindly oblige me by performing a circle,' said Sammy.

Susie did a slow, self-conscious about-turn.

'Well?' she said.

'Crooked seam,' said Sammy, a perfectionist.

'Oh, no,' wailed Susie. She bent her right knee, lifted her leg and looked over her shoulder at the stocking seam. It was quite straight. She inspected her left stocking. The seam deviated a little. 'But that's got nothing to do with the dress.'

'Just thought I'd mention it,' said Sammy.

'Is that all you're going to say?' asked Lilian.

'I like it,' said Sammy. 'We'd better talk about a campaign, right?'

'Right,' said Lilian.

'Gambling's goin' to cost us.'

'But you know what you're gambling on.'

'Yes, the 1926 look,' said Sammy. 'Let's talk about it. Then I've got to get back to Camberwell, which hasn't seen much of me this week, and where I'm all behind, like the cow's tail. Sit down, Lily. You too, Susie.'

'Not in this dress,' said Susie.

'Susie, legs are going to be the thing in 1926,' smiled Lilian.

'Well, mine aren't goin' to be the thing in here while it's still 1925,' said Susie. 'I'll change. Mister Sammy, would you kindly go away for a little while?'

Sammy went outside. He regarded the drab street, grey in the misty morning. Tommy appeared. He had gone to his stall first, to make sure the temporary help promised by Sammy had arrived, and to talk to her and Mrs Walker about keeping the takings up.

'This is prospective?' he enquired, looking at the entrance to the office and factory and conscious more of a surrounding dinginess than of bright hopes.

'All right, some paint's needed, but you got to look farther than that,' said Sammy. 'I'll take you in as soon as Susie's finished dressin'.'

'Finished what?' Tommy grinned. 'What's she been suffering, a fate worse than death? Chinese Lady'll kill you, Sammy.'

'Kindly grow up,' said Sammy, and took his brother in. Susie was herself again. Tommy was introduced to Lilian, then to the workshop, where the Shoreditch seamstresses eyed him with delight.

'Yer new manager, ladies,' said Sammy, 'Mister Tommy Adams.'

'Well, I ain't never seen a more manly pair of trousers,' said one woman.

'I'm all yours,' said Tommy amiably, eyes already on the sewing-machines.

'No, she's 'ad 'ers,' said Gertie. 'That's Flora, and she 'as 'ers reg'lar every mornin'. It's Glad who don't get none, 'er old man's got a hurt back. Tell 'im, Glad.'

'You 'old 'is trousers, Glad, and I'll mind yer drawers,' said another woman.

'I'll mind me own drawers, if yer don't mind,' shouted Glad.

'Just can't satisfy some women, that yer can't.'

'It's occurrin' to me,' said Sammy in a deep growling voice, 'that yer beginnin' to think yer'll get paid just for being here. Well, yer won't. Any one of yer that doesn't reach her minimum quota will get her pay docked accordin', and will also receive the sack. Yer got that, I hope?'

'Gotcher, Mister Adams,' said Gertie.

In such fashion was Tommy introduced to the atmosphere of the workshop, and it did not take him long to discover that these skilled East End seamstresses, who worked for a pittance, never quite lost hope, any more than the hard-pressed people of Walworth did. There were little differences between the people of the East End and the people of South London, but they all shared the same kind of cockney resilience.

He acquainted himself with the workshop machines. They were all fairly ancient, but every sewing-machine in the world was built to last a lifetime. Three machines here were out of action. He saw at once that as soon as he put them right, he could overhaul every woman's machine in rotation. That was a job to give him pleasure and satisfaction. He discussed with Sammy the office work required in all its aspects. Susie agreed to spend the rest of the week at the factory to help with current mail not yet attended to, and to start a filing system, a petty cash book and a sales ledger.

Sammy and Lilian agreed that various of her designs were to be made up and shown to buyers around the time when the French collections were on display in Paris. That was to impress buyers with the fact that Adams Enterprises were not offering copies of any Paris models, but the exclusive range inspired by their own designer, Lily Dupont. Lilian was high on adrenalin, totally captivated by Sammy's personality, his eccentric euphemisms, his belief in himself and his faith in her. They spent the whole morning in discussion. Susie opened outstanding mail and Tommy used the telephone where answers were needed, Sammy telling him what to say in certain cases. Sammy also saw to it that Tommy made his status known. Tommy obliged.

'This is Mr Adams, manager of Adams Enterprises in Shoreditch, speakin'.' So he opened each phone conversation. When he had finished with all necessary calls, he went back into the workshop to look at the three machines that were out of action, and to see if he could put one to rights for Lilian's use. Which he did. By the afternoon, Lilian was using it, her adrenalin higher. Sammy had given her an advance on her agreed salary; the workshop and its stock of materials were at her disposal, and she was in sheer pleasure at putting some of her own designs together. Not, however, any of the more audacious creations. The machinists would be bound to notice, and however much they were sworn to secrecy, one tongue would inevitably wag.

Gertie did what she rarely did. She left her machine to go to the office. Susie was out, buying books for the office, including a wages book. Sammy was at the desk, writing out an order for materials suggested by Lilian.

'Yer'll pardon me, guv,' said Gertie.

'What'll I pardon you for?' asked Sammy.

'That woman, the one you said's our designer. She's a seamstress?'

'Why you askin'?'

'It ain't right 'er makin' up samples if she ain't.'

Sammy cottoned on.

'She's a seamstress.'

'Worked in a registered fact'ry, I mean?'

'Of course.'

'Yer sure?'

'I'm sure,' said Sammy.

'It ain't fair if she ain't.'

'You've already said that. Don't say it again, Gertie. She's all right, you're all right. Push off now, you got work to do.'

'Well, if you say so, Mister Adams, good enough. I'll pass the word.'

Gertie went back to her machine. She had made her gesture, but Sammy knew the threat of a strike had not been present. None of them could afford to strike, and even if they did, it could easily be broken by simply taking on unemployed seamstresses. But they might have been awkward, they might have come up with sloppy stitching in a crafty way, a way that meant a finger could not be pointed at the guilty. If they were satisfied Mrs Hyams had been one of them in the past, they'd be happy. He had a word with Lilian later. She was able to inform him she had worked as a seamstress from the age of fourteen until she was married. She named three sweatshops. They might have been registered with the Inspector of Factories and they might not. There were any amount of tiny, back-street places in the East End unknown to the Inspectorate. It did not matter. Lilian had worked in sweatshops and that was good enough.

'Glad for you,' said Sammy.

'You're a welcome change as a boss, you are,' smiled Lilian. 'By the way, do you know any big buyers?'

'For West End stores and chain shops? No,' said Sammy frankly.

'We ought to know who they are by name,' said Lilian. 'It'll help if we don't look as if we've just come in from the outside.'

Sammy thought about his contacts. Mr Greenberg came top of his list.

'I'll make enquiries, Lily.'

'My life,' said Lilian, 'you're bouncy, aren't you? You don't mutter and scratch your head.'

'I've heard him mutter considerable,' murmured Susie, who was entering names from a list into the new wages book.

'I don't think I caught that, Miss Brown,' said Sammy.

'I didn't say anything, Mister Adams,' said Susie. 'Well, nothing of importance.'

Lilian smiled. They had an engaging freshness in their relationship, this extraordinary young boss and his attractive, articulate assistant. And there was something else between them. What was it now? Of

167

course. They were in love. Were they keeping it from each other? If so, why?

'Are you married, Mister Adams?'

Sammy looked for a moment as if the question hurt him. He was making notes on a scribbling pad of a hundred and one things he had to do. His pencil stopped moving.

'Pardon?' he said.

'No, he isn't married,' said Susie, neatly inscribing one more name.

'I happen not to have had time to go courtin',' said Sammy.

'It's expensive too,' said Susie.

'What is?' asked Lilian, fascinated.

'Courtin' and gettin' married,' said Susie. 'And it interferes with business.'

'Miss Brown, would you kindly not put uninformed words into my mouth?' said Sammy.

'Oh, dear, so sorry, Mister Adams, do pardon me, I'm sure,' said Susie, tongue in cheek.

'And speakin' of business,' said Sammy, 'could you come up with a few French words, if needful, Madame Dupont?'

'A few,' said Lilian, 'like *oui*, *merci* and montsewer.'

'Not too good,' said Sammy frankly. 'How about English with a French accent?'

'Do you mean Jewish English with a French accent?'

'You got it,' said Sammy. 'That's a winning combination in the higher ranks of the rag trade. Let's hear a sample.'

'Ze pen of my Aunt Fifi is in ze garden wiz ze fairies,' said Lilian.

'Promising,' said Sammy.

Lilian laughed, liking Sammy very much.

'You want I should go to French classes for you?' she asked.

'You do that, Mimi,' he said.

'Mimi I am now?' Lilian laughed again.

'Glad you mentioned it,' said Sammy. 'Mimi Dupont. I regard that highly. More French feeling to it than Lily Dupont.'

'I'm not sure I shouldn't put trousers on and call myself Raymond Dupont,' said Lilian. 'I've mentioned before, haven't I, that French designers are all men?'

'Not my mother's kind of men,' said Sammy, 'and accordingly of small account to me. It shouldn't be too injurious to our manly chests to mount a frontal assault on them and split their ranks wide open.'

'Ours?' said Lilian. 'Mine, Susie's and yours?'

'I was being figurative,' said Sammy. 'You keep your flag flying high, Lily. You've got Adams Enterprises behind you, which includes Miss Brown, whose audacious tongue ain't unbeknown to you.'

'Flattered, I'm sure,' murmured Susie.

'Don't mention it,' said Sammy. 'Lily, it has just occurred to me, we need a trade mark. Could you design one?'

'Eiffel Tower?' suggested Lilian. 'Little deep blue silhouette on a white silk label?'

'Proud of yer,' said Sammy, 'glad we met.'

'It's bliss to me,' said Lilian. 'Must get on now. Ta for the tea.'

Saturday morning. Ned arrived home from his half-day's work just before one. His children greeted him boisterously, Lizzy with a kiss. Lizzy, unlike her mother, was demonstrative. Ned announced that through the good offices of a colleague he had arranged to rent a seaside bungalow for two weeks in August next year. At Selsey in Sussex. The property was on the sea front, overlooking the sandy west beach. There was a long time to go before next year's

169

school holidays arrived, but these seaside places were popular and needed to be booked well in advance.

'All in favour put their hands up,' said Ned.

Lizzy, Annabelle and Bobby put their hands up. Emma, three years old, thought about it. Edward, one year old, was interested only in winding his arms around his father's trousered tin leg.

Emma, having thought, said, 'Will there be donkey rides?'

'Oh, there's donkey rides at every seaside,' said Lizzy.

'A'right,' said Emma, and put her hand up.

'We'll call that unanimous,' said Ned.

'I call it spiffing,' said Annabelle. 'A seaside bungalow all to ourselves.'

'There's another next door,' said Ned. 'Eliza, d'you think Boots and Emily and their lot would like to rent it for the same fortnight?'

'Mum and Dad as well?' said Lizzy, meaning Chinese Lady and Mr Finch. 'I bet they'd all love it, and we can all afford it. It's time everyone had a real proper holiday.'

'Well, I don't suppose anyone's too keen on an improper fortnight,' said Ned.

'Funny ha-ha,' said Lizzy.

Boots and Emily liked the idea very much. So did Chinese Lady. And Rosie thought it sounded awfully imperious.

'Imperious?' said Boots.

'Yes, isn't that a ripping word?' said Rosie.

'Is it the right one?' asked Boots.

'Of course it is, Daddy, it means urgent.'

'I thought it meant haughty.'

'Oh, bless me,' said Rosie, 'how can you call a holiday haughty? You can call it urgent when you can hardly wait for it, only imperious sounds better.'

'All right, I'll tell Uncle Ned to ask his friend if he'll put our names down for an awfully imperious bungalow holiday.'

'Daddy, you're so comical,' said Rosie. 'Can I phone Annabelle and talk to her about it?'

'About my being comical?'

'No, about the holiday. Goodness, I don't know sometimes what we're going to do with you, do you, Mummy?'

'Live in hope, that's all we can do,' said Emily. Rosie darted out of their sitting-room to use the phone. 'Boots, I think we're bringing her up quite nice, don't you?'

'Well, she hasn't complained yet,' said Boots, 'and neither has her natural grandfather.'

Rosie's grandfather, Mr Tooley, visited once a month, on Sunday afternoons. His invalid wife had died two years ago, since when, with the agreement of Emily and Boots, he had kept in touch with Rosie by way of these monthly visits. Rosie liked him and behaved very nicely towards him, but Emily felt there was always a little apprehension below the surface, as if the girl suspected her grandfather might one day take her away. Emily assured her she need not worry. Mr Tooley was a man of integrity, a staunch friend to Boots, whom he liked and admired.

The woman in a dark brown cloche hat and a brown belted leather coat peered at the door in the afternoon darkness, took hold of the latchcord and pulled it. The door opened and she stepped into the passage, illuminated by a gas mantle in a pearly globe. She called in a gentle voice.

'Mrs Adams? Are you home?'

In the kitchen Freddy and Daisy were sitting at the table playing *Ludo*. Mr and Mrs Brown were down the market, Susie was out shopping for new shoes, and Sally was at the Brixton roller-skating rink with a girl friend.

'Who's that?' asked Freddy.

'It's someone in the passage,' said Daisy.

Freddy went to take a look. He saw the woman. She smiled kindly at him, her eyes softly clear behind her spectacles.

'Is that you, Sammy?' she asked.

'What, missus?' asked Freddy.

'Is your dear mother at home? She is such a good friend of mine.'

'Me mum's Mrs Brown, and I'm Freddy, yer know.'

'I wanted to tell your mother it will be all right for me to come in for Sunday tea tomorrow,' said the woman. Her smile faded and a little frown arrived. 'You aren't Sammy,' she said.

'No, I just said, I'm Freddy, and me mum's—'

'Everything is such a worry,' said the woman and murmured to herself. Then she said, 'Mr Finch will be coming to tea as well? Is he here?'

'Mr Finch?' said Freddy, bemused. 'Missus, 'e don't live 'ere no more, nor Mrs Adams. You said Mrs Adams first orf, didn't yer?'

'Dear Mrs Adams,' murmured the woman. 'Where is Mr Finch?'

'Dunno 'is address,' said Freddy, beginning to feel the caller wasn't all there, 'but yer could ask at the shop at Camberwell Green, the Bargain Bazaar. Me sister Susie knows the address, but she's out. Yer see, Mr Finch an' Mrs Adams, they're—'

'So kind, Mrs Adams, such a dear friend. Such a worry, to be without a husband. I must go. People look, you know, people look.'

Daisy ventured out from the kitchen. The woman smiled vaguely at her.

'She's Daisy,' said Freddy.

'Lizzy is such a sweet girl,' said the woman. 'Oh, dear,' she said, and murmured worriedly to herself, then turned and left. She wandered murmuring up the street.

'Cor, what a funny woman,' said Freddy.

'I dreamt a funny woman was in our 'ouse the uvver night,' said Daisy. 'Well, I fink I did.'

'Dreams is funny too,' said Freddy. 'Would yer like a cup of tea, Daisy, and a slice of me mum's fruit cake?'

'Oh, crumbs, not 'alf,' said Daisy.

CHAPTER FOURTEEN

'I still can't hardly believe it,' said Mrs Brown at Saturday suppertime. 'Our Susie bringing home three pounds a week as Mister Sammy's personal and private assistant, and goin' every day to Shoreditch with him to help with his new fact'ry and everything. I don't know when I've been more proud.' Mrs Brown smiled fondly. 'How much do bank managers get, Jim, and people like Navy captains?'

Mr Brown thought. 'Oh, four or five quid a week, I reckon,' he said.

'Fancy that, and our Susie gettin' as much as three. Ain't you grown up clever, Susie? Wait till I tell your brother William in the next letter I write to him.'

'I don't think I'll tell no one,' said eleven-year-old Freddy, whose brown hair always flopped over his forehead no matter what he or his mother did to it with a comb and brush. 'It's a bit embarrassin', y'know, Dad, 'aving a clever sister when all me best friends 'ave all got soppy sisters. Soppy sisters is more natural.'

'Oh, yer cheeky monkey,' said thirteen-year-old Sally, 'I bet all soppy sisters 'ave got even soppier brothers, I bet no girl's got a soppier brother than you. Can't we change 'im, Mum?'

'Oh, we wouldn't want to change Freddy,' said Mrs Brown, 'he's a nice boy, really.'

'Yuk,' said Sally, enjoying her hot faggots and pease

pudding with gravy from the pie shop at the end of East Street market. There was usually high tea on Saturday evenings, but Mrs Brown had treated her family on this occasion to celebrate Susie's promotion. A supper of faggots and pease pudding really was a treat, especially as there were two faggots each and a mountain of pease pudding.

'I been nearly all week gettin' the room next to Mister Sammy's office cleared and ready for Susie on Monday,' said Mr Brown. He applied himself with gusto to all the work he did for Adams Enterprises as their full-time odd-job man, despite his gammy leg, and he had added pride to gusto in preparing an office for Susie. 'Yer goin' to start work formal there on Monday, Susie?'

'I shall have that honour,' said Susie.

'Cor, yer do talk swell, Susie,' said Freddy, fond of his elder sister. 'Don't she talk swell, Sally?'

'I dunno where she gets it from,' said Sally, 'and I dunno I want 'er talkin' like that in the street to me with people listening. And I dunno it's fair 'er wearing silk stockings with me in rotten old socks or cotton stockings.'

'It's imitation silk, lovey, I've told you,' said Mrs Brown placidly. She was very much the indulgent mother, and always left it to her husband to apply the heavy hand, if the heavy hand was necessary. Unlike Chinese Lady, she could never have brought herself to box her children's ears, but Chinese Lady, of course, had had to be both father and mother to her four.

'Anyway, Susie's got ravishin' legs, which you ain't, Sally,' said Freddy.

'Oh, I don't have no legs at all, I s'pose,' said Sally, 'I s'pose I just walk about on me knees.'

' 'Old 'ard,' said Mr Brown, 'what was that word you used about your sister's legs, Freddy?'

'Ravishin',' said Freddy, looking pleased that he could pronounce it.

'I don't know I like it,' said Mr Brown.

'It's what the older boys say about 'em,' explained Freddy.

'Saucy devils,' said Susie.

'Well, Susie do have very nice legs,' said Mrs Brown. 'Modern fashions do suit yer, Susie love, but I don't know your grandparents wouldn't turn in their graves to see how short ladies' skirts is these days. My mother never showed any of her legs all her life.'

'P'raps she didn't 'ave any,' said Freddy.

'P'raps she was like me,' said Sally, sensitive about being short. ' 'Cording to Freddy, I don't 'ave any, neither.'

'Course you have, Sally,' said Mrs Brown, 'and pretty ones.'

'Yes, course you have,' said Susie, and ruffled her sister's curly hair. The kitchen was a warm and cosy place. She always felt they had inherited its welcoming family atmosphere from the Adamses. The range was glowing, the wooden bunker in the yard containing five hundredweight of newly delivered coal, all because she and her Dad were bringing home good and regular money. Pictures danced for her in the fire.

'Sally's gettin' very pretty, ain't she, Jim?' smiled Mrs Brown.

'She's me pretty little fairy,' said Mr Brown.

'I ain't noticed it,' said Freddy.

'Well, boys never notice how pretty their sisters is,' said Mrs Brown.

'Girls notice their brothers is little 'orrors,' said Sally.

'I don't mind being an 'orror,' said Freddy, 'but I ain't little.'

'You goin' out this evening, Susie?' asked Mrs Brown.

'I've got a library book to read,' said Susie.

'That young man from Brixton not goin' to call any more?' asked Mr Brown, wondering if his wife was right about Susie being in love.

'I hope not,' said Susie. 'I happen to have acquired distinctive uninterest in him.' A little laugh escaped her. Verbally, she was a faithful echo of Sammy sometimes, and she knew it.

'Still, it's a shame you don't have no one to take you out on Saturday evening,' said Mr Brown, and it occurred to Susie then that Sammy had never even offered. It was criminal. What was he doing now? Probably studying the accounts books his brother Boots kept for him.

'If you're all finished, I'll make a pot of tea,' said Mrs Brown. At which point the front door was opened by a pull on the old latchcord, also inherited from the Adams family. A voice called.

'Freddy? Can I come in?'

'Course yer can, Daisy,' called Freddy.

' 'Ere comes 'is sweet'eart,' said Sally.

Footsteps sounded over the floor of the passage and down the step into the kitchen. Ten-year-old Daisy Cook put her head in. From beneath her woollen hat shining black hair escaped, and her button-bright brown eyes beamed at the family. Her coat, run up by her mother out of a navy blue blanket, cuddled her plumpness, and her little nose was pink. Knitted black mittens showed pink finger tips.

' 'Ello,' she said, 'can Freddy come an' play?'

'If 'is legs ain't fell off,' said Sally. ' 'As yer legs fell off, Freddy?'

'Not lately,' said Freddy.

'I don't 'ave none meself,' said Sally in a bitter aside.

'What d'yer want to play, Daisy?' asked Freddy, getting up.

Daisy came right in and breathed a little excitedly.

'I got conkers, me dad give 'em me,' she said, and dug her hands into her coat pockets. She brought out four huge glossy horse chestnuts, two in each hand. 'An' I got two more besides. Yes, I got six, I fink.'

Freddy, impressed, gave her a pat.

'Crikey, they look like champions, Daisy,' he said. 'I'll get some string and a meat skewer.'

'You can 'ave four, if yer like,' said Daisy, 'an' I'll keep two.'

'No, three each, that's fair, and I'll conker with yer,' said Freddy.

They went out into the street and began their game of conkers under the light of a lamp-post. Daisy closed her eyes as she held the string of one conker and Freddy took a swipe at it with his.

'Oops,' she kept saying, each swipe striking a hit. Then came a miss.

'Your go, Daisy,' said Freddy, 'and I still ain't cracked yer.'

'Oh, lor',' said Daisy, and took her turn. Freddy's conker took a biff and cracked. The audience of street kids yelled.

'Yer done 'im, Daisy, yer done the champion conker of the Place.'

'Crikey,' said Daisy.

'Go on, Daisy, yer still got another go,' said Freddy, 'yer keep goin' till yer miss.'

'Oh, corks,' said Daisy, not sure she wanted to completely shatter the conker of the champion in front of the other kids. So she took a blind swipe. Her tough horse chestnut struck home, all the same. Freddy's conker split apart and fell from the string. The kids yelled in delight.

'Yer done 'im right up, Daisy, yer got a seconder!'

'Yer the champ now, Daisy!'

'I dunno she is. Freddy's 'it oners to make 'isself champ. Daisy's only 'it a seconder.'

'That don't matter. If yer beat the champ wiv a seconder, yer beat 'im.'

178

'But it don't make 'er champ, not till she beats 'im wiv a oner. Freddy being a oner champ don't give up being champ till 'e's beat by a oner. Yer got to be fair. Still, yer can do it, Daisy, yer got a real champion conker there.'

'Oh, I don't mind Freddy's still champ,' said Daisy.

'Give over, Daisy, don't talk like that, and yer still got a right to go first when 'e strings up a new conker.'

'You Jimmy! You Cissie!' A mother was calling from a front door. 'Come on in now!'

The kids began to melt away in case other mothers had the same idea. Cold or foggy, hot or rainy, the street kids still preferred to be out of doors most of the time.

'The kids was right, Daisy,' said Freddy, 'yer got a champion conker there.'

'Can we go an' sit on yer doorstep while yer put anuvver one on yer string?' asked Daisy.

'All right, come on,' said Freddy. 'I've got a gobstopper in me pocket, I'll share sucks with yer, if yer like.'

'Oh, I ain't tasted a gobstopper for ages,' said Daisy, 'I put all me 'a'pennies away for the country 'oliday fund.' The country holiday fund was something sponsored and organised by schools. Pupils who could afford it paid sixpence a week during term times, and were rewarded with a fortnight's summer holiday in a country village, boarding with villagers. It was a fortnight's bliss to Walworth kids.

'Come on,' said Freddy, and they went and sat on his doorstep. Daisy was Freddy's mate. They had once done *Knocking Down Ginger* together, all along King and Queen Street, and knocking on every door, Daisy in exhilaration and all flying feet as irate residents yelled after them. ' 'Ere y'ar.' Freddy fished the gobstopper out of his pocket. It was pink-tinted. He wiped flecks from it. 'You can 'ave first go, Daisy.'

Daisy popped the large sweet ball into her mouth and sucked in rapture. It rolled around her tongue and puffed out her cheeks. She gurgled something.

'What?' asked Freddy, working a meat skewer through a new horse chestnut.

' 'S'nice,' slurped Daisy. She took it out. It was all white. 'Oh, I been an' sucked all the pink off.'

'I don't mind,' said Freddy. He took it from her. It was shining wet. He put it into his mouth and sucked with boyish relish.

'Yer ever so kind, sharin' yer only gobstopper wiv me,' said Daisy.

'Well, you're me mate,' said Freddy, driving the skewer right through. He disgorged the sweet into the palm of his hand. 'Your suck, Daisy.'

'Fanks,' said Daisy blissfully, the gaslight of the lamp-post reaching out to faintly touch them. The gobstopper spilled sweetness down her throat.

'I s'pose we could get married later on,' said Freddy.

'If yer like,' said Daisy. 'Your turn, Freddy.'

Freddy rolled the gobstopper thoughtfully about inside his mouth, took it out and said, 'Can yer make apple dumplings and 'ot custard?'

'Course I can,' said Daisy. 'Well, not yet, not exactly yet, not exactly now.'

'It don't 'ave to be now,' said Freddy, 'I just 'ad faggots and pease pudding. Later on.'

'Yes, a'right,' said Daisy.

Freddy looked at the gobstopper, slightly decreased in size. 'Whose turn is it?'

'I fink it's mine,' said Daisy.

A shadow fell across the faint light. They looked up.

'Hello, Freddy,' said Sammy, spruce in overcoat and trilby hat. 'Who's yer lady friend?'

'Crikey, it's Mister Sammy,' said Freddy. He liked Sammy, although he had only met him a few times, when Susie had been working in the Camberwell shop.

'I was just passin',' said Sammy, 'and thought I'd take a look at the old place. How's the fam'ly?'

'In the pink,' said Freddy. 'This is me friend Daisy.'

' 'Ello, mister,' said Daisy.

'Yer best go in,' said Freddy, 'they're all 'ome.' He pulled the latchcord and opened the door. 'They're in the kitchen. Yer goin' to say 'ello to 'em, Mister Sammy?'

'Well, now I'm here,' said Sammy, and went through and knocked on the kitchen door.

'Who can that be?' asked Mrs Brown, about to pour tea.

'Daisy, I expect,' said Susie, and opened the door. Sammy offered a slight smile and cleared his throat.

'Good evening,' he said. Susie stared at him. He took his hat off. 'I just happened to be passin',' he said.

'I thought it was just happening to be an emergency,' said Susie, 'that the fact'ry had fallen down and you required me to help put it together again.'

'Now would I ask that of yer on a Saturday evening?' said Sammy.

'Yes, you would,' said Susie, hiding the delight she felt in seeing him.

'Mister Sammy, come in now,' said Mrs Brown. 'I don't know what Susie's doin', keepin' you standin' in the doorway. I just made tea, you must have a cup.'

Susie stepped aside, watching Sammy as he entered the kitchen. His tallness made the ceiling seem lower. She tried to catch his eye. He avoided the attempt. Oh, you Sammy Adams, you wait, she said to herself, I'll make you look me straight in the eye one day, I'll make you tell me you love me. You'd better love me when I've given you the best working years of my life, or I'll kick you to death.

'All very cosy here,' he said, 'just like the old days.

Pleased to see you, Mrs Brown. You all right, Jim? And how are you, Sally? Haven't seen you since you were in Peabody's. Little terror you were then. Now look at you. Pretty as a picture.'

Oh, the swine, thought Susie, all that cheerful chat for them, and not a word to me about my divine beauty.

'Do honour us by takin' a seat,' she said.

'Well, I was only passin',' said Sammy.

'You already said that.'

'Mister Sammy, you can sit next to me,' said Sally, who had developed an instantaneous crush. 'Yer ever so welcome to 'ave a cup of tea with us, and Mum's got some 'ome-made cake as well.'

'Well,' said Sammy.

'Yes?' said Susie, the light in her blue eyes a little dangerous.

'I happened to be on my way to the Tivoli in the Strand,' said Sammy, 'where there's this monster Hollywood film showing. *Ben Hur*. Featuring a popular Hollywood geezer name of Ramon Novvaro.'

'Ramon Navarro,' said Susie.

'Funny name, that, sounds Eyetie,' said Sammy. A cup of tea was pushed across the table to him. He was still standing. He accepted the cup and saucer. He sipped the tea. Susie watched him, eyes simmering. 'Well, in passin' I thought – this is first-class tea, Mrs Brown.'

'You thought in passin' that my mother's tea is first-class?' asked Susie.

'I was makin' a complimentary comment on the spot, Miss Brown,' said Sammy, who had come to a final conclusion for the twentieth time. 'What was I saying before that?'

'Lord knows,' said Susie, 'I don't.'

'Ah,' said Sammy. 'Ah, yes,' he said, and drank more

tea. He looked at the clock on the mantelpiece. Ten past seven. The last performance at the Tivoli began at eight. 'I thought as I was passin' I might look in and request the pleasure of knowing that if you weren't otherwise engaged, Miss Brown, you might consider—'

'Thank you, how kind, I won't be a minute,' said Susie.

'Pardon?' said Sammy.

'I'll just get my hat and coat.' Susie disappeared. She was laughing to herself as she ran lightly up the stairs to her bedroom.

'What's she done that for?' asked Sally.

'To get ready to go to the pictures with Mister Sammy,' said Mrs Brown, quite sure she'd been right in the first place about who Susie was in love with.

'But Mister Sammy didn't accherly say so.'

'On the tip of my tongue,' said Sammy.

'Yer very welcome,' said Mr Brown.

'I heard it's a highly remarkable film,' said Sammy.

'I 'eard there's always queues,' said Mrs Brown.

'I happen to have acquired circle tickets,' said Sammy. 'It wouldn't look right, standin' in a queue with a young female woman as ladylike as Susie.'

'Crikey, can't yer talk 'igh-class?' said Sally, faint with admiration.

'Well, y'know, Sally,' said Sammy confidentially, 'when you get out into the world you meet all kinds, and it's needful to know how to talk to them. Me brother Boots, he can talk to anybody and not turn a hair. He learned, when he was being educated, that if you talk right, then people'll listen to you. If you talk slipshod, they mark you down as slipshod. I'm cockney all over, I got a feeling for Walworth and me hallowed years here with me fam'ly, but it's needful for me to offer the world a bit of style. And there's Susie, she's got style. She didn't have when she first started to work for me, which I hope don't offend you, Jim, but in five years she's collected as much style as if she'd been born a lady, which is a credit to you, Mrs Brown. You'll get style, Sally, when you're older. Being born poor don't mean you've got to stay poor, we've all got something we can offer, and it's up to us to see it don't go to waste. You're pretty, and you've got lovely curly hair and a sister who's an example to you. Your mum and dad'll help yer, like they've helped Susie. Don't get stuck in a ditch, just find out what you're best at and go to work on it.'

'But I'm growin' up all short,' said Sally.

'You've hardly started yet,' said Sammy.

'But I'm thirteen,' said Sally.

'All right, so you're thirteen. And you're something else. You're dainty. Not every girl is, and really dainty girls make good dancers.'

'Mum, that's it, I'll be a dancer!' cried Sally rapturously.

Susie returned in her blue cloche hat and a blue coat. She was freshly made up, new lipstick moistly glimmering.

'I am quite ready, Mister Adams,' she said.

'There, see what I mean, Sally?' said Sammy. 'That's style.'

'Have a nice time, Susie,' said Mrs Brown.

'So long, fam'ly,' said Sammy, 'I'll bring her back.'

Walking to the Walworth Road bus stop with him, Susie, who had decided just how she would conduct herself, slipped her arm through his. She felt him quiver a little. She smiled.

'Do you go out often?' she asked.

'Not often,' said Sammy. There was no fog, the street lamps glowed clearly, and the lights of trams, buses and the Walworth Road shops created a picture of brightness quite different from the greyness seen by day. 'Still, it's a nice evening tonight.'

'It's a surprise,' said Susie.

'What is?'

'The evening,' she said. 'Who'd have thought you'd take me out? I wouldn't. You haven't been drinkin', have you? I don't want to go to the Tivoli Cinema with a drunk.'

'I am mystified by such remarks, Miss Brown.'

'No, you're not, and don't call me Miss Brown. It's my belief you must have been drinkin' or a brick must have dropped on your head for you to actually invite me out.'

'I have not been drinkin',' said Sammy, as they crossed Walworth Road, 'and I do not recall any brick droppin' on my loaf of bread. It happened to occur to me that as you've been a good and helpful girl this week, it would become me to show me heartfelt appreciation.'

'Bless the man,' murmured Susie, 'I'll get a pat on the head next.'

'I didn't catch that,' said Sammy, as they arrived at the bus stop. The right bus came along almost at once, a number 68. It was packed with people going up West for the evening.

'Room for two only,' sang the conductor. 'One short, one long, one up, one down. You takes yer pick. Suit yer, mister and missus? You can cuddle up later.'

Sammy perforce had to separate from Susie. He went up to the top deck, Susie boarding the lower. 'I'll pay for Lady Hortense,' he said to the conductor.

'So yer should, me lord,' said the conductor, and winked at Susie.

'He's so kind,' said Susie, whose unexciting evening had turned into one of exhilarating cut-and-thrust.

They joined up again in the Strand, and made their way to the Tivoli. There were long queues slowly moving forward for the last performance. Sammy produced tickets obtained from Keith Prowse, agents, and Susie forgave him everything for the moment as they were led up to the circle by an usherette. The Tivoli was the handsomest cinema in the West End. To add to her excitement, Sammy bought her a box of chocolates from the tray of another usherette.

'I don't know I can hardly believe this,' she said, quite giddy.

Sammy, settling into the comfortable seat beside her, murmured, 'Well, it's like I said, Miss Brown, you've been a good, kind and helpful girl this week.'

The lights were up, the circle filling, and Susie kicked his right ankle with the side of her left shoe.

'Take that,' she said.

'Ouch,' said Sammy as an afterthought.

'Did it hurt?' she asked. They were whispering.

'Well, pain does happen to hurt a bit,' he said.

'Good. It was for callin' me Miss Brown. And I shan't offer you a chocolate.' She opened the box of Cadbury's King George chocolates while the lights were still up. She selected one and ate it. Delicious. She had never been happier.

'I'm partial to chocolates myself, y'know,' said Sammy.

'Oh, dear, hard luck, then,' said Susie. 'Oh, all right, just one.' She offered the box. Sammy took one with a caramel centre. 'Put it back,' she said, 'I like caramel centres myself.'

'It's upsettin' me,' said Sammy, 'you not givin' me a bit more kindness and gratitude.'

'I suppose,' whispered Susie, leaning close, 'I suppose you couldn't just say you're takin' me out and treatin' me and buying me a lovely box of chocolates because you happen to like me a bit? Oh, no, you couldn't say that, not the highly reputable Mister Sammy Adams. Give that chocolate back.'

Sammy popped it into his mouth, turned his head and looked at her. Susie held his glance. He saw her deep blue eyes bright with silent laughter, her lips slightly parted as if that laughter was about to spring forth. Sammy's confused emotions crystallised into one clear certain emotion as he fell hopelessly, helplessly and inescapably in love with her. Their eyes locked, faint colour flushed her face and a little pulse beat. The huge buzz of a thousand people waiting for the performance to start receded from their own little world of the moment.

Then Susie looked to her front, to the blank silver screen, her flush visible. The lights dimmed, the audience became still and sighed itself into expectant silence. Sammy sat back, arms folded. Susie sat breathless with the certainty that he loved her.

Ben Hur, with Ramon Navarro in the leading role and Francis X. Bushman playing Messala the Roman, was as powerful and moving a film as the critics had said. Dramatic, stirring and spectacular, the tale of a great wrong and a great revenge, it unfolded silently on the screen, but was accompanied by the telling virtuosity of the pianist. The chariot race, a pitiless contest, reached its terrible climax with Messala crushed and broken beneath iron wheels. At the crucifixion of Christ, the sky darkened to blackness, the blackness was sundered by the lightning of God, and Susie's tears ran as the dreadful scourging sores of leprosy vanished from the faces of Ben Hur's mother and sister because of their belief in the Son of God.

Susie's face was still wet, and women in the audience were dabbing their eyes, as everyone stood for the pianist's last piece of the evening, the National Anthem.

The bus back to Walworth was crowded with home-going cockneys. The continuing post-war depression was trying the people, and there were ominous rumblings from trade unions, but somehow London's cockneys endured and survived, and they flowed into the West End on Saturday evenings to enjoy themselves, even with no more than a few bob in their pockets.

On the packed bus, Sammy said, 'Enjoy the film, Susie?'

'Oh, yes.' Susie was still in the land of Christ and Ben Hur, still emotional. 'I think I'd like to see it again.'

'Whenever you say,' said Sammy.

She wanted to tell him what a lovely evening he had given her, but the crowded lower deck was a discouragement to heartfelt talk. She was glad when they reached Browning Street and alighted from the bus. She said then, 'I've had a lovely evening, it was the best film I've ever seen, I don't know how to thank you – oh, I'm sorry I was so mean about the chocolates, except I was only teasing, really I was.'

'I know you were,' said Sammy, who was examining his feelings. 'Regular little tease you are, Susie. I don't know why I—' He broke off.

'Why what?'

'Pardon?'

He was doing it again, thought Susie, he was backing off. She ought to go to Boots and ask him to hit his brother over the head. Boots, she knew, was on her side.

'Never mind,' she said, 'you can have a chocolate when we get home.' She hadn't touched the chocolates all through the drama and emotion of the film. Nothing had diverted her attention from the screen. Sammy had sat quiet and absorbed beside her, and not once had he attempted to touch or grope. She had a feeling Sammy and Boots and Tommy were all like that, they'd all been brought up to respect girls, and they respected the mother who'd been responsible for that. But sometimes, of course, a girl wanted to be touched. Only by someone special, of course.

Reaching her front gate, she turned to Sammy.

'Same old house,' he said reminiscently.

'It's a happy house,' she said. 'You made it like that, you and your family. It sings sometimes, specially at Christmas. Houses are like that, aren't they? They never let go of the people who've made happy places of them. There's two families there at Christmastimes, yours and ours.'

'Susie?' Sammy's commercial soul was strangely touched.

'There is, you know. Oh, am I being silly? I expect it's the film. But you'll come in, won't you?'

'Is it a bit late?' Sammy had emotions of his own to contend with, because of his absolute certainty of what Susie meant to his life. At this particular moment she even meant more than his business. The realisation was quite shattering. So was the possibility that Susie's feelings for him might not be the same as his for her. Never having taken women seriously, except to make sure none got too close, Sammy was now on such unfamiliar ground that it was making him lose his way. His self-confidence as a businessman took him along sure-footedly, but his self-confidence as a man in love was almost nil.

Everybody said yes to Sammy, either at once or eventually. He was not equipped to cope with the devastating blow of having Susie say no to him. She could get vexed with him, haughty with him, and even answer him back. She'd ground him into the dust that foggy morning at the factory. He would have lost her if he hadn't gone after her and eaten humble pie. He'd never had to do that before, not with anyone, and especially not with a female woman.

I'll leave it, he said to himself, I'll work up to it. Yes,

that's what I'll do. I'll see if she comes over a bit loving now and again. Best to be a bit sure, best not to rush her.

Rush her? If Susie, who had known him over five years and was now twenty-one, could have read his thoughts, she would have hit him over the head herself, and without any help from Boots. As it was, she pulled on the old latchcord, opened the door and said, 'Of course you must come in, it's not as late as that, and Mum and Dad will still be up.'

'My pleasure,' said Sammy, feeling that a coward's decision had been a wise one.

Mr and Mrs Brown were waiting to hear how the evening had gone. Mr Brown had talked about what a surprise to have Mister Sammy call and take Susie out, and how educating he'd been in the way he spoke to Sally. It had done Sally no end of good. Mrs Brown had remarked what a clever girl Susie was, she'd played it very cool with Mister Sammy.

Susie recounted details of the film. Sammy interposed relevant comments. Susie said she'd make a nice pot of hot tea for all of them, and sandwiches for herself and Mister Adams, who had been very gracious taking her to the Tivoli and buying her a box of chocolates as well. Sammy said he'd only been given one chocolate and accordingly fancied a fried bacon sandwich. Mrs Brown said there were only streaky rashers. Sammy said streaky were best for sandwiches and that he'd fry them himself, which he did. The old gas stove was still being used, still in its place in the scullery. Susie, waiting for the kettle to boil, watched him. There were four rashers in the pan.

'You can cook as well?' she said.

'Being a bachelor, Miss Brown, I have—'

A kick arrived, from the toe of her shoe.

'Take that,' said Susie.

'What, again?' said Sammy, feeling it was definitely not loving.

'I mean it,' said Susie, 'I'll do it every time you call me Miss Brown. I don't mind at work, it's proper at work, but not at sociable times. Can you cook?'

'Being a bachelor,' said Sammy, turning the sizzling rashers, 'I have learned the needful necessity of cookin' for myself, and regard myself as comin' up to a highly competent performer. D'you like your bacon crisp, Susie?'

'In a sandwich, yes,' said Susie. A little smile showed. 'You're actin' like you're at home.'

'Oh, well, the feel of the old place, y'know,' said Sammy.

'Mum keeps it nice.'

'Well, you're a nice fam'ly,' said Sammy.

The kettle boiled and Susie made the tea, thinking how much she liked having him here. If he was smart and shrewd, he wasn't conceited. He had bounce and he had belief in himself, but he didn't go about full of conceit. He was still ever so droll. She supposed he would kiss her before the evening was over. He had better.

Everyone had a cup of tea. She and Sammy ate their bacon sandwiches. They all talked around the kitchen table. To Sammy it was a little like old times, even without Chinese Lady's searching eye and quick admonishments. The Browns were a happy family and knew how to make the kitchen a place of warm, homely hospitality. And that Susie. Remarkable. The style she had. She and Lizzy, two Walworth cockney girls who had known what real poverty was, had bloomed like flowers, Lizzy vivid as a rose in her colouring, Susie as fair as May.

It was almost midnight before he left. He said good night to Mr and Mrs Brown, and Mrs Brown said, 'It's been a pleasure havin' you, Mister Sammy.'

'Glad you and Susie picked yerselves a good film,' said Mr Brown.

'Oh, we're goin' to see it again,' said Susie, 'I happen to have received a kind promise from Mister Adams for next Saturday week.'

'Was it Saturday week we mentioned?' asked Sammy.

'You're so kind, thank you,' said Susie, and saw him to the front door.

'Been a nice evening,' he said.

'Lovely,' said Susie, lifting her face.

'Yes, well, see you Monday morning at the Camberwell offices,' said Sammy. 'Good night, Susie.' He put his hat on and left.

Susie, watching him go, breathed, 'Oh, I don't believe it. Not even a peck. Sammy Adams, you wait, you just wait.' She closed the door and leaned against it. She laughed.

There was still next Saturday week. And every day at the office.

Life was utterly wonderful.

CHAPTER FIFTEEN

There were five rooms directly above the clothing and linen shop by Camberwell Green. They had all been turned into offices. Sammy occupied one office, Boots another. The two largest offices housed the staff, four general clerks in one, three copy typists and a Jill-of-all-work in another. They were all girls. Sammy stuck to his opinion that girls were more adaptable and less demanding than young male clerks. And they cost less in wages.

There were further rooms on the second floor, all available for staff expansion. At the moment, Sammy had his flat up there.

At five minutes to nine on Monday morning, Boots put his head round the door of the little room that had just been turned into an office for Susie.

'Good morning, personal assistant,' he said. Susie, in a neat dark blue dress with a white collar, was regarding her little sanctum. It contained a desk, a chair, a filing cabinet, an Imperial typewriter, a wastepaper basket, two wire trays, empty at the moment, a telephone and two or three sundries. The window overlooked the main road and an inner door opened on to Sammy's office.

Susie, turning, gave Boots an affectionate smile.

'I'm so glad to see you, and over the moon to be back here,' she said. 'I just hope I can live up to my promotion.'

'You'll walk it,' said Boots. 'You're a treat. Glad to have you back with us.'

193

Impulsively, she said, 'Are you really? It's bliss to me.'

'Welcome home,' said Boots, and stepped in. He placed a wrapped sheaf of chrysanthemums on her desk. 'From the garden, and with Emily's good wishes as well as mine. You only need to pinch a vase from the typists' office.'

Susie, overcome, said, 'Oh, I could kiss you.' And she did, very warmly, with her arms around his neck. The inner door opened and Sammy addressed her.

'May I enquire, Miss Brown, as to the nature of the business you happen to be conductin'?'

Susie, startled, detached herself. And it mortified her to know she was turning a hot pink. The lurking smile in Boots's eyes reached his mouth. If no one else knew of Sammy's weakness for Susie, Boots had spotted it long ago.

For once Susie was unequal to the situation. Further, Sammy had a glint in his eye and was very straight-faced. All she could say was a limp, 'Boots brought me flowers.'

'We're not holding any horticultural show,' said Sammy, 'there's work to do. Kindly see me in my office.' He disappeared.

'Oh, lor', that's done it,' said Susie in dismay, 'my first day here and I'm goin' to get the push before I even start.'

'Well, don't forget to mention that as you're salaried, you're entitled to either a month's notice or a month's pay,' said Boots.

'Oh, don't,' begged Susie, 'it's not funny.'

'Yes, it is, it's very funny,' said Boots, 'but you'll win, Susie. Just look him in the eye.'

Susie went in. Sammy, seated at his large desk, had an enormous backlog of mail in front of him. All letters had been opened by Boots while Sammy had been busy at Shoreditch, and all mail requiring Sammy's attention was what he was going through now, a pencil in his hand. Susie presented her defensive self.

'Mister Adams?'

'Brixton,' said Sammy abruptly, scanning a handwritten letter from a supplier. He liked to see every letter that arrived. It kept him up-to-date with everything that was happening.

'Brixton?' Susie sagged for a moment, then pulled herself proudly upright. 'The shop or the prison?'

'Prison?' muttered Sammy, keeping his head down.

'If it's back to the shop it's as good as the prison,' said Susie.

'Kindly be your age, Miss Brown,' said Sammy, refusing to meet her eye. He was suffering slight trauma. Susie and Boots kissing. Everyone knew ladies took a fancy to Boots. Was that why Susie had wanted to return to Camberwell? 'Did I say I was sendin' you back to our Brixton shop? I was merely about to inform you that the new manageress took over on Thursday and is doing very nicely.'

'I still don't like your growling look,' said Susie.

'My what?' Sammy leaned back and fixed his eyes on her white collar. 'What did you say?'

'You're wearing your growling look, that's what I said, Mr Adams.'

'I must point out, Miss Brown, that I am considerable shook up to catch my personal assistant disportin' herself in the arms of my office manager, whose name we both know but won't mention out loud in case Mrs Em'ly Adams gets to hear, which if she does will cause horrendous ructions. I don't want your fatally dead body littering up these offices. That's all, Miss Brown.'

'No, it's not, Mister Adams,' said Susie. 'I merely happened to give Boots a grateful kiss for welcomin' me with a gracious bouquet of flowers. I don't know anyone nicer than Boots, who's a pillar of shinin' light compared with

195

someone else I know but won't name in case he gets more growling.'

'I will choose to ignore that,' said Sammy, compulsively raising his eyes to hers. Hers were a scornful dark blue. I knew it, he told himself, I knew I'd get turned upside-down and my business as well. And what does she mean by coming in on a cold November morning looking like a summer day in June? 'Just do me the favour, Miss Brown, of conductin' your kissin' out of office hours.'

'Shame on you, Mister Adams.' Susie had not only recovered, she was enjoying a sudden certainty that Sammy was jealous, actually jealous. 'I won't tell Boots what you said about him and me disportin', because we weren't, and because I don't want him givin' you a black eye. It wouldn't do the business any good, everyone seeing you goin' around with a black eye as if you'd been gettin' mixed up with hooligans.'

Sammy wondered what good it was doing him, being hopelessly in love with a girl who had a talent for giving him headaches.

'Go away,' he said, 'I'm havin' a fit, and I'd like to have it in private.'

'Yes, Mister Adams. Is there any work for me?'

'Work?' said Sammy vaguely. He felt floored. Susie regarded him tenderly. He caught the look. She smiled. His mouth twitched, just as Chinese Lady's did when she wanted to smile at something she should be frowning at. 'Work?' he said, rubbing his mouth.

'It's what I'm here for, isn't it?' said Susie.

'Yes. Right.' Sammy became brisk. He picked up a pile of letters he had already examined. 'Take these, read 'em, regard my pencilled notes, write out answers and get Lottie to type them. If I'm not here when they need signing for the afternoon post, you sign 'em as personal assistant to S. W. Adams, managing director. There'll be more comin' your way all day. Shoreditch has put us behind here. You'll see I've suggested on some letters that you answer by telephone. They're the ones that concern prices, and such prices I've pencilled in. The first job I want you to take off my hands is answering correspondence. I'll help you with details until you're into the swing of things. All right?'

'Very good, Mister Sammy. There's files I can refer to?'

'These here offices happen to be full of well-kept files.'

'Very good, Mister Sammy. Who is Lottie?'

'Senior copy typist. The one with the Friday night Amami shampoo look.'

'Very good, Mister Sammy.'

Suffering cats, thought Sammy, I'm going to eat her in a minute.

'What's all this very good lark?' he asked.

'It's for formal business hours,' said Susie. 'Oh, can I take that vase on that sideboard there?'

'Pardon?'

'Thank you, Mister Sammy, that's very obligin' of you. It's for the flowers your kind brother graciously presented me with.'

Sammy muttered something highly uncomplimentary about his kind brother. Susie smiled, picked up the vase, and went back to her office singing to herself. Not until the door closed behind her did Sammy let a huge grin spread over his face. The monkey. He ought to sack her. He couldn't. It would be like cutting off his right arm.

Susie, at her desk, the chrysanthemums in the vase which she had placed on her window ledge, thought that working like this with Sammy was going to be joyful. Life was hard, especially for the really poor people, but even for them there were some happy days. But oh dear, for Sammy to have caught her kissing Boots wasn't the best start she could have made to this day. Never mind, he had finished up trying not to laugh.

Her telephone extension rang.

'Hello?'

'Are you Miss Brown?' It was a girl's voice.

'Yes.'

'I'm Doreen. I do everything, like. D'you want Camp coffee or tea in the mornings, d'you take how many lumps of sugar and d'you want to pay tuppence a week for biscuits with your afternoon tea like everyone does?'

'Oh, thanks,' said Susie. 'I'll have Camp coffee in the mornings, one lump of sugar and, yes, I'll pay tuppence a week towards the biscuits.'

'A'right, Miss Brown. I do the telephone switchboard as well, and Mister Sammy said you'll be taking all calls for him when he's not here. I also do the correspondence filing and you can ring through if you want me to bring any file any time. I don't do errands, though, we don't have an office boy like we should.'

'I've got the picture, Doreen, thank you.'

'Yes, Miss Brown. Goodbye, Miss Brown.'

Susie heard giggles in the background before the line went dead. She smiled. She was past giggles herself. Happily she went to work on the letters.

At coffee-time, Boots introduced her to the rest of the staff, girls and young women. They all seemed very nice, even if their interest in her as personal assistant to Mister Sammy drew covert looks. Lottie, senior copy typist, was a blonde young woman, her bobbed hair too frizzy to lie in disciplined neatness around her head. She was the only one who was a little cool towards Susie. At eleven, she walked into Susie's office bearing letters and written answers. She put them down on Susie's desk.

'I can't read your writin',' she said, 'so I can't type what I can't read.'

'Just a moment,' said Susie, and called one of the other typists in. 'Norah, would you read that?' she asked, giving the girl one of her hand-written answers.

Norah quoted. 'Dear Sirs, In answer to your kind letter of the 9th of November, we confirm receipt of all goods except the knitwear for our Kennington and Peckham shops. Please telephone—'

'Yes, thank you, Norah,' said Susie, taking the answer back, and Norah went back to her work. 'It doesn't seem like my handwriting's all that bad, Lottie. You don't need glasses, do you?'

'Course I don't,' said Lottie.

'Well, I tell you what,' said Susie, 'I'll get Norah to do them, shall I?'

'But I type all Mister Sammy's letters,' protested Lottie sulkily, and Susie recognised a girl with her nose out of joint. She might also have seen her as a rival had she not been sure there were never going to be any. That telling moment at the Tivoli on Saturday, when she had held Sammy's eyes at last, had given her a breathless certainty that he was hers alone. Lottie Miles was just a silly girl. 'I'm his personal typist, I am, Miss Brown.'

'I know you are.' Susie gave the girl a winning smile. 'He told me to give these only to you. Could you manage them with a bit of a push?'

'Well, all right.'

'Thanks ever so much.' Susie smiled again, and that hurdle was cleared. It was odd but true, most girls didn't like women being in charge.

On the stroke of noon, Mrs Rachel Goodman entered Susie's office. Rachel, in a black astrakhan coat and a silver-grey fur hat, looked a warmly clad winter beauty. Susie knew her, having seen her several times in previous years. She would enter the shop, exchange light patter with Boots and then make her way up to Sammy's office. Boots had eventually come up with the information that she had been Sammy's only girl friend, but had inevitably married a man of her own race.

'Hello, Susie.' Rachel's greeting was a smiling one. 'Boots has just told me Sammy's appointed you as his personal assistant. My life, that's a promising curtain raiser to a career for a girl, isn't it? Best of luck.'

'Thanks,' said Susie, and Rachel crossed to the inner door in gliding grace, knocked and went into Sammy's office. The door closed on her. Seven minutes later, Sammy appeared.

'I'll be out for a while, Miss Brown. I am takin' a business acquaintance to lunch.'

'Yes, very good, Mister Adams,' said Susie coolly, and made a pencil note in a red-covered desk diary.

'What's that you're writing?'

'Oh, just a diary entry, Mister Adams. Twelve-five. Mister S. Adams, lunch with Mrs R. Goodman, a married woman.'

'What?'

'I won't tell Mr Goodman.'

'Oh, my suffering ears,' said Sammy, 'is that you saying that, Susie?'

'It's a diary for all your appointments, Mister Adams.'

'Well, you can rub that one out,' said Sammy.

'Very good, Mister Adams.'

'Jesus, you saucebox,' said Sammy, and went back into his office. From there he took Rachel across the road to Camberwell Green's high-class pub. At the marble-topped food counter, he surveyed the joints of cold meat available for sandwiches. Roast beef, pork, mutton and York ham were on offer. The white-capped chef, an array of carving-knives to hand, smiled at him.

'Mornin', Mister Adams.'

'How's yer luck, Ernie?' responded Sammy.

'So-so, yer know. Can I pleasure yer with a prime cut or two?'

'That yer can,' said Sammy. 'Ham. And kindly apply

unsparing mustard. Any kosher beef?'

'Don't upset me, Mister Adams. That joint is fresh kosher.' The chef pointed to a cold roast rib of beef. 'Or where would I be with some of me valued customers?'

'Only askin' on behalf of me business friend,' said Sammy. Rachel was seated at a table in the far corner. 'And she'd like mustard pickle of gen'rous proportions on a separate plate. Also, do us proud with your crustiest bread, Ernie.'

'Got you, Mister Adams.'

'Good on yer,' said Sammy. At the mahogany drinks bar, he ordered a dry cider for Rachel and a Guinness for himself. He carried the drinks to the table while Ernie prepared the sandwiches. He sat down beside Rachel on the leather-backed wall seat. Rachel slid herself gently close.

'Sammy darling—'

'Now, Mrs Goodman, try to remind yourself you're a wife and mother.'

'And could I remind you to come to Rebecca's next birthday party and do funny faces for her?'

'Cheers,' said Sammy, taking up his Guinness.

'Cheers, lovey,' said Rachel, and sipped her cider. 'And what's the idea of having Susie as your personal assistant instead of taking on a male manager?'

'I don't need a male manager, not in the offices. Boots is the Lord Factotum there.'

'Well, no funny business, Sammy.'

'Eh?'

'I'm all teeth when I'm jealous, lovey.'

'Here, hold on,' said Sammy, 'your life's your life, my life's my life. Am I jealous of Benjamin?'

'Yes, of course you are, aren't you?'

Sammy looked into deep, sultry brown eyes. It wouldn't do any good not to humour her. Rachel and her father meant much to him in his business world.

'Considerable,' he said, 'but I wasn't brought up to uncover me aching heart. Me old lady expects me and Boots and Tommy to stand up courageous to hurt and sorrow. Burnin' arrows pierced me to me vitals, Rachel, when yer married Benjamin, but did I reproach yer? I can say with remarkable integrity that I did not.'

'Ain't you the one and only?' murmured Rachel in delight. 'Sammy, I could eat yer. Now, tell me more about Adams Enterprises as fashion designers.'

'I have already informed you we are intendin' to manufacture our own designs,' said Sammy. 'It's now my pleasure, sport, to further inform you that all I need is a couple of grand.'

'That's all? Two thousand pounds?' Rachel shook her head. 'That's a fortune, sweetie. My daddy will have a heart attack.'

'Your daddy is a friend of mine. It's against my principles to be fatally injurious to my friends.'

'Ain't yer lovely, Sammy?' Rachel's velvet laughter softly bubbled. 'You want I should break it to my daddy gently?'

'A touch of lovin' preparation might help,' said Sammy. Then Ernie the chef arrived, bringing the tray himself. He set out the plates containing the sandwiches and the plate containing a generous portion of mustard pickle. He produced napkins and cutlery. Sammy gave him the customary sixpence for carving the meats.

'Pleasure, Mister Adams.'

'Mutual, Ernie.'

Ernie departed. Rachel and Sammy began to eat. They both had good appetites, and the large crusty sandwiches of new bread and fresh meats were works of art.

'Sammy, why aren't you asking me for the loan?'

'I am dead set on not askin' you, Mrs Goodman. It ain't right. It's takin' advantage of yer warm and noble heart, which kind of advantage has been known to happen before. And yer warm and noble heart is something I hold in affectionate reverence, like I do your melting peepers and your highly good-lookin' female legs.'

Rachel, mouth full of new bread and kosher beef, pressed her napkin to her lips to stifle choking laughter. She chewed and swallowed.

'Oh, you crafty demon, Sammy, I could listen to you all day and you know it, even if you don't mean a word of it, you old ratbag.'

'Steady, Rachel, this here public house is now full of listening earholes.'

'I should blush after hearing you talk of your affectionate reverence for my highly good-looking female legs? Sammy, Sammy, tell me everything about your new venture and your faithful Rachel might buy a piece of it for two thousand.'

'You'd buy in on a gamble?' said Sammy, a gleam in his eye.

'I want to know what kind of a gamble it is, I want to know who this fashion designer is, what her credentials are. She's news to me. A woman fashion designer? Crazy. It's bitter to say so, but it's men who've got the gift for dressing us.'

'Never heard of men like that myself,' said Sammy, the mustard hot to his appreciative tongue, 'only heard of French poofs.'

Rachel's soft laugh arrived again. Every minute she spent with Sammy was delicious entertainment to her.

'All the same,' she said.

'Never mind all the same, Rachel, there's a first time for everything. Mimi Dupont's going to first-time the fashion world.'

'Mimi Dupont? She's French?'

'Well, I'll tell you, Rachel, but keep it all under your tit-for-tat. There's a shockin' amount of underhand goings-on in the rag trade, which me old lady would call

203

implorable, but I favour you with me deepest trust.'
Sammy could be very close-mouthed about his business,
but he trusted Boots, he trusted Susie and he trusted
Rachel. He gave her the details of his new venture,
including those concerning the fixed belief of Lilian
Hyams that her 1926 look was going to anticipate Paris
ideas.

'Bobbed hair, strings of beads and two inches above
the knee?' breathed Rachel. 'And frilly garters?'

'Sent you dreamy with bliss, has it?' said Sammy.
'Well, it'll suit a young Yiddish beauty like you, with
your remarkable handsome limbs.'

'I'm a wife and mother,' said Rachel. 'Benjamin probably wouldn't notice, but my daddy would, and he'd
have a fit.' But her eyes were a gleaming velvet. 'Sammy,
of course. The flappers would consider it the last word.
They'll trample each other to death to be first in the night
clubs with it. You'll form a subsidiary company? I'll buy
thirty-three per cent for two thousand pounds, lovey.'

Sammy considered it.

'It's fam'ly, Rachel,' he said.

'I know. I'll buy into your family, Sammy darling.'

'Why?'

'It's a dream of mine.'

'Twenty-five per cent,' said Sammy. He was incurably family-minded. Boots, Tommy, Lizzy and Chinese
Lady all counted. Ten per cent each for Boots and
Tommy, ten per cent each for Lizzy and Chinese Lady,
and thirty-five per cent for himself, giving him a needful
advantage over Rachel, whose warm and noble heart
didn't get in the way of her shrewdness. Adams Fashions
Limited might well make the rest of the business look
puny.

'Thirty,' said Rachel.

'Agreed at twenty-five, yer sweet and lovely song of
me heart,' said Sammy.

'Oh, my God,' breathed Rachel, but shook her head and laughed. 'Why didn't I do it when I was fifteen?'

'Do what?' asked Sammy.

'Make you make love to me.'

'I didn't hear that,' said Sammy, 'and I am, in any case, dead against performing illegal activities with under-age female persons. Handshake, Rachel, on twenty-five per cent?' Rachel moved closer and they shook hands. 'Kindly lift your hip off my lap,' said Sammy, 'there's people lookin'.'

'People,' said Rachel, 'are spoilsports.' But she smiled. She was very pleased with things. She was in Sammy's business now. She was part of his life.

Mr Barry Somerville, son of the senior partner of Somerville & Partridge, Estate Agents, said, 'Thanks, Emily.'

Emily, having placed an up-to-date list of properties available for purchase or rent on his desk, said, 'I haven't had time to check it, I've only just finished typin' it. But it's just gone one and I must go, my mother-in-law always likes me home punctually to have lunch with her.'

'I know.' Mr Somerville, thirty and dapper, smiled up at her. He liked her efficiency, her willingness. He also liked her figure, her legs and her green eyes, even if she wasn't a raving beauty. 'Keep working on her. We really could do with having you full-time, and I'd like to teach you to help with valuations.'

'No chance, not till my little boy gets to school age,' said Emily.

Mr Somerville got up, saw her to the door of his office, touched her shoulder lightly and said, 'Well, keep working on her, all the same.'

Emily's quicksilver smile flashed in response to his encouragement, and she went. She was quite aware Mr Somerville fancied her. He was already talking about bringing mistletoe to the office at Christmas. She supposed it was flattering to be fancied at her age. She was twenty-seven and had been married nearly nine years. She'd given up her previous job in 1921 when she was expecting Tim. The man she worked with, Mr Simmonds, was very down in the mouth about her going. She had come to like him very much, and let him kiss her goodbye on the day she left. A light kiss had been intended, but it became warm and lingering, and a second kiss followed, and even a caress of her breast. Alarmed at her response, she hastily said goodbye and left. She was Boots's wife, and faithful to him, but the moment showed her that temptation could exist even for a faithful wife. She must make sure temptation did not arise with Mr Somerville, who was a dashing bachelor and liked her to use his Christian name when they were working together in his office. To call him Mr Somerville was so stuffy, he said, that it made him wince. He did not hide the fact that he liked her in the modern fashions, for legs as good as hers, he said, should be seen, not covered up. She told him he ought to keep such remarks to himself, specially as she was married. Nor would her husband be too keen.

But she liked him, he was breezy and outgoing, and he didn't actually pester her, he just had a frank eye for her and kept it that way. And he was set on getting her to work full-time. She had dropped various hints to Chinese Lady. Chinese Lady was not too responsive. For one thing, although she did not say so, she thought a wife and mother's place was at home. For another, Emily didn't need to be out working. Her job ought to go to some poor woman who really did need it.

When Emily got home on this particular day, she raised the subject again over their light lunch. Tim had had his meal earlier and was playing on the hall floor with his clockwork train set. It gave Chinese Lady the necessary privacy to speak her mind firmly at last.

'Em'ly Adams, I don't know what's gettin' into you. You've got a nice home, two nice children, and a hard-workin' husband. I wouldn't like to think you're dis-remembering your blessings, that you're thinking tappin' a typing machine all day would be more of a pleasure to you than your home and fam'ly.'

'But Boots is out all day, and Rosie's at school most of the day,' said Emily.

'Tim's here, so am I, so's the house. You can't expect to have everyone round you every hour of the day, but you can expect all of them to like comin' home to a place that a wife and mother's made warm and welcoming for them, which you can't do if you've only just come home yourself. Men have got their duty, and women have got theirs, and them duties is different, Em'ly, or a house wouldn't be a proper home any more. I don't like saying so, but it seems to me Boots ought to have a firm talk with you.'

'Mum, Boots hasn't ever minded me havin' a job.'

'You mean he's never said anything to upset you. Well, he wouldn't, love, would he? Boots likes peace and quiet, he likes it because peace and quiet is a godsend to him after all them guns and shells when he was in the trenches. Em'ly, you're a good girl, but be careful you don't take Boots too much for granted.'

'Well, I like that,' said Emily, getting cross with Chinese Lady for the first time ever, 'it's wives that get taken for granted.'

'It can happen the other way, Em'ly, and if Boots comes to feel you like your job better than your home and fam'ly, you might just lose his best affections.'

'What d'you mean?' demanded Emily.

'Boots is attractive to women, and I mean women, not flighty girls.' Chinese Lady thought of Miss Simms, the lady teacher who was always asking Rosie about her father, and who had suddenly become cautious during a

207

certain conversation. Very striking to look at, she was, and high-class too, and wasn't she the daughter of an aristocratic lady who still did business with Sammy concerning an orphanage? Miss Simms must have known Boots as well as Sammy before she became a teacher. Chinese Lady thought there was a strong possibility that she was very partial to him. 'It's best to make sure you do the right things, Em'ly, and not the wrong ones.'

'Mum, I think you're being very unfair,' protested Emily. 'All right, suppose I do like my job? Boots likes his job, don't he? But he's not goin' to be told he's puttin' his home and fam'ly second, oh, no.'

'Em'ly love, I don't like to hear you not being sensible. A man's got to have a job, he's got to provide for his fam'ly, it's what a man's made for, and it gives him self-respect. I dare say Boots does like his job, but what he likes better is comin' home from it. Boots is a fam'ly man. I don't want to interfere, I'm only just saying be careful.'

'I don't see why—' Emily broke off as Tim came into the kitchen, his clockwork engine in his hand.

'Mummy, it won't go,' he said.

Emily turned in her chair and opened her arms to him. He scrambled willingly up on to her lap and she hugged him.

'You're not second to me, Tim love, you're first,' she said.

'Can you mend it?' asked Tim hopefully, offering the engine. Emily took it, looked it over and tried the key. It wouldn't move. 'I fink I overwound it,' said Tim sadly. 'Can you mend it?'

'I don't know it can be mended, darling,' said Emily.

'I best ask Daddy, then,' said Tim, and slipped from her lap. 'I'll just have to push it till he comes home.' And he went back to the hall.

'That's put me second to Boots,' said Emily wryly.

'Course it hasn't,' said Chinese Lady. 'Boys need their

mothers for some things, and their fathers for other things.'

'Well, I want you to know none of my fam'ly come second to my job,' said Emily.

'That's nice, Em'ly, I'm glad to hear you say that.'

Emily, of course, mentioned the matter to Boots, first asking him a direct question.

'Boots, do you or don't you like me havin' a job?'

'What brought that up again?' asked Boots.

'Just tell me.'

'I'm in favour of you doing what you like to do,' he said. 'I did say so before.'

'And supposin' I did it full-time?'

'If that's what you want,' said Boots.

'You don't sound too keen,' said Emily.

'Well, you don't need to do any job, and there's Tim and Chinese Lady, and the housework.'

'I could still do my share of the housework.'

'I know you could, lovey, but it wouldn't give you much time to yourself. Anyway, what brought it up?'

'Chinese Lady went and gave me a lecture,' said Emily. 'She told me I'm puttin' my home and fam'ly second to my job.'

'Well, you know Chinese Lady. She's got very fixed ideas about marriage, and about the ordained roles of husbands and wives.'

'It's 1925, not 1890,' said Emily firmly, 'and I don't like havin' to listen to a Victorian lecture. You better tell her that.'

'Pardon?' said Boots.

'Tell her,' said Emily. 'It's your place to stand up for your wife.'

'Don't be silly,' said Boots, 'just laugh it off.'

'You don't mind I'm upset?'

'I mind you taking Chinese Lady too seriously. She

209

might not be in favour of mothers going out to work, but she loves you, Em. That's all you need to remember, that she cares for you. Just settle for doing your job part-time until Timmy goes to school. It's a ready-made compromise.'

'Oh, you sound so upper-class sometimes you make me feel I'm not good enough for you,' said Emily crossly.

'That's even sillier,' said Boots. If anything was notable at the moment, it was Emily's improved speech. She was no longer a gabbling cockney, rushing her words, she had benefited from the way she had applied herself to her jobs, first in the town hall and now at the estate agents.

Her mood changed. She smiled ruefully.

'Oh, I'm sorry,' she said, 'it's just that I want you on my side.'

'Forming sides, taking sides, that's the start of family divisions,' said Boots. 'Not good, Em. Better to laugh some things off. Better to remember, as I said, that Chinese Lady loves you.'

Emily, touched by that, said, 'Well, I love her too, don't I? That's why it upset me.'

Boots gave her a cuddle. She pushed herself against him. When Rosie entered the sitting-room a moment later, she found them kissing.

'Golly,' she said, 'are you having happy ever after?'

'Yes,' said Emily.

'Spiffing,' said Rosie, pleased for the two people she loved the most.

CHAPTER SIXTEEN

The December day was murky. At eleven o'clock, Sammy entered Susie's office, his overcoat on, his hat in his hand.

'I am about to make a call, Miss Brown.'

'On the telephone, Mister Adams?' enquired Susie, busy with a heap of correspondence.

'I do not regard that as amusing,' said Sammy. 'I have in mind an important conversation with Mr Eli Greenberg at his junk yard off Newington Causeway.'

'Yes, Mister Adams,' said Susie, and consulted the desk diary. 'I don't have it recorded. I've got down that tomorrow Mr Entwistle of Manchester is comin' to see you at eleven-thirty, and on—'

'Turn it up,' said Sammy.

'But, Mister Adams, as your personal assistant it's highly needful for me to know your present and future whereabouts each day.'

'I do not consider it needful for you to give me sauce,' said Sammy, sternly hiding a grin. 'I think you'd better come with me and learn how to extract confidential information from Mr Greenberg without it costin' yer a packet.'

Susie's eyes lit up. Sammy had ways of making her very happy.

'Yes, Mister Adams.'

'Lottie's workin' on some letters?' he said.

'Yes, and I've most of these ready for her. I've got phone calls to make with some, I can do that when we come back.'

'Well, jump about, Miss Brown, I'm standin' here waitin' on yer competence.'

Susie could hardly believe her eyes when she and Sammy stepped through the door of the high wooden gates fronting Mr Greenberg's covered yard. She was confronted by great piles of every conceivable kind of household goods, some dating back to Queen Victoria's heyday.

'Jesus,' said Sammy, 'do my mince pies glimpse pianos as well under this lot, Eli?'

'Vun or two, Sammy, vun or two,' said Mr Greenberg, beard and hat both nodding in welcome to Susie. 'Vhat's your pleasure, my poy, a Bechenstein? You vant a Bechenstein, I got a Bechenstein. Sammy, vhat a cheering thing it is to have you visit me in company vith your lady friend. Vhy, never before has it happened, and do I remark her to be a sweet friend of mine too? Susie?'

'Miss Brown happens to be my personal assistant,' said Sammy. 'Give her your respects accordin'.'

'Ah, my respects, dear young lady,' said Mr Greenberg, lifting his hat to Susie, who smiled.

'Mister Sammy has been most kind,' she said.

'Ah, vhen vas Sammy not kind?' said Mr Greenberg. 'It has cost me money, my dear, but vhat is an emptied pocket compared vith the blessings of such kindness?'

'Your compliments, Eli,' said Sammy, 'are a pleasure to me ears, which have been suffering unbelievable lately.' Susie gazed in innocence at a stack of dismantled bedsteads. 'Well, now,' said Sammy for openers.

'Ah,' said Mr Greenberg in pleasurable anticipation.

'I wish to converse with you,' said Sammy.

'And vhy not, Sammy?'

'At no charge.'

'Of course, my poy. I vill forget time is money,' said Mr Greenberg, with Susie listening fascinated. A train rumbled by over the nearby railway bridge on its way to Blackfriars. A mountain of chairs trembled and quivered. Stacked saucepans vibrated. 'Come into my office, ve don't vant the next train to bury Susie under my stock of valuable brass fenders.'

His office was a small wooden hut that had been painted green twenty years ago. But its interior was surprisingly neat. He extracted a large red handkerchief and dusted the seat of a chair for Susie, who sat down.

Sammy said, 'My desire for converse concerns some friendly information I require, Eli.'

'Friendly?' Mr Greenberg looked cautious.

'Helpful,' said Sammy.

'Friendly information that's helpful I should supply free in times like these? Sammy, Sammy, vhat are you askin' of such a friend as I am? Already I am standin' here losing money.'

'I am only requiring names,' said Sammy, 'the names of buyers of ladies' wear for West End shops and stores.'

'The Vest End?' Mr Greenberg smiled in delight. 'Sammy, you are goin' to dig for gold?'

'Branching out, Eli, branching out with quality garments. Observe that I do not want to go into a class store and ask to see Mr Whatsit or Madam Howjerdo. I want to know names, I don't want to look like a pushing elbow. I want to sound familiar.'

'Familiar, Mister Adams?' enquired Susie.

'Familiar with the buyer, Miss Brown. Meaning I am able to ask to see Madam Hilda Ponsworthy or Mr Lionel Spriggs, giving the impression we are close to

213

bosom friends. First names accordin' are also required, Eli.'

'Ah, vhat is called vun foot in the door,' said Mr Greenberg.

'You got it, old friend,' said Sammy breezily.

Mr Greenberg raised his hands high.

'Sammy, Sammy, all this for friendship?'

'All what?' asked Sammy, and Susie thought oh, ain't he priceless?

'My life,' said Mr Greenberg, 'ain't vun foot in so many doors vorth a mite?'

'All right, how much?' asked Sammy. 'I know yer've rubbed shoulders with the trade for more years than I've been born with, I know yer can point yourself at an informative geezer.'

'Vell, now,' said Mr Greenberg, 'it might be I know a certain gent. But he von't expect friendship to interfere with business. It ain't done, Sammy. Did my father leave Russia vith the help of friendship or business? Business, my poy, vhich he expected. Vell, then, vhat d'you say?'

'Two quid,' said Sammy, 'one for your certain gent, and one for you, and I can't say fairer, not without it hurtin' me considerable.'

'Sammy, Sammy, are you trying to kill me vith kindness?'

'All right, you kill me,' said Sammy.

'Shall ve say tventy?'

'Twenty what?'

'Green vuns?'

'Oh, my bleeding heart,' said Sammy, 'did you hear that, Miss Brown? Now look what you've done, Eli, you've turned Miss Brown dead faint. All right, I forgive yer, old cock, I realise you spoke unthinking, only don't make it so that I can't afford to pay Miss Brown her wages. Use your smelling salts, Miss Brown.'

'Yes, Mister Sammy, thank you for your kind concern,' said Susie, 'but I am overcomin' my faintness.'

'There you are, Eli, now can you think up a friendly figure?' said Sammy.

'My poy, ain't tventy single smackers friendly?' countered Mr Greenberg. Sammy winced.

'Twenty smackers for names?' he said. 'That's fatal, and dying hurts, yer know. Moses would have left yer to the Egyptians, Eli. I tell you what, I'll double me original offer. Four quid.'

Mr Greenberg's red handkerchief reappeared. He blew his nose on it.

'I'm veeping for yer, Sammy, veeping. But I'll take three vhite vuns.'

'Fifteen nicker? Not from me you won't. All right, I'll give yer six quid, plus me trust and faith, which means six quid in yer mitt now.'

'Done,' said Mr Greenberg. 'I'm a poor man, Sammy, and times is hard, my poy, hard.'

'Don't I know it,' said Sammy, 'it's hardly worth being alive sometimes. Still, friendship keeps a bloke going.' He handed the money over.

'Vell, it's a comforting thing, friendship,' said Mr Greenberg, 'except vhen it pushes a poor man under a tram.'

'They're a sign of hard times too,' said Sammy.

'Trams?' said Mr Greenberg.

'Funerals,' said Sammy. 'I'll expect the list of names some time next week, Eli?'

'I'll ride up special, my poy.'

'Love yer, Eli. Well, come along, Miss Brown, and I'll find out if I can treat you to lunch. I might have enough for a stale loaf and some cheese.'

'Oh, just a crust will do for me, Mister Sammy,' said Susie.

He took her to the little SPO cafe under the bridge at

Waterloo Station, where they each had a plate containing sausages, mashed potatoes and fried onions, and the onions were truly luscious.

'Mister Adams, poor Mr Greenberg,' she said.

'Now, Susie, Mr Greenberg ain't poor.'

'I meant the way you teased him.'

Sammy popped sausage into his mouth and chewed with thoughtful relish.

'No, no teasing,' he said, 'just accepted custom, Susie love.'

Her blue eyes danced.

'Pardon, Mister Adams?'

'Pardon?' said Sammy.

'Yes?' she said.

'What?' he said.

'You spoke familiar, Mister Adams.'

'I accord you me respectful apologies, Miss Brown.' A kick arrived under the table. It struck his shin. 'Would you mind keepin' the pain out of my legs except for when we're socialising?'

'We're socialising now,' said Susie, and gave him a sweet smile. Their eyes met across the table. Sammy fell into hers, they were so vividly blue and large. He drew a breath. He looked at his fork. There was another piece of sausage on it. He muttered at it. Susie wanted to shriek with laughter. He was still doing those things. Looking, dropping his eyes, and muttering. It was hysterical, Sammy not knowing how to tell her he loved her. Sammy of all men. 'When we're socialising, Mister Adams, I'm goin' to kick you every time you call me Miss Brown or talk about respectful apologies.'

Sammy ate the piece of sausage, and followed with a forkful of fried onions. Then he said, 'I appreciate your sentiments.'

'I bet,' said Susie.

'But regardin' Mr Greenberg. My dialogue with him

is mutually harmonious. It is the agreed form of bargaining. It is a considerable pleasure to them to have a conversational carry-on when doing business. And you mustn't think, Susie, that the mention of friendship is all my eye and Betty Martin. It ain't. It is genuine. I've known Eli Greenberg all my life, also Isaac Moses, known as Ikey Mo, and his daughter Rachel. All lifelong friends, Susie, all genuine and reliable business contacts.' Sammy finished his tasty meal. The little cafe, clean and quite attractive, was a long-standing retreat for those who enjoyed a well-cooked, homely repast. It was full, but he and Susie had a small table to themselves. 'If I ever have to ask you to conduct a matter of business with Mr Greenberg on our behalf, you'll know how to talk to him and how to bargain.'

'Yes, Mister Adams, I'll tell him he's ruining us,' said Susie. 'By the way, I happen to have heard you used to go out with Mr Moses's daughter Rachel.'

'Just roller-skatin',' said Sammy.

'Yes, well, I don't think you should go out with her now she's a married woman,' said Susie, trying to catch his eye. 'It just don't look good, Mister Adams, not now you're a business gentleman of high repute.'

'My hearing's gone up the spout again, the ringing in me ears has come back,' said Sammy. 'I'd better ask you to repeat that piece of unsolicited wordage in case I got it wrong.'

'I was speakin' to your dear brother Boots—'

'My what?'

'Oh, he is a dear, Mister Adams, and he agreed with me that as your personal assistant one of my most important personal responsibilities was to protect your high repute. We'd best not take married women out to lunch any more, Mister Adams, we don't want people talkin'.'

'I ain't here,' breathed Sammy, turning his eyes up to

the ceiling, 'I'm somewhere else, havin' a fit. Have you finished them satisfying eats, Miss Brown?'

'Yes, Mister Adams, and I don't mind Miss Brown now we're talkin' about business.'

'Then perhaps you'll kindly accompany me into Waterloo Station. I desire to fall under a train.'

'Very good, Mister Adams.'

Outside he stood on the pavement with her. He looked at her through the murk of the day. Susie smiled.

'Susie Brown, you'll be the death of me,' he said. His mouth twitched, and as they walked to the bus stop he was laughing. Susie, laughing herself, thought the dismal day gorgeous.

That evening, Mr Finch had a private word with Boots, the one person in the family who knew his true background and his secrets.

'In a week's time, Boots, I shall be going to Belgium, and from there into Germany. With a German passport. I've told your mother I've a job to do for the Government in Belgium, of indefinite duration. I am, of course, being sent back into the field by Intelligence.'

'British Intelligence?' enquired Boots, his pipe going. They were in Mr Finch's study.

'A fair question,' said Mr Finch with a slight smile, 'but yes, you can believe it, old chap, British Intelligence.'

'As a former member of German Intelligence, you'll be going into the lions' den,' said Boots. 'Can I ask why?'

'Oh, to acquire information. Isn't that what it's all about for every agent?'

Boots looked slightly sceptical.

'What's important about information on Germany, a country down and out?' he asked.

'Down, Boots, but not quite out. And have you heard

218

of a political gentleman called Adolf Hitler?'

'I've heard of him,' said Boots. 'It's news to me that he's a gentleman.'

'A dangerous nationalist,' said Mr Finch, 'with a flair for oratory and rabble-rousing, and peculiar ideas about the superiority of Germanic people.'

'You've orders to take a close look at him, to join his political party, perhaps?' said Boots. 'That'll mean months in Germany for you, won't it?'

'I shall be sorry to miss Christmas with you,' said Mr Finch. There was more to it than an investigation of Adolf Hitler and his National Socialist Party. There was a certain General Hans von Seeckt, a Prussian of the old military caste, whose record during the war had been highly distinguished. He was now Commander-in-Chief of the limited German Army of 100,000 men allowed by the Allies. He was training that army of long-term officers and men to become an elite force of the finest soldiers in Europe, or so it was whispered. Its attitude, so it was said, was based on the principle of Aryan supremacy.

Mr Finch was to find out what General von Seeckt might be up to, to discover what, if anything, was being kept from the eyes and ears of Allied military observers.

'I thought you'd finished field work,' said Boots. He knew Mr Finch to be over fifty now.

'I had thought so too,' said Mr Finch, 'but when one's country calls, Boots, one does what one can.' He gave another slight smile. 'This is my country now, England is where all my affections lie. Believe that too. And it's a pleasure to know I shall leave your mother in the good hands of her family.'

Polly visited the house every Tuesday and Thursday evening to give Rosie tuition in French. Mr Finch let them use the quietness of his study. He was abroad now, in Belgium, everyone thought, except Boots. Christmas was close, and in the study one evening Rosie was persisting with the complexities of French grammar, an important part of the written exam she was to face in the future.

Boots put his head in.

'Camp coffee, Miss Simms?'

'Oh, very welcome, Mr Adams,' said Polly, finding it difficult always to be fairly formal with him in front of any member of his family.

'And tea for you, Rosie?' asked Boots.

'Oh, ever so grateful, ta,' said Rosie. 'It might save my life, you know. French grammar is killing.'

'You'll win,' said Boots, 'and I'll decorate you myself.'

'What with?' asked Rosie.

'Cocoa tin lid on a piece of string?' suggested Boots, and withdrew.

'Is your daddy fun, Rosie?' asked Polly.

'Oh, Nana always says he's always saying things no one ever understands except himself.'

'Well, that's fun, isn't it?' said Polly. 'Now, how about trying to paraphrase, "*Notre maison est assez grande pour nous*"?'

'Crumbs, Miss Simms, I don't even know what it means.'

'Yes, you do. "Our house is big enough for us." '

'Help,' said Rosie, but went to work.

Chinese Lady had made the inevitable pot of evening tea. Tim was enjoying a cup before being put to bed. He didn't like cocoa, he said it was yukky. Boots made a cup of Camp coffee for Polly, who had become addicted to its chicory flavour during her time in France and Flanders.

'Is that for Miss Simms?' asked Emily, seated next to Tim and caressing his tousled hair.

'She likes Camp,' said Boots.

220

'Well, it's nice she comes to the house to help Rosie,' said Emily, thinking of what Chinese Lady had said about Boots being attractive to women. 'But you don't have to run about for her.'

'Who's running about?' asked Boots mildly. 'Just performing a small service.'

'Still, it's my job really,' said Emily, 'I'm the skivvy.' Chinese Lady looked pained.

'Oh, I've skivvied a bit myself in my time,' said Boots, and took the coffee and tea to the study.

'*Merci, mon père,*' said Rosie.

'Lovely,' said Polly, turning on her chair to receive the steaming cup. Her dress was hitched, knees showing, legs gleaming in her silk stockings. Boots thought about Sammy's new venture, Adams Fashions, soon to be launched as a limited company. Polly, slim of figure, neat of bosom and long of leg, was a natural for Lilian Hyams's 1926 look, though not during her school hours. She caught his brief glance at her legs. It induced excitement in her. She had thought, at her teachers' training college, that time and absence would cure her of her love for him. Instead, the moment she first saw him again she knew her feelings were incurable. She would have given a whole precious year of her life to have him make love to her. Just once, only once. Only once? How absurd.

'Daddy,' said Rosie, 'Miss Simms just told me I'd split a French infinitive.'

'Good for you,' said Boots, 'that's stupendous progress. Split a French infinitive? Amazing. Remarkable. Well done, kitten. And I suppose I ought to thank Miss Simms for helping you achieve it.'

'But it's not an achievement, Daddy, it's a howler,' said Rosie. 'Isn't it, Miss Simms?'

'Of a kind,' said Polly, 'and forgivable.'

Boots saw her out later. Parked in the road was a

high-bonneted Bullnose Morris, its hood up. It was Polly's car, a present from her father.

'You wouldn't like to whizz off with me into the dark yonder, would you?' suggested Polly, warmly wrapped in a winter coat of black leather.

'Ask me another,' said Boots.

'Aren't you ever going to make love to me?'

'Is it necessary? Won't someone else do? One of your many friends?'

'Oh, you sod, that's below the belt,' said Polly.

'Language, Miss Simms, language.'

'Pompous prig.'

'Fair comment,' said Boots amiably. 'But you're a lovely girl, Polly. Don't go to waste.'

'I'm not going to waste,' said Polly, 'I'm living a worthwhile life. Or haven't you noticed? Or do you mean I ought to be someone's wife? Well, I would be, you stinker, if that someone hadn't married some other woman when my back was turned. Why couldn't you have waited for me?'

'Never having met you, I'd no idea you existed. Come on, I'll crank your car for you.' Boots went to the car with her. She got in and switched on. He cranked. The engine spluttered. He tried again, vigorously. The engine fired. He put the starting handle back into the car. He leaned in under the hood. 'Good night, Polly, and don't think I don't appreciate what you're doing for Rosie.'

Polly kissed him full on the mouth.

'Love you,' she said, and drove off into the damp, misty night.

Boots went back into the house. He put his head into the study, thinking to ask Rosie how her cramming was going. Rosie, however, had already joined Emily and Chinese Lady in the kitchen.

The doorbell rang. He answered it, suspecting Polly had forgotten something.

It was a woman in a dark brown cloche hat and a brown leather coat. She wore spectacles. She had a soft enquiring expression on her face, and her face looked cold and pale.

'God Almighty,' he said.

The woman was Elsie Chivers. He had last seen her at Lizzy and Ned's wedding in March 1916, nine and a half years ago. Elsie Chivers, tried for the murder of her mother at the Old Bailey, and acquitted. And he had committed perjury on her behalf because at that time he was fascinated by her, a woman of soft myopic loveliness without her glasses, her voice a caress. Nearly ten years older now, she had changed little, except for a slight twitch and tremble to her mouth. He stared in helplessness at her. She smiled, a softly sweet smile.

'How tall you are,' she said. 'Such a fine young man, Boots. Oh, dear, it has been so worrying. Is my husband here?'

'Husband?'

'Mr Finch. Edwin.'

'Jesus Christ,' said Boots.

She was a woman tired and drained. Seated in an armchair in the sitting-room, her gloved hands hung limply over the sides, her body slightly drooping. Her head nodded. Her coat was off and he saw that her body was thin in its brown skirt and beige jumper. She was vague now, and incoherent, her answers to his questions making no sense.

'Where are you living?'

Her head came up.

'Hotel. Yes, hotel.' That was her first coherent reply. 'But with no one, you see, no one. I must find my husband.' The worried look appeared. She murmured to herself, and her head nodded again.

'Hold on,' said Boots, who now had worries of his

own, catastrophic worries. 'Hold on now.' He went into the kitchen and quietly advised Emily and Chinese Lady that Miss Elsie Chivers had turned up out of the blue. They gaped at him. Rosie looked puzzled.

'Who's Miss Chivers, Daddy?' she asked.

'An old neighbour of ours,' said Boots. 'She's not too well. I think—'

'You're jokin',' said Emily.

'He better not be,' said Chinese Lady.

'I'm not joking,' said Boots, 'I think she needs some strong coffee and a brandy. She's worn out.'

'Well, I'm amazed,' said Chinese Lady. 'Miss Chivers? I can't credit it. I'd best go and see her.'

'Could you make the coffee, Em?' asked Boots.

'I'll bring it in,' said Emily, charged with intense curiosity. Boots knew there was no way he could keep Miss Chivers to himself, but there had to be a way of preventing her from telling Chinese Lady she had come in search of Mr Finch, and that she had named him as her husband. Mr Finch, Boots remembered, had told him that Miss Chivers had married a Bavarian land-owner.

He went back to the sitting-room, Chinese Lady with him, and his mother took a long look at the woman in the armchair. Miss Chivers was leaning back, her eyes closed, her lids heavy.

'Miss Chivers?' said Chinese Lady, who had thoughts of her own. 'Miss Chivers?'

Miss Chivers opened her eyes. She blinked through her spectacles.

'Oh, my dear friend,' she said. Chinese Lady studied the pale face.

'Lord,' she said, 'what brings you here, Miss Chivers?' she asked.

'It is so nice to see you, so nice,' murmured Miss Chivers, who was not Miss Chivers, thought Boots.

224

'Where have you been all this time?' asked Chinese Lady, who always went straight to the heart of things.

'Boots is such a fine young man, isn't he?' said Miss Chivers, and lapsed into vague, wearied murmurings again. Emily came in with a cup of hot Camp coffee, strong and black. She gazed in intrigued wonder at the visitor.

'Miss Chivers, it really is you,' she said. 'Oh, you do look tired. Here's a cup of coffee.'

Miss Chivers took it. The cup and saucer trembled a little in her hand.

'How kind,' she sighed, 'how kind.'

'Steady now,' said Boots, and poured brandy into the coffee. He'd drunk coffee and brandy, or coffee and rum, in the trenches when there was a treat on, the spirits usually emanating from the company commander, Major Harris, a man of grey granite but, to Boots, an incomparable soldier.

Miss Chivers sipped the laced coffee. The slight tremble afflicting her mouth caused the liquid to spill a little down her chin. Chinese Lady looked distressed at that.

'Oh, poor woman,' she whispered to Emily.

'She's ill,' whispered Emily. 'Where's she come from?'

'I just don't know, and she don't seem in the right kind of way to say.'

Miss Chivers slowly drank the coffee, her chin wet and stained. Boots, taking the cup and saucer from her, wiped her chin clean with his handkerchief. She seemed not to notice.

'Can you tell me the name of your hotel?' he asked.

She lifted her head and looked up at him. He saw the eyes that had once held so much fascination for him, eyes so clear when seen through her spectacles and so soft, peering and myopic without them, holding even more fascination. She smiled.

'You're Boots,' she said. 'How is your dear mother?'

'Oh, lor',' breathed Chinese Lady, 'she's really in a bad way.'

'Boots, I think she'd better stay here for the night,' said Emily, 'we can let her have the spare room.'

Miss Chivers sank back. Her head dropped and a tired sigh came from her.

'Emily,' said Boots, when they were eventually in their own bedroom, 'would you go and bring me her handbag?'

'What?' asked Emily. She had looked in on Miss Chivers and found her fast asleep. After Rosie had gone up to bed, they had all talked about their unexpected visitor, although Boots had not talked quite as much as Emily and his mother. 'What d'you mean, her handbag?'

'I'd like to see what's in it.'

'You know what Chinese Lady would say to that, don't you? She'd say a man goin' through a lady's handbag is desecratin'.'

'I know, Em. But I have to tell you what I couldn't tell Chinese Lady, that Miss Chivers made a fairly lucid statement when I opened the door to her. To the effect that she was looking for Mr Finch, her husband.'

'Oh, my God.' Emily whitened with shock. 'No, it can't be. Boots, it can't be.' She went into painful thought. 'But I remember – oh, Lord, no – we all said at the time that she and Mr Finch had eloped. Boots, it'll give your mum heart failure, it'll give her a terrible time.'

'So would you go and get the handbag? I will, if you'd rather. There might be something in it, something a woman might carry about with her if the rest of her possessions were in an hotel.'

Emily stared at her husband.

226

'Yes,' she breathed, 'a marriage certificate. Yes. Wait.' She hurried out. She was back in quick time, with a brown handbag. She opened it and spilled the contents out on the bed. There were all kinds of things. A purse, a bottle of aspirin tablets, two crumpled hankies, make-up items, bus and tram tickets, loose coins, a spare pair of spectacles in a case, a fountain pen and other innocuous things. But no papers, no letters, no certificate. Boots turned the handbag inside-out without result.

'Hell,' he said, 'nothing. In the morning, Em, I'll take her with me when I leave for work. I can't leave her alone with Chinese Lady.'

'Yes, we can't risk that,' said Emily, green eyes enormous with worry. 'It might be something she made up about Mr Finch, but all the same we can't risk her repeating it to Mum. Oh, God, I hope she did make it up. Well, she's wandering in her mind, you can tell, so she might have. But suppose it's true?'

'Shattering, if it is,' said Boots. Tight-mouthed and grim, he thought. 'I'll have to try to get the name of the hotel out of her. There must be some clue in her possessions.'

'Yes, if she's married there has to be a certificate,' said Emily. 'Lord, if it is Mr Finch, he must have deserted her – Boots, he couldn't have, could he?'

'And committed bigamy with Chinese Lady?'

'Oh, God,' said Emily.

Boots returned everything to the handbag and Emily took it back to the spare room, placing it on the chair beside the bed. Miss Chivers was sleeping heavily. Emily and Boots had hours of broken sleep themselves, waking up and whispering worriedly to each other. Boots said it would be wise to give Miss Chivers breakfast in bed, not to let her come down and have Chinese Lady ask her questions. He'd get her out of the house as quickly as he could, on the grounds that he was going to take her back to her hotel. He'd name one.

They slept fairly soundly in the end.

Boots, woken by the alarm, came to with a start, and went at once to the spare bedroom in his pyjamas. He knocked. There was no answer. He put his head in. The room was empty. He went all over the house.

Miss Chivers was gone.

'Thank goodness,' breathed Emily.

'Only up to a point,' said Boots.

'Pretend she never came.'

'She's a wanderer, Em. She's only half in the real world. But she may wander back here again. How, I wonder, did she get to know our address?'

'Don't think about her, pretend she never came,' said Emily.

'Well, there's nothing we can do as things are,' said Boots, 'except wait until Edwin Finch returns.'

'Yes, we'll do that,' said Emily, 'we'll wait.'

Boots wondered how it would all work out. He wondered exactly what had happened between Mr Finch and Miss Chivers when they went off together in 1916. Both had had more on their minds than a thousand other people put together.

228

CHAPTER SEVENTEEN

Boots spent some time out of his office during the next few days to look for Miss Chivers. Sammy, with Susie looking after so much of his office work, was busily out and about, but still managed to find a moment to ask his eldest brother what he was up to. Family business, said Boots. What family business? Boots said he'd let Sammy know if he had to, but would keep it to himself if he didn't. Very informative, I don't think, said Sammy, and what about the real business, the business that paid a handsome salary? Boots said not to worry.

Chinese Lady, of course, was worrying at the mystery. Boots had noticed that the bus and tram tickets in Miss Chivers's handbag all related to journeys in South London. They pointed to the possibility that she was living in the area, but he could think of no hotel in places like Walworth, Kennington, Bermondsey or Camberwell. But he spent time looking for her there, searching the streets she had known so well for many years. A woman with a wandering mind might be drawn back to the environment of her past out of strange compulsion. He had reached the conclusion years ago that Elsie Chivers was guilty of the murder of her mother. It was not a conclusion of absolute certainty, but of suspicion and painful deduction.

He searched Walworth Road and the East Street market more than once in his attempts to find her. He walked around the little streets surrounding Caulfield Place and St John's Church. He went into the church, thinking she might be there.

He was in Caulfield Place one day. The kids were just coming home from school. They were sprightly. Christmas was coming. That always put a spring in young feet.

Freddy Brown saw the tall man in hat and overcoat, and recognised him, even though he had only seen Boots once. Susie often spoke of him and how nice he was.

' 'Ello, mister,' said Freddy.

'I think I know you,' said Boots.

'I'm Freddy, Susie's brother. We live in yer old 'ouse, yer know.'

'So you do. Is it all right, Freddy?'

'You bet, Mister Adams.'

'Freddy, have you recently seen a certain woman?' Boots described Miss Chivers, and also mentioned her cloche hat and leather coat.

'Crikey, yes, I seen 'er all right,' said Freddy. 'Ain't she a funny old girl?' Miss Chivers was in her early forties. 'She come and asked questions, yer know.' Freddy told Boots of the time when the woman had appeared in the passage and asked about Mrs Adams and a Mr Finch, and talked about coming to Sunday tea and didn't listen to nothing he said.

'I'd like to get in touch with her,' said Boots, 'I'd like to find out where she lives. If you see her again and your time's your own, is it possible you could get someone to ring me at the shop from the Walworth Road phone box while you keep your eyes on her? If it's out of shop hours, have the phone call made to my home. There's a couple of bob in it for you, and two extra pennies to keep in your pocket for the phone call.'

'Two bob?' Freddy's eyes lit up. 'Yer on, Mister

Adams. I'll keep me eyes on 'er, I'll keep 'er talkin', I'll invite 'er in, that's what, and me mum'll keep 'er talkin' as well. Me mum's a dab 'and at keepin' anyone talkin'. Course, I could just ask 'er where she lives, if yer like.'

'She might not tell you.'

'See what yer mean, Mister Adams, she's a bit funny all right.'

Boots took out his wallet, found a scrap of paper and used his propelling pencil to write down the relevant phone numbers. He gave it to Freddy, together with a florin and two pennies. He had a feeling that it was here, in Caulfield Place, that Miss Chivers was most likely to reappear. Was it the grisly and macabre nature of her conscience that had driven her to return to Walworth? He experienced a sense of deep pity.

'Right, Freddy, keep your peepers peeled, then, eh?'

'You bet, Mister Adams,' said Freddy. He could buy Daisy a Christmas present now, out of the two bob. A fair-sized rubber ball, which they could both kick about.

That evening, Boots advised Emily of his arrangement with Freddy Brown. Emily said that was a long shot, if you like. Better if Miss Chivers just disappeared again, and for good. Boots thought not every sleeping dog ought to be left to lie.

The following day was crisp and bright with winter sunshine, shop windows decorated for Christmas. At ten o'clock, a small dark blue motor van stood outside the Adams's shop at Camberwell Green. On each side it bore the painted inscription, 'JAMES BROWN & CO – FAMILY BAKERS – DAILY DELIVERIES'. Boots was inspecting it in company with an old wartime comrade, ex-Corporal Mitchell of the West Kents.

'I'm leavin' it with yer, guv,' said the driver.

'Fine,' said Boots, and gave him a tip.

231

'Bless yer, guv, merry Christmas to yer,' said the driver and went off.

'Well, there you are, Mitch,' said Boots, 'all yours, job and the van.'

'Ain't many sergeants like you,' said Mitch.

'We're all sods,' said Boots.

'Gettin' a permanent job ain't something I don't like to mention,' said Mitch, 'specially at Christmas time. Me old lady don't know if she's comin' or goin', she's that tickled. I've had bits o' jobs, I 'ad one that lasted six months once, so yer won't mind me mentioning this 'ere permanent job's a godsend.'

'Works both ways,' said Boots. 'You need us, we need you. All right, Mitch, hop up and try it.'

'I ain't 'andled four wheels since me Army days,' said Mitch, 'but this runabout won't give me no trouble.'

'Take it for a run round the block,' said Boots.

Mitch climbed up into the driving seat. Sammy came out.

'What's this?' he asked.

'A delivery van,' said Boots. 'Needs a sign-writer to work on it, that's all.'

'You crafty bleeder,' said Sammy.

'Now, now, sonny, it's a bargain buy at forty quid,' said Boots.

'I don't recollect signing no indent approving same.'

'Don't worry about that now, I've sent the cheque to Browns, and it's still a bargain. Remark the condition, my lad.'

'Sometimes,' said Sammy, 'I can hardly believe you're me own brother the way you slip in unapproved transactions when I've got me back turned.' But he walked around the van with a slightly proud look of ownership. He spoke to Mitch at the wheel. 'You from Browns?' he asked.

'No, from fifty-four Rodney Road,' said Mitch, 'and

was instructed to present meself 'ere by Sergeant Adams to take on the job of driving this box for 'is firm, which is Adams Enterprises.'

'I see,' said Sammy, 'you're an old Army mate of his, are you?'

' 'E's me sergeant,' said Mitch.

'Well, I'm Adams Enterprises,' said Sammy, 'and Sergeant Adams is me brother and manager.'

An open Morris car came rushing up. It jerked to a stop behind the van. From the driving seat, Polly Simms gestured frantically to Boots, who strode up to the car.

'Where's the fire?' he asked.

'Oh, God, it's Rosie,' gasped Polly, pale-faced. 'She fell down some steps at school. She's unconscious. I've just driven her to King's College Hospital. She's in casualty. You must come.'

Boots, stunned for a moment, shook himself and leapt into the car.

'Pick up Emily, at the estate agents,' he said.

Polly, teeth biting bottom lip, drove to the estate agents. Boots jumped out and ran in. A young woman in the front office looked up.

'Sir?' she said.

'My wife, Mrs Adams, where is she?'

'She's out with Mr Somerville, Mr Barry Somerville.'

'Where?'

The girl, seeing the look on Boots's face, said, 'She's gone to help with a valuation at fifty-four Denmark Hill—'

Boots was out and away. He gave Polly the address, and Polly, her mouth compressed, drove there at speed. It wasn't far. Boots leapt out again. Polly followed. The front door of the house was open.

'Emily!' Boots shouted from the hall. There was no answer. He looked into one room, then another. He entered the living-room, Polly behind him. Through the window he saw Emily. She was in the garden with Mr Somerville. He was kissing her, his arms around her. Polly sensed Boots turning rigid. She herself felt frozen with shock. She wished herself a thousand miles away.

Emily put her hands on Mr Somerville's chest and gently pushed him off.

'That's your Christmas come and gone,' she said.

'Emily!'

She turned her head, and she too froze in shock then. Boots was looking at her from the window he had opened.

'Oh, my God,' she gasped.

Boots, his face expressionless, said, 'Break that up, will you? Rosie's had an accident. She's in King's College Hospital. I'd like you to come. Miss Simms is here with her car.'

It was a short ride but a traumatic one. Emily did not know what to say. For the first time in her life her ready tongue lay helpless. It was impossible, the situation, because of the presence of a third party. Boots was curt in telling her about Rosie's fall. And Emily found herself saying, 'But she'll be all right, won't she, she'll be all right?'

Boots did not answer.

And Polly said nothing. She was angry now, and suffering. She was totally unable to understand why the wife of a man like Robert Adams could indulge in cheap kisses with another man. Polly had known a thousand cheap kisses herself, every one of them instantly forgettable. If the actions of Emily Adams made her angry, the humiliation Robert had endured in seeing his wife in the arms of another man made her suffer. She felt intensely for him.

She heard him speak then, quite quietly.

'Just say a prayer, Em.'

And Emily said huskily, 'Yes. Yes.'

At the hospital they spoke to a doctor in casualty.

'Severe concussion, of course, Mr Adams. But we'll see what the X-ray says. If there's a fracture, it'll show up.'

'A skull fracture?' said Boots.

'There may be no fracture at all. Call in later this afternoon.'

'Can we see her?'

'She's sleeping. We've given her a sedative. Best thing.'

'Is she sleeping, or is she unconscious?' asked Boots.

'Oh, she came to, but with a terrible headache, of course. She's a brave little girl. Yes, she's sleeping.'

'Can we see her?' asked Emily.

A nurse took them to the ward. Rosie lay asleep, with a huge black bruise disfiguring her forehead. Emily suffered distress, unhappiness and pain. She glanced across the bed at Boots. He looked tragic. He took life mostly in a whimsical way, as if he found its ups and downs amusing. An old comrade of his, a man called Nobby Clark, blind from the war, had once said to her when she asked him how he was getting on, 'Well, it ain't a garden of roses, Mrs Sergeant Adams, but it's good to be alive.' That was how it was with Boots, of course. It was simply good to be alive. It was painful to see him so set-faced, so sombre, his eyes on Rosie. She wondered if he loved Rosie more than he loved her. The thought that perhaps he did twisted the knife. Had she been taking him for granted? Whenever she did anything special for him, he'd say, 'Love you, Em.' Or, 'Love you, old girl.' She could not remember the last time she'd said she loved him. Now, on a day when Rosie had perhaps fractured her skull, he had caught her being kissed by Barry Somerville, an irresponsible bachelor. And so soon after this awful problem with Miss Chivers.

'Boots?' She spoke in a whisper.

235

'She's so young,' he said.

'Yes. I love her too, you know, and I am praying.' She reached out a hand across the bed, and emotions welled as he took it and squeezed it.

Leaving the hospital, he said, 'I'll call in again this afternoon, they'll have examined the X-ray by then.'

'Yes, I'll call in too.'

Polly, who had spoken to the casualty staff, was outside, in her car. Boots thanked her for everything and told her he and Emily would walk back to their work. Polly said nothing, she drove away, eyes burning.

Emily watched her go, then turned to Boots.

'Don't say anything,' said Boots.

'I must. It was only a stupid Christmas kiss. He brought mistletoe.'

'Yes, all right. Leave it, Em.'

'I can't. It didn't mean anything. He gets silly ideas. It would only mean something if I got silly ideas myself. Did she see too, that woman?'

'Leave it, Emily,' said Boots, as they turned left into Denmark Hill, in the direction of the shop.

'We've got to talk,' said Emily.

'I don't see why, if it didn't mean anything.'

'I just want to know you believe that.'

'I believe you.'

'I want you to believe something else, something important,' said Emily. She stopped, took his arm, and made him stop too. 'I want you to know I love all of you. Rosie, Tim, Chinese Lady, Dad, and you. It wouldn't matter if I had the best job a woman could ever have, and all the money in the world, my fam'ly would still mean more to me than all of it. Only no one believes me. I just like being busy, doing things. Oh, men are so stupid.'

'You've set yourself up, have you, Em, as an expert on our imperfections?'

'I'm unhappy, I'm suffering for Rosie, I'm mad at myself and that stupid, stupid man. And don't be upper-class with me. Hit me.'

'Do me a favour,' said Boots. His mind on Rosie, he was not disposed to discuss who was stupid and who was not. 'Give Somerville a message from me. Tell him you're my wife. Tell him that if he's that much in need to get one for himself.' A little gleam of the hidden steel surfaced. 'Tell him that if he continues to fancy you, I'll knock his bloody head off. You got that, Em?'

It shocked Emily. It almost frightened her. Boots meant it. She had never heard him speak like that before, nor had she ever seen his eyes look so steely.

'I don't like this,' she said, oblivious of people passing by.

'Tell him, Em.'

'I'll tell him.'

'You'd better,' said Boots.

'Then I'm going home to talk to Chinese Lady.'

'Why?'

'Because she's the fam'ly, because I've got to, and because I don't like you like this.'

'You're my wife,' said Boots, and went walking on to the shop. Emily had a terrible feeling that in some way she was going to lose him. She crossed the road, she walked fast to the estate agents. Mr Barry Somerville was back. She marched straight into his office, and word for word she delivered her husband's message to him.

Mr Somerville sat up.

'Emily—'

'And what's more, I'll kill you too. If you've done anything to my marriage, I'll kill you!' She marched out and she went home to talk to Chinese Lady.

Chinese Lady listened in silence, then regarded Emily a little sadly.

'I'll get my hat,' she said.

'Your hat?'

'I'm going to the hospital to sit with Rosie. Rosie's a child, and she's hurt bad. You and Boots, you're grown-ups. What's happened was bound to happen, with you comin' home each day with tales of Mr Somerville saying how good you are at this, how promisin' you are at that, and what he's got in mind for you, and Boots lettin' it go on and not seeing what it was goin' to lead to. Well, he's been pulled up with a jerk, I'll be bound. Of course you didn't like him speakin' to you like that, but what did you expect? Did you expect a bunch of roses, Em'ly Adams?'

'Oh, that's not fair,' protested Emily.

'You said that to me once before,' said Chinese Lady. 'I told you then, and I'll tell you again, you and Boots got duties to each other, and responsibilities, and it's not responsible for him to be so airy-fairy about things and for you to encourage men to kiss you. Now don't tell me there was no encouragement, it might not have been deliberate, like, but it was there, it's no good always blaming the men and calling them stupid. There's stupid women, Em'ly, as well as stupid men, so don't go about thinkin' it's all on one side.'

'Oh, anyone would think I went to bed with Mr Somerville!'

'Well, that's usually the next step. I'll get my hat and coat and go and sit with Rosie. You stay and look after Tim.'

'Mum, you're being awfully hard on me.'

'Wait till I see Boots, I'll be a lot harder on him. It's his fault mostly. If either of you think I'm goin' to sit back and see a fam'ly marriage break up, you've both got another think comin'. There's goin' to be no broken marriage in my fam'ly, nor broken Commandments.'

'I'll come down later meself,' said Emily. 'Oh, it's a

238

rotten rotten day, Rosie looks so bad. Mum, I don't want a broken marriage, honest to God I don't. I never seen Boots look at me the way he did.' She put her face in her hands.

There was the lightest pat on her shoulder.

'There, he'll get over it, and there's wives who've done far worse things than you, Em'ly love.'

Emily, strong-minded though she was, burst into tears. Chinese Lady comforted her.

'I'm afraid you can't, Mrs Finch,' said the ward sister.

'Don't be afraid, because I'm goin' to,' said Chinese Lady. 'She's my granddaughter, she's a hurt child.'

'She's still sleeping, and the visiting rules—'

'I won't interfere, I'll just sit with her. She ought to have someone there when she wakes up. I'll stay until her father gets here.'

'Matron will have my head.'

'I don't want to get you into trouble,' said Chinese Lady.

'Go in, Mrs Finch.'

'That's kind of you. Well, it looks a nice cheerful ward. And there she is. You just get on with things, sister.'

The ward sister smiled resignedly. Chinese Lady, seating herself at Rosie's bedside, gazed in concern at the huge black bruise. Rosie lay with her eyes closed, her breathing interspersed with what sounded like the sighs of troubled dreams. Chinese Lady removed her gloves and took hold of the still hand that lay over the blanket. She held it gently throughout her vigil, discouraging talk from any of the other patients. She did not want to be obtrusive, only to be there if Rosie woke up.

In the middle of the afternoon, the girl's hand lightly stirred and her lashes lifted. Chinese Lady thought her eyes looked blurred.

'There's a good girl,' she murmured.

239

There was a faint, painful sigh from Rosie. Her heavy lashes blinked.

'Nana?'

'Yes, it's me, Rosie.'

'Nana—' Another sigh. 'Oh, I've got an awful head.'

'Bless us, that's a nuisance.'

'Yes. Awful.' The lashes dropped and the sedated girl went to sleep again.

Chinese Lady looked up as someone looked in. Sammy. The ward sister was shaking her head at him.

'Just a quick peep, be a sport,' said Sammy, and crossed to the bedside, hat in his hand. 'Mum? I heard, of course. How is she?'

'She just woke up, then went off again. We just have to wait and hope, Sammy. Nice you've come, nice you remembered Rosie.'

Sammy looked down at her girl. He frowned.

'Boots is regular cut up,' he said. 'He'll be here soon, he's been frettin' all afternoon. Have they looked at the X-ray yet? Boots'll burn his top if they don't have the result when he gets here.'

'I didn't think.' Chinese Lady relinquished Rosie's hand and got up. 'You sit with her, Sammy, while—'

'I've only got a few minutes.'

'I didn't finish speakin'.'

'Sorry, old girl.'

'You sit with her and hold her hand. I'll go and see a doctor or someone. If that X-ray's been done, I want to know what it says. It's no good you goin', you'll try to sell them sheets and blankets. That won't do Rosie no good.'

Sammy sat down and Chinese Lady went in search of up-to-date facts. She looked for the ward sister. She might know by now. The ward sister was missing for the moment. Chinese Lady went to casualty.

Sammy took hold of Rosie's hand, thought how

warm it was, and how ugly and painful the bruise looked.

'Buck up, Rosie love, you'll win,' he said, 'your mum and dad are counting on that. So am I.'

The next one to arrive was Polly. She had had a terrible afternoon. The ward sister, around again, was very firm this time. Sammy got up and joined Polly in the corridor.

'Sammy, you're here?' she said. 'God, does that mean she's bad? Does it?'

'Steady,' said Sammy. 'I don't really have time to be here, but I made time. I don't know if she's bad or good. I'm just hoping. You don't look all that good yourself.'

'Thanks very much,' said Polly, 'but I've had a bloody awful day, and I feel responsible.'

'Now, Polly, don't say things like that. You can't stop kids from falling over. Not even God can. Kids are always falling over.'

Polly, trim but haggard in a cloche hat and buttoned coat, smiled wanly, then bit her lip as Boots appeared.

'I had to come,' she said.

'I'll take a look at her, then find the doctor,' said Boots. The ward sister reappeared.

'We really can't have this,' she said, 'so many of you.'

At which point, Chinese Lady returned, her back straight, her step sprightly.

'So there you are,' she said to Boots. 'And good afternoon, Miss Simms.'

'I'm so terribly sorry about Rosie,' said Polly.

'It's bad concussioning, that's what it is,' said Chinese Lady. 'I just seen the doctor.' The ward sister exclaimed and departed with a swift rustle, wanting to find out for herself. 'Rosie don't have a fracture, Boots. She'll be kept in a few days, but she'll be all right. What a blessing.' Chinese Lady raised an eyebrow as Polly turned away, biting on a lip that was actually trembling. One never thought of weakness in a woman who had seen the hell of France and Flanders as an ambulance driver. 'There's a—'

'It's official?' said Boots. 'There's no fracture?'

'I don't like this interrupting,' said Chinese Lady. 'Still, I can understand. No, there's no fracture. There's a place where we can all have a cup of tea – Boots, what're you doing?'

Boots was giving her a warm kiss on her cheek.

'Good on yer, Granny,' he said.

'There's no need—'

'I got you, Boots,' said Sammy, and kissed her other cheek.

'That's it, make exhibitions of yourselves and me too, never mind it's a hospital.'

'Love yer,' said Boots, and slipped into the ward to take a look at Rosie.

'I don't know what you must think, Miss Simms,' said Chinese Lady.

Polly faced up to the emotional problems she experienced so often in her relationship with this family. Their background was plain, simple and unvarnished cockney, their love of life extraordinary. In going regularly to the house to cram Rosie, she had come to know their enthusiasms, their laughter and their loyalties. For her, Boots stood out, of course, an ex-Tommy, a man of infectious whimsy who could pass muster in any house in the land. His mother was a reactionary Victorian, an incredible character, with searching eyes and knowing eyes. Polly was sure that Mrs Finch, formerly Mrs Adams, was aware of how she felt about Boots. She stood up to that awareness now.

'I think, Mrs Finch, that people who make exhibitions of themselves on occasions like this are the best kind of people. I'm so relieved about Rosie, so glad for all of you. I feel I shall never let Rosie out of my sight again.'

Chinese Lady gave her a kind but level look. The vitality of Rosie's teacher looked as if it had taken a drubbing. Chinese Lady did not know Polly had witnessed Emily's indiscretion. Emily had left out any mention of Polly. Chinese Lady only saw a woman whose feelings had badly suffered solely on account of Rosie. For all that she felt Polly Simms needed watching, Chinese Lady could not help liking her.

'I think you need a cup of tea too, Miss Simms,' she said. 'Come along, we'll go to the tea room. My hooligan sons can join us there.'

'I don't know I've got time,' said Sammy.

'I'm not havin' any argufying, I want to speak to you. I'm hearing tales about you designing ladies' clothes. I don't like the sound of that, it don't sound decent or proper. When Boots comes out, bring him with you. Come along, Miss Simms.'

Sammy grinned and waited for Boots. Polly went with Chinese Lady, and by the time they reached the tea room Polly had a curiously tingling feeling that this resilient and protective Victorian mother had accepted her as a family friend.

Chinese Lady, of course, believed in keeping close to anything that might be a threat to family unity.

'We'll walk part of the way home,' said Chinese Lady later. 'We can talk better than on a bus. Em'ly should be with Rosie now. You didn't wait for her, I noticed. She'll have had Tim with her.'

'We'll go together this evening, at visiting time,' said Boots.

'Still,' said Chinese Lady, walking through the darkness of the cold, crisp December evening in her proud, busy way, 'I think you might have waited, just to please Em'ly.'

'I'm seeing you home.'

'I'm not an old woman yet, I can see myself home.'

'It's not the kind of thing I promised your husband.'

Chinese Lady reflected, little knowing Boots was wondering if she had a husband.

'Well, it's nice Edwin was thoughtful concernin' me,' she said. Boots silently winced. The situation was playing havoc with his peace of mind. He had got to find Miss Chivers. 'Still, you mustn't think it's the cold air that matters, it's the fog. And it's not foggy, and I've got something to say to you.'

'Yes, Emily spoke to you. She said she was going to.'

'Yes. Well, it wasn't a great sin she did. I don't want you to go about thinkin' it was. Men have always got an eye for women. Most men have got respect for married women, but some haven't. Some think married women get taken for granted by their husbands and will enjoy being flirted with. The trouble with married women goin' out to work is that they come up against men like that Mr Somerville of the estate agents, and it makes them lose their heads. Not that Em'ly's a woman who'll lose her head easy, but you know she don't think much of her own looks, specially not when she puts herself up against our Lizzy and our Vi, or that young lady who's come back to work for Sammy in Camberwell. I disremember her name—'

'I don't think so, old girl, I think you know she's Susie Brown.'

'Oh, yes, that's her. I went to the shop yesterday and happened to see her.' Chinese Lady was casual, so Boots, of course, knew how her mind was working. 'I noticed she speaks much better and has got very elegant, like.'

'I'm with you,' said Boots, 'I'm following. Have you told Sammy you've decided?'

'I don't know what you mean. It's a grief to me you still say things no one understands except yourself. I hope you get to understand about Em'ly, she was very upset when she got home. I wouldn't like to think I brought up my only oldest son to be uncaring. Now, I don't want any nonsense from you about all this. It was silly of Em'ly to go to an empty house with that man and let him kiss her there. In an office or a fact'ry at Christmastime, well, people do bring mistletoe, but lettin' it happen at an empty house, it was wrong of Em'ly and she knows it. Em'ly's a good girl, really, and a lovin' mother, even if she has got strange ideas about she ought to have a job when she shouldn't and needn't. I been surprised all along you wasn't more firm with her, a man's got a duty to be firm with his wife sometimes, same as a woman's got a duty to put her husband in his place when he's lordin' it. I don't hold with men actin' like lords of creation, and never will. Well, I was saying before you interrupted me about Em'ly not thinkin' much of her own looks – Boots, now what're you doing?'

'Taking your arm, old lady. It's dark along here.'

'No, it isn't.' The window lights of houses emitted a cosy glow. 'I'm not ninety yet, so stop your fussing.' But she let him take her arm. 'Where was I? Yes, our Em'ly. Not thinkin' herself much to look at, and havin' a husband who's so airy-fairy she thinks he don't mind what she gets up to, she's bound to let herself be flattered by a man like Mr Somerville. I don't hardly know any husband more airy-fairy than you, Boots. Em'ly can't know where she is with a husband who don't do his duty by being firm, it's like children get when no one tells them what's right and what's wrong, they don't know where they are. Em'ly's been talkin' all the days God's give her about havin' a full-time job, and I been sorely grieved to see you sittin' there and not puttin' your foot down like a proper husband should. What you saw goin' on between Em'ly and that Mr Somerville is your own blame. Boots, you listening?'

'I'm listening.'

245

'Well, I can tell you Em'ly went back to her office and give Mr Somerville an earful, like you asked her to, but when I heard what shockin' language you used to her, your own wife, as well as givin' her a very nasty look, I near fell down with shame. What your dad would of said, or Edwin either, don't bear thinkin' about. Speakin' like that and lookin' at Em'ly so nasty, it's near to hooliganism and it upset her something chronic. You sure you're listening?'

'Carry on, old love.'

'If I thought you had one of them sly smiles of yours on your face, I'd give you a real talking to. Now, I don't want you ridin' no high horses, my lad, I don't want no unpleasant atmospheres. I know it's not been the best day you and Em'ly ever had, but God's still been good to you by makin' sure Rosie wasn't fractured. When we get home I'll start doing the supper, and by the time we're sittin' down to it I want to see you and Em'ly lovin' each other.'

'Over the supper table?'

'What? Is that one of your low music hall jokes at a time like this and you my own son?'

'Yes, all your own work, old lady. And Dad's too, of course. Come on, there's a bus on its way and here's the stop. You've walked far enough, and I promise Emily and I won't disgrace the supper table.'

Her mouth twitched. Standing with him at the bus stop, she said, 'I don't know how I ever come to have a son who's always saying one thing and meaning another. Anyway, Boots, I'm not havin' no fam'ly upsets, I'm not havin' any of my fam'ly being fractious with each other. It's not good for none of us, specially not for the children.'

'You're a wise old girl, old lady.'

'You and your old lady. After supper, you and Em'ly can go and see Rosie together. Together. Have you got that, my lad?'

'Yes, got it, Mum. I'll be firm.'

The bus pulled up. Chinese Lady boarded it with a satisfied look.

Emily arrived home with Tim not long after her husband and mother-in-law.

'Boots is upstairs,' said Chinese Lady. 'Did Rosie wake up?'

'Yes, she kept wakin' and goin' off again,' said Emily. 'It's such a relief it's only concussion.'

'She'll be more awake later, they won't give her another sedative yet awhile. There, I'll see to Tim. You go upstairs and take your hat and coat off.'

'Yes, upstairs where Boots is. The penny's already dropped, Mum.'

Boots had washed and freshened up. Emily entered the bedroom resolved to stand up for herself. Boots regarded her soberly. Her mouth tightened.

'Did Rosie wake up?' he asked.

'On and off, like I just told Mum.'

'We'll go and see her together after supper.'

'Will we?' said Emily, stiff-faced.

'Yes. Orders from Chinese Lady. Come here.'

'That's another order?' said Emily, taking her hat and coat off.

'Yes. Come here.'

She approached him, tense in defence of herself. He put his arms around her.

'What's this for?' she asked.

'Christmas,' said Boots and kissed her firmly on the mouth. Emily collapsed against him. 'All over, lovey,' he said.

'Oh, I been havin' a rotten day.'

'All over,' he said again, 'and we have to love each other over the supper table.'

'Oh, don't joke.'

'No joke,' said Boots, 'it's another order. From

247

Chinese Lady. We talk rhubarb, Em. She talks sense. She made me realise our little troubles hardly rate a mention compared with what might hit her if Miss Chivers does turn out to be the first Mrs Finch.'

'I've got a terrible feeling that if Mr Finch is a really dark horse, Miss Chivers might not be the first herself,' said Emily.

'Jesus Christ,' said Boots.

CHAPTER EIGHTEEN

Rosie's one concern, while recovering, was that she might not be home for Christmas. The school had broken up, and Annabelle and Aunt Lizzy were visiting.

'Of course you'll be home, darling,' said Lizzy, 'the nurses told us so.'

Rosie, still with a tender head that went thump if she moved it too quickly, said, 'Oh, but they have to say gracious things, Auntie, it's in case they don't want you to know you're next door to death.'

'You're not next door to death,' said Lizzy, looking like a Christmas card in her deep blue cloche hat and warm red winter coat.

'No, but I'm next door to not being home for Christmas, Auntie, and that's death,' said Rosie.

'Oh, I'll come and spend Christmas Day in here with you,' said Annabelle, 'and we could—'

'Don't say it,' said Lizzy, 'you're not goin' to die together in here, you pair of pickles. We'll all be with Granny Lady and bursting with health unless some I could mention eat too much and get sick.'

'Auntie, I haven't bought presents yet,' said Rosie. 'Oh, what a blessed nuisance having a head like this. I just hope it didn't knock my brains about and get them all mixed up. Auntie, I've got saved-up money, really, and I made a list. Could you—' She winced as a little

249

dart of sensitive pain struck. 'I expect you're awfully busy, but—'

'I'll get them for you,' said Lizzy.

'Oh, and could I whisper to Annabelle?'

'I won't listen,' said Lizzy.

Rosie whispered to Annabelle.

'Goodness,' said Annabelle, 'she'll like that. I know where to buy one.'

Lizzy affected innocence.

Going down to the shops at Camberwell Green after leaving the hospital, Lizzy stopped with Annabelle outside the theatre. Camberwell Green still boasted a theatre, and still promoted mainly music hall turns. Now the annual pantomime was being advertised. This year it was *Dick Whittington*. Annabelle eyed the posters excitedly.

'Oh, there's a conjuror too, Mummy.' Conjurors fascinated her. Rabbits out of a hat were simply spiffing.

Lizzy noted the fact that, along with other turns in the pantomime, Rainbould the Master of Magic and his assistant Vivette would be performing.

'Annabelle, let's,' she said. 'A fam'ly pantomime party. We'll go and see Uncle Boots and Uncle Sammy, and we'll get tickets for Uncle Tommy and Auntie Vi, and Granny Lady too. We'll all go, the whole fam'ly.'

Sammy, arriving in his office from Shoreditch, was a man perpetually busy. He looked lean, fit and clear-eyed, for perpetual motion that related to business, his business, did for him what climbing a mountain did for other men. Boots came in as soon as he sat down.

'Ah,' said Sammy.

'Ah?' said Boots. 'I believe that's an interjection mainly used by bank managers.'

'That's educated talk, Boots. You're good at that.'

'You're not short of your own kind of chat,' said Boots.

'I do me best, y'know. Now, it's me pleasure to inform you that Christmas Eve – oh, how's Rosie?'

'Out in two days,' said Boots.

'I'm joyful,' said Sammy. 'Well, on Christmas Eve, Madame will be here to show us samples of her first collection.'

'Madame?'

'Madame Mimi Dupont, called Lily Hyams previous. Camberwell, I thought, not Shoreditch. Yer can't believe the eyes that creep up around Shoreditch. We shall have the honour of receiving our benefital shareholder, Mrs Goodman—'

'Rachel, your old love, you mean, and beneficial, not benefital.'

'Same difference,' said Sammy, 'but kindly don't pain me with references to what ain't relevant. Also, do me the favour of remembering I'm your own brother, and refrain accordin' from acquaintin' Chinese Lady with details of the Christmas Eve display, or she'll come round and set fire to everything.'

'If you don't refrain from trying to teach me how to suck lemons,' said Boots, 'I'll break your leg.'

'Granted,' said Sammy. 'We shall discuss the samples and prospects, you, me, Mrs Rachel Goodman and Fifi—'

'Fifi?'

'Mimi. My personal assistant, Miss Brown, will also be present on account of if she's left out I might not get to see Christmas Day.'

'Pardon?' said Boots.

'Did I say something?'

'Nothing that I don't understand. Christmas Eve, right, I'll be here.'

'You certainly will,' said Sammy.

'New Year's Eve, you'll be there,' said Boots, and placed two tickets for the pantomime on Sammy's desk.

251

'What's all this?' asked Sammy.

'Tickets for this year's pantomime. New Year's Eve performance. Two bob each. Four bob for the pair. Pay Lizzy. She bought them for the whole family, this afternoon.'

'Well, I like a panto, I won't say I don't,' said Sammy, 'but I don't know I'll have time.'

'You'll have time. The evening is by royal command.'

'Whose command?'

'Chinese Lady's,' said Boots, 'as spoken by her herself when Lizzy phoned her from my office earlier.'

'All right,' said Sammy, 'but I don't need two tickets.'

'Yes, you do. One's for Susie.'

'I do not recall—'

'Nothing to do with your memory,' said Boots. 'It's orders.'

'Orders?'

'Chinese Lady's. Tell Sammy he's not to come by himself, it won't look sociable, she said. Tell him to ask that nice young lady who works privately for him.'

'She's pushing me,' said Sammy.

'Susie is?'

'No, yer clown, Chinese Lady. She'll have me churched the day after if she can.'

'I don't think so,' said Boots, 'I think she favours a spring wedding.'

'Kindly note I am not in the mood for comic chat of a highly personal fashion,' said Sammy.

'It's no joke, Sammy. Chinese Lady passes on those kind of orders directly from God.'

'What kind of orders?'

'Spring weddings.'

'I'm hysterical,' said Sammy.

Susie knocked and came in, looking the impeccable secretary in a stylish white blouse and dark blue skirt. She consulted her wristwatch. An air of reproof arrived. Boots studied the ceiling.

'You're late back, Mister Sammy,' she said. 'It's four-fifteen, and you told me half-past three.'

'My movements happen to be elasticated, Miss Brown.'

'Yes, Mister Sammy, very well. Christmas week is very elasticated, of course. I've ordered the port for Christmas Eve. There are forty letters waitin' for your signature.'

'You sign 'em,' said Sammy, regarding her cautiously and looking for a sign of a little loving. 'And ah, yes, let me see. Now what was it?'

'It'll come to you, with the assistance of the nice young lady who works privately for you,' said Boots, and went back to his office.

'May I enquire who this young lady is?' asked Susie. In the office, she conducted herself to plan, exercising a businesslike air that sometimes induced that muttering mumble in Sammy, much to her delight. 'I do not recollect being told about her.' She could take him off with no effort at all.

'Listen,' said Sammy, 'that high-falutin' gent, who happens to be my only eldest brother, has a nasty weakness for failing to be serious at times, which is every day.'

'I won't hear a word against him, Mister Adams,' said Susie, 'he's adored by all of us.'

'Oh, he is, is he?' growled Sammy. 'Well, if I catch him being adored in office hours there'll be ructions that'll blow the roof off.'

'Really, Mister Adams, such a fuss about our hero-worship, I'm surprised at you,' said Susie.

It wasn't possible, thought Sammy. She'd been a woebegone, hungry-eyed, skinny young cockney waif five years ago. Look at her now. And listen to her. The Queen of Sheba couldn't have been more regal. Gawd help me, if I ask her and she does say yes, she'll have me on toast for the rest of my life. I won't be able to say no to anything she asks for, she'll end up with all I've got, including every shirt off my back.

'Where was I?' he asked.

'You were going to tell me who the young lady is who works privately for you,' said Susie.

'Didn't I make it clear Boots meant you?'

'Oh, the dear man,' said Susie, 'to call me nice, would you believe.'

'I'll remind you, Miss Brown, that on a considerable number of occasions I've called you nice myself. Also good, kind and helpful.'

'Yes, Mister Adams, thank you. I want you to know—' Susie paused.

'All right, let's hear it, I know it's goin' to make my ears ring,' said Sammy.

'I want you to know I'm very very happy working here,' said Susie. Sammy coughed, rubbed his mouth and looked at his desk. He had a thousand things to do, and as always she took his mind off all of them. Susie's eyes grew warm and loving. He was a terrible coward, but such a darling. 'I'll go and sign the letters. Oh, that list on your desk is of people you have to phone.'

'Yes, right,' said Sammy. 'By the way, I happen to have acquired tickets for the Camberwell theatre pantomime on New Year's Eve. Would you care to accompany me?'

Her eyes danced.

'New Year's Eve? The pantomime? Oh, Mister Sammy, I'd love to.' Susie lost her businesslike mask.

'It's with the fam'ly,' said Sammy, 'we're all goin'.'

'Oh.' Susie adored his family. His brothers were gorgeous, and she didn't know anyone more loveable than his mother, nor anyone lovelier or more infectious than his sister Lizzy. 'The Tivoli again with you tomorrow, and the pantomime New Year's Eve? Mister Sammy, why are you so lovely to me?' That was a request to him to declare himself.

Sammy coughed again and said, 'Well, I was thinking that in appreciation of your considerable worth—'

'Oh!' Susie, in spirited vexation with him, stalked out. Sammy's phone rang, and he was immediately wrapped up in a profitable business conversation.

She forgave him again during the second visit to the Tivoli, which was even more exciting than the first. He actually called for her in a taxi, bought her an even sweller box of chocolates, saw her settled comfortably in her seat, and even went so far as to tell her he was highly gratified to know she was the most stylish young female woman in the audience.

'Mister Sammy, you can have a chocolate for that, a caramel centre. Oh, lor', though, the money you're spending on me when you've got all those ruinous business expenses.'

'You saucebox,' said Sammy, 'I'll take two caramel centres for that.'

She laughed. She liked him so much when he was droll. She looked at him as he helped himself from the proffered box of chocolates. She liked his clean look very much, and the manly lines of his face. She liked the way he challenged life, the way he bargained, and the way he left competitors trailing in his wake. The people who worked for him really did have to work, but no one ever complained, because if you did a good job for Sammy Adams, you had a job for life. The Shoreditch machinists were stitching for their lives, for their promised bonuses, and Sammy kept them going not only because of the bonuses, but because of the way he talked to them. He gave them cockney talk, and he laced all his threats with a mixture of sugar and vinegar that made them shriek with laughter. Susie liked going to the factory with him, to see how improved in look it was, and to see Tommy, for whom she had much affection.

The lights went down, and Susie absorbed herself again in the tense and emotional drama of *Ben Hur*. At the end, when the whole audience was charged with emotion, she found she was gripping Sammy's hand tightly. She could not remember when she had taken hold of it. She felt his fingers press hers as the screen went blank.

They stood for the National Anthem. When it was over, Sammy handed her something. His handkerchief.

'Blow your nose, Miss Brown,' he said.

It was a taxi again for the journey home. As it carried them over Waterloo Bridge, Susie kicked his ankle.

'You did that last week,' said Sammy.

'Yes. I never makes promises I don't keep. You're terrible, takin' me out, being lovely to me, and then calling me Miss Brown.'

'Well, Susie—'

'Yes?'

'You're nice to be out with.'

'Yes?'

'I won't come in when we get you home—'

'You will,' said Susie.

'I've got some multiple financial figuring to work on.'

'No, you haven't, you've just made that up. Besides, Mum's doing us a late supper of eggs and bacon.'

'Eggs and bacon? That's different,' said Sammy.

Susie smiled. Everything was fun when she was out with Sammy.

At midnight, with the weather chill and damp, they were at the open door and Sammy was about to say good night.

'I was thinking,' he said.

'Yes?' said Susie.

'Yes, I've been thinking.' He had. He had made his

decision. He would ask her Christmas Eve. Christmas Eve was always a time of goodwill, when most people had loving feelings towards each other, and some port inside them as well. And he could fall back on more port if she said no. 'I'll have to speak to you some time, Susie.' He lightly patted her arm. 'Good night, Susie.'

He'd done it again, thought Susie. He'd left her unkissed. But he was going to speak to her some time? When was some time?

CHAPTER NINETEEN

On the day before Christmas Eve, Boots's office phone rang. He picked it up.

'I think Oliver Twist wants to speak to you, Mr Adams,' said Doreen.

'Who?'

'Well, it's some boy.'

'Put him through,' said Boots.

' 'Ello?' said a young voice.

'Is that Freddy Brown?'

'Yerse, Mister Adams. Cor, ain't phones funny? Mister Adams, she's been again. Me mum's out Christmas shoppin', yer know, so I couldn't get 'er to talk to the lady. She kept saying she was goin' to come to Christmas dinner, an' I kept saying won't yer come in, so's I could get me sister Sally to phone yer. Only she just stood on the doorstep talkin' away till she said she'd got to see to 'er muvver and then go an' see Mr Finch—'

'And she's gone, Freddy?'

'I got 'er address, though, Mister Adams. I just said to 'er, "Where'd yer live, missus?" An' she come right out an' said, "Twenty-one Westmoreland Road." So I fought I'd phone you right away. Cor, Mister Adams, fancy talkin' to yer like this, I never used no phone before.'

'Freddy, have you told your family about this lady?'

'I ain't told no one. Well, I felt she was trouble to yer,

like, and I wasn't goin' to say anyfink unless she turned up again—'

'Good on yer, Freddy, you've earned that two bob. Leave it with me now, and thanks a lot. Merry Christmas.'

'Yer a sport, Mister Adams,' said Freddy and hung up.

Boots rang Emily at home. It was three in the afternoon. Freddy, of course, had broken up for the Christmas holiday.

'Boots?' said Emily.

'Listen, love. Our lady of trouble may be on the way to you right now.'

'Her?' said Emily.

'That's the one. Don't let her get inside the door. I'm afraid that means you'll have to put your hat and coat on and intercept her at the end of the road.'

'Yes, love,' said Emily. 'I'll take Tim for a walk. I know what to do if she turns up. I'll handle her, I'll put her on a bus. Trust me.'

'I'm going down now to Westmoreland Road. Young Freddy Brown has found out where she's staying. There's a chance she may have gone there first, and another chance she may have forgotten about visiting us again.'

'Yes, go there, Boots, see what you can find. Lord, I hope you don't find the worst.'

'We've got to know, Em.'

'Yes, we've got to, but I don't want to.'

'We'll see.'

It was not far to Westmoreland Road. A tram got him there in minutes. The street lamps were alight, the afternoon damp, and little eddies of shifting fog swam in the dusk. He knocked on the door of number twenty-one. He knocked twice without getting an answer. The latchcord, such a familiar thing in Walworth and

Camberwell, invited a tug. He tugged and the door opened. The passage was gloomy. He closed the door and made his way up the stairs. The house smelled of polish, a sure sign that the tenants were people of pride, however poor. Having made up his mind that Miss Chivers was a lodger here, he made straight for the upstairs back room. The landing was dark. He struck a match, turned the handle of the door and went in. The match went out. He struck another and lit the gas mantle. The room sprang into light. There was no fire burning and the room was cold. He saw the bed. It was neatly made, and the room was perfectly tidy. He had felt he might find untidiness and some neglect. One could relate that to a woman not quite right in her mind. He doubted then if this was her room. This might not even be where she lived. The address she had given Freddy might easily have been something she pulled out of her vague mind. Certainly, it was not an hotel. That too could have been a vague something.

An item standing on the mantelpiece caught his eye. It was the back of a photograph frame, a small frame. He picked it up and turned it, and a snapshot of Mr Finch came into sharp, clear being. He put it down and closed the door. He looked around. He opened a cupboard. A suitcase stood on the floor. He brought it out and placed it on the bed. He sprang the locks. He lifted the lid. Possessions. Little delicate ornaments, carefully wrapped in tissue. Little jewellery boxes. A ribboned bundle of letters. A flat inlaid box containing a manicure set. A leather wallet. He opened it. He saw German banknotes. He extracted two folded documents of fine, thin paper. One was Miss Chivers's birth certificate, the other a marriage certificate, issued in Munich in the Republic of Bavaria, and dated 21 September 1917. There was her name, Elsie Maud Chivers. And the name of the bridegroom, Walther Hirst Lansberg.

Except that this had been crossed out by a single, wavering line of ink, and above it, in equally wavering fashion, had been inserted, '*Edwin Finch*'.

That, thought Boots, in great pity, was the wishful thinking of a woman who had married a German called Lansberg, but would have preferred Mr Finch, a lapsed German and a man who had given her all the supportive strength of his being after the murder of her mother.

Boots's relief was intense. The foundation of his trust and belief in his stepfather had proved solid. And his mother had no worries. He tidied up, and he left, catching a bus that would carry him straight to Emily. Miss Chivers had not turned up. Nor did she at all.

Christmas Eve morning.

Emily was at work, Mr Barry Somerville subdued and quietly businesslike, Emily cool, efficient and thinking of a happy family Christmas.

Chinese Lady was mixing the Christmas pudding, using rich old ale to bind everything. Lizzy was in the kitchen with her, making stuffing for a gigantic turkey. A turkey. Some people sometimes ran to a chicken for Christmas, but only the rich were known to have turkey. Sammy had been presented with this twenty-six-pound bird by a customer who supplied lingerie to his ladies' shops. Sammy had presented it in turn to Chinese Lady, for the family's Christmas dinner. Chinese Lady had asked him how much he was charging her for it. Sammy said that was the kind of question that gave him a pain. Chinese Lady said it never used to. Sammy said he was profoundly pleasured to hand it over free and for nothing. Chinese Lady said she'd always known he was really a good boy at heart, and that she hoped some nice girl would recognise it.

'I'm on to you, Ma,' said Sammy.

'I don't know what you're talking about,' said Chinese Lady.

All the family would be there for Christmas dinner, including Aunt Victoria and Uncle Tom. Only Chinese Lady's husband would be absent. She hid her little sadness about that. No one knew just how much she liked having a husband again. To make up for his absence, she had just received an affectionate letter from him.

Rosie was home and taking it quietly. She was under strict orders from Boots. Annabelle was with her and they were writing their Christmas cards in Chinese Lady's little sitting-room. Tim was in the other sitting-room, playing with his cousins Emma and Bobby. Three-year-old Emma was giving the two boys a terrible time. Tim and Bobby both felt girls ought to be sent to live on a desert island.

Lizzy's youngest child, Edward, was toddling about in the kitchen, making use of his grandmother's skirts and his mother's legs to steady himself whenever the floor didn't behave as his childish mind thought it should.

Vi was out shopping with her mother, and her mother was proudly wheeling the pram in which infant Alice lay warmly covered up to her button of a nose. Uncle Tom was at his work, laying gas pipes in Peckham.

Tommy was at the factory in Shoreditch, keeping one eye on the machines and the other on the machinists. He had confiscated a bottle of gin.

Polly was at home, going restlessly from one room to the other. Her father, General Sir Henry Simms, who had once had the audacity to argue with Field Marshal Douglas Haig during the war, asked her why she wasn't out and about. Polly usually spent Christmas Eve rushing around London with long-established friends, friends who thought her enthusiasm for teaching fiendish kids a scream.

'Is that a serious question?' asked Polly.

'Best I can do,' said her father, tall and iron-grey.

'Well, look, old bean, you'll make more of a success reading your *Times*.'

'It's bad, is it, Polly?'

'You don't require an answer to that, do you?'

'Gad, no. Treat it as an expression of sympathy. But would you like to go to India for a year?'

'To get over my blues?' said Polly. 'Yes, I'd like it very much. It's a ripper of an idea. I'd love to go and eat my heart out with the flies, the punkah-wallahs and the Indian elephants. There's only the school and the kids to leave behind.'

'It's not on?' said General Simms.

'It's not on,' said Polly.

Lady Simms put her head in.

'Diana's on the phone, Polly. She'd like you to lunch with her at Romano's.'

'I'm not in,' said Polly.

'Where shall I say you are?' asked Lady Simms, step-mother.

'Purgatory.'

'Very well,' said Lady Simms pacifically. 'You can come and help me decorate the orphanage Christmas tree this afternoon.' And she went to advise Polly's friend that Polly had a headache.

Sammy spent the morning in his office with Boots, Rachel, Lilian Hyams and Susie. His office was radiant with colour, for Lilian had brought the best part of her collection. She met Rachel and Boots for the first time. She thought Rachel sultry and striking. She thought Boots fascinating. 'One mother to have two like Sammy and Tommy, and another like Boots, I should believe that?' she said to Rachel. And Rachel replied, 'Yes, I have asked myself, is it fair?' She recognised the fashion

263

designer as a re-charged live wire, a woman who, discouraged by fixed attitudes, had had the good fortune to encounter Sammy, a man who could infect people of promise with his own energy, vitality and enthusiasm. Sammy could identify winners and losers. He had seen the woman, Lilian Hyams, as a winner. He had seen the promise in the girl Susie Brown even when she had been all huge eyes, sharp cheekbones and skinny frame. He had hung on to Tommy, a young man of honesty and skill, until he could place him with advantage in a job in which he could excel. Tommy could manage machines, and Rachel had no doubt he could manage the machinists. Boots, of course, had been a winner from the beginning. Sammy was the creative builder, Boots the one who held everything together. Sammy, a dynamo, electrified people. Boots could get all he wanted with a sly smile and a whimsical comment.

Rachel felt nothing could stop Adams Enterprises becoming big business. Their ladies' shops were already well-known, their scrap yards run by astute men whom Sammy seemed to have plucked magically out of the air. Men who ran scrap yards for a parent company could fiddle with ease, but Sammy rarely made a misjudgement, and in any case the man in overall charge of the yards was Fred Scribbins, Sammy's most loyal servant.

As for Lilian Hyams's collection, Rachel considered it original, imaginative and colourful. She asked, however, why Sammy had not arranged for the hire of a mannequin. Sammy replied that mannequins talked, and that in any case Miss Brown's kind services were available. Susie said she did not recall being asked. Sammy told her to have another port. (He had ideas of getting Susie mellow.) Susie said too much port went to her head. Sammy said he was pleased to hear it. Susie made a face. But Sammy had made her part of the team, and although she did not really like taking on the role of mannequin, for she was no exhibitionist, she consented to model a number of the designs. Rachel made comments that were shrewd and generally enthusiastic. Sammy's comments increased Lilian's belief in him as a man who could meet a challenge. Boots put in a word or two from time to time. Rachel had only one real criticism, of a spring coat, which she dismissed out of hand as being too fussy. Lilian listened to all comments. She was there to listen. Listening was more beneficial than arguing. She was not showing her collection to acknowledged experts of fashion, but Mrs Rachel Goodman was a woman who dressed beautifully, Sammy had a natural eye for what would sell, and his eldest brother, she felt, would know what looked good on a woman. Sammy had put his faith in her, and she was willing to put her hopes in the judgement of the three of them.

In respect of the star dress of the collection, the short purple dress with the fringed hem, Susie modelled it a little self-consciously. Going into her own office with Lilian to put it on, she said, 'Oh, lor'. Well, if I die, you'll send me a wreath, won't you, Boots?'

'Two,' said Boots. 'One out of affection, one out of admiration for your bravery.'

'I like the first reason best,' said Susie.

'I am not in approval of funeral talk,' said Sammy, who really meant he was not in approval of a flirtatious exchange between Susie and his brother.

The dress evoked a low, warm whistle from Rachel. Long strings of beads adorned neck and bodice, and reached to the waist. The purple silk shimmered, and a narrow matching bandeau with a single black feather encircled Susie's fair hair. Frilly garters peeped through the fringed hem of the dress. She was pinkly self-conscious about the garters, not her style at all, but

Sammy thought her irresistible in Lilian's 1926 look. Boots thought her delicious but sensitive. Rachel took a very long look, then said, 'My life, should we worry that in the country women will still wear tweeds? In London, the flappers will scratch each other to be the first to wear this. It's audacious, Sammy, and that is the rallying flag of the flappers, audacity. You're certain, Lilian, that it's going to pre-empt the French designers?'

'It's a feeling I have,' said Lilian.

The atmosphere was one of exciting challenge. Sammy poured more port. It was midday. Boots, declaring himself impressed, went to his office to make a phone call.

The butler, finding Polly in the conservatory, informed her she was required on the phone. There had been six previous calls for her from friends, and she had been unresponsive to all.

'I'm not at home,' she said.

'Very good, Miss Polly. Hi will advise the gentleman accordin'.'

'What gentleman?'

'A Mr Robert Adams—'

'I'll take it. In the library.' Polly was swift in getting to the library extension. 'Hello, is it true?'

'Is what true?' asked Boots.

'That you've actually phoned me. God, I hope it's not to do with orphanage business. I'll kill you if it is.'

'Merry Christmas,' said Boots.

'As if you care.'

'I care enough to ask if you'd like to share a turkey sandwich and a bottle of French wine with me at the pub. It'll be crowded out, but they're holding a table for me at one o'clock in the sandwich bar. It's not the Savoy, and it wouldn't surprise me if you were already fixed up, but—'

266

'Are you inviting me out? Am I actually listening to an invitation? I never have before. I think you'd better start at the beginning again, old love.'

'If you can't manage it—'

'Don't spoil it with negative speech, darling. I'm tottering with rapture.'

'Is that what a turkey sandwich on Christmas Eve does to you?'

'It's what an invitation from you does to me.'

'One o'clock, then, in the sandwich bar?' said Boots.

'Yes, if I can get up. I've fallen to the floor. But don't go, I've plenty of time to get there by one. Talk to me. You can't be busy. Nobody does much business on Christmas Eve. God, I've been so bored. No school, no kids, no dreams.'

'What sort of dreams have you been looking for?'

'Don't ask dreary questions, sweetie, that makes you too much like other men. Be what you always have been, provoking, frustrating, stinking and adorable.'

'D'you think, over our sandwich, we can have a sensible conversation?' suggested Boots.

'Hell, I hope not,' said Polly, revitalised. 'I like our kind of conversation. I can have sensible conversations with MPs, archbishops and other boring people, I don't want them with you. I'd like a lifetime of our kind of dialogue, with not one sensible word spoken by either of us.'

'You'd like me as a village idiot, would you?'

'Join the club, darling, I'm one myself.' Polly paused. 'Is it intruding too much to ask about you and Emily?'

'Emily's fine.'

'Hate her,' said Polly, 'hate her for what she did to you.'

'When you get to know Emily, you'll find you can't hate her.'

'You clown,' said Polly, 'I'll never like any woman who sleeps with you.'

'See you at one,' said Boots, and rang off.

At ten to one, Susie was in her office, trying to come to terms with the effects of three glasses of port and the necessity of preparing letters for Lottie to type. Lilian had returned to Shoreditch with her collection, ex-Corporal Mitchell driving her in the firm's van. Rachel, much though she would have liked to lunch with Sammy, knew she must go home and take her little girl Rebecca off her father's hands.

'*Shalom*, Sammy. Good luck.'

'Likewise, and spoken from me heart, Rachel.'

'Bless you,' murmured Rachel, and kissed him and left.

Sammy entered Susie's office. It was colourful with little Christmas decorations. So were the offices of the typists and clerks.

'Ah, Miss Brown,' said Sammy, 'I thought on this auspicious occasion of Christmas Eve, it behoves me to ask me invaluable personal assistant to lunch at the expense of my private pocket. In the upstairs room of the pub, where there is an aspidistra and a potted palm.'

'Upstairs room? The private room? Mister Adams, really, should you? Lord above, Mister Adams, what will people say?'

'I am indifferent to un-Christian gossip,' said Sammy who, having made his momentous decision, was accordingly firm.

'But my mum's not, nor my dad,' said Susie. 'I just simply couldn't, not a private room, Mister Adams. Private rooms are for fast women.'

'Eh?' said Sammy.

'Well, all right,' said Susie, the port making her feel

268

warm and rosy with well-being and entirely capable of holding her own with Sammy. 'But I'd best cover my face and head with a scarf when we go in and come out.'

'None of your sauce, Miss Brown,' said Sammy. 'I am not noted for escortin' young ladies into dubious places. Kindly put your hat and coat on.'

'Yes, Mister Adams.' Susie smiled. Sammy saw blue eyes swimming with dreams, or so they seemed to him. He wondered if his future meant he would be waking up to them each morning.

He took her across the road to the pub. Susie bobbed and danced on high heels, humming 'Miss Peggy O'Neill' to herself. They entered the pub by a side door and climbed the stairs to the upstairs room, reserved for small private gatherings. Usually, it was never used on days like Christmas Eve, when the pub was far too busy coping with bar trade. Ernie, the sandwich bar chef, had put in a word on Sammy's behalf, however. In the window, draped by green velvet curtains, stood a huge aspidistra on a bamboo table. In a smaller side window stood a potted palm. In the middle of the room a mahogany table was laid for two.

'Be seated, Miss Brown,' said Sammy.

'Excuse me, I'm sure,' said the rosy Miss Brown, 'but are we socialising, Mister Adams?'

'It's my pleasure,' said Sammy, as she sat down.

'I hardly like to kick you at Christmastime,' said Susie.

'None of that, Susie. I am in a considerable serious frame of mind.'

'Oh, lor',' said Susie, 'it's goin' to be lecturin' and growlin'.'

Ernie came in bearing a tray containing two plates of a hot turkey lunch. He set the plates before the customers.

'Yer'll excuse me hurry, Mister Adams, I got a bar that's bustin' at the sides, like. I'll send Johnny up with any drinks yer want.'

'Susie?' enquired Sammy.

Susie, trying to focus on her turkey lunch, said murmurously, 'I'll 'ave a port, if you'd be so kind.'

'You sure?' said Sammy.

'A port,' said Susie.

Sammy ordered a beer for himself. A little man brought the drinks up, and left them to their lunch. Susie had no trouble with the port, but seemed vague about the exact purpose of her knife and fork.

'Merry Christmas, Susie,' said Sammy, and cleared his throat and drank some beer.

'Oh, same to you, Boots, I'm sure,' murmured Susie, and managed to fork a piece of turkey into her mouth.

'Pardon?' said Sammy.

'You're sweet,' said Susie, and blinked to focus on him. 'Oh, lor', you're Sammy.'

'It is my good fortune to be my dear old lady's favourite son on account of my kind nature. I ain't Boots. You got that, Miss Brown?'

'Who said Miss Brown?' Susie drank more port.

'Now, Susie, kindly pay attention. We'll be busy this afternoon, I'm takin' you round our shops, to the stall and to Fred's scrap yard, and then to the fact'ry. We are droppin' in on one and all, as is my custom at Christmas, bestowing good wishes and bonuses, which is done in appreciation of their work, but not forgettin' to tell some there's room for improvement. It will take time, and I am accordin' sharing this table with you for thirty minutes in order to acquaint you beforehand with certain feelings of mine, not excludin' my honourable intentions. I am hopin' – Susie?' He stared at her across the table. She was sitting back. Her chin had dropped, her head and hat bent. She was gently asleep, lulled into dreams by the morning's port. 'I don't believe it,' breathed Sammy. 'It wouldn't happen to a dog, but it's happened to me, Sammy Adams. Is it right? No, it ain't, and it's not even decent. Chinese Lady, she's done it on me. How'm I goin' to get her back to the offices?' He put his knife and fork down, got up and went round to Susie. He lifted her chin. Beneath her cuddling cloche hat her fair hair peeped and her sleepy eyes opened. She smiled dreamily.

'Oh, I do feel lovely,' she murmured and drifted off into warm seas again.

'Done it on me,' said Sammy.

The port.

He laughed.

In the sandwich bar, Polly sat with Boots at a small corner table. The place was loud and hearty with Christmas spirit, and there was a crush of people at the marble-topped sandwich counter. Polly's friends might have thought it screamingly bourgeois, but to Polly it was life among the people, just as her time in France and Flanders during the war had been life and death close to the raw, earthy Tommies of the trenches. If it had made a brittle woman of her, it had also taught her what ordinary men and women were made of, except that she had long given up thinking them ordinary. Nor was it remotely ordinary to be eating turkey sandwiches with Boots in a Camberwell pub. It was rescuing her from restless boredom. So many things were boring that did not have anything to do with Boots or Rosie or the school. Her knee touched his under the table.

'Am I crowding you?' he asked, refilling her wine glass.

'Please do,' said Polly, refusing to take her knee away. 'Exactly why am I here? Oh, I'm not complaining, old bean, far from it. But why am I here?'

'So that I can thank you for all the private tuition you're giving Rosie, and for taking such good care of her by getting her to the hospital so quickly.'

'Have you forgotten I was an ambulance driver for four years?' Polly's smile was brittle. 'I love Rosie. If I had a small share of her, I'd have a large share of you. You can have all of me.'

'That's far too much,' said Boots.

'You've forgiven Emily, haven't you?'

'We haven't quarrelled, no.'

'You mean you've settled for peace and quiet,' said Polly, maroon coat unbuttoned, round black fur hat softly crowning her head. 'You're an old softie, Robert. You're all the same. My father's the same. It's a form of cowardice. You should all have gone to war on the politicians after the last man had got back from the hellholes. Everything to do with blood and guts you all left behind, buried in the trenches. I'd have marched with you on Parliament, so would a thousand other women like me.'

'Are there a thousand like you? As many as that? Terrifying.'

Polly laughed, then put a hand on his arm. A man not far from them got up and left the bar. 'Listen, darling, could we have a lifelong friendship? It need not be platonic, I'm very easy about that, but I'd like it to be lasting.'

'Is this a serious conversation?' asked Boots.

'Well, it's not a boring one, at least. No, really, dear old sport, if you ever need silly old me, just call and I'll come. God, is that hackneyed?'

'Not to me,' said Boots. 'What are you doing over Christmas?'

'Participating in the rites of being utterly charming to a select gathering of ancient relatives on Christmas day. On Boxing Day, my father and step-Mama are off to Nice for a month.'

'In that case,' said Boots, 'my mother would like to know if you'd care to join us for Boxing Day tea.'

Polly stared and said, 'Would you mind repeating that?'

'She feels the family should show its appreciation of the way you're giving up your time to cram Rosie. It's not been enough to give you coffee on those evenings. Boxing Day tea will be like Sunday tea. It's a religion with my mother. Everyone sits up straight and no jam is allowed until you've eaten at least one slice of bread and butter. And you must pass the cakes or jam tarts before you take one yourself. Do you like winkles?'

'Oh, my God,' said Polly, big-eyed and fascinated.

'Pins are provided with the winkles. Do you like toasted crumpets with butter? It used to be margarine. It's butter now.'

'What are you doing to me?' asked Polly.

'Boring you and putting you off?'

'Darling, I'm entranced.'

'About pins and winkles?'

Polly laughed.

'Love the thought,' she said.

'It's a cockney feast,' said Boots.

'I'll come,' said Polly.

'You can say no.'

'I'm not going to say no.'

'You're for it, then. You'll have to wear a party frock—'

'A what?'

'Party frock. We always have a Boxing Day party as well as a Christmas Day one. The kids insist. After tea you'll have to play party games, like Tail the Donkey, Hunt the Slipper, Forfeits—'

'Forfeits?'

'The men like Forfeits. The girls usually find they have to do things that make them show their legs. My

273

mother allows this, as legs are traditional at party games.'

'Crazy,' said Polly.

'You're not keen?'

'I can't wait. I'll put my legs up against Emily's any day. Or is it all a joke?'

'It's no joke, it's dead serious. And there are no exceptions. Rosie and Annabelle won't allow them. Nor will I. And we usually finish with a knees-up.'

'Say that again.'

' "Knees Up, Mother Brown," ' said Boots with a straight face.

'Hysterical,' said Polly.

'And watch out for Postman's Knock,' said Boots.

'I haven't played Postman's Knock since I was ten.'

'Being rusty is no excuse. Rosie and Annabelle won't accept that. Nor will I. In between, a hot supper will be served. Don't call it dinner or my mother will think you're trying to turn things upside-down. Have you got a party frock with a red sash?'

'I had one when I was eight.'

'Well, make do with one of your Bond Street creations. Rosie and Annabelle might pass it.'

'I think I'm going to love Boxing Day,' said Polly.

Mrs Brown, opening her front door in answer to a knock, found Mister Sammy standing there, one arm around Susie, whose head was resting on his shoulder.

'Sorry and all that, too much port, Mrs Brown,' he said. 'My fault, but I'd be grieved if you thought I'd been careless about Susie. It's just that we do pass the port round at Christmas.'

Mrs Brown, seeing a taxi outside the house, its driver waiting, said, 'Oh, but it's kind you brought her home in comfort, Mister Sammy, and only two o'clock as well, when she should still be at work.' Mrs Brown was too philosophical a woman to make a fuss about Christmas drinks, even if it was a little bit of a shock to know Susie had had one too many. 'Susie, you been havin' too much port and no lemonade with it? Susie?'

'Been lovely,' murmured Susie.

'I'll see to her, Mister Sammy.'

'I'd be gratified,' said Sammy, 'I've got a hundred calls to make. I'd also be obliged if you'd tell her my mother's invited her to tea on Boxin' Day, which if she can come will be a pleasure to one and all. I've put her Christmas bonus in her coat pocket, I don't think she knows it's there.'

'Been lovely,' murmured Susie, as her mother took hold of her.

'Merry Christmas, Mrs Brown,' said Sammy. 'Must push off, I'm considerable belated with my calls. Susie?'

'Mmm?' said Susie, befuddled with an excess of well-being.

'Merry Christmas, Susie.'

'Been lovely,' said Susie dreamily.

'It's no blame to you, Mister Sammy,' said Mrs Brown, 'when a girl's come of age, like, it's her own blame.'

'Did it on me,' murmured Sammy wryly.

'Pardon?'

'So long,' said Sammy, and went.

'Oh, Mum.' Susie, having come to by half-past three, was aghast at herself. 'Lord above, what'll he think of me? I left all that work not done. I don't know how I'm goin' to look Mister Sammy in the face. Did he really say his mum's invited me for Boxin' Day tea?'

'He said his fam'ly would be that pleasured to have you, love. What got into you, all that port and all?'

'Everything was so exciting,' said Susie. 'I bet he won't even look at me on Boxin' Day. He took me to lunch, and then I didn't remember anything. Oh, he's goin' to be all growling, I'm sure he is. Me, his private secretary, goin' one over the eight. I'll have to cut my throat or take poison. It's awful, he'll never—' Susie, looking down at the kitchen range, broke off.

'Never what, lovey?' said Mrs Brown, mixing the pudding.

He'll never ask me to marry him now, thought Susie, I know he won't, he'll never marry anyone who gets tipsy in his offices on Christmas Eve.

'Oh, it doesn't matter,' she said.

'That's yours,' said Mrs Brown, pointing to an envelope on the mantelpiece. 'Mister Sammy put it in your coat pocket, and I took it out for you.'

Susie opened it. She drew out two crisp white fivers and a note written in a hurry by Sammy.

My compliments, and your bonus, Miss Brown. That's business. S. W. Adams.

Merry Christmas, Susie, see you Boxing Day for tea at my mother's, if you're free. Four o'clock. That's socialising. Love, Sammy.

Love, Sammy? And a whole ten pounds bonus? Ten pounds?

'Mum, look, a bonus of ten pounds.'

'Lawks alive,' gasped Mrs Brown, who had never seen two five-pound notes all at once.

'I'm goin' back to work,' said Susie, 'I've got to, it's only fair. I can work till six and do some late shoppin'.'

'Susie, I don't think Mister Sammy wants you to—'

'No, it's only right,' said Susie, and she went back to Camberwell, where the other girls were in high spirits and Boots was at work in his office. No one asked where she'd been. She sat down and attended to a stack of letters, writing out replies that Lottie could begin typing first thing after Christmas.

Love, Sammy.

Her head was a little like a floating puffball from the after-effects of the port, but was back to normal after Doreen had given her a strong cup of tea. Boots sent all the girls home early, electing not to argue when Susie told him she was staying until six. She was secretly hoping Sammy would be back. He wasn't. She left with Boots at five-past six, all the letters ready for Lottie.

'Did you receive an invitation for tea on Boxing Day?' asked Boots.

'Oh, yes. I'll love to come.'

'Love to have you. Merry Christmas, Susie.'

'Oh, you too, and all your fam'ly.'

Sammy left Shoreditch a little after six, in company with Tommy and Lilian. The machinists had left at six in rapturous disbelief, each with a bonus of five bob. Money of this kind left the firm's till as an outgoing investment.

Tommy took Lilian and Sammy home with him, where Aunt Victoria gave everyone a supper of poached fresh haddock with two poached eggs for each, and a great pile of crusty bread and butter. Lilian was touched. Tommy just didn't like to hear she was living on her own in one room in Battersea, and Vi and Aunt Victoria had happily arranged to entertain her for supper. She stayed on a while. Extrovert, she took the atmosphere of a Christian family on Christmas Eve in her stride, and liked the gentle nature of Tommy's wife.

It was Vi who saw Sammy out at ten to nine.

'Well, I tell yer, Vi, yer a treasure,' said Sammy in old-time fashion, 'and you got another little treasure in Alice. And yer mum's turned out a real homely female woman. You and Tommy all right?'

'Tommy's a dear,' said Vi, as placid as Emily was spirited.

'I'm considered fairly kind and lovin' meself,' said Sammy.

'You're considered smart,' said Vi.

'Kind of yer to say so, Vi.'

'Gertcher,' said Vi. 'Oh, but me and Tommy'll have enough saved by the spring to put down a big deposit for a house mortgage. We've been saving for ages, and now he's got his new job – Sammy, thanks ever so for that, and Mum couldn't be more proud now she's got a son-in-law who's a manager.'

'Well, Vi old girl, I didn't do Tommy any favours. It's fifty-fifty and mutual as well. Tommy knows what doing a good job's all about, and I know when I'm gettin' a good return. Also and further, I like his wife considerable, which is you, Vi. I like havin' yer in the fam'ly.'

'Oh, I better give you tuppence,' said Vi.

'What for?'

'Well, you still charge for getting a kiss, don't you?'

Sammy grinned. In his boyhood he had never kissed or allowed himself to be kissed without charging a penny.

'Merry Christmas, Vi, see you at dinner tomorrow,' he said, and kissed her. Then he went back to his office. It did not worry him that the place had a hollow ring, that he was the only one there, that it was Christmas Eve, some shops still open, carol singers abroad with their lanterns and pubs alive with revelry. Business fascinated him. He sat down at his desk to commence work on a multitude of matters. A letter stared up at him from his blotter, a letter from Susie.

Dear Mister Sammy, I don't know how to thank you for such a generous bonus, I really don't, but I'm terribly grateful. Also, Boots told me I'm invited to Boxing Day tea with your mother and family, which overwhelmed me with pleasure. I came back to the office at four, I felt I had to, I wanted to show I'd forgiven you for getting me drunk. I'm sure your intentions weren't dubious, which they are with certain men who've fallen from grace, I'm sure you're a trustworthy business gentleman as well as a reputable one, so I'm not going to say anything about how you poured all that port wine into me. I've done all the letters and they're ready for Lottie as soon as she gets in after Christmas. I wish you a very happy Christmas and I really do forgive you, Yours sincerely, Susie Brown.'

Sammy grinned. That Susie. The saucebox. She was trying to turn him upside-down.

I'll get you, Susie, I'll make you Mrs Sammy Adams, even if it costs me the lifeblood of my business.

CHAPTER TWENTY

Chinese Lady had her own reasons for inviting Miss
Simms and Susie to the Boxing Day party. She did not
divulge them, but at a quarter to four she addressed her
family. They were all in the large sitting-room, where
the old piano stood in the corner.

'Now, when our lady guests arrive, we won't have
any larks, if you don't mind,' she said. 'Miss Simms is a
respectable teacher and high-class, and that nice Susie
Brown is comin' on to be as ladylike as our Vi, which
I'm pleased Tommy noticed in good time. So we won't
have any larks, I don't want Miss Simms or Susie to
think I've got hooligans in my fam'ly.'

'Larks? What larks?' asked Ned.

'In my position, I can't afford larks,' said Sammy. 'It
might get about.'

'Vi and me haven't met Miss Simms,' said Tommy.
'Would she do Bible readings?'

'Bible readings?' said Annabelle. 'At a party? Ugh.'

'We could ask for the Old Testament,' said Boots,
'there's blood and thunder in that.'

'I'll give you Old Testament, my lad,' said Chinese
Lady.

'Nana, we could have some small larks, couldn't we?'
said Rosie, her forehead showing the receding bruise.
'Only small ones. Daddy was splendiferous yesterday,
doing Pass the Orange with Auntie Vi.'

'We don't want your Auntie Vi lookin' like she's been dragged through a hedge backwards again,' said Chinese Lady.

'Hooligan, that's what your daddy is, Tim,' said Lizzy.

Four-year-old Tim looked at his father and gave him a shy grin. Boots responded with a wink.

'Granny Lady,' said Annabelle, 'I quite like our hooligans.'

'Yes, they've all got saving graces, haven't they?' said Rosie. 'We have to count our blessings, Nana. About their saving graces, I mean.'

'I haven't noticed any,' said Emily.

'Nor me,' said Lizzy, giving toddling Edward a cuddle.

Vi said, 'Isn't it awful, Bobby, your daddy and all your uncles goin' to perdition one day?'

Five-year-old Bobby thought. Tim asked, 'Have they got train sets there?'

'Course they have,' said Bobby. 'My daddy said so. We're going there together.'

'Who said you was?' asked Tim.

'My mummy,' said Bobby.

Emily's laughter pealed. They had all enjoyed an hilarious Christmas Day party, and Emily was quite ready to enjoy more fun at this Boxing Day get-together. Her quicksilver energy always unleashed itself at family parties. During the progress of this one she was to make friends with Polly Simms. Chinese Lady had advised her to. Emily, of course, was going to make up her own mind about that.

Boots, answering a ring on the front doorbell, admitted Susie into the hall. Outside, the afternoon was dark, damp and foul. Susie compensated with her glowing colour.

'You're in the pink, I see,' said Boots, taking her hat and coat.

'Pink?' said Susie, thinking the hall and the house grand.

'Your nose,' said Boots.

'Oh, it's not, is it?'

'Fashionable at this time of the year,' said Boots, 'but cover it up, or all the girls will want one like it.'

Susie laughed and Boots gave her a Boxing Day kiss. Susie, in impulsive affection, hugged him for it just as Sammy appeared.

'Again?' said Sammy.

'Oh, don't be mean,' said Susie, 'it's Christmas.'

'It seems to be goin' on all the time, Miss Brown,' said Sammy. 'I'll see to her, Boots, I have formally informed the company I am takin' her to inspect the kitchen of this palatial residence. This way, Miss Brown.'

'Pardon?' said Susie.

'You're surprised?' said Boots. 'Don't be. We always insist on new visitors inspecting the kitchen.'

'But I haven't paid me respects to your mother,' said Susie.

'Later,' said Sammy. 'Kindly accompany me, Miss Brown.'

Boots, his smile close to the surface, went back into the sitting-room. Susie, wearing an ultramarine dress quite new, lifted cool blue eyes to Sammy.

'Very well, Mister Adams, but I hope you don't have any ideas about growling at me.' She went with him. The handsomeness of the kitchen made her sigh. 'Oh, I never saw any kitchen so posh,' she said.

'Never mind that,' said Sammy. 'What I am concerned about, Miss Brown, is my shockin' discovery that you're a little Turk.'

'Well, I don't know what my parents are goin' to say to that,' said Susie. 'I wasn't found in some Turkish baths, you know.'

'Kindly don't give me no innocent looks,' said Sammy.

'Really, Mister Adams, you're conductin' yourself very growling, and I don't know what your mother must be thinking, me not paying respects to her.'

'I have informed my mother I am obliged to deal severely with you,' said Sammy sternly, who thought that in ultramarine blue and with her hair newly shingled, Susie could knock 'em for six down the Old Kent Road.

'Oh, you're goin' to hit me now, are you?' she said.

'You saucebox,' said Sammy, 'what d'you mean by writing down in black and white that I poured a gallon of port wine into you?'

'Really, Mister Adams, I thought that was over and done with after I'd forgiven you for makin' me unconscious with drink.' Susie put her nose in the air, giving not the slightest hint of how much she was enjoying herself. 'It's not hardly my fault if it's still on your conscience.'

'See that?' said Sammy, pointing upwards. Susie lifted her eyes and found mistletoe depending from the ceiling. Sammy swooped. 'Oh—' He cut her off. Susie went dizzy. He was kissing her. It lasted for ever, or almost for ever. Bliss and colour suffused her, and when the end of the world had been reached her face was as flushed as the sky at final sunset. 'Oh,' she gasped faintly, 'did you hit me, then, was that what it was?'

'My eye and Betty Martin,' said Sammy, 'you're still at it, you're still banging my ears about.'

Susie, exhilaration overcoming faintness, drew herself up and said, 'Sammy Adams, you kissed me.'

'Yes, and I'm likely to do it again, any minute, Susie Brown.'

'Very well, Mister Adams, I'm only your helpless employee and a defenceless girl, and if I don't let you I suppose you'll sack me and really hit me. I hope you'll be able to live with your unChristian conduct, makin' me drunk on Christmas Eve and hittin' me on Boxing Day.'

'Oh, my achin' head,' said Sammy, and roared with laughter.

Annabelle put her head round the door.

'Uncle Sammy, Granny Lady says if you don't kindly come and present Miss Brown to the family, she'll come and see what you're up to. Hello, Miss Brown.'

'Hello, Annabelle,' smiled Susie.

'We're comin',' said Sammy.

'Uncle Sammy?'

'What's up?' asked Sammy, ushering Susie to the door.

'Uncle Sammy,' said Annabelle gravely, 'you've got lipstick. And you're ever so pink, Miss Brown.'

Susie knew all the family. They greeted her like an old friend, and she felt quite swamped by the warmth and affection. It made her eyes misty. Sammy's mother was very kind and welcoming, and said how pleasured she was that Sammy had such a ladylike assistant. Tommy kissed her very affectionately. So did Ned. Emily was sparkling, Lizzy vivacious, Vi charming. And Susie thought what a lovely young girl Rosie was, despite her forehead still showing a faint bruise.

Chinese Lady intended to serve tea at four-fifteen, but by four-thirty Polly had still not arrived. At twenty to five she asked what had happened to her.

'She's forgotten, I expect,' said Emily.

'Oh, she wouldn't be casual like that,' said Lizzy, who liked the schoolteacher because she was so good with the schoolkids.

'Well, we can't wait and do nothing,' said Sammy crisply. 'Phone her, Boots. If she's forgotten, I recommend a large helping of tactfulness. We don't want to lose the orphanage business, it's a steady income for the Camberwell shop.'

'You and your business,' said Lizzy, 'you ought to be hung out to dry with the orphanage blankets.'

'She might of had a collapse comin' here,' said Chinese Lady.

'I'll phone,' said Boots. He and Sammy both had the number of Lady Simms's house. The butler answered, informing Boots that Miss Polly had left in her car at just after four. Boots disliked the sound of that. Her family's mansion-like house in Dulwich was no more than a six- or seven-minute drive away. She was half an hour late. Boots asked the butler if he knew whether Polly had intended to drive straight to North Dulwich.

'I was hinformed by Miss Polly at where she would be at this evening, sir, and was not given no himpression she was hobliged to call in somewhere else on her way. May I henquire if we are to be in concern?'

'I'll let you know,' said Boots, and hung up.

'I don't like it,' said Chinese Lady when Boots recounted the conversation.

'Boots, didn't you speak to her parents?' asked Ned.

'They left for the South of France today,' said Boots.

'Which they won't get to until tomorrow morning,' said Ned. 'It's in our lap.'

'I'll get my hat and coat,' said Boots.

'I'll come with you,' said Sammy.

'Yes, you best go and see,' said Chinese Lady.

'I'll go with them,' said Tommy.

'We don't want everyone leavin', Tommy,' said Chinese Lady, but saw Boots give him a nod. Yes, Tommy knew most about cars, of course, being an engineer.

Boots took a torch, and the three brothers, overcoated against the damp cold, made their way along the road in the direction of Dulwich. Street lamps cast misty light. Behind drawn curtains, house lights dimly glowed. There was no one about. People were tucked into their homes, seated around their coal fires, the toys

285

and games given as Christmas presents the focal point of family enjoyment.

At the end of the road they turned into Half Moon Lane, eyes peering and searching the darkness. Boots stopped.

'Half a minute,' he said. They had just passed a half-demolished house at the end of the road. The remains of the residence stood in a third of an acre of overgrown grounds. He turned back, Tommy and Sammy with him. He switched on the torch and flashed its beam over the road. The beam swept the immediate stretch of road, then the pavement. He held the torch steady. The wet pavement was marked by the muddy streaks of skidding tyres. The beam traced the course of the streaks to the open front of a neglected garden. A forest of weeds lay crushed in two parallel lines.

'God,' breathed Tommy.

Boots moved forward, and the beam of light played over tangled undergrowth and came to rest on the back of a car, its bonnet close to the rubble of demolishment. Boots knew what had happened. It was so typical of Polly. Only at school was her behaviour constrained. Outside of it, she was as mad as ever. The misty darkness of the wintry afternoon and the greasiness of the roads would have held no terror for a woman who had driven her great square box of an ambulance over the torn, muddy roads of France and Flanders. She had taken this corner in reckless defiance of conditions and she had run out of road. No one had seen her, no one had heard her. These were not the crowded, close-packed streets of Walworth.

The thoughts travelled fast through his mind as he ploughed his way around the crashed car, the wet undergrowth soaking shoes and trousers. He pulled open the driving door. Sammy was behind him, Tommy on the other side of the car. He played the torch. There she was, huddled over the steering wheel, arms limp, round fur hat squashed down over her head. Fragments of glass glittered in the fur. The windscreen was smashed. The passenger door, slightly buckled, was wrenched open by Tommy.

'Won't be moved, Boots. Hit the rubble. I think the front axle's gone. Hell, she looks bad.'

'Run back home and phone, Tommy. Call an ambulance.'

An ambulance for Polly.

Tommy dug himself out of the undergrowth and ran. Leaning in, Boots carefully brought Polly back against the seat, Sammy holding the torch. Polly's face was white and waxy, eyes closed.

'Don't like it,' said Sammy tersely.

Boots said, 'Polly?'

She opened her eyes. Cloudily, they saw him.

'Been a hell of a day, old sport . . . and so cold . . . so cold . . .'

Her eyes closed. Boots felt a strange, intense affection for this brittle, extrovert woman who had lived with the sound of the guns for four long courageous years, and conceived a lasting love for the bitter, caustic men of the trenches. Her Tommies, she always called them.

'Watcher, Polly, old girl, come to pick up Bert, 'ave yer? Well, there's 'is left leg and there's 'is tin lid. Dunno where the rest of 'im is.'

Boots had heard that kind of comment from soldiers to women ambulance drivers.

There was no blood, but he could smell some. Blood he could always smell.

'Sammy, get round to the other side. Give me some light from there. She's bleeding and we've got to find where.'

'Got you, Boots,' said Sammy, and tramped his way round to the open passenger door, from where he gave

287

Boots light from the torch. Polly was inert, her head heavy, shoulders sagging.

'Hold her, Sammy – gently now.'

Sammy, reaching in, pressed Polly's left shoulder back, keeping her upright in the driving seat. He shone the torch over her. Boots's nostrils tracked the blood. He opened up her fur coat. She was wearing a plain russet-coloured dress of simple style, not a creation to stun. Boots saw wetness. He drew dress and slip up. Blood pulsed. There was a savage gash above her left knee, the stocking ripped. The gear lever, he thought.

'God,' said Sammy, 'her life's running away, that's a foot long, that gash.'

'Hold her, Sammy.'

Sammy held her, gently but firmly, and left the rest to Boots. It was Boots's moment. He was a man who had been wounded three times, and then blinded. Sammy saw the soldier in his brother go to work. He took Polly's shoes off. He unclipped her stockings and removed them, working fast. He discarded the soaked one. He tore a large button from her fur coat, his wrench savage. With the button and the right stocking he made a tourniquet around her left thigh, above the gash. He used a propelling pencil from his inside jacket pocket to tighten the stocking. It bit into Polly's strong, smooth thigh.

'Hell, that's tight, Boots,' said Sammy.

Boots held the tourniquet and watched. The slowly pumping blood from a ruptured artery gradually diminished. He made another turn. The pumping stopped, to become a small seeping. He tightened a little more and fixed the tourniquet.

'Hold on, Polly,' he said. Sammy gave him a look. Boots's expression was a strangely bitter one. Boots was thinking of Major Harris, his commanding officer, who had bled to death in Trones Wood on the Somme because that German grenade had blasted fiery light before he could apply tourniquets to legs riddled above the knees. He covered Polly's legs, drew her fur coat to and buttoned it up. Polly did not move or speak or moan.

'Worth saving, if we can, Sammy,' he said.

'I know,' said Sammy. 'Up to Tommy now.'

Boots sucked on his pipe and watched Polly. Sammy lit a cigarette.

Tommy had been quick, literally barging his way into the house the moment Emily answered his summons. The ambulance arrived not long after Tommy got back to the car. It rushed Polly to hospital. Boots went with her. Sammy and Tommy both thought he should. They returned to the house, where Sammy phoned Lady Simms's butler. Everyone was upset by the news, but Emily understood about Boots going with Polly to the hospital.

'Yes, someone's got to decide if her parents need to come back,' said Chinese Lady. The evening was any old how. 'I'll put the kettle on. I hope some of you will sit down to a bit of tea.'

Rosie and Annabelle shed a little tear for their teacher.

'Well?' said Boots.

The doctor on duty in casualty looked him over.

'What's your blood group?' he asked.

'It was A positive when I was in the Army,' said Boots.

'Good. Come this way. You don't mind, do you? She needs a generous transfusion. She'll have a chance then. Who applied that tourniquet?'

'I did,' said Boots, going with the doctor.

'Well, if she lives, she can thank you.'

The evening was well advanced, and the damp mist had turned into wet fog as a million chimneys emitted the smoke of coal fires into the cloudy sky. But there was some faint colour back in Polly's cheeks. Her neatly bobbed hair looked dark against the white pillow, and her eyes were open.

'Good as new,' said the doctor, and left Boots to have a couple of minutes with her. She looked vaguely up at him, she focused, and a little smile touched her mouth.

'Did it in,' she said. Boots nodded. She smiled again, faintly. 'What've I got?' she asked.

'A hundred stitches and two ruined stockings. And they think you've caught Rosie's complaint. Concussion. Your fur hat saved you from worse.'

'My head's lousy,' said Polly. She frowned and thought. 'Stupid wheels left the road,' she said. 'Who dug me out?'

'Sammy, Tommy and self,' said Boots.

'Good old sport,' she sighed.

'There's a silver lining,' said Boots, 'you've missed the torture of Forfeits and Postman's Knock.'

'I was counting on not missing that.'

'Time's up, Mr Adams,' said a nurse. 'That's all.'

'Except for this,' said Boots, and gave Polly what she had missed in Postman's Knock, an affectionate, comradely kiss on her lips.

'There's a good old scout,' she murmured, and her eyes closed.

Sammy took Susie home after a somewhat disjointed evening, although it had been a relief to all when Boots returned with the news that Miss Simms was recovering, not dying. Emily had asked why he had been so long at the hospital. Boots said it wasn't every day that Polly made a mess of herself and her car, so he'd stayed to hold her hand. In a manner of speaking. Emily gave him a searching look. Boots gave her a smile. But she knew that smile of his. It didn't always mean what it seemed to. For the first time the firmness of their marital ground felt a little unsteady beneath her feet. She supposed if she could be tempted, so could he, and that Polly Simms, with her glittering, artificial smile and her silk stockings, was a temptress all right.

Oh, blow and bother, am I going to have to watch my husband and that Polly Simms?

Susie and Sammy caught a bus. It trundled slowly through creeping, rising fog. Susie said she was so sorry about Miss Simms. Sammy said no, be glad for her, she could have been a goner and would have been if Boots hadn't done a fast first-aid job on her.

'Some people think Boots is airy-fairy, but don't you believe it. He only seems as if he is. Well, all right, he does take most things a bit easy, but not when the kettle's boiling over. Dubious geezers is well advised to stand clear then.'

'I think he's lovely,' said Susie.

'Well, I know you're on a kissing relationship with him, of course.'

'I'll kick you, Sammy Adams, and on this public bus too.'

'Which behoves me to say, Susie Brown, it's a grievous pain to know my own kind self has to put up with you being on a kickin' relationship with me. It ain't partic'larly Christian, y'know.'

'Really, Mister Adams, I don't know anyone who sometimes deserves kickin' more than you. And I bite as well. Sometimes.'

'Fares, if yer please, and if it ain't disturbin' yer too much,' said the conductor, making a sudden appearance. Sammy fished out coppers and the conductor clipped tickets. 'Is the young lady yer Christmas present, guv?'

'Not yet,' said Sammy, 'and she's still givin' me problems.'

291

'I got some of them. Me feet's perishing, to start with. And me missus put burnt Yorkshire pudden on me plate with the Christmas beef. I dunno, life don't 'ardly seem worth gettin' up for sometimes. Still, I've 'eard it's an improvement on being dead.' The conductor moved along. 'Fares, if yer please, ladies an' gents.'

'Cheerful old Charlie, that one,' observed Sammy. He was sitting with Susie at the back of the top deck, a dozen other passengers way down from them. He felt a little sober on account of Polly and her crashed car, but it did not affect the pleasure of being with Susie. 'It occurs to me,' he said, as wet fog and the dim glow of street lamps slid by, 'that new plans for you next year is needful and likewise necessary.'

'What plans?' asked Susie.

'Pardon?' said Sammy.

'What plans?'

'New Year's Eve,' murmured Sammy, talking to himself.

'New Year's Eve?'

'Highly appropriate now Christmas Eve's been and gone,' said Sammy. Yes, he thought, the pantomime and the revelry. But no port, not for Susie. By New Year's Eve, he'd be in firm command of himself, and have the right words ready. *I am concerned to know, Miss Brown, if you would do me the honour of becoming my wife.* No, considerable honour? No, great honour? No, loving honour. Right. Loving honour. There ought to be a touch of that. 'Yes, New Year's Eve,' he said in decisive cowardice.

'Pardon me, I'm sure, for not knowing what you mean,' said Susie. If the evening had not been hilarious, because of poor Miss Simms, there had been all the pleasure of being with the family she liked so much. And Sammy had given her the kiss of a lifetime.

The trundling bus began to pull up.

'Our stop, Susie,' said Sammy. He was off the bus first. He gave her his hand. She liked that. He was well brought up. He took her cautiously across the foggy road to Browning Street. She put her arm through his.

'You haven't said what plans you've got for me, or what New Year's Eve means,' she said.

'I'm just hoping, Susie Brown, that on New Year's Eve you'll lay off the port.'

'And I'm just hoping you won't pour none down my throat,' said Susie.

Sammy laughed. He guided her through the fog to her door. He kissed her, lightly this time.

'You're a lovely girl, Susie. Good night,' he said, and left her glowing.

CHAPTER TWENTY-ONE

Emily, back at work the following day, took completed letters to Mr Barry Somerville at twenty past twelve.

'Thank you, Emily. Enjoy your Christmas?'

'Yes, thank you.' Emily, in a dark green costume and neat white blouse, had an acquired elegance that took Mr Somerville's eye as usual. Her trim figure, her personality and her marvellous green eyes discounted the plainness of her thin cheeks and pointed chin.

'I saw your husband on Christmas Eve, in the sandwich bar of the pub,' he said in friendly fashion. 'He seemed to be enjoying himself too.' He felt, of course, that if Emily's husband had a piece of stuff on the side, it was an infernal cheek for the man to take umbrage with him.

'With drink?' said Emily, eyes cool.

'With a rather attractive lady,' said Mr Somerville junior.

'Yes, I know,' said Emily, coolness changing to contempt. 'A friend of ours. He was invitin' her to tea with us on Boxing Day. Good morning, Mr Somerville.'

She left his office. She put her hat and coat on. The other girl said, 'Where you going?'

'Home,' said Emily.

'But it's not one o'clock yet.'

'Tell Mr Barry Somerville hard luck,' said Emily.

She crossed the road. The day was misty again, but

not wetly misty. High above, the sun was trying to break through. She walked to the Bargain Bazaar and through the shop, saying good morning to the manageress on the way. She went up the stairs and into Boots's office. He was at his desk, his hand in his hair, fiddling with his scalp, a fountain pen in his hand. He turned his head.

'Emily?' He came to his feet. Emily realised her husband had very nice ways with him. He always came to his feet for a member of her sex.

'Boots.' She went close to him and kissed him.

'What's that for?'

'Oh, just to show you. Boots, you offered for me to work for the firm. Is it still on? Oh, just mornings, of course, just something more than all-day housework.'

'You'd really like that?'

'Ever so much. It's safest.'

Boots smiled.

'Does safest appeal to you?'

'Yes, it does, when it's safest for me and you.'

'Well, I suppose we ought to take care of what we've got,' said Boots.

'And we've got a good marriage really, don't you think so?'

'Good enough for us to keep working at it,' said Boots. His phone rang. He picked it up and answered it. Emily quickly recognised there was someone obstreperous on the line. Boots didn't get vexed or impatient, even though he obviously kept being interrupted by the angry voice. He calmed the caller down in the end.

'What was that all about?' asked Emily.

'Oh, a supplier trying to suggest we'd promised to pay on delivery instead of asking for the usual twenty-eight days' credit,' said Boots, and Emily wondered if all her husband's calmness and airy-fairy front didn't hide a

295

much deeper man than she'd thought.

'I been a bit worried about you lately,' she said.

'Worried?'

'Yes. Boots, you're not in love with Polly Simms, are you?'

'Not yet,' said Boots.

'Oh, what d'yer mean, not yet?' she flashed.

'I'm not in love with Polly Simms yet.'

'That's not tellin' me what you mean!'

'Yes, it is. It's telling you I'm still in love with you.'

Emily shook her head at him and smiled wryly.

'Oh, yer cuss,' she said, 'you're always doing that to me.'

'Doing what to you?'

'Takin' the ground from under me feet,' said Emily, and kissed him.

A tap on the door preceded the entry of Doreen, carrying a file.

'Oh, sorry, beg yer pardon – oh, sorry, Mrs Adams.' She fled.

'She's not used to seeing us rubbing noses,' said Boots.

'I don't care,' said Emily.

'About the job,' said Boots.

'Yes, I'm serious, honest,' said Emily. 'Is there one for me? I mean a proper one, not one that isn't.'

'We don't place lady applicants in improper positions, Em. Sammy wouldn't allow it, and Chinese Lady would pull the place down.'

'You'll be the death of me and Chinese Lady with your comic stuff,' said Emily. 'Boots, I do shorthand-typin' now, you know.'

'I do know,' said Boots. 'You're going to be a godsend. We're expanding fast. Sammy wants to transfer the shop below to other premises and convert the space into more offices. The Council's refused permission. They won't allow change of usage. Sammy's still going to transfer the shop business to other premises. Just around the corner of the Green, in Camberwell New Road. Then he'll cut the shop space down to a third and just sell children's clothes. That'll take care of no change of usage. It's a large shop and deep. Two-thirds of it will convert to two offices. For more staff.'

'But how long will that take?' asked Emily.

'Oh, you can start now,' said Boots. 'In here, with me. I'll order a desk for you, and a typewriter, I'll give you dictation and also a little bookkeeping work. I'm run off my feet, and you'll be our first shorthand-typist. I'll talk to Sammy about what we'll pay you. Sammy might want to grab you for your shorthand-typing, but with Susie in charge of all his correspondence, it won't do for you to take dictation from her.'

'I don't mind working with a woman,' said Emily.

'You'll be working for her. You're the wife of a director. You can't work for an employee, Em. For Sammy and me, yes. Got that, lovey?'

'I got you, Boots,' said Emily. That was something Boots and Tommy and Sammy often said to each other. It went back to their days as Walworth cockneys.

'Well, stick with us, Em, and you'll be a director yourself one day.'

'Me a director?'

'You've got brains, love, and Sammy likes as many family brains in the firm as possible. In addition, a fancy dress and an elegant pair of legs on the board will make it better-looking.'

'Lucky for you you mentioned my brains,' said Emily, 'or I might've thought you was lookin' forward to the Can-Can at directors' meetings. But I can really start next Monday week, say?'

'You're on,' said Boots.

'Bless yer. Yer still good for a girl, ain't yer, Boots?

I'm off home now. I'll tell Chinese Lady I'm comin' to work for the firm. In the mornings.'

'I think in my lunch hour I'd better pop in to see Polly.'

'Yes, well, all right,' said Emily, 'but don't get into bed with her or I'll kill you.'

'You can't,' said a nurse.

'Can't what?' asked Boots.

'You can't visit a patient, not at this time of the day.'

'I keep having these problems,' said Boots.

'We keep having ours,' said the nurse.

Boots rubbed his chin. The nurse eyed him warily. He smiled.

'Mine give me a headache,' he said.

'So do mine,' she said.

'Well, I'll only be a minute,' said Boots.

'You won't,' said the nurse.

'I'll just slip in when your back's turned.'

'I'm not turning my back.'

'Don't blame you,' said Boots, 'you've got a perfect front.'

'My word, that's too much,' said the nurse. 'Sister is with Matron. I shall go and report you to both of them.' And she turned her back and walked crisply down the corridor. Boots slipped into the ward. Several female patients, sitting up in digestive repose after their lunch, eyed him with interest. Another nurse eyed him with suspicion.

'Dr Adams,' said Boots, 'to see Miss Simms. Ah, there she is.' His hat in his hand, his overcoat over his arm, he approached Polly. Polly, who had seen him and heard him, wanted to shout with laughter. Shock and concussion were going to keep her hospitalised for a few days. Her head still felt a little tender, her leg a little sore. Otherwise, she was fine, apart from being bored out of her wits. The arrival of Boots charged her with adrenalin. She lay with her head and shoulders resting on heaped pillows.

'Oh, good morning, Dr Adams,' she said.

'How are we today?' asked Boots.

'You'd better take a look,' said Polly. 'Nurse, would you put the screens up, please?'

The nurse came over.

'Well, I don't know—'

'What d'you mean, you don't know?' asked Polly. 'I'm not going to be examined in public, I hope.'

'But I don't know Dr Adams, and no one's said—'

'Well, I know him,' said Polly, 'he's my personal physician.'

'But Sister James hasn't said—'

'Look, don't muck about, darling. What kind of a hospital is this?'

The nurse looked at Boots. He responded with a nod of gravity.

'I'm sorry, Dr Adams,' she said, and wheeled the screens into position around the bed. Boots looked down at Polly, her bobbed hair slightly ruffled by the pillows. Her smile was full of silent laughter.

'Monkey,' he murmured.

'Monkey yourself, you started it. I heard you. Oh, joy. Besides, you look like a doctor in your grey suit. My, how very distinguished. You can examine me now. Not all over. Just my bosom. It's slightly bruised but otherwise perfect. Do examine it thoroughly, won't you?'

'We're better, are we?' said Boots.

'Certainly not. I'm ill. My leg's a swine. Oh, hell, I think I'm going to have a scar. I'm badly in need of your bedside manner. It's bliss to see you, darling, really. Are you going to examine me?'

'Not today, Miss Simms, I'm pressed for time, but glad you're all in one piece.'

'Your doing, darling. They told me about the tourniquet, and the blood transfusion. You gave some of yours. I'm joyful. You're going round and round in my veins. Jolly giddying that is, old sport. Were my legs a mess, or did you like them?'

'Did it all with my eyes shut, Polly. I've had your car towed away for repair. Your butler's got all the details. But ride a bicycle from now on or I'll worry about you.'

'I like the idea of you worrying about me.'

Whispers outside the screen suddenly culminated in the rise of a sharp voice. The screens were opened up and the formidable presence of Matron Ramsey was revealed.

'Must dash, Miss Simms,' said Boots, 'I've got my surgery and an outbreak of mumps.'

Polly, the silent laughter bright in her eyes, watched him sidle adroitly past the Matron and two nurses. One nurse was trying to hide a smile. Boots was out of the ward before the Matron could catch her outraged breath.

'Miss Simms,' she said.

'Sorry, old thing,' said Polly.

'I won't have this kind of behaviour.'

'Sorry, dear lady,' said Polly.

'Who was he?'

'No idea,' said Polly, 'never seen him before.'

'But you said he was your personal physician,' protested the second nurse.

'I wasn't seeing straight. Isn't concussion rotten on the eyes?'

The outraged Matron said, 'Good heavens, did he examine you?'

'No,' said Polly. 'Worse luck,' she murmured.

'Pardon?'

'What a bounder, though,' said Polly. Matron quivered. 'My father, General Sir Henry Simms, may be

300

visiting tonight. He's on his way back from the South of France. Fred telegraphed him.'

'Fred?'

'Our butler.'

'Ah,' said Matron, 'I see. Yes, very well.'

Polly smiled. It was quite useful sometimes, her father being a baronet. She hoped her leg wouldn't be badly scarred. She always felt both her legs belonged to Robert. In a certain way. One day that certain way would arrive. One day. Or one night.

Susie had a busy day. Sammy was conspicuous by his absence. He was with Lilian at the Shoreditch factory, absorbed in the promise and potential of his biggest venture, and pouring all available capital into Adams Fashions. He did not appear in his Camberwell office until nearly five-thirty. Susie went in to see him.

'Good evening, Mister Adams.'

'Good evening, Miss Brown,' said Sammy at his desk. He glanced up. 'Is that a new office dress?' It was dark blue with white cuffs and white collar.

'I have only worn it on and off for several months, Mister Adams, includin' when I was banished in Brixton.'

'Well, it suits you on, I won't give an opinion when it's off.'

'I am gratified you noticed it, Mister Adams,' she said. 'After several months,' she added.

'Quite so,' said Sammy, leafing through papers in his Gladstone bag.

My, thought Susie, we are getting a posh man of business, aren't we, Sammy Adams darling.

'It suits you,' she said.

'What does?' asked Sammy.

'Quite so,' said Susie.

Sammy, extracting papers and keeping his face

301

straight, said, 'I am takin' no notice of that, Miss Brown. I happen to have concluded it don't advantage me to exchange verbal wordage with a female woman.'

'Well, no, of course not, Mister Adams, us female women are ever so much smarter, aren't we?'

'I didn't hear that, Miss Brown.' Sammy perused the papers.

'You ought to see a doctor about your ears, Mister Adams.'

'I know that. They're full up with ringing bells. But I haven't got time. Madame Dupont sent her regards, by the way.'

'Yes, thank you, Mister Adams.' Susie felt that in leaving Brixton she had exchanged dull old routine for moments of heavenly delight. 'I'd like to tell you before I go that all outstandin' letters have been done and signed and put in the post. And my new typewriter's come and—'

'What new typewriter?'

'Oh, Mister Adams senior ordered it for me.'

'Mister Adams who?'

'Your eldest brother, Mister Adams. Boots.'

'I'm watching you, Miss Brown, and I'm listening to you, and I've got ringing bells again.'

'Oh, dear, couldn't you try cotton wool soaked in warm olive oil?' asked Susie, looking earnest with concern.

'No, I couldn't. I'll just cut me head off and throw it away. Regardin' the typewriter, I don't recollect signin' the indent.'

'Oh, I'm so sorry, Mister Adams, I think Boots just went and ordered it. I've bought myself a Pitman's Typin' Manual, and I'm staying on each evening to teach myself touch-typin'. Touch-typin's best, Mister Adams, and I can learn it quicker this way than at evening classes. It's ever so consid'rate of you to let me practise here in my office.'

302

'Susie Adams—'

'Pardon?' said Susie.

'Now what've I said?' Sammy was past all help. The pangs of love were crucifying him.

'You called me Susie Adams.'

'It's all that ringing,' said Sammy. 'It makes me unconscious.'

'Oh, Susie Adams come out unconscious, Mister Sammy?' she enquired, blue eyes wide and innocent. She could have told him how much she liked the sound of Susie Adams.

'Never mind,' said Sammy. He muttered a bit. Susie smiled. He looked at his pocket watch. 'It's too late, I suppose, for someone to make me a cup of tea and find me a biscuit?'

'Yes, everyone's just goin',' said Susie.

'All right, never mind,' said Sammy, and got down to his papers again. Susie gazed lovingly at him.

'I'll do it,' she said.

'You're a lovely girl, Susie.'

It caught at her breath, that endearment, it was spoken so easily, so nicely, and with a little upward glance and a little smile before he bent his head again. Susie knew then that she loved him very much, because it almost hurt. She made him a pot of tea, took it in on a tray, with several biscuits, and placed it on his desk. He was so absorbed by then that he only murmured his thanks. She didn't mind. He was always going to be a man of business, but what you had to remember about him was that for all his ambition he didn't tread people into the ground, and however high he rose he was never going to leave his family behind.

Susie very much wanted to be part of that family.

In her own office she began to teach herself the first basic rudiments of touch-typing.

* * *

303

'Tommy?' said Vi, when he arrived home from work the following day.

'Watcher, Vi,' said Tommy, kissing her.

'I just missed,' said Vi. 'Well, nearly three weeks, actually.'

'Missed?'

'Oh, you know, silly. Tommy, I think we might be goin' to have another baby.'

'Help,' said Tommy.

'Aren't you pleased?'

'I ought to be, it's a consequence of me virile manhood.'

'You can say that again,' said Vi.

'You're welcome, Mrs Adams. Give us another kiss.' Vi, always responsive, kissed him warmly. 'But it's a bit soon for you, Alice only being seven months.'

'Just tell me, are you pleased?'

'I'm gladsome for both of us. Yer a lovely wonder, Vi, you're me own private Empire Day and me own Vilma Banky.' Vilma Banky was a film star who had played opposite Rudolph Valentino.

'All that?' Vi laughed.

'I'll do the cookin',' said Tommy.

'I shan't tell Mum and Dad till I know for certain.'

'That makes sense,' said Tommy. 'Still, I think I'll go and tell Alice.'

'She's in her cot – wait a minute, what d'you mean, you'll tell her? She won't understand a word you're saying, not at seven months, you silly.'

'Course she will,' said Tommy, 'she's an Adams. Chinese Lady don't allow any Adams to be born that don't understand another Adams.'

'I think all the Adams are a bit barmy,' said Vi.

'Who said that?' asked Tommy from the door.

'Me,' said Vi. 'Barmy nice, though, not barmy peculiar.'

'I'll tell Alice that as well. Good on yer, Vi love.'

'Good on you too, Tommy love.'

CHAPTER TWENTY-TWO

On New Year's Eve, the whole family attended the pantomime at the Camberwell Palace Theatre, except for little Alice and young Edward, both of whom were with Aunt Victoria and Uncle Tom. Aunt Victoria had actually invited everyone round after the performance was over, and to have a drink and see the New Year in.

The pantomime, *Dick Whittington*, was like all of its kind, full of nonsensical dialogue, terrible jokes, tinselled costumes, foul villainy, traditional songs and contrived absurdities, all of which delighted the audience, especially the children. Everything was magic to the children. Minor music hall stars played the main parts, but the cat, of course, was everybody's favourite. There was a magician too. He came on while the rest of the cast and the scene shifters prepared for the entry of Dick into London. He was dressed in black, with a top hat and black stick. He did conjuring tricks and made magic, producing things out of nowhere, even out of the ears of little girls and boys whom he induced to come up on the stage. He had a lady assistant, Vivette, who wore a kind of basque that shaped her voluptuous form, and flesh-coloured tights that sheathed her legs and handsome thighs. Chinese Lady, Tim on one side of her and Bobby on the other, took silent umbrage at such a revealing costume, and thought the people who whistled at it very common and vulgar. Vivette was very sweet to the boys and girls who let the magician pull cards or eggs or pennies out of their ears. Her smile for them was flashing, and she gave each of them a sweet as she led them off.

Boots thought the magician past his best. He fumbled some of his sleight-of-hand stuff, and his disappearing tricks were very old hat. His lady assistant's permanent smile looked very fixed at times. She wore a tinsel star in her wavy mass of auburn hair. Boots found himself watching her, wondering why he thought there was something familiar about her. The auburn hair, as darkly fiery as Emily's, ought to strike a chord, but didn't. He concentrated more on her round face and round eyes.

The familiar something resolved itself just as the act came to an end. He glanced at Rosie beside him. She was clapping, her face alight with the pleasure of a girl entertained. Rainbould the Master Magician bowed, then turned and flourished a hand at Vivette, who responded to applause and more whistles by blowing kisses. Rosie clapped her too, then whispered to Boots.

'Eyes off, Daddy, Nana's going to have something to say about her not wearing a blouse and skirt.'

Boots gave his foster daughter a smile. Rosie winked at him, and Boots knew she had not recognised her natural mother. The auburn hair was a wig, of course, and beneath it was the round face of Milly Pearce, the woman who had deserted Rosie, her illegitimate daughter. Boots was sure he was making no mistake. Rosie had been a mere child of five then, and her picture of her mother would have quickly faded. He wondered if Chinese Lady had recognised the woman. Or if Emily had. Or Tommy and Sammy, for that matter.

As the magician and his assistant began to withdraw to the wings, the theatre manager came quickly on to the stage.

'Ladies and gentlemen, a moment, please. If Mr Samuel Adams is in the house, would he be so good as to come to my office immediately. Thank you, thank you, the show will now go on.'

'Excuse me a tick,' said Sammy to Susie, and Susie nodded, wondering what could be up.

In the theatre office, the manager advised Sammy that the Shoreditch police had telephoned to say his factory was on fire.

'Eh?' said Sammy.

'They thought you should know. One of your workers reported it to the police.'

'Christ,' said Sammy, and ran, just as he was, in his suit, with no hat and no overcoat. Outside the theatre, he was lucky. It was New Year's Eve and there were London taxis about. One took him all the way to Shoreditch, and at speed under the promise of a generous tip.

Gertie, thought Sammy. She lived nearest the factory, and he had told her only this afternoon that he was going to the pantomime. He fretted and he worried. He had to rest his hopes in the quickness of the fire brigade. All the machines and the collection, all that material, material that was awaiting the first orders he and Lilian hoped to obtain for her collection. And many completed garments in cheaper material for his own shops, but not to be released to them until the Paris show began.

He saw the glow in the sky before he reached the factory. As the taxi turned the corner of the street, he saw the flames and the hoses of the firemen spouting arching streams of water. A policeman stopped the taxi before it reached the edge of a watching crowd. Sammy got out, quickly paid the driver and pushed himself through the crowd.

Gertie, the senior machinist, saw him. She hurried up to him.

307

'Oh, gawd 'elp us, Mister Adams, it's goin' to burn to the ground. That Daft Dick, the bleeder, he ain't never been safe with matches in 'is mitt. Morris did it on yer when 'e sent Daft Dick along to keep the yard clean. 'E's kept it clean all right, and 'e's made 'is bonfire 'eaps all right with cardboard boxes and every bit o' stuff Ma's swept orf the fact'ry floor. Mister Adams, is it goin' to sink yer?'

Sammy, watching the blazing factory and the playing hoses, felt as sick as a dog. Adams Fashions was all going up in fire and smoke.

'Bloody hell,' he said.

'Me too,' said Gertie, hair a tangle, arms crossed over her chest, hands clasping and digging at her thin arms. 'I'm cryin' me bleedin' eyes out. Yer didn't deserve this, Mister Adams.'

Sammy watched the high, leaping flames that shot sparks and smoke, flames that were consuming and destroying building, machines, benches, stockroom, everything. The hoses played, but he knew the firemen were fighting a losing battle. The factory was a roaring furnace. Glass exploded.

The faces of the crowd were lifted to the blaze, eyes glittering in red reflection of the blaze. There was something horribly fascinating about a fire such as this. It drew people and it held them mesmerised and rooted. It even excited some, such was the awesome spectacle of elemental destruction. The sparks soared in mockery of the firemen's efforts, and the heat scorched the night. A remaining section of the roof crashed inwards and a million fiery sparks leapt upwards.

'Jesus Christ,' said Sammy.

'I never seen nothink more crool,' said Gertie. 'No fact'ry, no jobs, no wages, an' yer losin' a packet, Mister Adams. There ain't no insurance can make up for this. Yer've only got the stuff.'

'There's no stuff I'm goin' to get out of this lot,' said Sammy.

'Oh, we got the materials out, an' the garments,' said Gertie, 'but the machines, there wasn't no time, and most was too near the fire.'

'What?' said Sammy. 'Say that again,' he said, and put an arm around the thin shoulders of the gaunt woman who had given him loyal service from the day he took the factory over. 'Say that again.'

'Me old man, 'e seen it first,' said Gertie, amid the shouts of the fire brigade chief and the roar of the blaze. ' 'E was comin' back from the jug an' bottle with our New Year's beer, 'e'd 'ad a couple of days' work at the docks an' said 'e'd treat. 'E saw Daft Dick runnin' away, the bugger come out by way of the office an' front door. Me old man smelled smoke. 'E went in, Daft Dick 'aving left the door open. 'E saw the fire right at the end of the fact'ry, a bleedin' great pile of rubbish flamin' away against the wall, an' 'e smelled petrol. 'E come runnin' across to me an' we got neighbours out an' some of the machinists, an' I told one of 'em to run an' tell the coppers to get the fire brigade. Then we all run into the fact'ry. It was goin' up down the end, Mister Adams, gawd, it was, an' me old man said buckets of water wasn't goin' to do no good. But the stockroom next to the office wasn't in no danger, not then, so I said let's get the stuff out while we can. So we did, we sweated blood, but we got it all out, all the finished garments an' the rolls of material, ev'rythink, we didn't leave nothink. It's all in our 'ouses, an' if anyone's nicked any of it, me an' me old man'll get it back for yer. Yer been a good boss to us, Mister Adams. Oh, I told Mrs Bernstein what run for the coppers to tell 'em to see if they could get a message through to yer at the Camberwell Palace, where you said yer was goin' for yer fam'ly New Year. Gawd, look at it, Mister Adams, don't it make yer 'eart bleed? We'd've got the machines out if we could, well, some of 'em, but they're bleedin' weighty an' the place was gettin' too 'ot by then, an' the smoke, I never seen smoke like it, we was coughin' an' spittin', an' me old man said right, ev'ryone out, and then the fire brigade come an' they 'ad us out sharpish. Is it goin' to sink yer business, Mister Adams?'

'No, it isn't, Gertie. Nor you.' Sammy had thought only the finished samples of the 1926 dress design were safe. Lilian had them at home. She had run them up herself at home. In secret. To know that the whole collection had been saved, that all other garments and all materials had been saved too, brought Sammy's resilient nature to the surface. There was nothing to be done about the factory and all the machines, except to pass the headache to the insurance company. But there was something to be done about Gertie and the machinists. 'Gertie, where's yer old man?'

' 'E's over there, tryin' to cheer Gladys up. I'll 'ave to watch 'im with Gladys.'

'What happened to the jug of beer?'

'Eh? The beer? Gawd, we didn't stop to drink no beer,' said Gertie. Other machinists, shawls over their shoulders, were edging up, shocked, shaken, and despairing of their jobs.

'All right,' said Sammy, 'let's go and have some beer now, and I'll talk to you. Let me meet yer old man.'

'Bert!' Gertie shouted. Her husband, in a flat cap, trousers, jersey and tied scarf, came across. He had muscular shoulders. The rest of him was lean and wiry. Physically, he was typical of a docker. His life was hard. Dockers were counted as casual labour. Sometimes there was work for many, sometimes for some, and sometimes for only a few. 'Bert,' said Gertie, ' 'ere's Mister Sammy Adams.'

310

' 'Ow is yer, guv?' said Bert. 'Yer bleedin' copped it tonight.'

'Nice to meet yer,' said Sammy, and shook the docker's hand vigorously. 'Nice to know yer. Yer got some beer, I believe. I'd be pleasured to participate.'

'It ain't much,' said Bert. 'Well, it ain't as much as it was, seeing what got slopped on me run across 'ome. Still, there's maybe enough for you, me an' Gertie.'

'That'll do me,' said Sammy. 'Could yer get someone to go to the jug and bottle for a large bottle of brandy? Here's a quid. Never mind the change. We'll dole the brandy out to whatever machinists are here, if they could come across to your house.'

' 'Ere, you all right, guv?' said Bert. 'You got yer fact'ry burnin' to the ground an' yer doling out quids for brandy?'

'I'm all right,' said Sammy.

One of the machinists went for the brandy. About to leave the scene with Sammy and her husband, Gertie suddenly said with bitter venom, 'There 'e is, there's Daft Dick. Look at the bugger.'

Sammy saw him. The man had edged his way to the front of the crowd. He wore an old shabby mackintosh, belted, but no hat. His shock of wiry hair stood up. His face was shiny, his expression exultant, his eyes on the flames.

'Leave him,' said Sammy.

'Aincher goin' to do the bleeder?' asked Gertie.

'Not now,' said Sammy, and went across the street with her and her husband to their small, flat-fronted house.

'It ain't no palace, Mister Adams,' said Gertie, 'and we only got the kitchen stove alight.'

'I was brought up in a kitchen,' said Sammy. 'Best place in a house. Lead the way.'

It was small, the kitchen, but the glowing stove and

311

the homely nature of the room were more than good
enough for Sammy. On the table, covered with green
baize, stood a brown jug, three-quarters full of ale. Bert
rushed his gawping children up to bed. Gertie put
cheap thick glasses on the table. Sammy sat down. The
machinists, a dozen of them, arrived to crowd into the
kitchen doorway. Gertie poured the beer, and she and
Bert sat down at the table with Sammy. The machinist
who had gone for the brandy returned with it, pushing
her way through. She placed the bottle on the table.

'Yer only got six bob change, Mister Adams,' she said,
proffering it.

'Well, that's seventy-two pennies,' said Sammy.
'Share it out among all yer kids. Can yer uncork the
brandy, Bert?'

Bert got a cheap corkscrew from a dresser drawer and
pulled the cork.

'There y'ar, Mister Adams is treatin' yer to a nip
each,' he said to the machinists. 'Do yer good, it ain't
been yer best New Year's Eve. But leave a nip each for
me an' Gertie an' Mister Adams, or I'll crown yer with
the bottle.'

The bottle was passed round. The pale-faced
machinists gulped from it. They coughed, they turned
red.

' 'Ere's yer good 'ealth, Mister Adams,' said Gertie,
lifting her glass of beer, 'yer need it.'

Sammy took a long swallow of the beer.

'Now,' he said. 'First, you got a job for as long as
yer want with me, Gertie, and so have the rest of yer. I
am in—'

'But you ain't got no fact'ry,' said Gertie, 'you ain't
got no place for us to 'ave jobs in, nor machines. You
ain't goin' to get no money from no insurance company
for months.'

'An' they'll fight yer for every penny you ask for,' said

312

Bert. 'They got more takin' ways than payin' ones, guv, I tell yer.'

'We'll see,' said Sammy. 'I am concerned now to advise yer all I am in considerable appreciation of what yer did in clearing out the stock room, and it won't do me any good not to say so. You all got the stuff in yer homes?'

'We 'ad to do our bit for yer, Mister Adams,' said Gladys, a woman of thirty-five and still with some of the prettiness she had owned as a young woman.

'We couldn't just stand about,' said another machinist.

'That Gert, she run us off our feet,' said another.

'An' Bert, 'e got all our old men sweatin' at it,' said Gladys, 'an' my old man with that back of 'is an' all. But we 'ad to save somethink for yer, Mister Adams.'

'Yer been fair to us, Mister Adams,' said Gertie, 'yer been the best bleedin' boss I ever knowed, an' yer give us a good manager in yer brother.'

'Lovely feller, 'e is,' said another machinist. 'Keeps yer at it, mind, but a lovely bloke. Pass the bottle back, Maggie.'

'Pass it 'ere,' said Bert. A few mouths took further swigs before the bottle reached his hand. 'Mister Adams?'

Sammy finished his beer, dried the inside of the glass with his handkerchief and Bert poured him a generous noggin. He poured Gertie one, then himself. He passed the bottle back to the machinists.

'You've got part of the stockroom stuff here, Gertie?' asked Sammy.

'Me livin'-room's full of it,' said Gertie, the brandy tinting her cheeks. 'Want to take a look at it?'

'I am acceptin' your word,' said Sammy.

'We rushed about with it,' said Gertie, 'but treated it gentle, like. There ain't nothink ruined, Mister Adams.'

313

'I believe yer,' said Sammy. 'Well, then, you all want to keep workin' and I want it selfsame. If I put machines into yer houses, could yer work at home?'

'I'll work in me coal-'ole,' said Gladys. 'I don't 'ave to, but I would.'

'We've got one problem,' said Sammy, 'a place for new cutting machines. A shed would do, but it's got to be central.'

'I'll get yer the 'ire of a shed, guv,' said Bert.

'You're on, Bert,' said Sammy. 'Now, I'll give yer the loan of our van an' driver. I want someone who's got the room available to keep all the materials. I'll pay rent for it. The driver will collect for cuttin' work and deliver to her or her or her accordin'. Savvy?'

'Got yer, Mister Adams,' said Gertie.

'It's not goin' to mean the kind of turnover I'd like,' said Sammy. 'It can't be expected when you're not all under one roof, but I have considerable faith in yer willingness and a high regard for your co-operation, which has been a credit to yer so far. With the assistance of a certain business acquaintance of mine, who is notable for his remarkability, I'll get the new machines delivered to yer houses as quick as I can, but yer'll understand I can't pay yer any wages till yer start workin' again. At home. However, to compensate for loss of business revenue in misfortunate circumstances like these here, there is an insurance clause—'

'What's a clause?' asked a woman.

'A bit of wise thinking when takin' out business insurance, which in this case will allow me to pay yer fifty per cent of yer wages while yer waitin' for yer machines to arrive.'

'We get paid while we ain't workin'?' said Gertie. 'Yer jokin', Mister Adams.'

'It occurs to me,' said Sammy, 'that I have had occasion more than once to advise all of yer I do not joke

314

about business. I need yer skill, you need yer wages. It is mutually serious. All right, now, you girls get off to yer homes and see the New Year in with yer fam'lies.'

'God bless yer, Mister Adams,' said Gladys, 'yer a gent, you are. 'E copped yer, 'e did, that Daft Dick, but yer still on yer uppers and smilin'.'

'I ain't smiling,' said Sammy, 'but also I ain't on me downers. Yer'll all get an extra bonus at the end of yer first week's work at home in appreciation of what yer did to save me stocks. And I'll leave it to yer to acquaint all the other machinists with me proposition about workin' at home. A happy New Year to yer.'

'An' to you, Mister Adams.' The relieved machinists melted away.

'The bleedin' perishers,' said Bert, 'they swiped the bottle.' He rushed after them and brought it back. 'Guv'nor?'

'I'll go another,' said Sammy, and Bert poured a little more for all three of them. He looked at Sammy.

'I know yer been good to me Gertie,' he said. 'She ain't said how good, and yer maybe let slip then what yer didn't mean to just now, about bonuses. Yer been doin' that, guv, paying 'em bonuses?'

'Givin' due regard to yer natural question, Bert, I'm obliged to answer that I ain't saying.'

'You Bert, you ain't saying, neither,' said Gertie, 'you forget you 'eard it, or I'll wrap yer Sunday braces round yer neck an' strangle yer.'

'She would too,' said the docker, 'so I'll tell yer, Mister Adams, I've clean forget you said anything. All the same, yer a gent. What yer goin' to do about Daft Dick?'

'I'm not goin' to do anything,' said Sammy, 'but you could maybe favour me. He's not daft, he's a firebug, he likes the feel of matches in his hand. I wouldn't be disagreeably surprised to hear you knew someone who'd hammer his fingers.'

315

'Got yer, guv,' said Bert. 'I'll lay 'e ain't goin' to be able to strike another match for the rest of 'is life.'

'Just his fingers,' said Sammy. 'I am averse to hearing his loaf of bread has been bashed in. My mother wouldn't like it.'

'That's lettin' 'im orf light,' said Gertie.

'Not when the coppers get after him,' said Sammy. 'How much, Bert?'

'Five bob,' said Bert.

Sammy gave him four pounds.

'You and Gertie keep the change,' he said.

'Look,' said Bert, 'what we done we did on account of Gertie saying we 'ad to, which was on account of you treatin' 'er an' the girls right.'

'I owe yer both,' said Sammy. 'You know it, I know it. Cheer up, Gertie, we'll get another fact'ry built.'

'I'm cheered up already,' said Gertie. 'Any more brandy, is there?'

They finished the bottle between them. Sammy sat talking and thinking. Then he said, 'Right. Been a pleasure, considering. Now I've got to go and let Mrs Hyams know what's happened and what's happening.'

Gertie and Bert saw him out. He shook hands with them, wished them a happy New Year, and went striding away south in search of a taxi. He had to let the family know, as well as Lilian. And there was Tommy, without a proper job for the time being.

It was late when he reached Aunt Victoria's. The family had had their New Year drink, but not in the most convivial of moods. Boots had gone to see the theatre manager and been told the reason for Sammy not returning to his seat.

Lizzie and Ned had taken their children home, but Boots and Emily were still there with Rosie and Tim. Susie had felt that under the circumstances she was outstaying her welcome, but it had been compulsive to stay in the hope Sammy would put in an appearance before time completely ran out on her. Tommy was sombre, Vi upset. Uncle Tom and Aunt Victoria were doing their best to be consoling. Chinese Lady was straight of face.

Sammy described the fire and the complete destruction of the factory. He recounted how all the stock had been saved and what he proposed to do to get production going again. Further, he and Lilian Hyams would proceed with the launching of Adams Fashions by introducing them, as planned, to West End shop and store buyers. That would take place in a few days. No one was to worry.

'What started the fire?' asked Chinese Lady.

'A box of matches in the hands of a dubious geezer,' said Sammy.

'I knew it,' said Chinese Lady. 'That's what comes of havin' a fact'ry in the East End.' Chinese Lady considered the East End was like foreign parts, and that Jack the Ripper's birth certificate was probably highly dubious.

'Sammy, you talkin' about the fact'ry handyman, Daft Dick?' asked Tommy.

'A misfortunate acceptance on my part of the previous owner's choice,' said Sammy. It was Reuben Morris who had sent Daft Dick along. 'Which grievous error I freely admit. Yer learn hard lessons in hard times.'

'But I thought he was harmless,' said Susie, suffering for Sammy.

'No, I'd say he was biding his time,' said Sammy.

Boots, looking thoughtful, said, 'Get yourself a car, Sammy.'

'How did that creep in?' asked Emily.

'Daddy's ticking, Mummy,' said Rosie. Tim, tired out, was asleep in an armchair.

317

'We don't want Sammy breakin' his neck in no car,' said Chinese Lady, 'specially after he might have just missed being burned alive.'

'The van's indispensable in its present use,' said Boots. 'Get a car, Sammy. You make a hundred journeys every month. Tommy will show you how it works, and he can use it, or you can use it, for carrying the cut materials to your machinists.'

'A car does sound nice,' said Aunt Victoria, already thinking of mentioning to her neighbours that her son-in-law's brother owned a car.

'Comin' up in the world, that is,' said Uncle Tom.

'You can talk about it at the office tomorrow,' said Chinese Lady. 'It's time now we all went home.'

'I'll take Susie,' said Sammy.

'I'll be all right,' said Susie, not her usual bright self because of the fire and the blow it must have been to Sammy. Also, he had been going to tell her tonight of the new plans he had for her. Everything had fallen flat, a bit like it had on Boxing Day evening. She hoped the Adams family hadn't entered a bad luck period. 'There's no need for anyone to come with me.'

'Now, Susie,' said Chinese Lady in a proprietary way. She had, of course, already made up her mind that Susie would make another ladylike daughter-in-law. 'Boots is seeing me and Em'ly and the children home, Sammy is just about fit to see hisself home, and Tommy will see you home.'

'Yes, I'll take her,' said Tommy, 'you look whacked, Sammy.'

'Yes, you go with her, Tommy,' said Vi.

'All right, see you in the morning, Susie,' said Sammy, feeling frankly drained, 'and you can come with me to Mr Greenberg, he being a very helpful gent who can lay his hands on anything, including best-quality second-hand industrial sewing-machines.

318

Which means, if you know Eli Greenberg like we know him, it ain't goin' to be necessary to buy new ones.'

'But my office work,' said Susie.

'I'll come in and help tomorrow,' said Emily.

'Yer will, Em?' said Sammy.

'The fam'ly comes first in a crisis,' said Emily.

CHAPTER TWENTY-THREE

New Year's Day, 1926, opened to rain. It had been raining buckets all over the Continent, and the rivers of Europe were flooding towns and villages. Chinese Lady, over breakfast, said that was what come of living in Frenchified countries instead of a God-selected country like England. And like Scotland and Wales too, she said, in her loyalty to the United Kingdom. But not Ireland. Ireland was a pack of trouble. She wouldn't be surprised, she said, to hear that all that Continental rain was falling on Ireland too, and that all them troublesome Irish were swimming for their lives. Boots said if they were, they'd all be swimming this way and probably end up on Blackpool beach. Tim looked awed at this. Rosie stifled giggles. Chinese Lady said someone whose name she wouldn't mention would be better getting off to his work before he brought the house down with his music hall jokes.

Emily left to go to the estate agents. She entered the premises in crisp fashion and said to her colleague, 'When Mr Barry Somerville comes in, Mary, would you tell him I won't be in myself, not this morning, we've got a fam'ly crisis. I'll hope to be in tomorrow.'

She had given in her notice, anyway. Umbrella up, she crossed the road and walked to the offices of Adams Enterprises, going up the side stairs adjacent the shop. She entered her husband's office.

'All right?' said Boots.

'What's it they say? See you got your priorities right? Yes, I've got mine right, Boots. You dictate and I'll do the shorthand-typin'.'

Boots had offered to look after Sammy's correspondence, with Emily's help, leaving Sammy and Susie free to devote themselves to the problems caused by the fire. The post was all opened, he had given out work to the copy typists, and had a pile ready for dictation. Emily was to use Susie's office and Susie's new typewriter. Emily, always brisk, wasted no time. Within two minutes she was seated, notebook open, pencil sharpened, legs crossed. Boots observed her legs and the sheen of her stockings. That, he thought, was probably one of the first reasons why Somerville had come to fancy her.

'You're showing off,' he said.

'I'm daft to ask,' said Emily, 'but what d'you mean, showing off?'

'Kindly adjust your skirt,' said Boots.

'Oh, yer chump,' said Emily, 'get on with it.'

Boots got on with it. After six letters, he said, 'How we doing?'

'I think I'm goin' to like it.' Emily smiled. 'I'm glad I think I'm goin' to like it.'

'It's to be your own choice, Em. No coercion. Right?'

'I got you,' said Emily.

'Good on yer, old girl.'

'Not so much of the old girl, old boy. Get on with it.'

Susie's first job that morning was to telephone the insurance company while Sammy was busy using the other line. She spoke to a clerk in the claims department, the policy in front of her. His first response was to say, 'Who?'

'Adams Enterprises,' repeated Susie, and went on to give details. To which he said, 'A fire? Well, I don't

321

know. A fire, you say?' Susie, in no mood to play second fiddle to a voice vague with doubt and laziness, said, 'Kindly don't waste my time. Mr Adams will expect a claims form by first post tomorrow, and the date when the fire assessor will inspect. Sorry to have woke you up, what a crying shame, but you can go back to sleep now.'

When Sammy had finished his own phone calls, he summoned her. Susie, hat and coat on, went into his office. Boots arrived through the other door at the same time.

'Morning, Susie. Listen, Sammy.'

'I'm in a hurry,' said Sammy, shovelling himself into his overcoat, 'but I'll spare you a minute of me valuable time.'

'I can only spare you thirty seconds myself,' said Boots, 'that's all Emily's allowing me. I haven't finished dictation yet. This fire. That firebug. Adams Fashions. Exclusive collection. Think about the possibility that someone put the box of matches into Daft Dick's hand. It's a cut-throat trade, sonny, and someone might be thinking there's not room for you in it. One more thing. Mitch is going to find you a high-class, first-rate and commendably desirable second-hand car. Take care of Susie. It's wet outside.' Boots returned to his office, leaving Sammy gaping. Recovering, he let a little grin appear.

'Who was that, Susie?'

'That was Mister Adams senior,' said Susie.

'You sure? I thought it was God havin' a sharp half-minute with me.'

'Yes, Mister Adams senior can be very impressive,' said Susie.

'I'm not being provoked by that, Miss Brown.' Sammy buttoned his coat up and put his hat on. 'Come on, let's catch a bus.' They left the office and descended the stairs, emerging into the street. 'There you are, one

322

comin'.' He walked smartly to the stop, Susie bobbing along beside him with quick clicks of her heels. 'Make a note, Miss Brown, that we're to enquire into the possibility of devious actions by competitors unknown. And make another note that if it's true we ain't goin' to take it lying down. Which means God might send his troops in.'

'God?' said Susie, their arrival at the bus stop coinciding with the arrival of the bus. 'God, Mister Sammy?'

'Boots,' said Sammy.

They boarded, seating themselves in the lower deck. Susie was stifling laughter. Sammy enquired what was funny.

'Oh, you are,' she said. 'I know it's serious, the fire and everything, but I'm so glad you can wake up laughing about it.'

'Who's laughing?' said Sammy. 'I'm not.'

But he was meeting the first day of 1926 in a challenging mood and was not without cheer. He had his worries, but he also had the uplifting knowledge that he had far more friends in the East End than he had thought. He also had Susie beside him. He could, of course, have dealt with Mr Greenberg on his own, but Susie's presence was a pleasure. Susie had never let him down. She's had funny moments, but so did all women. It was a paralysing weakness, being in love with her. He had never included that kind of thing in his calculations. Other men got hit by a hammer, but it had never occurred to him he'd get knocked flat himself. It took his mind off business. It made him think of coming home at night to Susie, Susie in a pretty apron and serving up steak-and-kidney pudding. Or Susie in a black silk nightdress – no, don't think of that.

A warm hip was touching his, a warm voice floating into his ear.

'Penny for your thoughts, Mister Sammy?'

'Pardon? Ah, yes, about Mr Greenberg.' He spoke to her about Eli and industrial sewing-machines.

They came off the bus and out of the rain into Mr Greenberg's covered yard. They caught the well-known rag and bone man before he took off with his horse and cart.

'Morning, Eli,' said Sammy.

'Good morning, Mr Greenberg,' said Susie.

'Ah, good morning, Sammy, good morning, Susie,' said Mr Greenberg from beneath his round black hat. 'A vet vun, ain't it? And a sad vun.' He pulled out his large red handkerchief and blew his nose sorrowfully. His beard curled in sympathy. 'Sammy, such a grievous fire I have heard about. Vhat can I say? Vas it insured, my poy?'

'Fully covered,' said Sammy.

'Vhat a relief to all of us, and vhat a pleasure to see Susie, ain't it? A picture, Sammy, a picture, ain't she? Such a sveet vife she vhould make, even for our Prince of Vales.'

'Leave off,' said Sammy, 'I ain't proposin' to introduce her to no Prince of Wales.'

'Very vise, Sammy. Vill you both step into my office?'

They entered the old green shed that served as his office. He dusted a chair and begged Susie to be seated.

'Thank you, Mr Greenberg,' she said.

'Now, my dears, vhat can I do for you? I am a poor man, but vhat is money between friends? Money ve can do without, ain't it? Did not Moses say the poor shall inherit the earth?'

'I thought that was Jesus,' said Sammy.

'Jesus or Moses, Sammy, vhat is the difference to you and me?'

'Don't worry, Eli old cock, we're not after a loan. We're here to put some valuable business in your way. Mind, I could negotiate direct with certain suppliers myself, but it would take time, and I don't have any to spare, I've got Adams Fashions takin' up all of it. Susie, acquaint our friend with details.'

'Oh, a pleasure,' said Susie. 'Dear Mr Greenberg, we've come to ask how long it will take you to acquire on our behalf fifty highly recommendable first-class second-hand industrial sewing-machines which won't fall to pieces at first go.'

Sammy grinned. Mr Greenberg peered.

'I should be hearing this from Susie?' he said in pleasure.

'Also, Mr Greenberg,' said Susie, blue eyes making him sigh, 'we'd be awf'lly obliged if you won't ask a price that will ruin us, as we're near to that already on account of the fire.'

'My life,' said Mr Greenberg, mittened hands waving about, 'vhat have you been makin' of a girl so young and pretty, Sammy?'

'We are also in the market for three cutting machines,' said Susie. 'In prime condition, of course. For everything, Mr Greenberg, we're open to an askin' price of two hundred pounds.'

Mr Greenberg clutched at his heart and turned pale.

'Susie, Susie,' he said hoarsely, 'I am hearing this from friends? Two hundred single green vuns for fifty sewing-machines and three cuttin' machines?'

'Yes, it's a valuable order,' said Susie.

'I ain't saying it ain't, Susie.' Mr Greenberg took his hat off and fanned his beard. 'But valuable ain't too valuable vhen it gives a poor man a heart attack.'

'Can you get 'em, and at express speed immediate and forthwith, that's the point, Eli,' said Sammy.

'I am acquainted vith promising sources, to be sure,' said Mr Greenberg, replacing his hat, 'but at a fair price, Sammy, a fair price. Shall ve say three hundred pounds, vhich vould include cost of time?'

'That's upping it considerable,' said Sammy, 'and I don't think me personal assistant is too impressed.'

'We could go to two hundred and twenty, Mister Sammy,' said Susie.

Mr Greenberg shook his head reproachfully. They began to bargain. Out in the street a taxi pulled up. Rachel alighted, paid the cabbie and entered the yard. She knocked on the shed door. Sammy opened it. Rachel, in a shining cream-coloured raincoat and matching rain-hat, looked up at him, the velvet lustre of her brown eyes reflecting the wetness of the day.

'Sammy, my God, your factory,' she said in pain.

Sammy turned. 'Take over, Susie. Excuse me, Eli.' He came out of the shed, closing the door behind him. Susie saw him through the little window, and she also saw Rachel, the woman who had once been his only girl friend.

'Sammy, I phoned your office as soon as I'd looked at our morning papers,' said Rachel. 'Boots told me I might find you here. I had to see you. I'm devastated. Has everything gone?'

'The fact'ry's gone,' said Sammy, 'and the machines. But not the stock.' He detailed events and what the machinists and their husbands had done for him. Rachel took a deep breath. 'We're not done for,' said Sammy, 'the investments are still good, Rachel.'

'I should stand here with tears in my eyes about money?' she said. 'They're for you, you idiot. Or they were. Now I don't have a breaking heart. You've still got everything that's important at the moment. I thought you'd been left with nothing except the insurance. Do you know what it means that you've still got what's most important?'

'Yes, I know,' said Sammy, 'it means I've got a staff of machinists that need taking care of. And I'd like to say, Rachel, that you're a love for comin' here to be consoling.'

Rachel smiled a little moistly.

'That's my Sammy,' she said. 'You're soft, aren't you, under all that flannel you dish out. You're a man, Sammy, you've been brought up as a man, and you belong to the best family that ever came out of Walworth. You're my kind, Sammy, and I'm your kind, and I'm going to be with you every step of your way up, without doing any harm to anyone. You get me, Sammy?'

'I get you, Rachel.'

'It's special, what we've got. Ain't it?' Rachel was what she was born, a Jewish cockney with a warm heart, and Sammy was what he was, a man of Walworth, and Walworth was the resilient heart of the cockney world this side of the river. 'Ain't it special, love?'

'Right,' said Sammy. 'Which means it ain't something you'd tell Benjamin or I'd tell me future wife.'

Rachel shook a gloved finger at him.

'Listen, you clown, don't talk to me about any future wife. When it happens, I'll come to the wedding, but I'll be wearing black. You hear that, Sammy?'

'I hear you, Rachel.'

'Good. It's so you'll understand. Never mind the fire, you can build a new factory and you can still pre-empt the French designers. Oh, and my daddy sends his sorrow and regards, and asks me to tell you a friend of his has vacant premises in Islington.'

'I'm beholden to Isaac,' said Sammy, 'but it's got to be Shoreditch. I've got fam'lies in Shoreditch, me machinists' fam'lies, and I owe 'em, Rachel.'

'Only round the corner, Sammy. Well, as good as. Cheap rent.'

'It's a thought.' Sammy's eyes gleamed. 'Got insurance cover for that too, as well as fifty-per-cent wages for the girls when they're not working on account of unfortunate happenings.'

'Who's a clever, thoughtful boy, then?' smiled Rachel.

'I'll speak to me chief machinist. She and the others might not mind walking the extra footage to the next parish till the new fact'ry's up. Tell Isaac I'll look in on him this afternoon.'

'He'll be able to tell you he knows of a lease on a shop in Oxford Street that will be on offer in two months' time.'

'Oxford Street?' The challenge of that brought the gleam back to Sammy's eyes.

'Near Selfridges,' said Rachel. 'I was going to phone you about it today. Adams Fashions in Oxford Street, Sammy, think of that. If it's not Regent Street or Mayfair, it's still the West End.'

'Tell Isaac I'll definitely look in on him this afternoon.'

'My word,' said Rachel, 'I like the way you're bouncing back, Sammy, and I like it that you know where you're going and how to get there.'

'I like it that you and your father have got consideration for a Gentile.'

'My daddy loves you, Sammy, and wouldn't care if you were a Buddhist monk with two heads. Do you mind if I rush now?'

'I'm touched to the cockles of me heart that you came, Rachel. Help yourself to my best regards.'

'Sammy, Sammy, I get best regards from my grocer.'

'I get groceries from mine.'

'My, aren't we witty? *Shalom*, lovey.'

'Bless yer, Mrs Rachel Goodman.'

She left, and Sammy went back into the shed, where Susie and Mr Greenberg had settled, of course, on two hundred and fifty pounds cash and no questions asked, particularly about Mr Greenberg's sources of second-hand supply.

'Ah, Sammy,' he said, 've are now comin' to delivery charges.'

'Yer pulling a fast one, Eli,' said Sammy.

Mr Greenberg spread his hands in gentle protest.

'Sammy my dear, for new machines, no delivery charges. For second-hand, nothing is for free, ain't it? Also, dear me, delivery not to vun single address, but many. Vell, I vill arrange it for fifteen green vuns.'

'Delivery's when?' asked Sammy.

'Three days vill do?' said Mr Greenberg.

'Three days?' Sammy regarded his long-standing friend fondly. 'That's a winner, Abraham old love. I ain't goin' to reproach yer for skinnin' us a mite, but I will tell yer delivery might be to just one address, an Islington fact'ry. I'll let yer know. Shall we say a fiver for same?'

'Two vould be sveeter and fairer, Sammy.'

'Oh, I think six pounds would be very fair, Mr Greenberg, don't you?' said Susie.

'Eight?' said Mr Greenberg.

'Very well, dear Mr Greenberg, seven,' said Susie.

'Done,' said Mr Greenberg, 've all know times are hard.'

'We're all suffering together,' said Sammy. 'Still, I'm proud of your influential talents, Eli.'

'Ah, my dear Sammy, vhat is the vorth of a deal when it ain't been conducted vith love and friendship?'

'There's the profit, that's always a consolation,' said Sammy. 'A happy Christian New Year to you, old sport.' Sammy shook hands. 'Shall we go, Susie?'

'Goodbye, Mr Greenberg,' said Susie, 'and thank you.'

'A pleasure, Susie.'

They left, making their way to a tram stop.

Susie said, 'An Islington fact'ry?'

'An empty one,' said Sammy, 'known to Mr Isaac

329

Moses, father of Mrs Rachel Goodman. We'll have to see if our machinists don't mind goin' the extra distance until we've built the new one. It's a hard life they live, Susie, and I ain't inclined to do any pushing. Well, let's get there.'

She walked through the rain in her brown cloche hat and her German-made leather coat, her umbrella a black, dripping shield that kept her glasses dry. She stopped at the entrance to Caulfield Place. It was wetly grey, its gutters running with water. She was talking vaguely to herself. Passers-by, hearing her, felt sorry for her. Some people got like that, they talked aloud to themselves.

She frowned and shook her head.

'Not now,' she said, 'not now, it's not the right time.' And she went on in a wandering way.

CHAPTER TWENTY-FOUR

In the wetness of the day they surveyed the sodden mounds of grey ashes. Twisted and contorted clusters of blackened iron and steel sprouted from the glistening grey heaps. The brick walls were devastated, fallen girders at obscene angles. Passing people, shabby with poverty, stopped to look and to mutter. A destroyed factory meant more unemployment.

Susie felt harrowed. Sammy felt philosophical. The temporary use of another factory helped, and so did the mental picture he was painting of a new building full of light, with decent amenities and radiators. Some schools had radiators and a hot-water plant. If schools could, his new factory could. He'd have to find out the running costs. But this lot had to go first. The damaged walls had to be pulled down and the site cleared. He had bought the freehold from Mr Morris on behalf of Adams Enterprises, the company's first venture into property ownership.

'It's awful,' said Susie, 'and so dispiritin'.'

'It's not good, but it could be worse,' said Sammy. 'It's a blow, I grant you, but there's consolations. Like Eli Greenberg and Isaac Moses both comin' to our rescue. And there's you too, Susie, which is a considerable consolation.'

'This is so sudden,' murmured Susie.

'Pardon?'

'Thank you, Mister Adams.'

'I'm on to you, Susie Brown.'

'On to me? I don't know what you mean.'

'Little Turk you are, Susie. It's leadin' you to a shockin' fate. Not today. Today's a bit mournful. But it could easily happen tomorrow, or the day after.'

'What shockin' fate?' asked Susie.

'You'll find out. I just hope it won't make you run a mile in record time. Come on, let's go across and see Gertie.'

Susie, now reading him like a book, went across the street with light dancing in her eyes, and hoping that her shocking fate wouldn't be too long delayed. Imagine he could be so dynamic in business matters and so hopeless about saying just a few special words.

Gertie was in. So was her husband Bert. He hadn't been called at the docks this morning, so he had come home. Gertie brought the visitors into the small kitchen. It was warm enough from the stove fire, but Sammy thought it had a kind of bare look, like Mother Hubbard's cupboard. That came, he knew, from poverty and a hand-to-mouth existence. The resilience of cockneys like Gertie and Bert would have surprised him had he not grown up among such people. He introduced Susie to Bert, who was down on his knees beside the grate. In the grate stood a triangular iron foot. On the upper foot was a boy's boot. There was a large square of boot leather on the floor, from which Bert had cut two soles. He'd got the leather from the docks. It had fallen off a ship. One sole was on the boot, a nail protruding. He got up to shake hands with Susie. His worn, rugged and lean face creased into an admiring smile.

'Blimey, it's a pleasure to meet yer, Miss Brown, yer the one I 'eard was the Lord Mayor's daughter.'

Susie smiled. 'I ain't no Lord Mayor's daughter,' she said.

'Don't you believe it, Bert,' said Sammy, 'she's given my ears more than a few tannings. No work today?'

'Dock labour's casual, bleedin' casual,' said Bert.

'Well, when there's no work for you,' said Sammy, 'would you do a job for me? That site's got to be cleared. I could use contractors to clear it in a few days. But there's no hurry until the insurance is settled and I know what I'm gettin'. You'll need a cart or a lorry, and some mates to help you. You can take your time. Give you forty quid to do the job, plus cost of hiring the cartage. You pay your mates out of the forty quid. What d'you say?'

'I'll say yer on, Mister Adams, that's what I'll say.'

'Also,' said Sammy, 'when the new fact'ry's built, I'll give you a job. That's if you won't mind handin' in your docker's card. You can be responsible for fact'ry maintenance, which will include keepin' it warm in the winter, decent all the year round, and makin' sure unpleasant geezers don't set fire to it.'

Bert's mouth fell open.

'Yer been an' poleaxed 'im, Mister Adams,' said Gertie, 'and 'e ain't goin' to get his breath back for a while. So I'll speak for 'im. Yer got yerself a man what'll do a good job for yer. 'E don't keep me in fur coats, like me old mum 'oped 'e would, but 'e can do a job good as any man. There y'ar, Bert, yer can straighten up now, Mister Adams don't want you lookin' as if yer goin' to fall over. Yer a gent, Mister Adams, an' I don't mean a fancy gent, an' when yer come up with them new machines yer promised, me an' the girls'll do yer proud workin' at 'ome.'

'Glad you mentioned that,' said Sammy, and put the alternative to her, the factory in Islington. It was a bit of a walk, but without the problems bound to be experienced by each machinist working at home. She could think it over, she could talk to the others, but he'd like a decision by tomorrow.

'We'll go there,' said Gertie.

'You sure? Look, tell you what, Gertie, I'll pay any tram fares that's necessary.'

'We won't say no to that,' said Gertie. 'It ain't the walkin', it's what it does to yer shoes. You take the fact'ry, Mister Adams, then yer'll get the turnover yer want.'

'Makes sense to me,' said Bert.

'Glad yer come to,' said Gertie.

'I'm all ears,' said Bert.

'Yer 'andsome brother come 'ere earlier, Mister Adams,' said Gertie. 'Lorst all 'is paperwork in the fire, yer see, all the order details specially. So he went orf to yer Camberwell office to telephone people an' yer shops, so 'e can get all them details, which we gotter 'ave. It won't be no use guessin'. Mister Adams, when will yer be puttin' the new machines into Islington for us?'

'Three days, I hope,' said Sammy, 'and I'll get you all back at work the day after, with brother Tommy's help.'

'Bleedin' lovely,' said Gertie. 'Oh, beggin' yer pardon, Miss Brown.'

'Don't mention it,' smiled Susie.

'Bert done a call on 'is way back from the docks, Mister Adams,' said Gertie. 'Like yer wanted, come tomorrer or the day after, Daft Dick ain't goin' to be able to strike no more matches. That right, Bert?'

'Right,' said Bert.

Susie gave Sammy a straight look.

'What does that mean?' she asked.

'No idea,' said Sammy. 'Didn't you make a note of something, Miss Brown?'

'Oh, about enquiring into things suspicious?' said Susie.

'That's it,' said Sammy. 'Listen, Bert, forget the aforementioned arrangement. It's occurred to us you

334

might instead like to enquire into what set Daft Dick off. Well, yer never know, someone might have put the matches into his hand, with the promise of a quid or two.'

Bert was on to that immediately.

'I gotcher, Mister Adams. The rag trade ain't never been like a dance of sugar fairies, not in the East End it ain't. It's more'n likely you been too good at it. Too good for other people, yer see. So I gotcher, Mister Adams. Leave it to me.'

'Good on yer,' said Sammy. 'We'll get all stock out of your houses, Gertie, on the day the machines are delivered to Islington. I'll phone Carter Paterson. They can pick up the lot at one go. And you better take this, Bert.' He took two fivers from his wallet and handed them to Bert. 'That's an advance for the clearing job. Start when you like, after the fire assessor's been tomorrow.' The insurance company had phoned after Susie's call. 'Leave it to you. Those brick walls have got to come down, of course.'

'No trouble,' said Bert.

'Good. I'll be coming around. So long for now. So long, Gertie.'

'Good luck, Mister Adams,' said Gertie. 'Oh, would yer like to know Mr Morris 'as started up again, in a fact'ry near 'Oxton Road?'

'Is that a fact?' asked Sammy.

'Did you squeeze 'im, guv?' asked Bert.

'He was in financial straits,' said Sammy. 'I favoured him with a deal. I do deals, I ain't partial to squeezin'.'

'I was just askin',' said Bert.

'I know yer was, Bert,' said Sammy. His little grin appeared. 'Good question, though. So long.'

Walking to the tramways, Susie said, 'Excuse me, Mister Adams, but I must ask what was meant about Daft Dick not being able to strike any more matches. I don't think I liked the sound of it. It didn't sound charitable or Christian.'

'I'm thinking at the moment about other things, Susie, such as calling on our Madame Dupont concerning arrangements to introduce our range to buyers in the West End. The Paris shows start soon.'

'Yes, but what about poor Daft Dick?'

'I've just been very considerate in respect of the bleeder—'

'Really, Mister Adams, I don't expect that kind of language from our managing director,' said Susie. The rain had stopped and two shawled women peered at them from an open doorway.

'My, yer a couple of fancies,' said one woman.

'Granted, missus,' said Sammy, walking on with Susie.

'Dolled-up rent collector and 'is bit of Sunday lamb, they look like,' said the second woman.

The street was a wet brown and grey, the flat-fronted dwellings grimy with London soot, the smoke from chimneys rising listlessly. A woman with a pillowcase full of wet laundry from the local bagwash fumbled for the latchcord of her front door. Sammy halted to oblige her. He gave the cord a tug and the door opened.

'Ta, yer a gent, mister, and a posh one too,' she said. She had the pale complexion of the East End, but her dark brown eyes were brilliant and her full mouth very kissable.

'Yer welcome,' said Sammy, lifting his hat to her.

'Same to you.' She winked at him. 'Knock any time yer like and ask for Amy. I'm Amy. Only don't knock Sunday afternoons, me old man's around then.'

'All right, no Sunday afternoons,' said Sammy. 'See yer Friday morning if it suits yer.'

'I can't 'ardly wait,' said Amy, and went in. Sammy resumed walking with Susie.

'You didn't say what time Friday morning, Mister Adams. Shall I put down eleven o'clock in your appointments diary?'

'It won't be Sunday afternoon, that's for certain. I'll get me livelihood injured. Right, now we'll take a tram to the City, find a JP eatin' house and partake of their individual steak-and-kidney puddings before goin' to Battersea to see Mimi.'

'Yes, Mister Adams, quite so.'

Sammy grinned. That Susie. Few people were going to get any change out of her. She was a ladylike knockout. No wonder Chinese Lady was regarding her as highly favourable.

In the restaurant in the City, where there were white cloths on the tables and the individual steak-and-kidney puddings were luscious with meat and gravy, Susie harked back to Daft Dick and her suspicions.

'I wouldn't like to think you'd do him bodily harm,' she said.

Sammy chewed and thought. He was not going to ask the police to charge the miscreant. If the fire brigade declared it was an arson job, the police could take it from there. But nobody had been doing any sifting work today. The insurance company would get interested if arson was mentioned. That would delay settlement. They'd investigate the affairs of Adams Enterprises. And they'd find those affairs far too healthy for him to need his factory being burned to the ground.

'I don't go in for doing bodily harm personally, Susie. My mother wouldn't stand for it. All I've done is arrange for Bert to take a look at Daft Dick. Now how'd you feel about Adams Fashions opening a shop in Oxford Street?'

'Oxford Street?' Susie's blue eyes sparkled. 'Oh, how excitin'.' The restaurant was almost full, City clerks predominating, the clatter of knives and forks a metallic accompaniment to the chatter of conversation. 'You're not kiddin', are you?'

'The lease is comin' up on offer in two months, or so I was reliably informed earlier by Mrs Rachel Goodman during my business conversation with her.'

'Oh, thank goodness,' said Susie. 'I was so embarrassed, thinking Mr Greenberg was thinking you were consortin' with a married woman in his yard.'

Sammy eyed her across the table. Susie offered him a look of innocence.

'Kindly note, Miss Brown, I don't like gettin' a ringing in my ears when I'm enjoying steak-and-kidney pudding. Further note, you saucebox, that I don't consort with any female woman of a married kind.'

'I should hope you wouldn't, Mister Adams,' said Susie. 'Oh, but a shop in Oxford Street, that's really excitin'.'

'Thought you'd like it,' said Sammy.

'Oh, yes. I—' Susie's fork halted halfway to her mouth, and she gave Sammy a suspicious look. 'Excuse me, I'm sure,' she said, 'but you're not goin' to ask me to be the manageress, are you? Because I won't. I've only been your personal assistant for five minutes. I hope the new plans you've got for me don't mean I'm being banished again, even if it is to Oxford Street.'

'I don't know where you get all these banishing ideas from,' said Sammy. 'Did I say Oxford Street was for you, now did I?'

'You'd better not,' said Susie, 'or I'll throw what's left of my pudding over your waistcoat.'

'Eat it up, Susie, it won't do my waistcoat any good,' said Sammy. He coughed to clear his throat. That made Susie give him a different look. 'I'm not in favour of deprivin' myself of your personal assistance. Far from it.' He eyed the cruet. Susie eyed him. 'By the way, I don't want you to think I'm askin' a nosy question, but are you a marrying young woman?'

'Pardon?' said Susie, slightly quivering.

'Are you in favour of gettin' married?'

'Not to anybody I'm not,' she said, 'but I am to someone special.'

'Well, yes, I can see that's a fair point.' Sammy cleared his throat again, the small residue of his meal lying neglected on its plate. 'It reminds me that my old lady is in favour of everyone gettin' married. Anyone who doesn't is a kind of untidy piece of furniture to her. Of course, we owe a lot to our parents for gettin' married, or we wouldn't be here.'

'Mister Adams, that's an awful shame.'

'What is?' asked Sammy.

'Your mother thinkin' you're like an untidy piece of furniture.'

'You saucebox,' said Sammy, and gave her a direct look then. It raised slight colour in her. 'I'd be obliged, Susie Brown, if your parents would invite me to tea next Sunday week.'

'Mister Sammy, you can come to tea any Sunday you like, you know that. You only have to say. Why d'you want to come next Sunday week?'

'Well, the Paris shows will be well over by then, and Adams Fashions will have got off the ground. Also and further, I'll be wantin' to speak to your parents.'

'Oh,' said Susie, quivering again.

'Oh what?' asked Sammy, optimistic rather than confident.

'I don't know. Just oh.'

'I thought of arrivin' at four, if that's convenient.'

'Four. Next Sunday week. Yes.' Susie actually felt a little dizzy. It lasted for the rest of the day. It was present while they were with Lilian Hyams in Battersea, and while Sammy was receiving details from Mr Isaac

Moses concerning the Islington factory and the lease on the shop in Oxford Street.

When she finally arrived home in the evening, her mother thought she looked as if something rather exciting had happened to her. Sally asked if she'd lost a penny and found the Sheik of Araby, popularised by the song. Freddy said the Sheik of Araby wasn't much of a find, he only had a tent to live in and his horse shared it with him. When Susie went up to her room, Mrs Brown, naturally intrigued, went up after her. Susie was looking into her dressing-table mirror.

'Susie, has something nice happened after that awful fire?'

'I don't know,' said Susie.

'Don't know?'

'Well, I know Mister Sammy's makin' light of the fire, Mum. He's bounced back so cheerfully you'd think it hadn't happened.'

'Well, I expect that's what you're pleased about, lovey,' said Mrs Brown.

'Oh, he did say he'd like to come to tea Sunday week, so I invited him.'

'Sunday tea? Mister Sammy?'

'He said he wants to speak to you and Dad.'

'Susie, oh, my goodness, what about?'

'Ask me another,' said Susie.

This is your last chance, Sammy Adams, she thought, before I take Dad's chopper to you.

CHAPTER TWENTY-FIVE

The Paris fashion houses opened their salons to the world. The trade unions of Britain, seething at the injustice of low wages, long hours and continuing unemployment, thought the interest in fashions disgusting. The flappers did not.

On Thursday, Susie bought all the morning papers on her way to the office and rushed into Sammy's sanctum with them.

'Sammy, look!' She forgot business formality in her excitement.

'Good morning, Miss Brown. You have arrived distinctly refreshin', I see.' Susie wore a bright yellow jumper and a dark blue skirt. Spring daffodil, thought Sammy. 'I'm already lookin', by the way.'

The morning newspapers were on his desk. He had bought them too.

'But can you believe it?' Susie was radiant.

'It's in front of me eyes,' said Sammy. 'Our Mimi Dupont's anticipated the Frenchies.'

'Well, say something human,' begged Susie.

'Eureka,' said Sammy.

There they were on the fashion pages of every newspaper, photographs and sketches of the 1926 look proposed and created by the designers of Paris, with descriptions of the colours, the styles, the materials and the innovations. The colours sounded dazzling, the day

341

dresses and dance dresses were all waistless, with rounded or pointed scalloped hems, or inserted flared pieces, like draped handkerchieves. And there were the abbreviated hemlines, the daring short-short look. Knees were in. Bobbed or shingled mannequins, poised on catwalks, were in haughty display of long legs and peeping knees.

Susie could hardly contain her excitement. Sammy was smiling. Lilian Hyams arrived, and she too was carrying the morning papers.

'Lilian, you did it, you were right,' laughed Susie, bubbling and sparkling.

Sammy, on his feet, said, 'I'm pleasured to congratulate you, Mimi.' And he kissed his designer. Lilian, no longer with hunger in her eyes, received the kiss enthusiastically.

'My life, such a smacker, Mister Adams.'

'Yer welcome,' said Sammy.

'You believed in me, you and Susie. And where's that handsome buck Tommy?'

'Islington fact'ry,' said Sammy, 'gettin' it fixed up. The machines arrive tomorrow.'

'Tomorrow's our day?' said Lilian.

'Tomorrow,' said Sammy, 'we go in and knock the West End buyers for six.'

That was Sammy's optimistic belief. But the day was a disaster, a fiasco. No one had ever said no to Sammy. At least, not for long. Lilian had harboured little doubts, little qualms, but had placed her trust and hopes in Sammy's infectious dynamism, supreme self-confidence and arresting personality. The collection was hung carefully in the van, and the van was driven by ex-Corporal Mitchell around the shops and stores of the West End. Lilian sat in the back, guarding the samples. Susie and Sammy sat next to Mitch, Sammy in his best grey overcoat and suit. Susie, hair newly dressed, looked lovely, but was all nerves. She was bravely prepared to model the collection, but was by no means an exhibitionist, nor could she contrive the haughtiness of professional mannequins.

She was not called upon to model a single one of Lilian's creations. Adams Fashions had never been heard of, nor had Mr Sammy Adams or Madame Mimi Dupont. Sammy had the list of buyers' names procured for him by Mr Greenberg, but for all the good it did him it might as well have been a list of East Street stallholders. Adams Fashions were plainly regarded as interloping amateurs whose rightful place was Petticoat Lane. Susie, introduced as the firm's mannequin, was stared at by buyers' assistants as if she belonged to a dubious second-hand clothes stall. However, even if Sammy had hired a professional mannequin it would have made no difference. Not one buyer bothered to appear. Most, in any case, were busy studying the implications of the new Paris fashions, and some, of course, were in Paris.

'Do go away.'

'Who are you?'

'We've no interest in you.'

'Don't be absurd.'

'Please leave.'

'Where is your fashion house?'

'You're wasting your time. And ours.'

'Do go away.'

By late afternoon, total failure was obvious. Sammy's teeth were gritted, Lilian was brooding, and Susie felt sick with acute disappointment.

'All the same,' said Sammy, 'I ain't done for yet. I can't afford to be done for, but I'll admit me pride is suffering.'

Lilian went home with a headache. Neither her

343

portfolio nor any of her designs had been given a glance. Mitch drove Sammy and Susie back to Camberwell. They arrived in the offices a little before five. Boots came in to enquire about results. Sammy, in a brief exposition, revealed that results were nil, nothing and bloody hollow. Boots looked at Susie. Susie looked a nicely dressed and charming young lady. But she did not, he thought, look like a mannequin of flamboyant gestures or haughty carriage.

'Wrong presentation, probably,' he said. 'New tactics required. I'll make a couple of phone calls.'

He made them from his own office.

Polly was home, her leg healing rapidly, the stitches out, and the school still on Christmas holiday. The phone rang in the drawing-room. She answered it.

'How are you, Polly?' asked Boots.

'Is that my hero?'

'D'you want one? I'll find you one. How's your leg?'

'Leg singular? I happen to have two, old bean, and they're both visionary. I'm visionary everywhere, except for an unfortunate contusion on my left thigh. Not my best moment, that, letting my snorting beast run away with me. I think I was in too much of a hurry to get to Postman's Knock. Aren't you sweet to ring me?'

'My motive's suspect,' said Boots, 'I'm after something.'

'At last,' said Polly. 'Where d'you want to have it? Brighton?'

'I'm after what you can do for me as a well-dressed flapper, Polly. I think you're a customer at some of the best shops and stores in the West End.'

'Oh, you're interested in my ravishing undies? That's naughty, Robert old sport, but so exciting.'

'Leave off,' said Boots, and explained in detail Sammy's venture into fashions and how it had culminated in today's fiasco. Polly, who knew nothing about

Adams Fashions, was vastly intrigued.

'So Sammy fell flat on his face,' she said. 'Hysterical, darling. Has it put years on him?'

'It will do if he can't solve the problem.'

'No problem, old love. Harriet. She's the answer.'

'Who's Harriet?'

'Well, you've asked me, haven't you, if I can wangle things. Harriet de Vere, chief buyer for Coates, the West End store. That's not her real name. It's Bird. Her husband was Lieutenant Clarence Bird, killed in the war, poor devil. We knew her family. My father helped her to get a job with Coates immediately after the war. He's a shareholder. Leave it to me, sweetie, I'll see that Sammy gets the right kind of introduction to Harriet.'

'Bless you,' said Boots. 'And there's something else.' He explained what the something else was. A mannequin job, not only for her but for Sammy's friend Rachel Goodman as well. Polly yelped with delight.

'Crazy,' she laughed, 'crazy. Utter fun. No, wait a moment, are you sure this woman Lilian Hyams can design wearable stuff? I'm not pouring my perfect body into rubbish, not even for you, Robert.'

'Come in tomorrow morning and see for yourself.'

'Love to. Do you like her designs yourself?'

'I like the fact that I know they'd suit you, and that you'd suit them.'

'Is that good or bad, I wonder? But look, can't you use professionals?'

'I think they'd turn their noses up at working for an unknown designer.'

'They would. I won't. Darling, what a lark. I'll slay Harriet. I hope.'

'Adams Fashions will think the world of you, Polly.'

'Blow Adams Fashions, I'm doing it for you, sweetie, you know that. Now tell me what I get out of it.'

'I'll ask Sammy.'

'Miserable beast. Some husbands like to be faithful, I know, but you're ridiculous. Oh, come on, hero mine, at least present me with the order of your number one concubine.'

'Order presented,' said Boots. 'Turn up tomorrow in seven small veils or transparent Turkish pantaloons.'

'And then?'

'Tales of Arabian nights on Saturday morning in Camberwell, what else?'

'No wonder your daughter Rosie says your mother has never known what to do with you,' said Polly.

Boots rang Rachel next.

'Hello, you dear man,' said Rachel, 'to what do I owe the pleasure? The triumph of Adams Fashions? But I thought Sammy was going to give me the news himself.'

'He's speechless at the moment.' Boots described Sammy's day of disaster. Rachel expressed bitter disappointment. Boots said there was still a ray of hope and told her about Polly, who was going to arrange for Sammy to see the chief buyer at Coates. 'I think it's got to be one step at a time, Rachel. If he can do a deal with Coates, that's as good a beginning as we can expect.'

'Coates?' said Rachel. 'I should say it was.'

'You can help.'

'How?' asked Rachel.

'Well, you're good to look at,' said Boots. 'Striking, in fact.'

'Steady,' said Rachel.

'You're a natural for catching the eye, standing, sitting or walking. So do a mannequin job for us at Coates. Not by yourself. With Polly. She's also striking.'

'You're joking,' said Rachel.

'You only need to be yourself. Polly will put on an act. You don't need to. Have you ever been to a fashion show?'

'One or two, by special invitation.'

'Good. Susie's a lovely young lady, but mannequin stuff isn't her style. She's charming, but not extrovert. Polly is totally extrovert. You're self-assured. You get that from simply being beautiful.'

'You old dog,' said Rachel. 'You want me in Lilian's designs? I should be so outrageous? My daddy will sorrow for me. My life, my legs.'

'Yes, nice and long. Exactly what's called for. Many thanks, Rachel.'

'I'm helpless,' said Rachel. 'Your mama has much to answer for. One such son is enough. Two are one too many. Three are impossible. So how can I not do it? Monday?'

'Can you be here by half-nine?'

'For you and your family, and for me too, yes.'

'That's what I call a friend,' said Boots.

'That's what I call a sacrifice,' said Rachel.

On Saturday morning, Polly purred, gurgled and exclaimed over Lilian's collection. She tried on a number of designs that fitted her. She adored the audacious 1926 look. The injury to her thigh, covered by lint and a plaster, did not obtrude, it was too high up. Susie thought her theatrical but utterly right. Sammy thought her exciting, and Lilian saw the difference her posturings and mannerisms made to each garment. She did not simply wear them. She exhibited them.

Won over to a Monday performance, she advised Sammy she had been in touch with Harriet de Vere, and Sammy was to be there, with Lilian, at half-past ten.

'And you'll be here at half-nine on Monday morning?' said Boots. 'That's when Rachel's arriving.'

'The other half of the act?' said Polly.

'You'll like Rachel,' said Boots.

'She must be as crazy as I am,' said Polly.

347

'You're both gilt-edged,' said Sammy, 'you're both good friends.'

'Friendship has a lot to answer for,' said Polly.

The night darkness had not yet lifted at seven o'clock on Monday morning. Caulfield Place lay in silence, its pavements damp, the lamp outside the printing factory casting a misty glow. Light glimmered behind the curtains of some bedroom windows, where men were sleepily rising to prepare for an early start to their day's work.

The latchcord of a house door stretched to a pull and the door opened. In the dark passage a match was struck and the flame applied to a candle upright in its holder on the hallstand. The holder was lifted, and the candlelight illuminated the passage and the stairs. Shod feet began to quietly ascend the stairs.

Daisy, a light sleeper, awoke to the sound of a creaking board. There were never any creaks at seven in the morning. The creaking began only when her father went down to the kitchen to make tea and bring it to everyone, which was never before half-past seven. Daisy's subconscious reacted to a change in the pattern. She sat up in the darkness, the bedroom chill with January cold. A landing floorboard creaked. She heard a murmuring voice, the tones the soft ones of a woman. Was that Mummy? What was she doing up?

Daisy scrambled out of her bed and pattered over the lino in her bare feet to the door. She opened it. She saw her then, a woman with a lighted candle in her left hand, a long knife in her right hand. She was at the door of the front bedroom, where Daisy's parents slept. She was muttering.

Daisy screamed.

'Mummy, Mummy! Daddy, Daddy!'

It was her brothers, one fifteen and the other seventeen, who appeared first, charging out of the middle bedroom in their nightshirts. The woman did not struggle. She merely looked perplexed as the knife was wrested from her hand.

The police came a little later in answer to a summons. And at the police station a doctor was called to examine a woman who did not know her own name, but whom Boots and his family would have recognised as Elsie Chivers.

Harriet de Vere, chief buyer for Coates, was changing expression. She had been guardedly tolerant at first in her willingness to do a favour for Polly, an old friend and occasional customer. She was beginning to stare now, and so was her assistant.

Polly, of course, was a natural. She could have asked for a more spacious stage than the chief buyer's office, but she nevertheless performed with a dramatic range of gestures and movements. Her long cigarette holder was like a slender wand of black and silver in her right hand, her left hand rippling along her strings of beads. Around her bobbed hair was a purple bandeau with a black feather. The waistless day dress of bright purple that draped her body had a fringed hem that flirted just above her knees. Her legs were clad in black silk stockings. Her chin was lifted, her expression fixed and haughty. She moved with theatrical deliberation, aloof and red-lipped. Rachel, lush and sultry, glided to meet her in a dance dress of blazing tangerine, its scalloped hem lightly moving around her knees. Her strings of beads swung in her left hand, her right hand caressed the air. Her bandeau was silver, her feather matching her dress. She eschewed fashionable aloofness in favour of her rich smile and white teeth.

Harriet de Vere, impeccable in a dark grey tailored costume and white blouse, had returned from Paris on

Friday evening. She looked now as if she could not believe her eyes. Her assistant was rooted. Lilian stood well back, other creations over her arm. Sammy stood beside the assistant, hat and overcoat off, watching with new-found optimism as his amateur mannequins for the day met in studied deliberation. Close to the window, they were as far from their audience as they could get. Polly planted a chaste and haughty kiss on Rachel's cheek, and they murmured to each other.

'Dear God, what am I doing?' asked Rachel.

'No idea,' said Polly, 'but you're doing it rippingly, old thing.'

'Is anyone laughing?'

'No one.'

'Looking?'

'Everyone. Delicious, don't you think?' Polly turned and glided towards Sammy. Rachel weaved a half-circle, her smile vivid. Each moved differently. Legs were brilliant. It was simply not possible to ignore the effect each woman created. If Polly was perfection as a flapper, Rachel was representative of beauty in dazzling colour. To Polly it was exhilarating fun, a gorgeous lark. To Rachel it was time for a prayer. Polly was a mannequin to the manner born. Rachel was a sultry, provoking exponent whose smile hid her feelings of sacrifice.

The chief buyer's assistant took a deep breath. Harriet de Vere caught Polly's eye. Polly smiled.

'You're surprising me,' said Harriet, a woman of thirty. She looked at Sammy. 'I'll give you ten minutes, Mr Adams.'

But Sammy, Lilian, Rachel and Polly were still in Harriet's office long after ten minutes had elapsed.

Polly and Rachel had lunch at the Ritz. They had established a rapport.

'How long have you known the Adams family?' asked Polly.

'Since I was fourteen,' said Rachel. 'I'm a Jewish cockney.'

'I'm upper-class,' said Polly. 'Cheers, old thing.' They touched wine glasses and drank to each other. 'What a performance. Why did you do it?'

'I'm a shareholder,' said Rachel. 'Why did you?'

'I was asked,' said Polly, 'and had no idea how to say no.'

'Ah, Boots, of course,' said Rachel. 'I have my own problems with Sammy.'

'Have you and I got something in common?' asked Polly. 'Do we both want something we can't have?'

'I should answer a question like that?' smiled Rachel.

'What a life,' said Polly, and they laughed together.

Susie had spent the day at the office, unable to bear the possibility of being present at another fiasco. For his part, Boots wondered if it wasn't time Sammy made up his mind about Susie. The bonehead was obviously besotted with her.

Susie felt more comfortable working at her desk. She had not felt at all comfortable about the possibility of exhibiting herself as a mannequin for Sammy. She prayed he would not come back today wearing his previous tight-mouthed look of failure.

He was not back at all by the end of her working day. She went into Boots's office to say good night to him. She felt very low at having to wait until tomorrow for news. When she mentioned to Boots she was going to have a rotten night worrying, Boots said, 'Well, while you're tossing and turning, Susie, think about what the inebriated general said when he was waiting to hear whether his troops were flat on their backs or still standing up.'

351

'What did he say?'

' "In my condition, no news is good news." '

'Oh, that old chestnut,' said Susie.

'It's all we've got, love, so hang on to it.'

The phone in the general office rang after Susie had gone. As everyone else had also departed, Boots went in to answer it, feeling it had to be Sammy.

'Adams Enterprises,' he said.

'Ugh to Adams Enterprises, Robert old darling.'

'Hello, Polly.'

'I hoped I might catch you. Pleased with Polly, are you?'

'Should I be? I'm hoping so.'

'Sammy hasn't phoned? No, I suppose not. He talked just before lunch of going to Islington with Madame Pompadour, the designer. There's a contract coming up from Coates of Knightsbridge.'

'Tell me.'

'I'm at the Ritz. I've just had a pot of tea and some rounds of toast. I'm wearing one of your designer's day dresses. It's a knockout. Everyone's been looking. The colour, you know, a purple gold. Sounds hideous? Well, it isn't. And over lunch here, Rachel was slaying upper-class flappers in fiery tangerine. Hers and mine were both presents from Sammy. Dearie, that brother of yours, what he can do with the English language has to be heard to be believed. Listen, sweetie.'

Boots listened. The buyer at Coates had fought a losing battle with her own reactions, with Lilian's portfolio and samples, and with Sammy's eccentric English. After fifteen minutes, she was no longer a free woman. She was trapped. But of course, said Polly, the fact was the captive Mrs Harriet de Vere knew the collection was irresistible. Polly and Rachel were requested to try on other designs. Lilian brought more from the van, parked outside the store. Sammy pointed out that if the collection as a whole didn't stand up to the new Paris fashions, he would eat his way through Tower Bridge, whether it was up or down. Polly thought that by this time Harriet, whose business name showed where her prejudices lay, had become a little stupefied. But she was still smart, and began to talk about an exclusive contract. Sammy demurred on the grounds that it would limit the horizons of Adams Fashions. Mrs de Vere, jolly handsome, you know, said Polly, confessed she was a war widow and suggested Sammy should call back when the store closed and accompany her to her Kensington flat, where they could continue discussions without interruption. Meanwhile, she would lunch with him and Lilian. She was set by then on an exclusive contract for Coates. She mentioned they had branches in the swankiest shopping areas of Exeter, Bristol, Oxford, Bournemouth, Eastbourne, Brighton, Guildford, Bath and God knows where else. It was an attempt to stun Sammy. Sammy, of course, could see the advantages. He couldn't possibly meet other contracts on his present basis of production. But he refused to be stunned. He simply said he'd spend the afternoon doing costing so that he could have figures to present to her at her flat in the evening. He not only had all the answers, he looked so distinguished he was hardly believable.

'Where did he get that look? He was only a flash barrow-boy a few years ago.'

'He decided to become a reputable business gent,' said Boots. 'Is there more to tell? If so, carry on.'

'Willingly, old love. My foot's in your camp.'

'Mrs de Vere suddenly said she didn't want to upset anyone, and then proceeded to upset Lilian by saying she had to be sure there was no possibility the designs had been copied from the French. Sammy asked if she meant pinched. Mrs de Vere said with respect that such things happened. Lilian said they hadn't happened in this case. Further, the Paris shows were only just over. Further, she had never been outside England. Sammy said behold, and took a letter from an envelope clipped inside the back of the portfolio. It was a letter from a solicitor stating in clear terms that the designs, twenty-four in number, had been inspected by him on 17 December 1925, that he had stamped and initialled each one in confirmation and had photograph copies in his office.

Sammy then showed Mrs de Vere that each sketch in the portfolio bore the solicitor's stamp and initial on the reverse. He said there were so many suspect characters operating in the rag trade that when he had taken on Madame Dupont it was needful to protect her honour and reputation. Polly said Rachel looked as if she was splitting her sides at this. Mrs de Vere looked satisfied in a jolly pleased way, she having taken to Sammy by then. It was odds on she might want to nibble his ears when she got him to her flat. Rachel said later, over lunch, that Sammy would fight anything like that.

'Now are you pleased with me, Robert old sport?'

'Enraptured,' said Boots.

'Well, then?'

'Love you, Polly.'

'Say that again.'

'Love you, just as much as I love Lizzy.'

'You swine, Lizzy's your sister.'

'You're not complaining, are you, Polly? I'm not.'

'Listen, stinker, I'll be a sister to you when I'm ninety, never before. Oh, well, see you Thursday evening when I restart cramming Rosie. Had fun today. Sammy's a knockout. Toodle-ooh, old top.'

'Many thanks, Polly.'

As Boots put the phone down, Mitch put his head in.

354

'I'm back, guv. I got to bring the stuff up from the van. I just come from Islington. Yer kid brother said I wasn't to take it 'ome. I dunno, it's all go.'

'All right, bring it up, Mitch. And look, on your way home, would you drop a note in at Susie's house for me?'

'Lay it in me mitt, sarge.' To Mitch, ex-West Kents, Boots would always be his sergeant first, his employer second.

Susie opened the delivered note.

'Susie. Have a sound night. Sammy won. But leave the port alone. Boots.'

The following day, florists deposited a huge bouquet into the arms of the butler at the residence of General Simms. The bouquet was for Polly. With it was a brief note from Boots.

'Thanks, love.'

A similar one, with a similar note, reached the arms of Rachel.

The same day, Boots, turning the pages of the *South London Press*, the local newspaper, came across a news item that reported the detention by the police of a nameless woman following a disturbance at a house in Caulfield Place, Walworth.

And later, Boots received a phone call from Freddy about the incident.

'They copped 'er, Mister Adams. Daisy told me last night. It was 'er all right. Daisy said she 'ad a knife, a long one. She went in Daisy's 'ouse an' Daisy 'eard 'er comin' up the stairs. Cor, ain't she a queer one? They'll put 'er in the mad 'ouse, I reckon. You there, Mister Adams?'

'I'm here, Freddy. Thanks for ringing.'

'I fought you might like to know.'

'Yes, thanks. I'll pay you for the phone next time I see you.'

355

'Oh, yer don't 'ave to worry about that, Mister Adams.'

'So long, Freddy.'

'Any time, Mister Adams.'

The call gave Boots food for deep thought. She'd gone right over the top. She'd taken a knife into the house in which she had lived with her mother, and in which her mother's throat had been cut. She had become a woman haunted by the event. His conclusion about her became a conviction. What did 'nameless' mean in that newspaper report? That her troubled, haunted conscience had taken refuge in forgetfulness? Amnesia? Was that the word? What good would that do her? Her possessions, her birth and marriage certificates were in an upstairs back room of a house in Westmoreland Road. The landlady there would not let that room stand empty for long, and the police, of course, would do their best to find out all they could about the woman they were holding. They would ask around in Caulfield Place, and some of them would recall the unsolved murder and the woman who had been tried and found not guilty. They would take another look at her. And her birth and marriage certificates would inevitably come to light.

What would he do?

He could help her no more. She would end up in an asylum, for the law could not try her again.

Remembering her as she had been, during the years of his youth, the long-suffering daughter of an intractable and impossible mother, Boots sighed for her.

CHAPTER TWENTY-SIX

The contract to supply Coates of Knightsbridge and all their branches had been agreed and was being drawn up at speed under the supervision of Harriet de Vere. Coates were to launch Adams Fashions and its label. The factory at Islington was working full out, Lilian was on the way to being made as a designer, and Sammy was on the way to making his fortune. Susie was ecstatic.

'I need a new secretary,' said Sammy.

'I'm unsatisfactory?' she enquired, knowing she wasn't.

'You're valuable as my personal assistant,' said Sammy. 'We can make a secretary of a shorthand-typist. A good shorthand-typist. All these offices are bunged up with work. Boots needs more staff, I need more staff. The secretary'll be for you, Miss Brown.'

'Oh, Sammy, stop calling me Miss Brown when we're together.'

'Very good, Miss Brown, quite so,' said Sammy.

'Now you're mockin' me. Oh, did you say a secretary for me?'

'Your forthcomin' status requires you to have a secretary.'

'My what?'

'You're not goin' to be just anybody,' said Sammy. She was going to be Mrs Sammy Adams, whatever it cost him. His phone rang. Doreen said Mrs de Vere was on the line, and put her through.

'Sammy?' said Mrs de Vere.

'Good morning, Harriet,' said Sammy, and Susie's eyes began to spark. That woman. She was always phoning Sammy. And there he was, calling her Harriet when he hadn't known her for five minutes. Susie listened to him answering unnecessary questions about production and delivery, which had been agreed on already.

When he put the phone down, Susie said, 'I'll talk to that woman in future, she's takin' up too much of your time.'

'Good idea, Susie. You do that. I got a horrendous feeling she's after my incorrupted body.'

'You don't fancy that?'

'She'll eat me,' said Sammy.

Susie laughed then. It pealed from her. Sammy grinned.

'Being eaten could be ever so painful,' she said.

'We'll handle her, Susie, between us. In the right way, mind. She's the icing on our cake now.'

'Duly noted, Mister Sammy. You mentioned my forth-comin' status. What's it mean?'

'I'll advise you at an early date.'

Early? Susie thought. Sunday tea? When he was going to speak to her parents?

Doreen knocked and put her head in.

'Someone wants to see you, Mister Sammy,' she said.

'Who?' asked Sammy.

'He just said he's Bert.'

'Send him in.'

Bert, Gertie's husband, came in, cap in his hand, suit shabby but shirt clean.

'Thought I'd best come an' see yer, guv,' he said. 'Morning, Miss Brown.'

'Good morning, Bert,' said Susie.

'Right, that's what you were, Mister Adams, right,' said Bert. 'The bleeder took a 'andful o' notes as well as a box of matches. I 'ad to tread on 'is plates o' meat a mite. 'E 'owled something shockin', but 'e come up with the goods. Wasn't Morris, guv. Two large geezers and a big fat one, the fat one in the background, like.'

'Fat Man?' said Sammy. 'Him again?'

'It ain't Morris's fact'ry what Morris 'as set 'isself up in, it's Fatty's,' said Bert. 'Morris is just runnin' it for 'im. I just found that out. I got eyes an' ears round corners, guv. I come to see yer on account of Daft Dick tellin' me, with tears in 'is eyes on account of his feet 'urting bad, that yer Islington fact'ry's goin' to get done. Goin' to be smashed up and set fire to. Tomorrer night.'

Sammy sighed. The Fat Man, Ben Ford, had tried to close him down when he first opened up here in Camberwell. Boots had used old comrades to prick the balloon. Fatty hadn't forgotten that, and now he was extending his business into the East End, he was after getting his own back. Dangerous, that was. For Fatty.

'Bert, yer a friend. Here, you've come all this way, so use this to buy yourself a pint and a sandwich across the road.'

'Don't want that, guv, I never come for it and I ain't takin' it.'

'Good enough,' said Sammy, and put the pound note back into his wallet.

'Gertie an' the girls is goin' great guns in Islington,' said Bert. 'Gertie says they're singing. See yer again some time. So long, Miss Brown.'

Sammy spoke to Boots, and Boots spoke to Mitch. Mitch began to contact old comrades.

'Just this one game, Daddy,' said Rosie that evening. She and Boots had settled themselves down in the sitting-room for a game of draughts. 'Then I'll do homework, I promise.'

She would keep the promise. But she would enjoy the game first. She enjoyed any activity with her foster-father. Emily and Chinese Lady were in the kitchen with Tim at the moment. Rosie had Boots all to herself. They began the game, Boots making quick moves, Rosie dwelling on hers. She had some of his men cornered after a while, and he did some dwelling then, one hand in his hair, the other on the table.

'Well,' he said.

'Got you there, Daddy,' she said. He smiled. She put her own hand over his and gave his fingers a love squeeze. She sometimes couldn't help demonstrative little gestures like that.

The doorbell rang.

'I'll go,' she said.

On the doorstep stood two people, a man and a woman. The man wore a black Bohemian hat and a flashy caped overcoat. The woman wore a fur coat and a green velvet hat. Her lips were red, her face heavily made-up. The time was seven-fifteen. They had to be on stage for their first entrance at eight forty-five.

'Good evening, young lady,' said the man, and the woman stared intently at the girl, noting her prettiness.

'Good evening,' said Rosie, disliking the way she was being looked at.

'Is Mr Adams home?' asked the woman, smiling with artificial brilliance.

'Yes, he's my father,' said Rosie.

'Is he?' said the woman, round face a trifle plump. 'Ask him if he'll talk to us.'

Rosie went to the sitting-room door.

'Daddy, a lady and gentleman want to talk to you.'

Boots went to the door. He recognised the woman at once. Milly Pearce, Rosie's mother. Her real name was

Tooley. He told Rosie to go and talk to Tim in the kitchen. Rosie, who had not seen her mother for well over five years and did not recognise her, went to the kitchen. Boots brought Milly Pearce and her male companion into the sitting-room.

'D'you know me?' asked Milly.

'I know you,' said Boots, 'and your friend. You're both performing in pantomime at the moment.'

'You've got my daughter,' said Milly. 'I saw my father last Sunday and he told me about Rosie and where she was. He had to, me being her mother. I was expectant of him caring for her.'

'Yes, I saw the note you left on your kitchen mantelpiece,' said Boots.

'Well, I was in great stress at the time, I couldn't take care of her myself, not then, which Mr Rainbould knows.'

'You're Mr Rainbould,' said Boots to the master magician.

'I have that honour, sir,' said Rainbould, 'I am he. I am happy to meet you, knowing you've taken good care of Milly's daughter. We can't, alas, stay long, we are due at the Camberwell Palace in a little while. You are probably well acquainted with my name and reputation. Milly is my well-known assistant, her stage name being Vivette. Ah, yes, and now that she's no longer pressed by ills and misfortune, she naturally wishes to have Rosie back.'

'We called tonight just to let you know,' said Milly, remembering how she had fancied Boots and how he had kept turning her down. 'We thought it was only fair to do that, to let you know. We'll come and collect her later, at the end of the pantomime run, near the end of the month. Rosie was always a dear pretty girl, I was tragic not havin' the means to provide for her, but I'm better off now, havin' paid all my debts, and

Mr Rainbould is natur'lly prepared to see she has a lovely future on the stage.'

Emily came in then, having talked to Rosie about the callers. Her quick eyes at once took in the overdressed look of the woman and the flamboyant airs of the man. She searched the woman's face, and her wide firm mouth compressed.

'You're Milly Pearce,' she said stiffly.

'And you're Em'ly Adams, I'd know your face anywhere.' Milly was vinegary in her snide reference to Emily's plainer features. 'You and your husband's got my little girl Rosie. I was telling him I'm in a position to take care of her myself now. I thought my parents would look after her, I was surprised to hear you two had her. I didn't give no permission for you to. Still, she looks all right, so I'm not goin' to complain. Of course, me and Mr Rainbould haven't come to take her right now—'

'You're not takin' her at all,' said Emily.

'Alas, dear madam,' said Mr Rainbould, holding his hat over his heart, 'her mother has prior claim to her under the law of the land.'

Boots, steely, regarded the prize pair in hard, sharp suspicion. He thought about their act, the man visibly past his best. Drink was probably something to do with that, if his florid complexion was anything to go by. And the woman had little to offer apart from her theatrical tights and her artificial smile. They were probably down on their luck, with engagements few and far between. The woman's round face was coarse beneath its powder, her mouth sullen. Boots reflected on what might be the real reason for their call and their threat.

'How much?' he asked.

'I beg your pardon?' said Milly, her aged fur coat bristling.

'How much?' repeated Boots.

'Don't offer them money,' said Emily, green eyes flashing. 'She doesn't even have a father for Rosie, nor a husband for herself. The courts won't take Rosie away from us and give her to a woman who works on the stage and doesn't have a husband.'

'Mr Rainbould is my husband,' said Milly.

'I do indeed have that honour,' said Mr Rainbould, running his tongue over his bottom lip as if in need of liquid refreshment. 'And I am willing, of course, to be a father to Rosie and to see to her future. It will be a privilege.'

'Very well,' said Boots, 'by the end of January, then. Bring clothes for her, and shoes. You'll naturally wish your privilege to extend to providing her with a wardrobe.'

'I must say, sir, that sounds a trifle small-minded,' said Mr Rainbould, 'and not in keeping with the handsomeness of this abode.'

'This abode belongs to my mother and step-father,' said Boots. 'If you'll call again at the end of this week, we'll have Rosie ready for you.'

'Here, look,' said Milly crossly, 'there's no call to be in a rush to settle things. We've come here friendly, just to talk about it, which you can't say's not fair. We don't mind comin' again to talk more about it and settle it so there's no hard feelings.'

'We must go now, Milly my love,' said Mr Rainbould, certain he was not going to be offered a whisky, a constant consolation for a master magician who had never been fully appreciated.

'I've got a mother's feeling for Rosie,' said Milly. 'I've suffered tortured times thinking about my little girl.'

That was too much for Emily.

'Oh, you cheeky bitch,' she said, 'you left Rosie alone in the house, you went off not caring a thing about her. This is the first time you've shown your face. Well, it's

363

not goin' to do you any good, you're not goin' to have Rosie, nor put her on any stage all painted up.'

'Really, my dear Mrs Adams,' said Mr Rainbould in a pained way, 'that is a little uncharitable. Milly and I will naturally sympathise with your desire to keep Rosie.'

'Course we will,' said Milly, 'but I hope I won't be spoken to in a common way again.' She addressed herself to Boots. 'We'll come again Sunday morning and have another talk, if that's convenient.'

'Yes, work out how much by Sunday,' said Boots.

'My dear sir,' protested Mr Rainbould.

'I'll see you out,' said Boots.

After the master magician and his powdered assistant had gone, Emily said fiercely, 'They're not havin' Rosie, she's ours. I feel like I gave birth to her myself. What got into you, talking about givin' them money?'

'It's what they came for, Em.'

'They didn't say so.'

'No. They went through the overture. On Sunday the curtain will rise and the performance will begin. They're down on their luck, old girl, and the last thing they want is to be lumbered with Rosie.'

'I'm not so sure, and you can be too clever by half sometimes,' said Emily. 'They could be thinking of using her on the stage now. She's such a pretty girl, they could be thinking of dressin' her up in tinsel and spangles and using her in disappearing acts. Help, they were the pair we saw at the panto on New Year's Eve, only her hair was different.'

'A theatrical wig,' said Boots.

'Look, don't count your chickens.'

'I hope they do want money. Legally, we've no hold on Rosie. But we would have if we adopted her by her mother's consent. Tarty Milly would have to sign her over, of course. How much, I wonder, is her signature on the dotted line going to cost us? She'll get nothing unless she does sign.'

'Just don't take it for granted she don't have her own ideas about Rosie, but if you're right, she might ask for what we can't afford.'

'We'll have to afford it,' said Boots.

'Well, I'm not partin' with her, not even if we have to go through the courts,' said Emily.

'Bless you,' said Boots. 'Not a word to her, of course.'

'As if I would. I'll go and make some coffee and tell Rosie she can come and finish her game of draughts with you. And when Tim starts school later this year, I'll come and work full-time for you. Well, up to half-past three in the afternoon, when I'll go and collect him and Rosie then. Chinese Lady says she don't mind me workin' for the fam'ly firm. I want to, anyway.'

'Sure?' said Boots.

'Yes.' Emily smiled. 'I likes yer for me boss.'

The ex-Servicemen of the West Kents and East Surreys, with a few Old Contemptibles, crossed the river by way of Blackfriars Bridge in the early evening, and reached Sammy's Islington factory just after the day's work was finished and the machinists had gone home to Shoreditch. Tommy had also gone. Boots had told him not to hang around. But Bert was there. The factory urn was full of freshly made hot tea. Mitch was in charge of the old comrades, who had done a job for Sergeant Adams once before. They drank tea and they waited. They did so in the darkness. They had to wait until after midnight. They heard the saboteurs then. They opened the main doors of the factory, poured out and met the enemy head-on. They used leather truncheons. They drew blood and they cracked a bone or two. No one came out of nearby houses. No one who woke up emerged to interfere. They all stayed put and minded their own business. It was over and the old comrades well away with Bert by the time the first copper's whistle sounded.

On Sunday morning, Boots opened the door at eleven o'clock to Milly Pearce and Mr Rainbould. Or perhaps it was Mr and Mrs Rainbould. If they were married, the significance of that to Boots was in the fact that it gave Milly a stronger claim to custody of Rosie. They assured him they were willing to be reasonable, although they protested the moment he asked them how much they wanted in settlement of the matter. Chinese Lady was at church with Tim and Rosie, and neither Boots nor Emily wanted to endure a prolonged discussion. They wanted it settled before church was over. So how much?

Mr Rainbould made pained gestures and Milly kept saying, 'Well, really.'

'Make up your minds,' said Boots.

Mr Rainbould managed to say that to deprive a mother of the pleasure of being reunited with her only child should mean offering her recompense. It was not what she had wanted, but if Mr and Mrs Adams were so set on keeping the dear little girl, Milly would not show a hard heart.

'Isn't that so, my love?'

'Well, yes,' said Milly.

'I repeat, we are prepared to be reasonable,' said Mr Rainbould.

'How reasonable?' asked Emily.

'Ah,' said Mr Rainbould.

'The thought of takin' money, well, I don't know,' said Milly. 'Like Mr Rainbould said, it wasn't what we had in mind.'

'It's a difficult decision to make,' said Mr Rainbould, and passed a silken handkerchief over his forehead.

'It's hardly decent,' said Milly, 'my own little girl and all.'

'Well, how decent is fifty pounds?' asked Boots.

'Oh, yer disgustin' man,' said Milly indignantly.

'Really, sir, that is farcical,' said Mr Rainbould. 'A moment.' He drew Milly aside and they whispered. She fished in her handbag, took out her hankie and dabbed her eyes. 'Don't upset yourself, my dear,' said Mr Rainbould, and looked up, his florid face shiny. 'My wife, Mr Adams, is heartbroken. What could recompense that? It hurts us both to concede a financial settlement, or to even think about it.'

Their performance, thought Boots, was first-class.

'Yes, of course,' he said, 'but give it a go.'

'If, sir, for the sake of not disturbing Rosie's life, there must be a settlement,' said Mr Rainbould, 'we suggest a thousand pounds.'

'You horrid creatures,' said Emily.

'Madam, it is not your heart that is broken.'

'Five hundred,' said Boots, 'and that's our utmost limit.'

'Ah,' said Mr Rainbould again, and Milly's floury face showed the glimpse of a quick, greedy smile.

But she said, 'Well, I don't know, I just don't know.'

'Make no mistake,' said Boots, 'it's take it or leave it.'

Emily eyed the pair in disgust. Boots was right, it was money they'd had in mind from the start. It's as plain now as the nose on my face, and that's as plain as anything could be.

'Allow us, sir, a natural distress,' said Mr Rainbould.

'I've never been more distressed,' said Milly, and dabbed at her nose. 'But – well, all right.'

'On condition you sign the necessary papers approving our adoption of Rosie,' said Boots. 'Otherwise, not a penny, and you can take yourselves off and apply to the courts.'

367

'Where we shall fight you,' said Emily.

'The courts?' Mr Rainbould permitted himself a shudder. 'Come, madam, do we wish to line the pockets of lawyers?'

'If you agree to the adoption,' said Boots, 'you have my word the money will be paid to you in full as soon as the papers are signed.'

'We don't want a lot of rigmarole,' said Milly.

'Just the minimum,' said Boots, 'and it won't hurt.'

'Oh, all right,' said Milly.

'Where we goin' to get five hundred pounds from?' asked Emily when she and Boots were alone. 'We only have about two hundred savings.'

'We'll borrow the rest from the firm,' said Boots. 'Sammy will agree to a director's loan. He's riding so high at the moment that he'll hardly feel the pain.'

'He had a flush and a bit of a cough yesterday morning at the office.'

'The flush of success and the strain on his vocal cords,' said Boots.

'Did you get Mitch up to something on Thursday?' asked Emily.

'Nothing out of the ordinary,' said Boots.

CHAPTER TWENTY-SEVEN

Just before Susie and her family sat down to Sunday dinner, a boy from Camberwell arrived with a letter. Susie, taking it from him at the door, saw that it was addressed to her. She recognised the writing on the envelope. Sammy's. She ripped it open and took out a brief note from Sammy.

'*Dear Susie. Laid out with a sore throat. Lost my voice. Can't come to tea. Regards and apologies to your mum and dad. Don't want to risk passing it on to everyone. Sorry, Susie. Love, Sammy.*'

'Are you goin' back to Mister Adams?' she asked the boy.

'Not likely I ain't, I'm goin' 'ome to me dinner,' he said.

'Did you see Mister Adams when he gave you this letter?'

'Only 'is bonce. Out of the top winder, it was. He dropped the letter down, wiv a tanner. He waved 'is 'and about. So I called up, "I gotcher, Mister Adams." I knows 'im, yer see.'

'All right,' said Susie, and the boy went off at the double. Susie addressed the printing factory. 'I'm not havin' this, Sammy Adams, oh, no. It's just one more way of being a coward. I'm comin' after you, Sammy Adams, and bringing my dad's chopper with me.'

* * *

It was half-past three when Susie, in her best Sunday coat and hat, entered through the door at the side of the shop, went up the stairs, passed the main door to the offices, and climbed the next flight to the second floor. There she knocked loudly on the door of Sammy's flat.

Sammy staggered out of bed, wrapped himself in his winter dressing-gown of dark blue wool with white piping, tottered into the lobby and opened the door.

'Oh, dear,' said Susie, 'oh, you poor thing. Oh, dear, I am sorry.'

Sammy, his hair tousled and untidy for once, his chin lacking the usual attentions of his morning razor, his face flushed, blinked at her in the way of a man who didn't quite know what had hit him.

'Go away,' he croaked.

'Certainly not,' said Susie. 'Oh, dear, dear, dear. Look at you. What have you done to yourself, left your vest off somewhere, I suppose. Not at Harriet's, I hope. Go on, back to your bed, and I'll take your temperature.' She stepped in and closed the door. Sammy backed off.

'Go away,' he croaked again, 'you'll catch me germs.'

'I'm not daft, I gargled with a throat disinfectant before I came out. Come along.' She took his arm. 'Where's your bedroom?'

'I ain't sure,' said Sammy, hoarse and husky, but he managed to find it. Susie hustled him in.

'Come along, back into your bed,' she said. She pulled the blankets and sheet down, and Sammy got in, still in his dressing-gown. She covered him up and tucked him in. 'Oh, dear, we are poorly, aren't we?' she said.

'I ain't a pretty sight,' croaked Sammy.

'Nor was I when I had mumps and you pushed your way in,' said Susie. She opened her large handbag and took out the family thermometer.

'Here, hold up,' said Sammy, sounding hoarser.

'Open your mouth.'

'I'm all right.'

'Of course you're not. Open your mouth.'

'Look, I—'

Susie popped the thermometer in. Sammy muttered around it.

'Don't start growling, you'll snap it,' she said. 'Or swallow it. Hand.' Sammy sucked ferociously at the thermometer. 'Hand,' repeated Susie. He gave her his hand and she felt for his pulse. She had no idea how to correctly check a pulse rate. She was simply putting Sammy through it. 'Oh, dear, if only Harriet could see you now, we really are poorly, aren't we? Now don't fidget. One, two, one, two – oh, lor'. Never mind, it's not as bad as mumps.' Sammy growled, and the thermometer rolled about. Susie smiled lovingly. 'I'm goin' to mix you two Beecham's powders and then make you a hot lemon drink. I've brought two lemons. Are you a bit feverish?' She placed a hand on his forehead. The coolness of her fingers was balm to Sammy's flushed brow. 'Well, you're not on fire,' she said. She took the thermometer out and peered at it. She could at least read a thermometer.

'Just don't worry,' said Sammy, 'I don't mind dying quietly.'

'I'll come to your funeral, if I've got time,' said Susie. He had said that to her once. 'But I think you'll be all right. Your temperature's short of the hundred.'

'Don't like you catchin' it,' he croaked, and glowered as she patted his pillows. She smiled. His little grin arrived. 'You Susie,' he said.

'You Sammy,' she said, and looked around the room. It was nicely furnished, if you liked mahogany. 'Well, I'll go and mix the Beecham's. I'll find the kitchen.'

She found it. It was surprisingly neat and tidy for a

bachelor. She warmed some water in a kettle, found a glass in a cupboard, and shook in the contents of two powders. She carried the glass to him.

' 'Orrible,' said Sammy, regarding the mixture with distaste. His voice was almost gone.

'Sit up,' said Susie, 'or you'll pour it all over your face.' Sammy sat up and took the glass. He drank the mixture at one go, to get it over with. 'There,' said Susie, taking the empty glass from him, 'aren't you a good boy?'

Sammy almost fell dangerously ill at being called a good boy.

'Susie Brown, I think you're comin' it a bit.' The words scraped his throat.

'Don't talk,' said Susie, 'I can't make out what you're saying, anyway. You sound like sandpaper fightin' a nutmeg grater. Just use this.' She picked up what she had seen on his little bedside table. A writing block and pencil. Typical. She could imagine him waking up in the middle of the night and jotting down a business idea or a reminder. 'While you're still sittin' up, just write.' She gave him the block and the pencil.

'Write what?' Sammy made himself heard.

'What you were goin' to say to me after you'd spoken to my mum and dad.'

'Eh?'

'Write it, then I'll go and make you the hot lemon drink.'

'Eh?'

'Just write it down, Sammy Adams.'

'Well, it hurts talkin', I can tell you,' he said, and bent his head over the pad. He wrote. Susie took the top sheet, ripping it off. She read his words.

'*Would you kindly marry me before I pass on?*'

'You'll be lucky,' she said.

'Pardon?' said Sammy in shock.

'It's not good enough,' said Susie, and gave the sheet of paper back to him. Sammy gaped.

'Susie, you turning me down?'

'I'm turning that down,' said Susie, 'it's just not good enough.'

The penny dropped. He had a headache and a fiery throat, but the penny managed to drop. He wrote more and handed her the sheet. She read the new words.

Dear Susie, business comes second to you. I loved you when I first saw you, it's given me a terrible time. Now it's making me ill. Do a life-saving job and marry me. You're an angel. Love, Sammy.

'That's better,' said Susie. She folded the sheet of paper and put it into her handbag. 'I'll make the hot lemon drink now. You can lie down again, you needn't sit up again until I come back. Oh, dear, how the mighty's fallen.'

Sammy watched her disappear again. That Susie. What was she up to? She hadn't said yes and she hadn't said no. He lay back. The Beecham's powders began to work. His headache slowly eased and the fire in his throat cooled a bit. Suppose she said no? Suppose she just said she was flattered to be asked, but didn't want to marry him? I'll jump off Tower Bridge. No, that wouldn't do the business any good, nor me either. Was there someone else? Did she have a crush on Boots?

She came back after ten minutes, her coat off, her blue cloche hat cuddling her bright hair, her royal blue dress new, her legs clad in dark blue silk. Silk. It's deliberate, that's what it is. Deliberate. She knows I can't talk, she knows I'm not myself, and she's brought herself here in a new dress and silk stockings.

'You Susie—'

'Stop croaking,' she said, the glass of hot lemonade in her hand.

'I'm croaking all right, I'll be gone in an hour.'

'I'll go and fetch the vicar,' said Susie, 'but first you'd better drink this. Sit up, come along.' Sammy perceptibly growled. 'Stop swearing. Sit up.' He heaved himself up and took the glass. 'You should drink lots, and stay in bed for a few days. Don't go out in the cold or you'll be worse before you're better. I'll see to things in the office and keep in touch with Tommy at Islington. I'll pop up here from time to time and nurse you a bit.'

Sammy, sipping the hot drink, almost choked on it.

'You'll what?'

'And I'll see you get some food. Bovril, porridge and rice puddings will be best. And lots of oranges. I'll make you a nice little tea in about an hour, and read to you as soon as you've finished the lemonade. Reading to the sick is soothing, I read that somewhere. Is the lemonade sweet enough? I found your sugar in the tea caddy. Your tea's in the sugar caddy.'

'That's it, drive me barmy,' said Sammy. The lemonade, tingling and biting, did wonders to his throat. He finished it. She took the glass from him and placed it on the bedside table.

'There, you can lie back again now,' she said.

'What's the point? I'm done for.' But he lay back and watched her. She took a book from her handbag, a book with a colourful picture on its cover. She sat down in a chair and crossed her legs. The silk stockings ran with gleaming light. Mother O'Reilly, thought Sammy, she's running rings round me.

She opened the book and leafed through it.

'Oh, here's a really nice story, with a nice endin' too,' she said. 'You'll like it, it's very soothing.' She began to read. 'Once upon a time in the land of daffodils and tulips, and of egg-cups made with marzipan, there was a Princess called Petal—'

'Bloody hell,' said Sammy.

The open book was lowered a fraction. Blue eyes looked reproachfully at him.

'Is that nice, Sammy Adams?'

'There's a lot more of it to come while I'm still alive. When I'm gone—'

'Don't be silly now,' said Susie, 'you can't go yet, not till after Easter.'

'Easter?'

'Easter Saturday.'

'That's a good day to go,' muttered Sammy.

'Not for you it isn't,' said Susie, 'there's the wedding.'

'Wedding?'

'Ours,' she said. Sammy stared at her. He knew then that she was laughing at him. Her expression was quite grave, but she was laughing all right, it was there in those eyes of hers. He knew something else too. The skinny waif he'd given a job to over five years ago had grown into a woman who was always going to be one up on him. It didn't bear thinking about. But look at her. She was worth every penny of a fortune, as long as there was some left for overheads.

'Susie, you witch.' He was croaking again. 'You've been havin' me on.'

'No, only hittin' you with me dad's chopper,' she said. She reached and squeezed his hand. She laughed. 'Oh, Sammy, you are lovely,' she said.

'Not by a long shot,' said Sammy, 'but I think I'm goin' to recover.'

Mrs Stubbs of Westmoreland Road, an honest woman, went to the police station to report that her lodger, a Mrs Adams, had gone missing and had left behind a suitcase containing valuables. Mrs Stubbs said she'd taken it on herself to open the case because she was worried, especially as her lodger had been a dreamy kind of woman. The police investigated, and turned the suitcase inside-out. What they found was of much interest to them. And Mrs Stubbs's description of her missing lodger pointed them to the woman they had released from custody into a hospital. They made no charges. She belonged where she was, in hospital.

The next edition of the *South London Press* carried a report that the nameless woman who had been arrested for disturbing the peace was actually Mrs Elsie Lansberg, formerly Miss Elsie Chivers, who had been acquitted in 1914 of the murder of her mother. She had suffered a nervous breakdown and was now in hospital.

Boots, for all his determination to leave things alone, went to the Walworth police station. Emily accompanied him. They had a very interesting conversation with a detective-sergeant, who informed them in the end that the matter was quite out of police hands now, and that Mrs Lansberg was currently an inmate at the Maudesley Hospital, Denmark Hill. Boots and Emily went there, and a doctor permitted them to see the former Elsie Chivers.

She was sitting beside her room window, hands in her lap and gazing at the wintry scene outside. She wore a soft brown dress that was a little loose on her thin figure. She turned her head as Boots and Emily entered. Through her spectacles her eyes were clear and untroubled, but unknowing.

Boots spoke.

'Hello, Elsie,' he said, and he smiled at her. Her brow puckered. She gazed up at him. 'Emily's here too,' he said. 'Old friends, you know.'

Her brow smoothed out, a little sigh escaped, and she gave him another look. Her eyes expressed recognition and delight. She came to her feet, took her glasses off in the way of a woman sensitive rather than vain, and placed them aside.

'Oh, dear, I'm not at my best, am I?' Her hands

fluffed at her hair and smoothed her dress. Again she looked at Boots, and he saw what had once been so familiar to him, and so enchanting, the myopic misty softness of her eyes. And if she was ten years older, she still had a loveliness. A smile of affection touched her mouth. 'Yes, it's Boots, dear dear Boots.'

And Emily stared in astonishment as she embraced Boots and kissed him full on his lips, like a woman whose inner anguish had dissolved in a flood of emotional and resurgent happiness. But Boots, of course, had always been her favourite, as well as the young soldier whose evidence at the Old Bailey had shown the court she could not have murdered her mother.

But everything had played on her mind, poor woman.

'It's all over, Elsie,' said Boots gently, 'it's all over. No more worries. You've people here to care for you now.'

'Why, look, and there's Emily,' she said, 'and such a picture.' She took Emily's hand and squeezed it, then kissed her softly on the cheek. 'You are Emily, aren't you?'

'Well, I always have been,' said Emily, 'and I'm so pleased to see you.'

'I've had so many strange dreams, Emily.'

'All over now,' said Boots again, and asked lightly and casually, 'What happened to your husband, Herr Lansberg?'

'Dead, you know. Oh, dear.' She sighed again. The dreams took hold of her. 'I must get on, I really must, there's so much to do at home, and my mother is never well. Oh, dear.' She took up her spectacles, put them on and sat down again to gaze at the wintry view once more. Boots, remembering his youthful love for her, felt pain. He touched her shoulder in the lightest gesture of good-bye, and then he and Emily left.

On their way home, Emily said, 'She'll always be in some strange world of her own.'

'I hope it's a kind world as well,' said Boots.

'Boots, you don't think perhaps she was guilty, after all, do you?'

'Perish the thought, Em,' said Boots, who was always going to keep certain conclusions and convictions to himself.

Chinese Lady and her grandson Tim got off the bus and walked towards the school, she holding him firmly by the hand. The March afternoon was crisp, bright and invigorating, and she had thought it would be nice to get out with Tim, meet the children from school and share the bus ride home with them. Emily was working on today, with her approval. That was much better, Emily working for Boots in the family firm and enjoying it. It was always better for any wife to work in her husband's offices, if she had to work at all. The firm was so busy, and Boots was being overwhelmed, all on account of Sammy's success with ladies' fashions. That Sammy, the things he got up to in ladies' wear. Chinese Lady paused in her reflections, thinking she hadn't got that quite right. Something told her Boots would show one of his sly smiles if she said it like that. Still, it was nice him telling the family Emily was a perfect godsend in the office. Well, she'd been that to the family for years. Mind, she and Boots had been given something to think about over that bit of silliness with Mr Somerville. It had pulled them up short. Emily might not be the best-looking woman in London, but she was very lively, and men liked that in a woman. She had a good figure too, and men liked that as well. Boots wasn't so airy-fairy about his marriage now. Good thing too. Wives gave a lot in marriage. Not many men gave as much.

Imagine Sammy coming to his senses at last. Making money was all very well, but it wasn't everything.

378

Well, he'd seen that, and he'd done himself proud in picking Susie. He'd never find anyone more suited to him, nor anyone who could handle him better. That young man needed handling or he'd start chasing the moon. An Easter wedding and all. He'd bought Susie a lovely engagement ring from one of Mr Moses's new jewellery shops, and Mr Moses himself was coming to the wedding, with his daughter Rachel. And Mr Greenberg, of course.

Vi and Tommy would probably always be the happiest couple in the family, because Tommy was the most considerate of the boys and Vi was so placid it didn't take hardly anything to make her contented. Tommy would get on well as the factory manager, especially when the new one was built. Sammy had had trouble getting the insurance company to settle. They'd said they weren't too happy about the cause of the fire. Sammy went round to their head office and told them not to lay that one on him or he'd sue them. Susie went with him, and said afterwards that Sammy paralysed them with a speech that lasted fifteen minutes. They were going to settle now. Chinese Lady thought she'd have to go and see the new factory when it was up, just to make sure it was a credit to the family and the workers. She'd heard tales about East End workshops and how machinists were paid starvation wages. No son of hers was going to be allowed to pay wages like that to his machinists.

It wasn't hardly believable, the name of his fashions company and the name of his designer actually being in the papers, on the fashion pages. Adams, that was the name at the top of one page. That was his dad's name. Chinese Lady felt sad that Daniel hadn't lived to see what his sons had made of his name.

Lizzy and Ned were doing fine. Lizzy was living all her ambitions as a wife and mother in her house with its own bathroom and garden. She'd been invited to go with Ned to a celebration of his firm, and Ned had had to buy her an evening gown, a real silk evening gown, for the occasion. Lizzy looked like one of them Buckingham Palace debutantes in shimmering gold silk, and you could see Ned was proud of her. Lizzy was scared that in her nervousness she'd drop her aitches, and Ned said that if she did he'd better drop his too, just to let people see they were two of a kind. But Lizzy rose to the occasion, apparently, and Ned said she was as good as Eliza Doolittle at the ball. Lizzy asked who Eliza Doolittle was, and Ned said she was a flower girl who turned into a duchess in a play by Bernard Shaw. Lizzy said she didn't want to be a duchess, just Mrs Ned Somers. She and Ned and the children were going on holiday in the summer with Boots, Emily, Rosie and Tim. Chinese Lady was going too, with her husband Edwin.

It was nice. Edwin was coming home at Easter, and in time for the wedding. He'd written to say so. The letter had come in a Government envelope, like others. She felt happy about that. She'd missed him. He'd be surprised to know Elsie Chivers had turned up. Poor woman, she was in hospital now with a nervous breakdown.

Sammy actually had a motorcar now. A new one. Chinese Lady wasn't sure she held with motorcars. Horses had always been all right as far as she was concerned, and a lot safer too. Nor did they break down or need filling up with petrol. Some man needed a good talking to for inventing motors. They weren't what a woman would have filled the roads with.

After Sammy's wedding to Susie at Easter, all her children would be married. She'd have no more worries on that score. They'd all be settled. Her boys had been fortunate. Vi, Emily and Susie, what mother's sons could have better wives? But all of them had had to be given a bit of a push. That was the way with young men, most of them couldn't always recognise the gold that was staring them in the face. Lizzy as a girl hadn't needed any push at all. Lizzy had known right from the time she first saw Ned. Still, everyone was right as rain now. Chinese Lady felt that Daniel would be happy and proud of all of them.

She stopped at the school gates, still keeping a tight hold of Tim's hand. The schoolchildren were just coming out of their classes. From the gates she watched them. Children. They were all precious, those who belonged to poor parents just as much as those who belonged to the better-off. They were walking or running or scampering, these children. There was Bobby, a bundle of energy, and there was Annabelle, such a bubbly girl and getting so like Lizzy in her looks. She was with Rosie, of course. They were always together.

And there was Miss Polly Simms, a lady's daughter who'd become a teacher and who had an eye for Boots. But Chinese Lady couldn't help liking her, especially as she'd been an ambulance driver during the war. Four years she'd spent picking up wounded soldiers. You could like any woman for that, but liking her for herself was something else. Life was strange, really, you could never tell which way it was going to lead men and women. Miss Simms came of an aristocratic family, and Boots was like his dad, a man of Walworth, a cockney, even if he did speak what Emily called upper-class posh sometimes. Being what he was, though, didn't make any difference to Miss Simms. Chinese Lady knew that. Miss Simms was often at the house, giving lessons to Rosie, and if you caught her off guard, when she was looking at Boots, you could see how she felt about him. Emily must have seen it too, because she was like a tigress sometimes when Miss Simms was in the house. But Boots had never been a man to lose his head. Except he had once, when he'd gone off to join up behind her back. But he wouldn't lose his head over Miss Simms, except over my dead body, thought Chinese Lady.

'Nana!' Rosie came running. She was the adopted daughter now of Emily and Boots. What a palaver it had been. All kinds of people poked their noses in when a child was being legally adopted. Rosie had put up with the fuss awfully well. Everyone could see she didn't even know her natural mother. Unnatural, more like. It was all over now, and Rosie knew what adoption meant. It meant no one could take her away from Emily and Boots, it meant they loved her and wanted her. She'd get to that advanced school all right, Miss Simms said she would walk the exam. The world was going to open right up for Rosie, and Rosie deserved it because she gave so much happiness to Emily and Boots.

'Hello, Rosie, love. And there's Annabelle. My, don't you both look pretty? Get hold of Bobby, Rosie, before he gets into a fight. You're all comin' on the bus with me and Tim. Oh, good afternoon, Miss Simms.'

Polly, arriving, at the gate, smiled and said, 'Good afternoon, Mrs Finch.'

'It's nice seeing you, specially as I wanted to ask if you'd like to come to tea on Sunday.'

'I'd love to,' said Polly, but her smile was wry as she regarded the children, Rosie, Annabelle, Bobby and Tim. They all belonged to this upright, old-fashioned and remarkable woman who still wore high-necked Edwardian blouses. Everyone who meant most to Polly belonged to Mrs Finch, particularly Boots, Rosie and Lizzy. Polly had a happy relationship with Lizzy, the mother of Annabelle and Bobby. But what was her life to be if she spent it merely in their shadows, more especially the long shadow of Boots? She must break the invisible chains. She knew famous men and notable women, she knew lords and ladies, yet she could not divorce herself from this family, Mrs Finch's family. After all those traumatic years in France and Flanders, amid the sound of the guns, she could have more than she was getting now, surely.

'Oh, could I come too, Granny Lady?' asked Annabelle.

'Everyone must come on Sunday,' said Chinese Lady, and smiled at Polly. 'Don't have another motor-car accident on the way, Miss Simms, my fam'ly don't like to lose their friends.'

'Specially not special friends,' said Annabelle.

'Am I special?' asked Polly, her smile brittle.

'Of course,' said Rosie. 'Isn't she, Nana?'

'Of course,' said Chinese Lady. That was the best way, to make a special friend of Miss Simms and see she didn't bring upsets to the family. 'When you grow up, Rosie, and you, Annabelle, you'll get to learn about the war and your soldier daddies, and what they owed to ladies like Miss Simms and their ambulances. Ladies like Miss Simms are very special. Come along now. Bobby, put your cap straight. I don't hardly know any time when it hasn't looked crooked. Don't fidget, Tim, we're goin' now. Goodbye, Miss Simms. Don't forget on Sunday. Four o'clock.'

'Goodbye, Mrs Finch, I'll be there.' Polly's smile was very brittle as she watched them go on their way, the children's grandmother holding the hands of the two small boys.

A special friend? Very special? Sunday tea with the family? Was that enough?

'Miss Simms?' A twelve-year-old girl, wanting to ask a question, came to look up at the popular lady teacher. 'Could I – oh, Miss Simms, you look like you've got something in your eye.'

'Oh, just a mote, Hilda.'

THE END